PEN

CHARLIE

Lesley Pearse's novels include *Georgia*, *Tara*, *Charity*, *Ellie*, *Camellia*, *Rosie*, *Charlie*, *Never Look Back*, *Trust Me*, *Father Unknown* and *Till We Meet Again*, all except the first five of which are published by Penguin. She was born in Rochester, Kent, but now lives near Bristol. She has three daughters.

LESLEY PEARSE

CHARLIE

PENGUIN BOOKS

PENGUIN BOOKS

Published by the Penguin Group
Penguin Books Ltd, 80 Strand, London, WC2R 0RL, England
Penguin Putnam Inc., 375 Hudson Street, New York, New York 10014, USA
Penguin Books Australia Ltd, 250 Camberwell Road, Camberwell, Victoria 3124, Australia
Penguin Books Canada Ltd, 10 Alcorn Avenue, Toronto, Ontario, Canada M4V 3B2
Penguin Books India (P) Ltd, 11 Community Centre, Panchsheel Park, New Delhi – 110 017, India
Penguin Books (NZ) Ltd, Cnr Rosedale and Airborne Roads, Albany, Auckland, New Zealand
Penguin Books (South Africa) (Pty) Ltd, 24 Sturdee Avenue, Rosebank 2196, South Africa

Penguin Books Ltd, Registered Offices: 80 Strand, London, WC2R 0RL, England

www.penguin.com

First published 1998
Published simultaneously by Michael Joseph
This Edition published for Index Books 2003
19

Copyright © Lesley Pearse, 1999
All rights reserved

The moral right of the author has been asserted

Set in 10.25/12.5pt Monotype Palatino
Typeset by Rowland Phototypesetting Ltd, Bury St Edmunds, Suffolk
Printed in England by Clays Ltd, St Ives plc

For Jan Miller, my friend, soulmate and the inspiration for the character of Charlie. Special thanks too to George Miller, for his loyal friendship and for not minding when Jan and I prattle on endlessly. I love you both.

And joyful thanks for my first grandchild, Brandon Jay, born 10 July 1998: the little boy I had always hoped for, a treasure beyond compare.

Chapter One

Dartmouth, Devon. July 1970

'Allison Proctor's going to enter the Carnival as Lady Godiva, on her horse,' Charlie remarked to her friend June, licking her ice-cream cornet in what she hoped was a sensual manner. Two boys had just sat down on the next bench, and although they were pimply-faced and weedy, probably no more than seventeen, they were better than no male audience at all.

'Not in the nude?' June exclaimed.

'Near enough,' Charlie replied, glancing sideways to see if the boys were listening. 'Just a flesh-coloured body stocking and a cloak.'

'Trust her! She always was a show-off,' June said indignantly. 'I bet she's only doing it because you've been chosen as Carnival Queen.'

It was only two weeks since Charlie had been picked for this role out of dozens of other hopefuls at the Queen's Hotel. She had thought of little else since, and she was delighted June had brought it up in front of these two boys.

'I admire Allison for being so daring,' Charlie replied. 'Everyone else in Dartmouth is so boring. If I wasn't going to be the Carnival Queen I'd enter as

1

something really shocking and make everyone sit up and take notice.'

The girls were sixteen. Their convent school had closed for the summer just the day before and although they were dressed almost identically in flared faded jeans and tie-dyed tee-shirts, the similarity ended there.

June Melling was a somewhat timid, blue-eyed English rose, her pale complexion prone to freckles, five foot two, prettily plump, with corn-coloured wavy hair. Charlie Weish was taller, slender, very pretty, and Chinese.

In point of fact she was only half Chinese, on her father's side, but her appearance was entirely Oriental and quite startling in a small town like Dartmouth where almost all the residents and visitors were of white Anglo-Saxon origin. Her sleek black hair was cut into a fashionable shoulder-length bob, her dark, almond-shaped eyes held all the mystery and fascination of the Orient, and her skin was golden-brown. She had inherited little from her English mother, aside from her long legs and slightly pouting lips. Her father laid claim to her intelligence too; she had taken seven 'O' levels just recently and she was expected to get mostly 'B's.

Even seen through the somewhat jaded eyes of two teenagers who'd never lived anywhere else, Dartmouth on a hot summer's day was at its most picturesque and vibrant. Yachts, ferries and fishing boats bobbed on the sparkling blue water of the river Dart, with a stunning backdrop of Kingswear with its pretty houses clinging seemingly precariously to the steep hillside across the water. Behind the girls' Embankment bench, the abundance of ancient buildings, quaint cobbled streets, the magnificent Naval College and a wealth of historical interest ensured Dartmouth's place as one of the most visited towns in Devonshire.

Charlie and June made a sport out of poking fun at the hordes of holidaymakers who thronged here each summer. They couldn't really understand why these people felt compelled to photograph each other outside every old building, take ferry rides to places they considered boring, or why they consumed such enormous quantities of cream teas and Devon fudge.

But this afternoon their minds weren't on ridiculing visitors, in fact they had been searching amongst them for boys who might brighten up the long holiday ahead. They had already made several slow trawls of all the moored yachts, hoping to spot a couple of bronzed Adonises with sun-bleached hair and fun on their minds. But everyone they'd seen had been either too old or ugly, or already with a girl. With Dartmouth Naval College dominating their town, and scores of young cadets milling around for most of the year, it seemed ludicrous to both girls that they were unable to find anyone even vaguely suitable, but the College had closed for the summer and suddenly there was a dearth of young males.

June had barely noticed the arrival of the two boys on the next bench until her friend began raising her voice and her conversation took on a more daring tone. She glanced across at them and decided that Charlie couldn't possibly fancy either of them, therefore she must have it in mind to tease them a little.

This meant she had to join in. She always followed Charlie's bold lead.

'People in Dartmouth are so behind the times,' she sighed, raising her voice so the boys would hear. 'I was telling Miranda Hutchings the other day that I'd smoked a joint when I was in London and she said, "I didn't know you could smoke meat, I thought it was only fish."'

Both girls sniggered at this joke they'd recently read in a much-thumbed old copy of *Private Eye*. Neither girl had even seen cannabis, much less had the opportunity to try smoking it.

'Miranda Hutchings is such a block-head,' Charlie said, flicking back her hair and casting a flirtatious sideways look at the two boys. Miranda was entirely fictitious, but a useful medium through which the girls could appear cool. 'I was talking about Woodstock the other day, she said she'd been there. Of course I didn't believe her and I asked her questions about it. It turned out she meant the Woodstock near Oxford. She'd stayed there with her auntie last summer. She didn't even know about the rock festival in America.'

June giggled. She thought Charlie was absolutely brilliant at this game, another five minutes and she'd be talking about the three-day rock event as if she'd actually been there. 'Shall we go down to the record shop and listen to a few sounds?' she asked. She actually liked the look of the dark-haired boy, even if he was spotty, but she knew Charlie would laugh at her if she admitted it, and what's more she'd want to back off immediately for fear of getting lumbered with the other one.

'It's too hot for that,' Charlie said with an exaggerated sigh. 'Besides, they'll never let us listen to Pink Floyd, they only like putting on "In the Summertime" or "Yellow River" because all the tourists like that rubbish.'

June was tempted to remind Charlie that she'd bought Mungo Jerry's 'In the Summertime' only last Saturday and couldn't wait to get home to play it. But along with always expecting, and getting, the first pick of boys, Charlie didn't like it when June pulled her up on a technicality. 'What do *you* want to do then?' she asked.

'I fancy going skinny-dipping down by the Castle,' Charlie said without any hesitation.

June might have gasped if she hadn't been so well trained by her friend to go along with anything, however outrageous, without showing the slightest alarm.

'Okay then,' she said, getting up from the seat. 'But we'd better get a move on, I'm supposed to be home by five.'

Charlie stood up, linked arms with her friend, and they walked on down the Embankment. She knew without a shadow of a doubt that the two boys would follow in a few minutes.

'Are you serious?' June said nervously once they were out of earshot.

'No, of course not,' Charlie sniggered. 'Do you really think I'd let two runts like that see me naked? What we'll do is get our bikes, then ride off towards the Castle. We can hide in the woods at Warfleet Creek and watch for them to come running past.'

'That's a bit cruel,' June, who was soft-hearted,

protested. 'It's far enough to the Creek without send-ing them on a wild goose chase all the way to the Castle.'

'I like being cruel to boys,' Charlie grinned impishly. 'It serves them right for thinking dirty thoughts, and for a couple of creeps like them to imagine they had even half a chance with us two.'

June didn't protest any further. Her father had often claimed she would jump off a cliff if Charlie told her to.

As the girls were unlocking their bicycles from the railings of the car park, half hidden by a tree, they saw the boys coming along. They were looking this way and that, clearly puzzled by the girls' disappear-ance. Seen on the move, they looked almost like Boy Scouts, with their khaki shorts, neat checked short-sleeved shirts and very short hair – they even wore socks with their plimsolls. Even June recognized them as 'mother's boys'. No normal boy of their age would be seen dead in any other kind of shorts than cut-down Levis, or with hair cut that short.

'I bet their normal hobby is train-spotting,' Charlie giggled. 'Come on, let's shoot past them and make them start running.'

The girls rode across the road, and as they passed the boys, Charlie tinkled her bell and blew a kiss in their direction, then turned her head to make sure June was right behind her.

June was pedalling for all she was worth to keep up on her mother's old black Raleigh with its big leather seat. Charlie's bike was a sleek, drop-handle-bar racing model, with white tyres and three gears. Before long, June was left way behind. Charlie liked to show off on her bike and rode like a mad thing, recklessly weaving in and out of the traffic. She was waiting by the wall at Warfleet Creek as June coasted down the hill, still panting from the steep climb up.

'What kept you?' Charlie asked with a trace of sarcasm. She looked as cool as when she'd set out this morning, there wasn't even a bead of perspiration on her dainty nose. 'You didn't go back to check they were following us?'

'No, I didn't, my bike hasn't got gears like yours, remember,' June retorted. 'Besides, why should I check? If you say they'll follow us, they will, you're always right, or so you keep telling me.'

Charlie just laughed at her friend's barbed retort. That was as nasty as June could get, she wasn't capable of real anger. 'I'll carry your bike down,' she said in an unusual effort to appear big-hearted. 'You look hot and mine's a lot lighter.'

It was cool down in the woods at the edge of the Creek. As small girls they'd often come here with June's parents for picnics, and it was still a favourite place to come to swim and sunbathe. They hid their bikes under a bush, then settled down on a con- veniently well-placed fallen tree trunk to wait and watch the road above them.

'If we had some binoculars we could probably see your mum in your garden,' June said after a bit as she gazed out across the river estuary to Kingswear. They both lived there, in Beacon Road, but while June's house was tucked away behind others, 'Wind- ways', Charlie's home, was ten minutes' walk further on and right on the cliff edge, with a spectacular sea

7

view that was the envy of everyone who visited the house.

Charlie didn't need binoculars to know what her mother was doing. She'd be doing exactly what she did every hot, sunny day, lying like a starfish on the lawn, her cigarettes and magazines close to hand. But she didn't say this. Her mother's total idleness was something of an embarrassment to her.

Ten minutes passed, fifteen and then twenty, but still the boys hadn't come along. 'I thought you said they'd run all the way?' June sniped.

'Actually I'll be very relieved if they don't come.' Charlie shrugged. 'It just proves they really were mummy's boys. Besides, they were foul.'

June knew that in fact Charlie was disappointed, not only because it suggested she wasn't as alluring as she imagined, but also because there was nothing she liked better than a good laugh at someone else's expense. By pretending she hoped they wouldn't come, she saved face. That was all-important to her.

June didn't feel any necessity to keep face, because she never really imagined any boy could fancy her. But then she didn't have that inner confidence Charlie had. To her mind her friend was perfection, with her looks, height, slender body and superb legs. Even June's own father had often remarked that Charlie Weish was a potential heart-breaker. On top of this she was effortlessly clever. June had revised for weeks before the exams and doubted she'd get more than one or two 'C's. Charlie larked about and hardly ever did her homework, but she somehow managed to retain everything she'd been taught. It wasn't fair really. Sometimes June felt she ought to hate the girl for showing her up.

But no one really hated Charlie. Most of the girls were a little jealous of her and often tried to put her down, but they still agreed she was fun. She made everyone laugh with her dry, often cynical wit. She charmed them with her bursts of generosity and enthusiasm; wilful, often callous, pampered and self-centred, yet still adorable. Right from the first day they'd met aged seven at Higham House Preparatory School, they'd been friends. June believed they always would be.

'Maybe they ran into their parents,' June said after another ten minutes had passed. 'Let's go home, Charlie. If we do bump into them before we get to the ferry we can just wave and make them sick they missed seeing us.'

Charlie agreed and got up to haul their bikes out of the bushes. As they struggled back up the steep steps carrying them, June asked if she could go home with Charlie to listen to her *Woodstock* album.

The three-day rock festival in America was one of Charlie's passions, which was why she'd brought up the subject earlier that day. Although it had in fact taken place in August of the previous year, news of it had only really filtered down to Devon once the film of it and the album of the soundtrack were released.

Charlie had been aware for over a year that there was something exciting and revolutionary going on elsewhere, in London, Amsterdam and America. She went to great lengths to find copies of *International Times*, *Private Eye* and any other underground publication which talked straight about Flower Children, rock culture and drugs. Although she wished she could have been one of those 400,000 people who had flocked to see Jimi Hendrix, Jefferson Airplane and all the other great rock bands at Woodstock, her interest wasn't merely as a frustrated groupie. It was something much deeper, and she was terribly afraid that by living here in such a staid little town she was missing out.

She knew there were conclaves of hippies moving out of London, setting up communes in Glastonbury in Somerset, or going on down to Cornwall. A few of them had taken root as close as Totnes, but they bypassed Dartmouth. Whether that was because they knew they wouldn't get a rapturous welcome in such a middle-class town, or just that it didn't happen to be on a ley-line, something which appeared to be part of the culture, Charlie didn't know. But apart from a few hippie beads and tie-dyed tee-shirts appearing in Dartmouth's one and only trendy boutique, Flower Power was not in evidence anywhere here. Charlie was frustrated by this. She had another two years of school to go and it was awful to think something so momentous might be over before she got a chance to experience any of it.

'Did you hear what I said?' June asked when they reached the top of the steps. They were both panting with the exertion and she thought this was why her friend hadn't answered her question. 'Could I come home with you?'

'I don't think you'd better. Mum was in one of her funny moods this morning,' Charlie replied hesitantly, pushing her bike up the hill as it was too steep to attempt to ride immediately.

June made no comment. Although Charlie rarely spoke about either of her parents, she had known for some time that Mrs Weish wasn't quite right. On several occasions she'd called round for Charlie to find her mother just sitting in a chair, chain-smoking and looking sullen. June's own mother offered the opinion that the woman didn't have enough to occupy her mind; her father said Sylvia Weish was neglected by her husband.

June wasn't convinced that either of these views was correct. It was true her own mother was un-usually energetic, always rushing around to PTA meetings, Women's Institute, baking cakes or redec-orating one of the rooms, but then she was ordinary, plump and mumsy, and perhaps a little jealous of glamorous women like Mrs Weish. As for her father's opinion, well, every time June saw Mr Weish he seemed to make a great deal more fuss of his wife and daughter than ever her father did of his wife and family.

Charlie realized June was waiting for some sort of an explanation. 'I think she's worried because Dad's been away so long. He hasn't phoned or written for ages, which is a bit odd.'

June's blue eyes widened. If her father was away for just one night he always telephoned, sometimes more than once. She paused in pushing her bike, very out of breath. 'Maybe he's gone somewhere remote where there aren't any phones,' she said quickly. 'He can't possibly find all those lovely things he sells in big cities.'

Jin Weish's real Chinese name was Jin Wing Wei Shi, but he'd adopted the abbreviated version when

11

he arrived in England in 1949. He was an importer of Oriental antiquities and rugs. 'Windways' was entirely furnished with such things.

'That's what I keep telling Mum, but I think she imagines he's got another woman,' Charlie said with a tight little laugh as if such a thought was utterly ridiculous. 'After all, if he did have a mistress somewhere, he'd be doubly sure to phone home, wouldn't he?'

June had learned to her cost that it was wiser to agree with Charlie, even when she sounded as if she wanted an honest opinion. 'Of course he would. Besides, he loves your mum dearly, anyone can see that. She's the prettiest woman in Dartmouth and Dad always says how much fun she is at parties too.'

Once at the top of the hill, the girls coasted down towards the ferry at Bayards Cove. It wasn't until they had reached the Kingswear side of the river and were once again having to push their bikes up the hill that they spoke again. June suggested that if the weather held out till tomorrow they could take a picnic and ride their bikes to Blackpool Sands.

'Okay,' Charlie agreed. 'Are you going to wear your new bikini?'

'I don't know if I dare,' June giggled. She always felt like a carthorse next to her slender friend. 'My tummy's a bit fat!'

'It's not,' Charlie replied. Although she was somewhat smug in private about her own body, she always made a point of hiding this from her friend. 'I wish I was a bit more womanly and curvy like you.'

They stopped to chat for a moment outside June's

12

house. It was a tall, narrow Victorian semi-detached, perched high on the hill with a long flight of steps up to it: one of the oldest houses in Beacon Road, and the least commanding. Mr Melling, who was a professor at Exeter University, had inherited it from his grandmother, and for years he'd been talking of selling it and moving to something modern, easily reached on a flat road. But he still hadn't put it up for sale, the steeply sloping garden at the side was like a jungle and the house hadn't had a lick of paint outside in decades.

'If Mum's okay when I get back I'll ask her if you can come up and stay the night,' Charlie said, leaning on her bike. 'I'll phone you and let you know. If she is still miserable, I suppose I'd better stay home this evening. I don't want her flying off the handle and grounding me.'

June sat on the steps as they made their plans for the next day. She wanted to invite her friend in, but only that morning her mother had warned her and her two younger sisters that she wasn't going to put up with the usual houseful of other people's children throughout the holiday.

Charlie pushed her bike the rest of the way home – it was too hot to make the effort to ride it. It was only four in the afternoon, and she dawdled, partly out of reluctance to get home early, partly to look at other people's homes and compare them with her own.

Every one was different: tiny quaint cottages squeezed up close to each other, then, here and there, an ultra-modern one with huge picture windows and glimpses of almost Hollywood interiors. There were several grand mansion-style houses with superb terraced gardens too, and when these came on the market they were always quickly snapped up by the very wealthy.

The most interesting thing about Kingswear, though, was that all the houses but the tiny old cottages faced the sea, and in the case of those which were perched on the cliff edge, like 'Windways', they could only really be appreciated from a boat down in the estuary. From the road they were mainly hidden by old stone walls and high fences.

It was said that 'Windways' had been built by a millionaire, but once they had moved in his wife became a nervous wreck because the huge expanse of sea from all the windows frightened her. Somehow Charlie doubted this. She couldn't imagine anyone not delighting in the view. Maybe it was a little bit scary in the winter storms, but you could shut that out with thick curtains.

She knew that one of the reasons June envied her so much was because her own home wasn't a bit luxurious. The Mellings weren't rich and what money they had was spent on their children's education rather than updating their home. Yet Charlie thought her friend would be amazed if she was to admit how often she wished her parents were as comfortingly ordinary as June's, and that she'd happily give up luxury if it would make her mother as happy and content as Mrs Melling.

But Charlie would never stoop to admitting such a thing. She was in many ways very Chinese – she believed in the necessity of keeping face, and tried to emulate her father's inscrutable manner. He had once made her look 'inscrutable' up in a dictionary, so she knew its real meaning. *That which cannot be penetrated. Wholly mysterious.* He claimed that cultivating such an image was to gain an invisible coat of armour, so that no one could wound you. Although Charlie hadn't always known what it was about her father that made him so different from other men, since she was a small child she had been taught and shown by both her parents' example that in public her behaviour must be unquestionably dignified, calm and polite.

She saw this at work when her parents hosted their many lavish parties, warm, gracious, totally charming and interested in their guests. No one would ever guess that when alone together they could be cruel, mean-spirited and swear at each other like troopers. Charlie had sometimes witnessed terrible rows, plates and pots being thrown, insults hurled, less than an hour before the start of a party. But the moment the doorbell rang and the first guest stepped over the threshold, they would be greeted with happy, welcoming smiles. Her parents could keep up this loving togetherness all evening, bandying tender little endearments to each other, praising one another, and doing it so effortlessly and sincerely that they were perceived as being on one long, loving honeymoon. But the moment the last guest had gone home, the fight would recommence and sometimes last for days.

Charlie had never been able to work out if there was a single serious underlying problem between her parents that caused these distressing rows. Sometimes they started over something as simple as her mother putting on a dress her father didn't like, or the wine merchant omitting to supply the expected number of bottles of gin. Charlie always fled to her bedroom when they started and vicious remarks overheard during the ensuing fights rarely made any sense to her. She comforted herself with the idea that perhaps all married couples were the same, but she didn't really believe it. June told her almost every last thing that went on in her house, including overhearing her parents making love, but she'd never mentioned any bitter rows.

'Why hasn't Dad phoned?' Charlie asked herself, stopping for a moment to catch her breath and look at the view of the estuary over a garden wall. The last time he'd called was the evening of her concluding exam at school. He had been away for some time even then, but he'd telephoned every single night to ask how she'd got on at whatever exam had been that day. That night he'd told both her and her mother that he was on his way to Rotterdam to chase up a shipment of goods. He thought he would be back within a week to ten days. But four weeks had passed since then.

Just a few days ago Charlie had suggested they call the police, but to her astonishment her mother had laughed at her. She said that was ridiculous and that he'd turn up soon with one of his plausible excuses. The sarcasm in her mother's voice had almost suggested she knew exactly where he really was. Charlie hadn't dared bring up the subject since.

It was that sarcasm and a kind of darkness in her mother that made Charlie sometimes reluctant to be at home alone with her. On the face of it Sylvia Weish had absolutely everything a woman could want: a beautiful home, enough help around it so she didn't need to lift a finger, money, jewellery and total freedom to do what she wanted. Considering the number of parties she threw and went to when Jin was home, she had enough friends to ask for some company if she was lonely. But all she did when Jin was away was stay at home. If it was cold or raining she sat in an armchair smoking and looking at a magazine. If it was sunny and hot she lay out in the garden. Nothing else – no hobbies, walks, chats on the telephone; she never even went shopping unless she was desperate for something.

Charlie wouldn't have objected to this if Sylvia had been content. But most of the time she looked downright miserable. In fact Charlie could sense her mother's mood the moment she opened the front door. It was like being enveloped in an invisible, cold fog. Even Mrs Brown, who came in three times a week to clean, had said she felt it too.

As Charlie approached 'Windways', she stood on tiptoe and looked over the wall down on to the side terrace, reminded that her father was always saying that one day it would be hers. Like most of the houses on the cliff edge it was remarkably unprepossessing from the road, but once you stepped in through the arched gateway and took the path around the side to look from the garden it was simply beautiful.

Built on three levels, each with its own terrace and huge windows, it was modern, yet timeless too. The outside was painted a soft cream almost yearly, with purple and blue clematis scrambling up as a vivid contrast. No wonder people constantly photographed it from their boats and glossy magazines often wished to feature it. But it was the spectacular view which had determined Jin Weish to buy it, back in 1956.

Charlie had no recollection of that time – she was only two – but she'd been told they lived in London, and while they were down in Devon on holiday, taking a leisurely walk towards the coastal path to Brixham, Jin had spotted the house. It wasn't for sale, but Jin was so determined to get a better look that he climbed down the steep wooded cliff by the Beacon and made his way back to the house and looked over the garden walls. He said he was moved to tears by the majesty of the panoramic view of the estuary, the old Castle on the opposite side and the lush green of the wooded cliffs. He made up his mind there and then that he was going to own it. Charlie had often heard his friends joke that he was the sort of man who got everything he wanted.

'I'm home!' Charlie called as she let herself in. Thursday was one of Mrs Brown's days, and she had clearly polished the parquet floor in the hall as the house smelled of lavender.

Charlie merely glanced into the drawing room; she didn't expect her mother to be in there on such a hot afternoon. It was a lovely room, decorated in shades of green and pale blue, with sliding patio doors on to both the side terrace and the one at the back over-looking the garden and sea. The blue and white canopies were pulled down outside to shade the room, giving it a curious, almost underwater appearance.

She went down the stairs into the spacious modern

kitchen, got herself a drink of orange squash from the fridge and a rock bun from the cake box, and went out through the back door. As she had expected, her mother was sunbathing on the lawn, tucked away down in her favourite corner between the small summer-house and the stone balustrading that ran along the cliff top, so that she couldn't be seen by anyone able to peer over the eight-foot walls. She was stretched out face down on a blanket, wearing just the bottom half of her turquoise bikini and a matching towelling turban covering her blonde hair.

It never ceased to surprise Charlie that Sylvia had kept her figure even though she took no exercise. She was still the same 36–24–35 she had been in her wedding photographs. Her fortieth birthday had been back in May, but she had virtually no lines on her face, no wobbly bits on her thighs or bottom, and her stomach was as flat as an ironing board.

'Hullo, Mum,' Charlie said cheerily. 'The tan's going well, you're catching up with me!'

Comparing sun-tans was a long-standing family joke. Both Jin and Charlie had only to sit out in the sun for a couple of hours and they turned brown. Sylvia, because of her fair skin, burned easily. Even if the sun shone non-stop for six weeks, she could never attain more than the light golden colour she was now.

Sylvia lifted her head and squinted up at her daughter. She had baby-blue eyes, framed by heavily mascara'd lashes. Even when she was alone she always wore mascara and lipstick, and her long nails were always varnished bright pink. 'What time is it?' she asked. 'I must have fallen asleep.'

'About fourish,' Charlie said. 'What are we having for tea?'

'I'm not hungry.' Sylvia fumbled beneath her for her bikini top and fastened it behind her back, arching her spine. She rolled over and sat up, adjusting the top more comfortably, then lit a cigarette. 'But there's some ham and salad in the fridge. You can get that yourself.'

Charlie knew that translated as 'Go away and leave me alone.' Sylvia didn't eat or cook when she was in one of her moods. She didn't ever eat much, but when she was normal she always made Charlie a good meal, even if she didn't share it.

'I'll go and have a bath first, I'm all sticky,' Charlie said. 'Shall I make you some coffee?'

Charlie's abilities in the kitchen didn't stretch beyond making instant coffee and sandwiches. Mrs Brown often said it was a disgrace and that all girls should learn to cook, wash, iron and clean. Charlie often wished she could learn to bake cakes, that looked like fun, but her mother hadn't the patience to teach her, Mrs Brown never had the time, and her school concentrated on academic achievements and sport.

Her mother lay down again, on her back this time, closed her eyes and took a deep drag on her cigarette. 'No, I don't think so,' she said eventually.

For a moment or two Charlie just sat beside her mother on the grass. She had a strong desire to punch her, anything to get some sort of real response. She wanted to be asked what she'd been doing all day, to be given some evidence that the woman was aware her daughter had been away from her since ten that morning. She wondered how much longer they could go on living this way, no real conversation, no interest, no affection. It was miserable, like living with a robot.

Her father wasn't like this. He wanted to know every last thing his daughter had done while he was away. He went out for walks with Charlie, looked at her homework, listened to her new records, asked about her friends. Yet for some unfathomable reason Charlie had never been able to discuss her mother's horrible moods with him. It seemed disloyal. Sort of sneaky. So she always pretended everything had been fine while he'd been away.

'I'll go and have a bath then,' Charlie said, getting up from the grass and looking down at her mother. She was tempted to try to ask what her problem was, but she didn't quite dare. She had tried in the past, but she always got fobbed off with excuses like being tired or having a headache. If she persisted, her mother was likely to withdraw even further into herself. It was clear to Charlie that wherever Sylvia Weish's mind was, she wasn't anxious to share it with anyone.

Upstairs in her bedroom at the top of the house, Charlie stripped off her jeans and kicked them across her immaculately tidy room with a touch of spite. It was a beautiful room, none of her friends at school had a bedroom to touch it. Peach and cream striped walls, soft peach carpet, and wall-to-wall cupboards stuffed with fashionable clothes. The four-foot bed had cream lace drapes around it, there was a padded window seat so she could sit and look at the view of the sea, and she had the best Pioneer stereo money could buy. But it felt worthless and somehow insulting

21

when the woman who'd chosen it all so carefully couldn't even be bothered to talk to her.

She thought she would try to get a summer job in the next day or so – anything was better than putting up with this all day, every day, for eight weeks. June would be going up to Scotland with her family in a couple of weeks' time, then there'd be absolutely nothing to do. If only her dad would come home!

Sylvia came to life when he walked in through the door. Suddenly there would be action, the radio playing, meals being prepared, chat and laughter. The telephone would begin to ring again, people ringing up to accept invitations to dinner, or to offer invitations to their house. There were the inevitable rows, of course, but even that was preferable to this stony silence.

'Windways' even had a different smell when Jin was home – fried bacon, his aftershave, freshly ironed shirts and shoe polish. He wasn't a big man, though tall for a Chinese, Charlie supposed, at five ten, but slender with small, delicate hands and feet. Yet he filled up the house somehow, made it a real home.

Charlie was in the bathroom running her bath when she heard a car pull up outside. The bathroom was on the side of the house, but because of its position and the high wall by the road, it was impossible to see anyone parking outside without leaning right out of the window. As she was naked this was out of the question, but she opened it wide and stuck her head out. As the car reversed into the space by the garage she saw the rear end of a dark blue car. She thought it was an old Consul or some similar model, but she didn't recognize it.

She waited a few moments for the front-door bell to ring, but it didn't. As she could hear the car engine still running, she thought it might be the gardener or his son perhaps dropping off some new plants or compost, so she got into the bath.

Some ten minutes later she realized the car engine was still ticking over, and curiosity made her get a move on. The gardener's son was a bit of a dish, all bronzed biceps and shoulder-length blond hair, and if he was out in the garden chatting to her mother it might be a good opportunity to get to know him better.

She dried herself hurriedly and pulled on some clean underwear, then ran into her bedroom to get a pair of shorts and a tee-shirt. Glancing out of her window, she saw it wasn't the gardener or his son, but two burly men talking to her mother as she sat on the rug.

From Charlie's viewpoint, her mother was partially obscured by one of the men crouching over her. It seemed to her, although she couldn't see properly, that he was holding her by the shoulders. The other man's back was also towards her, and he was bending over Sylvia as if questioning her. Both men wore dark blue overalls, like mechanics, and their stance appeared rather threatening.

Curious as to what was going on, and a little concerned, Charlie snatched up her discarded jeans from the floor and jumped into them, but as she struggled to pull up the zip, she heard her mother scream. Yet even before she got back to the window the scream was abruptly cut off.

What she saw made her gasp with horror and her

blood run cold. The man who she had felt was holding her mother before, was now forcing her back on to the grass and had one hand over her mouth. The other was holding a thick stick or rod across her knees, at first glance as if just to stop them thrashing about, but as Charlie watched, to her consternation he jumped heavily on to either end of it, clearly with the intention of breaking both her knees.

Charlie's frenzied yell was involuntary. Much later she wished she'd kept silent and merely run to telephone the police, then found a safe place where she could view the men for identification purposes and take the car number or anything which might have helped in their capture. But her reaction was instinctively protective.

Both men turned in her direction. As they were some twenty-five yards away from the house, and the sun was in her eyes, Charlie couldn't see them clearly enough to note their features, only that they were similar to each other, with close-cropped dark hair. Her mother was screaming again, this time in pure agony, and with that the men let her go and ran towards the house as if they were coming after Charlie.

She snatched up her top, raced along the landing and into her father's study, locked herself in and dialled 999. Her heart was thumping like a steam-hammer, as she expected that any minute the men would break down the door and grab her too. Although it couldn't have been more than a few seconds before her call was answered, it seemed like forever.

'There's two men hurting my mother,' she managed to get out. But even as the woman on the other end of the line was asking her to give her name and address, she heard the car engine revving up outside and the sound of tyres spinning on the gravel, and she dropped the phone and ran to the spare bedroom which had a view of the road. She was too late to get the number or make of car, all she saw was its rear end shooting down narrow Beacon Road at high speed.

Going back to the phone, she hastily explained the situation and where she was. Then she fled down the stairs and out into the garden to her mother.

For one brief moment she thought the whole terrible scene had been the work of her imagination. Sylvia was lying there on the rug as silent and still as she had been thirty minutes earlier when Charlie arrived home. Her blue towelling turban was still in place, her sun-glasses and packet of cigarettes were lying untouched on the blanket beside her. Birds were still singing in the woods on the cliff at the side of the house. Only the iron rod lying abandoned on the lush green grass proved that what she'd seen had really happened.

Sylvia must have slipped into unconsciousness with the pain, but as Charlie knelt down beside her, so she opened her eyes and groaned. 'My legs,' she croaked out, 'my legs.'

'Who were those men, Mum?' Charlie asked frantically, tears streaming down her face. 'Why did they do this to you?'

Sylvia writhed with pain, clutching at her daughter's arm, but didn't appear to be able to answer the question. Charlie could see an angry red weal, seeping with blood, across her knees. Unaccustomed as she was to seeing serious injuries, she could feel by the

25

strange jutting of bone in the kneecaps that they were crushed. She could only guess at how painful it must be and she didn't know what to do to help.

She hoped the police and ambulance would get there quickly. Kingswear was not easily accessible because the roads were so narrow and winding, and their house was at the far end of it.

'Stay very still,' she ordered her mother. 'I'll just go into the house to get you some water and something to put over you. Don't try to move, the police will be here any minute.'

To Charlie's amazement, Sylvia's eyes opened wide with a look of terror and she struggled to sit up. 'You called the police?'

Charlie pushed her mother back down. 'Of course I did. I dialled 999. They'll send an ambulance too.'

When Sylvia didn't answer, just turned her head away from her daughter and lay there sobbing, Charlie was totally baffled by her reaction. But assuming Sylvia was in deep shock, and too badly hurt to be rational, she ran back to the house.

After the heat of the garden, the kitchen felt very cool. Charlie splashed her own face with water, filled a glass, and seeing the long cotton shirt her mother usually put on after sunbathing hanging over a chair, snatched it up. The shock of what she'd witnessed was making her shake, but struggling to control herself, she went back outside.

Her mother had moved. She was now half sitting, leaning back on her elbows, looking at her knees in stunned horror, tears rolling down her face and staining it with mascara. Charlie knelt beside her and

26

supporting her with one arm, held the glass to her lips for her to sip it. 'Do you think you could manage to put your shirt on?' she asked gently as she put the glass down.

To her surprise her mother silently lifted one arm and allowed Charlie to slip the shirt on. This was heartening, suggesting her injuries were not quite as serious as she first thought. But as the second arm went into the shirt Sylvia screamed out again in agony, so Charlie laid her down gently, buttoning up the shirt round her.

'Don't try to move again,' she said. She could hear the siren of a police car in the distance and hoped it was coming here. 'The ambulance men will give you something for the pain, just hold on.'

'What did you tell the police?' Sylvia asked in a strangled tone, clutching Charlie's hand so tightly it hurt.

'Only what I saw from the window, the two men hurting you. Who were they, Mum?' she repeated. 'Were they something to do with Dad?'

Sylvia groaned again. Charlie could see by the way her forehead was furrowed with lines that she was struggling not to scream aloud with the pain and her heart went out to her. 'I love you, Mummy,' she whispered. 'Try to tell me what this was about.'

Her mother looked at her, her eyes bleak and agonized. 'I can't. I don't understand it all myself,' she said in a whisper. 'All I can say is that your father is in bad trouble. It's been coming for years and now it's finally caught up with him. But you must say nothing about him to the police, Charlie. Promise me?'

*

27

The police and ambulance arrived simultaneously just a few minutes later, and as their first priority was to get Sylvia into the ambulance and off to hospital, Charlie wasn't questioned in any depth. She related only what she had seen through the bedroom window, and as her mother lost consciousness while she was being lifted on to a stretcher, she couldn't be asked anything.

But once at Dartmouth Hospital, after Sylvia was first x-rayed and then taken away to the operating theatre, a policeman who introduced himself as Detective Inspector Willows took Charlie into a small office to talk to her. Although he was a local man, judging by his strong Devonshire accent, Charlie had never seen him before. He was a very big man, at least six foot, with the kind of powerful physique she associated with rugby players. He had a red face, shiny with perspiration which he kept mopping up, and he seemed puzzled rather than angry that something like this had happened on his territory.

'You say the men didn't ring the front-door bell but came straight through the gate and round the side of the house to the garden. That suggests to me that they had been to the house before and knew your mother and her routine well. Are you sure you haven't seen them before?'

Charlie shook her head. She had been very shaky and frightened back at the house, but now, mostly because of her mother's plea for her to say nothing about her father, she felt even more frightened and menaced. She began to cry again.

'There, there.' The policeman patted her shoulder comfortingly. 'I know this has been a terrible shock to you, Charlie, but it's important we catch these men as quickly as possible and we can't do that unless you give us some detail. Now, how tall were they, were they fat, thin? Did they have a beard or moustache? How long was their hair?'

She felt so foolish being unable to describe them in any detail. 'Burly men in dark blue overalls' could be absolutely anyone. When she said she thought they were tall, Willows asked her how she could judge that if she was looking down at them. When she said they looked alike, both with very short dark hair, he pulled her up again and asked if she was sure about that.

'I don't know,' Charlie sobbed. 'I couldn't see them that clearly, the sun was in my eyes.' She said she guessed them to be in their thirties, and they were both clean-shaven.

'They weren't Chinese then?' he asked.

'No, of course not.' She was surprised by such a question. Apart from her father she didn't know any Chinese people.

The man shrugged. 'That's a shame, they might have been easier to trace. Where is your father, Charlie?'

Charlie faltered. 'I don't know exactly, he's away on business.'

'When are you expecting him home?'

She had no choice but to say she didn't know that either, and by the time she had admitted she had no contact telephone number for him, or even an address, and he had been gone for some weeks, she knew it was as obvious to this policeman as it was to her that Jin's long absence and the attack on her mother were inextricably linked.

'Has he ever been away before and failed to contact you and your mother?'

'Yes,' Charlie said weakly. This wasn't strictly true, a week was the longest they'd ever gone without contact, but in the circumstances she thought it better to lie. 'He goes to places it's difficult to phone from.'

'Did he take his car with him?'

'Yes, he always does.'

'Well, where does he leave it when he goes abroad? At the airport, a friend's home, or does he drive it across to the Continent?'

'I don't know.' She shrugged. She'd never thought of that before, all she ever saw was him driving off in it, and coming back in it. His navy-blue Rover was as much part of her father as his dark suits and briefcase. 'I think he takes it on the car ferry sometimes, but I don't know for certain.'

The questions went on and on and most she had no answer for. Did her father have an office in London? What shipping company did he use for his imports? Did he have any business partners? Who was his closest friend?

'You are sixteen, Charlie,' the policeman said at length, looking at her intently. 'I find it very strange that you know so little about your father's business. Can you tell me why this is?'

'Dad doesn't talk about business when he gets home,' she said indignantly. She felt the man was suggesting she was stupid as well as a liar. 'Sometimes he talks about the things he has bought, like a new batch of rugs, or where he's been, but that's all. There are so many other things to talk about.'

*

By eight o'clock that evening Charlie was beside herself with anxiety, fluctuating between bouts of pacing up and down the small waiting room and sinking into a chair and sobbing hysterically. Her mother was still in the operating theatre and the nursing staff were unable to make any predictions about whether she would ever be able to walk again unaided because all the bones in her knees had been shattered.

Would she be able to stay alone at 'Windways' while her mother was in hospital? Would she still be able to be the Carnival Queen?

Detective Inspector Willows had gone away, but before he left he said he would return in the morning to question Sylvia and get her permission to go through her husband's private papers to find out more about his business interests. Charlie had a sickening feeling this would bring even more trouble.

On her own, with nothing else to do to distract her from thoughts of what she'd seen for herself and heard from her own mother's lips that afternoon, she knew those two men were almost certainly trying to find out from her where Jin was. As their attack on her was so brutal, it followed that Jin must have done something nasty to them.

Adding that to all the questions she had been unable to answer adequately for the police, her mother's dark moods, her fear of the police, and the rows between her parents, it became increasingly obvious to Charlie that her father couldn't possibly be the respectable businessman she'd always believed him to be.

That thought hurt her the most because she loved him. She supposed she loved her mother too, but she never *felt* it the way she did with her father. He was the one she ran to, the one she confided in, played with, laughed with, who provided the sunshine and warmth which were lacking in her mother.

He was her rock, unfailingly good-humoured, comforting, stable and dependable. He spoke often of honour, he despised liars, bullies and thugs, in fact to her mind he had all the virtues gentlemen were supposed to have.

It was as if she was standing on the edge of a cliff, and the ground was slowly slipping away beneath her feet. As she tried to pull herself back by clutching on to good memories of her father, so they seemed to shrink and slip through her hands. All at once she sensed that everything she had taken for granted in her life was under threat.

Just before ten the ward sister opened the door of the waiting room and beckoned for Charlie to come with her. 'You may see your mother now, just for a few minutes,' she said.

'Is she better?' Charlie was still enough of a child to imagine nurses and doctors could accomplish miracles.

Sister half smiled. She had a worn-looking face, and a soft Welsh lilt to her voice. 'Well, she's conscious again, that's something. She won't be up to talking much until tomorrow, but she'll feel better for seeing you.'

The sister led Charlie along a corridor, explaining her mother was in a room on her own. Charlie had never been inside Dartmouth Hospital until today, even though it was situated right on the quay and as familiar a building as the post office and bank. Other people had said hospitals made them feel sick, but she hadn't felt that way, despite the peculiar smells and the serious business of tending the sick going on all around her; yet as she walked into her mother's room and saw her lying flat on her back with a drip in her arm, and a sort of cage contraption holding the bedclothes away from her legs, Charlie suddenly felt faint.

For the first time ever Sylvia looked forty. Her tan seemed to have faded, without lipstick her lips were bloodless, her blonde hair appeared greasy and lank.

'It's me, Charlie. How are you feeling?' Charlie whispered as she approached the bed. Sylvia's eyes were closed; her lashes without the usual thick mascara were thin and very fair.

Her eyelids fluttered and opened just a crack. 'Poorly,' she said as if with great effort. 'My legs!'

Charlie glanced at the cage under the covers. Sister's words earlier about making no predictions for the future still rang in her ears.

'They'll be fine, Mummy,' she lied. 'You'll be walking and dancing again in no time.'

Her mother's eyes opened just a little wider, they looked like cold blue glass. 'I won't count on it,' she said and closed them again as if dismissing her daughter.

'I'll come and see you tomorrow and bring you a nightie and stuff,' Charlie said, fighting back tears. 'Don't worry about me.'

It struck her as she left the ward that her mother hadn't said goodbye, or even asked if she had somewhere safe to stay for the night. Maybe it was all part of the effects of the anaesthetic, but it felt like she didn't care. Tears trickled down Charlie's cheeks as she made her way along the corridor. She wasn't used to making decisions for herself, not about important things. Who was going to look after her?

Chapter Two

'You poor darling!' Mrs Melling exclaimed, jumping out of her armchair as her husband led Charlie into her sitting room. 'Why on earth didn't you phone us earlier? We saw the ambulance and police car of course, but we never guessed it had come from your house. We would have come straight down to the hospital. But how is Sylvia? Come and sit down and tell me all about it.'

Charlie's misery had increased after seeing her mother, with the realization that absolutely no one had considered her needs. The police had been quick enough to take her keys to the house, but hadn't asked if she had anywhere else to go. She didn't even have any money for the ferry across the river or a phone call. She had to ask if she could use a hospital phone and then had the acute embarrassment of trying to explain to the Mellings what had happened.

'I'm sorry I had to bother you,' she said in a small voice, fighting back tears. She was suddenly terribly ashamed. Whatever she said about this attack on her mother, the Mellings were bound to imagine her father was involved in something shady.

'Bother me!' Mrs Melling's voice rose to an indignant squeak. 'We've known you since you were

35

a little girl and I'd have been very hurt if you *hadn't* come to us for help. Why, this is almost your second home!'

Such warmth was typical of Diana Melling. Charlie had always thought of her as a *proper* mother. Although she was no older than Sylvia, she looked more like fifty, comfortably plump, with an old-fashioned wavy hair-style and no more than a faint hint of lipstick. She usually wore an apron over rather shapeless cotton dresses and she seemed entirely content cooking, cleaning and ironing for her family. Mr Melling was a jolly sort too, most of the time, a tall, gangly sort of man with a bushy beard and untidy, too long hair. When the children were younger he organized games of cricket or rounders, fixed dolls' legs back on bodies and liked to read them stories.

It was very true that the Mellings' was a second home. Charlie had spent a great deal of time in it over the last nine years. It was only when she reached adolescence that she realized the Mellings were poor compared with her parents. As a child she had never noticed the decor or furniture, only delighted in the fact that here she was allowed to spread toys on the floor, build tents with the clothes-horse, and make as much noise as she liked with June and her younger sisters Nicola and Susan. She had climbed trees in their garden, played in the sandpit, and made shops in the kitchen using the entire contents of Mrs Melling's cupboards.

Sitting on the settee beside June (the two younger sisters were already in bed), Charlie told them about her mother's condition, giving a little more detail than she had on the phone as to how it had all come about.

But she said nothing about her father, other than that he was still away from home. She sensed that Mrs Melling had dozens more questions, and dreaded them, but thankfully her husband intervened.

'Charlie's had a tough time. I think she should have some hot milk and a sandwich and get off to bed,' he said, patting her shoulder. 'I put the camp-bed in June's room for you.'

Mrs Melling took Charlie out into her kitchen and began to rustle up food. June came too and perched on a stool at their rather elderly and rickety breakfast bar, her wide blue eyes full of unasked questions.

'It was a good job you didn't stay here this afternoon,' she remarked. 'Imagine if your mother had been lying all alone out in the garden until late tonight! I bet the burglars would have taken just about everything in your house if you hadn't called out of the window to them.'

Charlie was on the point of saying she didn't think robbery had been the men's motive, but she stifled it. Maybe it was best to let them think that.

Mrs Melling put a ham sandwich, a banana and a glass of milk in front of Charlie. 'I don't suppose you feel much like eating, but try, dear,' she said persuasively. 'You'll sleep better on a full tummy and tomorrow morning when we phone the hospital we might find your mother is a great deal better. There's every chance the police might have managed to contact your father by then too. So eat up and then off to bed.'

Charlie didn't find it easier to sleep on a full tummy, in fact she felt sick most of the night. The camp-bed was uncomfortable, it wobbled every time she turned over, and her mind was stuck on what she'd seen those men do to her mother.

Odd things, seemingly unrelated to the day's events, kept popping into her head. Like her parents discussing the London gangland killers, the Krays. Their trial had been a couple of years ago. She remembered how both her parents had seemed obsessed with it, almost as if they had known the men. Looking back, her father had never shown much indignation about crime. He didn't even get worked up about drugs the way her friends' parents did. She had always prided herself that this was because her father was a very liberal man, but now she saw that it might well be because he was, or had been, something of a villain himself.

Charlie tried to think back to when they lived in London. She vaguely remembered a small terraced house which she'd been told was in Hammersmith. She recalled that in those days Jin went out to work in the evenings. She had a distinct mental picture of him tucking her into bed and kissing her goodnight before he left. He always wore a bow-tie and his hair was slicked back with some kind of perfumed oil.

So what did he do at night in those days? Neither of her parents had ever said.

Charlie was glad the Mellings got up early. She might have fallen asleep for an hour or two, but the night had seemed endless. As soon as she heard Nicola and Susan talking to their parents downstairs, she got up too, washed, dressed and went down, without waking June.

'Hullo, dear.' Mrs Melling smiled brightly. 'You're up early. Couldn't sleep?'

Charlie nodded. She had a strong desire to fall into her friend's mother's arms and sob her heart out, but such displays of weakness went against the grain.

'Well, sit yourself down here.' Mrs Melling patted a stool. 'Sue and Nicky have gone out to feed their rabbits and Herbert's in the breakfast room reading the paper, so you can talk freely if you want to.'

Charlie had already made up her mind that she wasn't going to be drawn into any confidences. 'I would like to say how kind it is of you to take me in,' she said. 'I'll try very hard not to be a nuisance.' She thought her father would approve of that, he had always said good manners were important. He had once told her that everything he knew, including his perfect English, he learned back in Hong Kong, from British naval officers. He said he had studied their manners, opening doors for ladies, walking on the outside of a pavement, how to hold a knife and fork correctly, and how to thank people graciously. He said that the Chinese were naturally polite, but their way was subservient. The British way was regal and he much preferred it.

'My dear, how could you be a nuisance?' Mrs Melling replied with a warm smile, even though she was a little surprised by the girl's chilly response. 'With all my children, one more won't make any difference to me! Until your father gets back, this is where you'll stay. Now, let's have a cup of tea before we start the breakfast.'

*

39

Five days later, on Tuesday morning, Charlie was feeling desperate, sick with fear and foreboding. Her father still hadn't turned up and down at the hospital the nursing staff were now very concerned about her mother's state of mind. Although the operation on her knees had been successful, Sylvia was sinking daily into a deeper and deeper depression. She fluctuated between wild bouts of anger directed at her husband, irritation at Charlie and extreme self-pity because she was convinced she'd never walk again. Yet for all this she still stubbornly persisted in saying she didn't know who her attackers were or why they came, and refused to tell either Charlie or the police anything about her husband which might help find him. Charlie was sure she knew quite a lot on both counts. So why wouldn't she talk about it?

Her life seemed to have turned upside down.

Until this awful thing had happened, everything was so orderly and predictable. A freshly ironed school shirt miraculously turned up on a chair in her room every morning, breakfast was laid on the kitchen table, and her dinner money in an envelope placed each Monday morning by her school bag. When she returned from school, tea was on the table, she did her homework on a desk that had been tidied during the day. Two evenings during the week she was allowed out, but she had to be in by ten-thirty.

This ordered life carried on even when her father was home. Charlie rarely saw how the house was run, it happened invisibly, just as she rarely saw cakes baked or shoes cleaned. They just were.

But here in the Mellings' home it was all noise and

frantic activity. Before and after every meal there were rows. Who was going to lay the table? Whose turn was it to wash up? They argued about when the rabbits were last cleaned out, who had left a ring around the bath. Nothing in this house happened by magic.

The police were in and out all the time with different questions relating to her father, and she sensed Mr and Mrs Melling were getting very irritated by that and by the publicity. Although the story about the attack was only a few lines on the inside pages of the national papers, the local press splattered it across the front page, and that had given rise to a great deal of gossip and speculation around the town. If her father had been English, maybe people would have been kinder, prepared to believe her parents were innocent victims. But because he was Chinese, wealthy and lived in one of the most envied homes in the area, it followed that there had to be something dubious about him. Judging by overheard conversations between Mr and Mrs Melling, Charlie guessed her father was being labelled as everything from a drugs baron to a member of the Triads.

Yet the most distressing thing of all to Charlie was that her mother showed absolutely no concern about *her*. She didn't ask if she minded being with the Mellings, or indeed if they minded having her there. She showed no sympathy when Charlie told her how the neighbours kept pestering her for information. Then when she asked if she could have some pocket money, her mother nearly bit her head off and said, 'Don't you think I've got enough on my plate already without you demanding money?'

Charlie felt almost suffocated by people and their

endless questions. Although in the past she had often envied June for being part of a big family, she had soon discovered they weren't as happy as she'd always thought. Mr Melling roared like an ogre. Nicola and Susan seemed to fight all day. Mrs Melling was shocked that Charlie hadn't the first idea how to make a bed, iron a dress or even wash up. Several times she had pointedly remarked that she had no room for ornaments in her home.

Even June, who she'd expected to be supportive and understanding, seemed sulky and cross. Charlie thought it was obvious why she couldn't wander about town chatting up boys, or go swimming while all this was going on, but June implied her holiday was being spoiled. Perhaps it was just because she had always relied on Charlie to make fun things happen, and now she was bored she had to blame someone for her disappointment. But the strain of sharing a small room with someone who flounced around making barbed comments made Charlie withdraw even further into herself. She found herself aching for solitude.

On Tuesday morning when Charlie woke to another fight between Nicola and Susan, she made up her mind she was going home if only for a few hours. The houseplants would need watering and she could sit peacefully in her own room.

She had been allowed to go back to 'Windways' the day after the attack, to collect some clothes for herself and nighties and toiletries for Sylvia, but she had been accompanied by a policewoman. The fact that her front-door key hadn't been returned to her made it clear she wasn't supposed to return there, but as she'd helped herself to a spare key in the kitchen, no one would be any the wiser.

She didn't go straight to 'Windways'; to do so might result in her being spotted by a neighbour. Instead she walked down the road, away from her home, then turned right up Ridley Hill and took a long and circuitous route to a footpath that brought her back to Beacon Road, far beyond 'Windways'.

Almost as soon as she set out she felt better, and when she got to a part of the footpath where she had a clear view of the sea, she sat down to look at it.

It was utterly peaceful, the sun warm on her face, birds singing in the trees, insects buzzing in the under-growth. The sea far below was azure blue, calm as a mill-pond, broken only by one lone speedboat pulling a water-skier. As she sat there thinking how often she'd stopped in this exact same place with her father, it suddenly occurred to her how little she knew about his background, or her mother's.

Her father had told her he was born about 100 miles from Shanghai, and he had been twelve when the Japanese invaded in 1932. His father and his elder brother were killed. He saw their tiny house burned down by Japanese soldiers, and his mother moved herself and the three younger children in with a relative. They were all starving and his mother urged Jin to leave, to find work in a city, so he trekked all the way to Hong Kong.

Until today that story had meant little to Charlie, but perhaps because for the first time in her life she was afraid and alone, it struck a chord. She wished now she had asked her father to tell her more about what happened when he got to Hong Kong, how he lived, how and when he got to England. Whether the rest of his family survived.

She knew even less about her mother. She once said she was secretary to a barrister, and that she'd met Jin when he first arrived in England. But that was all. Charlie didn't know where she was born, if she still had living parents or brothers and sisters.

Charlie thought about this deeply, trying to analyse why she'd never asked questions. When the answer came to her, it shamed her.

She was too self-centred.

June had accused her just yesterday of being spoilt rotten, and although Charlie had vigorously denied it, she knew in her heart it was true. If she wanted something, be it a bike, roller-skates or new clothes, she got it. Other kids at school had to do paper rounds for their pocket money, she got hers dished out without any suggestion she should work for it. It was for much the same reason that she couldn't cook, make a bed or even clean a bath properly. She'd never been made to do anything she didn't want to. They had Mrs Brown who cleaned and washed. Charlie Weish was a little princess who didn't need to be useful, because she was clever.

Tears sprang into her eyes. In the last few days in the Mellings' household she had become aware that being clever at school, being pretty and having good manners wasn't enough. What if her mother's knees didn't get better and she became a cripple? Who would look after her? Her father? But what if he never came back?

She began to sob. Yesterday she'd had to back down from being Carnival Queen because Mrs

Melling said she didn't think it was an appropriate role to play when her mother was in hospital. The summer holidays were ruined. Now it looked as if every plan she'd ever made was going to be dashed to pieces.

It was an hour or so later when Charlie approached 'Windways'. She paused by the steep wooded cliff with the navigational beacon on the rocks below and considered whether it might be better to enter her garden that way, however dangerous, to avoid being seen.

'Don't be ridiculous,' she told herself, walking on, holding her head high. 'It's your home, you have a perfect right to go in there.'

She stopped short as she rounded the bend and saw two cars parked by the garage. One was a new dark blue Rover which looked vaguely familiar, the other was a dark green Morris Minor. Obviously the owners were in the house. A sudden surge of irrational anger rose up inside her. The police had got her mother's permission to go in there the day after her attack, but Charlie didn't think they had any cause to return. And even if they had, surely they would have informed her of it?

Full of indignation, she opened the gate, marched up to the front door and let herself in with her key. To her astonishment the house was clearly in the process of being thoroughly searched. The book-shelves in the small sitting room to the left of the front door were bare, the books lying in piles on the floor. In the drawing room to the right, the bureau was open and letters and bills had clearly been leafed through.

Only her parents' bedroom appeared untouched, and male voices were coming from upstairs.

Charlie faltered for a moment, afraid it might be the men who hurt her mother, but her anger was much stronger than her fear. Pinpointing the voices as coming from her father's study, which was next to her bedroom, she picked up the cast-iron doorstop and crept up the stairs, then kicked the closed door open, brandishing the doorstop.

Two men were bent over the filing cabinet. 'What do you think you're doing in my house?' she shouted.

They both looked up. One was so surprised he dropped the batch of letters in his hands. She was relieved they weren't the same men who hurt her mother, they were much too small and old.

Before they could reply, the door partly closed again, then to her surprise James Wyatt appeared from behind it. 'Charlie!' he exclaimed. 'What on earth are you doing here?'

James Wyatt was a friend of her parents, she had met him at several parties here at the house. Now she remembered that the new blue Rover was his. 'I just came to water the houseplants,' she said, feeling a trifle foolish. 'This is my home, remember! What are these men doing?'

'We're police officers. CID,' the smaller and older of the two men said, his face cold and clearly irritated by the interruption. 'We do have a search warrant and Mr Wyatt is accompanying us because he is your father's lawyer.'

Charlie's stomach lurched. The man's curt manner implied he was searching for evidence of a crime and she had no business to be here.

'I thought you said Miss Weish had been informed about the search?' Wyatt said to the men. He came right out of the room and took the doorstop from Charlie's hand, putting his arm around her shoulders in a protective gesture.

'We thought she had been too, must have been a slip-up,' the policeman shrugged. He managed a tight smile. 'We're almost through here anyway, miss.'

'But what are you looking for?' Charlie asked.

The other man picked up the papers he had dropped, not even glancing in her direction. The older one gave a sort of shrug and looked at Wyatt as if expecting him to explain.

'Come downstairs with me, Charlie,' Wyatt said. 'We'll make some tea and have a chat while they finish up.'

Down in the kitchen the blinds were drawn and the table was strewn with the contents of a drawer Sylvia used for odds and ends. There were letters, odd bills and receipts, rubber bands and pieces of string.

Mr Wyatt let the blind up at the window and put the kettle on. Charlie looked at him curiously. He was dressed in a dark pin-striped suit with a stiff collar on his shirt. On all the other occasions she'd met him he had been casually dressed and she hadn't known what his profession was. He was a tall, well-built man with a hearty voice and a face to match. She remembered he shared her love of tennis; the last time he'd called at the house they had talked about Wimbledon.

She didn't know him very well, any more than she did most of her parents' friends, but the impression she'd got of him on several meetings was favourable – he wasn't snooty and he'd always been nice to talk to. Charlie thought she could trust him because her father obviously had.

'I'm very sorry you had to walk in and find all this,' Wyatt said, scooping up the contents of the drawer and putting it back where it belonged. 'After all you've been through already, this must seem appalling. I was intending to call at the Mellings' this evening to talk to you, after I'd seen your mother again. But maybe it's best that you are here now, at least we'll have some privacy.'

He turned away for a moment to make the tea. When he got milk from the fridge he sniffed it to make sure it hadn't gone off.

'Good old Mrs Brown's been in,' he said with a boyish grin. 'It's as fresh as a daisy. I shall have to pop up to see her too today. It's not fair on her to be so unsure about her position here.'

They sat down at the kitchen table and Mr Wyatt cleared his throat and took a sip of tea before speaking. 'What I need to tell you is going to be difficult, Charlie,' he said apologetically. 'Now, if I seem brusque, it's not that I don't care about your feelings, just that I want to explain it all as simply and clearly as possible.'

Charlie nodded.

'Your father is a friend along with being a client and as such it's my duty to protect you and your mother to the best of my ability in his absence.'

Charlie felt sick; that word *protect* suggested he

knew something even worse was going to happen soon.

'While the police's primary concern was with catching the two men who attacked Sylvia, your father's continuing absence has changed the direction of their investigations,' he went on.

'You don't mean they think he had something to do with it, do you?' Charlie interrupted him.

Wyatt looked apprehensive. 'I'm quite sure he wasn't responsible for it,' he said quickly. 'But the two things must be related in some way. I'm sure you can see that?'

'I think those men came here to find Dad,' Charlie said. 'Might they have found him and hurt him too?' Just voicing this tiny fear she'd had in the back of her mind made it seem larger and more plausible.

'I think that's unlikely,' Wyatt said. 'But trying to find your father has made it necessary for the police to look into his business interests. Unfortunately, some unexpected and very significant details have come to their notice which put a whole new slant on their investigation.'

'I don't understand. What details?' Charlie asked. 'Do you mean they've found he's been doing something bad?'

Wyatt looked uncomfortable and ran one finger round the collar of his shirt.

'Not exactly. It's more like odd things which don't fit into the image we all had of your father.'

'Like what for instance?' she asked with some indignation.

'Well, that he used to be a club owner in Soho?'

Charlie's eyebrows shot up into two inverted 'V' shapes.

'So you didn't know either! Oh dear!' Wyatt grimaced. 'I was shocked myself. In all the ten years I have known him as a friend and a client, he never even gave me a hint about it. I imagined he'd been in the importing business all his life.'

'What's wrong with owning a night-club?' Charlie was instantly on the defensive.

Wyatt looked even more uncomfortable. 'Well, discovering something like that, Charlie, is a bit like finding a locked box. If we could find the key to open it, we might find something inside which would help us to understand why those men hurt your mother.'

'Can't Mum help?'

Wyatt sighed deeply. 'I have tried to talk to her, but I didn't make any headway. She's so very angry. Of course that's understandable under the circumstances, she's in pain, her husband has disappeared, and her future looks grim to her.' He paused and frowned. 'She claims she knew nothing about his business, she even denied all knowledge of any clubs. I can't tell if she's speaking the truth or whether she's trying to shield Jin.'

'But why, and from what?' Charlie asked. Her stomach was churning, she could feel a cold sweat trickling down the back of her neck.

Wyatt shrugged. 'That could be what's in the locked box! Maybe she only suspects something and someone, and she's playing for time hoping Jin will get back to sort it out. But the most worrying thread in all this is money.'

Charlie was confused and frightened now. 'Money?'

'Yes, Charlie, money, or rather the lack of it. Now, forgive me if you don't understand all this, stop me if you want something explained more fully.

'Last year your father borrowed a great deal of money against this house. It was free and clear before that as he'd bought it with cash. He said he needed capital to expand his business and I handled the legal side of it for him. The mortgage company checked his accounts and as they were entirely satisfied with his credit-worthiness he received the money he needed in the early part of this year.

'When someone disappears, Charlie, one of the first things to be checked is a bank account, to see when and where it was last used. It was while doing that that the police discovered he had drawn out sixty thousand pounds in cash, plus everything from a savings account, and indeed almost emptying his current account, some months ago. He arranged it through a bank in central London.'

'Well, that's no one's business but his,' Charlie said indignantly. 'It's his money after all.'

'Of course it is,' Mr Wyatt said quickly. 'But in the light of his disappearance, and added to other things the police have found, it is rather suspicious.'

'What other things?' She didn't like the way this 'chat' was going at all.

'Well, they've found several unpaid bills, and it seems Jin is seriously behind with the mortgage payments on the house too. In fact the only thing we can find which has been paid was his life insurance, that was by standing order at the bank.'

Charlie gulped. She didn't fully understand what a mortgage meant, but she had the gist of what Mr Wyatt was getting at. Her dad had robbed Peter to pay Paul, but he'd overlooked the bills back home.

'What happens if someone doesn't pay their mortgage?' she asked, her voice trembling.

Wyatt sighed. 'Well, the very worst thing that can happen is that the mortgage company repossesses the house. That means they take it back. Of course, if Jin gets back in time and pays the arrears, everything will be fine.'

At this point they were interrupted by the police calling to him from the middle floor. Wyatt went up to speak to them. Charlie crept out to listen, but apart from hearing them mention some papers they were taking with them, the rest of their conversation was too muffled to follow. They left then and Wyatt came back downstairs into the kitchen looking extremely worried.

He sat down at the table again.

'What is it?' she asked after what seemed to be an interminable silence. 'Did the police find something else?'

He looked at her, and his eyes dropped from her firm gaze. 'Yes, Charlie,' he said at length. 'Something I hadn't anticipated and it's very serious. The last thing I want to do now when you already have so much anxiety is add to it. But as your family lawyer I would be derelict in my duties if I kept you and your mother in the dark about what is happening. What the police have just found was a registered letter. It was signed for by your mother, but unopened amongst a batch of others. It was from the Inland Revenue, warning your father that a bankruptcy order would be issued against him unless they received what he owed them within ten days.'

Charlie didn't understand. Bankruptcy was a word she'd read occasionally in the papers but she didn't know its real meaning.

Seeing her bewilderment, Wyatt explained it in simple terms. He also stated they had found other demands for this amount earlier in the day.

'I don't suppose he imagined they would press him for it so quickly,' he went on. 'I expect this deal he had up his sleeve was intended to sort everything out. Unfortunately the Inland Revenue do not wait indefinitely. As far as they are concerned, when the ten days are up and no payment is on their desk, that's it. That ten days passed some time ago.'

'But surely if we explain to them that my dad didn't see it and that we don't know where he is, they'll understand?'

James Wyatt was moved by the girl's naïvety. Just one look at her was enough to know all she'd ever had to do was ask and she received it. From her stylishly cut hair, trendy mini-dress, confident manner and cultured voice, everything about her said 'money'. But if the money was gone, she had some hard knocks coming to her.

James Wyatt was just a family lawyer, he handled wills, divorces, trusts and house purchases in the main, bankruptcy or criminal law wasn't his bag. What he'd stumbled on here now was well out of his sphere, and if he was honest with himself, he didn't want any part of it.

When the police called on him immediately after

Sylvia's attack and asked for his assistance, he'd steadfastly refused to believe Jin's disappearance was anything other than a coincidence. Jin was something of
a dark horse, he rarely spoke about his business and
never about his personal life, but in Wyatt's book
those were admirable qualities, he had no time for
men who boasted about their wealth and success.

Yet as the days had passed and disquieting facts
surfaced, so he'd begun to have his doubts about the
man he'd always trusted implicitly.

It looked very much as if Jin was an unscrupulous
bounder. He might not have anticipated the Inland
Revenue would take such action so soon, but he had
known the tax was well overdue, and that he hadn't
met the mortgage payments and other bills. Why,
then, had he drawn out all that money in cash and
disappeared?

To the police it had begun to look as if he'd hired
those men to hurt his wife, perhaps hoping it would
lead them to believe he'd been murdered by the same
gang and his body disposed of. As they had said so
succinctly, Jin wouldn't be the first man to go to such
lengths to start a new life, with a new identity.

On top of his anxiety about becoming embroiled in
a case which might affect his own standing in the
community, Wyatt was very puzzled by Sylvia
Weish's attitude. Her anger and distress at being
crippled were understandable enough, but why
wouldn't she speak out about what she knew of her
husband's business, unless she knew for certain that
to do so might precipitate more trouble and hurt for
herself? She was such a difficult woman to read, on
one hand she seemed entirely self-centred, com-

plaining loudly about her treatment in hospital and demanding to be moved to a private nursing home, on the other she seemed terrified of everything and everyone.

Charlie wondered why Mr Wyatt was taking so long to reply to her last question. 'What if I telephone the Inland Revenue myself and explain?' she suggested. 'I'm sure they won't do anything to Dad if I ask them not to.'

Wyatt shook his head at her innocence. 'I'm afraid you are wrong there. You see, they have to do it. They will make every effort to find him. Bankruptcy notices will be put in newspapers where he might see them. But if he doesn't come forward very quickly, the order will be made in his absence, his possessions seized by the Official Receiver and his creditors paid. It has to be, otherwise anyone who wanted to evade paying their debts could just skip off.'

Charlie fell silent for a moment, thinking about what that actually meant. Wyatt had said there were several debts apart from what her dad owed in tax. He hadn't paid the mortgage, and there was no money in his bank account to pay it either.

'They can't take the house surely? Where will we live?' She looked fearfully about her, she loved this house. She had believed it would one day be hers. 'What will Mum do if she can't walk again? She'll go bonkers if you tell her any of this!'

James didn't relish being the one forced to tell her. He could imagine her screaming so loud Jin would hear her wherever he was in the world. And what of Charlie? She was such a beautiful and intelligent young girl, spoiled maybe, but that wasn't her fault.

How was she going to cope when 'Windways' was taken and she had to try to rebuild her life with a bitter, crippled mother in tow?

'If the worst happens and your father doesn't return, I will of course act on your and your mother's behalf,' he said, choosing his words carefully. 'I will endeavour to get some financial provision made for you both. The house is in your father's name only I'm afraid, but should it be taken, I'll also do my best in helping find you somewhere else to live. So please don't think you are alone. As for essential household items, clothes, etc., they won't be taken by the Receiver.'

Charlie heard the word 'essential' and it seemed to have great significance. 'What does essential mean exactly?'

Wyatt heard the alarm in her voice and felt for her. 'Beds, bedding, table and chairs, a cooker, that sort of thing.'

Charlie felt as if someone had kicked her in the stomach. She had never paid much attention to the many beautiful artefacts around the house, but she knew they were valuable and none would be considered essential.

'And the rest of the stuff? They'll take that too?' she whispered.

'I'm afraid so,' he said wearily. 'You see, in bankruptcy everything is sold off and the money goes into a pot to be shared out to the creditors.'

There was utter silence for a moment. Wyatt looked at her stricken face and felt an absolute heel. He knew only too well what happened in cases of this kind. Between the Official Receiver's fees, the auctioneers' and lawyers', including his own, everyone stood to gain something, often far more than the creditors got. It was a shabby business, the goods in this house would be sold for a pittance to slimy dealers who plotted between themselves to keep the bidding ridiculously low. The person who would buy this splendid house would almost certainly have someone on the inside in the palm of their hand and get it at a rock-bottom price. Charlie and her mother's needs would be entirely disregarded. He felt he must do something to salve his conscience.

'If I give you a little tip, Charlie, will you promise me you'll keep it just between ourselves?'

Charlie nodded. 'Go on,' she urged him. 'I can be as secretive as Dad.'

Wyatt half smiled – her bland expression which gave nothing away reminded him strongly of Jin. He had a feeling she was capable of learning to be just as cunning too.

'Let's just say that no one yet has made an inventory of things in this house,' he said. 'They will of course, and possibly very soon, and at that time the doors will be sealed and no one will be allowed to take anything away. But right now there is nothing to prevent you taking some small pieces away to safety.'

She didn't understand what he meant exactly. Yet she sensed he was trying to help her. 'Like what for instance?'

He shrugged. 'I don't know what's here, do I?' he said pointedly. 'I do vaguely remember some rather fine miniatures once, though of course your father might have sold them. A quick look through your mother's jewellery box might be in order. It wouldn't do to take anything away that is too large to carry with you. Now let's have another cup of tea and then I'll leave you to water those houseplants.'

When he dropped the subject and moved away to make a second pot of tea, Charlie knew he had gone as far as he could for her and he would never mention it again. Over a second cup of tea she asked him if he thought she should forget going back to school in September and find herself a job now.

Wyatt had forgotten until that moment that she went to a private school, and that she was intending to take 'A' levels with a view to going to university. That threw up even more difficulties for her.

'I think it would be an excellent plan for you to get a job,' he said thoughtfully. 'But hold fire about school for a while, there's always a possibility they might offer you a free place, especially if your "O" level results are good ones. How are you getting on with the Mellings? Can you stay there indefinitely?'

'I don't know.' She went on to explain she felt the atmosphere was becoming a bit strained. 'Maybe if I found a job I could get a room of my own somewhere?'

Wyatt had been impressed by her poise and good manners on previous meetings, today he'd been touched by her innocence. But it was only now that he saw her courage and her intelligence.

She hadn't dissolved into tears or even bitter re-criminations. Every question she'd asked was relevant and showed a fine grasp of reality. He wondered though if she was capable of looking after herself – according to Mrs Brown the old housekeeper she couldn't even boil an egg. But maybe she needed to try. It might be the making of her.

'That sounds like an excellent idea to me,' he said.

'But find the job first. You can't pay rent without money coming in.'

He left soon after, warning her to double-lock the front door behind her and the outside gate. The moment she heard his car pull away Charlie went up to her bedroom, lay down on her bed and burst into tears.

She had cried many times in the last five days, but never like this – hot, bitter tears that seemed to come from some hitherto untapped well. She had never before felt such an overwhelming sense of isolation, grief, fear and betrayal. She had loved, trusted and looked up to her father, yet he had callously gone away, taking with him all the money, knowing full well it would be his wife and daughter who would be punished and publicly ridiculed when his debts were called in.

Why had he done it? Surely if he was in some sort of trouble he could at least have warned them? Now as a result of his cowardice, her mother was crippled, his daughter's life ruined. How could any man do such a terrible thing?

She knew that she would never again sleep on this big comfortable bed with its peach drapes, never lie and sunbathe in the garden, or curl up with a book on the settee downstairs. Common sense told her that wherever she and her mother ended up, it would be tiny and grim. As from today she was going to have to learn to live without all the luxury she'd taken for granted up till now.

How could she return to school in September? Even if it were possible to get a scholarship she wouldn't want to face the other girls' pity. She certainly had no intention of going to the comprehensive. She'd heard those common girls who went there calling her 'Chinky Charlie' behind her back. If she was suddenly flung in there they'd probably say worse.

The tears gradually dried up and she lay there sniffing. It was almost half past two and she knew she must get back to the Mellings' before long. But first she had to find the things Mr Wyatt spoke of. Right now she didn't really want anything of her father's, but then she and her mother might need the money from them later on. If she didn't do it today she might never get another chance.

The gilt-framed miniatures were where they'd always been, on either side of the bureau in the small sitting room. Six in all, of old-fashioned ladies. It had never occurred to her before that they were valuable, but Mr Wyatt obviously knew best. She took them down and put them on a tray. Next she moved into the drawing room and unlocked the glass cabinet. She knew the twelve small jade animals were good ones, her father wouldn't have had them in the house otherwise. There were four small silver photograph frames, all containing pictures of herself from two until ten. She would take those too.

It became harder after that. Her mother liked trinkets and there were many small things which might be valuable but more likely were not. She took a tiny enamelled snuff-box, a couple of old, small porcelain figurines and a collection of minute silver animals.

She wondered where the bulk of the treasures in this house would end up. Jin had often mentioned that the Chinese lacquered cabinet decorated with birds was worth a fortune. The Oriental rugs on the floor were exceptionally fine ones. It struck her as ironic that these things she'd always been so casual about suddenly seemed so dear to her. She bitterly resented that someone else would own them one day, while she and her mother had nothing.

Upstairs in her mother's jewellery box there were few pieces of any real value. Her good things were kept in a velvet roll tucked into a secret place in the wall. Jin had made the hidey-hole himself. She remembered him chipping out a brick and making a little box to put in its place. When the room was wallpapered next time it was almost completely invisible but for a tiny plastic tag.

She pulled at the tag and the box slid out. To her surprise and delight the red velvet jewellery roll was still there, along with a wad of banknotes beneath it as well. At a quick count there was nearly £200. Inside the roll were all the pieces she remembered her father giving to her mother for birthdays and Christmas, a gold linked necklace, a gold snake bracelet, diamond earrings and a platinum and diamond brooch were safely intact. There was a gold cocktail watch with tiny rubies marking the hours too, and two pairs of antique earrings, one set with emeralds, the other with pearls. She had always liked to put these on herself as a little girl because they were clip-on ones; Sylvia had hardly ever worn them because she said they were too grand for most parties in Dartmouth.

As Charlie tapped the empty box back, she wondered how many years would pass before anyone found it. She couldn't imagine a new owner hurrying to strip off the beautiful cream silk wallpaper.

Downstairs she found a strong, square plastic cake box in one of the kitchen cupboards. Wrapping each item in a tissue first, then in a plastic sandwich bag, she finally packed all the goods, including the money, into the box. They fitted well, and once the lid was back on, she sealed it round with sellotape and tied it up tightly with string.

After locking the front door, it suddenly occurred to her that it would be folly to take the box of treasures back to the Mellings', someone was bound to ask what was in it. For a moment or two she considered hiding it in the garden. But on further reflection that wasn't too smart. If she was seen in the garden after the front door was sealed, she might find herself in trouble, and have the things taken from her.

'Bury it,' she said aloud, and for the first time in days she managed to laugh because it seemed a bit like something the children in the Famous Five books would do. She found a small trowel in the summer-house, then without any hesitation climbed up on to the side wall which backed on to the wooded cliff beyond.

The view from the wall was just of dense trees and bushes, there wasn't even so much as a glimpse of the sea down below to her right, or of the Beacon in its rocky cove. Nor could she see the road to her left, although it was only twenty-five yards or so from where she sat. In fact it could have been any old wood, with no suggestion that just ten or twelve feet in front of her perch was a sheer cliff face. Charlie had been warned again and again throughout her childhood never to venture over the garden wall, yet unbeknown to her parents she had explored the dangerous route back to the road dozens of times and knew every inch of it well.

Using a tree to help her, she dropped on to the soft loamy soil below, and staying close to the wall, wriggled through the bushes until she came to a small clearing. Then she began to dig.

It took some time. Once through the thick layer of leaf-mould the ground was very hard and dry, and she had to stop frequently to listen for anyone walking along the road. But fortunately no one came by and once the hole was some three inches deeper than the box, she placed it inside, scraped the loose soil back around and over it, then stood on it to compress it. Finally she hauled a rotten log on top of it, scraped a little more soil around it, and satisfied, stood back to admire her work.

Even if some other foolhardy person scrambled through the bushes, her treasures would be safe. One shower and there wouldn't even be a footprint to show anyone had been this way. She tucked the trowel under an evergreen bush and turned and went back the way she had come, dropping silently back into the garden.

The following afternoon Charlie set off to visit her mother in hospital with some trepidation. She was tired after another sleepless night worrying. Anxious too about the jewellery she'd taken. Knowing her mother as she did, it was probably the first thing she'd ask about. Should she reassure her that she'd hidden it away? Or was it better to say nothing for now?

'Your mum's been moved into the big ward now,'

a small blonde nurse called out to Charlie as she came along the corridor carrying a bunch of flowers.

'Why?' Charlie asked as she got nearer. She had seen this young nurse on previous visits, in fact she'd stopped to comfort her when she saw her crying once as she was leaving.

'We need that single room for emergencies.' The nurse had a wide smile and sparkling brown eyes. 'Your mum's on the mend now, and once she's settled down, she'll be less depressed too with other women to talk to.'

Charlie doubted that. 'What's she been like today?' she asked.

'Down in the dumps, I'm afraid.' The nurse made a grimace. 'I offered to wash her hair, thinking it might make her feel better, but she nearly bit my head off.'

Charlie's heart sank. 'I'm sorry,' she said, embarrassed that her mother seemed set on upsetting all the nursing staff. 'She doesn't mean to be nasty. It's just that she's in pain and worried.'

'We understand,' the nurse said brightly, but Charlie sensed that this particular nurse had almost run out of sympathy. 'Go on in and see her. She's right down the end of the ward.'

The ward seemed huge, with six beds on either side. Almost all of the patients were very old. Some smiled at Charlie, perhaps curious because she was Chinese and wondering who she was visiting, others just lay there, their eyes dull and lifeless. It was a bright ward, overlooking the harbour, yet despite the many vases of flowers it still had a nasty sickly smell and it was very hot.

Sylvia was propped up into a semi-sitting position, but she didn't even turn her head as Charlie approached. Even from a distance her sullen mood was obvious.

'Hullo, Mum!' Charlie said cheerfully, bending to kiss her mother's cheek. 'I brought you some flowers from the garden. Mrs Melling made you some cakes too.'

Charlie thought her mother looked ghastly. She was haggard, her skin yellowish and her eyes dull. Her hair was so greasy it was stuck to her head with rat's tails around her shoulders, but worse still, it was as though all the years of constant smoking and eating too little had finally caught up with her. Her mouth was puckered by tiny lines, her neck was scrawny. Charlie doubted if any of their old neighbours would recognize her as the glamorous blonde from 'Windways'.

As Sylvia said nothing, Charlie put the bunch of flowers and the small tin of butterfly cakes on her locker. 'It was a surprise to find you'd been moved! How're the legs today?'

Sylvia turned her head slightly towards her daughter. 'My legs are hurting like hell. This ward is hell too. And I don't eat cake. I'd have thought you'd at least remember that!'

Charlie gulped. She was tempted just to turn around and walk away, but she didn't quite dare. 'I didn't like to tell Mrs Melling you don't eat cake,' she replied instead. 'I thought it was kind of her, besides I'm sure some of the old ladies in here who don't get visitors would appreciate them.'

'You get more like your father every day,' Sylvia

65

snapped. 'Always the smart answer. If it wasn't for him I wouldn't be here now.'

'Look, Mum, do you have to be so horrid?' Charlie pleaded with her. 'I know what happened was terrible, our life has been turned upside down, and it looks like it's going to get worse unless Dad comes back soon. But I'm not responsible for any of it, so please don't take it out on me.'

'But you'll be all right,' Sylvia sniffed. 'You can get a job, move away from Dartmouth if you want to. I'm a cripple now. I'll never walk again, everything I own is about to be taken away from me. I've got nothing to look forward to, I won't even be able to look after myself, I might as well be dead.'

Charlie thought that was all true, but she didn't think an adult should wallow in self-pity. 'I'll look after you,' she said, pulling up a chair and sitting down beside the bed. 'And if you make up your mind that you will walk again, you probably could. So we might lose the house, but we'll get somewhere else. Why don't you let the nurse wash your hair, put your makeup on again and do your nails?'

'Do my nails!' Sylvia shrieked, making several of the other patients sit up and look round. 'You want me to do my nails and put makeup on after what has happened to me?'

Charlie was horrified. Right from a small child she'd been taught by both her parents never to make a scene in public. She couldn't believe that her mother would change the habit of a lifetime, even if she was in pain.

'Please don't show yourself up, Mum,' she said in a hushed voice. 'I only meant it might make you feel better if you looked like your old self.'

'You're as cruel as your father,' Sylvia hissed at her, blue eyes blazing. 'Do you know what that bastard's done? He's robbed us. Cleaned us out, every last penny. All I've got is about a hundred pounds in my savings account. There's nothing left for your school fees, nothing even to pay the electric or gas bills. He's off with another woman, making a new life for himself. He hadn't even got the guts to tell me he didn't want me any more. Will putting makeup on make that go away?'

'I don't believe he's gone off with another woman,' Charlie said indignantly.

'How would you know?' Sylvia sneered. 'Since when did you become an expert on men?'

'I know Dad.' Whatever she thought about her father privately she wasn't prepared to admit it to anyone, not even her mother. 'He believes in honour and good manners. If he wanted a new life with someone else he would have said so.'

'You pathetic, stupid little fool. Honour and good manners! Your precious father has been a crook all his fucking life, my girl. He made his pile from running strip clubs, call girls and selling drugs. The only reason he bought "Windways" and started importing all that fucking shit he calls antiquities was because he wanted a legal front to hide behind.'

Charlie felt as if someone had just thrown a bucket of icy water over her. Yet she could do and say nothing, only stare at her mother open-mouthed with astonishment. She had never heard her swear publicly before and to hear her using such words, now with old ladies lying just feet away, somehow was confirmation she was telling the truth.

'Mum, don't,' Charlie whispered, catching hold of her mother's hand. She wanted to hear what had been said retracted, but even in her distress she was aware this wasn't something which should be aired here. 'People will hear!'

'Does that matter any more?' Sylvia slumped back against the pillows and turned her face away from her daughter. 'It will all come out before long anyway. You won't even want to keep his name, let alone try to stick up for him. I bet that shit has taken my jewellery too. I never thought to check if it was still there.'

Charlie thought quickly before answering. Her mother was so angry that one small piece of good news couldn't possibly calm her down. Besides, she might just give the game away to someone by accident.

'I'll check if I get the opportunity to go back to the house,' she said, hoping her face wouldn't give her away. 'Don't mention it to anyone though, Mum, otherwise they might look for it. Anyway, I don't think Dad would take presents he'd given you, even if he is as bad as you say.'

'You don't think about anything, do you?' Sylvia sniffed. 'Not what it's like for me in here, or what will happen when they chuck me out. All you care about is yourself, you're just like Jin, in looks, ways and character. Why don't you run off too?'

Charlie had heard more than enough for one day. Seething with anger, she got up, pushed the chair back and leaned over her mother.

'I do think a great deal,' she said in a low voice. 'I've already worked out for myself that both you and Dad have hidden a great deal from me. Now you've brought up Dad's past, it makes me wonder why you've never told me anything about yours. Could that be because you're ashamed of that too? As for being like my father, well, right now I'd rather be like him than you, at least he's got some guts!'

Sylvia's eyes opened very wide and she seemed to cringe back into the pillows. 'How dare you talk to me like that?' she said, but her voice trembled.

'I'm not going to run off too, even though I wish I could,' Charlie went on. 'But I am going to find myself a job, and somewhere of my own to live. So just watch what you say to me in future, otherwise you might very well find yourself entirely alone with no one to take care of you.'

She dropped a kiss on Sylvia's cheek, purely for propriety's sake. 'I'm going now,' she said. 'Ask the nurse to wash your hair. It's disgusting.'

Charlie couldn't bring herself to go back to the Mellings' immediately. Instead she walked to Warfleet Creek, found a log to sit on amongst the bushes and stared across the estuary to 'Windways'. It looked so very beautiful bathed in afternoon sunshine, and as she looked at it, bitter tears sprang to her eyes. It was only six days since she was here before, yet it seemed almost a lifetime away now.

Everything was smashed to pieces. From her mother's knees to her beliefs about her parents. Her father was a crook, her mother was a bitter harridan who couldn't even find a gentle way to break such terrible news to her daughter.

How was she going to live with this? She had always been so certain about herself. Top of the class, captain of the netball team, the popular, pretty girl everyone invited to their birthday parties. Just last week she had confidently imagined that she could choose any career she wanted too.

Sylvia had said, *It will all come out soon.* It was bad enough already with neighbours waylaying her, knowing the answers to their questions would be embroidered before being passed on again. Once the truth got out, who would want to know her? Certainly not her friends from school – their parents wouldn't want their precious daughters mixing with a villain's child. And what sort of a job could she get? Anything decent would be ruled out.

'It was all very well saying you'd look after Mum,' she whispered to herself. 'But how? You can't cook, you've never washed or ironed anything.'

Despair overwhelmed her and she put her head down on her knees and sobbed.

An hour or so later, Charlie was stiff and cold from sitting for so long in deep shade. She stood up and looked across the estuary again at 'Windways' and it seemed somehow symbolic that the sun was still blazing down there.

'You've got to forget that,' she whispered to herself. 'You've got to find a new patch of sun for yourself.'

As she walked back up the hill towards the ferry she mentally listed the things she didn't have. There was no one to turn to, she had no qualifications and no real skills, and apart from that money hidden in the box, no money either.

As the ferry moved out from the Dartmouth side over to Kingswear, and the sun struck her arms and face again, she listed the things she did have. A keen brain, youth, health, good looks and determination.

'It's enough,' she murmured to herself as the ferry docked on the other side and she moved to walk off. 'Dad made it all the way from a village in China to England with nothing more than that.'

Chapter Three

'Any luck, dear?' Mrs Melling asked from her position at the kitchen sink, as Charlie came in. It was the day after she'd visited her mother and she'd spent the whole day looking for a job.

Charlie shook her head, she wanted to cry, but she was determined not to give into it. 'I tried absolutely everywhere. The shops, hotels, pubs and guest-houses. No one wanted me.'

'I expect they've already got fixed up with students,' Mrs Melling said comfortingly, drying her hands on a tea towel. 'Something will turn up though, it always does.'

'It won't, not here in Dartmouth,' Charlie said with resignation. 'There were jobs going, they just didn't want *me*. I suppose they think I'll run off with the takings or the bed linen.'

Mrs Melling wanted to deny this, but she couldn't. Gossip about Jin Weish was rife all over town, and even people who didn't actually know him would immediately guess by Charlie's appearance that she was his daughter.

'It will blow over soon,' she said instead. 'Now, sit down and I'll make you some tea. You must be worn out.'

'I'll go and change first,' Charlie said. She was wearing her smartest outfit, a red mini-dress and matching jacket. She had been unbearably hot all day and her feet were killing her.

Diana Melling sat down for a minute once Charlie had gone upstairs. She too was very disappointed Charlie hadn't found a job today, she'd been banking on it, for she thought Sylvia Weish was taking advantage of her generous nature.

The woman had never been a friend, in fact over the years Sylvia had given Diana the distinct impression she considered her to be on the same social level as Mrs Brown, the Weishes' housekeeper. She might have crushed knees, but there was nothing to stop her asking for the telephone trolley in the hospital, or writing a letter to say she appreciated Diana and Herbert taking Charlie in.

For someone who had always prided herself on being so correct, it was insufferably insolent to expect a neighbour to take responsibility for a teenage girl indefinitely, to say nothing of offering some money for her keep. University professors were not very well paid, and she and Herbert had three children of their own to feed.

Charlie wasn't any trouble, even if she did have fancy ideas about having a bath and clean clothes every day and couldn't so much as make a pot of tea without supervision. But she and her problems were putting a strain on the whole household. Herbert was getting increasingly nervous since one of the policemen had told him Jin had once owned Soho night-clubs; he thought the man was most likely involved with organized crime. He was afraid too that

73

the men who attacked Sylvia might storm into his house for Charlie as well.

June was fed up too because Charlie wasn't any fun any longer. She wanted her bedroom back to herself, and she was jealous because Charlie's clothes were nicer than hers. She and the two younger ones had been very rude many times, purely because they knew their mother wouldn't give them a clip round the ear while they had company. On top of that they were going on holiday in a week's time. Were they supposed to squeeze Charlie in the car too, and pay for her food and accommodation for a fortnight?

But aside from all these considerations, Charlie unnerved Diana. Until she came here to stay, she had seemed an ideal friend for June. Charlie's confidence had brought shy June out of herself, she helped her with her schoolwork, and she was so well-mannered and intelligent that she and Herbert had never had a moment's anxiety that their daughter might be led astray.

But now, in the light of all this trouble, Charlie seemed to pose some kind of threat. The girl's dark eyes were on Diana constantly, making her feel as if she was under close and critical observation. Charlie rarely showed her feelings, never took Diana into her confidence and remained unnaturally cool and polite. Herbert said this was just her nature, being Chinese, but that didn't make it any easier to live with.

While Diana wasn't heartless enough to push Charlie out, it had occurred to her that once she found a job it might be fairly easy to suggest she found new lodgings too. Now that hope was dashed.

*

Upstairs Charlie slunk into the bathroom to have a cry. Even though Mrs Melling had been very nice, she sensed the woman's disappointment that she hadn't come back with a job. Then when Charlie went into the bedroom to find June, she studiously ignored her and went on reading a book. Once she would have tackled her friend openly about why she was being so nasty, but she knew why it was. June had spent most of her life basking in Charlie's limelight. Suddenly there was no limelight, only dark shadows, and June was afraid she'd be ostracized as well if she stood by her. Perhaps, too, it was a way of getting back at Charlie for all the times she'd felt second-rate.

But understanding why June had turned against her was the last straw after all the other humiliation she'd had today.

In one café she went into to inquire about a job the man there had said, *Sorry, we don't have an opium den upstairs.* That was his idea of a little joke. In the Royal Castle Hotel the housekeeper had said, *I couldn't take you on, dear, you'd be too much of a liability.* Charlie had to suppose she meant that men might come after her with iron bars. But the most crushing remark of the day had been from the ice-cream man in his kiosk on the harbour. He actually had a sign up saying 'Help needed' and when she'd offered her help he said, *You could make more money stripping, love. Can't your dad give you a job in one of his clubs?*

Mr Wyatt had only said her father once owned night-clubs, it had been her mother who had revealed what that really meant. So how did all these other people find out so soon? She'd never be able to hold her head up in Dartmouth again.

Two days later, on a hot sunny afternoon, Charlie was scouring nearby Salcombe for a job. She was now so desperate she was prepared to do absolutely anything, however awful, just to get out of Dartmouth.

The previous day she'd tried Paignton, this morning she'd tried Kingsbridge, but although she didn't feel her failure to find a job was due to her father in either of these places, merely that students had beaten her to it, that didn't make her feel any better.

Yet she couldn't help feeling optimistic here in Salcombe as it had always been her favourite place from childhood. It was sleepier than Dartmouth, kind of dreamy quaint with its pretty little harbour and dear little cottages. She knew she looked nice in her white sleeveless mini-dress. Someone must need her here.

Three hours on, however, Charlie was thoroughly dispirited and on the point of going home again, when she called into a sweet shop in Fore Street to buy an ice-cream. She had tried all the hotels, restaurants, cafés and shops, but no one needed any staff. As she bought her ice-cream she told the chatty old lady behind the counter her problem. The old lady said she knew Ivor Meeks wanted help in his fishing tackle shop on the harbour, but added that he really wanted a boy.

Charlie didn't think it sounded the least bit hopeful, especially as she knew absolutely nothing about fishing, but she thought she might as well give it a try anyway.

The harbour was surprisingly quiet for such a hot day. A couple of small boys were sitting on the wall throwing stones into the sea, an elderly couple were sitting on a bench eating ice-cream, watching a few seagulls fight over scraps of fish; but apart from them, the only other person about was a big red-headed, bearded man sitting on an upturned tub smoking a pipe, a black and white dog sitting beside him. Even though the name 'Meeks' didn't fit his appearance, she thought it must be the man she was looking for.

If she had been a tourist she might very well have photographed him because he looked so at one with his surroundings. His bushy beard was as fiery as his hair and his upturned nose gave him an almost Dickensian comical air. As she got closer she saw his huge arms were covered in tattoos. He wore baggy shapeless shorts almost to his knees and a kind of loose, smock-like top made of canvas. It was impossible to guess his age, he was as timeless as the harbour.

She didn't see how anyone could call his place a shop. It was just a wooden shack. Fishing rods, children's buckets and spades and rubber rings hung outside, and a dilapidated sign claimed 'Boats for Hire. Mackerel Fishing. Bait and Fishing Tackle'.

Charlie was aware the man was watching her as she approached him. She blushed because she sensed he was amused by the way the cobbled path was making her teeter on her platform sandals.

'Are you Mr Meeks?' she asked when she was some ten yards from him.

'That's me,' he said in a booming voice. 'What can I do for you, my dear? You don't look the kind to want a bit of bait. Let me guess, you want a pair of shoes you can really walk in?'

Charlie giggled. Although she was so dispirited and weary and she doubted very much that he would give her a job, it was nice to meet someone jolly, and a touch of her old boldness came back.

'No. I want a job, please,' she said cheekily. 'I hear you need someone to mind your shop.'

'Well, you'd make it prettier, my dear,' he said, rolling his Rs in a rich Devonshire accent. 'But I can't see you putting those dainty hands in amongst my maggots.'

'I'm not squeamish,' she said, giving him her best and most vivid smile. 'Go on, give me a try?'

He looked appraisingly at her for a moment, his eyes were greeny-blue like the sea, beautiful eyes for such an odd-looking man.

'Right then, try putting some in a bag,' he said. 'The tub's just inside.'

Charlie had always enjoyed a challenge and rarely backed down from a dare. Without any hesitation she stepped up into the shack. After the bright sunshine it was dark inside, but she smelled the maggots even before she saw them. It was a horrible pungent smell, far worse than rotting meat, and she gagged. She was backing away in disgust, but something halted her. 'Do it,' she whispered to herself. 'Show him!'

Holding her breath, she advanced on the tub.

It was the most disgusting thing she had ever seen, millions of yellowy maggots all squirming and heaving. She felt her breakfast coming up, but she fought against it.

'Where are the bags?' she called out, holding her nose.

'By the side of the tub, the scoop's in there with them,' he replied and smiled to himself because he was sure she'd come running out any minute.

She took a paper bag first, opened it wide and then transferred it to her left hand. Hesitantly she reached down into the tub, her hand wavering as there were maggots all over the wooden handle. She flicked the handle with her fingers so they fell off, then, holding her breath, dug into the stinking, squishy mass.

As she tipped the contents of the scoop into the bag, a couple of maggots fell against her fingers. It was all she could do not to drop the entire thing and run out screaming.

Dropping the scoop back into the tub, she bravely gave the top of the bag a quick twist as she might a bag of sweets, then turned out into the fresh air.

'There we are,' she said, handing them to Mr Meeks.

Ivor Meeks was flabbergasted. All day throughout the summer months he saw scores of pretty girls around the harbour. They came with their parents, with boyfriends and with groups of other girls, but whether they were sailing enthusiasts, city girls down on holiday or even country girls, there were few that weren't utterly repelled by maggots. He couldn't count the times girls had run out of his shack squealing; he remembered how one high-spirited young lad had once put a handful down the back of a girl's dress and she'd been so terrified Ivor had thought she might have heart failure.

He knew this girl was equally horrified by them and he was intrigued as to why she'd go to such lengths in order to impress him. Her white dress looked like an expensive one, so why should a girl who came from a comfortable background want a job working for him?

Her looks intrigued him even more. He didn't think both her parents were Chinese, her almond eyes were too open and she didn't have flat cheekbones. She reminded him of the Anglo-Chinese girls he'd seen in Malaya and Hong Kong. He had to find out more about her before he sent her on her way.

'Tell me about yourself,' he said, pulling up a stool for her. He turned around and tossed the maggots back in the tub.

'My name is Charlie Weish. I'm sixteen and I need a job desperately because my mother's ill in hospital,' she blurted out without drawing breath. 'I'll work hard, I promise.'

'Charlie's a boy's name,' he said with a smile, sitting down again.

'It was intended to be Cha-Lee,' she said, breaking up the syllables. 'Cha is tea, a revered plant in China, Lee a family name, with a hyphen in between. But my parents got tired of explaining how it should be spelt so they changed it to the English version. Dad had already shortened his family name Wei Shi to Weish anyway, when he first came to England.'

Ivor nodded. 'Well, Charlie, I'm sorry about your mum and I'm sure you would work hard. But I can't take on a girl. I need a lad that knows about fishing and boats. A pretty little thing like you should be in a hotel or a shop. Go on up to the Marine Hotel. They might have something.'

'I've already tried there, and everywhere,' she said. 'Oh, please give me a try. I pick things up really quickly, I can learn about fishing and boats. I wasn't scared of the maggots. And I'm strong too.'

Ivor looked at her long slender legs, her arms no

bigger than bean sprouts and her carefully manicured nails. He couldn't for one moment imagine her being strong enough to secure his boat in a high wind, or tough enough to deal with the many difficult customers he got in the high season.

'I'm sorry, you just aren't suitable, my dear,' he said, wishing he hadn't teased her by making her scoop up the maggots.

Charlie had bitten back tears of disappointment many times in the last two days, but this time she couldn't stop them. She was so tired, dreading going back to the Mellings' again, and she hadn't the first idea where to go from here.

Ivor was alarmed when her face crumpled and tears rolled down her cheeks. 'There's no need for tears,' he said. 'You wouldn't like working here anyway. It's good on a nice sunny day like today, but quite different in the rain and wind. Now you run along home, something will turn up for you. Where is your home anyway?'

She didn't answer, but covered her face with her hands, and Ivor thought she could be a runaway.

He had met a few runaways over the years. Mostly boys that had got themselves into trouble in London then hitchhiked down to Devon with the romantic idea of getting jobs crewing on boats and the like. Almost all of them had got themselves into worse trouble while they were here. He'd befriended one once who had then skipped off the first time he took a party out fishing, taking the day's takings with him and leaving the shack open for anyone to help themselves to his stock.

The thought of any young girl sleeping rough, at

the mercy of any unscrupulous man, frightened him. He felt compelled to do something, even if it was only to find out the truth about her and march her along to the police station.

'Sit down here,' he said, indicating a small stool beside him. 'And tell me the whole truth about yourself, Charlie,' he said gruffly. 'If you aren't prepared to do that, then clear off right now.'

'He's a tough old bugger' was a phrase often said of Ivor Meeks by the locals. Except for a few short weeks in summer when he made a few bob from tourists, and sat in the sun on the harbour puffing on his pipe, only the most foolish or romantically inclined would look at him in envy. His tiny cottage behind the shack had no comforts, it was a cold, damp place, battered by wind and sea spray. His life was hard, he took his small boat out in all winds and weathers, and the catches of fish, crabs and lobsters were sometimes barely enough to pay for his nightly drinks in the Victoria Inn.

He was something of a paradox, a loner whose brusque manner and somewhat frightening appearance didn't win him many new friends. But those who had had some reason to get a little closer to him discovered to their surprise that he had an underlying gentleness; he was a compassionate man who could be counted on in times of trouble. As such he was accepted by the community, and in the absence of any confirmation about his past, colourful rumours abounded about him, and he'd won his place in people's affections for being an eccentric.

Ivor was born in Plymouth in 1912, one of seven children, their father a fisherman. He married Sarah in 1933 when he was twenty-one and a year later their son John was born, followed later by a daughter, Kim. Life was extremely hard for them, they were very poor, the two rooms they lived in were damp and cold and when John died at only three from diphtheria, Ivor became fiercely determined to do better for his wife and daughter, so he sent them back to Sarah's parents in Lynmouth and joined the merchant navy.

He had had only two years at sea making good money to send home to Sarah and Kim when war broke out. Like so many men of his class and background he felt compelled to fight for his country, so he joined up in the Royal Navy.

After the war he went back to join Sarah and Kim in Lynmouth. Sarah's father had died a couple of years earlier, and now with people from the war-torn cities wanting holidays in picturesque seaside villages, Sarah and her mother were embarking on a plan to take in paying guests. For Ivor, however, things were not so rosy; he soon discovered that if he went back to fishing, with no boat of his own, he could only expect to scrape a living from the sea. With a long-term plan in mind for making enough money to buy his own boat and extend his mother-in-law's cottage to make room for more guests, he signed up in the merchant navy again.

The years between 1946 and 1954 were happy ones for all of them, despite the long separations while he was at sea. Kim was a delightful child, she had inherited Ivor's red hair and Sarah's sweet nature and she grew into a pretty and confident young woman. When Ivor was home between trips to Australia, China and India he took her fishing and sailing with him, and their close, warm relationship was something Ivor valued above all else. As the family nest egg grew, Ivor promised that in two more years he would come home for good, and he and Sarah discussed having another child.

But this dream was cruelly shattered. In January 1955, when Sarah was only thirty-eight and Kim nineteen, they were killed. Mown down by a lorry as they walked down the hill into Lynmouth one icy afternoon.

Ivor was on his way back from America when he received the news, and the funeral was delayed until his return. Sarah's mother died just three weeks later – her heart gave out from the trauma of losing her beloved daughter and granddaughter. Ivor had no wish to go on living either; he was forty-three, his wife and daughter had been his whole life, and without them he could see no future. He went back to Plymouth and fishing, but his bitterness and the tendency to fight anyone when he'd had a drink lost him the last friends he had there.

Ivor was in a low state when he finally arrived in Salcombe in the summer of '56. He had moved from one fishing village to another, getting drunk and fighting in each one. All the money he'd saved was gone, and he felt in his heart that he was finished. But fate took him in hand. Joseph Fear, the old man who then owned the cottage and fishing tackle shack, recognized Ivor as a wounded man who needed help and as he too needed assistance with his business, he offered him a job and a roof over his head.

There was a great deal of gossip in Salcombe that summer about the big, surly, red-headed man living with Joseph Fear. Many people feared that Joseph, who was over seventy, was losing his mind letting a stranger into his home. But as time went by they were reassured. Ivor cared for Joseph when he was sick, he repaired the shack and Joseph's fishing boat. It was he who worked while the old man sat and watched.

Two years later Joseph died of pneumonia following a bad attack of bronchitis. Ivor was the only person who was surprised that he left his shack, cottage and business to him; everyone else considered it appropriate. To a man who once felt he had no wish to live, such generosity was proof there was every reason to. For Joseph's sake he determined to put his bitterness behind him and start afresh. Now, some twelve years later, he rarely thought about the past. He had learned the simple art of being happy with what he had.

'Come on,' Ivor said impatiently. 'Either tell me the truth, or ship out.'

At this somewhat callous command Charlie withdrew her hands from her face, wiped her tears away with the back of her hand and braced herself to tell him to mind his own business. But as she opened her mouth to speak out, the man's greeny-blue eyes halted her. His appearance might be fearsome, his facial expression one of distrust, but his eyes were full of compassion, and she felt she was looking into his soul and seeing a good, kind man.

She was beyond hoping for a job now. Her only motivation in telling him the whole sorry story was the need to unburden herself. She held nothing back, everything – her mother's spiteful revelations about her father, the impending bankruptcy, even the situation back in Dartmouth – came out in a torrent.

'So that's why I've got to get a job,' she finished up, and found herself crying again.

Ivor had heard many sad stories over the years, but he didn't remember ever being quite so moved as he was now. She was only a child, it wasn't just a job she needed, but a caring adult to help and advise her. From the way she'd described her home life until all this happened, he could see exactly why there was no stalwart friend of the family to take her under their wing.

That she'd broken down on his doorstep seemed like fate. He could remember pouring his heart out to Joseph Fear, here in the same place, and Joseph hadn't turned him away, but offered a hand of friendship, knowing even less about Ivor than he did now about Charlie.

'Even if I was to give you a job,' Ivor said cautiously, 'I couldn't pay you enough to find somewhere to live.'

'I could try and find another job too,' she said quickly. 'Maybe as a waitress in the evenings. I have to stay somewhere near Dartmouth so I can visit my mother.'

Her desperate plea twisted Ivor's insides. Was it because of Kim, his own daughter? Or could it be that Charlie reminded him of some of those pretty young Chinese girls he'd met in Hong Kong brothels all those years ago, who if they'd had someone to lean on, might not have ended up in that dangerous trade?

'What's your dog's name?' Charlie asked, interrupting his thoughts. His dog was a good judge of character, she rarely made a fuss of anyone, but she was sitting now with her chin on Charlie's lap, looking adoringly at the girl as she stroked her.

'Minnie,' he said. 'Looks like she's decided you're a friend.'

'I love dogs,' Charlie said. 'Mum would never let me have one, she was too houseproud.'

It was that little remark which made up Ivor's mind. Somehow it encapsulated everything he sensed about this girl's childhood. 'I'll tell you what I'll do,' he said, compassion elbowing out common sense. 'I'll take you on for a trial period, and meanwhile I'll ask at the pub tonight and see if anyone there can put you up. But I'll tell you now, if you aren't any good, I'll have to send you packing. There isn't room in this business for passengers.'

Her expression drove away the last of his reservations. Her smile spread from ear to ear, her eyes were alight with joy. She reached out and caught hold of his hand, squeezing it tightly. 'Thank you so much, Mr Meeks. You won't be sorry, I promise you.'

Minnie seemed to appreciate a bargain was being struck. She put her paws up on Charlie's thighs and began licking her face rapturously.

'Let's hope not,' he said with a wry smile. 'Well, Minnie's clearly decided you are here to stay, so you'd better call me Ivor. Now, how's your tea-making? We can make a start with that. But then you'd better go back to Dartmouth and pack your things. Make sure you come back in the morning dressed in something practical. What you're wearing now won't do at all.'

As Charlie rode home on the bus in the early evening, for the first time since the attack on her mother she felt like smiling. It might not be much of a job, it only

87

paid £10 a week, but it was a start and she'd be away from Dartmouth.

Going into Ivor's tiny cottage to make the tea had been an awful shock. She'd never seen anywhere quite so, well, bleak was the only word that sprang to mind. It was clean, but there was no comfort in the one room downstairs. Just a sink, cooker, two upright chairs, a small table and an easy chair. He didn't even have a bathroom, only an outside lavatory. Charlie had never met anyone before who lived with so little.

But odd as Ivor was, she'd felt comfortable with him, he wasn't the least bit creepy. He really listened, and even though she'd told him all that stuff about her father, he hadn't uttered one judgmental word. She thought he could be described as inscrutable. Minnie was lovely too, so quiet, obedient and affectionate. She hoped Ivor would let her take her out for walks.

She hoped too she could really learn everything about the fishing and boat stuff – those maggots had made her feel quite ill. She wondered too if Ivor knew that she'd bluffed her way through the tea-making, calling out to ask how many spoons of tea he liked in the pot, then trying to remember everything she'd seen Mrs Melling do, like warming the pot. He'd probably think twice about taking her on if he knew how few practical skills she had.

'You're going to work in a fishing tackle shop?' Mrs Melling looked appalled when Charlie broke her news that evening. 'And where are you going to live?'

'Mr Meeks is going to arrange a room for me at the Victoria Inn,' Charlie lied. Ivor had hinted he might be able to arrange it, but it wasn't definite. She wasn't going to admit either that the 'shop' was in fact a wooden shack on the harbour. She had a feeling that if the woman knew what Ivor Meeks looked like she'd blow a fuse.

'I don't think your mother will approve.' Mrs Melling shook her head. Her mouth was pursed up like a cat's behind. 'But I suppose I can't stop you.'

'Mum is in no position to disapprove,' Charlie said tartly. 'And I can't keep sponging off you. You've been so kind, Mrs Melling, but it's time I looked after myself.'

'Charlie, you can't do the simplest thing for yourself!' Diana forgot she had wanted Charlie to leave and her maternal instinct took over. 'Do you know how to wash and iron your clothes? Can you cook anything?'

'I can make sandwiches, cups of instant coffee, and I mastered tea-making today. As for the washing and ironing, I'll just have to learn, won't I?' Charlie said defiantly.

Diana looked doubtful. 'You can do a bit of ironing for me tonight to get a bit of practice, once you've packed your things,' she said. 'And I'll try to explain to you which things need cool water, and which need hot.'

It occurred to Diana as Charlie ran away to pack that the Weishes hadn't prepared their daughter in any way for the outside world. It made her feel quite ill to think the girl would be living above a public house with no proper supervision. But then she wasn't responsible for Charlie, her mother was, and it was a relief that she was finally off her hands.

*

89

'My word, you come with a lot of baggage,' Ivor joked as he took Charlie's two large suitcases from her the following morning. Minnie jumped up and gave her an enthusiastic welcome. 'And to think that yesterday I thought you were a runaway!'

He had been getting his stock outside as Charlie came staggering around the corner with her luggage. He'd rushed along to help her, amazed that she had so much. He doubted he could fill one carrier bag with his stuff.

Charlie was just about to say these were merely her summer clothes, that she had as many winter clothes again back at 'Windways'. But she stopped herself, she must forget she was once spoiled rotten. 'Mr and Mrs Melling are going on holiday next week. I think they wanted me to take everything,' she said instead. This was true, she'd had the distinct feeling they had closed the door on her for good.

Ivor normally slept very well, but last night he'd hardly closed his eyes for worrying about what he'd taken on. He might have arranged a room for Charlie, but ultimately she would be his responsibility. What if she spent the time when he was out on the boat chatting up young men, or worse still got herself into trouble?

Still, he was pleased to see she'd dressed sensibly – she was wearing jeans and a pink tee-shirt, with plimsolls on her feet. She still looked like a young model though. He hoped she wouldn't distract the young men from buying their bait and other fishing tackle.

'I'll put it out back for now,' he said, humping the suitcases in through the shack. 'I've spoken to Beryl

Langley at the Victoria Inn opposite. She'll give you a room in return for a bit of washing-up in the evenings. You'll be safe with her, Charlie, she's a good sort. I'll take you over there at the end of the day.'

Charlie was surprised to find the morning flew by. She spent most of the time inside the shack, helping Ivor tidy it up and sticking price labels on everything so she would know what to charge when he went out on the boat later in the day. When someone came in, Ivor stood back and let her serve them and as they were mostly just holidaymakers with time on their hands it didn't matter if she was a bit slow.

'What's this for?' she kept asking, holding up all sorts of odd things she found lying on dusty shelves.

Ivor seemed pleased by her enthusiasm, and explained things very clearly. 'If it's a fine day on Sunday, you can come out fishing with me. That way most of it will just fall into place for you.'

She was helping some children pick out buckets and spades when the men booked for the afternoon fishing trip arrived. They were Londoners, in their late twenties, and rather rough types she thought, with sleeveless singlets showing big bellies and the sort of nylon shorts that footballers wear. They had a crate of beer with them, but it looked as if they'd already had a few pints in the pub, and all of them leered at her and made suggestive remarks.

Ivor took Charlie to one side. 'Don't mind them,' he said. 'They're harmless really, they only go on that way because they're mob-handed. Now, keep the money drawer locked, and stow the key away in your pocket. I'll be back by five.' He looked over his shoulder at the men, one of whom was passing out bottles of beer, and grinned wickedly. 'Maybe earlier if they're all sick. Keep an eye out for me coming in, I might need you to help with the mooring. I doubt if any of them will be capable.'

Suddenly Charlie was nervous about being left alone. 'What if someone wants something you haven't told me about?'

Ivor shrugged. 'Use your initiative,' he said. 'You seem pretty smart to me. Minnie can stay with you today, she'll look after you.'

There was little to do once she was on her own, most of the customers were just children wanting fishing nets or buckets, and she sold three pairs of rubber sandals too. Between customers Charlie sat outside on the stool, petting Minnie, watching the boats going in and out of the harbour, and tourists wandering aimlessly past. She wondered how Ivor was coping with those drunken men.

It was about four-thirty when she became aware of a young man watching her. He was on a very sleek yacht moored further along the harbour wall. He was deeply tanned, with fashionably long blond hair, wearing nothing but a pair of cut-down Levis, the sort of man she and June had so often dreamed of being chatted up by.

Just thinking of her friend made Charlie feel desolate again. She hadn't been much of a friend recently, but they had shared so much, for so long, she couldn't really believe it was over for good. Charlie wondered whether her life would go back to being just as it was before if her father was to come home and sort everything out, and her mother's injuries miraculously healed perfectly.

Somehow she knew it wouldn't. Overnight the giddy, spoilt Charlie had been forced to grow up. Adults were fallible, friends were fickle, and most people were quick to condemn on just the flimsiest of evidence. Where were all those so-called friends of her parents? Those people who had accepted so much generous hospitality in the past? Not one of them had called at the hospital to see Sylvia, or made inquiries to see if they could do anything for her. As far as Charlie could see there was only one person she could depend on now, and that was herself. Even if a miracle did happen, and she could return to living at 'Windways', go back to school, and her parents became the happiest, most loving couple in the world, she had a feeling she would still never really trust anyone, or anything, implicitly again.

The young man disappeared below decks, some twenty minutes passed and Charlie had almost forgotten about him when he suddenly reappeared and leapt off his boat on to the quay. As he walked towards her with a springy athletic step, smiling, Charlie gulped: close to he was even better-looking, with angular cheekbones and bright blue eyes.

Minnie barked furiously. 'It's okay.' Charlie bent down and patted her. 'It's just a customer.'

'Hi there,' he said as he reached the shack. 'I say, can you help me with a fishing rod?'

He had the kind of plummy accent so common to the yachting fraternity in this area. She wondered if it was his boat or his father's. Minnie slunk away, taking up a position out on the quay where she could watch.

'I will if I can,' Charlie said, hoping she wasn't blushing. 'It's my first day minding the shop for Ivor and I don't know too much about rods yet. Take a look at them and see if there's one you like.'

Ivor had said which ones were for sea fishing this morning, but she couldn't remember which were which. She made a mental note to ask him again.

He went over to the rack where all the rods were kept, touching each of them and occasionally getting one out as if to feel the weight.

'What did you want to catch?' she asked, feeling she must say something.

He turned back towards her. His smile was slightly lopsided and very attractive. His teeth were dazzling against his tanned skin. 'Something about five foot five, with black hair and almond eyes,' he said with laughter in his voice. 'I think her name must be Suzie Wong.'

Charlie had been called Suzie Wong derisively many times before, and knowing it came from a book about a Chinese prostitute, she found it very insulting. 'You'll need the most expensive one to catch her,' she said haughtily.

'Oh will I?' he laughed. 'Well, I guess I'd better take this one then,' and to Charlie's amazement he picked one from the rack which cost £60 and pulled a wallet from his pocket.

Ivor had said this morning that he rarely sold any expensive rods, and for a moment Charlie almost took it from the man's hands and urged him not to be silly. But he was looking her up and down with pure arrogance, the yacht he'd come from said he could afford it, and besides, she was here to sell things, not to advise against them.

'Sixty pounds please,' she said, trying very hard to appear casual about it.

His wallet was stuffed with money. He made a great play of showing her just how much he had as he peeled off six crisp £10 notes.

'Would you like to join me for dinner later tonight?' he asked as he handed it over, his hand lingering on hers. 'I'm Guy Acton-Bond by the way, and you?'

'Suzie Wong,' she replied with what she hoped was a deadpan expression. 'And I'm sorry I can't tonight, I've already made some plans.'

'That's a shame, I'm off to Cornwall at first light,' he said, his tone cooler now. 'Maybe some other time.'

In her dreams Charlie would have said, *Don't count on it* but all she did was smile a little foolishly.

'I'll be off then,' he said.

'Have fun fishing,' she said, and as he walked away she had a tinge of regret that she hadn't been warmer. June would have said she was crackers.

It was only a few moments after she'd locked the £60 in the drawer that she saw Ivor's boat the *MaryAnn* coming into the harbour. She ran along to the mooring and waved. Minnie raced along with her, barking with joy at her master's homecoming.

'Can you catch the line and pull it in?' Ivor yelled out. Charlie felt quite confident about this, she had been sailing a few times with her father and seen him do it.

'Ready when you are,' she called back. All the

Londoners looked green, one was out cold in the bows. To a man they all had sunburnt shoulders and arms.

Ivor threw the rope, she caught it, and winding it round a cleat she pulled the boat in.

'Good girl,' Ivor called out. 'Now the stern line.'

Minnie sat by Charlie's legs and they watched as one by one the Londoners came unsteadily up the ladder. There were no leers now, they just looked grateful they were back on dry land. Ivor had some difficulty assisting the last one up, his legs appeared to have turned to rubber. But at last they were all out of the boat and Ivor leapt nimbly out holding a plastic bag of mackerel.

'Your fish,' he said to the men. But they shook their heads and made the kind of gestures with their hands which said they never wanted to see another fish or boat as long as they lived.

'Looks like we'll have to eat them then,' Ivor said as he walked back to the shack with Charlie. 'Do you like mackerel?'

'I don't know,' she replied. 'I've never tried it.'

'Well, you soon will,' he said with a wide grin. 'I'll cook some for you before we go and see Beryl at the Victoria.'

An hour or so later, Charlie found herself wondering how a meal of plain fried fish with bread and butter could taste so wonderful, and why the company of a man old enough to be her grandfather and his scruffy mongrel should be so much fun. He had made her laugh fit to bust when he said how he'd purposely taken the Londoners further out to sea than he normally did.

'They were so know-it-all and flashy,' he said, and

his eyes twinkled with mischief. 'They spoke to me as if I was some dim-witted yokel who'd never been out of Salcombe. But by the time I had them all throwing up yesterday's dinner, they were a little more humble. With luck they'll take their holidays in Benidorm in future, that's where they belong.'

He was amazed that she'd sold the fishing rod, and laughed heartily when she told him what had passed between her and the man called Guy Acton-Bond.

'We get a lot of his type down here,' he said. 'Public school prats with fat wallets and nothing between their ears but air. I expect dozens of them will chat you up, my dear, but just take a word of advice from an old codger. Watch your step with them. It's easy for a young girl to be swayed into thinking a man really cares for her when he lays on the charm with a shovel. But some of these chaps are rotters, and you, my dear, are a little vulnerable right now.'

Charlie smiled. She thought she knew how to handle men.

At half past seven Ivor took her across the road to meet Beryl Langley, Minnie following them with the calm assurance of a dog who was used to shadowing her owner.

'This is my new first mate,' he said by way of an introduction to the woman behind the bar. 'And I can boast that today she's already trebled my usual takings.'

'Well, my lover,' Beryl said to Charlie in a similar Devon accent to Ivor's, 'you're a pretty little flower and no mistake. Let me show you your room. It's not much to write home about, I'll warn you, just a little old attic room. But if you'll put in a couple of hours a night for me when we're busy, you're welcome to it.'

Charlie felt she was going to like Beryl. Aside from her warm smiles and welcoming manner, she had a rather amusing appearance which reminded her of a pantomime dame: about fifty, slightly overweight, with tightly permed orange hair which vied for attention with her shiny pink, ruffled dress. Just the way she came rushing round the bar, picked up one of Charlie's suitcases, then admonished all her customers to behave themselves while she was gone, suggested she was a fun-loving person.

'Watch yourself on the stairs,' she said as she swept out through a back door, leaving Charlie to follow with the other case. 'The stair carpet's as old and worn as me.'

The inn seemed like a rabbit warren with its narrow dark passages, winding stairs and dozens of doors. Beryl led her to the top floor and a room at the back.

'This is it,' she said. 'Sorry it hasn't got a sea view, but then you'll be looking at the sea all day over at Ivor's.'

'It's lovely,' Charlie said weakly. In fact she had never seen such a tiny, cheerless room before. All it held was a single bed, a narrow wardrobe and a chest of drawers. The ceiling sloped so steeply it was only possible to stand upright in the middle of the room. But she reminded herself that she was lucky to be offered a bed at all. 'It's very kind of you to let me have it, Mrs Langley.'

'Beryl's the name, Beryl the Peril to some,' she laughed. 'I'll throw in an evening meal any time you want it,' she added, humping the case she carried up on to the bed and opening it. 'You'll have to help yourself to a bit of breakfast, I'm not usually about early in the morning. Oh, what nice clothes you've got!'

Charlie might have been offended at anyone else opening her case and pulling out items unasked, but the woman did it in an almost motherly way and her approval was welcome.

'My parents were rich,' Charlie said, feeling she had to give some sort of explanation. 'But everything's gone wrong for them. Did Ivor tell you about it?'

'All Ivor told me was that you needed a home,' she said, patting Charlie's shoulder. 'I put two and two together when he said you were Chinese, because I read about your poor mother in the paper. But I don't pry, my lover, if you wants to tell me anything, I'll be all ears, but don't feel you've got to. From what I can see, I reckons you've had a basin full of people poking their noses in.'

'You're very nice,' Charlie said, and suddenly her eyes were prickling with tears. In just a few words this woman with her odd dress and hair had made her feel at home and secure. She was so very glad she'd come to Salcombe. 'Shall I come down now and do some washing-up?'

'Certainly not, tomorrow will do for that,' Beryl said firmly. 'You stay and unpack, make yourself at home. If you want to pop down later for a cup of tea or anything, you know the way.'

Charlie got into bed at ten. From down below she could hear the sound of laughter and clinking glasses and bottles. Although it was dark outside now, people were still walking about. She could hear the sea in the distance and it was a soothing sound.

Her clothes were all unpacked. Her little radio, alarm clock and a photograph of her parents were placed on the locker by her bed. Beryl had popped up just once to bring her a cup of tea, cake and some clean towels. She used the excuse that she'd forgotten to tell Charlie where the bathroom was, but Charlie guessed the woman wanted to make sure she wasn't sitting up here alone and crying.

She did feel tearful, but only because she'd been made so welcome by both Ivor and Beryl. She wondered why some people could be so kind, yet others so cruel. Were the kind ones like that because they'd had some period of terrible unhappiness in their lives too?

She picked up the photograph of her parents. Charlie had taken it last Christmas with the camera she'd been given. They were cuddled up together on the settee in the drawing room with the Christmas tree behind them. It was often said by other people what a striking couple they were, her mother's silky blonde hair and fair skin a perfect foil for her father's olive skin and jet-black hair. In this picture Sylvia was wearing a pale grey cashmere dress, her father a maroon jacket, and they both held glasses of champagne.

At the time when she got the photograph developed Charlie was pleased with the sophistication of the picture. But in the light of recent events, it looked phoney. Everything, the adoring way they were looking at each other, the elegant glasses of champagne and the tree behind them, was posed. Until she suggested taking the picture they had been sitting on opposite sides of the room. It wasn't representative of how they really were alone at home with one another at all.

Why was it that with such a wealth of evidence, her mother's strange moods, her father's long absences, and the rows she overheard, she had continued to believe her parents were deeply in love with one another, and that their life together as a family would never change?

Now she was here in a funny little room above a pub, working in a fishing shack. Mum was in hospital and would perhaps never be able to walk again. And Dad, where was he? Was he, as her mother believed, off with another woman, financing a new start with the money he'd cheated his wife and daughter out of?

Charlie knew this was the most likely scenario. She could even see for herself that Jin might have got so tired of Sylvia's moods and her ever-increasing dependence on him that he felt he had to walk away. If he'd also fallen in love with someone else he could be really happy with, maybe he thought it was right to take everything he'd worked for too.

Yet however likely that was, she still didn't believe it, not deep down inside. Her father just wasn't a callous man. Besides, he had loved 'Windways'. Charlie could remember the many occasions when he'd just come back from abroad. The first thing he would do was insist Sylvia and Charlie join him in wandering around the garden. He would smile with delight over each new flower, drink in the sea air and cuddle them both as they all admired the view. Would any man willingly walk away from something he loved that much?

'Come back, Daddy,' she whispered in the dark. 'Even if it's only to see me and explain.'

Chapter Four

On Charlie's third day working for Ivor, he came into the shack around three in the afternoon and announced it was her turn to make their evening meal.

'Me?' she said, dropping the pile of sun hats she had in her hands in surprise.

Ivor was pleased at the way Charlie was shaping up in the shop. She had a nice manner with the customers and she was so enthusiastic to learn about boats and fishing. He'd fed her for the last two evenings because it was as easy to cook for two as it was for one, and he enjoyed having her company, but if a shared meal was to become a regular thing, he thought she should take her turn cooking too.

'Yes, you,' he grinned. 'I'm not your slave. Go over to the butcher's and get some pork sausages. I've already got potatoes in.'

He shoved a 10-shilling note into her hands and sat down outside to fill his pipe. Charlie didn't have the nerve to tell him she'd never cooked a sausage in her life.

She reasoned with herself as she went over to the butcher's that it couldn't be that hard, she'd seen her mother do it often enough. You just put them in a pan and fried them till they were brown. And potatoes only had to be peeled and put in water.

Ivor was outside talking to one of the boatyard men when Charlie started to cook. She got out the frying pan, put a lump of fat in it, then dumped in the sausages. It was a great deal harder to peel potatoes than it looked, and she was so engrossed in it that she didn't notice the kitchen was getting smoky.

Ivor came rushing in, followed by Minnie barking loudly. 'You'll set the house on fire! You've got the gas on too high,' he yelled, grabbing the pan off the cooker. 'My God, they're burnt to a crisp. Is there something the matter with your eyes and nose?'

'I was doing the potatoes,' she said indignantly.

Ivor dumped the sausages into the rubbish bin. Minnie put her nose in after them, but even she moved back in disgust when she saw the burnt offerings. 'We can't eat those. Go and get some more,' Ivor bellowed at Charlie. 'Be quick before they close.'

While she was gone, Ivor found she had only managed to peel two potatoes, and they looked like a small child's first attempts, heavily gouged with stray pieces of peel all over them. In a flash he realized it was something she'd never done before, and that shocked him. His first reaction was to do them quickly himself, but after a moment's reflection he saw that wouldn't teach her anything.

When Charlie came back five minutes later, he was standing in the kitchen, hands on hips, looking fearsome. Minnie had retreated to her basket as if she sensed trouble. 'Potatoes take longer to cook than sausages, so you peel those first and put them on to boil,' he said curtly.

Charlie sullenly returned to the peeling, but she was aware Ivor was watching her closely. 'What sort of a way is that to hold a potato peeler?' he asked, coming up behind her and grabbing her hands. 'This is the way you do it.'

She thought he would get tired of instructing her and take over, but he didn't, he just stood over her, criticizing the eyes she'd left in, and her slowness. It took her nearly half an hour to peel them all.

'Have you put salt in?' he asked as she lit the gas under them. 'Not that much!' he yelled as she dug a spoon into the china pot he kept it in. 'Only a pinch.'

Charlie wanted to cry. He kept shouting at her for not pricking the sausages, for not keeping her eye on the gas under the potatoes, for not turning the sausages, and for scalding herself when she tried to strain the potatoes.

'You've never cooked anything before, have you?' he said eventually, when she finally admitted defeat and said she didn't know how to mash potatoes.

'No, and I don't want to,' she said and burst into tears. 'Mum or Mrs Brown always did it.'

Ivor smiled to himself. He rather admired the fact she'd had too much pride to tell him so in the beginning. He smeared some butter on her scalded hand, but forced himself not to be overly sympathetic. 'Well, there's no mum here. You like to eat, don't you? So you have to learn to cook. It's as simple as that. So I'm going to teach you.'

He didn't let her off anything. She had to mash the potatoes, and he stood over her instructing her at each stage. Finally they sat down to eat, but by that time Charlie wasn't hungry and all Ivor did was go on about how meat had to be cooked gently otherwise it burned on the outside while the inside remained raw.

'Don't be so mean to me,' she burst out eventually. 'It's not my fault I don't know.'

Ivor wanted to laugh. Scowling didn't suit her, it made her look like a Pekinese.

'Quite so. But it's no good just bleating about it, you have to make up your mind to learn,' he said evenly, reaching over and taking her plate. He cut up her leftovers for Minnie who wolfed them down appreciatively. 'Cooking's a skill even the most stupid person can master, and you aren't stupid, just stubborn. And by the way, your washing-up is hopeless too. So we'll put that right tonight, we don't want Beryl sacking you.'

When he finally let her go back to the Victoria at half past seven, Charlie was livid with rage. He had humiliated her, made her burn herself and implied she was worthless. She hated him.

Beryl came into the kitchen later that evening and found Charlie crying as she washed glasses. 'What's the matter?' she asked.

Charlie blurted it all out. To her surprise Beryl laughed.

'So the old dog's teaching the new one tricks,' she said. 'Can't say I approve of his brutal methods, but it is pretty shocking that a girl of sixteen doesn't even know how to peel a spud.'

Charlie cried harder. She had expected Beryl to be on her side. 'Now, now.' Beryl put her arms round her comfortingly and drew her against her shoulder. 'Ivor's a good man really, just a bit crusty. But he's right, you must learn these things, or how will you manage when you get a place of your own?'

'I can't go back there tomorrow,' Charlie cried. 'He thinks I'm stupid.'

'He doesn't think anything of the sort, you should have heard him in the bar last night, praising you to the skies. And you will go in there tomorrow, my love. You'll march in there proudly with your head held high. Ivor will be sorry by now that he was so fierce. Let him teach you to do things, he's a good cook, nearly as good as me, but I haven't got the time to teach you. In a few weeks you'll be laughing about this.'

'I won't,' Charlie said stubbornly. She was embarrassed now that she'd allowed herself to be caught crying.

'You will when you can cook a whole meal all by yourself,' Beryl said, patting Charlie's back. 'Just you wait.'

Five weeks later, on a wet Thursday afternoon in August, Charlie got off the bus at Kingsbridge. Ivor had given her time off to visit her mother who had recently been transferred to a nursing home there. He said there wouldn't be any customers because of the rain, and there wasn't much point in both of them sitting idly watching it from his shack.

Charlie would have much preferred to spend a lazy afternoon chatting with him than with her mother, who was still being extremely difficult, and she'd said so, but Ivor gave her a pretend slap across the bottom and said, 'Duty comes before pleasure.'

Beryl was right when she'd said that in a few weeks

Charlie would laugh at her hapless first attempts at cooking; she did think it was funny now. But then she felt she was a different person now to the snooty, spoilt kid who'd actually expected her employer to cook her a meal every night. Who would have thought that in just five weeks she would have progressed from burnt sausages to making a chicken casserole from a recipe book without anyone standing over her?

She thought she had learned more useful things in a few weeks from Ivor than in her whole time at school. Every day there was something new, whether it was boiling up her white shorts and blouse in a bucket on his stove to get some stains out, sewing a button on, using Cardinal polish on the red tiles on his kitchen floor to make them gleam, or the correct amount of bleach to put down the lavatory to keep it hygienic. In the shop she'd learned the differences between fishing in the sea and fresh water, which bait had to be used depending on what the customer wanted to catch, and indeed how to handle customers and pick up hints from the ones who were experienced fishermen and sailors.

But it was more than new skills she'd learned from Ivor. In his often brusque manner he'd knocked the corners off her, made her aware of her arrogance and the need to look around her and take in how other people lived and learn from them too, because it was unlikely she was ever going to return to her once pampered life.

Although Charlie still yearned for the comfort of her old life, especially when she was tired in the evenings and still had to do two or three hours of washing glasses and clearing up in the pub before she could go to bed, mostly she loved being in Salcombe. If it hadn't been for the anxiety about her mother, who was still deeply depressed and utterly convinced she would never walk again, and the fact that her father still hadn't surfaced anywhere, she could have been ecstatically happy.

There was the colourful bustle of the harbour on hot days, the peace and tranquillity on wet ones, walks with Minnie and the joy of bringing order to the cluttered shop. She enjoyed talking to the many children who bought buckets and spades, and flirting with boys who came to buy bait. In the evenings at the pub as she collected glasses, she could moan about the strange habits of tourists with other locals, and late at night Beryl would give her a glass of cider with a dash of lemonade and they'd chat about everything from clothes to the latest news in the papers.

But as each day passed, she saw how much she owed to Ivor. He had so little money – what he made in summer had to last right through the winter – yet he shared everything he had with her, whether it was a catch of mackerel, a cake, or just his time. He made her laugh, he entertained her with stories of when he was in the navy, he listened when she needed to air her fears and anxieties about her parents and the future. His advice and teaching were always practical. But above all he made her feel safe and cared for.

Charlie put the hood up on her raincoat and hurried up Westville Hill towards Franklin House. Mr Wyatt had telephoned her a few days earlier at the Victoria to tell her the almoner at Dartmouth Hospital had managed to get Sylvia into this nursing home.

Wyatt felt it was a good move, easier for Charlie to visit, as it involved only one bus, and a calmer, more pleasant environment for her mother to regain her health. It wasn't a private home, just a council-run one, but Mr Wyatt had said it was every bit as good.

The last time Charlie had spoken to the surgeon who operated on her mother's knees, he'd said they were mending well and if only she would do the exercises the physiotherapist had recommended, he saw no reason why she shouldn't become mobile again. But so far Sylvia wasn't making any effort, not with the exercises, or trying to accept what had happened to her. She seemed to be almost enjoying her misery.

Charlie's spirits lifted when she got to the gate of Franklin House. It looked like a big private house with well-kept gardens, overlooking Kingsbridge School. It was painted white and the front door was a cheerful red, which she thought might have cheered her mother too.

A middle-aged nurse answered the door. 'I've come to visit my mother, Mrs Sylvia Weish,' Charlie said.

'Come in, dear. I'm Staff Nurse Dodds,' the woman said with a cheerful smile. She was a big woman with cheeks like russet apples. 'I'll take you along to the day room. Your mum's along there with some of the other patients. Would you like to hang your wet coat up out here? It will be quite safe.'

As Charlie took off her coat and hung it on a row of pegs, she looked around her. The home was as pleasant inside as it looked from without. No grim institutional cream and green paint, but attractive wallpaper and carpet on the floor. It even smelled nice, of flowers, fresh air and polish.

'This is a lovely place,' Charlie said. 'I do hope Mum's appreciating it.'

Just the slight clouding on the nurse's face told Charlie this wasn't so. 'Don't tell me she's being a pain here too?' Charlie blurted out. It had become increasingly embarrassing to visit Sylvia in Dartmouth Hospital; she had alienated herself from just about every member of the staff with her constant complaints and rudeness.

Staff Nurse Edith Dodds had been working at Franklin House for over ten years. Yet in all that time she hadn't met any patient who came close to being as difficult as Sylvia Weish. Today was only her fourth day at the home, yet she had already upset just about every member of staff, and most of the other patients. She complained about the food, that her bed was too hard, that the nurses weren't giving her strong enough pain relief. Another patient in her room snored, she had a crick in her neck from a draughty window, she even accused a nurse of stealing one of her nighties, when in fact one of the voluntary visitors had kindly taken it home and washed it for her.

Edith was aware that Mr Weish was the Chinese businessman who'd mysteriously disappeared, and therefore common sense told her the daughter would have some Chinese characteristics. Yet in her mind she'd pictured the girl as a younger version of Sylvia, and equally difficult.

To be faced with this radiant and polite young girl was quite a shock. She didn't think she'd ever seen anyone quite as lovely, with her jet-black shiny hair,

111

soft dark almond eyes and golden skin. She was wearing a navy and white mini-dress, and her long slender legs were tanned a dark brown. Edith could imagine what prompted Mr Weish to run away from his wife – she would try the patience of a saint – but she couldn't imagine any father wanting to leave a daughter like this one.

'I'm afraid she's not settling down too well,' Edith said with some reluctance. She didn't want to burden such a young girl with more worries. 'But I'm sure you'll cheer her up.'

Charlie half smiled. 'I've never managed to do that yet on a visit,' she admitted, 'but I can but try.'

Staff Nurse Dodds led Charlie down a wide corridor to a large room at the end of the building. It was almost like being in the garden, for there were large windows on all three sides of the room and the carpet was grass-green. Unlike in the hospital, most of the eighteen or so people in the room were under sixty, three or four probably only in their twenties, about a third male, the rest female. Some were recuperating from operations and illnesses and sat in armchairs and wore everyday clothes; a couple of them had a leg in plaster and sat with it out in front of them on a stool. Then there were three or four, including Sylvia, who were in nightclothes and sitting in wheelchairs. Everyone except Sylvia smiled at Charlie as she walked in. Sylvia pointedly turned her head away.

Since Charlie had taken her mother to task about her appearance in hospital, Sylvia had taken note. She allowed the nurses to wash her hair, she did her nails and her makeup every day. Yet she wasn't the glamorous woman she had been. Her nightdresses

112

might be exquisite dainty ones from an exclusive lingerie shop, her slippers rose velvet and her dressing-gown silk, but the misery inside her showed in her face. Daily, the lines around her mouth and eyes were getting deeper, there was a grey tinge to her skin that no amount of expensive cosmetics could conceal.

Charlie saw immediately that this visit was going to be potentially embarrassing. She turned to Staff Nurse Dodds and quietly asked if there was somewhere private she could talk to her mother.

'By all means,' the nurse said, and grabbing the handles of the wheelchair, turned Sylvia around and pushed her towards the door. The room she took them to was only next door; it was tiny, with just a couple of chairs and a small table.

'Well, Mum,' Charlie said as soon as the nurse had gone out, 'this is better, isn't it? I don't suppose you wanted to talk to me in front of all those people.'

'You took your time getting here, didn't you?' Sylvia whined. 'But I suppose your mother is a hindrance now.'

'Don't start on that tack,' Charlie said impatiently. Sylvia said the same thing every visit, like a stuck record. 'I'm working as you well know. I can't come and see you every five minutes. Now, how are you feeling?'

'Like death,' she said gloomily, and fumbled in the pocket of her dressing-gown for her cigarettes. 'I hope you brought me some more of these, I've nearly run out.'

Charlie opened her bag and brought out three packets and a copy of *Woman's Own*. She had given up trying to sweeten her mother with little treats.

Sylvia only ever wanted cigarettes and magazines.

Sylvia didn't thank her, not even with a smile. Instead she looked right into Charlie's eyes and made a sort of growling noise. 'You look just like Jin,' she said venomously. 'I suppose you know the bankruptcy hearing's next month? I'll be finished then. That idiot Wyatt is as crooked as your father. I bet he'll make a fortune out of it!'

'Please don't say nasty things about Mr Wyatt, Mum, he's the only person out there who is trying to help us,' Charlie pleaded with her.

'He's a pompous twat. He would drop our case like a hot brick if he could, but he's stuck with it.'

Charlie felt there was a certain amount of truth in that – he often cut her short when she telephoned him and he certainly wasn't as kind as she had thought at first. 'Well, even if he is pompous, he can't make a fortune out of it, there is no fortune to be had,' she said.

'I don't see why they should take *my* house. It isn't fair. I'm not responsible for what that bastard's done,' Sylvia bleated. 'Isn't it bad enough that Jin took my jewellery as well as all the money?'

Charlie was stumped for a moment. Surprisingly, her mother hadn't mentioned it once in all these weeks, clearly she was totally convinced in her own mind it was gone. Charlie hated Sylvia thinking Jin would stoop that low, but to tell her the truth might be dangerous. She could just imagine her mother insisting she brought it to her and indeed wearing some of it, if only to show off. Perhaps it would be best just to ignore the last question?

'But the house belongs to the mortgage company,'

she said with all the weariness she felt. She had accepted this now. She didn't like it, it made her angry just to think about it. But as Ivor had said on several occasions, 'Acceptance is the first step towards recovery.'

'Even if they let you keep it, you couldn't afford to run it anyway,' Charlie went on. 'They'll let you keep the furniture and stuff. Mr Wyatt said he would help us to find somewhere else to live. We can make that nice wherever it is.'

'What rot you talk,' Sylvia snapped back, her blue eyes as cold as a January sea. 'Do you know what they'll give me? A poky council place surrounded by all sorts of riffraff. What will I do all day in a place like that?'

'The same as you did at "Windways". You'll sit in a chair chain-smoking and reading magazines.'

'How can you say things like that to me?' Sylvia seemed to puff up in her chair, her eyes flashed dangerously. 'I've given you everything. You were treated like a princess. If it wasn't for you I'd never have been buried in the country in the first place.'

'So you didn't want to move to Dartmouth? Is that what you're saying?' Charlie thought that now her mother was good and angry she might let slip a few old secrets. 'You wanted to stay in London? Didn't you work in one of Dad's clubs?'

'Work in them! Without me behind him he wouldn't have even thought of owning one!' she spat out. 'I was the one who knew everything.'

'So why did you tell the police you knew nothing about them?' Charlie said indignantly. She was tired of her mother making things up to suit herself. Just a week ago, for no particular reason, she'd suddenly admitted Jin had never been a drug dealer. Charlie didn't know what to believe sometimes.

'Of course I knew about them. But I wasn't going to tell them, was I?'

'I suppose you'll be telling me next that Dad forced you to strip in those clubs?'

Charlie said that only as a ruse to aggravate Sylvia enough for her to respond. Yet it didn't have the desired effect, she just looked confused and wary, and suddenly clammed up.

'Why don't you tell me about those years?' Charlie pleaded. 'It might help me to understand you and Dad, and why everything went wrong.'

To her surprise her mother slumped back in her chair, her lips quivering. She looked as if all the fight had gone out of her.

'Mum, if you and I are going to have any sort of future we'll have to face up to things,' Charlie said in a low voice, moving closer to her and taking her hands in hers. 'We're losing our lovely home, we've lost Dad. You are sitting there in that chair and unless you make a real effort, you'll remain in it. All we've got left is one another. If I'm going to care for you, the least you can do in return is tell me the truth about your past.'

There was a long silence. Sylvia snatched her hands away from Charlie's and lit up yet another cigarette.

'You think you're so bloody clever,' she said eventually, her tone crackling with spite. 'But you would, wouldn't you? Private schools, the best clothes and toys, adored by everyone just because you look like a little Chinese doll. You might be more intelligent

116

than I ever was, Charlie, but there's one fatal flaw in you.'

'What's that?' Charlie had found so many flaws in her character in the past few weeks she wondered which of them her mother was going to pick on.

'You haven't a clue what poverty is like. Or the lengths people will go to to get out of it.'

Charlie's eyebrows arched in surprise. She believed she did know, after all she had to watch every penny she spent now. She couldn't afford to smoke, or even buy a new lipstick.

'I do,' she said indignantly. 'I spent the last of my wages on those cigarettes for you. All I've got is my bus fare home.'

Sylvia snorted, but there was a touch of amusement in it. 'I'm talking about real poverty,' she said. 'The kind when your stomach aches constantly with hunger, when there's holes in your shoes, and the only dress you have is the one you stand up in. You've never experienced that and I doubt you ever will.'

'No, but –'

Sylvia cut her short. 'I spent my childhood in an orphanage,' she said. 'My mother dumped me there in 1933. I was only four, she sat me down on the doorstep, pinned a label to my dress with my name and age on it, and told me to wait there. She skipped off and I never saw her again.'

Charlie gasped with horror. This was a real revelation and one she'd never imagined. 'Oh, Mum! Why didn't you ever tell me this before?'

'Because I've spent most of my life trying to forget it,' Sylvia said waspishly. 'Anyway, that isn't the point. That orphanage was a terrible place. We got beaten, half starved, and we knew there was nothing better in store for us when we left either. I was fourteen when I got chucked out, it was 1944, the war was still going on and I got sent as a maid to a house in Kensington. I had to get up at five to light fires, I had to clean the entire four-storey house alone, help the cook, clean shoes and do the washing. But I was grateful because I thought I was going up in the world!'

'That's terrible, Mum.' Charlie's eyes filled with tears. 'But were the people kind to you?'

'Well, they didn't beat me, and I got fed, never mind that I finally fell into my bed at after twelve every night and lived in terror of the doodlebugs and V2s. But like I said, when you've known real hunger you'll do anything for food. Even put up with a pervert.'

Charlie blanched. She wanted to know about her mother, but she had a feeling she'd just opened Pandora's Box. 'A pervert, Mum? Do you mean the man you worked for?'

'Yes. He was a barrister, one of the top ones in London. I was a poor little fool, as hungry for affection as I was for food, and he took advantage of it. It started off with him sitting me on his lap and fondling me when his wife was out. I suppose I knew it was wrong, yet I let him, because in my stupidity I thought he must love me.

'The war ended and I was still there, he had his hands up my dress every five minutes by then, and then one day when his wife had gone off to the country he raped me.'

'No, oh Mum,' Charlie gasped.

Sylvia shrugged, her face was expressionless. 'It

wasn't so bad, at least not after the first time, but he told me if I kept quiet about it, he would *see me all right*. I believed him too, God I was so trusting. I thought it meant a little house somewhere, money and nice clothes. Until I found I was pregnant.'

Charlie's eyes filled with tears. She reached out for her mother's hand and squeezed it, not knowing what to say.

'Do you know what that bastard said when I told him? He said I had to tell his wife it was by a boy I'd met in a dance-hall on my night off. He said if I did that he'd make private arrangements for me. Like a fool I did exactly that, trusting him to keep his end of the bargain. But she threw me out immediately, saying I was a dirty little slut. She wouldn't even give me a reference. As for *him*, well, I never saw him again.'

Charlie's tears were cascading down her face now. 'What happened to the baby?' she cried.

'I lost it at seven months or so,' Sylvia said in a cold voice. 'I was too dumb even to know exactly how far gone I was, and I'd been sleeping rough. A group of sailors caught me one night and had me one after the other. I started bleeding then, someone got me to a hospital, and the baby was born but it was dead already.'

Charlie's stomach lurched at such further horror. She knew without any doubt that this was the truth. 'How old were you, Mum?' she whispered.

'Seventeen. Not much older than you. When I got better I made up my mind I was going to use men in future, not the other way around.'

Everything unusual Charlie had ever noted about

119

her mother came sharply into focus. The cold, calculating way she appraised men, the flirtatious way she always approached them if they were rich, influential or she wanted something from them. The way she maintained a glamorous appearance whatever else was going on around her. Now Charlie understood the root cause.

She knew her parents had married in 1952, she had looked at the photographs so many times as a child. What happened in the five years before '47 and then? Something told her it was better not to ask, but she had to.

'I got a job in a café in Soho for a while. But I made so little money I knew I'd have to find something else. I watched the prostitutes and thought about that, but I couldn't stomach it. Then I got asked to strip in a club. So I did.'

Such unabashed honesty floored Charlie. Her mouth fell open in shock.

'Why not?' Sylvia said in defiance. 'I had a good body, lovely legs and I was pretty. I enjoyed it too. Somehow every night I was getting back at that rotten bastard who'd made me pregnant. Those sad, pathetic men who were cheating on their wives by looking at other women's bodies were paying. They could watch, ogle me, but they couldn't touch me. I liked it. I had power over them.'

Put like that, Charlie could understand.

'So when did you meet Dad? Did he come to the club?' Oddly enough, although she could accept her mother's reasons for being a stripper, she found it a lot harder to cope with the idea of her father hanging around in such places.

'No. He was never like those men. I met him out in the street in January of 1949, he asked me the way to China Town in Soho. He'd only just arrived in England.'

'Did he know what you did for a living?'

'Not at first. I told him I was a secretary. But as time went on and I fell in love with him I admitted everything.'

'So you did love him then?' Charlie's heart leapt absurdly at this. She'd been afraid she was going to hear he was just another man her mother used.

'Oh yes. Jin was the only man I ever loved. I would have died for him.'

'So why are you so nasty about him now, then?' Charlie asked, but the moment the words came out she knew she'd said the wrong thing.

It was as though a steel shutter had come down between them.

Sylvia had been relaxed, she hadn't lit another cigarette. Her voice had softened as if she was relieved to talk. But that was gone now. The tension was back in her face, her eyes were cold again.

'He cheated me,' she said in a low growl. 'That's all you need to know.'

Charlie sensed her mother wasn't prepared to say anything more, and in all probability she would start finding fault with her if she stayed any longer.

'I'm glad you told me all that,' she said cautiously. 'Perhaps next time I come you'll feel up to telling me a bit more. But I have to go now, Mum, Ivor's expecting me back. Shall I wheel you back into the day room?'

'No, leave me here,' Sylvia snapped. 'I can't stand any of those morons, they're all so fucking cheerful.'

Charlie shook her head sadly. She didn't like her mother swearing, she'd always been so ladylike before she was hurt. ' 'Bye, Mum,' she said, bending to kiss her. 'I'll come again next week. Try not to be grumpy with the nurses. They are trying to help you.'

'Grumpy! Who do you think you're talking to?' Sylvia snapped back. 'Do you know what it's like to be in pain constantly, to be dependent on someone for everything, even going to the toilet? How dare you swan in here when it suits you and tell me not to be grumpy?'

Charlie tried to calm her mother down, but she couldn't. She left after a few minutes with a tirade of abuse following her – that she was heartless, selfish and just like her father.

Staff Nurse Dodds came into the hall as Charlie was putting on her coat. By her sympathetic expression Charlie guessed she'd heard the shouting.

'Don't take it too seriously,' she said gently. 'She doesn't mean it.'

'I think she wants me to run out on her too,' Charlie said, and a tear trickled down her cheek. 'What do I do?'

'You give as good as you get, but still keep visiting,' the nurse said. 'I think she'll run out of steam before long. I just wish she'd put a bit of that energy into helping herself. She could walk again, you know. She just doesn't choose to try.'

'Thank you for being so patient with her.' Charlie wiped her eyes with her hand. 'If I was in your shoes I'd slap her.'

'I've been tempted.' Staff Nurse Dodds smiled and patted Charlie's shoulder. 'Now I've found what a

122

lovely daughter she's got I'll be tempted to shake some sense into her. But a psychiatrist is coming to see her tomorrow. We have every hope he'll sort her out.'

As Beryl had told her that morning that she wouldn't need any help with washing-up in the evening, Charlie went round to see Ivor rather than returning to the pub. All the way home from Kingsbridge she'd been crying. It was lucky there were so few people on the bus.

Ivor took one look at her pink-rimmed eyes and gave her a hug. He smelled terrible – fish, bait and pipe tobacco – but it was his reassuring usual smell and his big arms around her felt so comforting.

'Just as well that I made enough fish stew for both of us,' he said, lifting her chin up and smiling down at her. 'It's one of my specialities and not to be missed. So sit yourself down and I'll see how it's doing.'

He made her a mug of coffee. Charlie had developed a real taste for his favourite drink. He used Camp coffee, which was made from chicory and in a bottle. He added a couple of large spoons of condensed milk, three spoons of sugar and gave it a vigorous stir. Ivor said it was even better with a tot of navy rum in it, but he claimed she was too young to try that.

Her feet were wet, she felt sad and dejected, but the coffee warmed her inside, and when Minnie came and sat by her, her chin on her knee, dark, soulful eyes fixed on her adoringly, she began to feel better. Little by little she told him about the afternoon. Although she had a natural reticence to discuss private affairs with anyone, especially such shocking things in her mother's past, she had to get it off her chest. Ivor never sat in judgment on anyone, he didn't divulge confidences, and he was the most worldly, understanding person she'd ever met.

'So what are you actually upset about?' he asked once she'd told him everything. He put a large bowl of steaming fish stew in front of her. Charlie sipped cautiously at the somewhat grey-looking mass. To her surprise it was delicious. 'Are you disgusted because she was a stripper? Angry that she didn't tell you about herself before, or just hurt because she rounded on you after revealing so much?'

Charlie half smiled. Ivor had an amazing knack of being able to lay things wide open.

'The last bit really. I thought we were really getting somewhere at last. If she'd told me about her past before all this happened I would have been disgusted, I expect. But looking at it logically, it explains a great deal about her. She didn't have much choice, did she? In her shoes I might have done the same.'

Ivor sat back in his chair and began to clean out his pipe, looking at her over the top of it. 'Exactly. Becoming an adult's all about learning to understand others,' he said. 'A few people are born with it, but most of us only learn that through having some sort of crisis ourselves. Looking back at when I was very young I can remember doing things that I'm a bit ashamed of now, but at the time it was the only course open to me.'

'Like what?' Charlie asked. He had told her a little about his life. She knew about him losing his wife and daughter, and that he sank very low afterwards. He'd often spoken too of the old man Joseph who used to own this place and had taken him in. But he'd never talked about when he was young.

'Well, I was born into a very poor family, in Plymouth,' he said with a bashful grin. 'Dad was a fisherman and Mum took in washing. There were seven of us, and not much to eat when Dad didn't get a good catch. One time when I was about nine it had been too rough for Dad to put to sea for days. There was absolutely nothing in the house to eat and the two youngest were crying with hunger all the time.

'I went out up on to the Hoe, there's a lot of fine big houses there and I had the idea of begging at doors. As I wandered around I could smell this wonderful dinner smell and I was so hungry I kept going up and down until I located it coming from a kitchen in a basement. I crept down the stairs and peeped through the window. There was this big fat cook with a bright red face just getting a huge pudding out of a pan. It was in a china bowl, tied up with a rag on the top. She lifted it out and put it on the table. I didn't stop to think when she disappeared out the back, I just slipped in through the door, grabbed the pudding and ran out with it.'

Charlie laughed. She could imagine the ragged little red-headed boy running through the streets holding the hot pudding by its cloth.

'Was it good?' she asked.

'The best thing I've ever eaten,' he said, rolling his eyes and rubbing his big stomach. 'It was steak and kidney. Mum never asked any questions when I ran in with it. Just divided it up between us all and we wolfed it down. Now the moral of that story is a bit shaky. It was stealing, by rights we should have all

125

got belly-ache, but we didn't. It stopped the little ones crying. It gave Dad enough strength to go out fishing the next day. It made Mum smile again. For all we know the cook up at that house might have got the sack for losing her pudding. But none of us thought beyond our own needs.'

'Surely you aren't ashamed of that now?' Charlie laughed. 'It wasn't so terrible.'

'Maybe not. But it made me steal other things after that. A dress for Mum off a washing line, vegetables down the market, milk off doorsteps. There but for the grace of God I might have taken to a life of crime and ended up in prison. Now your Mum's situation wasn't so very different. She only did what she did to survive. So maybe dancing without any clothes in front of men shocks you, but as she so rightly said, you've never been that hungry.'

'But I didn't like what she said about using men,' Charlie said. 'That's horrible.'

'What she said is honest,' he said gently. 'And it's the same the world over. Women use men as providers, men use women to give them comfort. While I was in the Far East I saw streets full of brothels and I have to admit I was like all the other sailors, I used to go in and buy a woman for the night. Maybe you think that men who do such things are animals and ought to control their urges, but if it wasn't for me and those other men, how would those poor girls and their families live? It's just the same up in Soho. The men go there for a good time, the women charge them for it. It's a fair exchange. '

Charlie pondered on this for a moment. She thought she'd sooner die of hunger than sell her body, but she could understand the point Ivor was trying to make. 'Mum said that Dad cheated her in the end. What do you think she meant by that?'

Ivor looked at Charlie and felt a deep sadness. It seemed to him that this innocent girl was in danger of having all her happy memories of childhood eroded beneath her, because her parents had built a life together which was based on dark secrets, underhand dealings and lies. It was like a dormant volcano. Today there had been a small eruption which had spewed up some of the muck below. He thought that before long the entire thing would blow up and then she'd find a great deal worse. He wished he knew a way to spare her that.

'I don't know,' he said honestly. 'Maybe when she fell in love with Jin she believed he was different to other men, and that he was free of any vices. But few men are entirely pure, Charlie, there is a darker side to most of us. You must remember that when you fall in love, and try never to place anyone on a pedestal. That way you spare yourself the pain of seeing them tumbling off.'

Back at the Victoria Inn later that night, Charlie lay in bed thinking about everything her mother had revealed and Ivor's words on the subject. She was aware she couldn't be totally objective, she'd never been hungry, or in love. She didn't suppose she could even think of herself as poor either, she might have absolutely nothing left in her purse right now, but tomorrow was pay day and she had a wardrobe stuffed with expensive clothes and shoes. On top of that she had the hidden box of treasures and money.

127

What was she going to do about it? Mr Wyatt had said the Official Receiver had placed a seal on the door at 'Windways' and no one but the officials would be allowed in there until after the bankruptcy hearing next month, so she was very glad she'd grabbed them while she had the chance, but when was she going to own up to her mother about them? She hadn't even dared tell Ivor.

Thinking back to his tale about the stolen pudding, she had a feeling it would have his full approval. Perhaps she should tell him tomorrow and ask his advice about telling her mother?

'No, you won't,' she whispered to herself, 'you've leant on him too much already. Grow up and work things out for yourself.'

A couple of days later, on Sunday morning, Charlie had the first real panic attack since she'd arrived in Salcombe. Ivor didn't expect her to work on Sundays and usually she stayed in bed until late, then collected Minnie for a walk, or caught the bus down to Slapton Sands if it was warm enough for sun-bathing. But it had been raining when she woke at about ten, so she'd walked along the main street to buy a newspaper. Suddenly she felt acutely lonely.

Despite the rain there were lots of people about, and everyone but her seemed to have someone. Young lovers holding hands, married couples with their children, even the old ladies going off to church seemed to be in twos or threes. She saw other girls around her own age, giggling and laughing as they dodged from doorway to doorway, keeping out of the rain. It struck her that she'd give anything to see June again, just to have one day being silly, laughing at everything, following boys and chattering.

She knew June would be back now from her holiday in Scotland, but she had a feeling she wouldn't really be welcome if she caught the bus to Dartmouth to go and see her. After leaving the Mellings', Charlie had written them a thank-you letter and enclosed her new address, but June hadn't even sent her a postcard while she was away.

Charlie's eyes prickled with tears. The saddest thing of all was that she knew in her heart that she and June had nothing in common any more. School had been the main bond between them in their long friendship, and now she knew it was unlikely she could return there in September, the cracks that had appeared while she'd been living in the same house had grown too wide to bridge.

But what was she going to do if she couldn't return to school? By the end of September Ivor wouldn't need her any more. Now she came to think about it, there wouldn't be any other jobs then either. Everything died in autumn, the hotels and shops would be sacking rather than hiring new staff.

It was then panic overtook her. What if she ended up sleeping rough like her mother had done when the barrister and his wife threw her out? Visions of her mother living rough on the streets of London came to her and her heart began to pound with fear. Instinctively she turned down towards the harbour to find Ivor.

As always, he was sitting by the door of his shack smoking his pipe and watching the boats coming into the harbour. Charlie ran to him like a child, for once

129

even ignoring Minnie who came hurtling enthusiastically towards her.

Ivor jumped out of his seat in alarm. 'What on earth!' he exclaimed, and as she threw herself into his arms sobbing wildly, he drew her inside the shack out of the rain.

'There, there,' he said holding her tightly. 'Now, calm down and tell me what's happened. Is it your mum?'

It was some minutes before she was able to tell him and almost as soon as she'd blurted out her fears, she felt foolish.

Putting his arm around her shoulder, he led her out the back of the shack, across the tiny yard and into his cottage. He sat her down and put the kettle on. Minnie sat looking at Charlie, clearly puzzled by her distress.

'I'm sorry,' Charlie sobbed. 'I'm being silly.'

'You aren't being silly at all,' he said gently. 'You had to look ahead sometime, and a wet Sunday is as good a time as any. So why don't we sit here and discuss all the possibilities, eh?'

He made her one of his coffees, but this time he did put a spot of rum in it, as he said, *purely for medicinal purposes.*

'Now, let's see what we've got,' he said, pulling at his beard. 'Right now you have a job and a home, but they will go by the end of September. That's five weeks away. Don't you think that's long enough to find some alternative?'

Charlie gave a weak shrug.

'I think it's a pretty long time,' he said. 'Considering during that time you are going to get your exam results, and you'll know the result of the bankruptcy hearing. I suspect too, though I can't be certain, the council will have found a place for you and your mother to live, because they can't possibly let her stay at the nursing home indefinitely.'

'But what if I can't find another job?'

Ivor looked across the table at her fear-filled eyes and smiled at her naïvety. 'The days of the workhouse are long gone, Charlie, we do have something called National Assistance these days,' he said. 'I suppose folk who've lived up on the hill in Kingswear wouldn't be aware of such things, but it means the government will give you and your mum money for food and to pay the rent. There's no question of you sleeping rough, or starving.'

Charlie smiled sheepishly at his teasing words. She *had* known there was such a thing as National Assistance, but it hadn't occurred to her that she and her mother would be eligible for it.

'That takes care of the immediate future,' he said seeing the relief on her face. 'But you should be thinking a bit further ahead, Charlie. What do you want to do with your life?'

'What's the point in even thinking what I want to do?' she said sharply. 'I've got no choice, have I? I'll have to look after Mum.'

'You don't *have* to.' Ivor shook his head. 'If you refuse they'll get her a home help. No one would expect a girl of your age to look after her alone.'

'She'll expect it,' Charlie said. Her lip quivered and Ivor knew then that this was the real reason behind today's panic attack, even if she wasn't aware of it.

Minnie moved to sit between Ivor's knees, but she

continued to look at Charlie, her head on one side, almost as though she understood what was being said.

'My father always expected I would stay fishing with him,' Ivor said, fondling his dog's ears. 'My mother thought I would always be around to mind the little ones. But I fell in love with a girl, married her and made a home of my own. They had to accept that.'

'But your parents had each other and neither of them was crippled.'

'No, they weren't crippled, but my father was getting frail and my mother's legs were so swollen that she couldn't climb the stairs, so I was in much the same position as you, and I had to choose. I chose to be with Sarah. I still helped out when I could, but I distanced myself, and they managed okay. You must do this too.'

'But I'd feel mean.'

'You'd *become* mean if you allow yourself to be forced into something which will make you unhappy. Perhaps that's the reason your mother is the way she is, Charlie. As you said yourself, she didn't ever get any choice about anything, did she?'

The sun came out later and Ivor suggested they went out in his boat. Charlie made some sandwiches and a flask of coffee and they set off. Once out at sea Charlie's spirits rose. The sea which had been a dismal grey just a couple of hours earlier was suddenly blue again, and the wind whipping her hair off her face was exhilarating. Ivor let her take the helm for a while while he fished for mackerel at the stern with Minnie sitting up beside him. The utter peace, broken only by the cries of seagulls and the slapping of waves against the bows, was very soothing.

They were just about to go about to sail back to the harbour when Charlie caught sight of a sleek yacht speeding in their direction. There was something about the scarlet flash across the white bows which looked familiar and she pointed it out to Ivor.

He shaded his eyes and looked. 'I've seen it moored in the harbour but I don't know who it belongs to.'

Charlie sat in the stern watching enviously as the yacht came closer to them. She could see two men wearing nothing but shorts leaning out on the port side as they flew along. She thought it must be thrilling to harness the wind to drive you. Ivor's little fishing boat was lovely, but even at full speed it only chugged along, it didn't have that excitement factor.

As the yacht came alongside them and sped on by, she suddenly realized why it looked familiar. The man she'd sold the fishing rod to was at the tiller. It was Guy Acton-Bond.

He must have spotted her at exactly the same moment for he turned and waved.

By the time she and Ivor had moored the *MaryAnn* and walked back to his cottage, Guy's yacht was already moored and there was no sign of anyone on it. Ivor asked if she wanted to stay and share the mackerel.

'No, you eat it all yourself. I've been enough of a burden today,' she said with a grin. 'Besides, my jeans are wet and I promised Beryl I'd be there at seven to help out. I'll see you later.'

Back at the Victoria Inn Charlie took a shower and

washed her hair. She didn't usually bother about her appearance in the evenings, in fact she usually did the washing-up wearing the same clothes she'd worn all day. But her mind was on Guy, and just in case he came into the pub later she was determined to look her best. She knew this was a bit silly as she only popped in and out of the bar to collect glasses, but she wasn't going to be caught out looking messy.

If she was to wear a dress, Beryl would immediately suspect she had her eye on someone. She decided on her best white shorts and a white sleeveless tee-shirt, with a red belt to give the outfit a lift. Then she blow-dried her hair carefully, turning the ends under in the now very fashionable page-boy look. Finally she put on several thick coats of mascara and some lipstick; her face was so tanned nothing else was necessary.

'You look pretty tonight,' Beryl said as Charlie came into the kitchen. 'What incredible legs you've got. Mine were never like that even when I was sixteen.' She lifted her dress enough to reveal sturdy pale legs with little shape. 'See what I mean?'

One of the things Charlie liked most about Beryl was her complete lack of vanity. She took the rise out of herself all the time, she even seemed totally aware she had awful dress sense. Her interest was people, she cared about each and every one of her customers, took their troubles to heart, shared their moments of good luck and happiness. She had a very big heart.

'They don't look too bad to me,' Charlie said. 'Besides, you've got a lovely face and that's all people see behind the bar.' This was true. Beryl wasn't a

134

beauty, she probably hadn't been even as a girl, but her happy disposition made her so.

'You little charmer.' Beryl pretended to swat her with a tea-towel. 'Then tell me why I don't get any proposals of marriage?'

Beryl was a widow. Her husband Roger had died of cancer some ten years earlier. She often spoke of him, never in a maudlin way, but with laughter and fond memories. It was her favourite long-standing joke that she was looking for a replacement, but everyone knew she was just joking. She was content running the pub alone.

'Because all the men in Salcombe are afraid you'd think they were after your money,' Charlie said with a giggle.

'Go on with you, everyone knows I'm as poor as Ivor,' she said.

'Well, marry him then.' Charlie laughed. 'You'd make a fine pair with your matching hair.'

Beryl laughed. Really laughed, holding on to her sides and making great snorting peals of raucous laughter. 'Oh, Charlie,' she said eventually. 'What a thing to suggest!'

Charlie was still giggling about this as she emptied the dishwasher from the lunchtime session. She had never laughed so much with an adult as she did with Beryl, and daily she was growing almost as fond of her as she was of Ivor.

Around eight Charlie made her first visit to the bar to collect glasses. The first person she saw was Ivor, standing at the bar talking to Beryl. But although they were laughing together and she suspected Beryl had told him what she said, her attention was distracted because Guy was at the other end of the bar with two other men, both with dark hair.

She had remembered him as being very handsome, but during the time that had elapsed since she last saw him, she had come around to thinking she was probably exaggerating his good looks. But there was no exaggeration, he was gorgeous. His long blond hair was streaked almost white in places from the sun, skin the colour of mahogany, and angular bone structure like a male model's. He wore a white short-sleeved, open-necked shirt and faded Levis; even his eyes were the colour of new denim. She grabbed some glasses from a table to hide her confusion.

'Hi there,' he said, raising one blond eyebrow. 'It's the fishing-rod queen! Don't tell me you work here too?'

'I live here, so I help out,' she said. She thought that was quite smart, he might think she was a relative of Beryl's.

She saw him glance along the bar to Beryl and Ivor. He obviously recognized Ivor as being the man she'd been in the boat with.

'He isn't your father, is he? he asked nodding towards Ivor.

'No,' she laughed, amused at such an idea. 'I just work for him. Do I look like him?'

'No, I can see no resemblance,' he said. 'Actually I can see no one in this bar beautiful enough to have been either of your parents.'

Charlie picked up a few more glasses. As she turned to a table she knew he was studying her bottom and legs and she blushed furiously.

'Back to work,' she said as she turned and found him staring at her. 'See you later.'

She had never found it hard to stay in the kitchen before. Mostly she disliked going out into the bar because she felt people whispered about her. But tonight she wished more than anything that she had a good excuse to go out there.

It wasn't busy in the bar, it didn't look as if it was going to get busy. She guessed that before long Beryl would come in and say she didn't need her any more. Sure enough Beryl came in around nine, saw that Charlie had cleaned everything in sight and suggested she had an early night.

There was nothing Charlie could do. Beryl had never said she couldn't stay in the bar, but somehow she knew she didn't really approve of under-age girls being there. To ask if she could stay would make her suspicious, and anyway she couldn't really talk to Guy under Ivor's watchful eye.

As Charlie went slowly up the stairs, she willed Guy not to disappear at first light. She felt she was being a bit silly, but just the thought of his tanned angular face made her go all hot and cold.

She was round at the harbour before nine the next morning and she smiled to herself when she saw Guy's boat was still there, and no sign of activity on it. Every other boat owner was busy. Getting ready to sail, taking fresh water and provisions aboard, swabbing the decks, painting or cleaning.

'Glad you got here early today,' Ivor said as she walked into the shack. 'I've got a party waiting to go out fishing. Can you cope on your own?'

She assured him she could, helped some children pick out buckets and spades, and as Ivor went off to the *MaryAnn* with Minnie to meet his group waiting further along the harbour, she saw Guy come up from the cabin.

He stood on the deck stretching. He was wearing what looked suspiciously like only a pair of under-pants; blushing, she looked away.

An hour later Charlie had tidied up the shack, blown up a few more swimming rings and tied them in a big clump to hang outside, and unpacked more buckets and spades. She was just going to nip into Ivor's cottage to make herself some coffee when Guy appeared in the doorway. He was wearing proper shorts now and a spotlessly clean white tee-shirt. He looked like an advertisement for a washing powder.

'Hullo, Charlie,' he said.

'How do you know my name?' she asked, thrown by his sudden appearance.

'The time-honoured method. I asked,' he said. 'I'm sorry I called you Suzie Wong when I first met you. I only knew the name, I didn't know who she was. You must have thought I was being insulting. I certainly didn't mean to be.'

Charlie's heart began to race. That meant he'd thought about her after he'd left. She was excited, nervous, embarrassed and thrilled all at once.

'It's better than calling me Chinky Charlie as people did at school sometimes,' she said.

'I wouldn't dream of calling anyone as beautiful as you something so rude,' he said. 'I was often called Guy the Gorilla at school and I hated it. If I'd been covered in black hair it would have made some sense,

138

I could have beaten my chest and roared at people. But as I looked like a weedy little choir boy it wasn't very apt.'

Charlie was even more struck by him now she knew he was well-mannered and had a sense of humour. She could imagine him as a little boy. She guessed he'd been angelic-looking.

'I was just going to make some coffee,' she said. 'Would you like a cup too?'

'Best offer I've had all week,' he said with an impish grin.

'Well, mind the shop for me a moment,' she said. 'I have to nip into Ivor's cottage.'

He was helping a small girl in a red swimsuit select a rubber ring as she got back with the coffee. Just the way he had put it round her waist, checking to see it wasn't too big for her, made Charlie's heart lurch.

'There we are, sweetheart,' he said, patting the little girl's head. 'Just right for you. But don't go out of your depth in it, rubber rings are only meant to help you learn to swim, you mustn't rely on them to keep you safe.'

Guy passed the money over to her. 'You like kids then?' she said as the little girl went running away still wearing the ring.

'Yeah, I guess I do,' he said. 'I've often thought of going in for teaching.'

'What do you do now?'

'I work in the city,' he said with a smile. 'The Stock Exchange actually.'

'Do you wear a bowler hat and pin-striped suit?' she asked, handing him his coffee. She couldn't possibly imagine him in anything other than jeans.

'Only the old chaps wear bowlers now,' he laughed. 'Could you see me with my long hair in one?'

'No,' Charlie giggled. 'Not unless you tucked it up inside.'

'I wear it tied back, otherwise I'd be out on my ear, sometimes I wonder how I get away with it. I've got the pin-striped suit, though. I look one hell of a prat in that.'

He liked Ivor's brand of coffee. He sipped it reflectively and said his nanny used sometimes to give him some of hers which was just like it.

Guy sat down on Ivor's upturned tub, Charlie took the stool, and they'd only been talking for a short while before Charlie realized he'd been born with the proverbial silver spoon in his mouth.

His father was a director of several large companies. He lived at home with his parents and two younger sisters in Henley-on-Thames. He had been educated at Eton, but as he wasn't particularly academic he'd been nudged into working at the Stock Exchange because his father wanted him to gain experience before finding him a position in one of his companies. Charlie got the feeling that Guy wasn't entirely happy at having his career mapped out for him. He didn't say so, but the way he preferred to talk about sailing at weekends and holidays gave her the idea he lived for those times.

The yacht, his father's, was named *Chloë* after his youngest sister who had been born just as his father bought it, five years ago. Charlie thought having a baby sister was probably another reason he had been so nice to the little girl earlier. Guy said she'd been something of a surprise to all of them, he was twenty-one, the next sister was eighteen and his mother had been forty-two when Chloë arrived.

Charlie told him very little about herself, just that she was working here for the summer, her father was away on business, her mother in a nursing home and her real home was in Dartmouth. If he got the idea that Beryl and Ivor were people she'd known since childhood, she didn't straighten him out.

'Aren't you going sailing today?' she asked when he showed no sign of moving on. He'd already said the other two men with him on the yacht yesterday were old friends from his schooldays.

'No,' he said with a shrug. 'Tim's gone off for the day with his girl. Owen's sleeping off a hangover. We thought we'd have a day on land and sail tomorrow.'

It was a busy morning at the shack, one of the busiest Charlie had ever had, but even though at times there was a queue waiting to be served, Guy stayed sitting outside. In the lulls between customers they resumed their conversation, and Charlie found herself dredging up funny stories Ivor had told her about people here in Salcombe, and things about her friends from school – anything to keep his interest.

She thought she'd forgotten how to flirt. It seemed years ago that she and June had waylaid boys and told them tall stories, but to her surprise she was still just as good at it, better perhaps because she really did like this one.

At one point she reminded herself of her own mother: she found herself touching his arm, looking deep into his eyes and asking him questions about himself, just the way Sylvia did at parties. It was a bit like the effect of a couple of Babychams, she felt all sparkly and fizzy inside. She just wished she knew how to engineer things so he would ask her out tonight and wouldn't sail away tomorrow for good.

When she spotted the *MaryAnn* coming in, her heart sank.

'That's Ivor coming in,' she said, pointing out the boat to Guy. 'I think you'd better go.'

He stood up. 'Okay. I don't suppose you could get some time off this afternoon and come swimming with me?'

'I don't like to ask him,' she said, but even as she spoke her mind was already on what she could say to persuade Ivor. Could she pretend she needed to see her mother? Could she play ill?

'Try and think of something,' Guy said, and leaning forward, kissed her cheek. 'I'll be on the boat if you can get off. If not, what about tonight?'

The *MaryAnn* was getting closer and Ivor had keen eyesight. It wouldn't do for him to see her talking with Guy if she was going to make up a story.

'I'm supposed to work tonight too,' she said hurriedly. 'But I'll work on it. I'll come along and tell you later.'

Guy went off then, and as Charlie watched his bouncing step up to his yacht she knew she was prepared to say anything, do anything to spend some time alone with him.

As Charlie watched Ivor bringing in the *MaryAnn*, her mind firmly on Guy and everything he'd said to her this morning, she suddenly realized something which made her squirm.

She had always thought confidently of herself as

upper-class. She spoke well, she had a first-class private education, and she'd been brought up in a luxurious home. But now after meeting Guy, who really was out of the top drawer, and hearing him talk about his Mini Cooper, social life in Henley, holidays in the West Indies and diving in the Red Sea, it occurred to her that her background was in reality only working-class.

In a flash of intuition she saw this was exactly why her father had bought 'Windways'. At some stage of Jin's life, in all probability soon after she was born, he'd decided to embark on a new way of life and gain respectability.

Putting Guy aside for a moment, she wondered if this could be why her father had set so much store by socializing in Dartmouth. She had always assumed he just liked to make new friends and have fun. But in the light of what she knew now, wasn't it more likely that it had been for *her* benefit? Perhaps Jin's whole aim, the nice clothes, the good schools had all been in the hope that his daughter would ultimately marry well and have the security he and Sylvia had never had when they were young.

The thought was chastening. It explained those overheard rows between her parents, why her mother was so often locked in silent misery. Jin's intentions might have been good, but he had a separate life elsewhere, where he could be his real self; poor Sylvia had to breathe, live and sleep the image he'd created for her. Was that why she wouldn't make any effort now, because she knew that without all those trappings and without Jin she had nothing to offer anyone?

*

Ivor came bounding along the quayside, his smile stretching from ear to ear. Minnie ran before him, her tongue lolling out so she looked as if she was smiling too.

'How's my first mate?' Ivor boomed out. 'And who was the young man I saw chatting to you?'

Charlie knew then she'd never be able to fool him. He had eyes in the back of his head. Besides, he had obviously had a good morning, he was positively bristling with glee.

'It was Guy from the *Chloë*,' she replied, patting Minnie who was jumping up at her. 'But tell me about your morning.'

'I got a twenty-pound tip,' he beamed. 'They were Yanks and they said they'd never had a better time. Tell me you've been busy here too and you can have the afternoon off to go and lie in the sun.'

Charlie burst into excited laughter. 'I've never been so busy. I think I've taken over eighty pounds.'

Ivor stopped in his tracks, still smiling. He knew Charlie was always pleased when they sold a lot of stuff. She felt it justified her wages. But Ivor guessed that her bright smile was due to something more than money today. It didn't take a great brain to work out that the chap from the *Chloë* was behind it.

'Has he asked you out?' he asked.

'Yes, he wondered if I could go swimming with him.'

'Well, you'd best put him out of his misery then,' he said. 'Push off and have a good time.'

Charlie ran to Ivor and hugged him. As she leaned against his broad shoulder she felt ashamed she'd planned to lie to him.

*

That afternoon was the best time Charlie had had since the night she was picked as Carnival Queen at the dance in the Queen's Hotel. Everything seemed magical. Guy held her hand as they wandered up through the High Street and he bought an impromptu picnic of tuna rolls, pork pies, fruit and lemonade. They caught the ferry to the small beach at East Portlemouth and lay down on a rug he'd brought with him.

Charlie was very embarrassed when she peeled off her shorts and tee-shirt to reveal her scanty red and white spotted bikini. But when Guy looked at her and whistled, suddenly she felt like a beauty queen.

The sun was so hot they were forced to go into the sea frequently. She didn't want to swim in case her hair ended up like wet seaweed, but Guy leapt in immediately and kept splashing her until she joined him.

He kissed her for the first time in the sea. It was the best kiss she'd ever had, he didn't force his tongue into her mouth like so many other boys had done, but just teased her with it, his lips warm and salty, and she thought she might die from pure bliss.

Other boys she'd met with June on beaches the previous summer had always been so rough. They horsed around, picking the girls up and throwing them in the water, sometimes they'd even tried to wrench off her bikini top. But Guy wasn't like that, he wanted to cuddle her, stroke her skin, and kiss her tenderly. She knew right away that this was exactly what she'd been waiting for. It felt like love.

When they came out of the sea they were cold. Guy wrapped her in the towel as though she was a child, and cuddled her dry on his lap. Charlie didn't care that there were people watching them, she wasn't even concerned that they might think it shocking to see two young people kissing with such abandon.

Guy licked the salt from her tummy later, and whispered that if they were alone he would lick every inch of her. Suddenly she knew what real desire was; this wasn't one of those slightly tingly moments she'd experienced with other boys in the past. She wanted Guy. To lie beside him completely naked, to fondle him and let him do the same to her.

'I've never felt quite like this before,' he whispered after yet another long, deep kiss. 'I wish I wasn't with the lads, then I could spend all the rest of my holiday with you.'

Charlie wished that were so too, but she was wary of admitting such a thing just yet. 'I've got to work anyway,' she reminded him.

In the morning their conversation had centred on getting to know about one another's background, but now as they lay in the hot sunshine, their feelings became the important issue. Guy told her his father was often very disapproving of him, he wanted him to get his hair cut, to think about his career and find a nice girl from a good family to settle down with.

'I want that too, eventually,' he said, his blue eyes looking right into hers as if he believed he'd found the right girl. 'But I want fun now, adventure and good times. Father doesn't seem to understand that things have changed since he was my age. Our generation didn't live through the depression or the war, we don't need to be so practical all the time. Why shouldn't we go sailing in the summer, pack a rucksack and go off to India if we choose to? My idea of heaven is to be lying out under the stars, smoking a joint with a girl I love, or climbing a mountain just to see the view at the top, to explore remote places, to experience everything. Do you think like that too, Charlie?'

Charlie had never seen a joint, much less smoked one. She'd never thought of climbing a mountain and visiting a remote place would worry her in case she couldn't have a bath and wash her hair. But she thought all that would be heaven if Guy was with her.

'Sort of. Until Mum went into hospital I used to want to be a hippie and go to rock festivals and stuff, in fact I used to get frantic in case it was all over before I got the chance. But I haven't had much opportunity to think more than a day ahead just recently.'

It was then she saw she couldn't tell him yet about her real situation, it was too heavy and it might spoil things. Besides, for this afternoon at least she wanted to believe she was free.

'Once Mum's a bit better, I was thinking of moving to London,' she said. 'I don't know that I could stand going back to school for "A" levels. I want to share a flat with some other girls, to be free to do whatever comes along.'

He looked pleased at this and moved closer to kiss her shoulders. 'Won't your parents kick up a stink? Or aren't they stuffy like mine?' he asked.

'Not in quite the same way,' she said carefully. She didn't want to tell lies which might trap her later, but at the same time she wasn't going to say anything which might alarm him. 'Mum's neurotic, kind of wrapped up in herself, and Dad's away a great deal.

But I suppose they want much the same for me as your parents do, a career, the right kind of husband. They'd probably have fifty fits if they knew I was lying on the beach right now with a man I hardly know, planning to pack in school and a wild life in London.'

'You want to be wild then?' he grinned.

'Oh yes,' she smiled, and meant it. 'Rock concerts, parties, going to clubs and stuff. Nothing ever happens in Devon. I want to be where there's excitement, where places are open all night. I want to dress as I please and see who I want.'

'I knew you were my kind of girl the moment I saw you,' he said, bringing his lips down on to hers for another long, lingering kiss that sent tingles down Charlie's spine.

'If you get a flat in central London we can have such good times,' Guy said later as they began to pack up their things. It was after five now and getting a little cooler. 'Had you given any thought to what sort of job you'll get?'

'I thought of banking,' Charlie said on the spur of the moment. She had never for one moment considered this before. 'I'm good at maths. Or something in the Civil Service.'

Guy looked surprised. 'I think you ought to try modelling,' he said. 'You'd make a fortune with your looks. Surely you don't want to work somewhere as dull as a bank?'

'I was only thinking I'd earn plenty of money,' she said quickly. 'Do you really think I could be a model?'

'I know you could,' he said, standing up and pulling her up into his arms. 'I can just imagine showing the

148

chaps at work a copy of *Vogue*, with you on the cover, I'd say "That's my girl. Isn't she something?" and they'd all be green with envy.'

It was ten past six when Charlie got back to the pub, but despite the early hour it was already busy. Her heart sank, she'd banked on it being quiet enough for Beryl to give her the night off. Guy had said he was going back to the boat to have a shower and change and he'd come round later to see if she could get away. He'd joked that if it was busy he'd let off a couple of stink-bombs to clear the place.

Worse still, Beryl looked harassed behind the bar. Charlie knew she couldn't add to it by asking to be excused tonight.

She shot upstairs, showered, washed the salt out of her hair, and changed into her white mini-dress. If all else failed she could still have an hour or so with Guy after closing time.

Right up until nine Charlie was run ragged, collecting glasses, washing and drying them and taking them back to the bar just to get them used all over again. Guy was in there, but she got no chance to speak to him and she was beginning to despair.

To her surprise and delight, at nine-thirty there was almost a mass exodus from the pub. Charlie wasn't sure if it was just luck, or whether there was something else going on in another pub. But suddenly the bar was almost empty.

'Thank God for that,' Beryl exclaimed as she brought a tray loaded with glasses in for Charlie to wash. 'I must be getting old because I don't get the same high as I did once from taking money.' She paused to look at Charlie. 'You're all dressed up tonight!' she said. 'Who's that in aid of?'

'The blond man at the end of the bar,' Charlie said with a giggle. 'He's lovely, Beryl. I spent the afternoon with him today at the beach.'

'Guy Acton-Bond eh?' Beryl looked knowing. 'He is a handsome devil, I'll give you that. But isn't he a bit out of your league?'

Charlie bristled. 'He likes me,' she said with some indignation.

'I'm sure he does,' Beryl said more gently. 'I'm getting old and crabby, dear, forgive me. It's just that I always found the handsome ones were the rotters. I wouldn't like you to get hurt.'

'He won't hurt me,' Charlie said confidently.

'Well, you'd better rush off and join him then, dear,' Beryl said with a smile. 'But mind you're back by twelve, or you'll find yourself locked out.'

Chapter Five

'I know I'm an old fogey, Charlie, and probably out of touch with the younger generation. But mind you don't get out of your depth,' Ivor growled.

It was Thursday morning, three days after Charlie spent the afternoon on the beach with Guy, and since then she'd spent every available free moment with him. Even now she was standing at the door of the shack bleakly watching him sail the *Chloë* out of the harbour, despite knowing he would be coming back tonight.

'Don't be silly,' she snapped impatiently without turning to face Ivor.

A few moments later she felt ashamed of herself. She came into the shack, over to where he sat mending a lobster pot, and put one hand on his arm. 'I'm sorry. I shouldn't have said that, you aren't silly. Just a bit of a worry-guts. It's just that everyone keeps warning me off Guy. I don't understand why, we're really alike and we're so happy together.'

Ivor patted her hand with affection. He wasn't going to attempt a lecture, he knew she was deaf to everything except the words Guy whispered in her ears.

Salcombe was a tight community. Everyone knew

everyone else and even in high summer when one would imagine the tourists would act as a distraction, still everything that happened was noted and gossiped about.

Charlie had been a source of great interest since she arrived in the town. Along with her striking appearance, there was the fact she worked for Ivor. Beryl had told him just a few nights ago that some people were actually claiming she was his daughter, a love child born to a Chinese mother when he was in the navy.

As Beryl was the soul of discretion when she cared for someone, she had merely laughed at this fanciful tale. As she'd pointed out to Ivor, such a rumour was in fact less potentially damaging to Charlie than the truth about her real father. She found it quite astounding that no one had yet made the connection between this girl and the brutally attacked woman in Kingswear, whose Chinese husband had disappeared owing a great deal of money.

While Charlie might be a bit of a mystery to the people of Salcombe, Guy and his family were quite well known. He'd been coming here for holidays since he was a small boy, and latterly sailing in, sometimes with his father, but more often with friends. On almost all the recent visits he'd managed to put people's backs up, rowdy parties on his boat, getting drunk, or acting belligerently towards other people moored in the harbour. And on each visit there had been a different girl.

Mostly the girls came with him, arrogant ones with plummy accents and braying laughter; they strutted around looking at ordinary folk as if they had a bad smell under their aristocratic noses. But Ivor had heard that on two occasions Guy had found a local girl to be his entertainment for the duration of his stay, and both girls had been heartbroken and humiliated when he shipped out without even saying goodbye.

So it was hardly surprising that all eyes were focused on his new romance with Charlie. They made a very attractive couple, but because of Guy's track record, everyone anticipated trouble. Just that morning Ivor had been informed by his next-door neighbour that Charlie had spent the whole night on the *Chloë*.

Ivor knew this wasn't true. He was still at the pub at midnight, talking to Beryl, when Charlie arrived home. She may very well have got up early and gone down to the yacht to see Guy in the morning, but that wasn't quite the same thing. Even so, his paternal instincts were aroused. Charlie might think she was an adult, but she was still a vulnerable child in his eyes and as such he wanted to protect her.

'Have you told him the situation about your father?' Ivor asked gently. He hadn't actually met Guy's parents, they weren't the type to buy anything from a harbourside shack, but he knew a little about them. They were extremely wealthy and both came from illustrious families. Ivor didn't think they'd take too kindly to their only son and heir taking up with anyone who wasn't out of the top drawer.

Charlie looked awkward, her eyes dropped from his and she shuffled her feet on the floor. 'Not exactly,' she mumbled.

Ivor kept quiet.

'Why does it matter anyway?' she said defiantly

after a few minutes. 'Guy isn't the kind of person who cares about class, money and all that. He likes me just for myself.'

Ivor sighed. He didn't doubt that Guy had made such statements, and indeed meant them, right now. But it could well be a different story once he'd introduced Charlie to his folks. People like the Acton-Bonds would want to know every last thing about any girl their son was keen on. They'd almost certainly be dubious about her because of her mixed race. If they were to discover the truth about her parents they would undoubtedly demand Guy dropped her.

Maybe Guy had fallen heavily for Charlie, Ivor thought proudly that it would be hard for any man not to. But would he see her in quite the same romantic light if his father curtailed his sailing, cut off his allowance, and told him to make his own way in the world?

'I'm glad you've found someone to care for,' Ivor said. He wasn't normally one for choosing his words carefully, but he knew he must while she was in such an emotional state. 'And I really hope it works out for you with Guy. But just try to keep your feet on the ground, sweetheart. Don't pin everything on him.'

Charlie felt aggrieved all day. She barely spoke to Ivor again. She didn't understand why he was so doubtful about her and Guy.

It was like they were made for one another, they made each other laugh, they had so much to talk about. He had only to touch her hand and she wanted him, when he held her in his arms she melted into him. Just an hour away from him was too long, and she knew he felt exactly the same. It was true love. It wasn't a silly girlish crush. Why did everyone keep making those dark hints about how rich his family were? Did they think that was the only reason she liked him?

Anyone would think she was a girl from the slums. Hadn't she been brought up surrounded by wealthy people, just like Guy? They laughed at snobs together, they found social climbers pathetic. They both wanted a life where class, money and the establishment meant nothing. To travel the world, to try everything, see everything.

Around eight that same evening Beryl went into the kitchen to make a ham roll for a customer. Charlie was standing at the sink washing glasses. She was wearing a slinky pink sleeveless maxi-dress. Clearly she was intending to meet Guy later.

'I haven't seen that dress before,' Beryl said. 'Come on, give us a twirl, is it new?'

Charlie spun round from the sink, she was flushed, almost as if she'd been woken suddenly from a dream.

'I didn't hear you come in,' she said. 'I must have been miles away.'

'I can imagine where you were,' Beryl said wryly. 'Under swaying palm trees with the man of your dreams.'

Charlie giggled. 'Not exactly,' she said. 'I was thinking maybe I ought to go up to London for the day soon and see if I can find a job there for the end of the season. What do you think of my dress then? I bought it in that boutique up the road.'

'It's super,' Beryl said with the utmost sincerity. Even at sixteen her own body had never been as firm and shapely as Charlie's. Her stomach was flat, her bottom like two grapefruits, and the slit up the front revealed those perfect long brown legs.

'I was a bit rash,' Charlie said shamefacedly. 'I just couldn't resist it. I read in a magazine that no one in London is wearing minis any more.'

'And you didn't want Guy to think you were a bit square?' Beryl said. 'Was that it?'

Charlie giggled. 'I suppose so.'

She turned back to her washing-up, and Beryl, sensing the girl wasn't in a talkative mood, got on with making the ham roll. Ivor had been expressing his anxiety about Guy to her over the bar just a few moments ago, but she wasn't exactly sure where her sympathies lay. Ivor was being protective, he had grown very fond of Charlie, so of course he was wary of anyone who might hurt her. Beryl had watched the lad with Charlie on several occasions, and she had got the impression he was every bit as smitten with Charlie as she was with him. Being something of a romantic, and somewhat charmed by Guy herself, she wanted it to work out for them.

On the other hand she knew both the other local girls who'd fallen for him in the past, and remembered how callous he'd been with them. Of course men could change when they fell in love, she'd seen it happen dozens of times.

But the main thing which worried her was that Charlie might give too much of herself, too soon. It would be understandable, the poor kid was so young and naïve. It crossed her mind that maybe she

156

ought to give her some advice about contraception.

But even as she thought it, she knew she couldn't. Charlie would be terribly embarrassed, and anyway kids these days probably knew more than she did.

Beryl put the roll on a plate and looked across at Charlie's backview. For some unfathomable reason she suddenly had a rush of unexpected tenderness for the girl. Perhaps it was just the combination of those childishly narrow shoulders, the glamorous dress, chosen to please a man, yet there she was up to her elbows in soapsuds like a scullery maid. She deserved better, Beryl thought. She had earned her keep five times over in the time she'd been here.

'Finish those few and then you can go and meet him,' she said. 'But make sure you put on some handcream before you go. Dishwash hands don't go with that dress.'

She wanted to add some warning about being careful, but she couldn't bring herself to. The young didn't heed warnings, and first love, as she remembered, was too heady and reckless to think of tomorrow.

The last rays of daylight were just fading in the sky as Charlie walked across the road into the harbour. To her delight the *Chloë* was back and Guy was just leaping from it to the harbour wall. Even before she could call out his name, he saw her and ran to her, arms open wide.

'Have you got off work?' he asked as he hugged her tightly.

'Yes. Beryl let me come and meet you,' she said. 'We've got hours together now.'

He kissed her then, there on the harbour, long and hard without any thought to the people bypassing them on either side.

'Come on to the boat then,' he suggested. 'The lads have gone off. They won't be back till late and I've got a couple of bottles of cider in the fridge.'

Charlie had been on the *Chloë* several times in the last couple of days. Guy had even taken her out sailing for an hour after she finished work the previous day. She had always liked boats; in Dartmouth they had the same importance to most families as cars. But this one was the nicest and most luxurious she'd ever been on.

Guy had gone to great pains to explain that it had been designed specifically for his father and a young family. So it could be sailed single-handed if necessary, sturdy enough to stand up to rough weather, and with all the home comforts his mother had insisted on. Charlie got the impression that Guy would've preferred to lose the comfort and sturdiness in favour of more speed. But she thought it was just perfect.

There was a small double bed fitted into the cabin in the bows, another cabin with single bunks, and the saloon had comfortable couches which could be used as beds too. It had a toilet, shower and refrigerator. The galley was beautiful, with the cooker and sink tucked away under real oak counters, and an abundance of cupboards with almost everything you'd expect to find in a normal kitchen.

The men kept it very clean and tidy considering there was no woman aboard to tidy up after them, but Guy had said this morning that was Tim's doing, not his. Tim by all accounts had spent three or four years at sea, crewing for anyone that would pay him to see the world. He'd got into the habit of being cook, cleaner and laundryman.

'That dress is something else,' Guy said once they were on board. 'You look a million dollars.'

Charlie glowed. It had cost an entire week's wages, in fact she'd got a sub from Ivor to pay for it and she didn't know how she was going to manage all next week without any money. But it was worth it to see Guy's appreciative smile.

They had a couple of glasses of cider each, and because Charlie hadn't had anything to eat since lunchtime, it went straight to her head. When Guy took her hand and led her into the cabin, she felt no alarm, she wanted to lie in his arms in comfort.

The lapping of the waves against the hull and the gentle rocking movement were in perfect time with the Beach Boys tape playing softly in the background. Guy lit a couple of candles and turned off the electric light.

'Don't let me fall asleep,' Charlie said with a giggle. 'Beryl will lock the doors if I'm not home by twelve.'

'Do you really think I'd let you waste this precious time together by sleeping?' He laughed and climbed on to the double bed and pulled her into his arms.

Charlie had lost touch with reality many times before when he kissed her. Just this morning when she'd come aboard to see him before he sailed, they had tumbled on to this bed and were almost swept away by instantaneous passion. But the other two men were in the next cabin then, she'd had only an

159

hour before getting to work, and Guy had a thick growth of stubble on his chin.

But Guy's face was smooth and silky now, he smelled of expensive aftershave and there were no reminders of duty or other people to help her keep her head. Within minutes her dress and his shirt were off, and with each kiss Charlie felt the last of her reservations about losing her virginity fading.

They had petted heavily before, and Guy was a practised and skilful lover. He didn't alarm her by being too hasty and as his fingers gently explored her, so he whispered loving endearments.

'I love you, Charlie,' he said as he nibbled at her breasts. 'I've never felt like this before. I want you so badly.'

'Do you really love me?' she asked, catching hold of his face with both hands and looking into his eyes, searching for any sign of insincerity. 'Really, really love me?'

'How can you doubt it?' he said, caressing her vagina so delicately that she found herself pressing up hard against his fingers. 'I love everything about you, your face, your body, your personality. The only way I can really show you how much, is to make love to you.'

Charlie knew she should ask if he had a Durex, but she couldn't bring herself to say something so coarse and unromantic. His breath was hot on her cheek, his penis was rock-hard against her thigh, even the rocking movement of the boat in the water was simulating the act of love. But it was the tenderness in his eyes which drove away any last uncertainty.

She was surprised that it didn't hurt, she had always

supposed it would. It was a bit uncomfortable, and it was disappointing that the feelings of intense pleasure she'd experienced earlier as he caressed her stopped. But her pleasure came from sensing his. He gripped her buttocks tightly, pushing himself into her, and as he moved faster, the boat rocked with them and the lapping of the water sounded like a symphony.

'It's fantastic,' he yelled out suddenly and bit into her shoulder, then he was suddenly still.

For a moment Charlie just lay there, her legs still clasped around his waist. He was soaked in sweat, sticking to her, and the cabin ceiling seemed to be revolving above her in the candlelight. Tears prickled at her eyes and she wished she could have gone to whatever place Guy had; she felt a bit cheated.

'I blew that, didn't I?' he said after a moment or two, and his voice was muffled because his mouth was still on her shoulder. 'I was too quick for you. I'm sorry.'

'Don't apologize, it was lovely,' she whispered back. She wondered how many women lied the first time. It seemed to be the kindest thing to do.

'I'm usually at my best after a couple of drinks,' he said. 'But I suppose it was because I wanted you so much.'

The tears prickled again. She didn't want to be reminded he'd done this before lots of times with other girls. She wanted to be first, the only one. She wanted reassurances she was special.

Those reassurances came later as he cuddled her. He spoke of all the things they could do together when she came to London, and said that next summer they would take the boat across to France and sail right down the coast.

'Father did suggest that I could sail her right round to the Med and find a berth there for her,' he said gleefully. 'You could come with me as crew. We could get summer jobs in Marbella easily, and find a flat together there.'

'Why couldn't we stay on the boat?' she asked, already mentally packing a suitcase.

'Well, Dad, Mum and my sisters would fly over to use it for most of August,' he said. 'We wouldn't want to be stuck with them, would we? We'd just sail it home in September. Wouldn't that be great?'

Charlie thought it sounded more than great. It was the most thrilling plan she'd ever heard. But over and above the adventure of it was the thought he loved her enough to think a year ahead. She hadn't dared think beyond next week.

He made love to her again later, and this time it was wonderful. Maybe she didn't reach those dizzy heights she'd read about in magazines, she was pretty certain orgasms were something you'd recognize if you'd had one. But it was lovely.

'If you want to go up to London to look around for a job, why don't you come with me tomorrow?' Guy asked as she was dressing to go home. He had tried to persuade her to stay all night with him but she didn't dare do that.

'You're going tomorrow?' she said, so shocked her legs almost gave way under her.

'Well yes.' He shrugged. 'I thought you knew that?'

'No,' she said, 'I thought you were staying till Saturday.'

162

'I said I had to *be home* on Saturday,' he said cheerfully. 'I'm only sailing as far as Southampton, mooring her there and going up to London by train. You could tell Ivor you were going to crew for me. You could stay the weekend with my folks, then on Monday you could come up on the train with me to the city when I go to work and you could look around for a job. Later in the evening you could come back here on the train. Oh, do come, Charlie. It will be such fun!'

It sounded like a dream come true to Charlie. 'But Ivor!' she said as she zipped up her dress. 'Who will help him? I can't just go off from Friday to Monday and leave him in the lurch.'

'I'm sure he'll understand. You told me yourself he thought you ought to go to London sometime to look around.'

Charlie thought hard. She knew if she told Ivor she was going up by train alone, he would send her off with his blessing. But it might be an entirely different matter if he knew she was going on the *Chloë*. Could she make up another story?

'What time are you going tomorrow?' she asked.

'Around midday.'

Charlie looked at her watch. It was five to twelve, she didn't have long enough now to think about anything. 'I'll come here tomorrow at half past nine and tell you,' she said. 'I must rush now, Guy. I don't want Beryl locking me out.'

'It might be easier if she did,' he laughed. 'That way you could do exactly as you pleased.'

As Charlie ran back to the Victoria she thought about Guy's last words and it occurred to her he was

163

right. She could stay out all night. What business was it of Beryl's? Likewise she could tell Ivor to stuff his job if he didn't like her going to London for the weekend with the man she loved.

She paused, tempted to turn back, yet she couldn't. The truth was she didn't want Beryl or Ivor to think badly of her, she cared about them.

Charlie barely slept a wink. One moment she was thinking about Guy, reliving every kiss, caress and endearment. The next she was picturing Ivor's face when she asked for time off. No good excuse sprang to mind. He knew she had no family other than her parents; if she suddenly invented an aunt, uncle or good friend he would know she was lying.

But she was determined to go with Guy, whatever Ivor or Beryl said. She loved him, he wanted her with him. She was going.

'Attack is the best method of defence.' Charlie had read that somewhere and as she went down to the shack at half past eight the next morning she kept repeating it to herself.

It was drizzling, one of those grey, miserable days which make people wonder why they thought they liked English seaside towns. Both the sky and sea were like lead, and there was a strong westerly wind.

Ivor was bringing out the buckets and spades. When he saw her he waved.

All at once Charlie did mind what Ivor thought of her. He had taken her in on trust, comforted and cheered her when no one cared about her. Yet it wasn't just that she owed him a great deal, she had grown to love him too.

'Quiet day ahead,' he said as she came nearer. 'This rain looks set in.'

'Then you won't mind if I ask for time off to go to London?' she said.

'Hell no,' he said, squatting down on his tub to light his pipe. 'What time train were you thinking of going on?'

Charlie gulped. It had seemed easy back in her bedroom, she would just say what she intended to do, then if he got angry or started a lecture she'd just walk away. But how could she do that? It wasn't right. Supposing the drizzle stopped, the sun came out, and people descended on the harbour? He relied on her to look after things when he took fishing parties out. Apart from that she might lose his friendship and she couldn't bear that.

She blurted out her intention. One long monologue, hardly drawing breath.

'I must go with him, Ivor, so please don't say I can't,' she finished up.

Ivor didn't reply for a moment. He wasn't angry with her, what she said had struck a chord within him. He could remember wanting to be with Sarah so badly that he would have killed anyone who tried to prevent it.

Yet he was frightened for her. Not only because she would meet Guy's parents, who might very well be hostile, or that things might come to a head while she was away, but because sailing up the coast could be dangerous if young Guy hadn't got his mind on navigating that yacht of his.

He looked at Charlie before replying, her dark eyes were pleading with him, her whole body was tense. He knew she intended to go whatever he said.

'I don't like it, Charlie,' he said eventually in a deep growl. 'Southampton's a long way away, and that stretch of water can be dangerous to someone who isn't an experienced sailor. But if you feel you must go, I can't stop you.'

Charlie thought getting his permission would make her happy. But faced with his obvious anxiety she felt bleak.

'Guy and his two friends are all experienced sailors,' she said. 'Especially Tim, he's been right across the Atlantic. We'll be hugging the coast all the way. I'm sure if the weather got worse they'd sail into a harbour. Please be glad for me, Ivor, I can't be happy if I know you are sitting here being cross with me.'

Her pleading reminded him sharply of an incident once with his own daughter. Kim had been seventeen at the time and she begged him to let her go camping in Cornwall with her boyfriend on his motorbike and a group of other friends. Ivor had refused point-blank.

Kim never really forgave him, her boyfriend met another girl while he was away, and she never met another boy afterwards that she felt so strongly about. It was one of those things he recriminated over a thousand times after Kim and Sarah's death. Sometimes he even thought that if he'd let her go, she might have ended up marrying that boy. She and Sarah might never have been on that hill in Lynmouth to get mown down and killed.

'I can't help worrying about you, sweetheart,' he said, softening his voice. 'I've grown so fond of you and I just want to keep you safe. Go with him and have a good time. But promise me you'll keep your life-jacket on, that you won't horse around on the deck and distract the men.'

Charlie's vivid smile came back, lighting up her eyes. 'Oh, thank you, Ivor. I will be sensible, I promise. And I'll be back on Monday evening.'

It was nearly eleven that same night when they sailed into Weymouth harbour. The men weren't very happy; although the wind had been behind them all day, they hadn't made the kind of speed they intended. They were tired, wet and cold, and they were disappointed they hadn't been able to make a harbour further up the coast.

Charlie was glad they'd reached any harbour. She just wanted to put her feet on dry land again.

For the first couple of hours after they left Salcombe, she had thought it was thrilling. The rain stopped, there was even some weak sunshine, and as they sped along the coast her mind had been firmly on the night ahead. But then the rain came down in earnest and Guy ordered her below decks.

Up on deck she could ride with the big waves, it was exhilarating and exciting. Dressed in a set of waterproofs, lashed by sea spray, she felt part of the team and was happy to do whatever the men asked her.

But down in the cabin she felt suddenly queasy. If she looked out of the porthole the up-and-down motion made her stomach lurch sickeningly. She couldn't seem to read, it was stuffy and a bit scary. Making mugs of coffee for the men was difficult, she swayed and toppled over constantly, she even scalded herself with boiling water a couple of times.

Before they'd set out, she'd had the idea that Tim and Owen would do most of the sailing; she also thought they liked her. Yet she soon found they were annoyed that Guy had invited her along. Neither of these two rugged, dark-haired men was the playboy type – Tim worked in a boatyard in Southampton, Owen ran a ship's chandler's there, and they were very serious about sailing. To them, girls belonged on dry land, and Charlie, who had little experience of sailing, was a liability.

Although in the first two hours Guy was by her side constantly, pointing out landmarks, chatting about other sailing trips, once he'd sent her below he forgot about her. Owen and Tim came down frequently, to get coffee or a sandwich, but not Guy, he remained at the helm.

Around six the rain turned back to mere drizzle again and Guy yelled down to her to make them all something hot to eat. Charlie was thrown entirely by this. Although she'd learned to cook with Ivor, there was a great deal of difference between doing it in a spacious kitchen where everything was static, and attempting it in a confined space where everything kept moving.

She thought she was very ingenious. She found various tins in the cupboards – stewed steak, new potatoes, carrots and peas – so she emptied them all into one large saucepan and heated it up. Tim came down for his first, wolfed it down with several slices of bread and butter and begrudgingly said it was good. Owen did the same, but made no comment. Yet when Guy came down he took one look in the pan and shuddered visibly.

'There were sausages and bacon in the fridge,' he said reproachfully, peeling off his waterproofs.

'I didn't think I could manage frying anything,' she said. In fact she'd assumed that those things were intended for tomorrow's breakfast.

'You're not the best galley slave we've ever had.' His tone was half joking but there was an underlying edge she didn't like.

He ate his meal, in fact finished everything in the pan without asking if she'd had some. She wasn't hungry, but she had intended some to be left for her later.

'Make me a cup of tea,' he said lying back on the couch and lighting up a cigarette. 'You can do the washing-up later.'

Charlie bristled. She wasn't used to people ordering her about. Even Ivor and Beryl always asked her politely and they were paying her to work for them.

'So I'm a servant now, am I?' she retorted.

He looked astonished, blue eyes opening very wide. 'Everyone has to pull their weight on a boat,' he said.

'I'm aware of that,' she said. 'But how about please? Or even thank you for the dinner?'

'The dinner was shit,' he said coldly. 'And I'm cold and wet and want a cup of tea.'

After a very disappointing afternoon, with the prospect of a long, lonely and boring evening ahead, such a hurtful remark was too much for Charlie. Biting back tears, she turned away from him to fill up the kettle, but just as she was about to light the gas, a sudden swell made her fall backwards hard against the table. Guy's plate was still on there, it fell to the floor and smashed. The kettle, still in her hand, spilled everywhere.

She couldn't hold back tears then, and slid down on to the floor sobbing.

Guy, to be fair to him, did leap from the couch. He hauled her up, rubbed her back where she'd caught it and told her not to worry about the water because he'd wipe it up. But Charlie was angry, and she pushed him away saying she'd do it.

'You're a strange girl sometimes,' Guy said a few minutes later. He'd refilled the kettle himself and put it on the gas, Charlie was on her knees mopping up the water and picking up the broken china. 'I can't quite make you out.'

Charlie sniffed and dried her eyes. 'Why? Because I think people should say please and thank you?'

'No, of course not. Sorry I was a bit rude to you. I didn't really mean it. I'm just grouchy because of the weather.'

Appeased, Charlie let it go, but some five minutes later, once she'd made the tea, she brought up the subject again and asked what it was he couldn't make out about her.

He shrugged. 'Just silly little things really.'

'Such as?' She was so glad he looked as if he was intending to stay with her for a while she didn't mind if he was going to be critical.

'Why did you take the summer job working for Ivor? I would have thought a girl with your looks and brains would've gone for hotel work or something.'

'It was the only job I could find,' she shrugged.

'But didn't you try in Dartmouth? There's more going on there than in Salcombe. Besides, you could've stayed in your own home then. Who's looking after that if your mum's in a nursing home and your dad's away on business?' He looked at her intently, and continued, 'By the way, what is the matter with her? You've never said.'

Charlie felt trapped. She sensed these questions hadn't suddenly sprung to his mind, but had been gathering importance in the last couple of days, perhaps even prompted by his friends. Her first instinct was to lie, yet he said he loved her. So the truth shouldn't make any difference to him.

'It's a bit of a difficult thing to explain,' she said carefully. 'You see, everything happened suddenly and unexpectedly.'

His expression hardly changed as she told him an abbreviated version of the story. His eyes widened at the men crushing her mother's knees and he raised an eyebrow when she spoke of the impending bankruptcy, but he didn't look horrified, just sympathetic.

'Hell's bells, Charlie, that must have been so tough on you,' he said when she'd finished. 'And you still don't know where your dad is?'

Charlie shook her head. She didn't feel able to say she feared Jin had been murdered. Nor had she mentioned his past life as a night-club owner.

'Now you know why I'm not so brilliant at cooking,' she said with a wry grin. 'Until I went to work for Ivor I'd never done a hand's turn about the house. But then I don't suppose you do either?'

'Certainly not,' he laughed. 'Though I can cook if pressed. I'm impressed that you've learned so much in just a few weeks. As for thinking about looking after your mother, you must forget that. It would be a living death. Now, come here and give me a kiss. You deserve a few hundred.'

He went back up on deck soon after, and once it grew dark, all three men stayed there. It was one of the longest evenings Charlie had ever known and she was overjoyed when Guy finally popped down to tell her they were going into Weymouth.

'Maybe it will be sunny tomorrow,' Charlie said after they'd been directed to a berth, secured the boat and were making their way to the yacht club as the harbour master had said it was the only place they would still get a pint. With all the time she'd had below decks she'd been able to shower, change her clothes, put on some makeup and even paint her nails. The thought of spending a whole night in bed with Guy had banished any earlier despondency.

'The weather forecast isn't very promising,' Tim said gloomily. 'We'll have to set off at first light if we're going to make it to Southampton.'

Once the men had downed their second pint of beer all three of them became cheerful again. They ribbed Charlie about her stew, and her painted nails, but all of them remarked on how clean the galley was, and promised that tomorrow she could stay up on deck. She didn't think she and Tim would ever really hit it off, he didn't talk much, and when he did, it was only about boats, but Owen unbent quite a lot, and told her stories about him and Guy at school. She thought they'd finally forgiven Guy for bringing her along.

Back at the boat, some four pints later, Tim produced

a bottle of whisky. But Guy declined to share it and led Charlie off to the cabin.

'We'll have to make the most of tonight,' he said, hurriedly undressing. 'Mother will make us sleep in opposite ends of the house, and probably hang bells on your door knob in case I try to creep in there. The thought of you in here with me tonight has been the only thing keeping me going today.'

All the emotion and passion that had been pent up all day was released the moment their naked bodies touched. Although they could hear Tim and Owen laughing along in the saloon, it didn't inhibit them in any way. The three vodkas and grapefruit Charlie had drunk at the yacht club had made her just a little woozy, the gentle rocking of the boat was soothing, and when she looked at Guy her heart filled up with love for him.

His hair was caked with salt, he smelled a little gamy and he needed a shave, but none of that mattered one bit. She wanted him, now and forever.

It was well after three before Guy fell asleep in the crook of her arm, his hand still cupping her breast. Charlie was exhausted by the frantic love-making. He had been right, he did last longer when he'd had a few drinks.

Guy woke as the first rays of daylight crept through the porthole. Charlie was almost moulded against his back, and he turned to look at her sleeping.

She was without doubt the most beautiful girl he'd ever seen. Her hair gleamed like the feathers of a raven, silky soft to the touch, yet so heavy it lay on the pillow like a slick of tar. Her complexion was flawless, golden-brown with a delicate sheen. Such thick long lashes, beautifully shaped eyebrows and lips so plump and pink. He suddenly felt a stab of sharp sorrow that he couldn't keep her with him forever. A girl who looked as she did would be an asset to any man.

He knew when she came leaping on to the boat yesterday morning to say she could accompany him to London that he'd been too impulsive suggesting it the night before. He hadn't given himself time to think things through.

As the day wore on it became even clearer to him that he'd made a mistake. Charlie was entirely different to the girls he usually went for. Aside from the fact that they were usually older, and toughened up by boarding schools, they knew exactly what they wanted from life. They had strong family ties, multitudes of friends and filled their spare time with sport. Such girls wanted nothing more than a good time, sex was just another sport to them, and they said he was good at it. He could pick these girls up, take them out to dinner or away for a weekend of sailing and lust, and they accepted he might not call them again for weeks. In fact breathing space was essential to them – most of them had several other men in tow.

Charlie might appear superficially to have much in common with glossy Berkshire girls. Her stunning looks, education and the way she spoke would open doors for her anywhere. But she hadn't got that enviable bedrock of confidence which came with an impeccable pedigree. It was like trying to train a terrier to be a gundog, or expecting a Morris Minor to drive like a Porsche.

When Charlie finally told him about her parents and their problems, everything fell into place. The father sounded suspiciously like a rogue. That didn't bother Guy unduly – his own father was ruthless in business and had sailed very close to the wind on many an occasion. What worried him more was the mother! She sounded dangerously common, and she was now crippled to boot.

There was nothing his own mother abhorred more than common women who set themselves up as society hostesses. She could smell them a mile off, even if they had learned all the social graces, dressed superbly and did good works. Within a few minutes of talking to Charlie, Guy knew his mother would suspect her background and if she imagined for one moment that Charlie had designs on her son, she'd move heaven and earth to uncover her family secrets.

How could he take Charlie home knowing his mother would be watching her every move, looking for evidence of bad blood in everything from the way she held her cutlery to how she wrote a thank-you letter?

He wished he was brave enough to admit this to Charlie now, to suggest they spent the weekend together in a London hotel, and resume their relationship well away from his mother's eyes once Charlie moved to London. But he couldn't do that. If he wasn't home by Sunday morning at the latest, his mother would be on to friends in Salcombe to find out what he'd been doing all week. One of them was bound to tell her something. He could just imagine her face when she heard he had been seen constantly with a

Chinese girl. From then on she'd be like a dog with fleas, scratching and scratching until she drew blood.

Sadly, Guy cuddled closer to Charlie. He did care deeply for her; maybe to say he'd fallen in love with her was stretching it a bit far, but he liked her more than any other girl he'd known. But was she worth having his freedom curtailed? To live with rancid disapproval from his parents?

A couple of hours later, just after seven, Charlie woke to find herself alone in bed, and thinking the men were getting the *Chloë* underway she rushed out into the saloon wearing only a tee-shirt and knickers.

Guy was sitting there alone, drinking a cup of tea, fully dressed.

'I thought we were supposed to be sailing at first light,' Charlie said.

'I overslept,' he said, rubbing his eyes wearily. 'I guess the others did too. I'll go and wake them now. There's more tea in the pot if you want some. Then you'd better nip into the shower before they want it.'

By the time Charlie was dressed both Tim and Owen were up on the deck with Guy. She could hear their feet on the deck above her and the sound of muffled voices. She climbed up the steps and poked her head out. It was drizzling again and the men appeared to be discussing something about the mainsail.

'Shall I cook you all some breakfast?' she called out cheerfully. 'I'll try to do better than last night's stew.'

Guy came over to her. 'I think we're all a bit too

hungover to eat now. We'll get some fresh air in our lungs and a few knots under our belts first. But we need some bread and milk. While we're getting ready to cast off, could you nip down to the town and buy some?'

'Sure,' she said, and went back to get her jacket. As she came up again, Guy handed her a £10 note.

'There should be a paper shop open in the street off the promenade,' he said. 'Don't kill yourself to get back, we won't be ready for a while.'

Charlie stood on tiptoe and kissed his stubbly cheek. ''Bye, Mr Bristles. See you in a minute.'

Despite the rain, the air smelled wonderful to Charlie as she bounded down towards the town. Every other time she had been to Weymouth it had always been packed with jostling crowds and it was peculiar to see it deserted. She couldn't see anyone, not sailors, holidaymakers or even the odd man walking his dog. As she reached the promenade a couple of cars went by, but shutters were drawn on shop windows, the heaps of beach toys, postcards and rock stands were all safely tucked away.

She walked for some ten minutes before she found a shop open, and paused for a moment to look at the newspaper stand outside. The headlines were mostly about a radiation leak at Windscale. This didn't interest her much, but she thought Guy might want to read about it, so she selected *The Times* and went on into the shop. She lingered for a little while looking at a display of ornaments made of sea shells. Then she found a sliced loaf and a pint of milk, paid for them and left.

With the milk in her jacket pocket and the loaf under

her arm, she managed to skim through the paper to find the fashion page. An article about the dangers of damage to ankles from wearing platform shoes caught her eye. She was so engrossed in it that she was half-way back up the harbour before she looked up again.

A yacht was sailing out. She stopped in her tracks, thinking it was just like the *Chloë*, and then to her astonishment she suddenly realized it *was* Guy's yacht, not merely one like it.

For a moment she was too stunned to do anything but stare. It was moving fast, right out of the harbour. They were going without her. Hastily stuffing the paper into her jacket, she ran along the harbour wall shouting. Her first thought was that they'd forgotten she wasn't aboard. But as she got closer to where it had been moored overnight, she saw her travel bag sitting there beside a bollard.

All at once she realized it was intentional. She'd been dumped like so much rubbish. Sent out on an errand while they cast off.

She was beside herself with rage. She stood on the edge of the wall stamping her feet, waving her arms and screaming out obscenities. But it did no good. She could see Guy's back in his familiar orange oilskin coat as he stood at the helm. He was purposely not looking back, even now he was probably laughing with his friends.

A man came up on to the deck of the boat berthed next to where the *Chloë* had been.

'What's all that noise about?' he shouted at her.

Charlie took one look at his angry red face and knew she'd get no sympathy from him.

178

'Bloody men!' she shouted back, and picking up her bag turned to walk back to the town.

Tears began to stream down her face after a few minutes' walking. She had been paid off with £10, not an explanation, or even a kiss goodbye. Ten pounds for risking her job, losing her virginity and having the nerve to think she was important to Guy.

He was a lying maggot, she hoped he'd drown at sea somewhere between here and Southampton. In fact she hoped he would be in the sea for hours before he finally drowned, freezing cold, terrified and with enough time to reflect what he'd done to her.

It wasn't until she reached the station and found there wasn't a train for over an hour that she noticed a piece of white paper sticking out of the side pocket on her travelling bag. She pulled it out and found it was a hastily scrawled note from Guy.

'I'm sorry, Charlie, I know what I've done to you is awful. I shouldn't have asked you to come with me and meet my parents, I know now they wouldn't approve of you and I thought it better this way rather than let you be embarrassed.

I really did care for you. I'm so sorry.

Love Guy.'

Charlie stared at the note for some ten minutes until she could no longer read it through her tears. Perhaps it would have been better if he hadn't tried to explain himself; that way she could have believed he was just a rotter. But his note suggested something far worse, that she was an embarrassment to him.

She had been brought up to think she was something pretty special. And she'd expected her life to be golden. It was bad enough to have all the material things snatched away, and to find her parents weren't the people she had believed them to be, but she'd managed to live with that. But now Guy had destroyed the only thing left. Her pride in herself.

Chapter Six

Charlie limped back into Salcombe at three in the afternoon soaked to the skin. As she had spent all her wages on the pink dress, she thought she ought to hang on to the change from Guy's £10 note, so instead of catching a train, she hitchhiked home.

She'd got to Torquay easily in two lifts, but then she got lost, ended up on the wrong road, and by the time she'd walked to the right one her feet were hurting and she felt like lying down and crying.

Yet a steely resolve kept her going, even though it began to rain heavily again. Guy might have made a fool of her, but he'd be the last man to do so. From now on her heart was going to be locked away. Any man who wanted her in future would pay, one way or another.

There were five more lifts before she was finally dropped on the outskirts of Salcombe, and in each one of them the driver had attempted to discover why she seemed upset. But she told them nothing, and she was determined not to reveal the truth to Ivor and Beryl either.

The door of the Victoria Inn was locked for the afternoon as she'd expected. She could have rung the bell, but Beryl often had a nap in the afternoon, and she knew that if she disturbed it, there would be no way to get out of talking. As it was still raining and she was so wet, Ivor's was the only place to go.

He was sitting on a stool mending a lobster pot in the shack as she walked in. As always Minnie gave her a big welcome, but today she couldn't respond, and pushed her away.

'Charlie!' Ivor exclaimed in surprise. 'What's happened?'

'Nothing, I just jumped ship in Weymouth,' she said airily. She had rehearsed this explanation all the way home and hoped her contrived bouncy manner was convincing.

'Why?' he asked, getting up.

'Make us a cup of your magic coffee and I might tell you,' she said, forcing a grin.

Ivor came back from his cottage with two mugs of coffee a few minutes later. Charlie cupped her hands round hers, she was very cold and a little shaky. 'Well?' he said, raising one bushy eyebrow.

'It was all a bit of a disaster really. It rained all day yesterday and I was stuck in the cabin. Guy was cross because we only made it as far as Weymouth last night, and then I blew it by telling him about my parents.' She paused for a moment to gather herself. 'He said it didn't make any difference but he went all quiet on me afterwards and I knew he was having second thoughts about taking me home with him.

'Anyway, this morning I decided it was better to slope off and save us both more embarrassment. From what he'd told me about his mother she sounded like a terrible snob anyway. So I came on home.'

Ivor knew this wasn't what had happened. She

wasn't meeting his eyes, her explanation was too pat, and he could see she was close to tears. But he decided against probing any deeper. From personal experience he knew it a darn sight harder to strive to retain some dignity when your heart was breaking, than to cry and gain some sympathy. He thought she had real guts.

'Well, I'm really pleased to have you back,' he said, putting one big hand on her shoulder and squeezing it. 'I missed you. And just by chance I've got enough mackerel for both of us for tea.'

Charlie didn't know how she managed to get through that long day without breaking down. After sharing a meal with Ivor she went back to the pub to find it was very busy. She had no choice but to pitch in and help. It wasn't until after closing time that Beryl asked why she'd come back two days early.

Although she was exhausted, drained and grieving, somehow she managed to give Beryl the same story she'd told Ivor, then pleading tiredness she managed to escape to her room before her bottled-up tears overflowed.

A strong wind was whipping up the sea and she could hear waves slapping loudly against the harbour wall, and that was another unwanted reminder of Guy. In reality she had known him for such a short time, yet she felt that in just one week she'd left her girlhood behind and become a woman.

How could she ever forget him? He had taken her heart, her soul and her mind. All the memories of him were so sharp. How could she go to the beach without remembering his salty kisses, or look in the high-street souvenir shops without thinking how he used to laugh at them? She could smell his skin, his hair, see his blue eyes and feel the silkiness of his blond hair. She would hear his deep tender voice telling her he would love her forever.

Why had he spun all those dreams for her about sailing to the Med, going to parties and rock concerts in London, if he didn't mean them? Why would anyone pretend to care so much then run away without even saying goodbye?

She could just picture what he was doing now. He'd be all cleaned up in a clean shirt and trousers, sprawling gracefully on a settee in the drawing room of his grand home, sipping a gin and tonic and spinning the kind of yarns for his doting parents that would make them think they were fortunate to have such an adventurous son.

Charlie had believed he was a real man, strong, dependable and courageous. How wrong she'd been. He was a mummy's boy. A cowardly, weak and lying bastard. She just wished she could think of something to hurt him twice as much as he'd hurt her.

But he'd burst her bubble now and she had to face reality. There would be no job, or flat in London. No parties, rock concerts, night-clubs or holidays in exotic places. The truth of the matter was that she'd been fooled into thinking she had some choice about her future. There was only one option, living in a council flat and looking after her mother.

On Monday morning Charlie received her exam results through the post, sent on to her by Mr Wyatt. Because of everything that had happened during the last week she had forgotten they were due. When she opened the envelope her mouth fell open in surprise.

All her teachers had assured her of good results, but they hadn't led her to expect more than a few 'B'-pluses. Yet she had five 'A's, two 'B'-pluses, and the lowest mark was 'C' for History. Never in her wildest dreams had she imagined getting an 'A' for maths. It was incredible.

After the last two long miserable days of feeling completely worthless, it was good to have something to distract her and feel proud of. Beryl was still in bed, and not liking to wake her, Charlie got dressed hastily and ran round to Ivor's.

As always, Ivor didn't let her down. He didn't reproach her for interrupting him washing, or dither about looking for his shirt and reading glasses. Bare-chested, he just hauled her into his cottage and demanded she read the results to him.

'You clever girl,' he exclaimed, and his wide smile was one of pride in her. 'Of course it's what I expected. I knew right from the start you were as smart as new paint.'

He put a spot of rum in their coffee to celebrate, and made her a bacon sandwich. Then, putting his glasses on at last, he read the certificate again.

'Well done, Charlie. These results will get you the kind of job you deserve. Something a great deal better than weighing up bait. I think you ought to get straight off to Kingsbridge and tell your mum. She'll be thrilled.'

Charlie's face fell. Having spent the whole weekend thinking about what living with her mother would really mean, she couldn't face her yet.

'She won't be thrilled. She'll just tell me not to be so smug.'

'Then you must tell her you have a right to be smug.' He waved the certificate at her. 'This is all your doing, sweetheart, your brain, your hard work. No one but you can take credit for it.'

Those last words of Ivor's warmed the icy place in Charlie's heart as she rode in the bus to Kingsbridge later on that morning. Maybe losing Guy was the last of her bad luck, and from now on things would improve.

Her mother was sitting alone in the day room. All the other patients were either receiving some kind of treatment or they were in the conservatory or garden. Her isolation was a bad sign, though; Charlie felt she must still be upsetting everyone.

Sylvia showed no surprise or pleasure at this unexpected visit. But undeterred, Charlie took out her exam results, along with more cigarettes, and gave them to her mother.

She did look pleased at the cigarettes and opened one of the packets with some eagerness. But Charlie had to draw her attention back to the certificate in her lap.

With only a very cursory glance at it, she sniffed. 'Very good, I'm pleased to see we didn't waste our money on your education.'

Charlie's heart sank. She hadn't expected her mother to go overboard with praise, but she had hoped for a little more warmth. 'It means I should be able to get into banking or something like that,' she said, kneeling down by her mother's wheelchair. 'I'll be able to help take care of you.'

Sylvia folded the certificate and handed it back to her daughter. Her blue eyes were cold and her mouth pursed. 'You'll have to do that sooner than you expected,' she said. 'I've been offered a flat. It seems they can't wait to get rid of me here.'

Charlie felt she'd been dealt another body blow. She might have been thinking about this eventuality all weekend, but she hadn't anticipated it happening for weeks, maybe even months. 'That's great news,' she managed to say, getting up and turning to find a chair. She wondered if Sylvia had engineered this herself, suspecting that Charlie might find another job and home if she was in here for too long.

'Great news?' Sylvia sneered. 'Expecting a crippled woman to cope with living alone?'

Charlie recognized this remark as an opener to moral blackmail. All her childhood she had seen her mother use similar wiles to get people to do what she wanted. If Jin wanted a night out with a few friends, Sylvia suddenly came down with a bad stomach upset. Mrs Brown was often coerced into working extra hours when she wanted to get home to her family. She knew she was expected to assure her that she'd be there too, but some perverse instinct stopped her.

'They'll give you a home help,' she said instead. 'Besides, you'll be a lot happier with your own things around you again.'

'You selfish little bitch,' Sylvia snapped viciously, rising out of her chair by her arms as if intending to box her ears. 'Don't for one moment think you're going to clear off and leave me on my own. You are only sixteen, remember, too young to leave home, and

187

I think it's time you repaid me for all I've done for you.'

A cold chill ran through Charlie's veins. She might have been fully intending to look after her mother, but she was not going to be forced into it.

'I didn't cause your injuries,' she retorted, gathering her fast-diminishing store of courage. 'I'm not in debt to you either, so don't try and blackmail me. You speak to me like that one more time and I'll walk out the door and you'll never see me again.'

To her astonishment her words had quite the reverse effect to what she'd intended. Her mother's face turned purple with instantaneous rage.

'I'll have you made a ward of court,' she screamed at the top of her lungs. Her eyes went dark, and even more frightening, there was froth on her lips. Charlie fully expected one of the nurses to come rushing in, the whole nursing home must have heard her.

As no one burst in, Charlie got up and made for the door. She was really frightened now, her mother was demented. 'You try and do it,' she said, poised ready for flight at the door. 'They'll have to find me first and if and when they do, I'll tell the court a few home truths about you.'

'Don't you dare walk away from me, you hateful little bitch!' Sylvia yelled.

Charlie ran as her mother screamed more abuse. Down the corridor, past a surprised-looking nurse and out the front door. She didn't stop running until she was some 200 yards away from Franklin House and she had a stitch in her side.

It was a warm sunny day, but Charlie was cold. Her hands were shaking and once she stopped running her legs felt as if they wouldn't move again. She wanted to cry but she was too angry.

She had no idea where she was intending to go, she was heading in the opposite direction to the town centre and the bus home, towards open countryside. But she carried on walking aimlessly until she came to a five-barred gate. She climbed over it, skirted round the edge of a cornfield, and once she was far enough away from the road she lay down and cried.

She couldn't understand why she was being singled out for so much misery. Every other old schoolfriend of hers had spent the summer enjoying themselves, while she had worked. She'd had her home, her father and school snatched away from her, the man she believed loved her turned out to be a rat, and now her mother was slowly going mad and threatening to keep her in some kind of slavery.

It seemed like hours that she lay there crying. The sharp stalks of the corn were digging in all over her, and ants kept crawling up her legs. Thirst and the lack of a dry handkerchief finally made her get up. She didn't want to return to Franklin House, yet she knew she must.

Staff Nurse Dodds was sorting out the post in the hall when she saw Charlie come back up the garden path. She had been making beds earlier when she'd heard Sylvia Weish's outburst and the screaming which followed. It had taken both her and Nurse Wilson to subdue the woman, and her language had been appalling.

She hadn't grown to like Sylvia however hard she tried. None of the staff had a good word for her, yet this time, once they'd got the woman calmed down enough to drink a cup of tea and take a tranquillizer, her anger turned to pitiful tears, and she'd revealed a side of herself they hadn't seen before. It seemed to the nurse that Sylvia's real problem was a total inability to express her real emotions. She did love her daughter, she was also very worried that Charlie hadn't got a real home and might drift into trouble, but instead of saying these things, she lashed out wildly and thoughtlessly.

As Charlie approached the open front door, Staff Nurse Dodds saw her red-rimmed swollen eyes and instinctively knew exactly what she'd been doing for the last couple of hours. Her heart went out to Charlie, and to her mother.

'I'm so glad you came back, dear,' she said. 'Your mother was very upset after you left, but I think she's very sorry now.'

Charlie sensed the nurse knew the root cause of the trouble. 'I always intended to look after her. But how can I?' she asked imploringly. 'She's as horrible to me as she is to all of you.'

'No one will force you to take care of her,' Staff Nurse Dodds said with deep sympathy, patting Charlie's shoulder comfortingly. 'You are too young for one thing. This flat she's been offered will be got ready for her with her disability in mind, and she'll get nursing and home support. If you can't face going there with her, don't do it. She'll just have to learn to accept it.'

'I'll go and see her again,' Charlie said with a sigh. 'But if she's nasty again, this time it really will be the last visit.'

*

Sylvia had been taken back to the bedroom she shared with two other women and put to bed. The curtains had been partially drawn, and as all the other patients were downstairs it was very peaceful.

'Hullo, Mum,' Charlie said tentatively. 'I'm sorry. I had to come back because I was worried about you.'

Sylvia was lying flat on her back. As Charlie approached her she lifted her head a little and gave a weak smile.

Charlie felt a surge of relief. Her mother's eyes were swollen from crying but it was clear the fight had gone out of her.

'I'm sorry too,' Sylvia said in a croaky voice. 'I didn't mean what I said, darling. You know I love you really. I don't know why I'm so mean sometimes. And I'm really proud of you for doing so well in the exams.'

Charlie's hurt faded. Sylvia had never been one for apologies, or saying she loved her, and to hear both made her glad she'd come back. She sat on the edge of the bed and took her mother's hands in hers. 'I love you too, Mum, for better or worse. I won't run out on you, I promise.'

Sylvia gave a deep sigh. 'Your father said that to me once,' she said in a small voice.

'Well, I mean it,' Charlie said stoutly, assuming this remark was caused by disbelief. 'When did he say it to you?'

'When I found out he was having an affair,' she replied, her eyes mournful.

Charlie's heart quickened. Since the day Sylvia blurted out the story of her childhood and the stillborn baby, Charlie had never managed to get anything further out of her about the past. 'He had an affair? Who with?'

Sylvia closed her eyes as if to shut out a painful memory.

'Mum?' Charlie shook her hand gently. 'Who was it?'

'DeeDee.'

The unlikely name came out like a pistol shot. The sheer force of it proved it was something Sylvia had bottled up for a very long time.

'Who was she?' Charlie probed gently.

'I thought she was my friend. We worked together long before I met Jin. When he got his own club I got him to give her a job too.'

Charlie could see the pain in her mother's eyes. 'Go on,' she whispered. 'It's better to tell me than keep it all inside you.'

Sylvia sighed and reached out for her daughter's hand. 'She wasn't just a passing friend, Charlie, we were as close as sisters. We had so many good times both before and after she came to work for Jin, we were making big money and everything seemed wonderful. When I stopped working because I was pregnant she took over all my jobs.' She paused for a moment, looking bleakly at her daughter. 'I never thought for one moment she'd get her hooks into my husband too.'

Charlie understood that a woman was hardly likely to forget such betrayal, especially at such a vulnerable time in her life, but she did think it a bit odd that she should still be so bitter about it after all these years. She had to get to the bottom of it. 'And that's what Dad said? That he wouldn't run out on you?'

'Yes. He didn't say he would stop seeing DeeDee. Just that he loved me, for better or worse, and he wouldn't run out on me. Funny you should use the exact same words, but then you are so like him.'

Charlie was a little confused. 'So are you saying he went on with the affair?'

'Oh yes.' Sylvia sighed and her eyes looked stricken. 'You were two when I found out about it, and he said that. Like a fool I thought that meant it really was over, and then of course we moved to Devon. We were so happy then, I managed to forgive if not forget. But the truth of the matter was that he wanted me out of London so he could carry on with her. He had two homes, one with me and you, and another one with *her* in London.'

Charlie was astounded. 'Are you telling me this went on from when I was a baby right up till he disappeared? Sixteen years!'

Sylvia nodded. 'More or less.'

'And Dad knew that you knew?'

'Yes,' she said, but her eyes dropped from Charlie's. 'Well no, not exactly. At first I used to gently hint that I knew he was still seeing her, but he always laughed it off. Later on I used to say sharper things about it and it always caused a row. He always said I was the only woman he'd ever loved. But he wouldn't talk about it properly, he'd just throw something in a temper and walk away. I was afraid that if I kept on about it he might leave me.'

Charlie nodded. This at least explained some of the rows she'd heard. 'But you might have been mistaken. What proof did you have?'

'DeeDee sent letters and cards to him occasionally.

I used to steam them open. She phoned too, she'd pretend she had a wrong number if I answered, but I'd know her voice anywhere. It was low and husky. Not like anyone else's.'

'Did you show these letters to Dad, tell him about the calls.'

'No,' Sylvia replied, looking furtive. 'I was too frightened to in case it forced his hand.'

All at once Charlie began to see a fuller picture. This was almost certainly the cause of those black moods her mother had suffered from. She couldn't imagine ever choosing to suffer in silence rather than risk losing a man, but then she and her mother had very different characters. Perhaps for a weak person who had suffered so much abuse as a young girl, half a husband, a beautiful home and financial security was better than gambling the lot by speaking out, and maybe risking losing everything.

'Did you tell the police about her?' she asked.

Sylvia's eyes opened very wide like a startled deer's. 'No, I couldn't.'

'Why not, Mum? Dad might be there with her now. Where was this other home?'

'I never found that out.' Sylvia turned her face towards Charlie and her eyes were beautiful, big, sad pools of blue, brimming with tears. 'She never put an address on her letters. But he wouldn't be there. He promised he would never run out on me.'

Charlie felt a surge of anger at her mother's inconsistency and stupidity. 'But he has!' she retorted. She wondered if she was losing her mind now. 'He has run out on you, hasn't he? Even if you don't know her address, if this woman worked for Dad and had been seeing him all these years, the police might be able to find her and question her.'

'I *did* believe he'd run out on me,' Sylvia said slowly and thoughtfully. 'I was convinced of it until a few days ago. But then I remembered what he'd said, and I knew he must be dead. You see, he wouldn't have broken his promise to me, darling.'

Charlie was stumped for a reply to such an irrational statement. Maybe a week ago she would have gone along with what her mother felt, after all her father had never broken a promise to her either. But Guy had changed her views on men, honour and promises.

'Well, maybe that is true,' she said carefully, not wishing to upset her mother again. 'But we have to tell the police about DeeDee anyway. Even if he isn't with her, she might know where he is.'

'No, we mustn't do that.' Sylvia's eyes widened with sudden alarm and she reached out to grab Charlie's hands, gripping them hard. 'I don't want her brought into this. Promise me you won't tell them?'

Charlie was so taken aback by this plea that for a moment she could only stare at her mother. 'Don't be ridiculous,' she said eventually. 'It's the obvious thing to do. I certainly won't promise.'

All at once Charlie saw that shutter coming down on Sylvia's face again. She let go of Charlie and slumped back on the pillows. 'You go to them with that story and I'll deny it,' she said in an icy voice. 'I have some pride left.'

The last thing Charlie wanted now was more conflict. Maybe in a day or two she'd tackle the subject again, but for now she thought she'd better move on to a safer subject. 'Okay,' she said with a shrug. 'Forget that, and tell me about this flat.'

Sylvia relaxed visibly. 'It's in Mayflower Close,' she said. 'Do you know where that is?'

'Yes, I do,' Charlie said with some eagerness. 'It's nice there. High up, above the Naval College, there's lovely views of the river, and it's right on the bus route. Those houses haven't been built that long either.'

'Maybe it won't be so bad then.' Her mother half smiled. 'If you ring Mr Wyatt he'll probably be able to arrange for you to see it. Maybe you could work out what curtains, carpets and furniture would fit too. He did say he would arrange for someone to take me there in a couple of weeks, and to take me to "Windways" to make a list of things I want to keep.'

Charlie's irritation about her mother's response to telling the police about DeeDee was banished by this enthusiasm for a new home.

'We'll keep as much as possible,' she replied. 'Even if it doesn't fit, we can always sell it afterwards.'

Sylvia smiled, the first real one in a long time. 'What a smart girl I've got,' she said. 'I wouldn't have ever thought of that. I think I'd better leave the whole list-making to you.'

Once again Charlie thought of admitting about the things she'd already got hidden away. But again she stopped herself. Her mother seemed sane enough now, almost like the mother she remembered from her childhood, before the black moods started. But that didn't mean anything, tomorrow she might go cuckoo again.

'I have to go now.' She bent to kiss her mother. 'I'll ring Mr Wyatt later on today. Now, you just concentrate on getting better, Mum. Do those exercises, let the physiotherapist help you. Please?'

Sylvia smiled again. She lifted her hands and cupped her daughter's face. 'You are a little treasure,' she said. 'Okay. I'll try harder.'

August ended with two of the hottest days of the year, then September came in with a downpour that lasted three whole days. With each day the holidaymakers became scarcer. Ivor was kept busy though, he took out fishing parties every day, and Charlie spent hers sitting in the shack reading, waiting for customers who were few and far between.

Beryl only really needed help at the weekends now, but Charlie always went downstairs in the evenings and did what she could, because even washing up was preferable to being alone with her thoughts.

They were mostly dark ones. The deep hurt at Guy betraying her kept coming back in waves. She felt sorrow because her time here in Salcombe was nearly up, but most of all she felt dread at what was to come.

The optimism she'd felt when she had left Franklin House on the day of her exam results had faded very quickly. By the time she visited Sylvia again, the mask was on once more, and she was once again sullen. She took no interest in what they should try to retrieve from 'Windways', and appeared to care even less about Charlie's future prospects, or their new flat.

Charlie had been pleasantly surprised by the flat. Although set amongst standard recently built council houses, it was purpose-built for someone disabled, on the ground floor, and the back windows had a fine view over fields down to the river Dart. The living room was large, with windows at either end, and both bedrooms, although tiny in comparison to the ones at 'Windways', had built-in wardrobes. It had a ramp for a wheelchair up to the front door, wide internal ones, and lower than usual worktops in the kitchen and central heating. At the time Charlie viewed it the painters were still there, giving it all a coat of magnolia paint. It even had a tiny back yard of its own.

But however nice the flat was, there was no escaping the fact that once they moved in, she might as well be locked up and the key thrown away. Sylvia would be utterly dependent on her, and she'd never be able to leave.

The thought of this woman DeeDee had plagued her too, so much so that on an impulse she went to see the police in Dartmouth and told them about her. Her initial fear was that they would go straight back to Sylvia for more information and upset her, but instead they seemed disinterested. They said that all Jin's known business associates and people he supplied with goods had already been interviewed; as they'd drawn blanks everywhere, they didn't bear much hope this would change anything. Charlie left the police station feeling even more discouraged and upset. It seemed that no one but herself really cared about what had happened to him.

Going back to 'Windways' with Mr Wyatt and a man from the Official Receiver's office was a further distressing experience. The *For Sale* sign outside, the dust gathering on the once gleaming dining table, and the chilly emptiness of the house without its usual flowers and smells of polish brought back pangs of unbearable nostalgia.

Before going there, Charlie had spent a great deal of time and energy compiling a list of things they wanted to keep. To be curtly told by the official that the dining-room table and chairs weren't a necessity, and that the gate-leg table in the hall was quite adequate for their needs was humiliating. He sniffed at her request for the cream three-piece suite in the drawing room, and insisted they must have the shabbier green one in the small sitting room. By the end of the morning's haggling Charlie felt entirely drained and close to tears. To know she was never going to see all those lovely antique pieces of furniture which her father had collected ever again, that some other family would be walking on the Persian rugs, was too hurtful. She had worked out for herself, just by checking antique shop prices, that the contents of their old home must be worth far in excess of her father's debts, yet the official just shrugged when she pointed this out and said the Receivers had chalked up considerable expenses which had to be deducted before anyone was paid out.

It was the day of the creditors' meeting that tipped Charlie over the edge. Mr Wyatt took Sylvia in her wheelchair with him, saying that although it might be harrowing for her mother to come face to face with the people Jin owed money to, he felt her presence was essential to ensure that some of the funds which had been raised by the sale of the house and effects should be set aside for her.

As Charlie wasn't allowed to attend, she spent the

morning of the hearing in the shack, on tenterhooks. She was afraid her mother might be abusive if things didn't go her way, and that afterwards she might just plunge back into even deeper depression.

To her surprise Mr Wyatt came into the shack at one o'clock, beaming from ear to ear, and insisted she came out to lunch with him so he could tell her everything. Charlie assumed this meant he had good news and her spirits rose.

It wasn't until they were in the King's Arms with steak and kidney pudding in front of them that Wyatt began to explain what had happened. 'Only three creditors turned up in person so it wasn't too bad for Sylvia. It was agreed that she was entitled to some of the funds, and two thousand pounds was set aside for that.'

'That's good?' Charlie said in surprise. She thought it should have been much more considering her mother's disability.

'Well, she was lucky to get anything, the Inland Revenue don't care for sob stories,' Wyatt said somewhat callously. 'But wait till I get to the good news! Miss Fellows, your headmistress, has granted you a free place to continue at school.'

Charlie stared at Wyatt in surprise. 'When did she contact you?'

'She was there today. The school was one of your father's creditors.'

Charlie felt herself blush with shame.

'Why didn't you tell me that before?' she asked.

'The creditors weren't your concern,' he said. 'You're too young to worry your pretty little head about that sort of thing.'

That condescending remark angered her and reminded her that she'd never seen any list of creditors, or even had any idea exactly how much her father owed. She wondered if her mother had been properly informed. Perhaps at another time she might have been pleased to think Miss Fellows thought enough of her ability, even in the face of unpaid bills, to offer her a free place, but coming at such a time it felt like the ultimate humiliation.

'I can't go back there, not now,' she said.

'Why on earth not?' Wyatt's schoolboyish smile faded and he looked churlish. 'I thought you'd be thrilled. It's a very generous offer under the circumstances.'

'I expect they said that sort of thing to people who got thrown in the workhouse,' she said tartly. 'It was very kind of Miss Fellows. But I have some pride. I couldn't hold my head up there with everyone whispering about me.'

'Why should they do that?' he asked. 'Young girls aren't concerned by such things as bankrupts.'

Charlie had begun to see some time ago that Mr Wyatt wasn't quite the fatherly figure she originally took him for. He had been so condescending and evasive about so many matters, and it had crossed her mind that they ought to have got a lawyer to act for them who was an expert in bankruptcy. None of that really mattered now, as it was over, but suddenly she saw that he was just like she used to be, so wrapped up in himself, so sheltered from real life that he had no real idea what the world was like outside his own front door.

'Young girls are concerned by anything which has

a breath of scandal attached to it,' she said archly. 'They are also cruel and will take any opportunity to kick someone when they are already down.'

'Come now, that's a bit strong,' he said, raising an eyebrow. 'These girls are your old friends.'

'And not one of those old friends has shown the slightest concern for me since all this started,' she said bitterly. 'Just as all my parents' so-called friends have abandoned us. A fine lot they turned out to be. They drank Dad's booze, ate his food, and the minute everything came crashing down, they pretended they never knew us.'

This was a direct dig at Wyatt's wife Rachel. She had been particularly friendly with Sylvia, yet she hadn't so much as visited her in hospital or sent along a bunch of flowers. Nor had anyone else in the same social set. 'In fact,' Charlie went on, 'things will be so bad for me in Dartmouth, I probably won't even be able to get a part-time job there. I think it might be better if I moved to London.'

'And leave your poor mother on her own? Charlie! I can't believe you could even consider something so callous.'

Charlie hadn't really meant to say this. It came out in the heat of the moment. But when Wyatt retaliated so strongly she saw that he was in fact a twat, as her mother had called him. Sylvia must have reverted back to her old act, the charming, flirtatious, helpless little woman today. That he was stupid enough to be taken in by it, when he'd already had plenty of evidence of how impossible Sylvia was, made her seethe.

'You can call it callous if you like,' she said defiantly.

'I'd like to see you put up with her for more than a couple of days without being tempted to do a runner.'

Wyatt changed after that. He dropped the caring, protective persona he'd been adopting all this time, and briskly ran through other minor details that had been brought up this morning. Charlie despised him then. He didn't care one bit, it was just business to him, and he wanted to wind it all up with all speed so he could claim his fees from the Receivers and bow out.

Charlie half expected him to bring up his advice to her about the miniatures, she was even beginning to think he might be low enough to sink to a spot of blackmail. But fortunately he didn't. She might have been tempted to tip the remains of her half-eaten lunch over his head if he had.

'Well, I have to say I'm disappointed in you, Charlie,' he said as he made a move to leave to go back to his office. 'I had prided myself on acting in your best interests today. Perhaps you should try to be a little less selfish and consider all those who have tried to help you.'

'You get paid for what you've done,' she snapped back. 'I don't actually remember any help coming from anyone else.'

Back in the shack, shaking with rage, Charlie told Ivor what she thought of Wyatt. 'He was so bloody pompous. How dare he think he knows better than me how it will be at school, or what Mum's like?'

Ivor put his arms round her; he had never seen her so angry and it frightened him. 'Lawyers are all like that,' he said. 'They live in ivory towers and haven't the first idea how it feels to be broke, hurt or confused. Blame him, but not Miss Fellows – she must be a decent sort, and she must have great belief in you to stick her neck out.'

'I can't go back to school. I don't know that I can even face Dartmouth again,' she sobbed. 'I dread even visiting Mum, so how can I possibly look after her?'

Ivor just held her and soothed her, every instinct urging him to say she could stay with him and let her mother take care of herself. He felt like sobbing too. He'd grown to love Charlie, his thoughts about her were as pure as if she were his own daughter. He wanted her to finish school, go to university and make something of herself. But to lawyers she was just a pawn they could push around their chessboard, and fit in somewhere it suited them best, regardless of what she needed. Like looking after a half-mad woman who they knew was going to be trouble.

'Just give it a try first,' Ivor said, feeling like Judas. 'Go and see Miss Fellows, and see how you feel about school while you're there. Settle your mum in that flat, and wait and see what happens. If it is terrible, at least you can say you tried. You can always come back to me. I won't ever turn you away.'

'But I'm going to miss you so much,' she said in a croaky voice against his shoulder. 'I'll miss being so close to the sea, the smell of this place, your cooking, Minnie and Beryl. But most of all you, Ivor. I don't know how I'm going to cope without seeing you every day.'

'Nor me,' he said in a gruff voice, and when she moved back slightly to look up at him, his eyes looked damp. 'It's a long time since I really cared for anyone,' he said.

Charlie had once thought he looked odd, but now his red hair, bushy beard and even his uptilted nose had become so dear to her, that other more conventional-looking men seemed bland. She remembered in her first few days here thinking he ought to wear smarter clothes and trim his beard because it would make customers less nervous of him. Of course in those days she was something of a snob, judging people by outward appearances. She hoped she'd never again judge anyone by their clothes, or the amount of money they had. Ivor would always be the man she measured others by.

Chapter Seven

The day after the creditors' meeting Charlie woke from a terrible nightmare. She had dreamed she was balancing on the stone balustrade in the garden at 'Windways', looking down at the sea below, and behind her people were shouting viciously.

She didn't dare turn to look at them for fear of falling. Her mother was screaming at her to get down and come and give her a bath. Mr Wyatt was shouting that she was selfish and cruel to neglect her mother, and Miss Fellows kept saying over and over again that she'd never make anything of herself unless she worked harder.

There were other softer, taunting voices too. One was Guy's – he was saying she was a liar and a fraud. June was saying she was spoilt rotten and too big for her boots. Ivor was there too, his gruff voice entreating her to hold on just a little longer.

As she teetered precariously, so she heard thundering feet running towards her. Her mother screamed as she had that day in the garden, and Charlie knew the two men had come back for her.

She jumped, down into the sea, and the dream went into slow motion then as she spun round and round, clutching at plants as she passed them, but they all came away in her hands. Below her she could see waves breaking on the rocks and she was heading straight for them.

Charlie sat up, soaking wet with sweat and panting as if she'd run a mile. It was just on daybreak, a grey, eerie light filling her small room and making it seem like a prison cell. She knew she had to get outside in the fresh air; if she didn't, she'd fall asleep again and the dream would come back.

She got up, pulled on jeans, a sweater and her plimsolls. The only clear idea she had was to walk until her head cleared of all those horrible images.

Ivor always got up at daybreak, summer and winter alike. It was a legacy left from his time as a fisherman. Now he was getting older and stiff, sometimes he wished he could break the habit and stay in his warm bed, but he found he couldn't. His routine was the same every day, out into the yard to the lavatory, then a swift walk along the harbour with Minnie just to fill his lungs with fresh air before he made his breakfast.

There was an autumn chill in the air this morning – almost, but not quite, an early frost. He noted there were far more seagulls than usual, wheeling around screeching, and that suggested bad weather was on its way.

He liked the harbour best at this time of day, deserted but for the birds and the odd prowling cat. On warmer days he liked to sit and watch the sun come up, to marvel how the sea turned from black to dark green and slowly to blue. But today the sea was determined to stay a sullen grey-green, and he decided to take the *MaryAnn* out now to collect his lobster pots rather than wait until after breakfast.

The pots were disappointingly empty, and as he turned the boat around to go back to the harbour, he spotted a figure in the distance, walking up by the Marine Hotel. He idly wondered why anyone was about so early; except in high summer he never saw a soul on his morning excursions. He came to the conclusion it was one of the hotel staff returning from a night on the tiles. The thought made him smile. He could remember a time when he too could stay out all night and still do a day's work after it.

Ivor had finished all his chores, washed his shirt and underwear, swept and mopped over the kitchen floor, and laid a fire for later. It was only the pips on the wireless that made him look at the clock. It was nine, and Charlie hadn't turned up.

He wasn't the least concerned as there was little for her to do now the only holidaymakers were a handful of pensioners; besides, it was raining now and that would deter any would-be customers.

Ten o'clock came, then half past, but there was still no sign of Charlie. He stood in the shack doorway looking out at the heavy rain, and wondered if she was still upset about the events of the previous day.

By eleven the rain was torrential, so dark Ivor couldn't see well enough in the shack to do anything, and as Charlie still hadn't turned up, he put his pipe in his pocket, locked up and walked over to the pub, Minnie padding silently behind him. Mrs Maggs the cleaner was just mopping down the bar floor as he stepped inside. 'We're not open yet,' she bawled at him, as if he didn't know the opening hours.

'Just wanted to see Beryl for a minute,' Ivor said. Maggs was a harridan of over sixty, she had only one brown tooth and the worst varicose veins Ivor had ever seen, yet she not only cleaned here, but in several private homes too. Beryl called her a treasure.

'She's doing some paperwork upstairs,' Maggs shouted as if he was deaf. 'You can go up, as long as you wipe your boots first.'

Beryl was sitting at her desk just inside her sitting room, with a desk lamp on. Her red hair was like a torch, contrasting vividly with an apple-green sweater. She looked round in surprise as Ivor came up the stairs with his dog.

'What brings you round here?' she asked. 'Want to borrow some money or a bottle of rum?' This was a long-standing joke between them. Once, many years ago, another regular drinker at the pub had suggested Ivor and Beryl were having an affair because Ivor always seemed to be the first in the bar in the evenings. Ivor had kept a straight face and said he always got in first to borrow a bottle of rum and some money.

'Neither today,' Ivor grinned. 'Just wondered how Charlie was. Is she sick?'

'You mean she isn't with you?' Beryl said in some surprise, and beckoned him into the room. 'She's not upstairs. I went up there earlier when it started to rain to check she hadn't left her window open.'

'Did she get a call or anything from her mother last night?' Ivor asked, mystified as to why she hadn't been round to tell him if something pressing had come up.

'I don't think so,' Beryl frowned. 'She went up to bed about ten. She seemed very down in the dumps.'

'She had a bad day yesterday,' Ivor said. 'Did she tell you about it?'

'Not a word.' Beryl shook her head. 'But then she's been kind of quiet and brooding ever since that business with Guy. What with that, and the prospect of moving in with her mum, I thought she had a perfect right to be a bit dejected. I didn't believe a word of her story about Guy. I reckon he dumped her.'

'Me too,' Ivor said ruefully. 'I didn't challenge her story at the time because I thought she was being very brave. Perhaps I should have.' He then went on to tell Beryl what had happened with the lawyer. 'I thought she'd come to terms with it all by the time she left me in the early evening. But maybe I was wrong.'

'Where could she have gone?' Beryl asked. 'She must have left before nine because I got up around then.'

Ivor sensed this was something more than a teenager suddenly bunking off work. He sat down with Beryl and they discussed the business of her meeting with Wyatt the previous day.

'If she was angry and felt cheated, perhaps she got the idea of going back to her old house,' Beryl suggested. 'I know I'd want to go and grab anything I could if I'd been treated so shabbily. Or could it be Guy? Could a letter have come from him in the post? If he apologized she may have gone off to meet him.'

'I think she would've left a note if she'd heard from Guy,' Ivor said. 'And however angry she was about the bankruptcy, she wouldn't dare break into the house to take anything, it would be a criminal offence.'

Suddenly Ivor remembered that figure he'd seen going towards the Marine Hotel. The person was so far away he had no idea if it could have been a girl. He told Beryl about it.

'Around five-thirty, you say,' she mused. 'Oddly enough I woke up around that time today. I could have been disturbed by the sound of the front door closing behind her.'

They went up into Charlie's room then to look around. Her bed was unmade, and her waterproof coat was still there, hanging on the back of the door.

'It's strange she didn't make her bed, she always does,' Beryl said, bending over and straightening it out. 'She told me once she didn't even know how to until she went to stay with that friend of hers. Apparently the mother laid into her about it, and said there was no housekeeper there to do it for her. She said she had to learn how to do it then, and never forgot again. I suppose she could have just gone out for a breath of fresh air, intending to come right back, then took shelter from the rain.'

'She always laughed at me going out early in the morning,' Ivor said. 'So I can't imagine her getting out of a warm bed for that. Besides, it didn't start raining until nineish. If she did set out at five-thirty she's been gone nearly six hours!'

Beryl made no reply. When Ivor looked at her he saw she was frowning.

'What's up? Have you thought of something?'

'You don't think she could be pregnant, do you?' she blurted out.

They stared at each other for a moment, united in

their anxiety for a girl they both cared deeply for. 'Good God! I hope not,' Ivor exclaimed.

'She couldn't really know yet, could she?' Beryl said breathlessly. 'I mean, it's only a month, isn't it? But what if she was worrying about it?'

'If you weigh up everything she's had to cope with since those men attacked her mother –' Ivor broke off, afraid to finish saying what he'd thought. A clap of thunder, quickly followed by a flash of lightning, made him look towards the window. 'And she's out there in that. She hasn't even taken her coat.'

'You don't think she might have planned to –' Beryl stopped short, her expression one of horror. She clapped her hand over her mouth as she remembered where the road Ivor had seen her on led to. 'The cliff path!'

'I'll go and look for her,' Ivor said. He suddenly felt sick with fear, just the way he felt when the *action stations* signal came on the ship during the war. 'Can I borrow your car?'

'But you can't drive!' Beryl wrung her hands.

'Yes I can, I just haven't chosen to for years,' he said. 'You ring the police, Beryl. I'll go straight along to Soar Mill Cove. If we aren't too late already, by my reckoning that's about where she would have got to by now.'

Ivor was right in his estimation, Charlie was near Soar Mill Cove. But at the point earlier in the morning when it began to rain heavily, she might as well have been in Outer Mongolia. She couldn't see more than a few yards ahead of her, and but for the sound of the sea crashing constantly against rocks below to her left, she might have been walking round in circles. She was also soaked to the skin.

She had no idea why she'd come this way, she'd just walked blindly, wrapped up in her misery, and found herself on the cliff path. As the rain got heavier, she thought she might reach shelter up ahead quicker than turning back, so she pressed on. But the path just went on and on, up and down, growing more slippery with each step. Her plimsolls were sodden, the stones dug right through the thin soles, and before long she was stumbling and crying with frustration. There were no houses, at least if there were any they were shrouded in mist. The only living creatures she saw were a few straggly, frightened-looking sheep.

Suddenly she saw she was back in her nightmare. She was right on the cliff edge looking down at the sea pounding on rocks below. Yet it didn't seem like a dream, she could feel the rain going right through her clothes, she was icy cold, and the wind was buffeting her, almost as if it was trying to assist her over the edge. Had the nightmare been a prophecy? A way of showing how she could escape her misery?

She wanted oblivion, nothing had ever felt so right before. To step out into nothingness, leaving all her problems behind. No more waking each day to a sick fear inside, no one could humiliate her again. Someone else could look after her mother.

She took a step backwards, poised herself to take a running jump. But just as she had lifted one foot to go forward, a voice shrieked out inside her head, asking who would look after Sylvia.

'I don't care who does it,' she shrieked back in answer. 'As long as it doesn't have to be me!'

213

The sound of her own voice above the rain, the sea and the seagulls was like an alarm clock going off, abruptly bringing her back to reality. She looked down at her feet in sodden, dirty plimsolls, saw they were less than six or seven inches from the cliff edge, and she felt again that absolute terror she'd woken with just a short while ago.

Yet as she shrank back from the edge to safety, anger supplanted terror. She wasn't even free to end her own life, she was bound too tightly by morality and duty. Shackled to her damned mother so there would be no escape, ever.

In her anger she yelled out, cursing her father for starting all this, cursing Guy for giving her the dream of freedom, and damned herself to hell and back for not having the courage just to leap forward into space regardless of the consequences to her mother and those who cared about her.

She couldn't even have the utter silence she needed. The rain was hammering down, the sea roared and boiled on the rocks below, seagulls squawked all around her, seemingly taunting her timidity.

Sobbing wildly, she went on, but the desperation which had driven her here was now focused only on getting back home, to be dry, warm and comforted by someone. Half blinded by tears, the path now just a slippery slick of mud, she wasn't watching where she put her feet. As she went down a steep section of the path, she lost her footing and fell backwards, shooting over on to the grassy hill as though she was on a toboggan run.

Her arms and hands flailed out, trying to snatch at the long grass, but this was wet and slippery too and

214

just slid through her fingers. She hit a large stone, but instead of breaking her fall she seemed to veer off to the right, down over more sodden grass and heather, and kept hurtling on downwards.

The last thing she saw was a large boulder looming up right in her path.

She came to to find herself lying at an acute angle, her head pointing down the hill and a terrible sharp pain in her back and shoulder. She thought she must have hit the boulder and been knocked out, for she was right beside it.

She didn't dare attempt to move, assuming by the pain that her back must be broken. The rain was lashing down on her, the wind icy through her soaked sweater and jeans, then a loud clap of thunder quickly followed by a flash of lightning frightened her still further.

'Help me!' she called out, but the futility of such a weak cry in the wind and rain made her sob with hopelessness. It was only when she instinctively lifted her arm to look at her watch, some minutes later, that it occurred to her she wouldn't be able to do even that if her back was broken. Surely she'd be paralysed?

That cheered her slightly, but she wasn't wearing her watch, she'd left it on the bedside table, and she couldn't even guess what time it was. She asked herself how long she might have to lie here before anyone found her. Hikers and bird-watchers used the path frequently in good weather, but not in rain like this. She might be here for hours.

Turning her head a little, she saw to her further consternation that if she continued to lie as she was

215

now, pretty soon the heavy rain would sweep her further down the hill. With her right hand, which she knew was unhurt, she reached out for a hand-hold on the boulder and slowly, inch by inch because of the pain, she managed to pull herself up and round into a sitting position.

Just the fact she could sit was proof her spine was intact, yet the pain was so bad she wanted to lie down again. She lifted one leg tentatively, then the other, and decided they were only badly bruised. But her left arm and shoulder hurt so much it was clear they'd taken the brunt of the fall. She might physically be able to walk, if she could get herself into a standing position, but common sense told her it would be folly to attempt to climb up that slippery slope to the foot-path. One more slip and who knows where she might end up.

There was nothing for it but to sit and wait for help to come. She would keep her ears open for footsteps, then yell if she heard anyone.

Sitting there in the rain soon became the worst kind of torture she could imagine. She was so cold she wasn't even shivering any longer, and the pain was growing ever stronger. She couldn't get even moderately comfortable against the boulder, and the prospect of a long wait grew ever more alarming.

If she could just see clearly she felt she'd be less scared; for all she knew there could be a house some-where near. But the visibility was limited to around ten yards or so through the rain and mist.

Yet over and above her discomfort she kept asking herself why she'd come up here in the first place. She couldn't really remember exactly what prompted it

– surely just a nightmare wasn't enough to make someone behave so irrationally? When she thought about it, the whole business, from dressing herself to finding herself here, was something of a blur. She'd often heard that phrase, 'While the balance of his mind was disturbed', and it was usually said after someone had committed suicide. Was that what had happened to her? Had she lost her mind for a while?

It occurred to her that for weeks now she'd been behaving as she imagined her father would under pressure, getting on with what had to be done, resigned to it all. Apart from the odd weep now and then she'd been quite tough. But today's events proved she was every bit as capable of loopy acts as her mother. Strange though it was, that almost pleased her. She didn't like to think she was entirely Jin, in the light of his behaviour. Anyway, she felt she was rational again now, it was ghastly to think that just a short while ago she'd been on the point of jumping from that cliff top, but maybe she had to go so far before she could see how things really were?

The bankruptcy had been finalized. She and her mother had a home again. Sitting here soaked to the skin, a storm raging around her, with no immediate rescue likely, looking after her mother and returning to school didn't seem so very terrible, in fact it felt comforting. So maybe Guy had let her down badly, but could she really have moved to London just to be near him? The men from the Receiver's office were a bunch of crooks, but she did have those treasures stashed away. If she went back to school and got her 'A' levels, maybe she could still go to university.

There was still a chance too that her dad might turn

217

up, she mustn't lose sight of that. She also wondered about her mother's fright at informing the police about DeeDee. Was it because Sylvia would rather imagine her husband dead than having it confirmed he had betrayed her trust? Or was there some more sinister reason for her fear? Charlie couldn't imagine what this could be right now, but once they were living together again perhaps she could get to the bottom of it.

She looked up as another flash of lightning flashed across the dark sky. Ivor would be looking out at it from the shack, he'd be wondering where she was. She knew with utter certainty that before long he'd start a search for her. Even if everyone else had failed her, she knew he wouldn't. All she had to do was wait.

In an effort to take her mind off the pain and cold, she tried reciting poetry aloud, forcing herself to remember things she'd learned when she was seven or eight. She tried singing, but nothing more came to her than 'Onward Christian Soldiers'.

After a while she felt as if she was drifting off to sleep. It was an extraordinary sensation, because common sense told her sleep was impossible when she was so cold and wet. Besides, even if it was possible, she knew she mustn't because she had to listen for people. Yet still she felt herself slipping away, and her whole being told her to lie down and let it happen.

Ivor drove Beryl's Morris Minor to where the narrow lane ended above Soar Mill Cove. He leapt out, Minnie following him, and strung the coil of rope he'd brought

218

with him diagonally across his shoulder and chest. Then, reaching back into the car, he took the rucksack he'd packed with a flask of hot tea, Charlie's coat and a blanket, and slid that on to his back. Finally he grabbed his walking stick, jumped over the stile and set off at a fast jog down the footpath through fields towards the sea.

'Find Charlie,' he said to Minnie, but she just barked and wagged her tail as if she thought she was in for a good day out.

This part of the Devon coast land was the most deserted and unspoilt: wild and rugged, a place for only sheep and wildlife. Ivor had often walked it when he first came to Salcombe.

On a warm summer's day it was probably one of the most beautiful places in all England, a valley between steep rocky hills, with a sensational view of the sea crashing on to the rocks down in the cove. But today in the heavy rain Ivor could see no further than forty or fifty yards, and the footpath had turned to thick, glutinous mud.

He felt the sea spray on his face even before he caught sight of the beach. The waves were mountainous, crashing over the mound of rocks in the centre of the cove. In high summer this was a bit of paradise, but today it looked forbidding.

Ivor stood by the path going down to the beach for some few minutes, trying to gauge whether Charlie would have got this far. He thought not. If she had, she would surely have gone up the way he'd just come, if only to find shelter. And if his worst fears were realized and she'd run off seeking permanent oblivion from her troubles, she would surely have done it at the first high point. Not kept on walking without a coat.

He set off up the steep rocky path back towards Salcombe, Minnie scampering up ahead of him. He wasn't as fit now as he had been, and he found the going tough, especially in an oilskin coat. His breathing was laboured, his boots slid on mud, but he kept going, calling out Charlie's name.

He didn't want to brood on pregnancy as a reason for her odd behaviour, he couldn't believe fate would deal her that many dud cards.

'Just keep her safe,' he muttered, looking skywards. 'Don't you dare take this one from me too.'

Charlie was dreaming. She was back at 'Windways', lying on the big settee in front of the fire, so comfortable she didn't want to move when she heard her father calling her name. She didn't even want to open her eyes.

But he was so insistent. 'Charlie,' he called. 'Charlie! Where are you? Answer me!'

She opened her eyes, then shut them because of the rain. She didn't want to feel cold, wet and the pain in her shoulder, she needed to get back to the fire. But the voice called out again, closer this time.

'Charlie, answer me if you can hear me. Just call and I'll find you.'

'I'm in here, Daddy,' she said sleepily. 'Don't bother me.'

But she couldn't get back to that comfort. She ached all over, she felt the cold acutely, and suddenly it was as if the mist around her parted and she remembered her father was missing.

'Daddy?' she called out. 'Daddy, is that you?'

She struggled to sit back up, but her hand was too cold now to hold the boulder and she slid a little way. Fright brought her to, and she remembered what had happened.

'Help me!' she screamed out, not knowing whether the voice she'd heard was reality, or just part of the dream. 'Help me! I'm hurt.'

A dog barked not far away, though she couldn't see it.

'Charlie, it's me, Ivor!' His familiar voice rang out loud and clear. 'Call Minnie, she'll find you. Keep calling. I'm coming.'

She called Minnie again and again, focusing only on that she would soon be safe, then suddenly through the mist and rain she saw Minnie haring joyously towards her, tail wagging, barking furiously.

'Oh Minnie,' she exclaimed as the dog came over to her. As if sensing Charlie was hurt, she slowed right down and crept forward to lick Charlie's face tentatively.

'Good girl,' Charlie said, patting her head. 'Go get Ivor, show him where I am.'

Minnie ran off, disappearing into the mist, barking fit to bust. A few minutes later Charlie suddenly saw Ivor coming down over the hill to where she lay.

Nothing and no one in her whole life had looked as good or as colourful as he did: his yellow oilskin and sou-wester, the bushy red beard and his face purple with exertion, framed by a leaden sky.

'Oh, sweetheart! Thank heavens I've found you,' he exclaimed. 'How bad are you hurt?'

'My shoulder,' she said weakly. 'But everything hurts.'

She learned a great deal more about Ivor's strengths in those next few moments. He was as capable as a doctor, running his hands over her arms and legs with clear medical knowledge. He was tender and fatherly, cutting off her sweater with a knife to save hurting her arm more, then wrapping her in her coat, he made a sling for her arm with a neckerchief.

After tucking the blanket round her, he gave her hot, sweet tea. Nothing had ever tasted so good, and she gulped it down eagerly.

'I got Beryl to call the police,' he said. 'So they should turn up soon, but do you think you could walk at least part of the way?'

She agreed to try and Ivor pointed out that just a few yards down from where they were was another rough path which also led back to the cove. 'Shuffle down on your bottom,' he said. 'I'll tie the rope around your middle and stay here to hold it till you reach the path. From there on I can probably carry you if you can't manage any further.'

It was just as well Ivor had her tied securely as she slid most of the way. But the pain was bearable now he was with her.

Their progress towards the cove was very slow. Charlie could walk but she was very unsteady, and Ivor held her round the waist to support her. As they approached the small beach, two policemen appeared through the rain, and after a hurried confab with Ivor, the pair of them joined hands and made a sort of seat to carry her up over the hill.

*

Ivor sat beside Charlie's bed in a curtained cubicle of Dartmouth Hospital. Nurses had stripped off her wet clothes, put her in a gown and tucked her under several blankets until the doctor finished with his previous patient.

Her hair was nearly dry now but she was very pale and still cold. The silence she'd sunk into since her admission was very worrying.

Ivor had never seen anyone looking so woe-begone as she did when he found her. Her face, hair and clothes were smeared with mud, her dark eyes looked haunted, and when he pulled her jumper off it was heavy with rain-water. Yet over and above the harrowing ordeal she'd been through, and the pain she was in, he sensed something more. Whether that was because she'd gone out with suicide on her mind, he couldn't tell. But he knew he had to get her to open up now, because if she didn't talk about what was troubling her, next time there might be no rescue.

'Charlie, I don't want to embarrass you, but I have to ask something. Are you pregnant?' He took her hands in his and looked deep into her eyes, daring her to lie to him. 'You might think it's none of my business, but if you are, we have to tell the doctor so he can check the baby is still okay.'

Charlie *was* embarrassed. She turned her head away from him and began to cry. Getting her period two weeks ago was the only luck she'd had in months.

Ivor let her cry for a few moments, gently stroking back her hair from her face. 'Are you? Because if you are I'll help you.'

'No, I'm not,' she said, shaking her head. 'Thank goodness. I wouldn't want to bring that creep's baby into the world.'

The vitriolic way she spoke was evidence of her deep hurt. Ivor wished he'd probed more deeply that day when she came back from Weymouth, some things were better brought out into the open. 'Well, that's one worry less,' he said with a gentle smile. 'Is this an appropriate time to ask what really happened between you?'

She turned her face back to him, tears welling up in her eyes. 'He abandoned me on the quay at Weymouth and sailed off,' she whispered. 'It hurt so much, Ivor. He didn't even have the guts to say goodbye.'

'Was it that which prompted the early morning walk?' Ivor asked. 'Or that chap Wyatt upsetting you yesterday?'

'I don't really know. A bit of everything I guess,' she said.

Ivor sighed. He'd lost more hours than he cared to remember in the weeks after Sarah and Kim were killed. But his problem had been grief, and agony though it was, it ran its course. Charlie had so many different things to cope with – a broken heart, missing father, crippled mother and any freedom of choice snatched from her.

'Don't you ever run off alone like that again if you are hurting or frightened,' he said reprovingly. 'The cliffs are dangerous places even on a warm sunny day. In rain they are treacherous. If you ever feel like that again, you come to me.'

'I didn't know what I was doing,' she cried, rubbing at her eyes like a small child. 'That was what scared me the most, Ivor. I think I just flipped, a bit like Mum does.'

There was nothing more Ivor could say. She was safe now. She'd even learned that the human mind can only take so much. And she'd proved she could take more than most.

An x-ray later proved no bones were broken. Charlie's shoulder was dislocated and she was badly bruised, but because she was in shock and suffering from hypothermia, the doctor insisted she stay in hospital overnight.

Ten days later, in Beryl's car, Ivor drove Charlie over to Mayflower Close. After she'd seen the flat he was taking her on to Paignton to Miss Fellows, her headmistress.

Charlie had gone down with a very bad cold soon after she'd left hospital. This, coupled with her injured shoulder and low state of mind, had forced her to stay in bed. Yet despite this, the Receiver's office had still callously insisted on the Weishes' belongings being taken out of 'Windways' on the original date they'd set. Determined that Charlie was to have no further anxiety, Ivor and Beryl had overseen the move without her.

As Charlie opened the front door of the flat she braced herself for piles of boxes and furniture piled up high. But as she walked in and saw the living room she gasped in astonishment.

The carpet was fitted, curtains were hung, even the furniture was arranged with a rug in front of the gas fire and a table lamp on a low bookcase. She could hardly believe her eyes. Apart from a stack of boxes up by the back window, the room was ready to live in.

'You did all this?' She looked about in absolute wonder. 'Oh Ivor, you're wonderful.'

'Beryl masterminded it, I was just the labourer,' he said, looking at his feet in embarrassment. Charlie rushed into each of the bedrooms. The beds were made, clothes hung up in the wardrobes, even her stereo was fixed into a wall unit. In the kitchen the refrigerator and cupboards were stocked with food and china. All the flat needed was for her to hang pictures and place a few ornaments.

'If it had been left to me, the kitchen utensils would be in the bathroom, and the beds in the living room,' Ivor called out from the living room. 'Beryl said you'll need to shorten the curtains. She'll sew them if you can't do it. And of course you'll want to rearrange the furniture to suit yourselves.'

'You were much more than a labourer!' Charlie came back into the room, sniffing and dabbing at her eyes. The carpets all looked as if they'd been bought for the rooms, he'd fixed up a mirrored cabinet on the bathroom wall and a tool rack in the kitchen. It looked like a real home; if they were to draw the curtains, Charlie could at a pinch pretend she was back at 'Windways'. 'It's such a lovely surprise. How can I ever thank you?'

Ivor wanted to hug her, but she still had a sling on her arm and she was badly bruised. 'By being happy here, sweetheart. Both Beryl and I were very glad to do it for you – it's our way of showing how much we care.'

Charlie thought they'd both already proved that by their concern when she went missing and the loving care they'd given her since.

She had turned a corner now, thanks to that care. These last few days of rest and peace had brought it home to her that she must accept what she couldn't change. Today she was going in to see when she could start back at school; in a few days' time her mother would come home.

Maybe the accident was a good thing. Sylvia had said during a recent telephone conversation that it had jolted her into thinking more positively. Perhaps she'd thought on what might have happened, because she now seemed to be more concerned about Charlie than herself. Just yesterday afternoon she'd said she was determined to try to walk, and she was looking forward to being together with her daughter again.

'It's a new start for both of you,' Ivor said, making her sit down while he put the kettle on. He thought she was still looking too pale. 'In my view tragedy can often be the making of people.'

If anyone else had said such a thing to Charlie she might have snapped at them. But Ivor spoke from experience, so she said nothing.

She looked about the room and felt a bubble of happiness growing inside her. It was just a very ordinary flat, as far removed from 'Windways' as it was possible to be, but maybe that was a good thing. She and her mother had to be ordinary people now.

It wasn't going to be easy looking after her mother and the flat and going to school. Six months ago she wouldn't even have known how to put a light bulb in, but now was her chance to show Ivor and Beryl just how much she'd learned from them.

'I'm determined to make it work,' she said firmly. 'You just wait and see what I can do when I make my mind up!'

Ivor smiled, but his heart was a little heavy. He had every faith in Charlie, but he wasn't so sure her mother was as deeply committed. He hoped he would be proved wrong.

Chapter Eight

Charlie staggered into the tiny hall with two large bags of shopping, pushed the door shut behind her with one foot, put the bags down, kicked off her wet shoes and then removed her dripping raincoat.

It was ten o'clock at night, March 1971, and she and Sylvia had been living in Mayflower Close for six months. Charlie had left home before eight that morning, bought the shopping after school, then gone straight to the Royal Castle Hotel on the harbour where she had a part-time job in the kitchens. She'd missed the bus and she'd had to walk all the way home up a steep hill in heavy rain carrying the shopping. She was exhausted.

The television was blaring out, and Charlie took a deep breath before opening the door to the living room. She knew exactly what to expect, an overheated room full of cigarette smoke, the remains of a Meals on Wheels dinner still sitting on the coffee table and her mother slumped sullenly in front of the television.

Although Charlie had embarked on living with her mother again with hope and determination that they would have a happy life together, Sylvia hadn't shared her commitment. She showed no appreciation for anything Charlie did for her. She grumbled incessantly and made no attempt to do anything for herself. Last month it had been Charlie's seventeenth birthday. Sylvia hadn't even remembered. The only greeting that morning had been a complaint that Charlie had forgotten to pick up her prescription for sleeping pills.

'Hullo, Mum.' Charlie forced herself to smile as she humped the shopping in. Everything was exactly as she expected, the mess, heat and smoke. 'Sorry I'm late, I missed the bus.'

Sylvia had given up on her appearance soon after she settled into her new home. Charlie's memory of painted nails, carefully set hair and makeup was so distant nowadays that she rarely even tried to persuade Sylvia to make an effort any more.

Sylvia tied her blonde hair back with an elastic band, and her skin was yellowy and puckered through lack of fresh air and too many cigarettes. As she ate much more now she had put on weight too, and she always wore baggy trousers to hide the scars on her knees. She looked old and slovenly.

She didn't even turn her head towards her daughter, just kept her eyes firmly on the television. 'There wasn't any bread left and I couldn't reach the crackers,' she said in a dull monotone.

Charlie bit her tongue. She had become a master at this for it was the only way to avoid ugly scenes. 'I've got some now,' she said, going on through to the kitchen. 'Would you like a sandwich? I bought some ham too.'

'I'm not hungry any more. Did you get my cigarettes?'

'Do I ever forget them?' Charlie replied. She pulled them out of one of the bags and took them over to her mother. 'But you must cut down, Mum, we can't afford so many in a week. Since this decimalization came in they are putting pennies on everything, thinking we don't notice. This week's shopping was over fifty pence more than it used to be. That's ten shillings in old money.'

Sylvia got through over forty cigarettes a day now. Back at 'Windways' she had limited herself to about twenty, and never smoked in her bedroom. But now Charlie often woke in the middle of the night to hear her mother coughing and she'd be sitting up in bed with a cigarette. Charlie hated it, her own clothes and hair stank of them, the walls and ceiling were turning brown, and she was worried in case her mother accidentally started a fire.

'It's the only pleasure I get, surely you aren't going to deny me that now?' Sylvia whined.

Charlie didn't bother to reply and just got on with unpacking the shopping. If she allowed herself to be drawn into an argument she'd never get to bed tonight.

The kitchen was messy, but then it always was. Sylvia could walk a little now with the aid of a walking frame, so she could go to the toilet alone, and take a bath just with help getting in. In fact there was nothing to stop her leading a fairly normal life, as all the doors were wide enough for her to get about in her wheelchair if her legs grew tired. But although she made tea and snacks for herself during the day, she never attempted jobs like washing up or wiping the work surfaces. She treated Charlie as if she was a servant.

One day a week she was collected in an ambulance

231

and taken to the hospital for physiotherapy, but even though she was always urged to walk and stand more, she ignored the advice. Charlie suspected that if she didn't leave her any cigarettes she could make it to the shop around the corner without too much difficulty. But she hadn't found the courage to be that ruthless yet.

'I think I will have a sandwich after all,' Sylvia called out, after Charlie had tidied up the kitchen. 'And a cup of coffee.'

Charlie gritted her teeth. It was tempting to tell her to make it herself, but she'd just make another mess.

She took it into her mother a few minutes later. 'I'm going to my room to do my homework,' she said. 'Is there anything else you need before I settle down?'

'No,' Sylvia said and looked up at her daughter with reproachful eyes. 'But I would have liked you to watch television with me.'

'Mum, I can't,' Charlie said in despair. 'I've got two hours of English to do and it's got to be in tomorrow.'

'Oh, please,' Sylvia pleaded, patting the seat beside her. 'There's a weepy film on and we can snuggle up here together the way we used to.'

Charlie was tempted, not so much by the film itself as by the good memories her mother's words brought back. They had spent a great many happy hours together that way once. She had almost forgotten how emotional her mother had been at sad films; perhaps it would take her out of her own problems for a while.

But she couldn't spare the time. The homework had to be done. 'I can't, Mum, not tonight,' she said.

'All you think of is work,' Sylvia said sulkily. 'I'm

alone all day and I want a bit of company when you come home.'

Charlie closed her eyes and counted to ten. She wanted to say that if her mother was to sort the laundry and put it in the machine, even sit and do the ironing or clean the kitchen, she'd have several free hours in a week to spend watching television. She also felt like adding that if Sylvia read books from the library instead of insisting on buying expensive magazines, cut down on smoking and didn't put the fire on full, Charlie wouldn't need to work so many evenings to make ends meet. But she'd said these things before and it always ended in Sylvia taking to her bed and playing ill. She couldn't face that right now.

'I'm not working tomorrow night, I'll sit with you then,' she said instead. 'And on Saturday morning, if it's fine, I'll take you down into the town in the wheelchair so you can look in the shops.'

It was hell taking her mother out. On the way down the hill it took all Charlie's strength not to let the chair run away with itself. Coming home was even worse because it was so heavy. But she was prepared to do it if it cheered her mother.

'What's the point? I can't afford to buy anything,' Sylvia retorted sulkily. 'Oh, go on and do your homework! You think more of that school than you do of me.'

Charlie sat at her small desk and tried to blot out the sound of the television. She had an essay on *Hamlet* to write and although she'd planned it all mentally while she was working in the hotel kitchen that evening, now her mind was fuzzy with weariness.

She had no time for herself now. It was just school, work, and looking after her mother.

It had all looked so rosy at first. She had been welcomed back at school by both the other girls and the teachers as if she'd just returned a little late from the summer holidays. Apart from an occasional curious question no one mentioned her father's disappearance, the attack on her mother, or even her old home.

She and June had picked up their old friendship, they even met every morning to travel together on the train. At first June used to urge her to come out dancing, she sometimes used to come round to the flat on a Saturday to play records too. But Charlie couldn't go out dancing, she had to work Saturday nights. Now June had a boyfriend and she spent all her spare time with him. They were still friends at school, on a superficial level, but in reality they had little in common any more.

Charlie hardly ever visited Ivor in Salcombe either. On the few Sundays she'd been over there, her mother invariably sulked for days afterwards. Ivor understood, so sometimes he borrowed Beryl's car and met Charlie in Dartmouth after school. They'd have a cup of coffee and chat, then he'd drop her home.

Last November he called at the flat quite regularly. At that time Sylvia welcomed him – he was handy for putting up shelves, moving furniture and other odd jobs. She even flirted a little with him the way she had done with men in the past. But by Christmas she was claiming he smelled funny, that he was uncouth and peculiar, and she was so offhand with him that Ivor suggested he met Charlie elsewhere.

It was very tempting to tell her mother that she smelled too. Except for the day she went to the hospital she didn't seem to care much about her own personal hygiene any more. Charlie had hinted about it, but Sylvia didn't respond to hints.

If it hadn't been for school, Charlie felt she might crack. There at least she had a strong purpose. While her classmates saw the sixth form as a continuation of their social life, she saw the 'A' levels at the end of it as a firm goal. Gone were the days she larked about, she knew her future career depended on good exam results, so she took every lesson and every piece of homework seriously.

Occasionally she'd listen to her *Woodstock* album and remember how she'd once yearned to be part of the youth revolution, and her main preoccupation had been boys, records and clothes. But that all seemed so long ago now. She had no money for new clothes or records, Guy had made her wary of boys, and she no longer cared about being revolutionary.

When she had time to dream, it was only of freedom. Of living alone, waking up each morning without hearing her mother coughing her lungs up, to have a job she loved, time to make friends, and to return at night to a clean flat without having to see that sour, embittered face wreathed in cigarette smoke, or hear that grating, whining voice demanding attention.

Sometimes though it shamed her to think it, let alone voice it, she wished her mother would die. At those times she cursed her father for leaving her with this terrible burden which made her think such wicked thoughts.

*

'I'll be home about six,' Charlie said the following morning as she was leaving for school. Sylvia was still in bed. She took sleeping pills every night and she was always groggy in the mornings. Charlie would make her tea and help her to the bathroom, then Sylvia went back to bed until eleven or so. 'I'm meeting Ivor after school.'

'What do you want to see that nasty old man for?' Sylvia asked, her once pretty face full of spite. 'There's something wrong with you.'

'But for that nasty old man I would have been jobless and homeless all summer. I might also have lain on those cliffs until I died of exposure,' Charlie said tartly.

She didn't wait for a reply, but closed her mother's door and promptly left the flat. It was eight o'clock, but she'd been up for two hours already, finishing the homework she was too tired to do last night. Now she was a little late and she would have to run all the way down to the ferry, or she'd miss the train from the other side of the river.

Ivor was waiting for her as she came off the ferry in the afternoon. Even though it was a very cold, windy day he wasn't wearing a coat, just a thick oiled sweater and corduroys. Just seeing his warm smile and his untidy red hair and beard cheered her. Ivor was as constant as the tide. A true friend and her only confidant.

'Hullo, sweetheart,' he said with his usual welcoming if somewhat fishy-smelling hug. 'How was school today?'

'Fine,' she said. 'Pretty good actually. Miss Endersleigh said my essay on *Hamlet* was first class.'

236

As they walked along towards the coffee bar in Foss Street, Ivor asked about her mother.

'Much the same,' Charlie said. She tried to avoid discussing her mother with him. If she told the whole truth it would only worry him, so she changed the subject as soon as they were sitting down.

Ivor told her all the Salcombe gossip, including how Beryl had become a blonde. 'It suits her,' he said with twinkly eyes. 'She said she was tired of being taken for my younger sister. And before I forget, she asked if you'd like to come and stay for a few days at Easter.'

'I'd love to.' Charlie's eyes lit up. 'It would be heaven.'

But then she remembered her mother and her face fell. 'But how can I, Ivor?'

'You can, and you should,' he said, reaching across the table to tweak her cheek. 'Sylvia's perfectly capable of looking after herself for a few days. She gets a dinner brought to her, and I'm sure if you spoke to her doctor he'd arrange for the district nurse to pop in just to check on her.'

'She'll play ill.'

'Well, let her.' He shrugged, his greeny-blue eyes sparking with indignation. 'You and I both know you are going to leave one day. The sooner she gets used to being alone occasionally, the better she'll cope then. Besides, if you don't get a rest soon, you'll get ill. And where would you be then?'

Ivor was always the voice of reason. Charlie knew he had a great deal of sympathy for Sylvia, but it was tempered with irritation that she made no effort to improve her situation. He understood and applauded

Charlie's sense of duty, but at the same time he felt it was time she stood up for herself.

'I'll speak to her about it,' Charlie said.

Ivor could see she was exhausted and it twisted his stomach to see her like that. She was too thin, too pale, and there was dark circles beneath her eyes. She had lost that chic, polished look she'd once had, her hair was straggly, her school uniform hung on her. All through January and February she'd had a series of bad colds, and he suspected she didn't eat properly. At times he wished he could storm in on her mother and tell her what he thought of her, but he knew Charlie wouldn't like that.

'What if I got Beryl to ask her?' he suggested. Oddly enough Sylvia got on well with Beryl. She had called in to visit Sylvia one day soon after she came out of the nursing home, and since then she often popped in during the day while Charlie was at school.

She never stayed long, but she always took a batch of magazines with her, and with her own special brand of persuasive charm, she had got the woman to open up about many things, including her relationship with Jin, and a little about DeeDee, the other woman in his life.

It saddened Ivor to think Sylvia could talk to a comparative stranger, yet refused to talk to her daughter about anything connected with either of her parents' past.

Beryl had gleaned that DeeDee was a strong, ambitious and very beautiful woman. She came from the East End of London originally, but had somehow managed to shed all trace of her humble beginnings, including her cockney accent. Beryl said that when

Sylvia spoke of their early friendship, despite everything that had happened, it was clear she still retained admiration, even some affection, for this woman. She spoke of DeeDee bringing up her two younger brothers single-handedly, of how she took Sylvia under her wing, gave her a roof over her head, taught her how to dress, and indeed how to fleece rich men.

Beryl had told Ivor on several different occasions that she'd seen how Sylvia must have been before the dark moods Charlie spoke of took over her life – a vulnerable yet vivacious and warm woman, who cared about other people.

In Beryl's opinion, Jin had cheated on Sylvia because her insecurity made her clingy and demanding. To her DeeDee sounded like perfect mistress material, passionate, wilful and exciting. What Beryl couldn't understand though was why Jin, who in so many ways sounded such a decent man, could plan and execute such a cruel and devious way to leave Sylvia, or why the woman who had suffered so much because of him wouldn't tell everything she knew. Beryl was totally convinced she did know a great deal more and that she was still, perhaps irrationally, frightened of DeeDee.

'I can't see Sylvia refusing Beryl,' Ivor went on. 'She'd be afraid Beryl would accuse her of being selfish, and stop visiting her.'

Charlie looked thoughtful. 'It might work, it's worth a try,' she said, her eyes brightening a little.

'Then I'll suggest it,' he said. 'So say nothing to your mum right now.'

They spoke of Charlie's job at the Royal Castle.

Charlie made Ivor laugh with stories about what went on in the kitchens. She only did the menial tasks, preparing salads and vegetables, but her interest in cooking had taken a leap forward since she'd been there. It was when she made a weak joke about smuggling home some leftover chicken and vegetables to supplement her poor wages that Ivor wondered if she was struggling to make ends meet.

'Are you short of money?' he asked. 'Because if you're worried about a bill or something, you've only got to say and I'll try and help.'

'That's very kind of you,' she said. 'But I'm coping okay.' Her eyes weren't meeting his and he thought she was lying to him.

'There is something wrong. I can tell,' he said firmly. 'So tell me?'

Charlie hesitated for a moment. She was worried, but not about money, she'd got used to having very little. It was the treasures buried up by 'Windways' which bothered her, and as each day passed she knew she had to do something about them, but she didn't know what.

'Come on, Charlie, tell Uncle Ivor, you know what they say about shared problems?'

Charlie decided to take the plunge. She blurted it out without drawing breath.

Ivor gave a low whistle as she finished. He hadn't expected anything like that. 'Well, that *was* a smart move, Charlie,' he said, looking at her admiringly. He couldn't imagine any other young girl keeping such a secret. 'Don't for one moment feel guilty about it, they are yours by rights. But you certainly can't leave them there much longer. For one thing damp might get in, for another a builder or someone might find them.'

'But what should I do with them? Should I tell Mum?'

Ivor gave this a moment's deep thought. Judging by Charlie's description of these items, they could be worth a great deal of money. Sylvia had long since decided that Jin had taken her jewellery, and she had everything she really needed already. In all probability, being entirely self-centred, and hardly the smartest woman in the world, she would either merely sit on them, refusing to sell even one item to relieve Charlie from the pressure of working so hard, or, more likely, she'd want to blow the lot on something very extravagant. If it was the latter, someone would find out and questions would be asked about where the money came from.

'I don't think you should tell her, not the way she is,' Ivor said firmly. 'At the moment she has her rent paid and enough money to live on quite comfortably, and you have a free place at school. All that would be in jeopardy if the Social Security found she had a nest-egg. And if they refused to give her benefits, any money from the sale of those items would soon be eaten up. I think you should find a really safe place for them. I can find out about that for you. Maybe once you've finished at school and got a decent job, it might be different, you could sell them then, and get a better place for your mother to live. But right now I think it's better to keep quiet about them.'

'But what if she accuses me later of deceiving her?'

Ivor shrugged. 'So what, Charlie? You had the presence of mind to take these things, not for yourself, but to help her. You've done everything possible to make your mum comfortable and secure in these past months. She is a very lucky woman to have you caring for her. It's time you stopped pandering to her every little whim and stood up for yourself.'

Two weeks later, in the Easter holidays, Charlie was packing a bag to go to Salcombe for a few days. Beryl had finally managed to persuade Sylvia that she could cope alone. The fridge was full of food, there was a pile of cigarette packets on the coffee table, and a selection of new magazines were sitting on her mother's bedside table. The district nurse and their next-door neighbour had promised to pop in each day. The sun was shining outside, with a real promise that spring was finally here. Charlie even had the treasures she'd recovered from their hiding place. They were now at the bottom of her bag to be taken first to a valuer Ivor had tracked down, and then to be put in a security vault.

She was very glad to be taking them somewhere safer. She had dug them up on the first day of her holiday, and she'd been terrified that her mother might poke around in her room and find them.

It had been scary creeping through the dense bushes by 'Windways'. As she dug them out, she had visions of someone popping their head over the wall and demanding to know what she was doing. But as there were no curtains in the front of the house and the windows hadn't been cleaned, she thought perhaps the new owners hadn't moved in yet.

She zipped up her bag and put a few clothes away. The bus to Kingsbridge was due in ten minutes, but she was worried about her mother. Last night Charlie had made a special meal for them both, helped her mother into the bath later, washed and set her hair, and Sylvia had been so cheerful that Charlie'd actually begun to believe she was happy her daughter was having a little holiday. Now this morning she wouldn't get up, she claimed she had a stomach ache and even suggested there was something wrong with the chicken Charlie had cooked.

'She's making it up,' Charlie told herself. 'The minute you've gone she'll be out of bed and checking to see what's on TV. Remember what Ivor said. You have to stand up for yourself.'

Picking up her small bag, she went out into the living room and looked around her. In the week she'd been home from school she'd done some spring-cleaning and the flat looked nice again. The net curtains were snowy white, she'd washed all the cushion covers and given the carpet a shampoo. Sunshine was streaming through the front windows and at the back the view down to the river was enough to lift anyone's spirits. A vase of daffodils on the coffee table looked cheerful and as the windows had been open for a while the room didn't smell of smoke.

She wished her mother would learn to appreciate that it was a nice flat, and how kind the neighbours were. They were only ordinary working-class people, with enough problems of their own, yet several of them went out of their way to call in on Sylvia when she was alone.

Charlie was wearing jeans and a red sweater, but as she looked at herself in the mirror she winced. Last year her jeans had been skin-tight, now they were loose, the sweater had bobbles on it through age and constant wear, and it was so long since she'd last had her hair cut that it looked bedraggled. It crossed her mind that if Guy turned up in Salcombe for Easter he'd get a shock to see her this way.

Sighing deeply, she turned away from the mirror and put on her coat, then went in to say goodbye to her mother.

'I'm going now,' she said. 'How's the tum?'

Sylvia just groaned. 'Terrible, I think I've got food poisoning.'

Charlie looked hard at her mother. Her colour was normal, the same putty shade as always. She hadn't been sick. She was definitely making it up. 'The nurse will be in around twelve and she might have some-thing she can give you,' she said in a crisp voice. 'Is there anything you need before I go?'

'No, you go. I wouldn't want you to miss your bus.'

'Beryl's telephone number is on the pad by the phone,' Charlie said. 'You can call me there in an emergency, but I'll phone you each night anyway.'

'I'd have to be dying before I'd spoil your holiday,' Sylvia said and a tear rolled down her cheek.

Charlie took a deep breath, leaned over and kissed her. 'If the tummy ache stops later why don't you sit outside in the sunshine for a bit? It's lovely out by the back door.'

She left then, but it was hard to walk away leaving her mother crying.

To Charlie's surprise, there was no frantic phone call that evening. She rang her anyway. Sylvia claimed she still had the stomach ache and she didn't feel like eating, but she seemed resigned to being alone and even said she hoped Charlie would enjoy herself.

It was so good to be back in the bar with Beryl and Ivor that first evening. Beryl looked very glamorous with her new blonde hair, and she glowed with delight when Charlie told her so. In no time at all it was as if she'd never been away, laughing, gossiping and teasing. Many of the locals had virtually ignored her last summer, but now they acted as if she had been bred and born in Salcombe. When she finally fell into her little bed at nearly one in the morning, it was wonderful to know she didn't have to get up early.

She and Ivor spent the following day together. It was too early in the year for him to open the shack, anyone who needed something just banged on his cottage door. They took Minnie for a walk in the morning and in the afternoon they went out in the *MaryAnn*. To know she had a few days' release from cooking, cleaning and schoolwork was all Charlie needed to bring back her sense of humour. It seemed as if she was laughing all day at Ivor's tales. The smell of the sea, the stiff breeze and the watery sunshine brought the colour back to her cheeks, and for the first time in months she had worked up a real appetite. Ivor had made her his special fish stew and she ate two large bowlfuls of it, relishing every delicious mouthful.

'That's better,' he said approvingly when she almost staggered to an armchair and Minnie climbed up on her lap. 'You look like my old first mate again. And to welcome you back you're excused washing-up duties.'

On the second day, Ivor drove her in Beryl's car to Exeter to meet Mr Craig the valuer. All the way there, despite Ivor's insistence there was nothing to be frightened of, Charlie felt very nervous. After all, Ivor had never met him, he'd only got his name and telephone number from an acquaintance. She imagined him to be a snooty, aristocratic type in an elegant showroom and she was uneasy about the story Ivor had told the man about how she'd been left these things by her grandmother.

Suppose those miniatures hadn't been bought fair and square by her father, but stolen from someone? She'd read in the newspapers that people did get caught sometimes when they tried to sell such things on. Surely if they were her grandmother's she'd know the background about them, like how old they were, who the women painted were?

The last thing she needed now was to be caught with stolen property.

Her fears turned out to be groundless. Mr D. F. Craig turned out to be a rather wizened little man of over seventy who had now retired from his position as valuer for a major auction rooms. The address he'd given Ivor was his own home, a charming old cottage crammed with antiques, just outside Exeter.

Over tea and cake he studied each of the items carefully. The miniatures, he assured her, were fine ones, he dated them at around 1820, and he thought that if they were put into a suitable auction they would collectively raise at least £5000, maybe more. As for the jade animals, the complete collection was worth in the region of another £1000, though he advised Charlie to seek out a specialist in jade to have this confirmed. He was less enthusiastic about the jewellery – he thought the stones were excellent but the settings a little too ornate. Yet he still valued all the pieces at over £3000. As Charlie had suspected, the other odds and ends, although pretty, weren't very valuable.

'Your grandmother left you a nice little nest-egg,' he said, looking at Charlie over his glasses. 'If you'll take the advice of an old man, I suggest you hang on to them for a few years. Interest is mounting in miniatures, as in jade, but the economy is a little shaky right now, unemployment is at its highest since 1940, and it's my experience that to sell at such a time is always a mistake. Five, even ten years on, they might be worth double what you'd get for them now. As for the jewellery, women's tastes have changed since these large, ostentatious pieces were made, small and delicate is now more in vogue, but there will come a time when they'll be fashionable again, be assured of that.'

He asked for only £5, his standard fee for people requiring a valuation for insurance purposes, and then with the business over, he proudly showed Charlie some fine water-colours he'd painted himself.

'I've spent my entire life dealing with other people's family treasures,' he said, 'and a great part of it also collecting things myself, but discovering I could paint has given me more pleasure than anything else. Just you remember that, my dear, and if you have a talent, make use of it now while you are young. It's more important to be happy and creative than it is to amass a fortune.'

*

Ivor took Charlie to a bank in Exeter afterwards. She opened a deposit account with the £200 which had been with the treasures, using his address. When she asked about placing some items with them for security, she found all she had to do was fill out a brief form, pay a nominal fee, and she was ushered down some stairs into the vault to lock her things in herself.

It was an odd feeling looking around this secure room with its hundreds of tiny numbered drawers, knowing that the others probably contained far more valuable things than hers did. She had seen similar rooms in films about bank raids. She hoped bank robbers didn't come to places like Exeter.

'Well, that's all sorted,' Ivor said cheerfully as she came back up into the bank where he was waiting. 'It wasn't so bad, was it?'

'Are you sure I've done the right thing?' she asked as they went back along the street to find a café to have some lunch.

'Of course you have,' he insisted. 'Any time things get tough, or your mother needs something, you can get those things out. It's like an umbrella, my dear. Always handy to have on a rainy day.'

The last two days of her stay flew by. On one she went out mackerel fishing with Ivor and a party of men down from London. They didn't leer at her like that first fishing party she'd met, but then she was wearing oilskins and Ivor spoke to her as if she was his regular crew. Once out into deep water some of the men turned green, and she felt proud of herself that she could bait hooks, haul in lines and take the helm like a real fisherman, while these city men floundered about like silly schoolboys.

'To think I was apprehensive about taking you on as help last year,' Ivor said thoughtfully as he was watching her later gutting the fish they'd caught. 'I think you could do anything you set your mind to, Charlie. I've never met anyone so determined.'

Charlie laughed. A year ago she wouldn't have wanted even to touch a fish, let alone gut it and cook it. 'I don't think I would have turned out the same without all the trouble. I suppose that's what people mean when they say, "Every cloud has a silver lining."'

Ivor had lit a fire in the kitchen and the warmth of its glow softened the stark whitewashed walls and the Spartan furnishings. Outside the wind had got up and the sea was rough, pounding noisily on to the slipway just a dozen or so yards away. Charlie had come to love this little cottage; it was here she had learned all her most valuable lessons and found new strength to live with all the hurts and disappointments.

'Do you still think about your father as much?' Ivor asked a few moments later. He was sitting by the fire, filling his pipe. He felt it was an appropriate time to ask this question for he sensed Charlie was in a reflective mood.

'Yes, all the time,' she said and there was a slight crack in her voice. 'It's like a sore place which won't heal, Ivor. People in Dartmouth don't ever speak about him any more, at least not to me.' She turned towards Ivor and he saw pain in her eyes. 'I wish they would, really. It would get it out in the open, wouldn't it?'

Ivor nodded.

'Sometimes I don't even know what to think about

him,' she said sorrowfully. 'Was he really the strong good man I believed in? Or was he as cruel and selfish as Mum would have me believe when she's having a bad day? If I knew why he'd gone, and where, or even that he was dead, maybe I could put it aside for good. But there's this sort of little candle of hope burning inside me. Do you know what I mean?'

'I do,' Ivor said sorrowfully as he lit his pipe. 'I wouldn't wish grief for a loved one on anyone, but it is a healing process and it does eventually fade. You're stuck in a void, Charlie, a kind of purgatory of unanswered questions.'

'One day I'll find out the truth, she said firmly, turning back to the fish. 'Perhaps Mum might start talking. I know there is a whole lot more she could tell me, but every time I try to prompt her, she just clams up and makes out she can't remember. It's very frustrating. Even the police seem to have given up now. I bet they wouldn't have if he'd robbed a bank or something!'

Ivor's heart swelled with sympathy as he looked at her backview, a slender little girl in jeans and a worn-looking sweater, her black hair gleaming in the soft light, the way the sea did at night. She had grown into an adult since she moved back with her mother – laudable perhaps, yet it made him sad to think her girlhood had been cut so short.

'It will come right,' he assured her. 'You are too brave and strong for it not to.'

'You are too,' she said softly, turning her head to look at him. 'I don't know what I would have done if I hadn't met you. You are so special and so very wise.'

Ivor chuckled. 'You wouldn't have said that in my

fighting and drinking days! What you see now is an old man who only gained the little wisdom he has from his own near self-destruction.'

Finally on Good Friday Charlie had to go home. 'You're to come regularly in future,' Beryl said firmly as she kissed her goodbye at the door of the pub. 'So don't you go making excuses. As for that mother of yours, be firm with her. Make her walk, insist she does a few chores, maybe even find out if there's any clubs she could join to make some new friends.'

Charlie felt so much stronger after her short holiday that she even believed she might be able to do this.

'Thank you for having me,' she said, hugging the older woman. 'I've had such a good time.'

Ivor and Minnie saw her off on to the bus. 'Happy Easter,' Ivor said as it came along. 'Just remember you've only got this one term to get through before the summer holiday. It's only really one more year until you'll be through with school for good.'

He hugged her then, and Charlie knew he felt as sad to be parting as she did. Just as she was about to get on the bus he pulled a chocolate Easter bunny from his coat pocket. 'I've been waiting a long time to find someone special enough to buy another one of these,' he said, looking shy.

As the bus drove away towards Kingsbridge Charlie looked down at the chocolate rabbit in her lap and knew that the last time he bought one was for his daughter.

Easter was later the following year, in April instead of March, but so cold it might still have been the middle of winter. Charlie was eighteen now and after the holidays she had only her final exams to do and then she could look for a job.

Yet a year hadn't brought much change to her life. Her mother could walk a little better, at times she made an effort with her appearance too. Some days she was just the way she'd been when Charlie was younger, chatty, giggly and interested in everything. Yet as if to balance these improvements, her bouts of severe depression were worse. At these times she was hell to live with, she stayed in bed most of the day, then stayed up watching television until it closed down. If Charlie ever asked her to turn it down, she turned nasty, shouting, throwing things and crying endlessly. She was on tranquillizers, but Charlie felt they were making her worse long-term rather than better.

Charlie had had a boyfriend back before Christmas; his name was Simon and she'd met him in the bar at work. He was an articled clerk with a firm of solicitors in Dartmouth and for a few short weeks Charlie thought he was pretty special. She never found out what his real reason was for packing her in. His excuse at the time was that he didn't want to get serious. She knew that wasn't true. But whether it was because she'd taken him home to meet her mother, because of her father, or just that she refused to sleep with him, she didn't know. Maybe it was all three.

Visits to Salcombe were the high spots of the year, although except for a whole two weeks in August when a local charity took her mother away to Cornwall, they were only weekends. The holiday in August was the best time she had ever known. She sailed almost every day with anyone who wanted a crew, went fishing with Ivor, even had a little light-hearted romance with a sweet young waiter who worked in one of the restaurants.

Since her eighteenth birthday back in March she'd progressed to being a waitress at the Royal Castle with a little more money and good tips on top. She was guarding this job carefully, not only for the money, or because the few vacancies that ever came up were always highly sought after, but because she liked the people who came to stay at the hotel, and the other staff. Their company was the nearest thing she had to a social life.

But now it was Easter again and she was off to Salcombe for another four days. Like last year she had tried to anticipate everything her mother would need in advance. And just the same again, she was playing ill.

'Charlie!'

She gritted her teeth at the whining cry. 'Yes, Mum,' she called back from her bedroom.

'There isn't any toilet paper!'

'There is, it's down beneath the cistern,' Charlie called back. This time Sylvia's complaint was chronic diarrhoea, and it was hard to prove she didn't have it without marching into the bathroom.

Sylvia had got quite clever at inventing new complaints; once she frightened Charlie with a high temperature. It turned out she'd put the thermometer on her hot-water bottle. She'd drunk salt water to make herself sick, taken an overdose of aspirin once, and both these last occasions had made sure Charlie couldn't go to Salcombe for a couple of days as she'd planned.

But this time Charlie was determined to go. She arranged four days off from work, Beryl and Ivor were expecting her. The doctor had called that morning and said Sylvia was fine. Nothing was going to stop her.

'Are you going to come out of there and say good-bye?' Charlie called through the locked door. 'I have to go now or I'll miss the bus.'

'I can't,' the plaintive voice came back. 'Go on, have a good time. Don't worry about me.'

Charlie leaned her head against the doorpost deject-edly. The woman was impossible, so utterly selfish it defied belief. Last year when she'd gone away to Cornwall with the charity, apparently she'd been the life and soul of the party for the whole fortnight. She'd charmed the helpers, joined in every game and sing-song with enthusiasm, and what's more she'd dressed up every day in some of her old glamorous clothes and given everyone the impression she was like that all the time.

The minute she got back here, she reverted to her old self. One of the helpers had called one day unexpectedly and was so shocked by Sylvia's slovenly appearance she'd scolded Charlie the moment she got back from school. It turned out Sylvia had told everyone on that holiday that her daughter cared nothing for her. And they'd believed her!

'Okay, I'm going then,' Charlie called back. 'I'll phone you later to see how you are.' She left then, slamming the door behind her.

This time she didn't go straight off to the bus, but stepped on to the paved area at the side of the living room window. She didn't feel she could walk away while her mother was still stuck in the bathroom.

A couple of minutes passed, and then she heard the bathroom door open and her mother come out. Peeping through a gap in the net curtains, Charlie could see her clearly. She wasn't using her walking aid.

To Charlie's absolute amazement she walked entirely unaided across the room. She was stiff and slow, but she wasn't even holding on to the settee for support. She then sat down, first grabbing the bunch of grapes from the fruit bowl, and swung her legs up on the settee, gobbling down the grapes like a greedy child with sweets.

Charlie's blood almost boiled with anger. She was on the point of going back in to have it out with her, but she stopped herself. At least it was proof her mother wasn't really ill. No one with a bad stomach would eat grapes like that.

She turned and hurried down the street towards the bus stop. For some time now she had suspected her mother could walk better and stand for longer than she let on. If she got out of bed during the night, Charlie rarely heard the clonk of that walking aid. On several occasions she'd made it to the local shop for cigarettes too, claiming later it nearly killed her.

If she could walk that well it was something to rejoice about, not hide. What sort of woman was she that she chose to pretend to be a cripple to get attention?

Charlie was still angry when she got to Salcombe, and as Ivor was waiting for her in the Victoria Inn, she blurted it out immediately to both him and Beryl. They exchanged knowing glances.

'Oh dear,' Beryl sighed. 'I suspected as much. Twice

255

recently I've called there to see her and she's got to the door a bit too quickly. I noticed too that she never has the walking frame near her; most people do when they really need it. I didn't say anything to you when we talked on the phone because I thought you might be wanting to surprise us with the good news.'

'But I don't understand why she's kept it quiet,' Charlie raged, her face flushed a bright pink. 'She's a cheat. Just like my father.'

'I expect it's fear that stops her telling you, more than anything else,' Ivor said gently. 'Fear that you'll leave home.'

'But don't you think it's despicable?' Charlie asked.

'Yes, I do,' he said. 'It's the worst kind of moral blackmail to make out you are completely dependent on another person. I think when you go home you must tell her that you know. But have a drink now and put it aside. Beryl and I want to hear about school and your new waitressing job.'

Two half pints of lager later, Charlie had stopped being angry. Ivor had suggested they went out on the *MaryAnn* in the afternoon and her mother's cunning ways had turned into something of a joke.

'No more for you,' Ivor said as she finished the second glass. 'Or you'll be reeling around my boat like the proverbial drunken sailor. Now, nip upstairs and put on some nice warm clothes. You'll need it out there, it's brass monkey weather.'

The cold wind, the sea and being with Ivor again worked its usual magic. At five as she came back into the harbour Charlie was exhilarated and giggly. Beryl had invited them both back to a meal with her, saying she had help in the bar so she wouldn't need to put in an appearance until much later in the evening.

'You go on back there,' Ivor said after they'd moored. 'I'll go home and get myself spruced up. I think Beryl's got a bit of a party in mind.'

Charlie walked into the kitchen to find Beryl drinking tea with a tall young man. 'This is my nephew Andrew Blake,' Beryl said. 'Andrew, this is Charlie. Andrew's my sister Dora's boy, and staying with me for the Easter hols. He's at City University in London studying electronics.'

Charlie just stared for a split second. She had heard Beryl talk about her nephew, but she'd never said he was such a dish. He had that winning combination of dark brown hair and bright blue eyes, and an embarrassed schoolboy grin.

'Now, I've told you about Charlie,' Beryl reminded him, nudging him to respond in a sensible fashion. 'She's my little friend, former kitchen slave, and as smart as you.'

'Hullo, Charlie,' he said finally, and despite his youth his voice was very deep and adult. 'My aunt *has* told me a great deal about you, I'm very pleased to meet you at last.'

Charlie looked at Beryl helplessly. She knew this was match-making, Beryl was that kind of person. Charlie was embarrassed yet pleased too. Few girls would object to anyone trying to fix them up with someone so handsome. Now she understood why Beryl was cooking dinner and why Ivor had been invited too. He'd known about this, the old rascal. So why hadn't he warned her?

'Would you mind if I just got changed?' Charlie

257

asked. She had left her oilskin coat on the boat, but her feet and old jeans were wet and she felt her hair must look like rat's tails.

'No, you go ahead, dear,' Beryl said and gave her a broad wink which implied she expected her to dress up. 'Andrew's giving me a hand with the cooking. It's one of his many talents.'

Charlie was as quick as she could be, but it was half an hour before she came back downstairs. She wished she'd had some previous warning about this, then she would have brought some smarter clothes with her. All she had other than jeans was a dark red maxi-skirt and a matching jumper. But at least her hair had been trimmed and after a shampoo it gleamed satisfactorily. Andrew had seen her at her worst, so things could only improve now she looked half decent.

Beryl and Andrew were sitting at a table in the snug. Ivor was there with them too, and Pamela, a woman in her thirties who often helped Beryl out, was behind the bar.

'Coo-ee,' Pamela called out as she spotted Charlie. 'How are you, dear? Nice to see you again. What would you like to drink?'

'A vodka and lemonade, please,' Charlie replied. Before she was eighteen no one ever offered her a real drink, yet since her birthday, which people couldn't possibly have known about, everyone kept plying her with alcohol.

Charlie went on into the snug. Ivor, Beryl and Andrew all turned as one to look at her. She blushed till she felt her face must match her outfit.

'Well, you look smashing,' Beryl said appreciatively. She turned towards Andrew who was staring openly at Charlie. 'Can you believe that both your mother and I were that slender once?'

'Get away,' Andrew laughed.

Suddenly Charlie knew this was going to be a good evening. She liked men who laughed and as it was clear he liked Beryl as much as she did they already had something in common.

It was such a good evening. It would have been enough just to share a meal with Ivor and Beryl, but Andrew added another dimension and turned it into a real party. They had two more drinks in the bar, then Ivor and Beryl disappeared into the kitchen to dish up the food and take it upstairs.

'Beryl's bought herself a heated hostess trolley,' Andrew confided once his aunt was out of earshot. 'She's giving it its trial run tonight. I'm not sure whether it's in your honour or mine.'

Charlie giggled. 'My mother had one of those,' she said. 'But she used to forget to turn it off or take things out of it when she'd had a few drinks. Once there was a terrible smell in the house, and no one knew where it was coming from. It got so bad Dad was walking around sniffing like a dog. Eventually he found it. She'd left the remains of a crown of lamb in there. It was rotten. You can't imagine how nasty it was.'

'I can,' he said, smiling at her. 'I live in a flat with three other chaps and we're always leaving half-eaten takeaways lying around until they go rotten. I don't know what it is about men when they live together, they turn into such hideous slobs, me included.'

He didn't look like a hideous slob. His open-necked pale blue shirt was well ironed, and his grey slacks pressed. His hair needed a better cut, it was a bit bedraggled around his ears, but it was clean and shiny. She thought his eyes were lovely – bright, twinkly and kind.

'Are you in your first year at university?' she asked. She didn't like to ask directly how old he was.

'Second,' he said. Charlie assumed by that that he was twenty. 'Just a year and a bit before they let me loose in the world of business and high tech. Always supposing I get a good degree of course. If I fail I'll have to get a job in a shoe shop or something. What about you? Beryl said you were doing "A" levels?'

Charlie nodded. 'I wanted to go to university, but I don't think that's feasible. Has Beryl told you about my mum?'

'Yes, well, a bit. I believe she can't walk and you look after her. I'm sorry, Charlie, that must be tough.'

'It's a chore rather than tough,' but she laughed as she said it, suspecting Beryl had given him the true low-down already. 'She's doing a degree herself.'

'Really?' He looked astonished. 'What in?'

'Whingeing. I expect she'll get an honours in it.'

He spluttered with laughter, and as Ivor was just coming back into the room followed by Beryl, they both wanted to know what the joke was. Andrew repeated what Charlie'd said and both Beryl and Ivor joined in the laughter.

'Come on now, it's time to eat,' Beryl said, and waved them towards the door.

Charlie had never seen the table upstairs in the sitting room laid for dinner before as Beryl always ate in the kitchen. It looked very attractive with a dark blue tablecloth, good silver, crystal glasses, candles

260

and flowers. She had lit a real fire, the curtains were drawn and the room was very cosy.

Charlie had always been impressed by Beryl's cooking. She had a knack of making even an ordinary dish like shepherd's pie something special, but tonight she'd set out to impress: avocados stuffed with prawns for starters, then *boeuf en croûte* for the main course. Charlie was starving after being out in the boat, and she concentrated on eating and listening rather than talking herself.

Andrew was very funny. He told stories about his flatmates' escapades which were so vivid Charlie could almost see fat, short-sighted Nigel dancing with more energy than style to James Brown, acne-suffering Dan who couldn't find a girlfriend, and weird-sounding Robert Battershill with his passion for making home-made fireworks.

She liked Andrew's honesty too. He didn't make himself out to be super-intelligent, and pointed out early on that he'd been brought up on a council estate in Oxford. There was a joyfulness flowing out of him, as though he'd looked around him and decided his life was far better than he ought to expect. So many of the students Charlie had met while working in the Royal Castle complained about everything: their grants weren't enough to live on, their parents expected too much, the government was failing them and they doubted they'd even get a good job when they got their degree.

By the time Beryl got up to bring in the pudding, they'd already drunk two bottles of claret between the four of them, and Charlie was just a bit tipsy. When Beryl came back into the room with a huge steaming treacle pudding and another bottle of wine, Charlie groaned.

'Now, don't look like that,' Beryl said with a grin. 'I know full well you are a treacle addict, and you'll find room for it somewhere. Besides, these boys need pampering. I doubt either of them's had a home-made pud in years.'

'Mum used to make this when I was little,' Andrew said as he gleefully tucked into a huge bowlful. 'She says she doesn't remember how to make it any more. She'd better come down here and take lessons from you.'

'Takes me back to my childhood too,' Ivor admitted. 'Mum made suet puddings all the time. Not just sweet ones, but savoury ones with bacon and herbs. She used to say, "It greases your lungs."'

Charlie squealed with laughter. 'What a disgusting thought!'

'It did seem to have some magic qualities,' Ivor said. 'I can remember going out fishing with Dad after one of those puds and not feeling the cold at all. Sometimes she gave us another lump of it to eat cold later. Nothing tasted better at four in the morning with a nice hot cup of tea.'

'So what food sticks in your mind from childhood, Charlie?' Andrew asked. 'Something that had special significance?'

She thought for a moment. Her mother's brand of cooking had always been rather fancy and very forgettable. 'Dad making Nasi Goreng,' she said.

'What on earth's that?' Beryl asked.

'A kind of mixture of different Chinese dishes,' Charlie explained. 'Noodles, rice, vegetables and any meat or fish you care to chuck in it. It's wonderful.'

Ivor nodded. 'I had it all over the Far East,' he said. 'I've tried to make it myself, but it never tasted the same.'

'I'll find out how to make it properly and I'll make it for all of us one day,' Charlie said with a smile.

Beryl and Ivor went down into the bar later, but Andrew and Charlie stayed upstairs, drinking and talking.

She had believed she and Guy were on entirely the same wavelength, but after a short while with Andrew she realized this was a fallacy. She had in fact adopted Guy's ideas; perhaps that was why she didn't tell him about her parents until right at the end.

It was effortless telling Andrew about herself, he was so interested. He wanted to know everything about her father, and Charlie wished she had more background detail to share with him, because it was obvious he liked a good mystery.

'If you do come to London after your exams,' he said eagerly, 'I could help you dig around. If you could find out from your solicitor which clubs your dad owned, we could go there and pump people for information.'

'Do you think they'd tell us anything? I mean, if the police didn't make any headway, why should we be lucky?'

He smiled. 'We won't steam in there asking what they know about Jin Weish. We could make out we're researching a book or something, ask them general questions about Soho in the Fifties. If your dad was a lead player in those days, someone is bound to mention him.'

'That's a brilliant idea,' she said, suddenly feeling very excited and hopeful. 'We might be able to trace DeeDee too.'

'I hope you will look me up,' he said, all at once more serious. 'I haven't got much to offer, just a grotty flat and a clapped-out Lambretta to get around on, but I'd love to see you again and introduce you to all my friends.'

Charlie thought about those words again once she was in bed, and they made her feel tingly all over. It wasn't anything like that heart-stopping stuff she'd felt when she first met Guy, yet knowing what she did, she preferred this warm, happy feeling.

She thought Andrew was lovely. But this time she wasn't going to rush into anything blindfolded.

On Good Friday, Charlie's last morning, she and Ivor walked along the harbour wall together, Minnie running on ahead. 'What a beautiful morning,' Charlie sighed. It was only seven, but she'd been unable to stay in bed another minute knowing she had to return home today, and as Ivor was always up and about early, she'd slipped out of the pub to join him.

It was still very cold, but the sun was shining, seagulls were squawking as they looked for their breakfast, and the boats were bobbing up and down on a brilliant blue sea.

'Is it love that got you up so early?' Ivor asked teasingly.

Charlie slipped her arm through his and cuddled up to his side. 'Love for you, do you mean?'

'You know perfectly well what I mean,' he growled.

'Maybe, maybe not,' she laughed. 'Andrew is gorgeous, Ivor, he's got all the qualities I admire. But I'm scared of getting hung up on anyone right now. I've got to concentrate on my exams.'

'As I remember, love chooses you rather than the other way,' he said. 'Anyway, it's been good to see you looking so happy these last few days. I just wish you could stay longer.'

'Me too,' she said, her mind slipping back to all the fun she'd had with Andrew. They'd been out fishing with Ivor, they'd taken long walks together and even dared each other to paddle yesterday down at Slapton Sands. That had been the best fun of all, the beach was deserted because it was so cold and they'd played chase, like a couple of children. He had kissed her there for the first time, a long lingering kiss that had brought back all those half-forgotten feelings of needing and wanting.

'Will you see him again?' Ivor asked.

'You're like a dog with a bone this morning,' Charlie giggled. 'Yes, if you must know, I will see him again, but not till after the exams.'

'I'm glad about that.' Ivor pulled her round by her arms and looked right into her eyes. 'He's a good chap, nothing hidden, a kind lad with a good future ahead of him and a great sense of humour. I knew you weren't ready emotionally for love when Guy came along, but you're a big girl now and the time is right. Don't be afraid, sweetheart, and don't consider your mother too much. Take what you want.'

Charlie laughed. She thought Ivor was so sweet when he gave her his fatherly lectures. Yet she liked it, and he was so wise she couldn't ignore his advice.

'What time are you going today?' he asked a few minutes later as they went back towards his cottage.

'About eleven. Andrew is borrowing Beryl's car to take me.'

'Are you going to have breakfast with me?' He raised one bushy eyebrow. 'A big fried one with sausage and black pudding to grease your lungs?'

She giggled. 'Yes, please. I'll even be able to tackle Mum after that.'

Chapter Nine

'Are you sure I can't persuade you to go off galli-vanting with me today?' Andrew asked as he drove Charlie home to Dartmouth. 'I'd love you to show me where you used to live and all your old haunts.'

'The spirit is willing, but the mother's influence is too strong,' she laughingly replied. 'If I'm not home when I said, she'll be hell all Easter weekend.'

'She sounds a real tyrant,' he said.

'No, she's not that exactly,' Charlie said thought-fully. 'When she isn't depressed, she's a weak, kind of fluffy person. Perhaps it's much harder for someone like that to cope with problems and disappointments. Unfortunately there's only me now to take the full brunt of her depression.'

'Being crippled would turn most of us into a depressive,' he said.

'She was one long before that happened.' Charlie shrugged. 'I called it "moods" and "nerves" then, because I didn't know any better. But it was the same thing. The funny thing is that if you were to meet her on one of her "up" days, you'd be charmed by her. She can be very good with men.'

'You take after her then?' he joked.

'No, I'm not a bit like her. More like Dad I'd say. Mum says I'm cold, she used to say that about Dad too. I don't think I am, do you?'

'No, not cold. But there is a kind of distance in you,' he said. 'Maybe that's what she means.'

'Chinese blood,' Charlie giggled. 'When I was at the infants' school I cut myself quite badly once. The girl who took me into the teacher to get me patched up was astonished that I had red blood like her. I suppose she thought it would be yellow.'

'I love the way you look,' he said, looking sideways at her. 'Your shiny back hair, golden skin, those exotic eyes. I'd like to pin a picture of you to the wall and just look at you all day.'

'I suppose it would beat a cheap print of rampaging elephants,' she giggled. 'But a bit too much like that dreadful *Woman with the Green Face* print of the Chinese woman that people used to be so fond of, for my comfort.'

'My mum's got that picture!' He made a mock-scandalized face. 'Don't you ever tell her you think it's dreadful, or she'll die of mortification. She sees herself as something of an art lover.'

Charlie smiled. She liked the way he dropped sweet things like wanting to pin up a picture of her into the conversation, but then turned back to ordinary things immediately afterwards. She wanted to feel she was special, but at the same time she didn't want too much intensity.

'Now, what do we do when we get to your house?' he asked a little later. 'Do I sweep in carrying your luggage like a bell-boy, doff my cap and leave? Do I drop you outside, or do we give the dragon a hint that I'm considering the possibility of enticing you off to London before long?'

'I think the first one, but no cap-doffing, trying too hard to please, or questions after her health.'

'Why not?' He faked surprise at the last request.

'Because, simple one, she'll bore you with the full nine yards. We'll just say you are Beryl's nephew, at university, you have a quick cup of tea and then you scarper. Furthermore, I warn you the flat will probably be fairly disgusting. Mum doesn't believe in clearing up after herself.'

'I'm glad you live in squalor at times. It'll prepare you for my flat. That is a health inspector's nightmare.'

'Is there a masculine version of "slut"?' she asked.

'Slutter,' he said immediately. 'Or slutteri if one wishes to use a collective noun.'

Charlie laughed. She was going to miss Andrew a great deal, especially his sense of humour. She wondered if she really could hold out until after the exams to see him again.

As they approached Dartmouth she directed him down Townstal Road, left into the crescent and then along Mayflower Close.

Andrew gasped as he saw the panoramic view of Dartmouth and the river between a gap in the houses. 'I was expecting you to take me somewhere grim,' he said, slowing right down so he could see it better.

'There are no grim places in Dartmouth,' she said with a smile. 'But try telling Mum that!'

The curtains in the living room at number sixteen were closed. 'What on earth has she got them closed

269

for? The sun isn't that bright,' Charlie said with some irritation as she got out the car.

'Maybe she's watching TV,' Andrew said. 'It's Good Friday after all. There's probably one of those creaky old films on.'

He got her bag from the car and they walked up the path together.

'I'm back, Mum,' Charlie called out as she opened the door. 'I hope you're decent because I've got someone with me.'

There was no reply, but that wasn't unusual and Charlie went on in, Andrew following her. Sylvia wasn't in the living room and it was so dark with the curtains drawn that they could see very little. Charlie swept them back and stared at the room for a minute.

It was just as she'd expected, strewn end to end with dirty cups, plates, orange peel and overflowing ashtrays.

'Looks like home,' Andrew said brightly.

Charlie was embarrassed, even though she had warned him what to expect.

'Hang on a minute, she must still be in bed. I'll just check she's okay and I'll make us all some tea.' She swiftly crossed the room and went into her mother's bedroom.

A sudden piercing scream startled Andrew. He was just going over to look at a photograph of Charlie as a baby on the mantelpiece.

'What is it?' he called out as he ran to her. But he stopped short in horror by the door.

Even though Andrew had never seen a dead person before, he instinctively knew the woman on the bed was, and his stomach turned over.

270

Her glassy blue eyes were open, staring towards the door as if she'd died hoping for help to come that way. Congealed vomit was stuck to her lips, hair and on the pillow beside her.

'How do we tell if she's still breathing?' Charlie gasped out, clutching at his arm. 'What do we do?'

Andrew pulled himself together. He nudged Charlie aside and felt for a pulse on Sylvia's neck. There was nothing and her skin was cold. He sensed she'd been dead for some hours.

'I'm afraid she's dead,' he said quietly. 'I'm so terribly sorry, Charlie. What a terrible thing to walk in on.' He glanced at the bedside table. An empty aspirin bottle was there, also another bottle with a few tablets left inside it. 'I think she might have taken those. I'll have to call the police, don't touch anything while I'm gone.'

'She can't be dead,' Charlie burst out, grabbing his arm as he turned to go out the room. 'She was fine when I phoned her last night.'

Andrew felt utterly helpless. This was so totally unexpected, and nothing in his life so far had prepared him for such a situation. He was frightened and horrified, but above that was anger. He couldn't credit that any mother could do such a thing, knowing her daughter would find her. Yet he could voice none of this. He had to be strong, do what had to be done and look after Charlie.

'Just hold on,' he said, squeezing both her hands. 'I have to phone the police first. I'll be right back.'

As Andrew went to the phone in the living room, Charlie looked down at her mother in horror. She felt she ought to be wailing, feeling nothing but abject grief, yet she could only feel repelled and disgusted. It wasn't because Sylvia was caked in putrid-smelling vomit, Charlie had coped with far worse than that in the past. It was because she was looking at the ultimate act of selfishness.

Yet even as she stood there, dry-eyed and angry, a small voice inside her reminded her that less than two years ago she herself had thought of suicide as a way out. The same voice also insisted that she was to blame for this. She shouldn't have just accepted her mother's depression, she ought to have insisted the doctor did something more to help her. Nor should she have gone away to Salcombe and left her mother alone.

Yet worse still, the thought crossed her mind that she was now free.

The callousness of such a thought cut her to the quick. She dropped down on her knees beside the bed and taking her mother's cold hand in hers, she sobbed.

Charlie knew both the policemen who came in answer to Andrew's call for help by sight. They drank in the bar of the Royal Castle Hotel quite often. The older one she knew as Roger often inquired after her mother because he'd been one of the officers who'd come in answer to the 999 call when Sylvia was attacked.

There was little they could do but confirm Sylvia was dead and offer their condolences. Roger stayed on with her and Andrew while they waited for the doctor to arrive.

Charlie stood at the window long after the ambulance containing her mother's body had driven away. She couldn't cry, she couldn't speak. She felt numb.

'Come and sit down and have this cup of tea,' Andrew said gently at her elbow. 'I'm going to clear up all the mess, then I'm taking you back to Beryl's. You can't stay here.'

Charlie did as she was told. She felt like a robot obeying instructions mindlessly. She looked at the overflowing ashtray on the coffee table and began counting the stubs.

It was some time before she fully appreciated what Andrew was doing. Only the sound of running water in the bathroom made her realize he was swilling the vomit off the sheets and blankets in the bath. Somehow that kind and thoughtful act soothed her a little. If Andrew hadn't come in with her today, how would she have coped?

As Andrew rinsed out the sheets and blankets he sniffed back tears. Just early this morning he'd been thinking how meeting Charlie was the best thing that had ever happened to him. She was so lovely, both in looks and character. Everything she'd told him about her background intrigued him, yet somehow he hadn't felt sorry for her, she was too bright, jolly and vivid somehow to bring out sympathy. When he'd kissed her yesterday on the beach, it had felt like the first warm day of spring, Fireworks Night, birthdays and Christmas all rolled into one. He'd had quite a few girlfriends, some of them he'd even been a bit soppy about, but with Charlie it was different, he wanted her passionately. Last night in bed he'd imagined seducing her, getting the other guys to go out one night, changing the sheets on his bed, planning the right soft music. He hadn't been able to sleep for his erection, and that seemed terribly shameful now.

Everything about finding her mother like that, this flat, and the ambulance men carting her away to the mortuary for a post-mortem, underlined the bleakness of Charlie's life. He might not have met Sylvia alive, but by just looking around him he felt he knew her, and what she'd put her daughter through in the last two years.

His own childhood and adolescence looked so idyllic in comparison. His father might only be a sheet-metal worker, his mother a very ordinary woman, yet their life revolved around their only son. He had only to walk through the door and they stopped whatever they were doing to hear his news. His bed was always aired and ready for him, Mum cooked his favourite meals to please him. Charlie might have been spoiled in the material sense as a child, but Andrew could see now that while he might have felt overlooked because he never got a new bike or roller-skates, he had enough love for several children.

Where would he and Charlie go from here? How could he even consider trying to court a girl who'd just suffered such a terrible shock? She might be free now, but neither of them could take any pleasure in freedom which had been acquired at such cost. What should he do or say? The only death he'd ever encountered before was his grandfather's, and that had been a neat, clean release for a sick old man who was ready to go. He couldn't begin to think what it would be like for her. Or how to tell her he would be there for her whatever she needed.

He wrung out the bedding as best he could and went back into the living room. Charlie was still sitting in the same place, her face stripped of any colour.

'Why didn't Mum tell me last night that she was desperate?' she asked him. 'She sounded so normal when I phoned. I would have come home if she'd asked me.'

'I'm quite sure she knew that,' Andrew replied. He didn't even know if it was appropriate to try to hold her in his arms. 'I think you have to accept that she'd already made her mind up to do this, and she really wanted to die.'

'But why? Things hadn't got any worse for her recently, in fact they were getting better.'

Andrew had no answer to that, he was out of his depth entirely. His parents were the kind of people who totally accepted their lot in life, finding their reward in seeing their only son at university, having enough money for a holiday and a bit put by for a rainy day. Even if they did have some sort of disaster, or even found they had a terminal disease, he doubted very much that either of them would consider suicide.

In the last couple of days, listening to what had happened to Charlie had already brought home to him how cloistered he was. He'd never faced any serious problems or heartache. Andrew liked to think he was humane and understanding, but as he hadn't met Sylvia Weish alive, and almost everything he'd been told about her led him to believe he wouldn't have felt much sympathy for her, he found he couldn't be objective.

'Who knows what goes on in someone else's mind?' He shrugged. 'It could be that she was thinking you'd have a better future without her around.'

'She never thought about my future.' Charlie's voice began to rise with a touch of hysteria. 'This was intended to frighten me. She thought she'd just be unconscious when I got home and I'd get her to hospital to pull her round.'

'I don't think so, Charlie,' he said, kneeling down beside her and taking her hands in his. 'The doctor said he thought she took the pills around ten last night. She took well over a lethal dose, and she knew you wouldn't be back until midday.'

'She was cruel and spiteful.' Charlie began rocking herself in the chair. 'She never thought about me, just herself. Now I've got to carry on with people whispering again behind my back. I don't think I can stand any more.'

'You can, Charlie, you can,' he said, putting his arms around her and drawing her to him. 'You're all mixed up now, you will be for some time I expect. But I know from what my aunt told me that you've got no reason to feel guilty. She said you did far more for your mother than they would have done in a nursing home.'

'But I've wished her dead, lots of times,' Charlie said in a whisper. 'Can you believe I could be that wicked?'

'I think I would too if I had to put up with everything you have,' he said truthfully. 'But you still looked after her – if this hadn't happened you would have gone on doing so.'

Charlie broke down then and cried for her sad, weak mother who chose death rather than try to make a new life for herself, and because she hadn't seen this coming and found some way to avert it. Andrew sat down beside her and held her tightly in his arms until her sobbing finally subsided.

'Come on now,' he said gently. 'Go and wash your face while I finish clearing up, then we'll go. I'll put the sheets and blankets in a bag and take them back to Beryl's to wash them properly.'

'I can't stay there,' she said in alarm. 'It wouldn't be right. I must be here in case the police need me.'

'They won't need you today,' he said. 'I told the police I was taking you back to Salcombe. Right now you need looking after.'

'Is she asleep?' Beryl asked Andrew as he came back down into the bar just after closing time that night. Ivor was sitting on a stool nursing a pint. He looked forlorn.

Andrew nodded. He felt very shaky and disturbed after listening to Charlie talking about her childhood.

It seemed to him that while Jin appeared to be the more caring parent, his habit of turning each visit home into almost a circus of indulgence, then suddenly leaving again, was in fact the most harmful force in Charlie's young life. She'd put her father on a pedestal, subconsciously blaming her mother for his departures. Yet in fact Sylvia had needed him there even more than her child.

Beryl poured him a large brandy. 'You look as if you need it,' she said. 'And I'll join you because I want to blot out the appalling things which keep happening to that poor kid.'

The last of the straggling drinkers left and as Andrew sat down beside Ivor, the older man turned to him, his face deeply concerned.

'Drink up, son. You look shattered,' he said.

Andrew downed the brandy in one and grimaced

as the spirits burned his throat. 'I was wondering if it might be better if I went back to London tomorrow,' he said.

'Don't be ridiculous,' Beryl exclaimed. 'You can't go now, Charlie would think you were running out on her.'

'I don't want to go,' Andrew sighed. 'But she's so very upset and I'm worried that she'll regret blurting out so much to me later.'

'It's a darn sight more healthy for her to talk than keep it bottled up, son.' Ivor shrugged. 'Of course there's a chance she might regret it later, but I think it's far more likely to make a stronger bond between the two of you. What you've got to ask yourself right now is whether you want that.'

'I do,' Andrew replied, looking Ivor straight in the eye.

Ivor felt a lump come up in his throat. He'd met Andrew many times before while he was staying with his aunt for holidays – even as a twelve-year-old he'd been a bright and amusing lad, so he'd been delighted when he felt the mutual attraction between him and Charlie. But it was only today that he'd seen Andrew had grown into a caring, deeply sensitive man, and he'd won Ivor's respect. 'Well, that's settled then,' he said crisply. 'No more talk of going back to London.'

'Hullo, sweetheart! There's a surprise,' Ivor exclaimed as he answered a tentative knock on his door and found Charlie standing there.

It was the following Thursday, six days since her mother's death, and the funeral was arranged for tomorrow afternoon.

'I felt I had to come out and get some fresh air,' she said. 'But once I was out I didn't know where to go.'

Ivor knew exactly what she meant. He'd been like that after Sarah and Kim were killed. There was only so much aimless wandering one could do, and always the fear of running into someone who'd ask questions you couldn't cope with.

'Well, I'm glad you came here,' he said. 'And so's Minnie.' Minnie was already sniffing around Charlie's legs, but because she sensed something was wrong, she wasn't jumping up as she usually did. 'Come on in and sit by the fire. It's too cold to go walking anyway.'

Charlie sat down in her usual chair, and Minnie sat beside her, resting her chin on Charlie's knee and looking at her mournfully.

Ivor watched Charlie petting his dog and wondered what he should say. Her face was set like pale concrete, cold and distant. He guessed she was wrung out with crying, talking, listening to platitudes, advice and sympathy. Maybe what she needed now was just peace to gather her own thoughts. He made her a cup of his special coffee and added a little rum, then sat down beside her and lit his pipe.

'If I hadn't been forced to get up each day to make the funeral arrangements and do all the other stuff like registering the death and telling the Council and the Social Security what's happened, I think I would have stayed in bed all this week,' she said eventually, and the eyes which turned towards him were bleak.

'It wouldn't hurt you to have a day in bed,' he said. 'After the funeral tomorrow you'll be able to.'

'You're the first person to even mention afterwards,'

she said. 'What am I supposed to do, Ivor? I don't know.'

Ivor's eyes prickled at her question. He knew from his own experience that would be the real test of her character. 'You try to pick up where you left off,' he said gently. 'You go back to school and prepare for those final exams. You'll get money each week from Social Security to keep you, so you mustn't worry about that. By the time the exams are over, you'll have your head straight again and then you can decide what you want to do. Are you nervous about staying in the flat alone?'

'No, not really,' she said with a big sigh. 'But it will be strange, won't it?'

Ivor agreed it probably would be and maybe very lonely. 'You can come over here every weekend if you want to,' he said. 'And I'm sure Andrew will want to come down and see you.'

'I don't know if I can cope with that,' she blurted out.

'Andrew is a sensitive lad,' he said carefully. 'He'll know better than to push you too hard. But if you'd rather he stayed away until you feel able to cope again, then you must tell him. He'll understand.'

'But will he? Isn't he more likely to be dreadfully hurt and think I don't care about him?' she whispered. She was so confused. One minute she wanted to be alone, then when she was, she got scared. Her heart said she wanted Andrew as a lover, yet her body and mind were shying away from it. At times she thought she was getting as crazy as her mother. 'You see, I couldn't bear to lose him, Ivor, he's the only good thing which has happened in a long time.'

Ivor thought it was time for plain speaking. 'I don't believe you will lose him, he cares too deeply about you, Charlie. But at the same time it isn't right to string him along with promises you don't know you can keep. Admit you are confused right now. Tell him you need time to sort out your feelings and in the meantime he must go back to London and pick up his life too.'

Ivor saw her face tighten. He guessed she was afraid Andrew might meet someone else while she was down here all alone. He wished he could promise her that wouldn't happen.

'You have to trust,' he said gently. 'Not just Andrew, but your own judgement too. It will come right in the end.'

She bent over Minnie to stroke her and Ivor sensed she was trying to hide tears. He wished he could find the right words to convince her that the sun would shine on her again, that one day soon she'd wake up to find the hurt was gone. But he knew only too well that would be a long time coming.

At four the following afternoon Charlie and Beryl were in the kitchen at Mayflower Close. Sylvia's funeral had taken place two hours earlier, first the service at St Saviour's in Dartmouth, then on to the burial at Longcross cemetery. The few people who had come back to the flat afterwards had now gone, and they were washing the last of the dishes. Ivor and Andrew were in the living room.

'The Mellings are nice people,' Beryl said more brightly than she felt. 'You heard what Diana said, didn't you? That you must go and have tea with them at least once a week.'

'Yes, I heard,' Charlie sighed. 'It was very nice of her. Now, stop worrying about me, Beryl. I am okay, really I am.'

Beryl was worried. She had never before attended such an emotionless funeral. Even Charlie had remained dry-eyed, straight-backed and composed throughout it.

It hadn't helped that the vicar had never actually met Sylvia. When he spoke of her fortitude in the face of her disability it sounded as if he had mixed up his notes with those of another person. Beryl was appalled too by how quickly afterwards some of the people scuttled away. She thought if they had that little interest in Charlie's welfare, they might as well not have bothered to attend at all.

Mr and Mrs Melling and their daughter June came back for tea, along with Mrs Brown, Sylvia's old house-keeper, and Reg the gardener. They at least had shown genuine concern and affection for Charlie. Yet Beryl couldn't help but think, if it hadn't been for the neighbours from this road, herself, Ivor and Andrew, to give some semblance of mourners, it would have been a very sorry affair.

'I wasn't so much worried as wanting to get some sort of response from you,' Beryl said sharply. 'It's not good for you to keep everything inside.'

Charlie shrugged. Her eyes gave nothing away. 'What is there to say, Beryl? What a shame a few more people didn't come? Why did Mr Wyatt leg it off so quickly? It's about what I expected.'

'Is it?' Beryl was surprised.

'Yes,' Charlie said. 'In fact I expected less. If the staff from Franklin House had come back here I wouldn't have known what to say to them, they didn't get on with Mum after all. All the people I hoped might come, like the Mellings, Reg and Mrs Brown, managed it. That's enough for me.'

'You're being very stoic,' Beryl said.

'I'd call it resigned,' Charlie said. 'My parents' friends were the fair-weather kind and if any of them had turned up after all this time and sobbed their way through her funeral I'd have wanted to punch them. And if you really want to know what I feel now, it's just relief that it's all over.'

Beryl thought that was perhaps a little *too* honest.

'Don't look like that,' Charlie said indignantly. 'You wanted to know what was going on inside my head. And that's it. Now I just want to be on my own and think things through.'

Beryl had always admired Charlie's dignity and control of her emotions. She had been at least thirty before she'd come even close to being poised. Yet today Charlie's control had been chilling rather than admirable. Even the black roll-neck sweater and long skirt she'd chosen to wear gave her a forbidding appearance. She was too elegant, too adult. Beryl pulled herself up sharply and decided she must say what was on her mind.

'You might think it's a bit odd, and a bit late for me to say this now. But I liked Sylvia,' she said bluntly. 'I didn't approve of the way she leaned on you, but I actually liked her for herself. I'm telling you this now, Charlie, because as far as I can see there isn't anyone else to speak out for her.'

Charlie looked staggered. She leaned back against

the kitchen sink and folded her arms across her chest. 'You only met her a few times!'

'I came to see her nearly every week since you moved in here,' Beryl said sharply. 'I should imagine that amounts to some sixty or more visits. I didn't tell you how often I came, because Sylvia didn't want me to.'

'Why?'

'You of all people should know how secretive she was!' Beryl half smiled: she had Charlie's full attention at last. 'Do you want to know what we talked about?'

'Yes. Yes, of course I do.' Charlie pulled out a stool and sat down. 'I can't imagine what you had in common.'

Beryl shrugged. 'Sometimes it's opposing viewpoints which make for a stimulating friendship. I've seen a great deal of life, but only from a safe viewpoint across the bar. Now, your mother experienced first-hand just about everything anyone could throw at her. I know she told you about her childhood and the tragic events when she was thrown out of her first job, but you and I, Charlie, can only empathize to a certain degree with that terrible ordeal. Neither of us knows what it's like to be raped, lose a baby, or to be that hungry and neglected. You can say you know how it feels to have your mother commit suicide, but not those other things.'

'Okay, I'll go along with that,' Charlie said. 'So what did you gather from her?'

'I'd say her biggest problem was that she actually believed herself to be utterly worthless,' Beryl said emphatically. 'To make up for this she became like a chameleon, changing colour to suit the people she became involved with. DeeDee was one of the strongest influences.'

'I should think she was, she stole Dad away!'

'I'm talking about long before she met him,' Beryl said. 'From what I gathered Sylvia was just a little grey mouse, hiding herself away until then. DeeDee took her in hand, showed her how to dress, style her hair, made her over if you like. Sylvia said she was the first real friend she'd ever had, she made her believe she could amount to something. They had a great many good times together and it was she who introduced her to night-clubs.'

Charlie sniffed disapprovingly.

Beryl looked at her sharply. 'Do you want me to tell you my views on your mother or not?'

Charlie nodded.

'Well, as I see it she tried to emulate DeeDee, made herself seem equally tough, bold and ruthless. But then when she met and fell in love with Jin, she changed again. She kept the glamour, but she became softer, generous, warm-hearted, and ambitious for him. I have no doubt that she was the driving force that made your father a successful businessman, Charlie, she'd learned a great deal from hard-headed DeeDee.

'Then when you were born, so was another Sylvia, a loving mother, dedicated wife. It's my belief that those early days in your childhood were the happiest, most fulfilling times of all for her.'

'She didn't seem happy to me,' Charlie retorted.

'She was,' Beryl assured her. 'I might not have known her then, but when she talked about that period in her life she glowed. There had been the hiccup when she found out about Jin's affair with DeeDee, but they moved down to Devon and it was all forgotten. Everything was fine right up till when you were about eleven. If you look back carefully I'm sure you'll have some memories of events at that time. She took you up to London for a shopping trip and you stayed in a hotel in Kensington.'

Charlie shook her head. 'I don't remember.'

'You may in a while, because that was when she found out DeeDee was still in your father's life,' Beryl said. 'I'm not going to go into that now, we can talk that through at some more appropriate time. All I'll say now is that was the time when things began to turn sour.'

Charlie frowned. She wanted to know more, but she sensed Beryl had started on this tack for another purpose than throwing light on the past.

'Go on,' she urged.

Beryl shrugged. 'I just felt that I couldn't let this day end without saying my piece about your mum. Sylvia *was* difficult, impossible sometimes, neurotic, selfish and often mean-spirited. But when you are thinking about her tonight, as I know you will, remember that chameleon. She had become like that because of circumstances. It was the only defence she had.'

All at once Charlie understood what Beryl was trying to do. The kindly woman had been distressed all day because no one, not even her daughter, had recalled any happy memories of Sylvia. All at once Charlie felt ashamed, and she stumbled across the kitchen to the older woman's arms.

'She did love you,' Beryl whispered as she stroked Charlie's hair. 'She wasn't much good at showing it.

But she often told me how she felt and I saw that love and pride in her eyes, the sorrow that she felt because she couldn't express it.'

Andrew came into the kitchen and stopped short when he saw the women embracing.

'I'm sorry,' he said, turning to go.

'It's okay, Andrew,' Beryl said. In her heart she knew Sylvia had killed herself to release her daughter from the burden of looking after her. She couldn't tell Charlie that, not now, it would be too disturbing, but perhaps in time the girl would come to see it for herself and appreciate it was done out of love for her, rather than self-interest. 'We're done here now, aren't we, Charlie?'

Charlie lifted her head, sniffed and wiped away her tears. 'I think perhaps you all ought to go now,' she said. 'You've got the bar to open, Beryl.'

Beryl slipped away into the living room to leave her nephew with Charlie for a few minutes.

'Do you really want me to go too?' Andrew asked, his blue eyes wide with hurt.

Charlie sighed. Just last night she had talked to him, explained how she felt, and she thought he understood. 'You came down here for a holiday,' she reminded him, 'but because of all this you haven't had one. You've got a few days left, so make the most of it.'

'But I'd rather be with you,' he said bleakly.

'No,' she said more firmly. 'I can't be what you really want, not yet, and it will just spoil things. So let me get back on my feet, on my own.'

'Can I phone you?' he asked. He sounded like a small boy.

'Yes, of course you can,' she said. 'But leave it till you're back in London. I'll write to you in a few days, maybe in a letter I can explain myself better.'

'You don't mean a "Dear John"?' he asked, but he smiled as he said it and his tone was teasing.

Charlie smiled too, for what she felt was the first time since she found her mother was dead. 'Of course not, silly. You've been the best friend any girl could have this last week. But all this has kind of distorted things, hasn't it?'

'I suppose so.'

'There's no suppose about it, it has,' she insisted. 'So let's just let time sort things out for us, shall we?'

As Charlie watched Andrew, Ivor and Beryl drive off, her heart swelled with gratitude and affection. She couldn't imagine what she would have done without them. She was especially touched by Beryl's attempts to make her understand her mother. She thought she must talk to Beryl again in a week or two when she was calmer and find out what else she knew.

The flat felt very eerie now. Apart from the day she'd first viewed it, she'd never been here alone before. She'd been in and out several times in the week, tidying and cleaning, but Andrew or Beryl had always been with her.

Now it was all hers. That little daydream which she had so often escaped into when things were bad had come true. She could move the furniture around to suit herself, get rid of anything she disliked, throw a brick through the television screen if she wanted to.

Yet as she sat on the settee, looking around her, she was surprised to find she felt nothing. No pleasure, no guilt or even sorrow. Just emptiness. The sympathy cards on the mantelpiece and window-sill, the vase of beautiful flowers which Andrew had brought her this morning and said were to stay here, rather than go to the cemetery, didn't seem to have anything much to do with her mother.

All the real symbols of Sylvia had gone. The walking frame and wheelchair had been returned to the hospital, the big, ugly glass ashtray had been thrown into the waste bin in a moment of rage, the piles of magazines were now being read by a neighbour. Maybe if she switched the television on and saw Hughie Green introducing *Opportunity Knocks*, Sylvia's favourite programme, she might just feel her mother's presence. But she had no idea what day of the week it was on, and besides, she had no wish to try that.

Beryl's description of Sylvia being a chameleon made a great deal of sense. It explained why she had always brightened up when Jin came home, how she managed to be such a vivacious hostess. Now Charlie could see too why Sylvia had always maintained a glamorous appearance back at 'Windways'; she had to, it was a way to disguise her sense of worthlessness.

Perhaps that was why she lost interest in her appearance once they moved here? A chameleon would take on drab colouring in drab surroundings. The only time she had sparkled in the last year was when she was taken away on holiday. Yet she must have had moments of her old gaiety and warmth when Beryl

289

and neighbours visited her, or they wouldn't have put themselves out for her the way they did.

It hurt to think Sylvia had never placed enough value or importance on her daughter to change her colours now and again for her. But that, Charlie knew now, was the real core of her pain.

'Well, it's all over now,' she said aloud, and her voice sounded strained and unnatural. 'You've got the freedom you always believed you wanted, so forgive her.'

She wandered around the flat for some time, picking things up, opening drawers and cupboards, then shutting them again without touching anything. She knew that soon she would have to go through her mother's things properly, take the clothes and give them to neighbours or a jumble sale, go through those boxes of letters and personal things which Sylvia had refused to unpack or even look at since they moved here. Maybe in there she'd find a few answers to all the many things which still puzzled her.

As she stood in Sylvia's bedroom she began to cry. Back at 'Windways' there would have been countless good memories trapped in the sunny bedroom, of lying between her parents as they planned the day ahead, or stormy nights when they'd let her come in with them, of pillow fights, being read stories, and opening her stocking at Christmas.

She wished she could lie down on the bed and draw on the comfort and security she'd felt as a child, but it made her shudder. It had been remade with clean covers, yet the image of her mother lying dead in it was imprinted on her mind. There was no whiff of perfume, no lacy negligée, manicure set and pots of nail varnish strewn around as there had been back at 'Windways', just Sylvia's hair-brush and mirror on the dressing-table, a wool dressing-gown hanging on the back of the door, two paperback books on the bedside cabinet and a faint lingering odour of vomit and cigarettes.

'Let me find some good memories,' Charlie pleaded aloud, her voice echoing in the clinical room. 'I want to remember you as you used to be at speech days in a lovely hat, or dressed for a party, not like this.'

It was homework that finally halted her tears. Back in her own bedroom, sitting at her book-covered desk in front of the window, with the door firmly closed on the rest of the flat, she felt safer.

There were no poignant reminders of the past in this room. The floral curtains had come from the spare bedroom at 'Windways', as had the matching cover on the single divan, but they were impersonal. The small desk was from her father's study, but he'd never used it as such, he'd had a much larger one he sat at, this one had merely been used as a surface to dump papers on.

Even the view from the window evoked no reminders of the past. The river Dart was a long way off, the green hills on the opposite bank she'd never explored.

In fact when she came to think about it, there was a whole world out there far beyond those green hills, waiting for exploration. Cities, towns, villages and other countries. She had one more term at school to get through, then she could leave Dartmouth for good. Sell up everything here, pack her bags, say goodbye and start afresh somewhere new. London, and

Andrew, might come first, she'd see how she felt when the time came.

With that she picked up her pen and began to tackle her maths.

Chapter Ten

Charlie walked slowly past number 12 Hazelmere Road, scrutinizing the big Victorian house carefully as she went. It was a bit neglected, and the garden was full of spilling bags of rubbish, but it wasn't as bad as some places she'd seen. Besides, the tree-lined road itself was very nice, so checking her watch first to make sure she wasn't too early, she turned back.

It was a Friday in mid-July, three months since her mother's death, and she was in Hornsey, north London, with a six o'clock appointment to meet three girls who wanted someone to share their flat.

Since sitting her exams and leaving school, Charlie'd also given up the tenancy on the flat in Dartmouth and her job at the Royal Castle Hotel. Many people including her employers and neighbours had expressed the opinion that she was being too hasty, disposing of the flat and selling the furniture, and advised her to stay on for at least the summer, but she knew the time was right to leave.

Few people knew just how desperately lonely and sad she'd been in these past few months. Her neighbours saw her going off to school and to work in the evenings and because she appeared so calm and hard-working, and rarely mentioned her mother, they believed she had put the past firmly behind her. But in reality there were few nights when Charlie didn't cry herself to sleep; just walking through the front door brought on searingly painful memories of Sylvia.

Beryl had been right in saying that before long Charlie would recall many incidents from her childhood. Some nights they came in rushes, tumbling over themselves as if asking to be examined. Sometimes they were funny ones, of her mum sitting astride the arm of the settee pretending to be Calamity Jane driving a stage-coach and singing 'The Deadwood Stage'. Sometimes they were sweet ones, like the time Charlie had chickenpox and Mum painted spots on her face too, in sympathy.

Then one night the memory of that incident in London which Beryl had mentioned came back. Charlie remembered a rather grand hotel suite, with a central sitting room cluttered with bags and boxes from their shopping spree. They were getting ready to go out to dinner that evening. Jin was shaving in the bathroom, Sylvia was still in a negligée, and Charlie was wearing a red velvet dress and patent-leather shoes, wriggling as her mother brushed her hair for her, when the telephone rang.

Charlie was never given any reason why that telephone call ruined the evening. All she remembered clearly was that suddenly Sylvia was screaming at her father at the top of her voice, they didn't go out to eat and she was sent to bed and her parents kept on shouting at one another.

Charlie's bedroom was the opposite side of the sitting room to her parents' one, but she heard her father go out later, leaving her mother still sobbing.

She lay in bed for some time listening, then eventually crept in to see her. Sylvia was lying across the bed face down, she didn't even seem aware her daughter was trying to cuddle and comfort her.

'I've lost him now,' was all she said, over and over again.

Sadly Charlie's memory stopped there, she couldn't even remember the next day, or the trip home. But Beryl was right; looking back, it was around that time when Sylvia's black moods began, the rows became more frequent, and her father stayed away more often.

Now, with the benefit of more information and more adult eyes, Charlie could understand what a terrible shock it must have been for her mother to discover Jin was still seeing DeeDee. Although Charlie still thought her mother was spineless not to fight back, bring it into the open and insist her husband made a choice between her and DeeDee, perhaps Sylvia thought having only half a husband was better than gambling the lot and ending up with nothing.

It was this thought which finally made her pluck up the courage to go through the many boxes of letters, papers and photographs that had been sent over from 'Windways', but what she found merely confused her further.

There were dozens of loving letters from Jin to Sylvia, some dated as far back as 1956, right up until the autumn of 1969. Some came from as far away as China, others on hotel notepaper from Harrogate, Bath and Winchester. There were Valentines, Christmas and birthday cards too. It didn't seem feasible to Charlie that any man would pen such emotional letters if he was living with a mistress.

There were dozens of old photographs too, apart from family ones, and some of these she felt were taken in one of his clubs. She wished she'd insisted Sylvia had gone through these boxes, maybe then she could have discovered who everyone was.

The only substantial thing she found was a small newspaper cutting about the opening night of Jin's first club, the Lotus Club in Carlisle Street. It was dated 14 April 1952 and there was a picture of Jin with Sylvia opening a bottle of champagne. Sylvia was described as his fiancée, Jin said they hoped to be married very soon.

It was this cutting more than anything which determined Charlie to go to London. Common sense told her she wasn't going to find her father if the police couldn't. Yet if she could just find a few answers to the hundreds of questions about her parents' earlier life together there, and this other woman, then maybe she'd find some peace of mind.

Then of course there was Andrew. He had written every week since Easter, telephoned her often too, and his warmth and jollity had kept her going when everything else seemed black. Whether or not their friendship could be fanned back into a romance, she didn't know. But she hoped it could.

The final reason for going was because she knew that in Dartmouth she would always be thought of as a tragic figure. Selling off the furniture not only provided her with a nest-egg, it was also like shedding an unwanted skin.

Ivor was storing the few items she wanted to keep. His little spare bedroom was hers now, for holidays and a base if she wanted it. The treasures taken from

'Windways' were still in the vault in Exeter and it was her intention to leave them there indefinitely. Ivor and Beryl were the only people she really cared about in Devon. If she could make something of herself in London it would be a constructive way to show her appreciation for all they'd done for her.

Unknown to Andrew she had been in London a week already, staying in an Islington guest-house. A rowdy end-of-term party had resulted in the boys being thrown out of their flat. Andrew had found himself a summer job, living in at a pub in Hampstead, but the last time they'd spoken on the phone and she said she was intending to come to London, he seemed harassed and anxious, reminding her how expensive and hard-to-come-by flats were in London. As Charlie felt she'd been enough of a burden to him in the past, she was determined to find a flat and a job before calling him. That way she'd be entirely independent.

Charlie's feelings about London were mixed. She loved the big shops and the feeling of being inconspicuous; she was also excited at finally seeing places like Carnaby Street where the small boutiques were stuffed with the kind of outrageous glam-rock clothes she'd only seen in magazines before. Rock music wafting out of shops and so many posters advertising concerts told her she hadn't arrived too late to experience some of the excitement of the youth revolution of the Sixties. Yet it seemed so peculiar and alien to see men like peacocks, wearing makeup, their hair dyed bizarre colours, girls of her age and even younger strutting about in six-inch platform shoes with yard-wide flares, feather boas and big hats. All at once she felt so very dowdy and out of touch with her own generation.

The milling crowds, the frantic pace and the sheer size of the city was at times frightening too. Getting from one place to another on the tube was much more difficult than she'd imagined and the maps only confused her more.

On her previous visits to London with her mother, they'd usually shopped in Knightsbridge and Kensington. She had started off looking for a flat around there, just because it was familiar, but she soon discovered that even a tiny bedsitter in that area was well beyond her means.

She couldn't stay at the guest-house for much longer. People had told her that £30 a week was cheap, but it was a fortune to her and it wasn't even nice. She had to ask permission to have a bath, there was constant noise of traffic as it was on a busy main road, and she couldn't even make herself a cup of tea in her room. It was imperative she found somewhere else to live, and quickly.

If this flat was only half decent and the girls nice, she was going to take it. She'd seen so many terrible places so far that she knew now she wasn't going to get the flat of her dreams.

Taking a deep breath and crossing her fingers, she walked up the path to the front door. The bell marked Flat 4 seemed to ring a great way off. As there was a pane of glass missing in the leaded lights either side of the door, Charlie peered in. The hall was wide, with old black and white tiles. A pram was on one side, a bicycle on the other. It looked mucky, but not impossibly so.

Hearing feet approaching, she stood back a little way. The door was opened by a girl wearing a flowing red caftan and a great many strands of beads. Her feet were bare and dirty, her long, dark, curly hair needed a wash too.

'I'm Charlie Weish,' she said. 'I had an appointment –'

'I'm Meg,' the girl replied, cutting Charlie short. 'You don't look a bit like I imagined, I expected a blonde. But come on in. We've tried to clear up a bit, but it's still a mess. I hope it won't put you off.'

Charlie followed the girl up two floors. She didn't need to speak because Meg gave a running commentary as they passed closed doors. 'Here's the bathroom, here's another loo. We've got one up on our floor too. But the one downstairs is old with lovely flowers on it. There's a girl with a baby downstairs front, next to her are two nurses. The first-floor flat is mixed, two girls and three blokes, they haven't been here long and I don't know their names. Where do you come from, Charlie, I can't place your accent?'

They'd arrived at the flat by then, and Charlie was out of breath. She guessed Meg was somewhat taken aback by her Oriental appearance, people always were. 'Devon,' Charlie said. 'I didn't know I had an accent.'

'Well, you don't sound like a Londoner,' Meg said, and with that drew Charlie in the door, straight into the living room.

To Charlie, who had only ever been in conventional homes, it looked bizarre. There were no chairs or settees, just mattresses covered in Indian-style cotton rugs and bedspreads. Even the central light was covered with what looked like several silk scarves. Right in the middle of the seating area was a low table. It looked very much like an old-fashioned dining one, but someone had cut off the legs and painted it red.

There was a peculiar smell too, not unpleasant, but a bit too strong. Dozens of large green plants everywhere, and the walls were covered in posters of Jimi Hendrix, Frank Zapper and several huge Day-Glo astrological signs.

'What sign are you?' Meg asked as she saw Charlie look at them.

'Pisces,' Charlie replied, wondering what that had to do with anything and where the other two girls were.

'Fab,' Meg exclaimed with a wide grin. 'I'm a Scorpio. Beth's a Cancer and Anne's a Taurus. That means you'll be compatible with all of us.'

'I don't know anything about astrology,' Charlie said. She felt instinctively drawn towards this chatty girl, even if she was a bit odd and grubby.

'You soon will if you come to live with us,' Meg laughed, then called the other two girls to come and meet her.

In the next hour Charlie found that the smell in the flat was joss-sticks, that all three girls were aged twenty, Londoners, and students at Hornsey Art College. They were vegetarian, smoked cannabis which they called 'dope', none of them believed in regular boyfriends or wearing bras, and the room on offer was shared with Anne. The girls had bombarded her with so much personal information about themselves that Charlie's head was reeling. Part of her was attracted to their hippie and somewhat irregular life-style – she had after all come to London looking for fun and excitement – but the other, more conventional side of her was wary. The talk of drugs made her nervous, the flat was a bit dirty and she wasn't sure she could learn to fit in.

Meg was very much their leader, outspoken, force-ful, with strong opinions about everything.

Although Beth was small, dainty and blonde, and by far the prettiest of the three, she was a true extrovert. Her rainbow-painted eyes were alight with mischief, and her zany patchwork trousers could only be worn by someone with a big personality. When she told Charlie it was her intention to become one of London's top fashion designers, Charlie had no doubt she would get there.

Anne was the most reserved and the plainest of the three – tall, a bit overweight, with long, straight, light brown hair which almost reached her waist. Meg rather unkindly likened her large, limpid brown eyes to a cow's, but in fact they were beautiful and very expressive. The Day-Glo astrology posters were her work, perhaps heavily influenced by Meg, rather than her own imagination, but technically brilliant. Inter-estingly enough, Anne was clearly the only do-mestically minded of the three. Several times in the hour-long visit she brought up the subject of a need for greater cleanliness in the flat, and looked to Charlie as if for support.

When she took Charlie into the bedroom at the back of the house that they were to share, this facet of her nature was proved. The large room was dark because a large tree was growing up in front of the window, but it was clean and tidy, and most of Charlie's reservations left her.

The furniture was very old and rather lovely. A huge carved fronted cupboard full of shelves and hanging space completely covered one wall; in front of the window was a matching large dressing-table. The two single beds were side by side with a small trunk between them. But what appealed to Charlie most was the way Anne had arranged strands of beads and old fans on the wall – there were dozens and it looked like a work of art. Anne warmed up considerably as Charlie praised it, and after discovering she didn't smoke, she was positively beaming. 'That's great. I couldn't bear to share a bedroom with a smoker,' she said. 'Beth and Meg's room stinks. I hate it.'

It seemed that Meg had already decided Charlie was to move in. She asked only the most casual of questions, informed her the rent was £3.50 a week each, to be paid to her every Saturday, and the gas, electric and phone bills were divided between them as they came in. She wanted £20 as a deposit against unpaid bills, and said they all bought their own food, but they each put £1 in the kitty each week for bread, milk and the other things they all used.

Charlie swallowed her anxiety about drugs, the squalid kitchen and the fact that the shared bathroom was out on the landing. It was a cheap place to live, Hornsey seemed a much nicer area than most she'd seen, the girls were warm and friendly. She decided it was an ideal place to shed her past and inhibitions, and arranged to move in the following day.

Before Charlie went back to the guest-house to

inform them she would be leaving the next day, she telephoned Andrew from a call-box at Jack Straw's Castle, the pub where he worked.

'You're here! In London?' he gasped when she finally got through to him. 'I thought you must be staying with Ivor when I found your phone had been cut off.'

Charlie told him she had wanted to surprise him and went on to give him her new address and telephone number. 'Fantastic!' he yelled down the phone. 'That's not so far away, not on my scooter. I've got Sunday off so I can come and see you. You do want me to come, don't you?'

'Of course I do, silly,' she laughed. 'I don't know how I stopped myself from coming into your pub during this last week. I can't wait to see you.'

'I work funny hours,' he said somewhat regretfully. 'Most evenings and lunchtimes.'

'Well, I've got an interview for a job on Monday too,' she said. 'It's in a photographic laboratory in Holborn, so if I get it, I won't be free much either.'

'Is it a good job? Do you know anything about photography?'

'You don't need to, and it sounds lousy, but it was the only job at the agency that said they take almost anyone on immediately and pay them well,' she said with a rueful laugh. 'Apparently no one stays there long, but you can do tons of overtime when they're busy. Its called Haagman's, and apparently if Mrs Haagman likes me she'll get me to start immediately. I thought it would do until I find something better.'

Suddenly her money had run out. 'It's really great you're up here,' Andrew said over the pips. 'I'll phone you at the flat tomorrow.'

Charlie arrived at Hazelmere Road by taxi at twelve-thirty the following day. Anne came down to let her in.

'Meg and Beth are still in bed,' she said as she took one of Charlie's two suitcases and went on up the stairs. 'And I'm sorry, but I've got to go and see my mum, so you'll have to settle yourself in.'

'That's okay,' Charlie replied. She had hardly slept a wink last night because she was so excited. She didn't expect or need a welcoming committee.

In the bedroom Anne showed her which drawers were for Charlie, and pushed her clothes along in the wardrobe to make space. 'Make yourself at home, help yourself to tea and stuff if you can stand the mess in the kitchen. I didn't make it, Meg and Beth did, and I'll be buggered if I'm going to make myself late for Mum by stopping to clean it up for them now. I'll be back about five, I expect.'

Charlie stowed her clothes away, made up her bed with her own sheets, then as Meg and Beth still hadn't surfaced, she went into the kitchen. Anne was right, it was even more disgusting than the night before, dirty saucepans filling the sink, piles of unwashed crockery and rubbish everywhere.

Looking at the room objectively, Charlie could see there was really no need for such squalor. It was a long, thin room, almost like a ship's galley, but the units all down one side were modern, imitation-wood Formica, even the gas cooker was quite new. If the big sash window at the end were cleaned, and perhaps pretty curtains or a blind put up there, it could be quite nice.

It occurred to Charlie as she started to clean it up that she was possibly making a rod for her own back, but apart from the fact that she couldn't bear even to make a cup of tea for herself there as it was now, she wanted the other girls' approval.

An hour and a half later it was finished. Every pan and plate had been washed and put away, surfaces cleaned, rubbish taken downstairs, and the filthy floor which didn't appear to have been swept, much less washed in weeks, scrubbed. She'd even cleaned the window inside and out, sitting on the sill and pulling the window down on her lap. Yet curiously it was the most satisfying thing she'd done in a long time. She just wished Meg and Beth would get up soon so they could see it.

At nearly five o'clock, Meg finally surfaced. Charlie was lying on her bed reading a magazine when she came in with two mugs of coffee.

'Hi there,' she said, yawned and handed one of the mugs to Charlie. She was wearing a yellow, very badly stained embroidered kimono, her dark hair was like a bird's nest and she had rubbed the previous night's mascara around her eyes. 'Sorry to leave you to settle in alone, but we didn't get to bed until five this morning. And you're a real angel cleaning the kitchen. I've never seen it looking so spick and span.'

Charlie glowed. She knew she ought to make it clear she wasn't going to do it all the time, but she couldn't bring herself to be officious just yet.

Meg sat down on the bed beside her, tucking her

305

legs under her kimono. 'So come on then! Tell me all about yourself.'

Charlie was surprised and pleased by such a direct approach. Messy as Meg was, there was something very compelling about her. She had rather bulbous dark brown eyes and her gaze was intense and un-wavering.

'There's not much to tell,' Charlie said with a smile. 'I'm eighteen, just escaped from school. My father is Chinese, mother English.'

'There's more,' Meg said with a shake of her head. 'I can read auras, and I knew the moment I answered the door to you that you'd recently come through a trauma.'

Charlie was very taken aback by this. She had read several articles in magazines about just this subject, and dismissed it as being even more far-fetched than palm reading or Tarot cards. Yet how else could Meg know about a trauma? Charlie hadn't said a word the previous day about her background.

'You might as well tell me,' Meg said with a smile. 'I'll winkle it out of you before long anyway. Besides, we're flatmates now, and for that to work well, we have to become friends.'

Charlie could see the sense in that, but her natural caution told her it wasn't a good idea to tell a complete stranger too much. 'My mother committed suicide three months ago,' she said. 'I expect it's that you picked up on.'

Meg looked shattered. 'I'm so sorry,' she gasped, putting her hand over her mouth. 'I didn't mean to be nosy, only friendly.'

'I know,' Charlie said. 'And I appreciate it. But I

came to London to put it behind me, so do me a favour and drop the subject?'

Meg looked at Charlie hard for a moment or two. 'You aren't a typical Piscean,' she said at length. 'Mostly they blurt everything out, whether asked or not. And they kind of wallow in their hard luck. I shall have to do your chart. My guess is that you have Leo on the ascendant, you have a great deal of pride.'

Charlie half smiled. She didn't believe in astrology any more than auras or ghosts. Her father, however, had believed in I Ching, and she knew quite a bit about that. She thought perhaps in a day or two when she knew Meg a little better, she might share it with her.

'Have you got anything planned for tonight?' Meg asked a bit later, after she'd looked at all Charlie's clothes and tried some of them on.

'No, I haven't,' Charlie replied, laughing as Meg held up a pink wool mini-dress against her. 'And as that looks so hopelessly old-fashioned, I think I'd better sit here and consider what new clothes to buy with my first wage packet.'

'No you won't, you'll come down The Fox with us,' Meg said. 'It's just a pub really, but it has a late licence and a live band. All the tastiest fellas get in there. As for your clothes, some of yours are pretty neat. I love that blue velvet jacket. You could wear that with jeans.'

When Meg went off to have a bath, Charlie took out the velvet jacket and looked at it. It was odd that Meg should pick that out, for it had been Sylvia's. Like all her clothes from before Jin disappeared it was an expensive one. Charlie had saved it and a few other classic items purely because she'd thought she might

307

be able to sell them later on. Until now she hadn't considered wearing any of them herself.

The big back room at The Fox was dark, smoky, sweaty and packed to capacity. On the stage, at the far end, a group who had clearly modelled themselves on T. Rex were playing 'Ride a White Swan' with more enthusiasm than talent.

Charlie had a pint of cider in her hand – her flatmates had told her she'd have to get used to drinking pints as it was too much trouble to keep queuing for drinks. She drank half of it quickly, partly to calm her nerves, partly so no one could spill it on her. She didn't want to spoil her jacket.

Looking around her, she felt she'd worn the right clothes. She was somewhere in between the girls who wore very dressy cocktail-type frocks, the glam-rock brigade with glittery jackets and enormously wide flares, and the more hippie element in their long flowing dresses, or tie-dyes and jeans.

The men were equally diversely dressed. Student types in denim or corduroy, Adam Ant look-a likes with painted faces, rockers in leather jackets, skinny hippies with tangled hair and beads, and a still larger proportion in smart suits, shirts and ties.

'Watch out for "the Suits",' Beth whispered in her ear. 'Most of them are villains. But they are always good for a few drinks, they've still got the old-fashioned idea that girls can't buy their own.'

It soon became apparent that her new friends' sole purpose in coming here was to pick up some men. All three had transformed themselves from how they looked a few hours earlier. Meg looked ravishing, like a gypsy dancer in a close-fitting long red swirly dress. Washed and left to dry naturally, her hair was a mass of corkscrew ringlets, with strategically placed glittery hair-slides. Beth looked like an angelic page-boy in tight velvet trousers, long boots and a man's frilly dress shirt. Even Anne, who had less to build on to start with, looked good in a long black embroidered dress. It was slashed open to mid-thigh and she had surprisingly shapely legs. The girls didn't stay in one place, but kept moving around the room, introducing Charlie to everyone they knew.

The music was so loud that it was impossible to hold a real conversation with anyone. Drinks seemed to appear from nowhere, and although a couple of years ago Charlie would have found a place like this absolute heaven and taken the opportunity to show off, now she wasn't so sure she liked being the object of everyone's attention.

She didn't like the way men openly stared at her, or all the cracks she heard about her being 'a Chink'. She felt incensed when one man pinched her buttocks and said something about 'I'll have the sweet and sour, with sauce.' She wanted to enjoy herself, after all she'd had precious little fun in the past two years, but the truth was, she felt threatened and out of her depth.

'Come on, pick out a man,' Meg said, as she returned from a sortie across the room, bringing back a third pint of cider for Charlie. 'Seen anyone you fancy?'

'I've already got a boyfriend, and he's coming round in the morning,' Charlie said nervously. She had a strong feeling whoever the other girls picked on tonight would be coming home with them. She wanted to fit in with the girls, but she wasn't prepared to sleep with a total stranger to do it.

'That doesn't have to stop you having a bit of fun tonight,' Meg said archly. 'Rob over there fancies you rotten. Come and meet him, he's nice, and harmless.'

Charlie shuddered as she looked to where Meg was pointing and saw a gangly-looking chap with long dark hair staring at her. He had pockmarked skin from old acne, his denim jacket was too big for him, she thought he looked awful.

'If I go and speak to him he'll think I fancy him,' she said.

'Of course he will, but there's no harm in you just stringing him along a bit,' Meg replied with a persuasive, wicked grin. 'We were all going on to a club later, so drink up and get in the party mood.'

'I'm already half cut,' Charlie said; she wasn't used to drinking. 'Look, it's really nice of you all to want to show me a good time on my first night, but I'm really not up to it. Stop worrying about me, go and have a good time. I'll find my own way home later.'

Meg gave her the oddest look, a mixture of disbelief and pique. 'Well, if you're absolutely sure,' she said.

'I *am* sure,' Charlie reassured her. 'Now go and enjoy yourself.'

Charlie slipped out while Beth and Meg were snogging a couple of men, and Anne was talking to someone else. Once away from the smoky pub and its loud music, she felt easier. It was a beautiful warm night, a million stars in the black velvet sky, and she was seeing Andrew tomorrow. Maybe in a week or two's time when she'd found her feet in London, she'd enjoy

310

nights out like this one. She hoped so, the other girls would think she was stuck up and strange if she didn't join them.

Charlie was dressed and ready to go out when Andrew rang the door-bell at eleven the following morning. She picked up her shoulder-bag, and ran down the stairs eagerly.

'Charlie!' he exclaimed as she opened the door. For a moment he just stood there looking at her. She was wearing her old white mini-dress, somehow she didn't think he'd care if it was old-fashioned, it was after all a hot, sunny day and she wanted to improve her sun-tan. 'You look even more gorgeous than I remembered.'

'And so do you,' she smiled. He was wearing a short-sleeved, open-necked shirt and jeans. His face and forearms were already deeply sun-tanned and his blue eyes were twice as vivid as the ones in her memory.

'Can I come in then, and inspect your new pad?'

Charlie blushed. 'I think we'd better do that bit later. The other girls are still in bed.' She didn't want to tell him that each of them had a man with them. Charlie had been woken around half past two by them coming in, they were all quite drunk and she'd felt intimidated by the rough male voices. They put a Rolling Stones record on very loud, and both Meg and Beth kept screaming with laughter about something. Fortunately it didn't last very long. Meg and Beth must have taken their men off to bed first, and Anne stayed in the living room with hers, turning the music down low.

Charlie had tiptoed through the living room this morning to go to the kitchen and bathroom. Anne was asleep on one of the mattresses, a fair-haired man with tattoos on his arms lying flat on his back beside her, snoring loudly. The whole room stank of stale sweat and it sickened her.

'Okay then, where shall we go?' Andrew asked. 'It's nice up on Hampstead Heath. I could take you to the pub at lunchtime so you can meet everyone.'

'That sounds super,' she said, and impulsively hugged him. His arms locked right round her, and his lips found hers.

His kiss took her right back to the day at Slapton Sands, before her mother's death. It was sweet and tender, re-awakening all those feelings she'd put aside and thought she'd lost forever.

'So where's this scooter?' she asked, once he finally let her go. She felt suddenly light-headed and deliriously happy. This was what she'd come to London for.

Charlie had never ridden pillion before, and she was just a bit scared as Andrew set off towards Highgate, but holding on tight round his waist she soon got over it.

'You don't have to worry about me doing a ton,' he shouted back to her. 'This is just about its top speed. We'll probably have a struggle getting up Whittington Hill.'

Charlie hadn't been to Highgate before, nor did she know that the hill up to it was named after Dick Whittington. But Andrew was a mine of information, pointing out landmarks like the cemetery where Karl Marx was buried, and slowing right

312

down so she could see all the pretty cottages in the Village.

He drove to Jack Straw's Castle where he worked and left the scooter in the car park, then they went for a walk across the Heath to see the Ponds. Charlie was amazed to find dozens of people were swimming in one of them.

'I should have thought of this yesterday,' Andrew said looking wistfully at a group of teenagers having a water fight. 'We could have brought our cossies and had a picnic.'

'Never mind,' Charlie said, sitting down on the grass. 'It's nice just to watch.'

Andrew sat down beside her and pointed out a clump of trees in the distance. 'There's a Ladies Only pool tucked away in those bushes,' he grinned. 'The other night some of us lads from the pub went swimming in there. It was great, as warm as bathwater. But the police turned up and we had to leg it, dressing as we went. John, one of my mates, lost his shoe. He came back the next day to look for it, but he never did find it.'

As Andrew launched into several more tales about the lads from the pub and his old flatmates who'd now gone off to France hitchhiking, Charlie became very aware of how isolated she'd been for the past months. She had no funny stories to tell him, she had lost touch with world news, fashion and pop music. Even if she was to tell him a couple of amusing incidents that had happened in the course of selling off the furniture at Mayflower Close, she felt that would only draw attention to how bleak her life had been.

Fortunately Andrew seemed unaware that she

wasn't reciprocating with any anecdotes, and he moved on to talk about his parents' annoyance that he wasn't prepared to come home to Oxford for the summer. 'My folks are cool in some ways,' he said. 'But as soon as I'm back there Mum treats me like a little boy and Dad badgers me to swot and stuff. It was a real drag getting thrown out of the flat, all three of us were intending to get labouring work on a building site for a few weeks so we could make enough money to pay the rent and save enough for a holiday later on. I hoped I could take you away somewhere. But I'm not really earning enough for that now. And I've got the drag of finding another place for us all in September.'

Charlie could at least relate to this, and described some of the awful flats she'd seen. 'They want so much money too,' she said indignantly. 'I don't know how they have the cheek to expect people to live in such damp, dirty places.'

'Nigel said before he left for France that he's got an uncle who might let us his house in Brent,' Andrew said, looking at her thoughtfully. 'That's part of Golders Green. His uncle's a Rabbi, and he's moving up to Newcastle, so he's going to let out his old home furnished. Nigel did say he might look on us more kindly if we had a girl sharing with us; apparently he believes girls are likely to create a little more order around the place.'

'Me, do you mean?' Charlie asked.

'Well, yes,' he shrugged. 'Does the thought appal you?'

Charlie giggled. 'No, not exactly, it's just a bit unexpected, that's all.'

314

A silence fell between them. Charlie wondered if he meant just sharing the house, or his bed.

'You think I'm being a bit previous, don't you?' Andrew said after a few minutes. 'I didn't really mean – oh hell, I've put my foot in it.'

'You haven't,' she said. 'It's just that we haven't had any time yet to see how things will work out between us.'

'I didn't really intend to sound as if I expected us to be, well, you know,' he said, blushing furiously. 'I was more thinking along the lines that all four of us would be friends, with our own rooms. Anyway, that's all in the future. Nigel won't be back for at least a month and his uncle isn't moving until September anyway.'

Andrew dropped the subject and moved on to ask about her flat and the other girls. Charlie explained a little about them, omitting that she suspected they slept with a different man every weekend. 'They are a bit wacky,' she said. 'But then they're art students. I'll just have to play it by ear and see how it goes.'

'Have the girls got summer jobs?' he asked a bit later.

'I don't know,' Charlie said thoughtfully. None of them had mentioned work, but then the subject hadn't come up. In fact she hadn't spoken of her interview tomorrow either. 'Why?'

'Just wondered,' he said. 'But it will probably be hell for you if they haven't. They'll be larking around half the night when you want to go to bed. I've had some of that in the past, it can be a real pain.'

*

315

Charlie must have fallen asleep lying on the grass in the afternoon, as she woke to find Andrew leaning over her, gently stroking her cheek.

'What time is it?' she asked. They had been to Jack Straw's at lunchtime to meet his employers and friends. By the time they came out at closing time, Charlie was a bit tiddly and they'd found a quiet place to lie down.

'Fourish,' he said, kissing her nose. 'You fell asleep on me almost as soon as we got here.'

'I'm sorry,' she said, sliding her arms around him and pulling him closer. 'It must have been those drinks. Were you really cheesed off?'

'No, I dropped off too,' he said. 'It's so nice just relaxing in the sun. I don't get much chance normally because even in the afternoons, the other guys pester me.'

'In what way?' She arched her eyebrows suggestively.

Andrew sniggered. 'Not *that* kind of pestering. I meant wanting to chat, play records, you know the stuff. At heart I'm a bit of a loner. I like to just lie about and think about things. Do you?'

Charlie nodded. 'Yes, I suppose I do. Though if you'd met me two years ago, you wouldn't have thought I was capable of thought. I was the original butterfly brain then.'

He gently kissed her lips, then drew back slightly, leaning up over her on one elbow, looking down at her. 'Tell me how it is now,' he asked. 'I mean, about your mum.'

She had glimpsed several new sides of Andrew today. The devil-may-care student bent only on

316

enjoying himself with the lads, a slick and charming barman, and the working-class boy who felt pressured to make good. But now as he leaned over her, his eyes showing his deep concern for her, she saw just Beryl's nephew, the sensitive boy who had put aside a budding romance, comforted and cheered her without any thought for himself.

'The pain has gone,' she said, looking up at him. 'Just a little dull ache inside, but I can live with that. This morning when I opened the door to you I felt as if I'd just come out the end of a long, dark tunnel.'

He smiled and stroked her cheek again. 'That's good. I've been so worried about you, Charlie. Afraid that you wouldn't return to being the girl I first met, scared too that I'd built up an imaginary girl in my head, and when I saw you again it would be all wrong.'

Charlie's thoughts about him had run along similar lines.

'Am I the same as the girl in your head?' she asked.

'Better,' he smiled. 'The Charlie I met back at Beryl's was a bit cool, she didn't give much away about herself. Then throughout that awful week before the funeral, you told me so much that it was like being with another quite different girl. Once I got back to London I couldn't sort out in my head which was the real Charlie. My heart told me one thing, my head said another. So many times I wanted just to charge down there and have it out with you. Sometimes I was actually angry that you were holding a bit of my heart, yet you gave me nothing in return.'

Charlie blushed. Looking back, she realized she was so hung up on her own problems and grief that she hadn't considered how he might be feeling. She'd lapped up all his concern and support, but never for one moment thought of offering him some too.

'June, that friend of mine you met at the funeral, always said I was selfish,' she said sheepishly. 'I believed I'd stopped being so, but I suppose it's hard to change your real character. But in my defence, I was so mixed up, I couldn't get my head round anything except my schoolwork.'

'And now?' he asked.

His anxious expression moved her. He wasn't an empty-headed waster like Guy. He might like rowdy parties, going out to get drunk and everything else that went with being a hare-brained student, but his consistency proved there was a great deal more to him.

'I want to start all over again as if we'd just met,' she said. 'To have fun together and see where that takes us. Is that enough to be getting on with?'

His lips quivered as if he wanted to laugh. 'Do we have to start right at the beginning?' he asked. 'I rather thought we might be able to pick up from the day on the beach, you know, when the kisses were getting a bit hot.'

Charlie giggled. 'We could try,' she said.

His answering kiss stripped away the last three months. A sweet and warm exploratory kiss quickly led to bolder, more passionate ones. The sun grew cooler, people around them packed up their rugs and picnics, but they stayed on, locked in each other's arms, shamelessly devouring one another.

It was after seven before they walked hand in hand back to the pub to collect Andrew's scooter. 'Let's go and have a meal to celebrate,' Charlie suggested. 'On me because I'm feeling rich.'

'Now, why are you feeling rich?' he asked, stopping to kiss her yet again.

'Because I'm with you,' she said.

He laughed and hugged her to him. 'I don't normally have that effect on people.'

'Well, you do on me,' she laughed back. 'I'm rich with tingles, rich with belief I'll get that job tomorrow. London suddenly looks wonderful. Is that enough reasons to celebrate?'

'More than enough,' he said. 'So where do we go? In the pub, or have you got something special in mind?'

'Chinese,' she said without any hesitation. 'We always went to a Chinese restaurant when Dad had something he wanted to celebrate.'

'Did I ever tell you it's my favourite food?' Andrew said, as he started up the scooter.

'No!' she said. 'But there's an awful lot I don't know about you, and it's my intention to start finding it out as soon as possible.'

He didn't reply to that, just squeezed her two hands clasped about his middle. As they drove down towards Hampstead Village, Charlie was suddenly aware she had never been this happy before in her entire life.

At nine-thirty the following morning Charlie arrived at Haagman's photographic laboratory in Endell Street, Holborn for her interview. It didn't look very prepossessing, plain concrete steps from the street up to an equally dreary reception area furnished with a

319

lone battered wooden bench and a dark-haired girl sitting behind a hatch which reminded Charlie of those in British Rail ticket offices. The girl slid back the glass partition only far enough to take Charlie's name and hand her an application form to fill in, then she disappeared through a door beyond her cubby-hole and didn't come back.

By quarter past ten Charlie was on the point of leaving, when a portly, middle-aged woman with a jet-black beehive, wearing a red suit and a great deal of jewellery, came through the door. 'Are you waiting for someone?' she asked.

Charlie stood up. 'Yes, for Mrs Haagman. I had an interview with her at nine-thirty. My name is Charlie Weish.'

'I'm Mrs Haagman,' the woman replied. She neither smiled nor apologized for keeping her waiting so long, just took the application form from her hands. 'Follow me!'

She led the way into a large first-floor room. One side of it was filled with large machines, which Charlie assumed processed the films; in the middle was a series of light-boxes, over one of which the girl she'd seen earlier appeared to be studying negatives. The remainder of the space was taken up by benches at which perhaps ten or twelve people were sitting or standing doing a variety of different jobs. There was no talking or laughter, only the buzzing and clonking sounds of the machines.

Although Charlie wasn't given much chance to study the place, she noted that everyone in the room was young, a balance of male and female. A boy with long brown hair tied back in a pony-tail grinned at her, then made a face at Mrs Haagman's back. Charlie had to assume that was some kind of warning.

Mrs Haagman went straight into an office and sat down behind a large desk covered with packets of photographs. She ordered Charlie to shut the door behind her, then indicated with one podgy, beringed hand that she was to sit down. She didn't speak again, but studied the application form.

'What is Charlie short for?' she asked without looking up.

'Nothing, that's it,' Charlie replied. 'It's a Chinese name.' She explained its origins. The only reply to that was a sniff.

'So you've just left school after taking four "A" levels,' the woman said after what seemed like at least ten minutes. 'Are you planning to go to university?'

'No,' Charlie said. 'I've just come to London to work.'

'What makes you want to work here?'

Charlie felt that was a trick question. She could hardly say she just wanted any job as long as it was well paid. 'It sounded interesting,' she said.

'There's nothing interesting about it,' Mrs Haagman said with yet another disapproving sniff. 'We process films quickly. The work is tedious and repetitive. But then I'm sure the agency told you that. So the truth. Why do you want to work here when you are clearly capable of something a lot more ambitious?'

Charlie was once again tempted to get up and leave, she thought the woman was insufferably rude. But she needed a job, the money she had saved wouldn't last long in London.

'I only just arrived from Devon,' she said. 'I need

time to think about what I want to do as a career, and I'm on my own, with rent to pay, so I need a job straight away. I was told I could earn good money here and I thought it would be a stop-gap until my exam results come through.'

'That's better,' the woman said, but she still didn't smile. 'I do pay well for those prepared to work hard. I do not tolerate bad time-keeping or absenteeism. My staff have no set jobs, I move them around during the course of the day whenever one section gets behind. I will not stand for anyone complaining about this. Now do you want the job?'

Charlie thought it would have been appropriate to show a prospective employee round before being asked that question. 'Yes, please,' she said anyway, thinking she could always leave if it was as awful as she feared.

'Right then.' The woman got up. 'You can start right away. The basic pay is fifteen pounds. It's a five-day week, from nine to five-thirty with half an hour for lunch. If I wish you to stay later or work on Saturday I will tell you by four in the afternoon. Have you got your insurance card with you?'

Charlie took it out of her handbag and handed it over.

Mrs Haagman didn't even bother to take her out into the main room and introduce her to any of the staff, she just yelled, 'Martin!' through the door.

Martin was the young man with the pony-tail. It seemed he could read minds because Mrs Haagman gave him no instructions, just announced, 'This is Charlie,' before retreating and shutting her office door dismissively.

'Well, that's it, Charlie,' he said, nodding back at the closed door. 'You are now one of the Hag's drones, and I'm supposed to show you around and put you to work. In case you didn't catch it, my name's Martin, I'm what passes for the supervisor, but only because I've been here longer than anyone else. The Hag is also Queen Bee, she sits in her office all day and counts her money.'

Charlie couldn't help but laugh. There was something so very surreal about this place, it put her in mind of weird Sixties films.

'It's not often people laugh in here,' he said. 'At least not when the Hag's in.'

Charlie managed to splutter out what she thought and Martin laughed too. 'You're right, it is a bit like that, a cross between an episode of *The Prisoner* and *The Avengers*. You couldn't be an Emma Peel, could you? Sent here to free us?'

Martin's tour was very brief, and he didn't bother to tell her anything about the film-processing machines because he said she would never be having anything to do with them. Instead he showed her a couple of girls in front of a small mountain of envelopes, taking the unprocessed films out, then moved on to other equally unskilled labour.

'Cutting the negatives,' he said, allowing her a glimpse of someone's holiday snaps on a light-box. 'That's a cream job, because it's the only one you get a whimsy of excitement from. Sometimes there's a few "rudies". Then there's lots of gory operation ones from the hospitals.'

'Do you really get rude pictures?' she asked as he took her over to where a handful of people were working out the price of the finished prints.

Martin nodded. 'Oh yes, but the Hag makes us separate them from the others. She says it's an offence to send pornography through the post. So if they want their dirty pictures they have to come to the office and collect them. But in our opinion she hangs on to them in the hope she might find someone she could blackmail.'

Charlie thought Martin must be joking, but if he was, she didn't know how he managed to keep such a deadpan face. But as he moved on to explain how the prices were worked out, and how to ensure that the right person received the right prints, she reminded herself to ask him again about that later.

She soon saw that the work would be tedious, the vast majority of the staff were either unpacking, or packing the prints up to post back to the customer. She hoped she might get to do the invoices, that at least required some brainwork.

Martin started her off with unpacking the unprocessed films, and showed the system of marking them. Some, it seemed, came direct from shops which collected the money directly from their customers; these were brought in daily by messenger boys, others came straight from the public, sent in special envelopes with a return address label.

Charlie was put to work beside Rita and Jenny. Rita was a small redhead with a big bust, and a good bit older than the rest of the staff. Charlie wondered fleetingly why she chose to wear middle-aged woman's clothes, no makeup and had her red hair tied back in such an unflattering way. With a bit of effort she could look very attractive, but instead she looked like a missionary.

Jenny was a student, working there for the holidays.

She was plain and thin with thick spectacles, and like almost everyone apart from Rita, she wore jeans and a tee-shirt.

Rita spoke first. 'Don't look so glum,' she said with a cheerful grin. 'Once the Hag's gone out it's not so bad.'

'Is she always so rude?' Charlie whispered. She had already worked out for herself that noise and chatter weren't approved of by the Hag.

'You haven't seen anything yet,' Rita whispered back. 'One blast of her breath would strip wallpaper.'

Jenny giggled at this. 'Rita's the only one of us brave enough to stand up to her. The rest of us grovel. Martin will train you in that, he's aiming at an honours degree in arse-licking and kow-towing.'

Charlie felt heartened by both the girls' sense of humour. Rita was particularly intriguing; her appearance was off-putting, but anyone who could make off-the-cuff, funny remarks and stand up to the boss, sounded worth getting to know better. She thought it might prove an interesting job after all.

At twelve-thirty the Hag came out of her office. 'Martin!' she bellowed.

Martin left his post at a light-box and hurried up to her. Charlie was too far away to hear what was being said, but when the woman came striding down the room, casting malevolent looks at anyone who dared so much as glance at her, Charlie saw Martin was grinning and surmised that meant the Hag was going out.

There was a deathly hush for a few minutes after the door slammed behind her. Charlie wondered why. She was soon to discover the reason, however, for

Martin crossed over to the window and looked out.

'She's getting in a taxi!' he called out. 'It's pulling away!'

Suddenly everything changed. The noise level went from utter silence to several decibels with chatter, laughter and chairs scraping on the tiled floor. Some of the staff picked up tiny catapults made from paper clips and rubber bands and began flicking scraps of paper around.

'Did she say how long she would be?' Rita yelled out across the room to Martin.

'She was her usual evasive self,' he shouted back. 'Said maybe an hour, but she'll be a lot longer than that because she sprayed herself with perfume before she went. That means she's off to get laid.'

'Who on earth would want to screw her?' a young lad with red hair working one of the processing machines yelled out. 'I'd turn queer if she was the last woman left on earth.'

Martin galloped across the room towards Charlie, caught hold of her hand and made her stand up. 'Never mind who's weird enough to fancy shagging the Hag, let's all welcome Charlie, the latest Christian to be thrown to the lions.'

Charlie could hardly believe what she was seeing and hearing. Everyone came crowding towards her, clapping their hands, stamping their feet and shouting things as diverse as 'Poor cow', 'Tell us about yourself' and 'What a pretty girl like you doing here?'

Martin rapped on the table with a pair of scissors for silence. 'You have to speak. It's tradition for new-comers,' he said, looking at Charlie. 'Don't flunk it and giggle. We want to know a little bit about you.'

Charlie felt as if she was blushing from her head right down to her toes, yet the warmth and camaraderie of this group touched her. 'As you can see for yourselves I'm half Chinese,' she said. 'I'm eighteen, just up from Devon. I'm living in a flat in Hornsey with three other girls. My interests are drinking cider, Pink Floyd, and finding out where my father is.'

She had no idea what made her say that about her father. It just sprang out from nowhere. On reflection later, she supposed it was perhaps the need to make herself sound interesting, and if that had been her aim, she was soon to find that it worked.

Martin ordered everyone back to work after a few minutes, but the room didn't return to silence. Jokes and gossip were shouted around the room, drowning the sounds of the machines. At first Charlie found it difficult to concentrate on marking the films while questions were fired at her from all directions, but when she saw everyone else was capable of working at their previous speed whilst talking, she soon made herself master it too.

Rita was clearly interested by Charlie's remark about her father, and insisted that she explained herself. Charlie kept the story as a simple mystery, she didn't mention the bankruptcy, or that her mother had since killed herself. Apart from being reluctant to discuss things she still found painful, she was determined that she wasn't going to become an object of anyone's pity again.

'I haven't actually got the first idea how to set about finding out the truth,' she finished up, rather surprised to find Jenny and Rita were both hanging on her every word. 'All I've got to go on is a newspaper cutting of

327

one of Dad's old clubs and the name of his mistress.'

At half past one, Martin told Rita and Charlie to have their lunch break, leaving Jenny to finish unpacking the last few films.

'What do you want to do?' Rita asked Charlie as she got up. 'I usually just go into the rest room for some coffee and a fag, but if you're hungry we could buy a sandwich and sit outside and eat it in the sunshine.'

Charlie was starving, she hadn't even bothered with any breakfast that morning because the kitchen was such a mess again. They bought corned beef rolls and cans of Coke, then went into St Giles's churchyard to eat them.

'How long have you been at Haagman's?' Charlie asked. She had already observed that almost the entire staff were students. It seemed peculiar that Rita, who was so very different to them, fitted in so well.

'Just three months,' she said. 'I was sent there by a temping agency, but I took a permanent job because the Hag offered me more money. I quite like it, we have a lot of laughs and there's none of that backbiting stuff you get in most offices. You see, I don't fit in many places.'

There was absolutely no reason for Charlie to ask why. The reason was as plain as the nose on her face. But she asked anyway.

Rita laughed. 'You'll understand when you know me better,' she said. 'You see, the inner me doesn't match my clothes, and it makes some people very uncomfortable.'

Charlie was puzzled. 'Well, why wear them then?'

To Charlie's surprise Rita stood up in front of her,

whisked the rubber band from her hair and ran her fingers through it. It was fiery and dramatic falling in waves over her shoulders. 'Do you see now?'

Charlie saw then what she was getting at. Setting aside the dowdy clothes, Rita was like a Fifties pin-up girl. Slim hips, tiny waist and big breasts, she looked undeniably racy.

'Yes, I can see, but if I had a figure like yours I'd show it off,' Charlie said.

'No, you wouldn't, you'd soon get tired of men pinching your bottom and trying to grope you,' Rita said with a shrug. 'How old do you think I am?'

'About twenty-five,' Charlie said.

Rita sat down again, took a brush from her bag and whisked her hair back into the original style. 'I ought to take that as a compliment, yet it doesn't seem like one. I'm thirty-two, Charlie. If I dress like this I look like I'm wearing my mother's clothes. Yet if I wear anything else, I look like a tart, and I attract the wrong kind of attention and women hate me for it. You're very lucky, Charlie, you're not only beautiful, but you have class. Men are a little in awe of that.'

'Oh, I don't know about that,' Charlie laughed.

'Well, I do. Sometimes I think I know everything there is to know about men. Your story about your father puzzles me though. From the little you said I can't imagine why he disappeared. Men don't usually leave their wives for a mistress, especially not when they've had her for years.'

Charlie wondered if she'd done the right thing telling this woman so much. She was very odd, in fact she'd never met anyone so forthright, and it made her a little nervous. 'What do you think happened to him then?' she asked.

'I couldn't possibly guess, not without knowing a great deal more about him, and your mother. But you're very young, Charlie, you're still hurt and puzzled by his disappearance, and you're trying to start a new life in London which is the best thing you could do. I doubt very much that you want a woman almost old enough to be your mother sticking her nose in. But I hope we can be friends and maybe in time you'll feel like telling me the rest of it.'

Charlie found herself warming to Rita as she went on to ask her about her flat and the other girls. As Charlie described her first night out with her flatmates she became aware by Rita's astute comments that she understood both Charlie's reservations and the other girls' attitude.

'You don't have to follow them to fit in,' she said. 'But on the other hand there's nothing worse in a flat-sharing situation where one girl is po-faced and disapproving, because it makes the others feel guilty. What you have to do, if going out and pulling men isn't your bag, is to avoid those kinds of nights out, but find some other time to spend with the girls and get to know them better.'

Charlie felt able then to admit to her embarrassment when she'd brought Andrew back to the flat the previous night. 'The whole flat was a tip again, aside from mine and Anne's room. Meg was walking around in something that looked like a petticoat, she didn't even have any knickers on.'

Rita smirked. 'I shouldn't worry about what Andrew thinks,' she shrugged. 'Men don't notice mess the way women do, especially when they're young. But the important thing to remember, Charlie, is that you didn't come to London to sink into some kind of middle-aged, suburban bliss. You came to have fun, to be part of a young scene. So forget about doing the washing-up, or hoovering the carpets, you can get into that when you're my age. Let yourself go, buy a few outrageous clothes, get off to those pop concerts and see the latest films. I don't want to hear you've been sitting alone darning your socks and waiting for Andrew to finish work.'

They chatted on until it was time to go back to work. But as they got up from the seat, Rita suddenly turned to Charlie and caught hold of her hand. 'You're going to think me very nosy saying this,' she said. 'But are you on the Pill?'

Charlie blushed. 'No, but then I don't need to be.'

Rita looked hard at Charlie, and saw her for what she really was. A young, somewhat innocent girl straight out of school. She wouldn't come to much harm at Haagman's, half the staff were much the same as her, but the girls she was flat-sharing with sounded a different story. She didn't know why she should suddenly feel involved, or so protective, but she did. Perhaps it was just because she could have done with some sound advice when she first left home herself.

'That sounds to me like I'm not doing that with him. But I can tell by the way you speak about Andrew that you soon will be. Get yourself on the Pill now, Charlie, don't wait until you find yourself in bed with him and hope he'll take some precautions,' she said with a smile. 'If I had a pound for every girl I know who's done that and found herself pregnant, I wouldn't be working at Haagman's now.'

Charlie swallowed her pride. She knew Rita was right. 'But how do I get it? she asked.

'Easily. There's the Brook Clinic or the Family Planning Association, either of them will sort you out. Or go to your doctor and ask him. I'd recommend the Brook, because they don't ask awkward questions. You can find their address and phone number in the phone book.'

'Okay,' Charlie said. 'I will.'

Rita grinned and took her arm. 'Not next week, or the week after, now, immediately. It takes time before it works and you have to start a course on the fourth day of your period. Now, let's get back into the madhouse and catch up before the Hag gets back and finds we've been slacking.'

Chapter Eleven

Three weeks after Charlie had moved into the flat in Hornsey, she was at Jack Straw's Castle in Hampstead, waiting for Andrew to finish work. She had arrived about one o'clock, imagining they would go out for the afternoon, but now at two-thirty it was raining hard.

'I think it's set in for the rest of the day,' Andrew said gloomily as he locked the bar door behind the last customer. 'I suppose we could go to the pictures.'

Charlie was sitting on a stool up at the bar; they were alone apart from John, one of the other barmen, who was wiping down tables and collecting ashtrays. 'We'll get soaked,' she said. 'I haven't even brought a raincoat or umbrella with me.'

Andrew didn't reply but opened the door which led to the public bar to check if Carol, the landlady, was in there. As the towels were over the pumps and all the lights turned off, he guessed she'd gone up to her flat.

'We could go upstairs to my room,' he suggested hesitantly.

Charlie knew the bar staff weren't allowed to have anyone up in their rooms. 'I don't want you to get into trouble,' she said, but her heart leapt at the thought of what being alone would mean.

Since her first weekend in Hornsey, they had snatched every available hour they could together, but because of Andrew's work, in practice this amounted only to afternoons at the weekends, and late-night visits at the flat. There was precious little opportunity for any privacy, the girls were always at the flat, usually with a crowd of their noisy friends.

'For you I'll take the risk.' Andrew grinned mischievously. He arranged the wet tea-towels over the pumps, then came back round the bar and went over to John. 'Don't let on to Carol if you see her, will you?'

John was another student, like Andrew working there for the summer. He was thin and studious-looking with glasses. 'My lips are sealed,' he said with a warm smile. 'If asked where you went I'll play dumb.'

It was scary following Andrew up the back stairs to the staff bedrooms in the attic. Their footsteps on the uncarpeted stairs sounded very loud and Charlie half expected Carol to come bursting indignantly out of one of the many doors and order them out.

'We're safe now,' Andrew said as they reached the dingy top floor. 'She hardly ever comes up here.'

'But how will I get out this evening?' Charlie asked nervously.

'That will be a doddle.' Andrew grinned as he opened his door. 'Carol always opens up alone at six. You can easily slip out through the back door to the car park, she can't see that from the bar.'

His tiny attic room was exactly as Charlie had

expected – strewn with books, records, clothes and dirty cups, the narrow bed unmade. One wall was almost completely covered in an *Easy Rider* poster.

'Sorry about the mess.' Andrew hastily snatched up a dirty shirt and a pair of socks, and pulled up the covers on the bed. 'Go and look out the window while I get this straight. I may live in a pigsty but the view makes up for it.'

Charlie did as he said. The view was superb, right across the Heath down to the Ponds in the distance. The heavy rain and the absence of people gave it a stark beauty. Each tree was swaying gracefully, the varied shades of green more vivid with the dark grey sky as a backdrop.

Andrew crept up behind her and slid his hands around her waist, leaning his chin on her shoulder. 'You should see it at sunrise,' he said. 'Sometimes the sky is pink and mauve, and the sun's rays are orange. Someone told me that it's more spectacular in London than anywhere else because of all the pollution and gases in the air. I don't know if that's strictly true, but whatever causes it, it's magic.'

'How come you're up at sunrise?' she asked.

'I'm an odd sort of chap,' he laughed. 'I always wake up then. Sometimes I do some studying, but mostly I make myself a cup of tea, look at the view for a while, then go back to bed to dream about you.'

'You don't,' she scoffed.

'Well, I don't always make a cup of tea,' he said with laughter in his voice. 'But I do spend a great deal of time dreaming about you, especially about being *alone* with you.'

'So what do you imagine?' she asked, a tremor of excitement running down her spine. Ever since she'd been to a clinic and got herself on the Pill, she'd thought of little else but making love. Every kiss, every touch made her ache for more, yet she'd been nervous of admitting her feelings in case he didn't feel the same way.

'Lying on the bed with you,' he murmured as he kissed her neck. 'Slowly undressing you, the feel of your skin under my hands.'

Charlie turned in his arms to kiss him and as his lips met hers she ran her hands down over his back to his buttocks, and drew him closer still. Andrew was a wonderful kisser, his tongue and lips so sensual that she had often found herself aroused even in crowded public places. But now, alone, knowing there was nothing and no one to stop them, she pressed her groin against his and delighted in feeling his erection.

One of his hands crept down to the crotch of her jeans, his fingers tracing the two small mounds inside. She ached for him to unzip her, to thrust his fingers right inside her, instead of just teasing her.

He moved back a little and with a lazy, sexy smirk he slowly and deliberately unbuttoned her shirt and peeled it off. 'No bra!' he whispered, raising one eyebrow. 'Why's that? To make it easier for me to touch you?'

Charlie nodded, she was both embarrassed and excited that he'd understood her motives. She held her breath, wanting his hands to caress her breasts, yet all he was doing was looking at them like a schoolboy.

'Do it then!' she said, taking a step nearer him, so her nipples brushed against his shirt. His two hands moved to cup her small breasts, he rubbed the nipples with his thumbs, but there was suddenly an almost fearful look in his eyes.

'I want you so much, Charlie,' he whispered. 'I've thought about nothing else but an opportunity like this. But I didn't expect it to happen today, and I'm a bit scared I might not be able to stop.'

Charlie frowned in puzzlement. 'Why do we have to stop?' she asked.

'I wouldn't want you to get pregnant,' he blurted out, blushing furiously. 'And I never thought to get anything.'

All at once she realized he wasn't as experienced as she'd imagined. Because almost everyone she'd met since coming to London slept around, she had just assumed he must have made love to other girls. Judging by his embarrassment he might even be a virgin, and he probably thought she was too.

'I want you too, Andrew,' she whispered back, undoing his shirt buttons and sliding her hands over his smooth bare chest. 'I have ever since our first date. But I won't get pregnant, because I went to a clinic and got myself on the Pill. I knew it would happen before long.'

He looked stunned for a second, then slowly a wide smile crept across his face. He cupped her face in his hands, his bright eyes searching hers for any lingering doubt. 'Really?'

'Yes, really,' she giggled. 'Rita gave me a lecture about "being prepared". I wanted to tell you before but I was too shy.'

He pulled her into his arms, kissing her with such passion she knew they had passed the point of

337

awkward questions, or even considering what might happen if Carol discovered she was up here in his room.

It felt like it was her first time, eager, fearful and embarrassed all at once. She wished too she'd worn something more suitable for seduction. Her jeans were so tight, and she was certain they would leave red marks all over her. She didn't think to remove her plimsolls first, and almost fell over when they caught in the legs of her jeans. Andrew was panting with eagerness as he stripped off his clothes, and he dived into bed, then lay there gazing at her as she bent awkwardly to take off her shoes wearing nothing but her knickers.

'I should have put some music on and undressed you myself,' he whispered, reaching out for her hand and drawing her back towards him. 'That's what they do in films, and I wanted it to be perfect.'

Charlie didn't reply, just slid into the narrow bed, but the moment he enfolded her in his arms and pulled the covers right up to their necks, suddenly it felt so right. The rain was splattering against the window pane, from somewhere along the corridor soft music was playing, and his warm, silky body felt so good against hers.

'I've done this in my dreams a thousand times,' he murmured as he caressed her. 'I can't believe I'm really touching you at last.'

His touch was delicate and hesitant as if he was afraid of hurting her, and that consideration for her feelings made her more excited than Guy with his thrusting demands had ever achieved. His whole body was throbbing with desire, his erection was rock-hard against her thigh, but still he held back until she was fully aroused.

When he did finally enter her, it was over too quickly, yet she felt no real sense of disappointment. 'I love you, Charlie,' he murmured into her neck. 'I never knew it would be so wonderful.'

She remembered then how when Guy had said he loved her she'd felt compelled to cross-examine him. She didn't feel that way with Andrew, her whole being knew he would never make such a statement unless he truly meant it.

'I love you too,' she whispered, holding him tightly and covering his face with kisses.

He was so sweet, half covering his blushing face with the blanket as he apologized for being so quick. 'It doesn't matter,' she assured him, thinking how lovely it was to have a man who could admit he wasn't perfect, rather than one like Guy who had to spoil it all by saying he was 'better after a few drinks'. 'We'll both get better with practice.'

She had thought she'd known Andrew so well that nothing about him could surprise her. Yet she had never seen his face so soft with tenderness before, never noticed how his lips curled at the corners as though in a permanent smile, the full length and thickness of his dark lashes or the way his ears fitted so snugly to his head.

Love welled up inside her as he held her in his arms whispering endearments to her. This was the man who had steadfastly stuck by her through tragedy, been her friend, her solace. Nothing had ever felt so right and beautiful, it was as perfect as the view of the sea on a summer's day, as serene as Exmoor under a blanket of snow, and as thrilling as sailing a racing dinghy in a gale. Outside on the Heath, the rain was still lashing down, but here they were in a little cocoon of their own making, warm, secure and so very happy.

They made love again later. This time it was slower, more sensual and experimental. She found that though Andrew might lack previous experience, his enthusiasm, a strong desire to please, along with a naturally sensual nature soon led him to find all the right places to caress. Under his sensitive and loving fingers she came to a shuddering climax even before he entered her again.

They must have fallen asleep in each other's arms, because all too soon it was half past six and Andrew said he had to get ready for work at seven.

'I can't bear to go home,' she said sleepily, pulling him closer to her. 'I'm much too snug and warm.'

'You have to,' he insisted, kissing her shoulders. 'Carol wouldn't like a stowaway in her tight ship.'

Charlie knew she must go, but it seemed so cruel after such a blissful afternoon. It was Saturday night, the other girls would be getting ready to go out; unless she went with them, she'd be alone.

'Will you come round after work then?' she asked. 'If we get into bed before Anne gets in, she'll sleep in the living room. I don't think I could get through the night without you.'

He kissed her tenderly, his blue eyes filled with the same yearning she felt. 'Nor me. I'll be watching the clock all evening. Let's hope it's a quiet night and I can get away early.'

*

340

Charlie didn't attempt to get a bus home, but walked instead. The rain had stopped while they were in bed and the Heath smelt fresh and clean. The sadness at leaving Andrew lifted as she walked, replaced by a feeling of joy that she was loved, and excitement for the future. London was a thrilling place, there was still so much more of it to explore with Andrew, maybe in September they could share a house with his friends, and they could spend every night together.

'What have you been doing today?' Meg asked as Charlie came in. Meg was sitting on one of the mattresses in the living room, rolling a joint; she looked ready to go out, in a long black dress. 'By the look of you I'd say you got laid!'

Charlie blushed. Meg was one for incisive remarks, and she made them regardless of who was listening. In the three weeks Charlie had been living here she'd been continually embarrassed by Meg. She liked her, admired her forthright manner and often wished she could learn to be so direct and sophisticated, yet it still made her squirm sometimes. Fortunately this time they were alone, Beth and Anne were in their bedrooms, and Charlie thought it might be a good opportunity to have a quiet chat.

'Maybe I did, maybe I didn't,' she giggled.

'Come and sit down and share this with me,' Meg waved the joint, 'and you can tell me all about it.'

So far, Charlie had resisted all the girl's attempts to get her to try some cannabis. It wasn't that she disapproved, everyone young seemed to be trying it, but Sylvia's incessant smoking had put her off

341

cigarettes, and cannabis had to be mixed with tobacco. But now, feeling happy after her lovely afternoon and the invigorating long walk home, she was prepared to try, if only to get to know Meg better.

'I'll give it a whirl,' she agreed, sitting down. 'Just don't laugh at me if I cough my lungs up.'

She took a few draws, coughed and handed it back. 'What's it supposed to do?' she asked. 'I don't feel any different.'

'It's a subtle buzz,' Meg said airily, tucking her legs into the Lotus position. She drew heavily on the joint. 'It doesn't hit you like three or four drinks, it just makes you mellow, softens the edges of every-thing. Now come on, tell me what's been going on today.'

Charlie leaned back on a cushion, she didn't know if it was the dope working or the after-effects of love-making, because normally she would run a mile from talking about intimate things. 'Andrew smuggled me up to his room,' she admitted. 'And we made love for the first time. He's coming back here tonight too. So would you hint to Anne that I'd like the bedroom to myself?'

'Right on!' Meg said jubilantly. 'Anything to further the path of true love.' She took several more draws on the joint and handed it back. 'You finish it,' she said with a grin. 'And as we're going to a party I'll roll you up a couple to share with Andrew when he gets here. That's when this stuff really comes into its own, it makes sex magic.'

As Meg rolled up a couple of very professional-looking joints, she talked non-stop about the man she'd slept with the previous night. 'He's got the biggest cock I ever saw,' she exclaimed. 'It was like a barber's pole. I could hardly walk this morning.'

Without drawing breath she went on to describe graphically the sex session she'd had with him including oral sex. Charlie blushed from her hair-line down to her toes; she was deeply shocked, and worse still, she was afraid she was expected to reciprocate with her experiences.

Anne came into the living room. She too was dressed to go out, in the same embroidered long black dress she'd worn on their first night out together, but her hair was still in rollers. She grinned at Charlie. 'Meg's not boring you with all that stuff too?' she said. 'You'd think a girl who had as much sex as her would be bored with talking about it, wouldn't you? Could you come in here a moment, Charlie? I wanted to ask if I could borrow something.'

Charlie excused herself and followed Anne. Once in the bedroom Anne closed the door. 'I didn't really want anything,' she said in a whisper. 'I heard what she was saying to you and I thought you needed rescuing. You see, she used to bang on like that to me when I first moved in here. I wanted to curl up and die sometimes.'

'It was a bit strong.' Charlie was hesitant about saying anything which might make the girls think she was a prude. So far her involvement with Andrew had given her the perfect excuse to remain uninvolved with the other girls' private lives, yet she was aware, too, that this might lead to her being alienated.

'She's a weirdo sometimes,' Anne said with a shrug of her shoulders. Her dark eyes flashed with indignation. 'She gets a kick out of talking dirty. Don't you

343

ever tell her anything about Andrew, if it's something bad she'll embarrass him with it. If it's good she'll be on to him like a rat up a drainpipe. I've lost two nice boyfriends that way.'

It was the first time Anne had said anything sharp about Meg. Charlie had noticed that she wasn't always quite in tune with her, but she'd assumed it was just because she was plainer and less extrovert.

Charlie sat down on her bed, wishing she hadn't asked Meg to speak to Anne about leaving her alone in the bedroom tonight. There was nothing for it but to broach the subject herself and apologize.

Anne laughed when she'd finished. 'You don't need to apologize, I don't mind. I'm not coming home tonight anyway. The party's by my mum's so I'll stay there. Anytime you want a bit of privacy just tip us the wink and I'll be off. Just you be careful with Meg, love, she's a typical Scorpio with a sting in her tail. She's a good laugh, nice as ninepence most of the time, but where men are concerned she's dangerous.'

'What do I do if she starts talking like that again?' Charlie asked nervously. 'I don't want to hear it.'

'I usually make up an excuse and walk away,' Anne said, turning to the mirror and taking out her rollers. 'The trouble is, you are a very different kettle of fish to me. You're very pretty, with an even better figure than Meg's, so she's a bit jealous, but what really bugs her is that she can't get into your head.'

'What do you mean, "She can't get into my head"?'

'That's what she does with everyone, whether it's with her astrology, reading auras or just embarrassing them with awkward questions until she finds their weak spot.'

344

'But why does she want to find that?' Charlie was baffled.

'Because it gives her a feeling of power over you. I'm a much better artist than she is, but I'm plain, so she can bring me down easily with remarks about my appearance. Beth's weak spot is that she's got no tits and terrible legs. You may have noticed she always wears trousers. I can't count the number of times Meg's dropped that into a conversation just because Beth has been getting more attention than her.'

'She must be very insecure herself,' Charlie said.

'She is. Her parents split up when she was eleven and I don't think either of them really wanted to have custody of her. She used to go from one to the other, like a yo-yo. Now they both give her money all the time so she'll stay away. She isn't very talented, all she's got is her sex appeal. She devours men but she can't keep any of them.'

'Do you like living here?' Charlie asked, suddenly realizing there was more to this conversation than a mere passing on of advice.

Anne turned back from the mirror, her long hair in fat curls from the rollers. 'I like it better now you are here,' she said with a smile. 'I was afraid Meg would pick someone for this room who is as impossible as she is. I've stayed this long because it's cheap and handy for college, but I don't like myself much for turning into almost as big a slag as Meg is.'

'You don't have to sleep with men just because she does,' Charlie said softly. She liked Anne and she was flattered that the girl appeared to trust her.

'I know,' Anne sighed deeply. 'But she put me under

345

a lot of pressure when I first moved in. Would you believe I was a virgin then?'

'Were you?' Charlie was surprised.

'I suppose I did it the first time just to appear cool,' Anne admitted. 'I wanted to be like Meg then, I thought she was very sophisticated. To be honest I don't even like sex much. I'd rather curl up with a good book. But you don't get much chance for that here.'

They were interrupted by Beth crashing in, wanting to borrow some hair spray. She was dressed in a skin-tight silver cat suit with flares a yard wide, and silver glitter on her cheeks. As always she looked sensational.

'Come on out with us?' she said to Charlie, dropping her head to the floor and spraying on the lacquer from an upside-down position. 'There's a party up at Muswell Hill, it's going to be wild.'

When she stood up her blonde hair was standing up on end; with the silver suit she looked like an alien from outer space. Charlie felt envious, this girl always seemed to have her finger right on the pulse of London.

'Andrew's coming round later,' she said. 'So I can't.'

'Come with him later,' Beth suggested. 'We'll leave the address. It's going to be a gas.'

'It will be for her, looking like that!' Anne said once Beth had rushed out again.

It was after ten before the three girls left the flat. Charlie tidied up, had a bath, put on the pink dress she'd bought when she met Guy and sat down by the open window in the living room to paint her nails. Hazelmere Road was at the highest point in Hornsey. The big trees in the road below grew to the level of the window-sill, and looking out she got a sense of being in a tree-house. It was dusk now, and she could see all the way across rooftops to Alexander Palace. As she sat there, street lights were switching on, and once it was completely dark it became a magical view, like looking at millions of candles in a distant shrine.

Charlie was glad to be alone. Several times in the past three weeks when she became irritated by the other girls borrowing her things without asking, or not cleaning up after themselves, she'd wondered if she was really cut out for flat-sharing.

Was that because she was basically selfish and liked everything her own way, or was it through being an only child? Yet she liked the idea of sharing with Andrew. They laughed about the same things, they had so much to talk about, everything was fun with him. Would it stay like that if they were together permanently?

She was absolutely certain she was in love with him. Her heart leapt every time she saw him, she thought about him almost every minute of the day. Time with him was always too short, but then she reminded herself she'd once felt that way about Guy too.

'You can't compare Andrew with him,' she told herself. 'You were only sixteen when you met him and you fell in love with the idea of escape. You really know Andrew, he's proved himself.'

Soon after twelve she heard the sound of his scooter coming along the road. Dropping the book she'd been reading, she ran downstairs to answer the door. The house was unusually quiet tonight, the nurses downstairs often had parties on Saturdays, but perhaps they were on duty tonight.

Andrew greeted her with a warm hug. His dark hair was windswept and he smelled deliciously of fresh air. 'I thought this evening would never end,' he said as they went back upstairs together. 'We had a crowd of Hooray Henrys in on a stag night. They poured beer over one another, threw up in the bog, shouted and bawled at one another. I hated every last one of them.'

Charlie laughed. She had watched him behind the bar many times. He managed to stay charming no matter how rude people were to him. It was no wonder Carol, the landlady, thought a lot of him.

'Who had to clear up the bog?'

'Thankfully, not me this time,' Andrew smiled. 'If I'd had to, I might have got one of those chaps and used him as a mop.'

Charlie put her Pink Floyd album on and got him a beer from the fridge. 'Would you like something to eat too?' she asked. 'I could rustle up a bacon sandwich.'

'All I want to eat is you,' he said, stretching out on one of the mattresses. 'How long have we got before the others get back?'

'I expect it will be hours yet,' she grinned. 'Anne's away for the night too. And look what I've got!' She held up the two joints Meg had rolled.

'Funny cigarettes I do declare,' he said. 'Since when did you indulge in such things?' He had often smoked cannabis at parties – his attitude to drugs was a mixture of curiosity and a touch of devilment because it was illegal.

'Only since tonight,' Charlie laughed, and sitting down beside him told him what had gone on between herself and Meg.

'You didn't tell her anything about us, did you?' He didn't really like Meg and he certainly didn't want her knowing anything personal about him.

'Nothing more than admitting we'd made love this afternoon,' she said. 'In view of what Anne said later I wish I hadn't even told her that.'

'She makes me feel uneasy,' he said, looking a bit sheepish. 'A couple of times when you've been out of the room she's asked me very rude questions. I don't like the fact she hasn't got a job either, it makes me wonder where she gets all her money.'

Charlie hadn't ever given this much thought before. Anne was doing temporary clerical work for an agency during the college holidays, Beth worked as a waitress most lunchtimes, but she had no idea how Meg filled her days. 'Anne said both her parents give her money,' she said.

Andrew just shrugged, Charlie wondered if he suspected Meg was up to something, but when she asked him he couldn't be drawn.

Later on Charlie thought Meg had a point about cannabis making sex extra special. They had smoked the two joints while listening to some music, and all at once she found herself totally relaxed, yet all her senses sharpened. Each kiss, each touch felt so slow and sensual, blending with the music. Her body moulded into Andrew's as if they were one person and she was transported away to another sphere where everything seemed liquid and dreamy. Even the living room looked beautiful, the red and pink scarves over the light cast soft shadows on to the ceiling and walls, the big plants creating a jungle effect.

Lost in the rapture of pleasing one another, they forgot that someone could come bursting through the door at any minute. It was only afterwards, trembling with spent passion and cold beneath the open window, that they were reminded other people lived here too.

'You've got the most perfect body,' Andrew said as he stood up and bent over her on the mattress to carry her to bed. 'It's golden all over, like you were sprinkled with gold dust at birth. I love you so much I can hardly bear it.'

He carried her effortlessly as if she weighed no more than a bag of shopping and after tucking her into bed he stood looking down at her for a moment.

'What are you doing?' she asked, holding up her arms to him.

'Trying to engrave you on my mind forever,' he said, bending to kiss her. 'So when you're old, wrinkled and fat, I'll still have this moment in my head.'

'I won't get fat,' she said indignantly. 'Maybe old and wrinkled, but not fat. And don't you get any ideas about growing fat either. I like you just the way you are.'

She thought he looked beautiful naked. Enough muscle in his shoulders and arms to look manly, but his tousled dark hair, the softness of his mouth and the adoring expression in his clear blue eyes were boyish and innocent.

'I want to marry you,' he said, kneeling down beside the bed and leaning his chin on her breast. 'I think I knew the day I met you that we were meant for one another. Now I know for certain.'

'Do you now?' she laughed. 'Well, get into bed and cuddle me.'

The speed he leapt in with made her laugh. 'Can I take that as acceptance?' he asked.

'No. You didn't ask me properly,' she replied snuggling into his shoulder. 'Besides, you've got your degree before we can talk about such serious things.'

'I suppose so,' he sighed. 'But that's not so long, only a year away.'

'A great deal can happen in a year,' she said sleepily. 'You might get bored with me, or meet someone else.'

'Never,' he murmured into her hair. 'I'm the constant type.'

They were awakened from a deep sleep by Meg and Beth crashing into the flat and it sounded as if they had a dozen people with them.

Andrew sat up and looked at his watch. 'God, it's four in the morning! Do they normally make so much noise at night?'

Charlie grunted that it was quite common and pulled him down beside her again. But there was no chance of going back to sleep, someone switched on the stereo and suddenly the whole flat began to vibrate with the sound of David Bowie's 'Ziggy Stardust'.

'Don't the people downstairs complain?' Andrew whispered.

'All the time,' Charlie said. 'Meg just laughs at them and calls them old fogies. But you must have been just as noisy in your flat?'

'Not at this time of the morning,' he said. 'It sounds as if they've got a complete rugby team with them.'

'They probably have,' Charlie sighed. She couldn't hear any female voices aside from Meg and Beth. 'Let's just hope they don't come bursting in here!'

As they lay there, the impromptu party got rowdier. Bellows of male laughter, shrieks from Beth and Meg, clinking of bottles, a shattered glass on the kitchen floor and people stumbling drunkenly into furniture. Charlie was embarrassed more than really angry, she sensed Andrew was thinking that if he hadn't been with her, the other girls might have dragged her out of bed to join in.

Suddenly their door burst open and a big man was illuminated in the doorway. 'Where's the little Chink then?' he shouted. 'Come out, Chinky, wherever you are!'

Andrew leapt out of bed before Charlie could even think what to do. 'Clear off,' he said in a loud, clear voice – he didn't seem worried that he was naked. 'People are trying to sleep in here.'

'Doesn't look like sleeping to me,' the man replied slurring his words drunkenly. 'Bin shagging the Chink, have you?'

Charlie's heart nearly stopped with fright, afraid that Andrew would punch the man and then the others would set about him. Quickly pulling her nightdress from beneath the pillow she slipped it over her head. But before she could get out of bed, Andrew was already poking the man in the chest and threatening him.

'Come another step inside this door and I'll knock you out,' he said.

Charlie leapt out of bed and pushed herself between Andrew and the man. Andrew might have a commanding manner, she'd seen it when he showed drunks the door at the pub, but he was no match for this gorilla.

'Meg!' she yelled at the top of her voice. 'Get this friend of yours out of here immediately.'

There were five men altogether, including the one in her doorway, all big burly types in their late twenties with close-cropped hair. A couple of them she recognized from her night in The Fox. They were the type Meg referred to as 'the Suits' and therefore far more dangerous than a group of hippie art students.

It was a horrible, terrifying moment. Andrew was trying to push past her, the man in front of her was staring at her lecherously. The rest of the group had got to their feet, their tough-looking faces menacing.

Meg appeared, quickly followed by Beth. 'Oh, don't be such a party pooper,' she said, smirking at Andrew's nakedness. 'Get your clothes on and come and join us.'

'We don't want to,' Charlie said angrily. 'Please make them go, Meg.'

The record came to an end, and as if prompted by the sudden silence Andrew forced his way past her. 'Out, all of you,' he said in the same firm voice he used in the pub. He'd put his jeans on, but his chest was still bare. He'd obviously sized up the problem and decided to try to tackle it without force. 'You've all had a lot to drink and I don't want it to turn nasty with three women around.' He glared at Meg and Beth. 'And if you two have got any sense you'll encourage them to go quietly before your flat gets ruined.'

The man who'd burst into the room backed off. He was very drunk, hardly able to stand, but his place was taken by one of the biggest men in the group, who looked distinctly threatening. 'You reckon you could throw us out?' he said derisively. 'You cunt, I could knock you over with one hand tied behind my back.'

Charlie held her breath, rooted to the spot with fear. She sensed men of their kind would think nothing of beating Andrew to a pulp, just for sport.

But to her surprise Andrew kept a steady gaze, showing absolutely no fear. 'I don't advise you to try. You see, I have a Black Belt in karate.'

Charlie gulped. She was certain he'd have told her if he really was a karate expert. But if he was bluffing, he was very convincing.

There was a palpable and dangerous current flowing between the big man and Andrew. In the utter silence Charlie could almost hear the bigger man's thoughts as he sized up his opponent. It would only take one of the others to step forward and all hell would break loose.

It was Beth who broke the deadlock. She pushed in between the two men, shoving the bigger one in the chest. 'That's it, go!' she yelled. 'I'm not getting my place smashed up. Go now or I'll ring the Old Bill.'

The men moved away slowly and reluctantly, watching Andrew for any sign of weakness, as if ready to come back and hammer him. But finally they were all out the door, the last one slamming it behind him, and they heard their feet clonking down the stairs.

Meg spoke first, turning to Andrew. 'Well, aren't

you the big man!' she said sarcastically. 'What right have you got to order people out of my flat?'

'Those men were animals,' he said quietly, crossing over to the window to check the men really had gone. 'If that's the sort you want to consort with, fine. But they came into Charlie's room, looking for her. If I hadn't been there, heaven only knows what might have happened.'

Beth looked crestfallen. 'Andrew's right.' She tugged at Meg's arm. 'They were all well out of line. It's a very good job he was here.'

Andrew drew Charlie back into the bedroom and closed the door. She got back into bed and waited for him to join her. 'Are you really a Black Belt?' she asked in a small voice. She was trembling with shock now it was all over.

'No, of course not,' he admitted, his voice a little quavery. 'I had a few lessons, that's all. But I reckon I must have the right mental attitude, sometimes I even believe I could smash a couple of bricks with one blow when I psyche myself up.'

'But what if they'd laid into you?'

'I'd be a bit of a mess now,' he grinned. 'What worries me more is that stupid Meg. What was she thinking of bringing a mob like that in here?'

Charlie didn't answer. She had seen the wolfish looks on those men's faces and even if she was relatively innocent still, she knew they hadn't come here for just another drink. She thought Andrew was the bravest man in the world.

After that Saturday night, Meg apologized. She said she was so drunk she hadn't thought where the

355

evening might end. Beth confided in Charlie that she'd laid down a few ground-rules herself the next day because those men were looking for a 'gang-bang', and if Andrew hadn't intervened, she might have been forced into it too.

Shocking as Charlie found this, as Meg seemed far more cautious who she brought into the flat after that, and Charlie was so happy in herself, she put the incident aside. With support from Anne, she often instigated mid-week all-girl nights out on warm summer evenings. Sometimes it was a swim in the open-air pool in nearby Crouch End, other times a Highgate pub with a garden, followed by fish and chips on the way home. Some Saturday mornings Beth and Meg took Charlie along with them to Portobello Road Market to pick through the antique clothes, and they never minded when she rushed off at two to meet Andrew.

She got into the habit of cooking a roast dinner for all of them on Sundays when Andrew worked. He would join them when he'd finished, always bringing a couple of bottles of cheap wine, and if he and Charlie disappeared into the bedroom later, the girls just laughed and teased them about being in love.

It was love too, growing deeper and stronger as the weeks went past. There never seemed enough time to spend together, often Andrew would collect her from work just so they could squeeze in an extra couple of hours. Charlie found she could hardly remember what it was like to be lonely, or isolated.

Even work at Haagman's was fun. All the staff had become friends, but Rita was the most important. She formed a very special relationship with this older woman – friend, but mother figure too. She could talk about anything and everything to her – the girls in the flat, her hopes for the future with Andrew, and her past. Rita was unique in that she was far more interested in others than herself, and she drew out confidences. Even though she was so much older and more worldly than Charlie, she wasn't judgemental. In fact when Charlie finally did tell her the full story about her parents she felt her friend related to it on every level, particularly Sylvia's suicide. They often went for a pizza or a hamburger after work, and it was then that Charlie discovered by chance that Rita had some knowledge of Soho nightlife. Disappointingly she didn't seem to want to discuss it in any depth, but maybe this was just because she was so much older and didn't want to encourage her younger friend's interest in such a seedy place.

They had celebrated Charlie's A-level results in a Chinese restaurant in China Town. To her delight she had 'A's in both English and geography, 'B+' in maths and science. Rita said that night that she must stop drifting now and think seriously about a career. Charlie had just laughed and called Rita a 'mother hen'. She knew in her heart that her friend was right, but her mind didn't seem to function beyond Andrew, or the holiday they'd planned in Salcombe for September.

It was the thought of that holiday which kept her smiling as she pushed her way into the packed rush-hour tubes during August. When the temperature at Haagman's rose to the nineties and sweat poured off her, she imagined paddling together at Slapton Sands, walking along the cliff top with Minnie, or taking the

357

helm of the *MaryAnn* as Ivor and Andrew fished for mackerel.

Andrew was going to leave Jack Straw's Castle then, leave his belongings at her flat, then, after the holiday, sort out getting a house to share with her and his friends for when his new term started in early October. A career could wait. Her love affair with Andrew was the most important thing in her life.

Chapter Twelve

The bus from Kingsbridge on the Friday afternoon was packed solid with holidaymakers for the August Bank Holiday weekend, and swelteringly hot, but as it pulled into the stop at Salcombe and Charlie saw Ivor waiting there to meet her, with Minnie lying at his feet, the weariness she'd felt on the long journey down from London left her.

She was alone. Andrew couldn't get any time off from the pub as it was their busiest weekend of the year, but the sadness she'd felt at going away without him was tempered by the knowledge he had only two more weeks before he left his job there for good and they would be down for their real holiday together.

'It's so good to see you,' Charlie shrieked as she hurtled off the bus and into Ivor's outstretched arms. 'I never knew a train take so long. I had my head out the window for the last few miles, taking in lungfuls of the lovely clean air. You can't imagine how excited I am.'

Ivor looked exactly the way he had the very first time she saw him. The same baggy shorts and faded shirt, plimsolls on his feet, hair and beard as fiery and untidy as ever.

'I can see,' he laughed, detaching himself from her so he could look at her beaming, flushed face. 'You look like Minnie!'

Charlie looked down at his dog. She had moved to a sitting position, panting furiously, ears pricked, paws twitching and her tail thumping on the pavement. 'Come on then, Minnie,' she said, crouching down beside her. 'Give Charlie a welcome home kiss!'

Minnie needed no further urging. She threw herself at Charlie, nearly knocking her over, and gave her face a rapturous licking.

Ivor was waylaid by a customer at his shack, so Charlie went into the cottage alone. To her delight absolutely nothing had changed. Ivor's chair was in place by the fire, the turquoise and green patchwork cushion she'd made in London and sent to him sitting on it. The old chiming clock, the ship in a bottle and the pipe rack still stood on the mantelpiece, along with odd fish-hooks, a skewer and a tin of shoe polish. Her chair was waiting too, the faded cushion plumped up as if no one had sat on it since she was last here.

Ivor had clearly gone to some trouble to make his home welcoming. The red and white checked tablecloth was spotlessly clean, a few wild flowers had been placed in a jam jar in her honour. The quarry-tiled floor had not only been swept and washed, but polished with Cardinal.

She took her bag upstairs to the small back room. Back when Joseph Fear was alive, this room had been his, but it had lain empty since his death. Ivor had repainted it white at the time Charlie was packing up the flat in Dartmouth, and insisted she brought her old bed, desk and other bits and pieces she might need later. At the time she had been dubious about this, believing she didn't want any reminders of the past, but now, seeing all her old things again in a new setting, so fresh and pretty, she felt very glad Ivor had been so long-sighted.

Downstairs in the kitchen, she opened the cupboard to get out the mugs, and laughed to see a new one saying 'First Mate'. She had bought Ivor a 'Captain' mug as a keepsake when she went to London, and she wondered how many shops he'd had to search through before he found the right one for her.

When Ivor didn't come back, she took their tea through to the shack. The customer he had been serving was just leaving.

'This is like old times,' Charlie said as they sat down outside together. 'And bless you for the mug, it was a lovely surprise.'

'I've missed you so much,' he said, his eyes looking a bit misty. 'No reason to go to Dartmouth, no one to share my catches of mackerel with. I had a young lad helping me until last week, but he was worse than useless, and I suspect he was taking money too. But however much I miss you, I'm glad you're happy in London.'

Charlie looked out across the harbour and her whole body seemed to swell with joy. The sea was even bluer than she had pictured it in her mind, the salty seaweed smell stronger now because she'd grown accustomed to London smells. There were more boats now too, many very smart ones. Two whole years had passed since she went off with Guy in the *Chlöe*; in many ways it seemed such a short while ago, yet in others, almost a lifetime.

'Come on, tell me everything,' Ivor said impatiently, 'particularly about the romance with Andrew.'

She caught hold of Ivor's big rough hand and smoothed it between her two small ones. She wanted to make him see how happy she was.

'That's the best thing that ever happened to me. I love Andrew so much, Ivor. I can't wait for him to go back to university in October so we can spend more time together. But then you must know how it is. I'm sure you were the same with Sarah.'

She couldn't possibly tell him about the joyful, tender and passionate love-making, snatched whenever an opportunity arose, or even explain that it was just *being* with Andrew that thrilled her. He filled a place in her heart and mind that until he came along had been so barren. No other friend had ever made her laugh so much, she had never felt so secure, inspired and so utterly happy with anyone. He made her feel beautiful, inside and out. The sad past was over, and the future looked golden.

Ivor looked at her glowing eyes, felt all the joy radiating from her and knew exactly how it was for her. 'I was just like you when I met Sarah. Walking on air, smiling at the whole world,' he said, patting her flushed cheek. 'That's why I was surprised when Beryl said you'd telephoned to say you were coming this weekend without him. I didn't think you'd be able to drag yourself away from him.'

'I suppose I should have just waited for our holiday next month,' she said. 'But it's so hot and kind of airless in London, Ivor, and Andrew will be working almost constantly because there's a big fair up on Hampstead Heath. I would only have been hanging around on my own.'

This was the main reason, but there was another too which she didn't wish to divulge. Meg.

Although Meg had calmed down for a few weeks after that middle-of-the-night incident with the five men, she was slipping back into her old ways again. It was wearing coming home from work and finding strange, half-naked men lying around in the flat. Charlie was sick and tired of clearing up the mess the girl and her friends made, and tired too of being woken in the night by loud music and frantic love-making.

But over and above that Charlie was anxious about a drugs bust. This hadn't occurred to her when she thought Meg was only bringing in cannabis to smoke herself, but a couple of weeks ago Charlie had discovered she was in fact a dealer. She bought a weight of cannabis, weighed it out into half-ounce portions and then sold it on to people who called during the day and evening.

If the police raided the flat, Charlie knew she might well find herself in trouble too. She had tried to talk to Meg about it, but it did no good. The girl had a good little business going, she certainly wasn't going to get a job like the rest of them. On top of this Charlie had also found out that Meg charged the rest of them enough rent so she didn't have to pay anything herself, and she shoplifted almost all her food and clothes.

There were times when the girl's personality reminded Charlie of her own mother's. Meg had extreme mood swings, changing from being a very likeable, amusing and stimulating companion to a foul-mouthed depressive. At these times she was best avoided, as it was impossible to jolly her out of it, and she usually came out with her most biting insults at these times.

But the most remarkable similarity was the way Meg played up to men. She switched on her flirting mode with any male, regardless of age, appearance and social standing. She touched their hands, stroked their hair, fluttered her eyelashes at them and boosted their egos. No one was safe from this. She played up to Beth and Anne's boyfriends, and Andrew. She would blatantly expose her body to them, she told embarrassing intimate stories about her sex life, and sometimes, though she always claimed it was a joke, suggested swapping partners. It had been the thought of being stuck with Meg for the whole long weekend which had decided Charlie on coming down here alone.

'Is everything all right with your flatmates?' Ivor asked.

'Mostly,' Charlie said. 'Meg's a bit annoying, and I get fed up with cleaning up after them sometimes. But I don't suppose anyone could expect to share a flat with three girls and find everything perfect.'

'And work, what's that like?' he asked.

'Great,' Charlie grinned. 'Once the Hag goes out, it's a riot. I've made some really good friends there. On Friday evenings we all go to the pub after work.'

'Won't it be different when all the students leave?' he asked.

Charlie knew he thought she should get a better job, with real prospects. When she'd telephoned him to let him know her exam results he'd asked if she was going to apply to any universities. Her answer had been that it was too late to apply for the coming year, and besides, she'd needed time to think about exactly what direction she wanted to go in. All this was true, but not quite the whole story; right now she just wanted some fun.

'Yes, it will be awful. Only Martin and Rita will be left. But I doubt I'll stay on anyway. I'll look around for a better job in banking or something, and then decide whether to apply to go to university next year.'

He smiled, he looked as if he knew the way her mind was working. 'Just make sure you don't distract Andrew in his final year, he'll need to keep his nose in his books.'

The weekend went past in a flash. On Saturday Charlie went off to Slapton Sands on her own, to sunbathe and read. On Sunday she had spent all day out on the *MaryAnn* with Ivor, and all three evenings had been spent in the Victoria Inn. She had turned as brown as a berry again, she felt invigorated by the rest and good food.

But now it was Monday and Charlie had to go home. She couldn't even hang on and get the last train to London, because that would be so packed with holidaymakers it would be hell. She telephoned Andrew at the pub and said she would be back by about seven. He said he would ask if he could have the night off, but he didn't hold out much hope. Charlie said she would phone him again when she got in.

The train journey was quite pleasant. Charlie read a little, snoozed for a while, then walked down to the buffet and bought herself a drink and some sandwiches. The train was right on time until it reached the outskirts of London, then it stopped. Twenty minutes passed before the guard came along saying there'd been a signals failure up ahead. Another half-hour passed and he came back to apologize again. Charlie tried to snooze and hoped Andrew hadn't managed to get the night off. At this rate she wouldn't be home until eight or nine.

Eventually the train started up again, but it chugged along slowly, coming almost to a halt many times. When she finally got to Paddington, it was half past eight and the whole station was so crammed with people waiting for delayed trains that she didn't even attempt to phone home, or the pub to speak to Andrew. She just wanted to get back to the flat.

She had to wait ages at Finsbury Park tube station for the Hornsey bus, and by the time she got to the front door it was nine-thirty and she felt completely drained, hot and sticky.

As she opened the door to the flat, she stopped in embarrassment. Meg was crouched over a man lying on one of the mattresses, wearing only a pair of black lace knickers, her hair hiding the man's face. The Eagles' 'Desperado' was blasting out on the stereo and the whole room stank of cannabis.

'Sorry,' Charlie said involuntarily. 'I'll –' The rest of the sentence about going to her room was cut off abruptly as Meg moved, for to Charlie's horror, the man she was making love to was Andrew.

For just one second Charlie remained rooted to the spot in shock. But as Andrew pushed Meg to one side, his eyes wide with fright and astonishment at her sudden entrance, she dropped her bag and moved.

'You bitch,' she screamed, running towards them, intending to claw the girl's eyes out. But she forgot the low table, banged her shins into it and fell sideways.

Andrew leapt to his feet. He was dressed, but he had several shirt buttons undone and red lipstick all around his mouth. 'It isn't like you think,' he said frantically. 'We had a few smokes while I was waiting for you, then she came in like that.'

Charlie got up and charged at Meg again. She was still on the mattress, half sitting, half lying in the same position she had landed in when Andrew pushed her away from him. She made no attempt to cover her bare breasts, or even move.

Charlie reached down, grabbed her by the hair with her left hand, and with her right smashed her fist into the girl's face. 'You scheming, rotten bitch!' she roared. 'You've had every other man in north London, why did you have to have him too?'

If Andrew hadn't caught hold of Charlie's right arm and pulled her back, she would have kept on punching until the girl's face was a pulp. Still holding Meg's hair tightly, Charlie tried to shrug him off, but Andrew was too strong. 'Enough, Charlie!' he yelled. 'Let her go.'

Charlie could do nothing more than yank on Meg's hair. As she forcibly pulled back, a great clump of it came away in Charlie's hand. But in her anger at not being allowed to hurt Meg further, she turned to Andrew and lashed out at him. 'Get out of here, you bastard,' she screamed at him. 'You said you loved me, how could you go with her?'

'I didn't, I wouldn't have,' he shouted back, pulling her further away from Meg. 'I was stoned and just lying there. On my mother's life I wouldn't have made love to her.'

'No one makes love to her. They screw her or fuck her, that's all she's good for!' Charlie screamed. 'Don't tell me you wouldn't have done it if I hadn't come in. Of course you would.'

'Don't you fucking well speak about me like that,' Meg shouted. While Andrew held Charlie she had managed to get up and make her escape towards her bedroom door. 'If you must know he's been sniffing around me for weeks. I only did it to put him out of his misery.'

'That's a bloody lie,' Andrew burst out, his face very flushed. 'Admit it, Meg. Or I'll smash your face in too.'

Charlie looked from one to the other in distress, not knowing which one to believe. Meg had blood running from her nose, her black curly hair was tousled, cascading over her naked breasts. She knew this girl was man-mad, but Charlie didn't think she was a liar. Andrew couldn't deny that was lipstick on his mouth. Why hadn't he got up and left the moment Meg appeared without her clothes?

'Get out of here, you bastard,' Charlie hissed at him, brushing off his hand on her arm. 'Go on, go, right now. And don't ever come back. I never want to see you again.'

'Tell her the truth,' he implored Meg. 'You got me stoned then leapt on me.'

Charlie looked again at Meg. She had her hands insolently on her hips, even now she wasn't attempting to cover herself. 'Fuck off, you jerk,' she said contemptuously. 'You were dying for it.'

'Get out now,' Charlie said, pushing Andrew towards the door. She was trembling and she felt nauseous. She knew any minute she was going to bring up the sandwiches and fizzy drinks she'd had on the train. 'You and I are finished.'

'No, Charlie,' he begged, his eyes wide with shock and dismay. 'Please come with me somewhere else and we'll talk. You can't stay in this flat with that witch.'

'Better a witch than a snake,' she snapped. 'Now go.'

He turned and left. The door slammed just as the record ended and it seemed to reverberate throughout the house.

Charlie turned menacingly towards Meg. 'You disgust me,' she said. 'No, disgust doesn't cover what I feel. You make me sick.'

She felt the vomit rise up into her throat, and she took one step towards the door and the bathroom outside on the landing. But she stopped as she suddenly thought of a way to get back at Meg.

Pushing the girl back against the wall as she passed her, she went straight into Meg's bedroom. Her bed, as always, was unmade, clothes strewn amongst the grubby, crumpled sheets.

She sensed Meg had followed her in, perhaps imagining she was going to destroy a few things, and that knowledge helped Charlie to control her nausea just that little bit longer. Stopping at the bed, she let it go, and vomited all over it. As if from a great distance she heard Meg gasp.

'There,' Charlie said in triumph, although she felt so weak all she wanted to do was slump down and cry. 'A fitting place for you to rest your diseased cunt.'

'You filthy cow,' Meg shrieked. She was really frightened. She had never seen Charlie lose her temper before, and she hadn't imagined she could be so violent.

Charlie surveyed the bed and the putrid mess she'd covered it in with some pride. 'Nowhere near as filthy as you,' she said. Then, tottering, she made towards the door where Meg was transfixed with horror.

'You can clean it up,' she yelled in a high-pitched shriek, trying to grab Charlie as she passed. But Charlie struck out with her fist again, and knocked her backwards against the door post.

'I'm going to call the police. I'll get them to throw you out on the street,' Meg screamed, but she backed into her room.

'Phone them if you want. But I'm going anyway,' Charlie said. 'I wouldn't stay under the same roof as you even if my life depended on it.' She turned and looked back at Meg. She was clutching on to a chair, as if she intended to use it to ward off any further blows. 'You know what you are, Meg?' she said with all the contempt she could muster. 'You're a slag! The Hornsey bike that everyone gets a free ride on. Why don't you go on the game? You could make a fortune.'

Back in her own bedroom, Charlie put a chair under the door handle, then began flinging her clothes into her two cases. She filled them to capacity, then shoved the remainder into her pillow-cases. She was scared now, the flat was silent and she had no idea if Meg was planning a counter-attack. She had to get out quickly.

It was a tense moment as she unlocked the door

and struggled out with a suitcase in each hand and the pillow-cases under her arms. But Meg wasn't out in the living room waiting for her. Charlie reached the outside door before the girl appeared again, now dressed.

'You owe me money for bills,' she yelled.

'You've got my deposit and this week's rent,' Charlie shouted back. 'Go and steal something if you haven't got enough, that's what you usually do, isn't it?'

Charlie was down the stairs and just about to open the front door when Meg's voice rang out again from the top of the house. 'I've had him already,' she called out. 'I had him Friday night, Saturday afternoon, and when he'd finished work he came back again for the whole night. He's got a nice big prick, hasn't he?'

Charlie didn't know how she managed to get to the phone box on Crouch Hill. Aside from the problem of trying to carry so much heavy stuff, she was blinded by tears and quivering with shock. She could only walk a few steps at a time before resting, then picked the cases up again. But she finally managed it and telephoned Rita.

The phone rang and rang, and Charlie was just about to give up in despair, when Rita answered it.

'Of course you can come here,' she said, without any hesitation even though Charlie wasn't able to explain properly through her tears. 'Now, just stay in the phone box and ring for a taxi. The address is 44 Church Road, Paddington. My flat is above a sweet shop.'

Two hours later Charlie found herself being tucked

into a narrow single bed by Rita. She was too exhausted from crying, too weary and distressed to ask any questions, but she sensed she was in a child's room. Rita had been so kind. She'd listened, let her cry, then run her a bath and given her some hot milk and a sleeping pill. By the time Charlie got out of the bath, Rita had hung up all her dresses, put the rest of her clothes in drawers, even the picture of her parents was beside the small bed.

'Sleep tight, lovey,' Rita said, bending to kiss her cheek. 'I know your heart feels as if it's been shattered, but it will mend in time. Tomorrow evening after work we'll talk everything through again and plan what you're going to do. But go to sleep now.'

'I thought he loved me. Why did he do it?' Charlie asked. She was groggy now, but the question was nagging at her.

'Because men think with their dicks more often than with their heads,' Rita replied. 'And that's why I don't bother with them any more.'

Rita sat deep in thought for some time after she'd put Charlie to bed. She knew why Meg had done what she did, because she'd been exactly like Meg herself when she was younger. Maybe it was because they were oversexed, or suffered from some deep-seated insecurity, probably a mixture of both. Rita remembered only too well what a thrill it was to steal another girl's man. Available ones were no challenge.

Yet she was puzzled by Andrew. Although she'd never met him, from things Charlie had told her, she felt she knew him. Why would a sensitive, intelligent man like him take the risk of losing a bright, lovely

372

girl like Charlie, to dabble with a grubby hippie art student? It wasn't as if Charlie had come back unexpectedly. He knew she might walk through the door at any minute!

But Charlie's distress about tonight's events wasn't all that was on Rita's mind. Charlie was young and resilient, in a few weeks' time she would be over the worst of it. But Rita knew from her own experience that when one door closes on a person's life, they usually look for another to open. Charlie had barely mentioned her desire to solve the mystery of her father's disappearance in the past few months, her mind had been purely on Andrew. But now, without Andrew around, she might very well turn back to it.

Right from Charlie's first day at Haagman's when she'd spoken of her father, Rita had an odd sensation of involvement. It was entirely irrational; she might know a great deal about Soho and its clubs, but she didn't know any Chinese men and she'd never heard of anyone called Jin Weish. But since the day Charlie had mentioned that her father's mistress was called DeeDee, she hadn't been able to get it out of her mind. The name reminded her of someone she would rather forget.

Common sense told her DeeDee was most likely a derivative of Diane or Diana, and she'd probably adopted it because strippers went in for cute stage names. The woman she knew, and had good reason to hate, had been called Daphne Dexter, and to Rita's knowledge she had never been known by her initials 'D. D.' But still the thought persisted in her mind and as the similarities mounted up, so the conviction that they were one and the same person had grown.

Rita had worked out that they must be around the same age. Daphne, before she owned a string of clubs, was rumoured to have been a stripper. DeeDee was reported to have come from the East End of London with two brothers. Daphne had hid her roots very well, but she had a faint East London twang to her voice, and Rita suspected the two men who had helped ruin her life might well have been her brothers.

Rita got out of her chair to go into the kitchen. Thinking about the Dexters would only bring nightmares on again.

'It was lucky you kept this flat on,' she said to herself as she washed up some cups and plates. 'You'd have been up shit creek without it.'

Back in 1961 when she found this unfurnished two-bedroom flat, Church Road and the surrounding area had been virtually a slum, with prostitutes, poor Irish and West Indian immigrants crammed into the many dilapidated houses. Time and again Rita had been tempted by more expensive flats in smarter areas, but because it was cheap and she'd spent so much money on making it nice, she always flunked out at the last moment. Now the dreadful old properties, many of them owned by the notorious Peter Rachman, had been renovated and their former tenants moved on elsewhere. Church Road was a decent address again, full of antique shops and smart boutiques, and she wouldn't move if anyone paid her to.

Looking critically back into her living room, she was pleased with what she saw. Going to so many wealthy people's homes in her youth had given her some taste, if nothing else. The green striped wallpaper looked classy, the plain green Wilton was as good now as it was when she had it fitted back in '62. No one coming in here now and looking at the lovely water-colours in their gilt frames, the elegant lamps and velvet curtains would ever imagine she'd been anything other than totally respectable.

A chill went down her spine, just as it had that day Charlie spoke of DeeDee and her father's club. Soho for all its international fame was just like a village, people who got sucked into it all knew one another, if not personally, by repute. The period they had been there made little difference, lives overlapped, and some people were so prominent they quickly became legends. Daphne Dexter was one of those.

'If only you'd heeded her warning,' she whispered. 'He wasn't worth a light as it turned out, and you might have known he wouldn't marry a club girl anyway.'

She opened the door to the spare bedroom and looked at Charlie asleep in the small bed and her heart contracted painfully. She was such a lovely girl, both in looks and manner. The light from the open door shone on to her coal-black hair and golden cheeks. She was at rest now thanks to the pill Rita had given her, but tomorrow morning she'd wake to face it all again.

Turning back to her chair, Rita sighed deeply. If she could have just one wish right now, it would be to save Charlie any more pain. Surely she'd already had more than her fair share? But life wasn't fair, as Rita knew only too well. And by getting involved with this kid, it might very well mean she would come face to face with her own past again too.

Closing her eyes, Rita let herself drift back to that

warm summer night in 1964 when she first met Daphne. She hoped she might remember something which would convince her that her suspicions were ungrounded.

Rita had called herself Suzie then; she was twenty-five, cheeky, fearless and a real little sex-bomb with her big breasts and flowing red hair. She and some of the other girls who worked with her at the Astor Club in Mayfair were invited by Stephen Brooks, a Harley Street surgeon, to his country house weekend party in Sussex.

It was the most beautiful old house Rita had ever been to, half timbered, polished wooden floors, mullion windows and furnished with antiques. But what she remembered most of all was the garden. It was huge, the kind you could almost lose yourself in as you wandered through the formal rose gardens, across lush smooth lawns to the shrubbery and the woods beyond.

The drawing room had French windows opening on to a terrace, from where steps led down to an ornamental pool and fountain. She remembered standing on that terrace around eight in the evening, a warm breeze fluttering her chiffon dress, the perfume of roses filling her nostrils, and wishing she could stay in such a place for ever.

Behind her the party was already in full swing. Many of the male guests were American doctors, here in England for a medical conference, and as usual when married men were on the loose, without their wives, and found an abundance of young pretty women more than ready to entertain them, they were in high spirits.

Rita had taken great care with her appearance that night. She knew she wasn't a real beauty compared with some of the other girls, without makeup she was pale, and her features insignificant. But she was pretty enough, she had a fabulous body, lovely hair, and her provocative style made sure she was never overlooked. She was wearing a short pale green floaty chiffon dress with a neckline which exposed both her back and her ample cleavage. She'd had her hair set that morning in curls on the top of her head, and a few ringlets left loose around the nape of her neck. She knew that by anyone's reckoning she looked sensational.

At that period in her life Rita had several wealthy lovers on a string. Granted, they were married men, but two at least of them would gladly have set her up in a little flat somewhere on the understanding she was theirs exclusively. But being a mere mistress wasn't her goal, she had her heart set on an extremely rich husband, a grand house and servants.

She had been to many similar parties, where the girls were paid a small fee to look pretty and make the party go with a swing. There was no obligation to have sex with any of the guests, though it often did occur, but daring acts, like swimming in the pool naked, or an impromptu strip-tease, were appreciated as it lifted the host's standing among his friends.

Around ten that same evening Rita was dancing with one of the American doctors in the drawing room, when she became aware she was being watched closely by a man standing out on the terrace. She was trying to show her partner how to do 'the Shake'. She was an expert at this latest dance, undulating her hips like a belly-dancer and making her breasts swing from side to side. But the doctor was hopeless, waving his arms and hips without any co-ordination.

Rita knew the man watching her wasn't one of the American doctors as she'd been introduced to all of them earlier. So she surmised he'd arrived quite recently and that he had a partner somewhere, because Stephen Brooks always made a point of bringing the available men to the girls' notice.

Rita wasn't often impressed by the men she met at this sort of party – usually they were overweight, balding and not very attractive. But this man was some six feet tall, slim, with rugged features and thick white, beautifully groomed hair. She thought he might be as old as sixty, but in his case, age was no barrier. He wore his dinner jacket with the kind of nonchalant style that showed events such as this were commonplace in his life. She made up her mind then and there that she was going to have him.

When the record finished she made the excuse to her partner that she wanted some fresh air, left him and went out on to the terrace. It was growing dark now, but there were lights in the fountain and still more in the trees.

'Isn't it a wonderful night?' she said breathlessly, and moving away from the French windows, she went over to the stone balustrade and she leaned over it as though admiring the garden below. 'Can you smell the roses?'

'I can indeed,' the man replied in a deep, resonant voice. 'It's a smell which always takes me back to my childhood. I used to gather up rose petals with my mother. She used to make pot pourri with them.'

Rita had no idea what pot pourri was, but just the way he said the word sent tingles down her spine. He reminded her a little of James Stewart, even if he did have white hair and a terribly upper-crust English accent.

'It's such a beautiful garden,' she said, turning to look at him. 'How about coming with me to explore it?'

'My dear, that would be a pleasure,' he said with a languid but very attractive smile. 'I'm afraid I'm not much of a party person. I don't like to stand around in smoky rooms making small-talk to people I have nothing in common with. Strolling around a garden in the moonlight is much more to my liking.'

They were gone for almost an hour. She discovered his name was Ralph Peterson and that he'd been widowed two years earlier. She didn't have to pump him for information to discover if he was rich; wealth seeped out of his very pores like a heady perfume.

Rita was very accomplished at pretending to be interested in everything men said to her – she'd learned to be in five years of working as a hostess in night-clubs – but for once she had found one who really was fascinating. He told her that his passion as a young man had been climbing, and as he spoke of mountains and faraway places he made her see them too.

'I haven't ever been outside England,' she said wistfully. 'In fact all I know is London.'

'Well, perhaps I could take you to Paris as a starting point?' he said. 'I have to go there on business next week. I've been dreading going, it was my wife's favourite city. But maybe with someone young like you I could see it all again through new eyes.'

Rita was astounded. As all her lovers were married men, even having dinner with them in public was difficult. She could hardly believe her luck, and she hadn't even tried any of her seduction tricks yet. 'I'd love that,' she said.

'Then we'll go,' he said, kissing her on the cheek. 'I'm afraid I'm actually with a lady tonight otherwise I'd be tempted to try and whisk you away somewhere right now. May I have your telephone number? I could ring you tomorrow evening to make some arrangements.'

He wrote it down in a diary, then they made their way slowly back to the house.

'Oh dear,' he said as they approached the stairs back to the terrace. A statuesque dark-haired woman in a long white dress was standing at the top, looking down at them. 'She looks cross.'

Rita wasn't often thrown by another woman, but she was by this one. Although she was old by her standards, perhaps in her mid-thirties, she was a stunning, classical beauty, rather like Elizabeth Taylor with glowing olive skin, vivid blue eyes and her dark hair in a sleek chignon. Her gorgeous white gown, diamond necklace and drop earrings all smacked of someone who came out of the top drawer.

'Where on earth have you been, Ralph?' she called out, giving Rita a cold, suspicious stare. 'I've been looking everywhere for you.'

'I'm sorry, my dear, we've been looking at the garden.' He looked at Rita, then back at the other woman. 'Do you two know one another at all?'

'No,' Rita said, and quickly held out her hand. 'I'm Suzie, a friend of Stephen's.'

'Daphne Dexter,' the woman said curtly, ignoring Rita's hand. 'Come along, Ralph. You wanted to meet Frank Southerby, and he's waiting for you in the library.'

It was around an hour later when Rita was upstairs in one of the bedrooms powdering her nose that Daphne spoke to her again. Rita guessed the meeting wasn't a chance one – the woman glanced in and when she saw Rita was alone she came right in, shutting the door behind her.

'Hullo,' Rita said. She was quite tiddly after innumerable glasses of champagne and prepared to be nice to anyone. 'It's a good party, isn't it?'

'I don't much care for this kind of party,' the woman said, looking pointedly at Rita's cleavage. 'There's always too many common little club girls on the hunt.'

Rita laughed. When another woman felt compelled to say such a thing, it meant they felt threatened. Clearly she wasn't entirely sure of her man. But another thing pleased Rita still more – she could hear a very faint twang of the East End in the woman's accent. As she came from a little village in Essex herself, that made them equals 'Yes, there's a lot of us about,' Rita said. 'Young ones, old ones and some plain cranky. Country house parties aren't what they used to be.'

Daphne's eyes narrowed. She took a step nearer Rita as if wanting to slap her. 'Don't even think of trying to hunt on my territory,' she hissed. 'Or you'll be very sorry.' And with that she walked away.

Chapter Thirteen

As Rita came out of Haagman's at half past five on Friday evening, a tall, dark-haired young man was waiting at the bottom of the steps. He looked quizzically at her, and when he moved to speak to her, she guessed who it was. Andrew had telephoned the laboratory several times in the past two weeks, asking for Charlie. Yesterday Martin had lied and told him she had given up her job so that he wouldn't call again. But clearly he didn't intend to give up that easily.

'Excuse me,' he said, 'would you be Rita?'

'Yes, I am,' she admitted. Charlie had almost certainly described her to him at some time, so it was rather pointless denying it. 'And who would you be?'

'Andrew Blake, Charlie's old boyfriend,' he said. 'I'm sorry to waylay you like this, but I didn't know what else to do. I'm so worried about her, and as I know you were friends I thought you might be able to tell me where she's living.'

Rita had no intention of telling the lad anything. Charlie was adamant that she didn't want to see or speak to him ever again. Rita had supported this decision, but now as she looked at him, her heart softened a little. She had expected an arrogant, plummy-voiced chap, but this lad was polite, softly spoken, and he looked so young and anxious. He had dark shadows beneath his lovely blue eyes, yet he was clean-shaven, his hair was neatly brushed, even his jeans and short-sleeved shirt were spotless. For someone to make such an effort with their appearance when they were clearly utterly miserable was evidence to her that he was a decent sort.

'I'm sorry, but she left while I was off work,' she said, lying through her teeth. Charlie was working overtime till ten tonight, and she was still staying with Rita. 'She didn't leave an address or telephone number. But she's got mine, so I expect she'll be in touch soon. You could give me a message if you like, and I'll pass it on to her when she does.'

'She'll just ignore it,' he said, and sighed deeply. 'Do you know what happened between us?'

Rita nodded.

'I honestly didn't do anything.' His eyes pleaded to be believed. 'It was Meg that did all the running. I didn't even like her. If Charlie had come in ten minutes later she would have found me gone. I certainly wouldn't have made love to Meg.'

'It was a shame then that you weren't tough enough to put her in her place immediately,' Rita said tartly. In fact she did believe him. Everything Charlie had said about Meg confirmed she was a man-eater, while Andrew looked about as worldly as a pet rabbit.

'If I had known how things would turn out that night I'd have ridden over to Paddington and met Charlie from the train,' he said fiercely. 'I'd walk on hot coals right now to put things straight. I love her, Rita. She means everything to me and I can't bear the pain of knowing she's out there somewhere, all alone and hurting. Do you know if she's got another flat? Is she safe?'

Rita had heard enough to banish any last suspicions about this lad. 'Come and have a drink with me,' she suggested. 'I'm tired and thirsty, and although I don't know where Charlie is right now, I might be persuaded to plead your cause when I do see her.'

They went to a pub further down Endell Street. There were no more than six people in there. One drink turned into two, as Andrew poured his heart out. Rita went so far as admitting Charlie had stayed with her for the first couple of days after she walked out of the Hornsey flat, but that was all.

'We were so happy together,' he said, his voice quivering with emotion. 'I can't believe it's really over. We had planned to go on holiday down in Salcombe this week. My aunt down there and Ivor, the man Charlie used to work for, are terribly worried about her too. They haven't heard a word from her.'

Rita knew that Charlie thought a lot of this man Ivor, and she was surprised her friend hadn't written to tell him not to worry about her. 'You can tell them both from me that she's fine, and when I see her I'll remind her to write to Ivor. I'm sure you can understand why she hasn't liked to contact your aunt, though?'

'Well, yes,' he agreed. 'I suppose she imagines Beryl would take my part. But you can tell Charlie she hasn't. She told me I was a damn fool and I deserved it. She's very fond of Charlie.'

'I am too,' Rita said. 'I took to her right from her first day at Haagman's. But I like what I see of you too, Andrew, and so I'm going to be straight with you. Charlie has immense pride, she won't come running back to you just because she misses you. You've hurt her too deeply.'

'But I didn't do anything,' he insisted. 'Meg came mincing into that room without her clothes, leapt on me before I even had a chance to move and kissed me. I didn't even kiss her back. If the roles were reversed and I caught Charlie with a friend of mine, I'd be prepared at least to listen before making a judgement.'

Rita thought he had a point, though she expected he'd be every bit as hot-headed as his girl. 'But you're forgetting that everyone important in Charlie's life has betrayed her trust,' she said. 'Her father, mother and her first boyfriend. She's strong, Andrew, but she isn't indestructible. You've got to give her time. I will try and talk to her, but you must learn to be patient.'

They chatted about other things for a little while. Andrew told her that he had stayed on at the pub in Hampstead, but that he had arranged to move into a shared house with his old friends at the end of the month. He spoke too of his final year at university and the need to get a first-class degree if he was to be taken on by a good company. 'IBM are looking for graduates,' he said earnestly. 'I really believe computers will change the face of business and industry within ten years or so. I want to get in on the ground floor.'

Rita's only experience of computers had been as a temporary filing clerk at the Egg Marketing Board a few years earlier. Their one was a vast machine taking up an entire floor. As she remembered, it was always going wrong and it appeared to be more trouble than it was worth. But she supposed Andrew knew what he was talking about, so she nodded in agreement.

'I hope this trouble with me hasn't stopped Charlie thinking about a real career,' he went on. 'She's so bright, I'd hate to think of her getting stuck in a dead-end job.'

Rita was just about to say how highly Mrs Haagman thought of Charlie. She was a rude, inconsiderate and totally ungrateful woman but Charlie appeared to have won her round. Only this morning she'd called Charlie into her office to offer her the chance to go on a training course for the technical side of film processing. But then Rita remembered Martin had told Andrew that Charlie had left the firm.

'I don't think that will happen,' she said quickly. 'She's got a very ambitious streak.'

Andrew looked harder at Rita. He had arrived at Haagman's imagining that the friendship between Charlie and this woman was a very casual one. Charlie had laughingly described her as 'a red-headed vamp in missionary's clothing'. He had wondered at the time why anyone could be bothered to spend their lunch-breaks with someone who sounded so weird and so much older than themselves. But now, after almost an hour in Rita's company, he understood the attraction, and why Charlie had confided so much in her. Her character was the same odd mix as her appearance. On the surface she was just a staid mother figure, warm, understanding and kind. Yet she was too aware, too free-thinking to be called ordinary. She was obviously very astute, and had studied Charlie very closely. And he thought she almost certainly knew exactly where Charlie was and what she was doing.

Andrew admired loyalty, and he felt that if Charlie had this woman on her side she must be safe. As he sensed he was not going to make any further headway tonight, he thought he'd better go, and leave her to confer with Charlie.

'I'd better be going,' he said, looking at his watch. 'I'm due behind the bar at eight. Thanks for listening to me, Rita, I hope you will press my cause with Charlie. If you have any news for me, could you phone me at the pub?' He jotted down the number for her on a piece of paper. 'By the way, before I go. I fully intend to start digging about her father, like we planned, with or without her. From next week I'm only working in the evenings, so I'll have plenty of time.'

He was out the door before Rita could say anything more. She drank the last of her gin and tonic and thoughtfully lit up one last cigarette.

Charlie had told her Andrew's ideas of how to set about tracking DeeDee down. Rita had wanted to laugh at the naïvety of a man who believed he could get information about anyone in Soho by pretending to be a researcher. There were only two ways she knew of extracting information from people in Soho. One was with money, the other was violence.

But now she'd met Andrew she couldn't laugh. He was a nice lad, as bright as a button, and handsome enough to persuade a few working girls to help him. And he had absolutely no idea how much trouble that might lead him into.

*

387

Rita was sitting in the dark by the open window, deep in thought, when Charlie came in.

'Has the electric gone?' Charlie giggled and switched on a lamp. 'Oh no, my nosy friend is just spying on people.'

'Hullo, love,' Rita said, her spirits lifted slightly by Charlie's cheerful tone. 'I must be getting old, I hadn't noticed it getting dark. How was work this evening?'

'So so.' Charlie pulled a face. 'The Hag came back at half seven and hauled me into her office to talk some more about that course. It's in York of all places and I've got to go there on Tuesday.'

'That's great,' Rita said. She could see by Charlie's expression that she was torn between apprehension and glee. 'A change of scene will be good for you. Is she putting you up in a hotel?'

'Yes, she said it was a good one too, and I wasn't to let her down by fooling around. But I expect you're right, a change will be nice, and I'll be out of your hair.'

Charlie disappeared into her room to put her night-clothes on. While she was gone, Rita made her tea and a sandwich. She didn't really know how to broach the subject of Andrew, but she knew she must tell her tonight.

'You are a love,' Charlie said when she came back out into the living room and saw the tea and sand-wiches waiting on the coffee table. 'You're so mumsy the way you look after me.'

'I enjoy being mumsy,' Rita said with a fond smile. It was actually far more than that. Having Charlie staying with her had filled a void in her life; for the first time in years she felt needed and useful.

She hoped her young friend might want to stay indefinitely.

Charlie was exhausted and she really wanted to go to bed, but she sensed Rita had something on her mind. 'I can't thank you enough for having me here. I don't know what I would have done without you,' she said. 'But I don't want to outstay my welcome, so just say the word when you want me to go and I'll find somewhere else.'

'Now, whatever brought that on?' Rita asked in surprise.

'Well, guests are like fish, after three days they begin to go off,' Charlie said.

'Is that what that smell is?' Rita sniffed the air in an exaggerated fashion. 'I've been wondering about it all evening.'

Charlie laughed. Rita was a natural comedienne, and it was mostly that which had helped her through these past two weeks. If she'd had too much sympathy she would never have got out of bed. But then Rita was a remarkable woman all round. She knew when to listen, when to offer a hug, and when to give a kick up the pants. Charlie had received several of those from her. One morning when she refused to get up for work, Rita pulled the covers off her and slapped a wet flannel on her face. The first Sunday here Rita had insisted they bought Red Rover tickets on the bus and went all over London so Charlie couldn't sit and brood. 'Stop wallowing,' she'd intuitively shout from the kitchen when a love song came on the radio, knowing it was likely to remind Charlie of Andrew. Often she refused to let Charlie talk about him, and insisted she told her about Guy, Ivor or even her old schoolfriends instead. It worked too – Charlie often found herself laughing over her reminiscences. She hoped that one day soon she'd find something about her time with Andrew to laugh about, rather than cry over, too.

'You *have* got something on your mind. If it's not throwing me out, what is it?' Charlie asked. 'You aren't peeved because the Hag offered me that course instead of you, are you?'

'Of course not,' Rita said, smiling at the idea. 'My brain is much too rusty to cope with all that technical stuff.' She thought Charlie was beginning to look and sound like her old self again, and she was wary of saying anything which might set her back again.

For the first week Charlie was with her Rita had been very worried. She hardly ate a thing, and when she did she was often sick. She lost her natural glow entirely, she was so pale and gaunt that even the Hag had noticed. Rita had to force her to wash her hair at one point because she'd lost all interest in her appearance. But in the last few days she'd started eating and sleeping again, and her colour had improved. Today she'd put on a dress, the first time she'd been out of jeans since she arrived here.

'I saw Andrew,' Rita blurted out. 'He was waiting for me outside Haagman's.'

'You didn't tell him where I was, did you?' Charlie said in alarm, rising out of the chair as if she was on a spring.

'Sit down, drink your tea and shut up,' Rita said firmly. 'Don't interrupt until I've finished.'

Rita told her the gist of what had passed between her and Andrew.

'You believe him, don't you?' Charlie's eyes flashed with anger. 'He's taken you in completely!'

'No one takes me in,' Rita said calmly. 'I must have met most of the lying, snivelling bastards in London in my time. So don't insult my intelligence, Charlie.'

Charlie blushed. 'I didn't mean to, but he's just playing on your sympathy.'

Rita was fast losing her patience. Charlie always thought she knew best about everything, but this time it was annoying.

'He didn't attempt to do that. He told the truth. He should have whacked that girl off him. It would probably have been wiser if he'd waited for you to phone him before going over to the flat. And maybe he shouldn't have sat there smoking dope with her. But ask yourself, Charlie, why didn't he wait for your call?'

'Because he fancied being there with her,' Charlie said sullenly.

Rita laughed. 'He didn't even expect her to be there on a Bank Holiday. And he certainly didn't go because he thought he might get his leg over before you got back. It was because he couldn't wait to see you. If there had been no one there he would have sat on your doorstep like a faithful dog waiting for his mistress.'

'But she said he'd been with her the whole weekend.'

'She would say that though, wouldn't she?' Rita shrugged. 'You'd caught her out, punched her and vomited on her bed. She wanted to hurt you back, so that was all she could think of saying. Surely even a five-year-old could see that!'

Charlie looked stubbornly at the ceiling, her arms

crossed. 'I'm not going to have him back,' she said.

'Did I ask you to?'

'No, but that's what you're thinking.'

'So you are a mind-reader now? My goodness, Charlie, you are a stubborn little minx. Let me put something to you. Just suppose it's Christmas, and we're having a party at Haagman's, Martin gets a clump of mistletoe and comes up to kiss you. He's just plonking one on your lips, when the door bursts open and in comes Andrew. Would you think that was just cause for him to cast you to hell and damnation?'

'I wouldn't let Martin kiss me!' she said indignantly.

'Oh, Miss Prissy Pants.' Rita grimaced. 'You would after a few drinks, so would anyone. But just because he kissed you, it wouldn't mean you'd have sex with him. Grow up, Charlie, and think about what you're chucking away.'

When Charlie made no response, Rita got up and collected the cups. 'That lad loves you. He's not some creep that you can replace easily, but a decent, bright man who would do anything for you. I can tell you, Charlie, and believe me, please, men like Andrew are scarce. They get scarcer still the older you get, because girls with any sense grab them and hold on to them. Give him up by all means if you don't love him. Let some other lucky girl have a shot at him. But if it's just hurt pride holding you back, then I'm sorry for you. Your pride won't keep you warm on a cold night.'

She stomped off into her bedroom then and left Charlie crying.

Charlie woke early the following morning. It was Saturday and as neither she nor Rita was working today it was going to be a strain being home together for a whole weekend. Her head said Rita had been taken in by Andrew's charm, and however many feminist views she upheld, in reality she still bowed to the idea of male supremacy. Charlie's heart argued with this, however – Rita was wise, a good judge of character, and she only really wanted what was best for her friend.

But whether to act on Rita's views or not wasn't the real problem. To save face it would be easy enough to agree to go and talk to Andrew, after she got back from the course. That wouldn't commit her to anything, and at least Rita would see she'd met her halfway. Yet however sound an idea that was, it still didn't address the really important issue which had come out of last night's heated talk.

Long after Rita had gone off to bed, Charlie had sat alone analysing just what had been said, and why. It occurred to her that the passion her friend had spoken with had to have come from a deep personal hurt. Thinking about what that might be had raised several questions in her mind.

Why hadn't Rita got married? Why was the spare bedroom done out for a child? Why did she really wear such frumpy clothes? She was still young, she had a good figure, and why, when she was so likeable, did she appear to have no friends aside from those at work? Could she have jacked someone in, and then come to regret it?

It was over two years ago when Charlie had suddenly realized she knew nothing about her parents, and discovered it was through being entirely self-centred. She'd prided herself on having become more concerned about people's feelings since then, but now to her shame she saw she wasn't much different.

Maybe if she'd studied Meg a bit closer she could have predicted what she might be capable of and warned Andrew not to be alone with her. She had known Rita for months now, yet she knew nothing of her past, not even where she grew up. Then there was Ivor, she loved him, but she hadn't written to him and told him she was safe. He must be so worried about her. What right did she have to expect these people's loyalty, when she was so busy thinking about herself that she never took the time to tune into them and consider their viewpoints or feelings?

Feeling very ashamed, she got out of bed and went into the kitchen. It was still only seven in the morning, but Rita usually got up early and she knew she would appreciate a cup of tea, even if she was still cross.

Rita's door was slightly open, so Charlie walked straight in to find her friend still fast asleep.

Her room was extravagantly frilly and feminine, yet although Charlie had been in and out of it dozens of times in the past two weeks, it was only now that she really looked at it. Almost everything was pink, shades from deepest rose to baby pink. Frilly-edged curtains, heaps of satin cushions, even the bedside rug, the lamps and the lace mats which covered the dressing-table were pink.

The big double bed was very much the centre-piece of the room; by day it was covered with a pink and white lacy cover, and strewn with the cushions and fluffy soft toys. But Rita had tossed off the bedcovers during the night and she lay there stretched out on her back, her nightdress riding up over her thighs. She looked very young with her long hair loose; its vibrant colour glowing against the white pillowcase made a very pretty picture.

As Charlie stood there, tea in hand, pondering whether to wake her or not, she noticed some curious chequered marks on Rita's thighs. At first glance it appeared to be a pattern made by the bright sunlight striking though the curtains, but as she moved forward to put the cup of tea down on the bedside cabinet, she saw it wasn't a shadow, but scars.

Rita woke at the sound of the tea-cup clinking in its saucer. She looked alarmed to see Charlie so close to her. 'What are you doing?' she asked, quickly pulling her nightdress down.

'I wasn't going to get into bed with you! Just bringing you a cup of tea,' Charlie replied.

Rita relaxed visibly, pulled the covers back over her, took the tea and sipped it, then glanced at her clock. 'You're about early, why's that?'

'I don't know,' Charlie said with a grimace. She sat on the bed facing Rita. 'Can you tell me why you can be so snug and comfortable in bed on days you've got to work, then on a day off you wake up at dawn feeling as if the same bed is full of nails?'

'Sod's law,' Rita chuckled. 'The same law which makes the tights you pull on in a hurry have ladders, or the cake you bake for someone special always sink.'

'I'm very sorry about last night,' Charlie said, glad to see her friend didn't appear to be bearing a grudge. 'You were right as always. I guess I ought to go and see him to talk.'

'Don't do it because of what I said, that would be self-defeating. Only go if you really think you must,' Rita replied. 'And I'm sorry too that I laid into you last night. It was wrong of me to air my views. I should have stayed neutral.'

'Did something similar happen to you once?' Charlie asked. 'When I thought about it afterwards it sounded like you were speaking from experience.'

Rita pulled a silly face. 'I've had all kinds of experiences, and been pretty daft in my time, but I don't think I've ever been guilty of chucking true love away.'

Charlie was disappointed. She'd hoped for some real revelation. 'Haven't you ever been in love then?'

'I can't say I have. There were a couple of blokes when I was very young that set my pulse racing, but that's not quite the same thing, is it?'

Charlie didn't believe this. In her opinion no one as warm and affectionate as Rita could have gone through her life without falling in love.

'I hope you don't mind me asking,' Charlie said tentatively, 'but I couldn't help but notice those marks on your thighs as I came in just now. What are they?'

To Charlie's surprise Rita blushed and stiffened. She pointedly turned her head away to put her cup down, and Charlie sensed she'd accidentally stumbled on something very personal. 'I'm sorry,' she said in a small voice. 'Forget I asked. I didn't mean to embarrass you.'

When Rita stayed silent, Charlie was even more puzzled. It wasn't like Rita, she always had a quick retort for any situation, and she wasn't bashful about anything. Charlie was just about to apologize again and leave the room when a long drawn-out sigh broke the silence.

'Those marks are scars. No one else has ever seen them before,' Rita said in a very low voice. 'I didn't want you to see them either, but now you have, I suppose I have to explain.'

'You don't have to,' Charlie said quickly. 'It's none of my business.'

Rita didn't reply, but got out of bed. Her nightdress was the kind old ladies wore, pink cotton, high-necked, with short puffy sleeves and buttons down the front. She undid the buttons, then slipped her arms out. Charlie turned away for a moment thinking Rita was going to get dressed.

'Look at me,' Rita ordered her. 'You might as well see the full glory and be done with it.'

Charlie turned, but gasped involuntarily before she could stop herself. 'Oh, Rita! What on earth happened to you?'

Her whole body was covered evenly in criss-cross marks about an inch apart. It looked for the world as if she'd been pressed on to mesh; no accident or operation could have achieved such a pattern. Rita remained silent and turned, lifting her long hair up to show Charlie her back. That was scarred the same way, from her shoulders right down over her buttocks and thighs. The marks stopped abruptly at her elbows and just above her knees.

'Now you'll understand why I keep myself covered,' she said, and hurriedly put her nightdress back on.

'How did it happen?' Charlie felt faint. The scars were old, faded to thin brown lines, but they must have been excruciatingly painful when they were made. Even sadder was that Rita's body was a perfect shape – full firm breasts, a tiny waist and a pert little bottom, and now it was disfigured.

'A punishment.'

'You mean someone did that on purpose? With a knife?' Charlie's voice rose to an outraged squeak. She could hardly believe what she'd just heard. It was like something out of a horror film.

'Yes, with a knife, coldly and deliberately. I was being punished for trying to steal someone else's man. I dare say you would have liked to inflict this much permanent damage on Meg. But eight years on, it still seems a bit extreme to me.'

Charlie's eyes welled with tears. It was typical of Rita to try and make a joke of it, even something so terrible. But who could laugh at such desecration of a perfect body?

'Can you bring yourself to tell me about it?' she whispered.

'I don't know, I've never tried before,' Rita said, getting back into bed. 'Like I said, no one but you has ever seen them. I didn't see a doctor then, and I doubt I could let one examine me even now. I used to try and invent a story about how it happened, a different kind of tattoo, or having some hot wire falling on me. But I couldn't even convince myself, let alone anyone else.'

Charlie lay on her side across the bed, and listened as her friend took her back to 1964 when she said the story really began.

'I thought I was a femme fatale in those days,' Rita smirked, tossing her hair back and pouting to make her point. 'A man friend once described me as a walking wolf whistle and I suppose I was, though I was later to discover he pinched that from the newspapers. It was in fact a description of Mandy Rice-Davies. Do you know who she was?'

Charlie nodded. 'The other girl with Christine Keeler in the Profumo scandal.' She remembered her parents discussing the girls' behaviour at the time of John Profumo's trial.

'Well, I was part of the same set, what you might call goodtime girls. We worked as hostesses in various high-class London night-clubs, we all had rich and influential lovers, and our lives were dedicated to being gorgeous, fun-loving Jezebels.' She paused and looked at Charlie as if to gauge her reaction.

'Go on,' Charlie smiled. Rita was being her usual jokey self, but Charlie sensed that was just a self-protective front.

'A great many people made damning statements about girls like us at the time of the Profumo trial. They implied we were prostitutes, but that wasn't true. We were just a bunch of girls who had little going for us but our youth and our looks, so we used them. Most of us were looking for the love and attention we'd never had as children.

'We were war babies, you see, brought up with blackouts, bombs and rationing, some of us were evacuated, some lost parents, all of us were deprived in some way. Even after the war, things didn't get much better, and the only real escape from the grimness of it all, for girls like us, was the cinema. I soaked up all those glamorous Hollywood films from the age of eight, I modelled myself on Rita Hayworth and

Lana Turner. I couldn't wait to leave school, I thought that sort of ritzy life was just a train ride away in London.'

Charlie wanted Rita to hurry up and explain about her injuries, but she realized that the background to this story was all-important, so she bit her tongue and listened.

'I was only sixteen when I left home in my little Essex village for London. It was 1955, pre-Pill days, and I fell for the first man who took me out in a car. I thought he was a real gent because he had a gold cigarette lighter and he introduced me to port and lemon.' She gave a wry little smile and leaned over to get her cigarettes. 'He never bothered to tell me he was married, not until I told him I was pregnant, then of course he disappeared.'

She lit her cigarette and leaned back against the headboard. 'I went home, I had nowhere else to go, Mum went mad, crying and screaming at me, Dad gave me a pasting. But once they'd calmed down, Mum said I was to tell no one and that they would bring up my child as theirs. They packed me off to a home for unmarried mothers in Colchester. When Paul was born my folks came and collected him. I was told I could come home just twice a year to see him, as his big sister, but that was all.'

Charlie's eyes opened wide with horror. 'But that's awful!'

'It was, but back then being an unmarried mother was about the worst thing in the world, and what they offered was better than handing Paul over to strangers.' Rita shrugged. 'But don't let me get side-tracked, I'll come back to that part later. What I want you to see is my state of mind when I had to set out again on my own.'

'You must have been desperately unhappy?'

'Yes, very, but it was more than that. I was kind of driven to make good. I had to redeem myself in my parents' eyes, and I guess I thought the only way I could do that was to make lots of money to send home for Paul. You see, my parents were poor, Dad was only a farm labourer, we lived in a tied cottage and I was the oldest of five. But I had no qualifications or training, all I had in my favour was my looks and my figure. I got a job in a London store, but I still wasn't earning enough to do more than keep myself in one tiny room.

'My parents were so cold with me. On the few occasions they allowed me home they made it quite clear they had no time for me, and my brothers and sisters just followed their lead and were much the same. Finally in 1959, when I was twenty, a friend got me an evening job as a cigarette girl in a London night-club. I had to wear a fancy costume with a short little puffy skirt and plunging neckline, and parade around the place all evening being sweet to men. I was working during the day too, so I was always tired, but that job changed my mentality. Suddenly I was mixing with girls in a similar situation to me, and by listening to them and copying them, I saw a way off the treadmill I was on.'

'Did you –?' Charlie stopped short, she couldn't bring herself to ask if that meant prostitution.

Rita half smiled. 'No, I didn't sell myself, if that's what you're thinking. Though there were several sugar daddies. The clubs I worked in were the very smartest places in London, you'd have soon lost your job if anyone found out that's what you were doing. I moved on from cigarette girl to waitress and then to hostess. I learned how to get big tips, and worked myself up to the smartest club of all, the Astor.'

'Did you make lots of money?' Charlie asked.

Rita nodded. 'All at once I had it nearly all. I was earning enough to send money home, I got this flat and furnished it, and I bought myself lovely clothes. I called myself Suzie, had dozens of admirers, and life was one long party. The only thing which was missing was my parents' approval.'

'They didn't like you working in a club?'

Rita grimaced. 'I didn't dare tell them that. They thought night-clubs were Sodom and Gomorrah! I made out I was a receptionist in a fashion house. But that made no difference to their attitude to me, they took the money I sent, but they still wouldn't forgive me.'

Charlie sighed. She knew only too well what it was like to want approval and affection. She could identify entirely with Rita.

'I suppose that was the real reason I became determined to find a rich husband,' Rita said sadly. 'I thought that would bring them round and make them proud of me.'

She went on to speak about the parties at country houses to which she and the other girls from the club were invited to make them swing. It made Charlie smile, as it was all very reminiscent of films she'd seen during the Sixties, pretty girls with bouffant hair-styles, false eyelashes and sparkly dresses, dancing on tables and around fabulous swimming pools.

'I met Ralph at one of these parties,' Rita said. 'He might have been sixty, but he was gorgeous, charming, rich and a widower. I made up my mind to have him, without even finding out a little more about him, or the woman he was with.'

Charlie's eyes opened wider as her friend went on to describe a weekend in Paris with Ralph, the first time she'd ever been abroad. Then the subsequent nights away in country hotels, the dinners, flowers and presents he lavished on her.

'He said he loved me, but looking back I suppose I ought to have had more sense than to think a man like him would want to marry a club girl less than half his age,' she chuckled. 'It's amazing how deaf and blind girls can be when a wealthy, attractive man showers them with affection. I didn't even care that he was still seeing that other woman. I thought it was only a matter of time before I knocked her out of the running.'

'Was he engaged to her?' Charlie asked.

'Not as far as I knew. But even if he had been, I was so determined I wouldn't have let that deter me. Several girls in the club warned me about her, they said she was a dangerous woman to cross, but I just laughed it off.

'Then one night in January of 1965, she came into the Astor Club and ordered me out into the powder room. She told me in no uncertain terms that I was to drop Ralph, or I'd be very sorry. Like a chump I slapped her round the face and told her Ralph had said she was like a sack of shit in bed. He didn't, of course, he was far too gentlemanly to speak of intimate

403

things to another woman. She left without another word, so I believed I'd won.

'Around a fortnight later when I'd almost forgotten about that incident, I came out of the club late one night and a black Bentley was waiting outside. The driver got out and said Ralph wanted to see me urgently, and he had been sent to take me to his country house. I never smelled a rat. In fact I was convinced Ralph intended to propose to me, and spent the whole journey wishing I was wearing something more glamorous than my black dress and that I'd had my hair and nails done that morning.'

She paused for a moment. 'It must have been about half past two when we drove up to the house,' she said in little more than a whisper. 'I was surprised it looked a bit dilapidated, not the grand place I'd expected.'

Charlie noticed then that Rita was getting agitated, she was picking at the bedclothes, and her eyes didn't seem to be focusing on her any more. She wanted to hear the rest but she was afraid Rita was getting too upset.

'Don't go on if it hurts,' she said. But Rita continued anyway, unaware now that she was still speaking. She'd slipped back in time, reliving every moment of that terrible night, just as it happened.

She saw the rusting iron gates in the beam of the headlights as the car turned into the drive. They looked as if they were almost propped against the posts rather than still being used. Huge trees hung over the drive, and branches swished over the car as they passed.

Rita leaned forward in her seat. 'It looks as if this

place needs a few gardeners,' she said through the glass screen to the driver. 'It's a bit overgrown, isn't it?'

'Mr Peterson spends more time in London than he does down 'ere,' the driver said in a cockney accent, without moving his head to look back at her as they drew up to the house.

Aside from a light in one downstairs window, and another in the large stone porch, it was in darkness. There wasn't enough light to see anything clearly, all Rita got was a vague impression of a rather Gothic style; she thought it was red brick, with a great deal of creeper growing up it.

The driver got out and opened the passenger door. As she got out he held her elbow, and he continued to hold on to it as they went up the few stone steps to the front door. It opened even before they reached it, and another man stood there. He was astoundingly like the driver, burly, with very short dark hair, wearing a similar dark suit.

'Are you two related?' she said, suddenly nervous. She knew they were in Kent from landmarks she'd noted, but she didn't know where.

'Brothers,' the driver said curtly, and all at once the gentle hand on her elbow tightened and he was pushing her through the door.

'Steady on,' Rita said. But the moment the door slammed behind them, she realized to her dismay that this was some kind of set-up. The hall was gloomy, lit by only one wall light, there was no furniture, not so much as a hall table or carpets, and it smelled musty, as if it had been unused for years. Before she could even gather herself to protest, the sound of feet

405

made her head jerk round to her left. Coming down the uncarpeted staircase at the side of the hall was Daphne Dexter. She wore cream jodhpurs, riding boots and a red sweater, her dark hair fixed up in a bun.

'Let me out of here!' Rita yelled in panic. 'How dare you con me into coming here?'

The two men each got hold of one of her arms and held her tightly.

'Still the same stupid little loudmouth,' Daphne said, and smiled sardonically. She walked right up to Rita, lifted her hand and slapped her hard across the face. 'That's repayment for the other night,' she said. 'You won't have long to wait for the rest of your punishment.'

Rita reeled back from the blow; if it hadn't been for the men holding her she would have fallen. One look at the two men was enough to know they were in Daphne's pay and likely to do anything she ordered them too. 'Look, I'm sorry I went for you,' she gabbled quickly. 'You caught me on a bad night. If Ralph means that much to you, you can have him. Just let me go.'

'I already *have* Ralph,' Daphne said haughtily. 'Do you really think you were anything more than a piece of fresh meat to him? Take her downstairs, boys.'

Rita screamed and tried to fight the men off as they manhandled her towards a door further down the hall, stripping off her coat as they went. But they were too strong, and they ignored her screaming. They pushed open the door which led to some steep rough wooden stairs, one grabbed her arms, the other her

406

legs, and they carried her down between them. Her shoes fell off and her dress rode up over her thighs, revealing her stocking tops.

The room they hauled her down into was a cellar; like the hall it appeared to have been unused for years. One wall held old empty wine racks covered with spider's webs. The only other item was a central work-bench with a large vice fixed on one side. The cellar was so damp and cold that Rita stopped screaming and began begging instead. 'Please let me go. I'll do anything you say. I'll even leave London if that's what you want. Please let me go.'

They ignored her pleas, just hoisted her up on to the bench like a side of bacon, and while one man held her firmly down, the other tied her wrists to the bench legs with some rope.

Daphne came down the stairs just as they were tying her ankles down too. She paused a few steps from the bottom and laughed. The laugh echoed round the empty room, adding further menace. 'You're quite used to that position as I understand it,' she said. 'So it shouldn't bother you too much.'

Rita lifted her head and stared in horrified fascin-ation as Daphne produced a large pair of scissors from the waist of her jodhpurs. She advanced on Rita and starting at the hem of her black dress, began cutting it right up the front. She pushed the fabric aside dis-dainfully, then snipped off Rita's suspenders, then through the band in the middle of her bra. She paused for a moment, sneering at Rita. The men both lunged forward and pulled the bra from Rita's breasts.

She was so scared now she could barely breathe. She'd had asthma as a child and she feared she would

407

have an attack again. But as Daphne laid the cold steel of the scissors on her groin, she screwed up her eyes in terror. When no pain came she opened them again. Daphne was calmly cutting up through her knickers and suspender belt; when she'd finished, she flapped the fabric back leaving Rita stark naked.

Rita assumed then that the men were going to rape her. That was bad, though not as bad as hurting her physically. But to her surprise they bent down beneath the bench and brought out white jackets, the kind chefs wore, handed one to Daphne and put the other two on themselves.

Apart from the absolute terror of these people getting ready for something barbaric in absolute silence, Rita was freezing cold. She tried pleading with them again, but they studiously ignored her.

'The gag now,' Daphne said, and one of the men pulled a strip of thick linen from his pocket. Rita bucked and shook her head from side to side as he tried to put it round her, but he slapped her face, shoved something which felt like a soft duster into her mouth, then tied on the gag, pulling it so tight round her head that it cut into the corners of her mouth.

She was completely helpless now, entirely at their mercy, and when Daphne bent down under the bench and came back with a long thin knife, the kind butchers used for boning meat, Rita wet herself with fright. Her urine was scalding hot on her thighs, steaming in the cold room, and it shamed her even more than her nakedness.

'Good job we planned to do it down 'ere,' one of the men said, and picking up a bucket of water, he sloshed it over her lower half. It was icy, but Rita hardly noticed it, all she could see was the knife in Daphne's hand and her gloating, demonic expression.

'I expect you'll pass out while I'm cutting you,' she said in a chillingly calm voice, bringing the knife close to Rita's cheek. 'So I'll explain now what we intend to do. I'm going to score your entire body with this knife, something like the way we score the skin on a leg of pork to make crackling. I'm not going to touch the parts of you which show in everyday clothes. Just that body you love to flaunt, that you use to make a living. But I'm going to make certain you never forget what happens to people who get on the wrong side of me.'

She put the knife first on Rita's breast, digging the point in just enough to draw blood. 'Before we start,' she said, 'when this is over, don't even think of running to the police, or to Ralph for that matter. Not unless you want something equally unpleasant to happen to your son.'

Rita bucked furiously against her restraints. No one knew she had a child, not even her closest friends. How could this woman have discovered that?

Daphne slapped at her thigh with the side of the knife. 'Keep still,' she said, 'or I might decide to re-arrange your face too. Now, as I was saying, you don't want something to happen to your son, do you? He's such a happy, bright kid, he showed me his train set and his pet guinea-pig. Your parents are so very fond of him too. We wouldn't want them upset, would we?'

Rita tried to shout, but the only sound to come from her was in her own head. Daphne began cutting then, as coldly and calmly as if she was carving a Sunday joint. She started at Rita's right shoulder, going diagonally across her breast, down her abdomen and finishing at her left hip. The knife was very sharp and the tip only went in a little way, and it didn't hurt very much either, not at first, despite the beads of blood popping out along the knife's path. But by the time Daphne had made three or four slashes across her, the first wounds began to sting and Rita was sobbing.

The two men, whose names were never mentioned, just looked on; they had cold blue eyes and thin lips. They rarely spoke and smoked incessantly.

On and on the torture went. When Daphne had finished the diagonal slashes from one shoulder, she moved to the other. There was no expression on her face, no glee, anger or distaste, she could have merely been doing some ironing. When she'd finished with Rita's torso, she moved on to her thighs.

Rita wished she could pass out, her entire body seemed to be on fire and each new cut added to it, but she remained stubbornly conscious. She could see Paul's small face dancing before her eyes, and she knew without any doubt that this fiendish woman really had gone to Felstead, the Essex village where her parents lived, and met the whole family. The knowledge that Daphne had gone to such lengths proved she fully intended to carry out her threat if Rita did go to the police.

She must have passed out finally when they turned her over to do her back. She remembered yelling with the pain, yet no real sound came out because of the gag. The next thing she knew was being drenched with icy water – they'd thrown a bucketful over her.

'That's it then,' Daphne said, and beckoned for the two men to untie Rita. She reached under the workbench and pulled out a towelling dressing-gown. 'Put this on. I don't want blood all over the car.'

The men hauled Rita to her feet and pushed her arms into the garment; it was yellow with age and stank of damp. She was too dizzy to feel the pain, but her legs sagged beneath her and the men had to grab her arms to support her.

'Now, remember what I said!' Daphne said, wiping blood from her hands on to her white jacket. 'One word to anyone, and Paul gets it.'

Rita was still gagged, she could only nod weakly in agreement. She glanced down at herself and saw her bloody stomach and thighs and she thought Daphne might just as well have killed her.

'Rita, are you all right?' Charlie's voice seemed to come from a great distance. 'Don't tell me any more, it's upsetting you too much. Let me make you some more tea.'

Rita hauled herself mentally back to the present. She was relieved to find herself in her own bed, sun streaming in through the window. Charlie was holding both her hands, but her face was as white as a sheet, proving that she hadn't been dreaming and that she had actually told the girl everything.

'Looks like you need the tea,' Rita said weakly. 'Your eyes look like piss-holes in the snow.'

Charlie moved closer then and hugged the older woman to her shoulder. She was so deeply shocked she couldn't speak for a moment. 'I don't know how you survived,' she whispered eventually. 'Did they take you home afterwards?'

Rita leaned against the girl. It was a long time since anyone had hugged her and it felt good to feel bodily contact. 'They dumped me here on my doorstep just as it was getting light. My body felt it was on fire, I've never known such terrible pain.'

Charlie went off then and hurriedly made some tea. She was afraid to leave Rita on her own; reliving that nightmare was enough to push anyone over the edge.

'How did you manage afterwards?' she asked a bit later. Rita's normal colour had come back, she was even managing a few of her jokes.

'It healed remarkably quickly, considering,' she said. 'I used to take salt baths and a sleeping pill, then cover myself with towels and get into bed. It stopped hurting as the scabs came. I used to hope that they would fall off and leave no mark, but of course they didn't.'

'Weren't you tempted to go to the police, despite what she said?'

'No. That woman wasn't human, Charlie, she wouldn't have thought twice about carrying out her threat. I stayed in here, eked out the few savings I had, then went through my wardrobe getting rid of all the clothes which wouldn't cover the scarred parts of me.'

'Oh, Rita! I don't know what to say,' Charlie said, tears running down her cheeks. 'It makes my troubles seem nothing.'

'I brought it on myself,' Rita said stoically. 'I hate that woman still of course, because she ruined my life.

412

I'll never fall in love, marry or have another child. She robbed me of my youth. All through the later part of the Sixties I used to look at the dolly birds in their mini-dresses and cry. I couldn't go out and have fun, I'd lost my confidence. The only consolation was that my parents became nicer to me.'

'You told them then?'

'Oh no.' Rita made a whistling noise as she sucked in breath through her teeth. 'I meant because of my change of image. I went home one day in the sort of clothes I wear now and it won their approval.'

'But weren't they suspicious?'

'I told them I'd started going to church,' Rita smirked. 'Well, it was the truth at the time. If it hadn't been for that I might have topped myself. Anyway, they let me see more of Paul after that, in fact he used to come for weekends sometimes. That's why I decorated your bedroom like that.'

Charlie nodded. She thought all her questions had been answered now. 'Does he still come?'

'No, he's got too big to stay with his big sister, he prefers his schoolfriends' company. He's sixteen now, at grammar school, and smart as new paint.'

Charlie saw the deep sorrow in her friend's eyes and hugged her again. 'He'll come back to you when he's older.'

'Maybe,' Rita said, and for the first time a tear trickled down her cheek. 'But he doesn't seem to like me much now. Last time I visited him he totally ignored me. I'd bought him some new football boots and he wouldn't even try them on to make sure they fitted.'

'Have you got a picture of him?' Charlie asked.

Rita pulled open the drawer of her bedside cabinet and drew out a thin album. She handed it to Charlie without saying a word.

Charlie felt a lump come up in her throat as she looked. There was just one picture for every year, marking his progress from a big, bald smiling baby of perhaps five or six months, right up to a somewhat gawky-looking teenager with straggly hair. They were all poor-quality black and white snaps, probably taken with an old-fashioned box camera. Charlie got the distinct impression that Rita's parents had begrudgingly given her these pictures, they looked suspiciously like ones they'd rejected.

'Is his hair red like yours?' she asked. She could see no similarity to Rita in Paul; his hair looked dark, he was skinny and foxy-faced.

'No, fortunately for him it's brown, he's a lot like my dad, tall, thin and wiry. I favour my mum, I suppose – her hair is red too, though more chestnut than mine. All Paul got from his real father was his nose, you can't see in any of those pictures, but it's kind of snub, like a boxer's.'

Charlie found the pictures too sad to look at any longer. They underlined the bleakness of her friend's life and her parents' lack of compassion. She closed it up and put it back in the drawer. 'Did you ever see that woman again?' she asked.

'I didn't ever see her, thank God, but then I haven't been to any of the old haunts or kept in touch with anyone from then. But I did read something in the papers about her. She owned some clubs in Soho during the late Sixties, the sort of places that cropped up like mushrooms when Flower Power was all the rage. One of them was raided by the police and she was charged with supplying drugs.'

Charlie's eyebrows shot up. 'Did she go to prison?'

'Did she hell!' Rita said scornfully. 'She wriggled out of it somehow. Her sort always does.'

'Do you think she's still around Soho?'

'I doubt it, she's probably moved on to somewhere with richer pickings.' Rita looked hard at Charlie. 'You wondered last night what I had on my mind. Well, it was this. You see, the last thing Andrew said to me yesterday was that he was going to find out about your father, with or without you. I'm afraid for him going around that area asking questions.'

'You don't have to be. He'll be careful,' Charlie said lightly.

Rita didn't reply. She was looking off into space as if deep in thought.

'What is it? Do you know something?' Charlie's heart quickened, suddenly realizing that during Rita's time in the West End she might very well have known people who did know her father.

Rita turned towards Charlie, saw that glimmer of excitement in her eyes and guessed its source. Her heart plummeted. She knew she must warn the girl and try to dissuade her from digging around. She caught hold of Charlie's hands. 'Did I tell you what the woman's name was?'

'Yes, Daphne.' Charlie frowned. She wondered why Rita should ask that.

'Daphne Dexter,' Rita said slowly and deliberately. 'Her initials are D.D.'

Charlie's mouth fell open. 'You mean that woman was my dad's mistress?'

'I don't know,' Rita said in a very low voice. 'It might be just a wild coincidence, but she's the right age, I believe she was once a stripper, and she had interests in several clubs. I hope for your sake that I'm letting my imagination run away with me.'

Charlie didn't speak for a moment, her mind whirling with all the fragments of information she had about DeeDee, and she tried to match it with what Rita had said about Daphne. She couldn't really believe her father could love someone capable of maiming another woman, yet Sylvia, who had known DeeDee well, was scared of her; she almost certainly knew who the two men were who attacked her too. Could they have been those two brothers?

She shook her head. 'She can't be the same person.'

'I hope she isn't,' Rita said, shrugging her shoulders. 'Because if the woman I know got your dad away from your mother, and you or Andrew cross her path, heaven only knows what might happen.'

Chapter Fourteen

Andrew felt very self-conscious as he walked up Wardour Street. It was only six-thirty, he thought far too early in the evening for Soho's night life to start, but there were girls and women watching him from almost every doorway.

It was the Monday after he'd seen Rita, and as he'd been given the whole day off he'd decided to make a start on finding out something about Jin Weish. He was very disappointed that there had been no telephone call from Rita over the weekend. On Friday evening he'd been so certain he'd won her round, but maybe Charlie hadn't contacted her yet.

Over the weekend he'd borrowed the pub typewriter and made a kind of handout, presenting himself as a freelance researcher requiring assistance in compiling information about Soho's characters during the Fifties. He'd used his friend John's Hampstead address as a temporary measure as he didn't have a permanent one of his own.

His first stop this morning had been at a small printer's where he had a hundred photocopies run off. Since then he'd been calling on every small business, cafés and shops, talking to people and leaving one of the handouts where they expressed any interest.

Andrew was elated by the response. Many of the older shopkeepers had been keen to chat to him, if only to pour out their complaints about the changing face of Soho. They were concerned by a rising tide of violence in the streets at night, the blatant prostitution and how decent shopkeepers like themselves were being squeezed out in favour of people selling pornography. They described Soho during the Fifties as glamorous, and spoke with some nostalgia of gentlemen frequenting the clubs, rather than the seedy riff-raff who came here now.

Two sixty-plus market traders in Berwick Street had been a great deal more specific. They had reminisced eagerly about the Maltese Messina brothers who ran most of the prostitution, the Sabina brothers who specialized in 'protecting' bookmakers, Billy Hill and Jack 'Spot' Comer who were undisputed gang leaders at that time, until they were ousted by the Kray twins.

Andrew found it quite amusing that these two garrulous old chaps were quite prepared to natter on about these thugs who had run Soho in those days, indeed to speak of people having their faces slashed with razors, kneecapping and other atrocities, yet when he asked if there were any major players at that time who were Chinese, they looked askance at him and said, 'Those Chinks are dangerous, son, you don't want to be messing with them.'

But one of the old men had given him the name of a man he thought might prove invaluable to Andrew, and he was on his way to the Black and White Café in Carlisle Street now, in the hopes of catching 'Spud' having his evening meal.

'Oih, son! Got time for a quickie?'

418

Andrew's head jerked round at the bawled question. It came from a grinning peroxide blonde in a short red dress with a low neck. She was standing in a doorway he'd just passed. She was over the hill, at least thirty-five, and he had a feeling it wasn't a serious attempt at soliciting, but more of a joke.

Andrew stopped, looked back at her and smiled. 'I can't do quick ones,' he said with a comic shrug. 'And I'm just off to meet someone.'

She laughed, and despite her somewhat desperate appearance – she had thick pink makeup, her dress was unbecomingly tight – it was a nice, jolly laugh. 'Story of me life,' she said. 'I spots a real tasty one and they're always in a 'urry.'

Andrew hadn't dared even think of speaking to any prostitutes, they scared him witless. But now this one had approached him, and seemed to have a sense of humour, he thought it might be worth his while to be friendly. 'I'll be back,' he grinned. 'Not for your body but to talk to you. I'm collecting information for a book, you see.'

'What about? Working girls?' She took a few steps closer to him, her face was alight with interest.

'Not just that, everything about Soho, you know, the characters, strippers, villains and stuff,' he said.

She looked at him appraisingly. Andrew guessed she'd been very pretty when she was younger, it was kind of still there, but camouflaged by extra weight and the awful thick makeup. 'I could tell you enough stuff to fill a suitcase, let alone a book,' she said. 'But you go careful, son, Soho ain't the kind of place to 'ang around when you're a bit green. Know what I mean?'

419

Andrew did. He'd been kind of aware all day that he was slightly out of his depth. 'Will you talk to me then?' he asked impulsively. 'I could meet you one afternoon and take you somewhere for tea?'

She smiled; one of her front teeth was broken, and it gave her mouth a slightly lopsided look. 'You sweet talker,' she said. 'Take me to Lyons Corner 'Ouse and buy me a Knickerbocker Glory and you're on!'

'Okay,' Andrew agreed. If she'd suggested taking him up to her room he would have been daunted, but a public place sounded safe enough. 'What about tomorrow afternoon at half past four?'

'Okay,' she grinned.

'I'll meet you outside,' he said. 'You're a diamond!'

Andrew was halfway up the street before he remembered he hadn't asked her name. He wondered if she really would come.

The Black and White Café would have been more aptly named Grey and Greasy. It was like a narrow corridor, stools along the counter; at the far end it opened up wider with half a dozen or so small tables. There were three men in total in there, two together at one table, the other alone. All three were middle-aged working men, so Andrew asked the woman behind the counter for a glass of milk and asked her if any of the men was known as 'Spud'.

'Over there,' she said, pointing to the one alone. 'He's just about to have his dinner.'

Andrew made his way over to the man, apologized for disturbing him and explained who had directed him to him and why.

Spud was as strange-looking as his name. His nose

was more like a huge growth, purple in colour and with lumps everywhere. His eyebrows were like an overgrown hedge, and he had extremely thick, wet lips, hardly any teeth and a bald head. He smelled of sweat and his shirt was filthy, but he was friendly, and insisted Andrew was welcome to sit down and ask whatever he liked.

'I used to be a boxer,' he said without waiting to be asked. 'My nose weren't too pretty before that, but it weren't as bad as this. That's why they call me Spud. When I gave up on boxing I worked for a time in the market, someone said it looked like a spud and the name stuck. Me real one is John Joe O'Neill. Me mam and dad were Irish.'

His meal arrived at that point, a gigantic cottage pie with chips, swimming in gravy. Attacking it with a spoon, he carried on talking as he ate. ' 'Course Soho ain't what it used to be,' he said, giving Andrew a disgusting view of his mouthful of food. 'It's all foreigners now and bleedin' tourists. The Fifties was its heyday. I used to stroll down through St Anne's Court in me flash suit, and I was cock of the walk. No one messed with me. They'd all seen me fight, and I could walk in any bar or club and get a drink on the 'ouse. I knew all the working girls by name, and most of them,' he paused to wink suggestively, 'well, you know, I knew 'em a bit better.'

Spud then went on to speak of the same people his two friends in the market had mentioned. Andrew listened politely to repeats of violent stories, and a list of celebrities he'd known well. He held up two fingers and claimed to have 'been like that' with the Kray twins. The boxer Freddie Mills was one of his mates and he said how Freddie had opened a Chinese restaurant, then later changed it into a night-club where he was subsequently found dead in his car in 1965.

'They said it were suicide,' he said, leaning closer to Andrew conspiratorially. 'That was tosh, he were a 'appy man, and 'appy blokes don't shoot themselves. I reckon it were the Chinks what done it, because he moved in on their territory.'

Andrew was very glad Spud had brought the Chinese into the conversation, even if he was talking about an event long after the time Andrew was interested in. 'Do you remember a club called the Lotus?' he asked hesitantly. 'I heard that was owned by a Chinese.'

'Yeah. It were just along the street 'ere,' Spud said. 'I 'ad some good times there. They always 'ad big girls.' He cupped his hands to his chest to show he meant big breasts.

Andrew wanted to laugh. He had never met anyone as odd as this man. His appearance might be utterly repellent, but there was a liveliness in his speech and facial expressions which made him fascinating. 'Someone told me there was something dodgy going on there. Would you know anything about that?' He was fishing in the dark, hoping to catch anything, however irrelevant.

'There was something dodgy going on in all the clubs,' Spud laughed cheerfully. 'They weren't like bleedin' Sunday schools. They was all smoking those reefers long before it was even illegal. There was gambling and God knows what else.'

'Was the owner Chinese?' Andrew said.

'Yeah, he was, decent bloke for a Chink. 'E 'ad a nice wife an' all. Blonde woman, pretty as a May morning.'

A tingle of excitement went down Andrew's spine. 'Any idea if he's still around?' he asked. 'I'd like to talk to him.'

''E's long gone,' Spud said. 'I ain't seen 'im in ten, maybe twelve years. I 'eard he went to live in the country. Funny you should ask about him, though, the boys in blue came around a couple of years ago asking questions. Seemed 'e'd disappeared.'

Andrew felt he ought to be pleased to have it confirmed the police really had looked around here; Charlie was of the opinion they hadn't really bothered. But if the police had made inquiries and found nothing, then he was hardly likely to do any better.

'Did you ever hear any more about him, you know, on the grapevine?' Andrew asked tentatively.

'A story went round that he was done in over in Holland. But then you 'ear all sorts round 'ere.'

'Well, I hope that's not true,' Andrew laughed. 'So when this man went off to live in the country, who took over his club?'

Spud frowned as if thinking hard. 'A woman that run the place for him kept it going, she might even 'ave bought it off him,' he said. 'I didn't go in there much then. Didn't like her. She 'ad a face like a bag of arrows.'

'Plain was she?' Andrew asked. 'And no tits?'

Spud burst into throaty laughter. 'No, she weren't plain, best-looking woman you ever saw in fact, and well stacked. No, what I meant about 'er was that one look from 'er was enough to send you running. She didn't want men like me in 'er precious club, she wanted big-spending toffs.'

'She sounds interesting,' Andrew said. 'What was her name?'

Spud said he couldn't remember, but Andrew was certain he could.

'It wasn't DeeDee, was it? That was a name someone told me.'

For the first time in their conversation Spud looked nervous. His eyes narrowed and he didn't answer.

'Well, was it?' Andrew persisted.

''Ow d'you expect me to remember someone's name that long ago?' he snapped. 'Whatcha want to know about that poxy place for anyway? It weren't famous.'

'Well, every book needs a bit of intrigue to make it more exciting,' Andrew retorted, wondering why the man should suddenly get needled by that question. 'Besides, all the better-known places have already been written about. I wanted a new slant.'

Spud finished up his vast meal in silence, belched, then downed a mug of tea in one. 'You're barking up the wrong tree, son,' he said eventually. 'If you wants a good story you'd be better off taking a trip out to Spain and talking to Billy 'Ill, 'e cleared off out there once the Krays took over the West End. But 'e was the governor round 'ere for a long time, and a nicer bloke you couldn't wish to meet.'

Andrew thought that meant Spud was trying to get rid of him. Whether that was because of his line of questioning, or just that the man had a low concentration span, he didn't know. Either way he thought he'd better leave him in peace. 'Well, thanks for your time. You've been very helpful,' he said. 'Can I pay for your dinner?'

'That's decent of you, son.' The man beamed again. 'It were nice to chat to you about the old times. I'm always in 'ere at this time of day if you want to talk some more.'

As Andrew was still wandering around Soho looking closely at all the clubs, and wondering if he dared go into any of them, Charlie was trying to telephone him.

'He's gone out. It's his day off,' she said glumly as she put the receiver down.

Rita sniggered. 'Friday night you said you wouldn't ever speak to him again, and now you're cross because he doesn't happen to be there when you want him. What a contrary person you are.'

'You know why I need to speak to him. I want to warn him to be careful in Soho.'

Rita raised her eyebrows, but said nothing. Charlie was very Chinese in her need to keep face. She'd spent most of the previous day writing a letter to Andrew, then tore it up because she said she was afraid it would give him the wrong signals. Now she'd changed tactics and was pretending her only interest in him was warning him of danger.

'I wish I didn't have to go to that course tomorrow,' Charlie said after a few moments of reflective silence. 'In fact I wish I'd turned the Hag down. I ought to be getting out and finding a better job, not learning something which will force me to stay there.'

'Learning something new is always worthwhile,' Rita said firmly. 'Besides, York is supposed to be a beautiful place, so it'll be a bit like a holiday. While

425

you're there you can think about what you'd really like as a career. But to put your mind at rest about Andrew, I'll phone him tomorrow morning if you like.'

'But what will you say? Martin told him I'd left Haagman's.'

'The truth. That you're away on a training course. I don't have to say who for, or where. I'll say we've talked, and that you will speak to him when you get back, but he isn't to go jumping the gun and thinking he's forgiven. Then I'll tell him to be careful.'

'Will you tell him about Daphne Dexter?'

'I can't, it's too complicated and delicate, and besides I'd rather he didn't know about my connections. I'll just tell him not to be too trusting with people. That's enough for now.'

Charlie's face brightened. 'I'd better go and pack then,' she said. 'Do you think I'll need my swimming costume?'

Rita chuckled. Charlie's habit of leaping from something serious to something absolutely trivial was very endearing. 'In my day a girl's travelling essentials were just a spare pair of knickers, a cardigan and her mascara,' she said. 'I can't imagine why you'd want a swimming costume in York, but you never know.'

Andrew got to Lyons Corner House by Charing Cross Station soon after four. To while away twenty minutes or so, he went across to Trafalgar Square and sat watching tourists feeding the pigeons and taking photographs. Rita had phoned him this morning and he was feeling much happier. Two weeks seemed a long time to wait before he could speak to Charlie but

426

with luck he might have some news about her father by then. He'd be moving into the house at Brent too. Maybe it was just as well she'd gone away, time was a great healer, or so his mother was fond of telling him. Perhaps they could start afresh when she got back.

Right on the dot of half past four, the woman arrived to meet him at Lyons, but Andrew had to look twice before he realized it was her. She looked completely different from the day before. She was wearing a floral dress, the kind his own mother would wear, very little makeup, and her blonde hair had just been neatly set.

'You look nice,' he said with a smile.

She tucked her hand through his arm. 'I don't advertise what I do for a living when I'm going somewhere posh.'

Andrew had never thought of Lyons Corner House as posh, but he was touched that she thought so. 'I'm Andrew,' he said. 'And I forgot to ask your name?'

'It's Angie,' she said and laughed. 'Well, me real name's Freda, but I like Angie better. I didn't think you'd turn up. If I 'ad a pound for every fella that's stood me up, I'd be able to retire.'

Andrew took her upstairs and over to a table by the window which overlooked Trafalgar Square. His parents had always brought him in here for a treat when they came up to London for a day, but he'd never seen it as empty as it was today. He thought it might be because it was so warm outside.

He ordered Knickerbocker Glories for both of them, then looked hesitantly at Angie, wondering how to start her talking as she was clearly a little nervous away from her own territory.

'I didn't ask you to meet me to poke my nose into your business,' he said gingerly. 'I'm just interested in Soho in general, and anything you might like to tell me will be in the strictest confidence.'

'Where d'you wanna start?' she asked.

'How about how long you've been working in Soho?' he suggested.

She sucked in her breath. 'Mind if I have a fag?' she asked.

Andrew got his out and offered them to her. He wasn't a real smoker himself, only the odd one now and then with a drink, but he'd bought a packet today guessing she was a heavy smoker.

'I've been working up 'ere for over twenty years,' she said after she'd taken her first drag. 'I came in the first place as a machinist at Cohen's, that was a ladies fashion 'ouse just off the Charing Cross Road. I was seventeen then, so that would make it 1952. It was a bloody awful job, us girls would start work at seven and we didn't finish until six, sometimes even later when they had a rush job on. We got paid piece-work and I weren't quick enough for the boss's liking. Some of the other girls started leaving to get jobs in clubs, and I followed them.'

Andrew listened as she gave him her views on Soho at that time. 'See, after the war, London was full of ex-service blokes, and lots of them couldn't really adjust to peacetime. They got jobs in insurance, banks and stuff, but they were bored silly. They used to escape after work to the little drinking clubs, meet up with mates they could talk to about the good old days and spin a few yarns.' She paused and laughed. 'Us girls used to hear some tales, every one of them was supposed to be a 'ero, but they was nice in the main, and it didn't seem so bad to us girls to take the odd one home for a bit on the side.'

'So that's how you got started?' Andrew asked, blushing scarlet.

Angie put one hand over his. 'Don't go bashful on me,' she laughed. 'Yeah, I became a tart, I'm not ashamed of it. I weren't forced into it, I was picky too in them days. I 'ad me looks and a good figure. It ain't like that now, it's a toilet out there. More weirdos to the square mile than normal blokes, and I can't be choosy no longer. But I make a good living. I've got a few bob tucked away and a little council place. I ain't complaining.'

The Knickerbocker Glories arrived and their conversation was halted. Andrew watched the way she ate hers and wondered at her almost childlike glee, suddenly aware how privileged he was. He broached the subject of the Lotus Club tentatively.

She stopped eating and looked at him in surprise. 'Fancy you knowing about that place! I worked there for a bit.'

'Did you?' Andrew could hardly contain his excitement. 'Tell me about it.'

'A Chinese bloke owned it,' she said without any hesitation. 'It was one of the first clubs I worked in and it 'adn't been open long. 'E were nice, always 'ad a laugh and a joke with us girls. I did me first strip there too.'

'You were a stripper too?' Andrew felt this woman must have been heaven sent.

'Not really, only did a few turns. I weren't any good at it. There was girls at that club who were the business,

429

next to them I didn't stand a chance. One of 'em – Sylvie 'er name was, she were the boss's bit of crumpet – was the best I've ever seen. Even the young girls now, proper dancers and stuff, couldn't hold a candle to 'er.'

Andrew gulped. For one brief moment he considered telling Angie that he'd found that same woman dead and that he loved her daughter.

'Don't suppose you know what happened to her?' he asked.

Angie giggled. 'She was the only girl I knew in those days who had her 'ead screwed on,' she said. 'Married the boss and turned respectable. That don't 'appen too often. They usually turn up again, but she never did.'

'What about her husband, your boss?'

'Now that's a funny story,' Angie said, glancing around her as if to make sure no one was eavesdropping. 'I 'adn't thought of 'im in years. Jin, 'is name was. Us girls used to call him gin and tonic. But a couple of years ago, the police came up 'ere looking for 'im. Seems 'e'd done a runner owing a lot of money. I never spoke to the fuzz, I wouldn't piss on them if they was on fire. But I 'eard the talk. Anyway, a mate of mine, who knows what's what, said they wouldn't find him however 'ard they looked, not in England anyway, because 'e'd been murdered over in 'Olland.'

Andrew felt a shiver go down his spine. Spud had mentioned Holland too, and Charlie had said that the last time she spoke to her father he was on his way to Rotterdam.

'Did you hear anything about why he was killed? Was he a villain?'

Angie gave him an odd pitying look. 'Blokes that start out in Soho aren't exactly straight,' she said. 'But Jin, 'e weren't a real "face", know what I mean? He'd been round the block a few times. Sharp as razors, but not a villain. He weren't the sort to get up people's noses either.'

'What do you think happened then?' Andrew asked.

'Buggered if I know,' she said, pushing aside her now empty glass and reaching for Andrew's cigarettes. 'I wonder 'ow his missis took it, she was mad about 'im and they 'ad a kid an' all. I was in 'is club the night she were born, what a party that was!'

Andrew almost held his breath as Angie spoke of Jin getting out bottle after bottle of champagne. 'It was the good stuff too,' she said, her blue eyes brightening as she remembered. 'Some people got so drunk they conked out on the floor.'

'Someone today mentioned a woman called DeeDee,' Andrew said. 'They thought she worked at the Lotus too.'

Angie began coughing violently. 'That bitch,' she rasped.

Andrew asked the waitress to bring a glass of water and ordered a pot of tea too. Angie's coughing gradually subsided after a few sips, but her face was still very flushed.

'Too many cigarettes?' Andrew said in sympathy.

'No, I reckon it was you bringing up that bitch's name,' she said. 'She got me the sack. But it's funny someone told you about 'er, no one ever mentions her name around 'ere.'

'Why?'

'Because she's real bad news.'

'In what way?'

'Keep on asking about 'er and you'll find out,' Angie said with a grimace. 'She's like a bleedin' octopus, with a tentacle in everything. But she don't call 'erself DeeDee no longer. 'Asn't called herself that since the days she stripped with Sylvie, and she's come a long way since that. Miss Dexter is what she gets called, and God 'elp anyone that forgets the Miss. But let's get off 'er, I'm not 'appy talking about that.'

Andrew felt as if his party balloon had just been pricked. He was certain Angie knew a great deal about this woman, possibly even where she lived and where she operated from, but he instinctively knew that if he persisted in asking questions she'd get up and leave.

Over the tea, he asked her about other aspects of Soho, and once again heard similar stories to ones he'd already been told.

It was nearly six when Angie said she had to go. Andrew thanked her for her help, and gave her one of his handouts. 'If you think of something more could you drop me a line there?'

'Okay,' she said folding it and putting it in her handbag.

Andrew didn't think she would write. 'Is there anywhere I could contact you again if I need something more?' he asked impulsively. 'I daren't go walking up and down that street to look for you.'

She looked apprehensive for a moment. 'Okay, I'll give you my home address,' she said. 'But I'm not on the phone, so drop me a line before you come, and best make it around two in the afternoon. Before the kids get home from school.' She scribbled down an address in Mornington Crescent.

'You've got kids?' He was surprised she hadn't mentioned them before.

'Three, two boys and a girl,' she said with a smile. 'That's another story for you. But they think I work in a pub, so if you should bump into them at my place, you mind your p's and q's.'

'Shall I walk back with you?' he asked. He assumed she was going to work.

'Not on your nelly,' she laughed. 'If any of the girls saw me they'd be pestering me all night to know what was going on.'

As Andrew rode back to Hampstead on his scooter, his mind was whirling with everything he'd been told today. He wished he could share it with Charlie and discuss where they should go from here. Maybe the police didn't know that DeeDee the mistress was now known as Miss Dexter, but it would be pointless for him to go and try to talk to someone about it. Charlie was the only person that could do that.

Chapter Fifteen

Spud staggered into his room in Berwick Street just after midnight. He was much drunker than usual for a Monday night, and he blamed that on the young lad who'd asked so many questions today.

Drink was the only way Spud had of blanking out how hopeless his future was. He might have been a courageous boxer once, and still remembered in boxing circles, but he'd only ever won minor championships, and was finished by an eye injury before he even got a stab at a big one. Two marriages down the pan. Both wives had run off when they discovered he was a loser. Even the jobs he once got as a doorman at clubs were closed to him now. Club owners didn't just want beef these days, they wanted handsome faces too.

Spud looked around his room dejectedly. He didn't really see the dirt, the filthy sheet on the unmade bed or the black mould on the walls; he'd grown used to that long ago. All he saw was the absence of comforts – no television, no soft armchair, not even a pair of curtains at the grimy window.

He got his dole money each week, and supplemented that with odd jobs, stacking crates in pub cellars, toting vegetables down the market, and on good days he told himself he still had his health and plenty of friends.

But talking to that kid today had brought back the good times, when he'd had flashy suits, a gold watch, money in his pocket and a girl on his arm. The lad had been fresh-faced, bright and eager, soaking up Spud's stories like a sponge. He'd got his whole life ahead of him and he'd probably make a fortune from writing a book about the characters of Soho. Spud was one of them, but what would he get? Nothing!

He fumbled in his pocket for the leaflet the lad had given him. The print was too small to read without glasses, and he'd lost those some time ago. But he could read the Hampstead address at the top, and that to his mind said it all.

'A big 'ouse, good schools, plenty of dosh,' he mumbled. 'You should'a got more than a dinner out'a 'im. You're a mug, Spud, you let people take advantage.'

He lay down on his bed and kicked off his boots. The room was like an oven and he wanted a piss, but it was too far down the stairs, and the lights had gone because someone had nicked the light bulbs. He could bet that kid didn't have to worry about his stairs being lit up, his folks probably had servants that put them on and off.

Spud reached under the bed for his emergency bucket. It was nearly full already and it slopped on the floor as he pulled it out. He flopped himself over the edge, relieved himself, then lay back on the bed.

'Strange he was so interested in the Lotus Club,' he said aloud. 'What did 'e want to know about that for?'

Spud fell asleep before he could think of any good

reason why anyone would want to know about one small cellar club owned by a Chinese.

It was early morning when Spud woke again. The market men were setting up below, clanking the poles from their stalls and shouting at each other, just as they did every day. The bucket stank, and he wished he'd had the presence of mind to chuck it out the window last night, as he usually did.

His head was surprisingly clear. And as he lay there wondering whether to get up and go and see if anyone wanted his help, Miss Dexter suddenly sprang into his mind.

She'd always been good for a few bob in the past when he had some information to pass on. She was after all Jin Weish's bird at one time, and she might very well be interested that someone was asking questions about him.

Spud smiled. It had to be worth a tenner. Besides, she might have some other jobs for him. The sun was shining outside, he'd go and see if anyone wanted any help, then nip down the baths and get spruced up to see her.

The man who marched briskly into the Mayfair offices of Eagle Incorporated at noon looked a great deal better than he'd looked at seven the same morning. In a dark suit, clean shirt and with his shoes cleaned Spud was almost smart. But the suit was threadbare with a pervading smell of mould, and his shoes had holes in the soles.

'Could I see Miss Dexter?' he asked the receptionist. 'She's expecting me. It's Mr O'Neill.'

'Would you like to take a seat while I call her,' the receptionist replied, trying hard not to stare at the strange-looking man, or wrinkle her nose at the smell of carbolic soap mingled with mould wafting from him. She'd only been working at Eagle Inc for two weeks so she knew nothing more about the company other than that they dealt in property, but she couldn't help thinking that for such a smart office, they had some very peculiar callers.

Spud sat and waited, his hands clasped between his outstretched knees. This office in Brook Street always intimidated him, it was too grand for his taste with its thick carpets, chrome and glass. Even the young receptionist looked as if she'd just stepped out of a fashion magazine.

'Miss Dexter will see you now, Mr O'Neill,' the girl said after a few minutes. 'Up the stairs and it's the room in front of you.'

'I know,' he said, anxious to make the girl see he was someone important. 'I've been here before, many times.'

Many times was stretching it, around three times including now, but then Spud always exaggerated.

'Good morning, John Joe,' Miss Dexter said as he opened her office door. 'Come in and sit down.'

Spud might not like her much, but he approved of her calling him by his proper name. Her office was just like her – cold, efficient and tasteful. A huge black desk, white walls and pale grey carpet, with black and white framed 'art' photographs on the walls. Her hair was black, fixed up in a tight bun, she wore a black suit and white blouse. The only scrap of colour in the room was her red lipstick.

'I hope you didn't mind me belling you,' he said. 'But like I said, I 'ad something I thought might be of interest to you.'

'And what might that be?' she said raising one thin pencilled eyebrow.

Spud explained as quickly as possible; he knew she thought her time too precious to waste on chit-chat. 'He might be kosher,' he said. 'Well-spoken, bright lad. But it struck me funny that he was so interested in the Lotus Club. He also asked if I knew a DeeDee.'

Spud knew that would worry her, few people knew she once went by that name.

'Did he now?' She put her elbows on her desk and rested her chin on her two clenched hands. 'And what pray did you tell him?'

'I said I'd never met anyone called that.'

'I see,' she said, staring at him coldly.

Spud observed that her blue eyes were the same colour as the sky outside the window behind her, her skin still as smooth as a child's. He had often wondered why such a good-looking woman could be so evil, for that was what she was.

'And what were you thinking this piece of news was worth?' she asked.

'That's up to you, Miss,' he said quickly. He slid his hand into his inside pocket and brought out the handout. 'Maybe 'e is what 'e says, but it's odd, ain't it?'

She gave it no more than a cursory glance and dropped it to her desk. 'I expect he's employed by one of those terribly dull film companies. They are forever sending out young people in the faint hope they might find something worth turning into a tedious documentary,' she said. 'But thank you, John Joe, for bringing it to my attention.' She opened her desk drawer and pulled out a £20 note. 'That's for your trouble, and of course it goes without saying you won't mention our little chat to anyone else.'

'Of course not, Miss Dexter, and thank you,' he said, pocketing the note before she could change her mind. 'I'll be off then.'

Spud almost ran to the nearest pub. He knew she was seriously rattled, or she wouldn't have given him a twenty. It had turned out to be a very good day.

Daphne Dexter studied the leaflet for some time after Spud had gone, wondering who on earth this Andrew Blake could be. If he had been working for a film company he would have used their headed paper, and his approach to Spud was far too amateurish for a detective, private or with CID. Of course he might be just what he said he was, a kid doing some freelance research work for a serious writer. But who could have given him that name DeeDee?

Only a handful of people knew it. The period she used it for wasn't more than eighteen months, and it was as dead as a door-nail by 1953, when she was twenty-four. That was nineteen years ago!

Daphne Dexter had got where she was today, the owner of an extremely successful company, by paying attention to small details. Back in the late Fifties when she was after buying a crumbling, rat-infested house in the back streets of Paddington, she made sure she knew all there was to know about the sitting tenants before buying it for next to nothing from the landlord.

Blackmail was a far easier way of persuading

someone to leave a property than violence. She used it quite casually at that time. Just a word in the Jamaican's ear that she knew he'd entered the country on forged documents, and he and his family disappeared the same day. The other family were obtaining National Assistance fraudulently, and that had the same effect.

Within three years she owned four such houses, and had them crammed with the kind of tenants who didn't complain about overcrowding, unsanitary conditions and high rents. They were all West Indians and grateful for anywhere to live.

Keeping an ear to the ground, checking people out became a way of life. And the East London thugs she'd known from childhood, and her own brothers, were invaluable to keep her tenants in order. People said she was lucky, but then they didn't know that what appeared to be luck was in fact often inside information. She heard a whisper that the notorious landlord Peter Rachman was about to be thoroughly investigated, long before he knew it. She emptied out her houses and sold them all. By the time his name became common knowledge throughout England, she was buying up other houses in more select areas and renting them out to young Australians, New Zealanders, and Americans, who wanted to sample 'Swinging London'. They had to get their friends to sleep on their floors to pay the high rents, but the 'Bleeding Heart' brigade didn't concern themselves with young visitors to England.

Then there were the clubs which turned over a small fortune, all of which went back into property. Daphne Dexter knew the club world inside out already, and each place she opened had a distinct style to appeal to a different kind of clientele. The traditional strip clubs were always a good money-spinner, the punters paid through the nose to get in, were fleeced on the price of drinks, but got a good show. She started the first peepshow place in Soho, and even though the thought of men masturbating in tiny booths while they watched a girl strip was nauseating, it was a brilliant money-spinner. Instead of a man being able to sit for the whole evening for the price of a ticket, he had to pay to watch each girl. There was no bar to stock, no waitresses, or tills to be dipped into. Just four or five girls doing the same routine over and over again.

Then there were the kids' clubs. Bare walls, coloured light shows and a hip disc jockey. Word of mouth brought the kids flocking, she could sell soft drinks at huge profits and the drug dealers had to pay a high premium or they didn't get in to sell their wares.

But all of that was over now. She sold up the clubs back in 1969 when she saw the writing on the wall. She'd managed to wriggle out of the charge of supplying drugs to her customers with a smart lawyer. But it had frightened her. The success of the Krays' conviction meant the police were getting sharper, kids were becoming a bit more discriminating about their entertainment, and she no longer had the stomach for sleaze and pornography. Now all the properties she bought, renovated and sold again were in smart areas, everything was above-board, right down to her tax returns.

The last thing she wanted now was old skeletons falling out of the cupboard.

*

The following Saturday afternoon Andrew called at his friend John's flat in Hampstead. It was raining hard, but he braved it in the hopes there might be a few letters for him, along with sharing a few cans of beer with his friend. They had been friends since they met as freshers at City University two years ago, and it was John who'd got him the job at Jack Straw's Castle. John had jacked in his job a few weeks ago as he needed time to study.

'There's two letters arrived for you,' John said as he let Andrew in. 'What are you up to, Andy?' he asked curiously as he handed them over. 'You're not having it off with a married woman or something, are you?'

Andrew laughed. John was a studious type, thin, glasses and a mop of hair that looked like dirty straw. Because he had so little success with girls and spent all his time thinking about them, he regarded any unusual behaviour on the part of others as evidence that they were having an illicit relationship. 'Certainly not. Would I use your address for that?'

They went into the living room. Andrew handed over the cans of beer, then sat down to read the letters. As always, the flat was like a show place, clean and tidy to the point of obsession. John's parents were wealthy and they'd bought the flat for their son as an investment. John fancied himself as a bit of an interior designer; all the furniture was Scandinavian design – bleached pine chairs and table, red and white checked armchairs and ultra-modern spindly lamps.

Andrew opened the handwritten envelope first, just because it looked more interesting, and in a woman's writing. It was only half a page, and very badly written, from an address he didn't recognize in WC1.

'If you want to now who killed Freddie Mills, I'm the persun who can tell you,' it said. 'I have to be carful because they wach me. But if you right and tell me were to meat you I can tell you then.' It was signed Julie and a surname Andrew couldn't read. At the bottom of the page was a postscript. 'Do not give my adress to aneone.'

Andrew sniggered. He didn't think he'd be taking her up on her offer! He opened the typewritten one. It had a Shepherd's Bush address.

'Dear Mr Blake,' he read. *'While in a sweet shop in Soho today, the owner showed me your handout because he knew I had a great deal of knowledge about Soho during the Fifties and he thought I could maybe help you. I worked as a living-in barmaid at the Garrick for some years, and as I was young then I visited all the clubs too, and knew most of the people who worked in them. The area has changed so much since then, but I could give you pointers as to what's still the same, what's missing now, and show you my collection of photographs.*

'I shall be home on Friday, 2 September and if you'd like to call at around three in the afternoon we could have a chat. I'm sorry if this time is inconvenient, but I'm working all this week until then, and afterwards going away for a little holiday.

Yours sincerely,

Martha Grimsby (Miss)'

Andrew gave a whistle of approval. She sounded perfect, the right age, the right type. And well away from Soho.

'Are you going to explain what you're up to?' John asked plaintively.

443

'Basically I'm trying to solve a bit of a mystery,' Andrew said. He was loath to give any detail, it was Charlie's business after all. 'Charlie's dad disappeared a couple of years ago and hasn't been seen since. I've been trying to find out what happened.'

'Oh, I see.' John looked disappointed it wasn't something more salacious. 'So who are those letters from?'

'Just people offering a bit of information. One's definitely a crank, but the other sounds hopeful.'

'But you've split up with Charlie,' John said. 'Why are you bothering?'

'To get her back of course,' Andrew said. 'Let's have a beer and put some sounds on.'

Almost a week later, on Thursday evening, Charlie was packing her suitcase in her hotel bedroom. She couldn't leave York until the course finished the next day at five, but she wanted to be ready to leave on the first train after that.

Despite her reservations about coming up to York, it had done her a power of good. She'd acquired a new skill plus the promise of a pay rise. But most of all she'd had time to sit back and look at her life as a whole, rather than just one piece of it.

She had found that the love she felt for Andrew was undiminished, despite all the protestations she'd made to the contrary. Her complete trust in him might be severely dented, but an inner voice kept telling her that she had over-reacted and allowed herself to be torn apart by irrational jealousy.

Rita had been right in saying men like Andrew were scarce. For the last two weeks she'd been thinking over all he did when her mother died, the support and friendship he'd offered in those black weeks that followed, and decided he deserved a second chance.

Even the change in weather seemed to bear out all she felt. The long, hot summer had ended suddenly two days ago, blue skies and sunshine being replaced with cold autumnal winds, rain and leaden skies. It was time to take stock of what was important, and what wasn't. And plan for the future.

At three the following afternoon, Andrew was in Shepherd's Bush for his appointment with Martha Grimsby. Tittmus Street was a very short street of small terraced houses, which led back on to the Goldhawk Road. After riding along it once and finding no room between the closely parked cars, he went back to the beginning of the street and left his scooter there. He took off his waterproof jacket and tucked it with his helmet into the box on the back of the scooter, combed his hair then made his way back to number 5.

'Miss Grimsby?' he asked when the door was opened by a dark-haired woman. 'Andrew Blake.'

'Yes, I'm Martha, do come in,' she said.

Andrew was surprised by her, he'd expected someone older, plump and brassily blonde. Martha was perhaps in her forties, but she looked younger. She was wearing baggy grey trousers, a hideous flowered smock-type garment on top, and her hair was scraped unflatteringly back off her face, but she had beautiful blue eyes, perfect, unlined skin and a kind of presence that suggested she had been, and could still, with a bit of effort, be something of a sensation.

'You must excuse the state of my home,' she said

in a low, husky voice. 'I've had some builders in doing work for me and they've gone off and left it in a fearful mess. We'll have to sit in the kitchen.'

Andrew could see what she meant. The two small rooms they passed by on the way down the hall had bare plaster and the floors were littered with tins of paint and bags of cement and timber. The stairs were bare too, the walls were in the process of being stripped.

'How much longer will they be doing it? It must be awful for you,' he asked politely. He hadn't imagined a barmaid who lived in Shepherd's Bush would be so well-spoken. But then he reminded himself that he shouldn't think in stereotypes.

'I hope it will be finished when I get back from my holiday,' she said, ushering him into a long, narrow kitchen. 'All my furniture is upstairs, and it's quite chaotic.'

The kitchen had clearly just been finished. It was all white with red knobs on the cupboards. Martha urged him to sit down at a small breakfast bar by the window and immediately offered him coffee.

'Nothing much else in the cupboards,' she said with a smile as she opened one and all there was inside were mugs, a bag of sugar and a jar of coffee. 'Everything's packed away upstairs. Of course when I suggested you came today I imagined at least the front room would be finished. I'm rather embarrassed to be only able to offer the kitchen.'

Andrew assured her he didn't mind one bit. As soon as she sat down opposite him they went straight into the conversation about Soho. 'I was just seventeen when I got the job in the Garrick,' she said. 'I made out I was eighteen and I used to put on lots of makeup to make myself look older. The first year I was frightened out of my wits most of the time. We used to get such tough types drinking in there.'

Andrew sat back and listened as she spoke of many of the characters he'd already heard about several times. Like Angie she mentioned the many ex-servicemen around in those days, but she claimed most of them were company representatives rather than in insurance and banking. 'Heaven only knows when they made their calls,' she said. 'They'd come in the bar around twelve, stay till closing time, then go on to afternoon drinking clubs. Most of them were very tedious, they talked constantly about their exploits during the war. But of course I was young, and I looked forward, not backward like them.'

She went on to explain how these men's drinking habits shaped post-war Soho. 'You see, the licensing laws were very strict, but operating a system where clubs opened and closed at different times, it was possible to drink solidly from noon until three or four in the morning. The men who owned the afternoon clubs were some of the very worst sharks. They not only fleeced the customers, but their staff too.

'It was very hard to get somewhere to live at that time, so they offered the girls who worked for them a flat above the club and charged them an exorbitant rent, and quite often the girls had to have sex with their boss too, as part of the deal. Of course it wasn't long before the girls found the only way to pay the rent was to charge customers for sex as well.'

Andrew was riveted by this candid exposure. It had no real bearing on what he wanted to know, but it

447

was giving him a real insight into the world Sylvia and DeeDee found themselves in.

'Now, when the afternoon clubs closed for the evening, those same girls would go on to other clubs, sometimes just to socialize, but often they might do a spot in a strip club as well. Later they'd go on to the night clubs. A really resourceful girl with stamina and determination could be making money from four or five different sources, and all within the law.'

Martha smiled at his shocked expression. 'They didn't consider themselves tarts,' she said quickly. 'That was a name only given to the women who touted for business on street corners. If you meet anyone who tells you she was a hostess, she was one of these girls.'

Andrew was warming to this woman. Unlike Angie she wasn't hiding behind euphemisms, she laid it right on the line. When he said this to her she laughed.

'Well, I was just an onlooker, Andrew. I worked at the pub for long hours and I'd dream of getting married, moving to a nice little house in the suburbs and having children. The more I saw of that world from the safety of the Garrick, the less Soho had to offer me. As it turned out I didn't get to move to the suburbs, I married a man in the licensing trade and we ended up in a pub in the Strand.' She paused for a moment. Andrew wondered what had happened to her husband. She'd put 'Miss' on her letter.

'The marriage didn't work out,' she shrugged. 'He drank too much and I cut my losses and then moved into office work. And here I am now, divorced, no children, but a nice little house of my own, or it will be when all the work is finished. I don't have any connection now with any of those people I once knew in Soho. It's a time I look back on with some nostalgia, but I'm very glad I got away from there when I did.'

Andrew suddenly felt very relaxed. He thought she was a nice woman, intelligent, and open-minded. It had been exciting talking to Angie, getting glimpses into her seedy world, but he felt a whole lot more comfortable with Martha.

He asked her then what she knew about the Lotus Club.

'Oh yes, I remember that one,' she said with a smile. 'It was a quite unique place. It opened about nine at night as I remember and it was primarily a drinking club, but they had strippers too. Some of the best in Soho, or so the men said. It had an excellent reputation, not one of the clip joints, a good atmosphere and a pianist and a bit of dancing. It was always packed. But why do you want to know about that club, Andrew? It wasn't a famous place, it certainly wasn't representative of the clubs of that time.'

Andrew took a deep breath before answering. His original plan to say nothing to anyone about his real motives for gathering information didn't seem to be getting him very far. All he really had was a lot of useless information about Soho in general and time was running out before Charlie got back. It would impress her far more if he had something solid and meaty to tell her, and maybe in her excitement she'd forget the past and let him back into her life.

Martha certainly didn't look or sound like a gangster's moll, she had no connections with Soho any longer. Just a middle-aged woman who would probably be intrigued to hear about the Lotus Club owner's disappearance, and it would focus her mind solely on the one place and the people who drank in there back in the Fifties and early Sixties.

'I'm not really researching a book,' he said. 'In fact I'm the boyfriend of Charlie Weish, the daughter of the man who owned that club. I'm just a student, and I'm sorry if I led you up the garden path at first, but I did have my reasons.'

'You'd better explain them then,' she said, but her smile was one of amusement, not dismay or annoyance. 'Come on, the whole story!'

Martha was very attentive as he explained, stopping him now and then to clarify a point, so that he found himself telling her everything even more fully than he'd intended. She seemed particularly shocked to hear Sylvia Weish had finally committed suicide.

'So I'm sure you can understand why Charlie needs to know what happened to her father,' he finished up. 'If he did make a new life with DeeDee, I think she'll accept it. But I'm inclined to believe he's dead and that this woman knows about it. If we could find something, who she is, where she is, anything, we could go to the police and get them to start investigating again.' He paused for a moment.

'Charlie doesn't actually know that I've started hunting around, we had a quarrel and I haven't seen her for a month now. But she's coming back to London tomorrow and I thought if I had something to tell her, anything, it might help put things right between us.'

'Dear me, Andrew! What a sad story,' she said, and patted his hand. 'The poor girl! What a terrible time she's had. I think you were very wise not to come right out and tell people your real interest, around Soho at least. The people there are always very cagey

450

about talking about their own. But I'm quite different. I'm just an office girl now.'

'But did you know Jin Weish back then?' he asked. 'Or Sylvia and DeeDee?'

'I remember Jin and Sylvia well,' she said.

'You do?' he gasped.

Martha half smiled. 'Yes. That's why it gave me such a turn when you told me what had happened to them. They were a nice couple. Jin came in the Garrick and told us when his daughter was born. But I don't recall DeeDee. Do you know what she looked like?'

Andrew shook his head. 'I've no real idea. Only that she was beautiful. Charlie has some old photographs, DeeDee may well be in them, but she didn't find them until after Sylvia died. There isn't anyone else she could ask about them.'

'I've got a few old photos upstairs,' Martha said. 'I haven't looked at them in years, but I'm almost certain there are some taken in the Lotus Club, you never know, looking at them together might jog my memory. Can you hang on while I go and try and find them?'

Andrew beamed, he was in no hurry. He didn't have to be back at the pub until eight. 'If you don't mind,' he said. 'Are you sure I'm not stopping you from doing anything more important?'

'What could be more important than helping a young girl find out about her father?' she said with a smile. 'You put the kettle on, Andrew, and we'll have another cup of coffee when I get back.'

Martha wasn't long. Andrew had put the kettle on and washed up their mugs in readiness when she came back in with a brown envelope in her hands.

'There's more than this somewhere,' she said. 'But they must be in one of the buried boxes. Still, we can search through those when I get back from my holiday, maybe Charlie could come with you then.' She passed the envelope to Andrew, urged him to open it up and turned away to make the coffee.

They were surprisingly good pictures for the period. The men were all very dapper with slicked-back hair and thin moustaches, either in dinner jackets or lounge suits, their women looking very dated in cocktail dresses with permed, stiff-looking hair.

'I've found one of Jin!' Andrew said jubilantly just as Martha was coming back to the table with the coffee. Even if he'd been surrounded by other Chinese, rather than a group of girls, and Andrew hadn't seen several photographs of the man he would have known him, he looked so much like Charlie. 'He was a handsome devil, wasn't he?'

'He certainly was,' she laughed. 'All the girls thought so, despite a natural prejudice against his race. Tall and slender, charming and always immaculately dressed. Now let me look at that one with you. Sylvia must be in there somewhere.'

She leaned over him. 'There she is.' Martha pointed out a girl standing slightly behind two bigger girls, looking over their shoulders.

Andrew had only ever seen pictures of Sylvia when she was over thirty, and although in those she'd always been so exquisitely dressed and unfailingly elegant, he'd always thought she looked cold and brittle. Yet in this picture he could see exactly why Jin had fallen for her rather than the other buxom girls in the group; she had an almost ethereal beauty, big eyes, a soft, childlike mouth, so very different to the only image he had imprinted on his mind of her.

Andrew drank his coffee while Martha rattled off the names of those she could remember and some potted history. 'This one,' she said pointing at a woman almost bursting out of a glittery evening dress, 'died a few years after this picture. Apparently she had an abortion that went tragically wrong. And that one,' again she pointed to a blonde, 'used to work as a nude model in one of those fake photographer's places, where men pay to take pictures.'

One by one Martha went through the pictures and the stories came thick and fast. 'That's Ruth Ellis,' she said, drawing his attention to another blonde in a glittery evening dress. 'You know, the last woman to be hanged. She shot her boyfriend. She worked the Little Club in Kensington, but she used to come over to Soho late at night to go dancing. She shouldn't have been hanged, her whole trial was a farce. Somewhere in these pictures there must be one of her boss, Maury Conley, he was a slimy toad, I hated him.'

Andrew found himself getting very sleepy. He thought it was because the kitchen was very stuffy. He kept jerking himself back to what Martha was saying, but each time it happened he felt he'd missed a bit.

'Are you all right?' he heard her say, but when he looked at her his eyes couldn't focus on her face. 'It is a bit stuffy in here. Why don't you put your head down on the table for a moment and I'll open the window.'

Andrew tried very hard to fight it off, but he couldn't. He had the strange feeling he was falling through space, and there was nothing else for it but to let himself go.

Charlie arrived back at Rita's flat just after ten-thirty that night.

'You look much better,' Rita exclaimed. 'See, I said a holiday would do you good.'

'Some holiday,' Charlie grinned. 'We were kept at it from nine in the morning until five. But the hotel was great, I ate like a pig.'

'Let's pop out and have a drink to celebrate your homecoming,' Rita suggested. 'There's half an hour till closing time.'

'Can I just phone Andrew?' Charlie said. 'I won't be a minute. I only want to say I'll see him tomorrow to talk.'

Rita raised one eyebrow. 'Absence does make the heart grow fonder then?'

Charlie giggled. 'I suppose so. I missed you too. You go on down to the pub and get the drinks in, I won't be two minutes.'

Rita picked up her bag and went out. Charlie dialled the number at Jack Straw's Castle and came through to the bar. 'Could I speak to Andrew Blake?' she asked. The bar sounded very noisy.

'He isn't here tonight,' the man said.

'He doesn't usually get Friday nights off, does he?' Charlie asked. She didn't like to ask who she was talking to, but she thought it was Stan, Carol's husband.

'He didn't get tonight off,' the man said stiffly. 'He just didn't turn up.'

Charlie thought that was odd – to her knowledge

Andrew had never bunked off work before. It was impossible to question the man further though; judging by the noise in the bar it was very busy. 'Will you tell him Charlie called?' she said. 'I'll come up tomorrow to see him.'

The man said something about he wouldn't have a job to come back to unless he had a good explanation and promptly put the phone down.

Charlie went downstairs and into the pub a few doors further along the street. It too was very busy but Rita had got her a half pint of cider.

'I expect he had a few drinks at lunchtime,' Rita replied after Charlie explained Andrew hadn't been there. 'He's probably at some mate's flat sleeping it off. Now come on, tell me about this course.'

Charlie was still talking when the pub closed, describing all the people she met and the places she'd been to.

When they got back to the flat, Charlie excitedly pulled a present for her friend out of her suitcase.

'You shouldn't have wasted your money on me,' Rita said, but her face lit up and Charlie knew she was touched. 'Oh,' she gasped as she unwrapped an emerald-green short-sleeved cotton jacket. 'Charlie, it's lovely. My favourite colour.'

Rita had been on Charlie's mind a great deal while she'd been away, and she had come to realize not only how much she owed her, but the full extent of her friend's trauma at the hands of the Dexters. She knew she couldn't wipe out what had happened with words, but she was determined to get Rita out and about more.

'I thought it was less frumpy than a cardigan, and

it will look sensational with your hair,' Charlie said as she tried it on. 'If it's the last thing I do while I'm staying here with you, I'm going to make you glamorous again.'

It was raining heavily again and quite cold, so Rita drew the curtains, lit the gas fire and opened up a bottle of cider. They sat drinking and talking for a couple of hours.

'I'm so glad to have you back here with me, I really missed you,' Rita said as they eventually got up to go to bed. 'And I'm really glad I told you about myself now. It's kind of pulled me together. I've been having all sorts of positive ideas for the future these last two weeks.'

Charlie hugged her friend joyfully, so very glad they'd helped one another and they were both on the road to recovery. She knew there wasn't any point in telling Rita that a man could love her even with a scarred body, she wouldn't believe it. But Charlie knew it was true and she hoped it would be proved before long.

Charlie woke the next morning to find it was still raining. She was very disappointed as she'd hoped she and Andrew could maybe walk on the Heath. But by the time she'd had a bath, washed her hair and dressed in a new black and pink maxi-dress, the sky looked a bit brighter.

'Now, just don't go rushing headlong back to him,' Rita said sternly when Charlie said goodbye to her. 'Try and be a bit cool, and don't make any rash promises.'

'What are you going to do today?' Charlie asked.

'I thought I'd do some shopping, get a joint in for tomorrow in case you want to invite Andrew over for lunch. Then later I'll go and see Paul and my parents. I won't be back until about ten. So the coast will be clear if you want to get up to some hanky-panky.'

'You said I wasn't to go rushing back to him,' Charlie giggled. 'What's sex during the day if it isn't rushing?'

'I know what human nature is,' Rita grinned. 'And quite often sex is the best healer of all.'

It was half past ten when Charlie arrived at Jack Straw's Castle and raining hard, despite her earlier hopes it might clear up. The saloon door was open, and she could hear someone vacuuming. She went in hesitantly. Carol, the landlady, was behind the bar polishing glasses.

Before Charlie had a chance to speak, Carol bawled out at her, 'If you've come to tell me Andrew's ill and can't get in tonight either, then you can pack up his stuff right now and take it back to him.'

Charlie was very taken aback. 'I just came to see him. Isn't he here?'

'Of course he isn't. Would I be grumbling to you if he was?'

Charlie just stood there, not knowing what to say. Carol was quite a formidable woman, even when she was in a good mood.

'I'm very sorry,' Charlie said nervously. 'But I've been away in York for two weeks and I haven't actually seen Andrew for a month. I don't know anything, other than that my friend told me he was expecting me to phone here last night. Do you mean he hasn't come home at all?'

Perhaps the woman knew why Andrew hadn't seen her for so long, and maybe she picked up the slight shake in Charlie's voice at the implications about him not coming home. Whatever the reason, her big face softened. She put down the glasses in her hands and came round the bar to Charlie.

'I'm sorry, dear, I knew you were away, but when he didn't turn up for work last night I just assumed he'd met you on your return and was skiving off with you. He wouldn't be with another girl, love, he was looking forward too much to you coming back. So I can't imagine where else he could be. He hasn't ever stayed out all night since you had your quarrel, and it's not like him to be unreliable. He's the best barman we've had in some time.'

Charlie asked when Carol had last seen him. She told her he'd left just after lunchtime closing, and that he hadn't said where he was going.

'Could I wait and see if he turns up?' she asked. 'I could do some jobs for you?'

Carol smiled with a great deal more warmth. 'That's not necessary. You just sit in the corner out the way and read the paper. I expect he'll come tearing in any minute with some excuse.'

An hour passed and he still didn't come. At twelve the bar was opened and Charlie bought a lemonade and went back to her seat. She stayed there till one when Carol came over to her.

'I've just been in Andrew's room,' she said. 'I went to look and see if I could find his mother's telephone number. I thought maybe he'd gone home. I couldn't find it, but I did pick this up off the table. Does it mean anything to you?'

She handed over one of Andrew's handouts. Charlie read it and looked back at Carol. 'Yes, it does. It looks like he's been trying to get some information about my father. You wouldn't know who the address belongs to, would you?'

Carol glanced at it again. 'Oh yes, that's John's. You remember him, the rasher of bacon with glasses that used to work here too.'

'I'll go and ask him then,' Charlie said. 'If Andrew should come back while I'm gone, tell him to wait here for me, will you?'

'I'll have him hung, drawn and quartered by then,' Carol joked. 'If he is at John's, make him phone me.'

John came to the door in his pyjamas; he looked terrible and told Charlie he had a bad hangover. Andrew wasn't there, and he hadn't seen him since earlier in the week. 'Come in, though,' he said. 'If you want to make a cup of coffee, I'll put some clothes on.'

Charlie was impressed by John's flat, she'd always imagined all Andrew's friends lived in squalor. When John re-emerged wearing jeans and a sweater, she handed him his coffee and asked about the handout.

'He didn't say much about it, just that it was to do with finding your father,' he said. 'Two replies came the other day. He said one was from a crank but the other sounded hopeful. All I know is that he was going to see someone in Shepherd's Bush.'

'When?'

John shrugged. 'He didn't say. He didn't even show me the letters.'

Charlie asked if he knew of any other friends Andrew might be with. John shook his head. 'It hit him very hard when you packed him in. So I couldn't see him going off to a party and getting wasted knowing you were coming back this weekend. Is his scooter back at the pub?'

'No. Carol said he went off on it after the lunchtime session yesterday.'

'Well, that rules out him going home to his folks, or anywhere further than fifteen or so miles,' John replied, scratching his head. 'He'd go by train if it was further than that.'

Charlie walked dejectedly back to the pub, she didn't know what to think. One side of her mind was telling her he was with another girl, the other side said that was improbable given that both Carol and John had said he was eagerly awaiting her return. He couldn't phone Rita because he didn't know her number. What if he'd had an accident on his scooter and he was lying in hospital somewhere?

Back in the pub Carol pooh-poohed the idea of an accident. 'We'd have heard by now,' she said. 'I doubt very much that he'd go out without any identification on him, he's the type that has his cheque-book, student union card and the works on him. Why don't you go up to his room and look around and see if you can find his diary or something? I don't like to poke around myself, but I'm sure he wouldn't mind you doing it.'

Andrew's room was exactly the way it was when Charlie last saw it over a month ago. Crumpled bedcovers, odd dirty socks lying on the floor along with his plimsolls, the poster from *Easy Rider* with Peter Fonda and Dennis Hopper on their Harley Davidsons, still with one corner flapping in the breeze. Even the candle she'd stuck in a straw-covered Chianti bottle was still there.

His collection of books stacked on the chest of drawers were a pointer to his diverse interests, everything from textbooks on electronics to steamy paperbacks, then Aldous Huxley's *Brave New World*, Salinger's *Catcher in the Rye* and a biography of Winston Churchill. A carefully arranged montage of photographs showed his affection for his family and old friends and his sentimentality about nights out he'd shared with her was apparent in a batch of programmes, ticket stubs and even beer coasters from various pubs.

It was the narrow bed that sent a pang through her heart, remembering all the times they'd made love on it on Saturday afternoons. She could recall stiffening each time she heard footsteps outside on the landing and even Andrew's assurances that the door was locked couldn't quite allay her fears that someone might burst in. She could almost hear his whispered tender words as they lay entwined afterwards and his promises he would love her forever.

One Sunday evening when he wasn't working there had been a summer storm and they'd sat by the window and watched forked lightning illuminating the rain-lashed Heath opposite. This was the tiny, somewhat grubby sanctuary they withdrew to as often as possible. It was here he told her he loved her for the first time, here they made love for the first time, and here she had her first orgasm. She remembered so clearly how she felt after it, the rush of emotion, the wonder and the conviction she'd become a woman at last.

She picked up an abandoned tee-shirt from the bed and sniffed it. It still held a faint whiff of Brut aftershave, and the poignant smell was one she recognized as one which often clung to her skin after bouts of love-making. As she held it to her cheek, tears welled up in her eyes. Carol, Stan and John might think he was off somewhere sleeping off a hangover. She knew better. A sixth sense told her he was in some sort of danger.

Chapter Sixteen

Charlie was up in Andrew's room for some time. She found his diary, but the only entry for the previous day merely said 3.00 Shepherd's Bush. For today, however, he had drawn a heart with the words *Charlie's coming home* inside it. Firm evidence, she thought, that he wouldn't disappear intentionally.

His home telephone number was in the front of the diary, but she was loath to rush into phoning his mother just yet. Then she found a notebook under the edge of his bed.

She might have just shoved it back imagining he was trying his hand at writing a play, for the first thing she read was: 'Alf – fruit and veg stall. 60ish. ex-bookie's runner'. But as she read on she realized this wasn't a fictional character, but someone he'd interviewed in Soho.

When she got to 'Spud', the ex-boxer, and discovered this man not only drank in the Lotus Club but knew her father and Sylvia, she felt elated. But Andrew's notes were too cryptic to follow, many names mentioned by 'Alf' being repeated. But, 'Didn't know DeeDee' and 'Holland' seemed to be of some importance to him because he'd underlined them. She wished he'd been more specific.

The next two pages were about 'Angie'. Judging by her potted history, from seamstress in Charing Cross Road in the early Fifties to finally ending up working as a prostitute in Soho, Andrew had spent some time with her.

Charlie had the feeling he'd liked this woman, even though his description – forty-plus, bleached blonde, blowsy, with missing teeth – sounded appalling. He'd even mentioned she had three children and her home address in Mornington Crescent.

His notes then went on to a list, clearly things Angie had told him which were particularly relevant. She knew both Jin and Sylvia. Worked at the club for a while. At the club on the night of Charlie's birth. Sylvia was the best stripper, better than any of the trained dancers. Said police came looking for Jin two years ago. Heard from a friend he'd been killed in Holland. DeeDee got her the sack.

The part about Holland made her turn back to the notes on Spud. She thought if two people had both specified the same place there had to be at least a grain of truth in it.

But when she saw the last underlined item on Angie's page, 'DeeDee calls herself Miss Dexter now', her elation turned to a chill.

During her stay in York Charlie had thought carefully about everything Rita had told her and she'd decided that Rita was probably letting her imagination run away with her, thinking DeeDee and Daphne Dexter were the same woman. It seemed too far-fetched, even a little hysterical. But now, faced with this confirmation, she was stunned.

Andrew had written a few footnotes at the bottom of

the page. 'Angie described Miss Dexter as an octopus with a tentacle in everything. Doesn't know where she is now. Refused to discuss her further. Afraid of repercussions.'

The only other thing of interest in the room was a badly written and misspelled letter from someone called Julie. Charlie thought it was almost certainly the one John said was from a crank. As he had said Andrew had received two letters, and she couldn't find the second one, it seemed likely the appointment he had in Shepherd's Bush was with the sender of the second. She was just about to go back down to the bar when she spotted his *A to Z* of London lying on top of the pile of books.

Andrew had once joked that London's *A to Z* was his bible, and she'd often seen him marking places he had to go to with a small cross. Turning to the Shepherd's Bush page, she scanned it quickly. There were three crosses on that page, one on the junction of Askew and Starfield Roads, one in Hammersmith Road and one in a tiny turning off the Goldhawk Road called Tittmus Street.

'Damn you, Andrew,' she said aloud. 'How am I supposed to guess which one you went to?'

Charlie went back downstairs with Andrew's notes and the *A to Z* in her handbag. Carol was busy behind the bar but she looked up as Charlie came in. 'Any luck?' she called out.

Apart from the fact that Carol was rushed off her feet, and probably would remain so until closing time, Charlie had already made up her mind that it wouldn't be a good idea to try to explain anything she'd found upstairs. Andrew might turn up, and if he did he wouldn't be pleased to discover his private business had been bandied around.

'I've found his mother's telephone number,' Charlie said, handing over a piece of paper with it written down, along with her own. 'I'm going to see a friend of his now, then I'll go on home. If you do hear anything, could you ring me?'

'I'm quite sure he'll be back this evening, so I won't attempt to phone his mum before that,' Carol said. She didn't look unduly troubled, perhaps because she'd been through this kind of absenteeism with other staff before. 'Andrew's normally a sensible lad, so I'm sure there's a very good reason he hasn't phoned in. So stop worrying about him. I'll get him to ring you the moment he comes in.'

Half an hour later Charlie was in Mornington Crescent climbing the stairs of a dismal block of council flats. The flats were relatively new, built in the early Sixties, but the lift was out of order and the stairs were rubbish-strewn, stinking of urine and stale vomit. From every direction her ears were bombarded with noise: children running up and down the concrete landings, loud music, people yelling, babies screaming. She was just stepping out on to Angie's landing when a small group of young louts came hurtling by her, pushing her hard against the concrete balustrade. She thought it must be a nightmare to live in such a place. Even looking down from the landing there was nothing to cheer her, just a view of many more huge tower blocks identical to this one, and bald, brown grass in between.

A little girl of about eight answered the door at number 140; she was a skinny blonde with blue eyes and a slight squint. She smiled shyly and revealed her front teeth were missing.

'Could I speak to your Mummy?' Charlie asked.

The girl didn't go back into the flat, but yelled to her mother from the door. Seconds later a woman appeared in the narrow hall, cigarette in hand, a questioning expression on her face.

Although Andrew's description of this woman had made her sound like a stereotyped ageing prostitute, to Charlie's surprise she looked no different to any other working-class mother. Her hair was in rollers, she wore no makeup, and her stretch ski-pants, slippers and shirt were comfortingly ordinary.

'I'm very sorry to call on you like this,' Charlie said. 'But I'm looking for my boyfriend Andrew Blake. I know he spoke to you just recently because I found your address among his things and I hoped you might know something which might help me to find him. He's gone missing, you see.'

'Whatcha mean, gone missing?' the woman said, staring hard at Charlie. 'Two days, three, or longer?'

'He went out yesterday afternoon to see someone, and he didn't go back to the pub where he works last night,' Charlie said. She felt nervous faced with the woman's hostile stare. 'I know that's not long, but it's a bit strange. You see, he's always very reliable.'

The woman didn't speak immediately, just drew deeply on her cigarette and frowned at Charlie. 'You look familiar,' she said at length, then quite suddenly and unexpectedly chuckled. 'I know! You gotta be Jin

Weish's daughter. So that's why Andrew wanted to know all that stuff about his club! I thought it were a bit funny. Well I never!'

Charlie blushed. Her Chinese appearance was unusual enough to focus anyone's mind very quickly, but she hadn't for one moment expected that someone who knew her father some eighteen years ago would instantly connect that she was his daughter. Yet it pleased her; judging by the warmth of the woman's smile, she must have liked Jin and known him quite well.

'You're pretty quick,' she said admiringly. 'I *am* Charlie Weish. Can you spare me a few moments?'

'Of course I can, ducks,' Angie said, then taking a step nearer to Charlie she whispered, 'But just mind what you say in front of the kids.'

Once inside the living room Charlie's nervousness vanished. It wasn't the kind of squalid place she'd expected, but clean, bright and very homely. The little girl was playing with a Barbie doll on the floor, a boy of about eleven who also had blond hair was doing a jigsaw at the table by the window.

'This is Tina, and that's Karl,' Angie said. 'There's Keith too but he's out playing football. He's fifteen and you can't keep them in at that age.'

Charlie sensed by that statement that Angie did her best for her children, and warmed to her. Before saying anything more she knelt down by Tina and admired her doll, then went over to Karl and told him she loved jigsaws too.

'Your mummy used to know my parents a long time ago,' she said, ruffling his hair. 'So I hope you don't mind me butting in this afternoon.'

'Of course they don't,' Angie said. 'Come out in the kitchen with me while I make some tea, love, we can 'ave a chat there.'

They went into the kitchen. Angie put the kettle on and then sat down opposite Charlie at the table. 'Now, before we go any further,' she said sternly, 'suppose you start by telling me the real reason Andrew asked me all those questions.'

Faced with someone who was clearly as sharp as razors, Charlie saw no point in prevaricating. She stated simply that she and Andrew had wanted to know the truth about Jin's disappearance and then went on to explain the events of two years earlier.

Angie looked stricken as she heard about Sylvia's legs being crushed by the men. When Charlie finally reached the point of her mother's suicide, she wiped a tear from her eye. 'I'm *so* sorry, love.' Reaching out she took Charlie's hand and patted it comfortingly between her two. 'That's just about the worst thing I've ever heard. But I 'ave to say right now, same as I told Andrew, I did 'ear a rumour that your dad got done in, in 'Olland. I really 'ope that ain't true for your sake, but to my mind that's far more likely than 'im running off with another woman. Your dad weren't the kind to do that, and he wouldn't run from trouble either.'

Charlie didn't really know how to take that. Was it worse to hear he'd been killed, or that he'd cast off his responsibilities and family to start a new life?

Angie seemed to sense what she felt because she patted her shoulder. 'There's always rumours in Soho, love. If I weren't seen for a coupla weeks they'd say I'd bin done in an' all. So don't take that as gospel.

But to get back to yer mum! Well, I'm 'eart-sick about 'er. I always liked 'er. She didn't deserve such an end. And you, you're just a kid yerself. 'Ow you been managing?'

'Not too bad,' Charlie said, touched that the woman had so much compassion when her own life fell very short of being perfect. 'I'm working and living in London now. But you see, I was away in York when Andrew started this, I suppose he wanted to surprise me, and now he's disappeared. I'm really worried about him, Angie. Did he mention anyone else he was going to see?'

'No love, 'e never.' Angie shook her head. ''E said when I first met 'im that 'e was on 'is way to see someone. But 'e never said who it were. I met 'im again the day after. He took me to Lyons Corner 'Ouse for an ice cream and we chatted. Lovely lad he was. 'E did ask if 'e could some 'ere to talk to me again. But that's all.'

'He had written some notes about you, that's where I found your address, and it said you got the sack from the Lotus Club because of DeeDee. Then he'd written that she's now known as Miss Dexter.'

Angie looked very uncomfortable suddenly, her eyes narrowed and she seemed to tense up.

'I'm sorry to bring it up. He's written too that you didn't want to talk about her. But was it Daphne Dexter?'

Angie looked startled. ''Ow on earth did you know that? I never told Andrew her Christian name!'

'A friend told me,' Charlie said.

Angie lit another cigarette and offered one to Charlie.

'I don't smoke, thank you,' Charlie said. 'Was Daphne Dexter my father's mistress?'

Angie got up to make a pot of tea and as she didn't answer the question and seemed very nervous, Charlie surmised she was stalling purposely.

'Anything you tell me is just between us,' Charlie reassured her. 'All I care about at this moment is what's happened to Andrew. I'm just trying to get the full picture because the friend who gave me her Christian name told me Daphne was dangerous.'

'So she is. My life wouldn't be worth tuppence if it got out I'd been talking about 'er,' Angie said sharply, putting the teapot on the table. 'When I first met yer mum, she and DeeDee, Miss Dexter, whatever you want to call 'er, were mates. Good mates, real close. So when I 'eard a whisper that yer dad was 'aving it off with 'er later on I didn't believe it. But then when he gave 'er his club, it seemed it could be true, and from then on she was off like a rocket, a finger in every piece of action going.'

'Is she still around? I mean, in Soho?'

Angie gave a hollow, humourless laugh, and took two mugs down off a hook. ''Er spies are still there,' she said. 'But she ain't got no business left in Soho now. Mayfair's more 'er scene.'

Charlie sensed Angie had no intention of telling her any more about the woman, so she thought she'd try another tack. 'Do you know someone called "Spud"? He's an ex-boxer. I think that's the person Andrew was going to see when he met you.'

'Blimey!' Angie exclaimed, clattering the mugs. 'I 'ope 'e didn't tell 'im too much. Spud'll grass up anyone for a fiver. 'E's a drunk, a loser and a slimy bastard.'

471

She poured out the tea in silence and Charlie sensed she was mulling something over in her mind. She thought she knew what it was.

'Look, Angie,' Charlie said in a small voice. 'Andrew didn't know about Miss Dexter, not until you told him, and that was the day after he'd seen Spud. In Andrew's notes he'd put that Spud didn't know DeeDee. Do you think Spud was lying?'

''Course he was!' she exclaimed. ''E were in the Lotus most every night in those days.'

Charlie mulled that over. 'Well, if Spud denied knowing her, perhaps that was because he didn't want to get in Miss Dexter's bad books either?'

'Sounds about right,' she said.

'Well then. Might he have gone to her and warned her someone was asking questions?'

'Very likely. Like I said, 'e's the sort to do anything for a fiver.'

'Do you think it might bother her enough to get hold of Andrew somehow?'

There was a moment or two of silence when Angie just stared at Charlie, her pale blue eyes suddenly darker with anxiety.

'I can't 'elp you. Go to the police.' She made a despairing gesture with her hands. 'Tell 'em everything you've told me. Once you've bin to the station, go 'ome and stay there. Don't you even think of wandering around asking any more questions. It ain't safe.'

Charlie was stunned. Although she knew nothing about London's underworld, she was aware women in Angie's position weren't normally inclined to suggest visits to the police. Was this because she knew

472

Daphne Dexter had a hand in Jin's disappearance?

'Okay,' she agreed, struggling to keep her composure. 'But if you hear anything more on the grapevine, will you ring me and tell me?'

Angie shook her head. 'No, I daren't. I've got my kids' safety to think of. Forget you ever spoke to me, don't come 'ere again, and don't you dare tell the fuzz you've bin 'ere either.'

As Charlie looked into Angie's frightened eyes, all at once she understood why Andrew had written that phrase *'having her tentacles into everything'* in his notebook. Daphne Dexter had got Rita's silence by threatening to hurt her son. Angie knew her children could be in danger too, because that's the way Miss Dexter controlled people. She was certain then that the woman had got hold of Andrew.

'I promise I'll never mention your name to anyone,' Charlie said in little more than a whisper. 'I can't thank you enough for your help.'

'I ain't done nothing to 'elp,' Angie retorted, finally pouring the tea.

'You have,' Charlie said. She was on the verge of tears now, because at last a shaft of light had been shone on the events of two years earlier. 'You see, Mum used to have these black moods, I always thought she didn't care about me much. When those men hurt her she made out she knew nothing, not who they were, or why they did it. I always thought she was protecting Dad. But she wasn't, was she? She was protecting me?'

''Course she was,' Angie said without any hesitation. 'I don't think there's a mum in the world what wouldn't fight to the death for her kids. And your mum put you first right from the start. She never worked in the club after you was born, she made sure you was kept right away from all that stuff. She wanted sommat better for you than what she 'ad.'

'I never realized that,' Charlie said, and a tear trickled down her cheek. 'I always had the idea I kind of spoiled her life.'

'That's rubbish, you made her life,' Angie said fiercely. 'I don't know what went on after 'er and Jin moved away from London, maybe she 'ad the black moods 'cos of what Jin were up to. But I can tell you she 'ad a good 'eart. See, I did see you when you was a baby, only once, but I ain't forgotten it.'

'Will you tell me about it?' Charlie asked.

'It were outside Dickins and Jones in Regent Street. Yer mum was pushing you in yer pram, you was about fourteen months. I was in a bad way then, drinking 'eavy, not looking after meself. I'd lost me first child, you see, just a few months before. Stillborn she was, they reckoned it was from a kicking I got from me old man, anyway I went up to yer mum and asked if I could 'old you. I thought she'd tell me to get lost, most would. But she didn't. She lifted you out and put you in me arms.'

Angie paused and lit another cigarette, her eyes were welling with tears.

'Go on,' Charlie urged her.

'I cuddled you, you was laughing and pulling at me 'air, and it made me cry 'cos you were so lovely and I wished you was mine. Anyway, Sylvie must'a known what was going on in me mind. She put you back in the pram and then cuddled me. I was dirty, Charlie, like a bleedin' tramp, and she were in nice clothes, her 'air all done nice and everything. But she still 'eld me, comforted me, and I never forgot it. Funny 'ow things work out, ain't it? 'Ere you are all these years later, in me kitchen drinking tea.'

Charlie had a big lump in her throat. It was the only story she'd ever been told about her mother that portrayed her in a compassionate role.

'I wish I'd known more about her,' Charlie said wistfully. 'You see, she never showed her feelings, not to me.'

Angie put one hand on Charlie's and squeezed it. 'Some people just can't, love. Maybe it's 'cos of the way they was brought up, or things what 'appened to 'em. But just 'cos they don't go round wif their 'eart on their sleeve, don't mean they don't feel.

'Look at the way you've turned out! You're a nice girl, nice manners, nice voice, smart as new shoes. Now, you didn't get that way all on yer own, did you?'

Charlie smiled weakly. She could see the point Angie was making. 'I can see why Mum cuddled you,' she said. 'I want to.' She got up from her chair and leaned over the older woman to hug her, resting her head on her shoulder for a moment. 'You're a really good woman,' she murmured, that didn't quite cover it but then she wasn't used to being emotional with strangers.

'And so was yer mum,' Angie said stoutly. 'Now, clear off and go down the police station. Then straight 'ome.'

'Which one should I go to?' Charlie asked. 'Just any one?'

475

'No, go to West End Central in Bow Street. That's where they came from when they was asking questions about yer dad. No point in farting around in places where they know nothing about 'im.'

It was after seven that evening when Charlie got home. Rita was out, the flat seemed cold and bleak without her, and after she'd telephoned Jack Straw's Castle and found Andrew wasn't back and his mother didn't know where he was either, she lay down on her bed and cried.

The police had been decent enough. They started out trying to fob her off with a young constable, but she'd stuck her ground and insisted she spoke to someone senior and eventually she was ushered into an interview room to speak to Detective Inspector Hughes.

He was a jovial man around fifty, with a bald head and a big stomach that strained his shirt buttons, but he was a good listener. He didn't seem the least bit confused that Charlie's story was part present, part events of two years earlier. She showed him the handout Andrew had made, and the *A to Z* he'd marked with small crosses, but because of Angie she didn't say she had Andrew's notes with her too. He took down the details of the scooter, and said he would get the police in that area to look for it.

'What makes you so sure this Daphne Dexter is behind his disappearance?' he asked. 'And how can you be so certain that she is your mother's old friend and father's mistress?'

'I just know,' she said stubbornly. She'd already told him all the many similarities, but she couldn't say that it had been confirmed by Angie. 'I feel it inside me.'

He laughed, but not unkindly. 'That's hardly proof,' he said.

'Maybe not, but don't you think it's significant that Andrew should go missing so soon after talking to people about my father in Soho? And ominous that people are afraid to talk about Daphne Dexter?' Charlie argued. 'And another thing. If I can put together that DeeDee and Dexter are the same person, why didn't the police uncover it while Mum was still alive? The woman took over Dad's club, and she was up on a drugs charge during the Sixties, I would have thought that made her pretty suspicious.'

'Can you tell me why you are hiding where you got some of your information from?' he asked, looking at her sharply.

'No, because some of the people involved have made me promise I won't.'

'Why?'

'Because they are afraid of her of course,' she said indignantly.

He smiled knowingly. 'That, Charlie, is exactly what makes police work so difficult. Almost every time a serious crime is committed we generally have a good idea of who is responsible, but getting people to speak up and act as witnesses is the tricky bit.

'We might very well have our suspicions about this woman, but without evidence she has committed a crime we can't put a case against her together. Being your father's mistress isn't a crime, and your boyfriend has only been missing for twenty-four hours, so he might well be off somewhere playing cards and drinking. So what possible reason could we have for bringing her in for questioning?'

'Do you mean you aren't even going to try and find Andrew?' she asked, tears spilling down her face. 'Can't you see if Daphne has abducted Andrew then it's certain she's got something she wants kept hidden? What could that be other than she knows exactly what happened to Dad?'

'Now, let's take it one step at a time. Of course we're going to try and find Andrew,' he said. 'But London's a very big city, so it might take some time. Now, you go on home now. The chances are he will turn up. When I was Andrew's age I disappeared regularly, sometimes I didn't even know where I'd been.'

Charlie had never felt so frustrated in her entire life as when she left the police station. She knew Hughes thought Andrew was off somewhere with another girl. How long would he have to be gone before anyone took any action?

She pulled herself together later and phoned Beryl on the off-chance he might have contacted her, but that made her feel even worse. Beryl told her he'd phoned during the week all excited about the information he'd got, and how she'd been scared for him and made him promise he wouldn't go back to Soho again. Now Charlie had to be the one to pretend she was over-reacting and play down how worried she was.

The telephone remained stubbornly silent on Sunday morning. Rita cooked roast beef and made a chocolate cake, but her attempts at being cheerful merely heightened the gloom rather than lifting it. It was raining again and a strong wind buffeted the windows. Charlie sat staring out at the road below, wondering why when just a couple of days ago in York she'd felt so full of life and optimism, she was suddenly thrown back to reliving the nightmares of the past.

The telephone finally rang in the middle of the afternoon. Charlie jumped out of her chair, Rita rushed from the kitchen.

It was Detective Inspector Hughes. 'We've found Andrew's scooter,' he said. 'It was in Tittmus Street, Shepherd's Bush, an old lady rang her local station to report it. I've just come back from seeing her. It seems she saw a young man leave it there on Friday afternoon. He then went into a house a few doors away from her. She thought he must be something to do with the builders working on the house and thought no more about it. It was only this morning when she saw it was still there, and no sign of the builders, that she thought it was odd. So she rang the police in case it had been stolen.'

Charlie's heart leaped with hope. 'Have you been to the house to see if he's there?' she asked.

'Of course,' he said crisply. 'There is no one living in the house, and hasn't been for six months. Tomorrow we'll make a check on who owns it. But meanwhile we've brought Andrew's scooter back here for safety.'

'Is that all you can tell me?' Charlie burst out.

'No, there is one thing more. In the locked box on the back we found Andrew's helmet, jacket and a letter. That letter appears to be a reply to his handout. It was from a Martha Grimsby who claimed she was a barmaid in Soho during the Fifties, inviting him to come and meet her in Tittmus Street.'

'So that's how she got hold of him!' Charlie exclaimed. 'It is Daphne Dexter, I know it is.'

'Maybe,' the policeman said more gently. 'We are checking the letter now for fingerprints, and to pin-point the kind of typewriter it was written on. We are also trying to trace the builders working on the house. If any further news comes in I will contact you immediately.'

'What about Andrew's parents?' Charlie said fear-fully. 'Have you told them yet?'

'Someone from the Oxford police is on his way to speak to them now,' he said. 'Do you have a recent photograph of him?'

'No.' Charlie felt her knees sagging under her and had to sit down. 'Neither of us had a camera.'

He must have heard the break in her voice and realized she was crying. 'Try and keep calm, Charlie,' he said gently. 'I know that's easy for me to say, but allowing yourself to get in a state won't help. We have no evidence that anything bad happened to him in that house, indeed he might very well have gone off somewhere else on an impulse. But you said you found some notes Andrew had made while he was in Soho. I think we'd better have those. I'll send someone round later to collect them from you.'

Charlie put the phone down and looked up in horror at Rita standing by her chair.

'Come on,' Rita said, stroking Charlie's shoulder, 'tell me what they said.'

Charlie related it all. 'How can I give him the notes?' she asked. 'I promised Angie I wouldn't tell them about her.'

Rita was surprisingly cool-headed; she got the notebook from Charlie's room, scanned through it, then calmly tore out the page about Angie. 'There,' she said, passing it back to Charlie. 'And you needn't feel guilty either, because you've told them everything she said.'

'But –' Charlie began.

'No buts,' Rita said. 'I know about working girls like Angie. They have a hard enough time keeping body and soul together without police harassing them. That bloke Spud and the other couple of market men are the ones the police need to question.'

'Have you got any idea where that house was you got taken to?' Charlie asked Rita later that evening. A policeman had called to collect the notes around six; since then Rita had done some washing and now she was ironing. Charlie had tried to distract herself by watching television and reading the Sunday paper but her mind refused to budge from imagining Andrew being tortured.

'Sort of,' Rita said, pausing in ironing a blouse. 'We went out of London on the A20. I know that road quite well because I had a boyfriend who used to do motor-racing at Brands Hatch. There's a fantastic view over a valley a bit further on. We often took a picnic there, so even though it was dark, I recognized it by the lights in the distance as we passed by. Just after that we turned off the main road, and it was only about ten more minutes before we got to the house.'

Charlie had never been south of London so she had no idea where Rita was talking about. 'Could you show me on a map?' she asked.

Rita gave her a sharp look. 'He wouldn't be there!'

'He could be, if it was her house. She might have just bought it to do up. The police said the house in Shepherd's Bush was being done up too. Besides, I'm just curious.'

Rita got a road map and pointed out where she meant. 'The house could have been anywhere around here.' She drew a big circle around a village called Borough Green with her fingernail. 'But it wasn't in a village, it was off the beaten track. I remember we went a long way up a winding lane with overhanging trees.'

Charlie found it impossible to sleep that night. All the different bits of information she'd gathered about Daphne Dexter from her mother, Rita, Andrew's notes and what Angie had said, were spinning round and round in her head. It didn't make any sense to abduct Andrew, then let him go; he would go straight to the police. The only reason she could have for snatching him was to kill him.

Andrew woke to find himself lying on the floor in total darkness. His mouth was dry and he had a headache. He thought he was on the floor in his room at the pub. But as he put his hand out, instead of finding the reassuring softness of a bed next to him, it met only cold stone.

He screamed involuntarily, but the sound of his voice brought him to and he realized this wasn't a nightmare but reality. He was lying on a thin, scratchy blanket, his shoes were off, and wherever he was it had a suffocating, musty, damp smell. The last thing he remembered was feeling sleepy and Martha saying she would open a window.

Assuming he was still in the same house, he got to his feet and fumbled blindly in the darkness. The coldness of the stone floor struck through his socks, but he came to a wall after a few steps. It was no ordinary inside wall, but rough stone and damp to the touch. He crept along it feeling for furniture, doors or windows, anything to give him an idea of where he was. He felt two corners before he came to something which felt like a metal stand of some kind, and then eventually to a rough wooden staircase. He hauled himself up it, and found a door at the top. It was locked.

He shook it first and called out, but when no one came he hammered, kicked and screamed at the top of his lungs. Then he stopped, struck motionless by a terrible fear. He could hear nothing beyond the door and there wasn't even a chink of light.

The fear grew stronger as he stood there, welling up from deep within him, intense and primeval, until he could smell it. He could hear his heart pounding, every hair on his body stood on end, and a cold sweat broke out on his forehead and trickled down his cheeks.

Afraid to go back down the stairs in the pitch darkness, he sank down in front of the door on to the top step, put his arms round his knees and sobbed uncontrollably.

The cold brought him to. As he hugged his arms around his body he suddenly remembered he'd been wearing his tweed jacket earlier in the day and now he wasn't. As his hands felt down his body he discovered he was now wearing a kind of boiler-suit. Could he have been sick and someone stripped him of his clothes?

Remembering the blanket he had woken up on, he stood up again, and holding the rail with his right hand, with his left on the wall, he took a tentative step down. At the second step his left hand brushed against a switch, and suddenly there was light. It was so unexpected he yelled aloud in relief.

The light was a dim single bulb and what it revealed did nothing to cheer him. He was standing on the second step of a crude staircase, looking down into a large windowless cellar, and all there was in it was a rusting wine rack against the wall to his right, and the blanket he'd been lying on in the middle of the stone-flagged floor.

Going on down the stairs, he picked up the blanket and wrapped it round his shoulders. Tucked under the stairs was a bucket and a bottle of water, but despite his dry mouth, and a need to urinate, these alarmed him even more as they suggested that who-ever had stuck him in here wasn't coming back for some time.

After closer inspection of his prison, he didn't think the cellar was beneath Tittmus Street. He'd never known a small Victorian terraced house have such a large, well-built cellar, and the kind of ordinary people who lived in such houses didn't go in for wine racks. So where was he?

Lifting his wrist to see what time it was, he found his watch was gone. All at once he realized that in taking his clothes and shoes they'd also taken the entire contents of his pockets, penknife, wallet,

484

address book, money and cheque-book. The only things of his own left were his underpants and socks. He broke down again then, crying like a child as it came to him that he had been drugged, stripped and redressed in this navy blue boiler-suit, then transported here unconscious.

Some time later, huddled in the blanket on the stairs, he forced himself to try and think rationally. He was still woozy from whatever he'd been given, and not knowing where he was, or what time it was, was in a way worse than physical pain. It prevented him from working out how much longer it would be before someone became alarmed at his absence. Nor could he consider how help might come.

There was a slim hope in his scooter. He hadn't told that woman how he'd got to Shepherd's Bush, so it might still be parked in that road. Maybe the police would find it. But how long would that take? In an area like Shepherd's Bush it might be there for weeks before anyone asked who it belonged to.

Stan and Carol would be angry when he didn't turn up for work. But they wouldn't be alarmed immediately. If Charlie telephoned and found he wasn't there, she'd believe he was off with another girl. In all probability it would be Sunday or even Monday before anyone got worried. And he didn't even know what day it was now!

He'd thought he was so smart acting out being a detective, but anyone with only half a brain would have taken the precaution of telling someone where he was going.

'Okay, so you've been a blithering idiot,' he said aloud. 'But you do have a logical mind otherwise

485

you wouldn't be any good at maths, physics and electronics. So use your brain now and at least try to work out why that woman drugged you and brought you here.'

Kidnapping for money as a motive could be discounted – it would be ridiculous as his parents had none. It had to be his inquiries into Jin Weish's disappearance. Obviously Jin couldn't have made off to escape debts or to start a new life with another woman, because no one would go to the trouble of abducting someone for that. So what would be serious enough for someone to go to such lengths?

'Only a fortune,' he said aloud. 'Or murder!'

Was it Jin who'd committed the crime and had orchestrated this? Or was he a victim of the same people behind it?

Looking at the cunning way Martha had got him to the house, her poise and charm as she'd won his trust and got him to reveal everything he knew and suspected, then calmly drugged his coffee while he studied the photographs, she wasn't some ex-barmaid who now worked in an office, but a scheming, clever and ruthless woman. Could she be Jin's mistress?

Andrew wished then that his mind wasn't quite so logical. No one would drug another person, take their clothes and shove them in a dark, damp cellar without evil intentions. If the crime these people wanted to keep under wraps was murder, then it stood to reason they would have to kill him too. What else could they do with him?

At five on Monday morning Charlie was still wide awake, and any further hopes of sleep were prevented by an idea which had popped into her head from nowhere. She tried arguing with herself that she should leave it to the police, that she ought to go to work. Yet she felt compelled to do something.

Five minutes later she was dressed in jeans and a tee-shirt, wearing stout flat shoes and carrying her waterproof jacket over her arm. She hastily scribbled a note to Rita asking her to tell the Hag she wasn't coming in to work because she was too upset, and besides the police might need her. She added that she'd just gone out for a walk to clear a headache and not to worry. Then she let herself out silently.

London was so different without the heavy traffic that would come in an hour or two's time. The rain and high winds of the previous day were gone, leaving a crisp nip of autumn behind. But the sky was light, and the chill air felt bracing as she scurried down towards Marble Arch.

One of the best things about Rita's flat was its close proximity to the West End and the ease of getting to anywhere else in London, by bus or tube. But Charlie wasn't intending to use public transport, she intended to walk to Charing Cross Station.

The walk took the best part of an hour, along Park Lane into Piccadilly and then through Green Park down to the Mall. She had a few misgivings about not admitting her real plans to Rita, but then she knew her friend would only have tried to stop her.

By seven she was at Borough Green. It wasn't a pretty village as she'd expected, just the station, a few dreary shops and very ordinary houses on two busy roads. All at once she realized that searching for a house that had been seen by someone in the dark, eight years ago, was going to be a tall order.

She stood for a moment outside the newsagent's shop and tried to assimilate all she knew. Gothic-looking and creeper-covered. Up an overgrown lane. Perhaps stables because Daphne had been wearing jodhpurs.

The newsagent, a thin little ferret of a man, was busy marking up his paper rounds and he looked none too pleased to be interrupted so early in the morning.

'You don't even know which village?' he exclaimed. 'It could be anywhere then – Ightham, Hatch, Stone Street or even Knole up towards Sevenoaks. Have you got a car?'

'No, I'm walking,' Charlie said. 'I thought you might have seen it as you deliver papers. Eight years ago it was a bit dilapidated, the iron gates hanging off. It might be really smart now.'

'Most of the houses out on the country lanes, except the farms, are smart,' he said grumpily. 'They come down from London, buy up these places for a song, and they never even use the local shops. What's the owner's name?'

'I don't know for certain,' she said, trying hard to keep smiling in the face of his displeasure. 'It might have been a Mr Peterson. Or a Miss Dexter. He's over sixty, tall with white hair. Miss Dexter is in her forties, and dark, a handsome woman. She rides horses.'

'So they all do,' he said dismissively. 'Can't say either of those sticks in my mind. Best thing you can do is go down the Maidstone Road past the recreation ground, then turn into the lane up beyond it. If you keep on going you'll come round in a big circle, and there's quite a few big houses that way. Ask a farmer if you see one. They know mostly everyone.'

Charlie bought two drinks and a big bar of chocolate. She thanked him and hastily left his shop.

Her spirits lifted as she turned into the lane the newsagent had spoken of; it was steep and overhung with trees. It smelled woody and earthy and reminded her poignantly of back home walking up Beacon Road towards the footpath to Paignton.

Common sense told her that even if she was lucky enough to be on the right road, what would be just a few minutes' ride in a car could be a very long walk. Finally the hill levelled out and seeing a footpath into a field, and a view of the valley she'd just climbed out of, she sat down to rest on the stile.

She was surprised by how much beautiful open countryside there was here in Kent. Back home in Devon people spoke about the South of England as if it was one gigantic housing estate. Looking down at Borough Green she could see its dreary straggly appearance was due to being cut in half by such a busy road. But sitting up high above it, watching a faint hazy mist rising from the fields, hearing birds singing and smelling the sweet fresh air, she could see exactly why people did rush out of London to buy up houses here.

Refreshed after a drink, Charlie walked on. There were a few houses, a cluster of old farm cottages here, a bigger farmhouse there, but nothing like the house Rita had described. She walked and walked but saw no one, and no cars passed her either.

At midday Charlie's optimism had left her entirely

and her feet were aching. As she stood at a crossroads, wondering whether she should give up and take the quickest route back to the station, a man on a tractor pulled out of the field to her right. He was young, possibly only in his early twenties, his face and bare forearms tanned a deep mahogany, and he looked questioningly at her.

As she walked towards him, he stopped his engine and jumped down. 'Are you lost?' he called out.

Charlie quickly explained what she was looking for and asked if he knew such a house.

'Oh, I know that one right enough,' he said in a rich country-sounding burr. 'It's a tidy old step to it, but go on straight ahead. Mind you watch out for it, though, the gates are almost hidden by big trees.'

Her heart quickened. 'Do you know the people who live there?' she asked.

He shook his head. 'I think they only use it for weekends and holidays. I've only ever seen a man cutting the grass.'

'Is he late sixties, white-haired and kind of distinguished-looking?'

'No, nearer forty or so. He's probably only the gardener,' he said, then pausing to look at her again and perhaps realizing she was tired, he smiled. 'If you can squeeze up on the tractor beside me, I'll take you there, I'm going down that way.'

Over the noise of the tractor it was impossible to hold any further conversation. After a couple of miles the man stopped by a gate and jumped down. 'This is as far as I'm going,' he said, holding out his arms to help her down. 'But it's only about a hundred yards or so further. Just round the bend. Sorry I can't take you the whole way, but there's nowhere for me to turn there.'

'It was very kind of you to take me this far,' she said with a wide smile as she reached the ground.

He swung the gate open and climbed back on to his tractor. Charlie stayed just long enough to shut the gate again behind him, waved goodbye and went off down the road.

The moment Charlie turned the bend and saw the iron gates and the house beyond, she knew with absolute certainty she was at the place Rita had described. Stepping back under the cover of some bushes on the other side of the lane, she paused to take a good look at it.

It wasn't dilapidated. The tall gates were newly painted, the drive was new-looking gravel, but the large trees Rita had spoken of still made an arch to drive through, and the house was kind of Gothic with its arched mullion windows, and covered in ivy. It was both splendid and chilling at the same time. The garden was manicured, neat box hedges of uniform size surrounded a lawn like a bowling green. Even a curved flowerbed up by the steps to the front porch was laid out with precision.

'The Manse' was the name on a discreet green plaque with raised brass letters attached to one of the gateposts. The gates were padlocked.

After such a long search it was thrilling to have finally found it, yet at the same time she felt a kind of dejection because she didn't know what she should do about it. Reason told her to go back to London, then ring Detective Inspector Hughes and ask him to check the place out. But what explanation could she offer for such a request? She had no proof Daphne Dexter owned it, and without telling him about Rita's ordeal here she had absolutely no grounds to claim Andrew might be being held here either.

Loath to return home without something concrete to offer him, she decided that a discreet look at the back of the house from the fields would do no harm. Yet after a long trawl around the wooded boundary she was even more disappointed. The trees and bushes were so dense and tall that even the barbed wire fence, let alone the house, was totally concealed. Then just as she was about to give up, she spotted a small gap beneath the wire. It looked as if it had been dug recently by badgers, and she couldn't resist crawling through it.

Getting under the wire was the easy part; from there, thick undergrowth, stinging nettles, brambles and piles of old sticks made it almost impenetrable. Yet having got this far, she inched her way forward until eventually she could see the garden and the house beyond.

To her astonishment this rear view was in complete contrast to the neat splendour she'd seen from the road. The garden was a vast jungle of waist-high weeds and clearly hadn't been touched for at least a decade. As for the house, that looked almost derelict and much larger than she'd expected.

Keeping well back in the bushes she studied the scene carefully, wondering at the mentality of the owner who had put all his or her efforts into keeping up a mere façade. From the road, she'd had the impression it was a typical early Victorian family house with just a few large rooms on two floors, but even that was a false one. The house had been extended at the rear at a later period, and judging by the ugly standardized metal window-frames it could have been used as some kind of institution in the Thirties. There were in fact four floors from this angle if she counted the basement and attics. She thought it might have as many as twenty rooms in all.

There were a great many outbuildings to one side of the house. From where she stood they could well be stables, though there wasn't even the faintest waft of horse manure to substantiate this.

Remembering that the front gates had been padlocked and there was no car on the drive, and seeing that all the windows were closed, she decided there couldn't be anyone in residence and perhaps no one lived here any more anyway. But her curiosity wouldn't let her turn and go, she felt she had to go closer and peep into some of the lower windows. Crouching down below the level of the tall grass, she made her way across the bottom of the garden to the far side, then up towards the house.

Close up she found there was a sort of narrow alleyway down in the basement. Apart from one window on the right, she couldn't get close enough to look in any of the others. That one window was a large kitchen. Its modern styling with cream Formica units and built-in double ovens suggested it was a recent improvement. But it was bare and clinical with not a pot plant, teapot or shopping basket to spoil the almost showroom image. She crept down the steps to the basement area to check that out.

The view through the wired glass on the top half of the door gave her no further insight to the owners of the house. She could see a bare, black and white tiled area, with only one door off it open. Through that she could just glimpse what looked like a laundry room. She came back up the steps and paused for a moment, torn between going back the way she had come and going on further round the house.

Going on won. So creeping on tiptoe across an area of broken paving stones, she made her way towards the side of the house and the outbuildings. A small barred window on the side caught her attention. It was just too high to see in, but spotting an abandoned beer crate nearby she pulled it up to stand on it.

The view through the window was partially blocked out by what appeared to be tea chests, but by clinging to the bars, she hoisted herself up a little higher to see past them. There were more tea chests, piled almost up to the ceiling, but curiously, on one of them was perched a large brass Buddha. Had it not been so similar to one they'd had at home at 'Windways' she probably would have jumped down immediately, but instead she scrabbled up further and saw other things very like those her father had dealt in: a red lacquered bureau partially concealed by the tea chests and in the far corner what looked like a heap of rolled-up Oriental rugs.

Curiosity overcame caution and she scrabbled higher still to see better, but her hand slipped on the bars and she toppled and fell back to the ground, knocking over the crate as she did so. The thump of the crate against paving slabs frightened her, and in alarm she leapt back to her feet and bolted, her heart thumping like a steam-hammer.

She heard something as she ran. A movement, a

door or window opening, she couldn't tell what, or from what direction it came. In her panic all common sense left her and instead of making off down the garden the way she had come in, she ran towards the outhouses instead.

'Oi, come 'ere!' a rough male voice called out behind her, and as Charlie turned momentarily to look, so she realized she was effectively cornered between walls and the thick hedge. She froze. The man looked like a gardener in a red checked shirt, soiled work trousers, heavy boots and a flat cap.

'What you up to?' he asked, and before she had a chance to even think about dodging past him, his arm shot out and he caught her firmly by the shoulder.

'I'm s-s-sorry. I got into the garden by mistake. I was walking in the f-f-f-field and I saw the woods. I thought it might take me back to the road,' she gabbled. 'I'll just go the way I came in.'

His other hand grabbed her other shoulder, and he looked her full in the face for a moment. His eyes were a cold blue and he had a missing front tooth. 'You were snooping. Suppose you tell me why?'

'I wasn't snooping,' she retorted, but her mouth was so dry she could barely get the words out. 'I was lost, I told you, I thought it was a wood.'

'Come off it!' he snorted. 'Do I look stupid enough to believe that? Come with me.'

It wasn't a request but an order. He twisted one of her arms up behind her back and pushing her in front of him nudged her back round the house towards the steps which led down to the basement. Charlie tearfully tried to plead with him, but he remained unmoved.

'Save it for the police,' he said, nudging her down the steps and into the black and white tiled hallway she'd seen earlier. Before she could protest any further he'd opened a door to the right, pushed her in, and slamming the door on her, locked it behind him.

Chapter Seventeen

As Charlie sat hunched on a chair, berating herself for being stupid enough to trespass on private property and wondering what on earth she'd say to the police when they got here, her jailer was equally deep in thought. He was sitting in a swivel chair up in a small study on the first floor. He'd taken off his boots and made himself a cup of tea. Now he was trying to weigh up what he should do about the girl.

With a deep sigh he reached for the phone and dialled his brother's number in Islington. 'Look, Baz, I've just found a chick snooping round the back,' he said. 'She claims she was trying to get to the road through the woods, but I don't believe 'er. I told 'er I was going to call the filth, and I've put 'er down in the old storeroom for now. Whatcha reckon I ought to do with 'er?'

'Dunno,' Baz replied unhelpfully. 'You'd better ask Daph. She's 'ere, just come round.'

Mick lit a cigarette as he waited for his sister to come to the phone. His stomach was rumbling, it always did when he expected trouble.

Michael and Barrington Dexter were identical twins and it was often said behind their backs that they had only one brain between them too. No one dared say such things to their faces, though, for what the boys lacked in intelligence, they more than made up for in aggression and strength. There was only one person who could insult them and get away with it, and that was their older sister Daphne.

In 1934 they were six, Daphne nine, when their mother ran out on them. Their home was two squalid rooms in Wapping in the East End of London. Their docker father, Danny Dexter, claimed his wife ran off with a fancy man, but young as the children were, they knew the real reason. Their father was a drunken brute, who when he did get a full week's work in the docks, spent most of his wages at the pub before he staggered home to beat their mother.

Even before their mother left, the children were already well used to extreme poverty. Quite often the only meal of the day was a slice of bread and dripping; shoes and clothes invariably came from charities. If Daphne hadn't been fiercely determined to hold things together in their mother's absence, she and the twins would have starved, or ended up in an orphanage, for even in an emergency it was clear to her that Danny wouldn't change the habits of a lifetime and provide for his family.

The twins had never forgotten how Daphne sat them down and explained the situation to them. She said they weren't to tell their teacher their mother had gone, nor were they to try and cadge food from neighbours, which might bring a social worker round. She said she had thought of a way she could make enough money to keep them. Her plan was that every day after school they would walk to the City to beg money from the toffs who worked in banks.

Her plan was an excellent one as it turned out. Few businessmen were able to resist the little girl with long dark hair, vivid blue eyes and a pale pinched face, who stood outside the banks in Threadneedle Street with her small ragged brothers. On a good day, if it was wet and cold, she'd get as much as ten shillings before the city emptied for the evening. They would ride home on the bus, buy saveloys and chips, and when they got home she'd light the fire to dry their clothes and all three of them would climb into the double bed they shared.

Young as she was, Daphne not only managed to meet the few shillings' rent each week and buy food, coal and clothes for them, but even managed to keep their father from giving them good hidings by slipping him a few bob to go down the pub. The boys would listen to her stories about how one day they would have a real house, with carpets on the floor and horses in the stables, and go into Bloom's in Mile End Road for hot salt beef sandwiches every day, and they believed her.

It was one freezing cold and foggy Saturday afternoon in February of 1939 when the twins were eleven, going on for twelve, that they discovered the real reason why Daphne hated their father. Until then they'd thought it was just his drinking and brutality and because he'd made their mother run away. But that afternoon as he gave the boys twopence each for sweets and ordered them out, Mick saw a look of terror on his sister's face. Down in the corner shop, he did his best to put that expression on his sister's face out of his mind, and concentrate on whether aniseed balls or coconut flakes were the best value.

But he found he couldn't, and even at risk of getting a good hiding from his father, he went back home, taking Baz with him.

The door was bolted on the inside, but there was a crack at the bottom where their father had booted it in one night. Mick peered in. He could see the old iron bed in the living room, and his father was lying face down on it, his naked backside pumping up and down. It wasn't until he heard a pitiful cry that he realized Daphne was trapped beneath him.

Mick was incensed. He had seen sailors doing this with tarts down by the docks, and then it was something for him and Baz to laugh about. But this was quite different, it was wicked for a father to be doing it to his daughter. He wanted to break down the door, scream and shout so neighbours would come and put a stop to it. Yet he didn't, just let Baz take a look, and then both of them ran away in horror to discuss what they were going to do about it.

Baz had remarked just a short while ago that the decision they made that Saturday afternoon was the only one they'd ever made in their lives without consulting Daphne. They resolved to kill their father.

Late that same evening when Daphne was fast asleep, they crept out of the bed they shared with her, let themselves out silently and went down to the Prospect of Whitby, their father's favourite pub on the waterfront, and peeped through a window. Even in a crowded bar he stood out because of his massive shoulders, big belly and the purple tinge to his face. He was very drunk already, swaying as he gulped down another pint. They knew he'd be the last person to leave at closing time. He always was.

The twins ran back up the alleyway, hid themselves behind some crates and waited. The fog was so dense now they could see only a few yards to either side of their hideout. A stream of drunken men came by later, shouting and bawling to each other. Many of them paused to urinate but the bitter cold soon had them moving on.

Danny came some time later – they heard him singing 'Danny Boy' long before he reached the alley. Mick tightened his grip on the stick, Baz crouched, holding the brick in readiness. Danny lumbered into the alley, caught for one brief moment under a weak gas lamp. His face looked yellow in the light, his jacket was slung over his shoulder, too drunk even to feel the cold. As he reeled towards the boys, Mick slid the long stick out, then as Danny approached it, he lifted it slightly, to trip him.

It worked. He fell flat on his face, cursing blue murder. Baz leapt out behind him and whacked him hard on the back of his head with his brick.

Looking back now as a grown man, Mick found it funny to think two skinny kids of eleven imagined they could kill a grown man with just one blow from a brick. But they believed they had, because Danny was motionless when they left him.

If it had been summertime when they chose to do it, he would probably have reeled in the next morning with nothing more than a bad headache. But as it was, the temperature was well below freezing that night, and wearing only a shirt and trousers he froze to death before his body was found next morning.

The policeman who called to tell them must have been surprised at the boys' lack of reaction to his news. They said absolutely nothing because they were too stunned to hear Danny Dexter had died from exposure rather than a blow to his head. Daphne actually smiled, offered the policeman a cup of tea, and said she hadn't got any money for a funeral so could he arrange for the Welfare to pay for it.

They may never have mourned their father, but his death was to have a dramatic and lasting effect on all of their thinking. Daphne was driven to find a better life for herself and her younger brothers. For the boys it was the inception of a career which would be based on violence.

'Who is this girl, Mick?' Daphne asked in her deep, husky voice when she came to speak to her brother.

Both Baz and Mick were very proud of their sister. Not only was she exceptionally beautiful and smart, but she had acquired class, taught herself to look and sound like a real lady. It didn't bother them that she passed off her brothers as mere employees. They understood what drove her.

'Dunno,' he said. 'I didn't want to get 'eavy till I'd spoken to you. She's probably just some nosy little bleeder.'

'Well, how old is she? What does she look like?' There was a note of exasperation in Daphne's voice as though she wished that for once he could make a decision for himself.

'Eighteen, nineteen,' he said. 'She's a Chink!'

His sister gave a sharp intake of breath. 'A Chink?' she repeated. 'Oh no!'

Mick was surprised by her reaction. 'Whatcha mean? D'you know her?'

'Is there anything between your bloody ears?' she snapped. 'Are Chinese girls so common in Kent that it didn't occur to you it might be Jin Weish's daughter?'

Daphne's insulting manner didn't bother him, she always spoke to him like that. But he was shaken by her opinion as to who the girl was. 'Weish's kid! No, it can't be, sis, 'ow the 'ell would she find 'er fuckin' way 'ere?'

'I can't imagine,' Daphne replied, and unusually, her voice wavered with uncertainty. 'No one knows about that place. No one.' She didn't speak again for some little time, and Mick could hear her breathing heavily.

'It might not be her,' she said eventually. 'So we've got to be very careful. Take her a cup of tea. Act like you're the caretaker, a real job's-worth, and tell her you've called the police and they are coming round to question her as soon as they can. But be nice to her, ask her name and stuff. That should keep her quiet until Baz and I can get there. You'd better give the boy tea and a sandwich too, but for Christ's sake be careful he doesn't get out. I'll make up my mind what to do when I get there.'

Mick's stomach was rumbling even more as he put the phone down. His memories of Jin Weish were disturbing ones. He was the only bloke his sister had ever tangled with that nearly made her come unstuck. If his daughter had found her way here, then it looked as if she could be every bit as smart as he was.

Both he and Baz loved their sister and they followed her orders out of loyalty, yet they both knew she was a witch. There had been many times in the past twelve years when they wished they could break the chains she held them with and start a new life without her.

Back in the old days when she worked the clubs and fleeced men, they'd both understood her motivation. She was fighting for a better life than the one she'd been born to and she used the only weapons at her disposal.

Yet somewhere along the line, around the time she'd bought her first house, she'd turned evil and it had gradually eaten away all the good in her. Nothing softened her now, not a starving child, a cripple or a blind man. Mick didn't dare contemplate what she might do to these two kids. Her usual tricks of blackmail or maiming those that got in her way wouldn't be enough this time.

The basement storeroom Charlie was locked in had once been servants' quarters. It was a long narrow room with two small barred windows up on ground level, with a lavatory leading off it. It was cold and damp and held nothing but two old easy-chairs and shelves along one wall. Mick approached it gingerly, holding a mug of tea in one hand, bracing himself as he unlocked it.

'I brought you a cuppa tea,' he said, barring the way out with his body so the girl couldn't dart out. 'I phoned the police to say I had a prowler and they'll be round to see you as soon as they can.'

He felt sorry for her once he got right into the room. She was slumped in one of the chairs looking forlorn and frightened, her eyes swollen from crying.

'Cheer up, girl,' he said, leaning back on the door. 'If you ain't got nuthin' to 'ide, they'll soon let you go. I 'ad to phone them, see. It's me job to look after this place. Mrs Randall would go spare if she found out I hadn't done me job.'

Charlie was cheered a fraction by the man's gentler attitude. Although he had the build and stance of a boxer, without the cap and jacket he'd been wearing earlier he didn't look so fierce. She thought he must be around forty-something and his strong cockney accent was kind of appealing. 'I was lost,' she repeated. 'I know I should have gone out again when I found I was in someone's garden, but I thought I could just nip round the side of the house to the road.'

Mick thought she was a pretty little thing, whoever she was, and he wished he'd sent her off with a flea in her ear in the first place. But now Daphne knew she was here, he had to do as he'd been instructed. He didn't dare disobey her.

'For all I know if you'd found a door or winder open you might 'ave nipped in and nicked sommat,' he said with a smile. 'Mrs Randall would 'ave me 'ung, drawn and quartered if that 'ad 'appened.'

'What's she like, your Mrs Randall?' Charlie asked, wiping her eyes. She thought the man was relenting a bit, he was even quite nice-looking when he smiled. Maybe if she got on the right side of him, he'd change his mind and let her off. He couldn't really be anything to do with Daphne Dexter or he wouldn't have called the police.

'A right old bag sometimes,' he said with a chuckle.

'How old?'

'Oh, about seventy,' he replied. That was his standard answer for anyone who asked him about his employer. 'Now, 'ow's about telling me yer name?'

'It's Charlie Weish,' she said. She didn't see much

point in lying, she'd have to admit it soon anyway.

Mick was stunned. Not only was Daphne right, but the kid hadn't got the sense to say another name. 'You're kiddin' me!' he exclaimed, then remembering he mustn't give the game away, 'Charlie's a boy's name,' he added quickly.

She explained its Chinese origins and he said it sounded pretty. Then he asked where she lived.

'In London. I had the day off from work and I thought I'd go walking in the country.'

Mick could think of nothing more to ask her. 'Well, I gotta go now, Charlie. I got loads of jobs to do,' he said, opening the door behind him. 'Drink yer tea and keep yer chin up. I kinda wish I 'adn't been so 'asty calling the boys in blue, but now I 'ave I gotta go through wif it, ain't I?'

Charlie nodded glumly. 'I suppose so.'

'Look at it this way, they'll probably give you a lift back down the train station once they've sussed you out.'

Mick felt shaky as he went back upstairs. It was bad enough that Daphne had dragged him and Baz into bringing the young lad here, in their view it was crazy and unnecessary. But now the girl had found her way here too, they had double trouble.

Hurting women wasn't his game, especially pretty young ones like her. But like it or not, he knew he'd soon be called on to do it, because Daphne couldn't afford to let her go. To top it all he had to go and take food to that lad too. The young bastard must have heard him come in this morning, he'd been hammering and banging on the door ever since.

*

Andrew had taken up a position on the top step of the cellar steps the moment he'd heard heavy male footsteps much earlier in the day, and he'd remained there, ears pricked for any further sounds.

The cellar door had become his only way of keeping track of days. He'd discovered that if he turned the light off for a moment, if it was daytime there was a weak glow at the top and bottom of the door. He'd done this at regular intervals since he'd arrived. Therefore, by his reckoning, it must be Monday now, and as the light was sharper today, sunny and bright outside.

He didn't think there had been anyone in the house above all weekend, because judging by the noise he'd heard this morning, a car scrunching on gravel, then a key turning in the lock and feet on what sounded like a tiled floor, it would be impossible for anyone to come in or out that way without him hearing them. Until then it had been as silent as a grave.

It seemed to him that the house must be very big, with thick walls, because after that initial noise today, he'd heard nothing more, not so much as a creak. All he could do was sit and wait, and hope that before long the man might come to him.

Mick came through the door to the hall carrying a small tray with a pint mug of tea, two thick rounds of cheese sandwiches and a plastic lemonade bottle of water. As there wasn't a sound coming from the cellar now, he guessed the lad was waiting behind the cellar door hoping to force his way out the minute someone opened it.

Mick smiled to himself. The kid couldn't know that

the door opened outwards, or that there was a chain on the outside, and besides, he had his flick-knife in his hand ready.

He put the tray down on the floor, turned the key in the lock and opened it with the chain still on. 'Oh no you don't, son, I've got a knife,' he said as the door shuddered against him. He made a slashing gesture down the crack with his knife to make sure he was taken seriously. 'I've got you some food 'ere. So if you try and act big I'll just take it away. I might even give you a stripe to remember me by. So move back down those stairs and let me put the tray in.'

Andrew could see no more of the man than half a shoulder and a powerful-looking arm, but the hand was the size of a ham, and the glint of the knife was enough for him to know he didn't stand a chance of getting out in one piece. Besides, he was weak with hunger, and he had to have that food. 'Just tell me why you've got me here,' he asked as he backed down the stairs. 'I haven't done anything to anyone.'

Mick took the chain off the door, opened it wider and swiftly slid the tray on to the top step. 'You'll soon find out,' he said as he closed the door again.

'People will be looking for me,' Andrew yelled back as the lock was turned. 'I gave the address in Tittmus Street to two friends. And I left the letter from Martha Grimsby with one of them. The police will have that by now.'

There was no reply. He heard the footsteps retreat and another nearby door close too. Once again the house was silent.

Andrew had convinced himself during the long weekend alone that these people were intending to leave him in the cellar till he starved to death. He had finished the bottle of water ages ago, and felt dizzy with hunger. Now that he'd been brought food and a fresh bottle of water, that was ruled out. Perhaps they weren't intending to kill him, or why bother to feed him?

Feeling a little more cheerful, after only the most cursory peering at and smelling of the tea and cheese sandwiches, he sat down and ate them, forcing himself to take it slowly, savouring each mouthful. They tasted wonderful.

The man's words *you'll soon find out* must mean something was going to happen shortly. Maybe with food inside him he'd be strong and alert enough to escape.

Andrew couldn't actually remember what he'd done with the letter from Martha Grimsby. It was most probable that he'd had it in his jacket pocket and they'd removed it with his other belongings, but he could have left it in his coat in the back of the scooter, or even in his room at the pub. He fervently hoped it was one of the last two possibilities, that way there was a chink of hope someone had already found it.

Being trapped in silence, cold and hungry for so long, had turned his mind in on itself. He had visualized every person that he cared about, listing their strengths and weaknesses, and then scrutinized his thoughts about them.

He had so often resented his parents for being so tight with money. All his friends got the odd tenner sent to them from time to time, but he never did. When he went home to Oxford, their council house seemed so poky and dull. He would sneer at his mother for her provincial ways, her lack of imagination and roll his eyes with irritation at his father's constant nagging to work harder, to stay away from drink, drugs and bad company.

Now, faced with the possibility of never seeing them again, what once seemed like nagging looked more like love and wisdom. He saw to his shame that he'd become something of a snob through mixing with students from wealthy, well-connected families. Why else hadn't he ever invited a friend up to Oxford for a weekend or during the holidays?

He saw now that honest, hard-working people like his parents were the foundations of a good, strong, law-abiding society. Certainly not something to sneer at. He felt heart-sick that he'd barely noticed all the many sacrifices they'd made for him. They'd never been able to afford a car, yet they'd paid for driving lessons for him. They never had real holidays, just a week in July with Aunt Beryl, yet he'd been sent on every foreign trip from school. He got a stereo when his father longed for a power-saw, his mother wore the same old clothes, week in week out, but her son got a whole new wardrobe when he went to university, just so he wouldn't feel out of place. Andrew vowed to himself that if he did get out of this, he would work harder, and make sure he got a first-class degree so that their selflessness would be rewarded.

He thought too about the heroic way his Aunt Beryl had managed to run that pub while nursing a sick husband for several years, without a word of complaint. Then there was Ivor, so much sadness in his life, yet he'd found room in his heart to help Charlie. He fervently hoped that he could acquire such compassion and be as content as they were.

But Charlie had dominated his thoughts. He thought back to all the trials she'd borne so bravely, her single-mindedness in working for her exams when she was all alone and hurting, her spirit of independence and her ability to charm everyone she met. He had fallen in love with her face, body and personality, and when she turned her back on him, it was those things he ached for and missed the most. Yet now he could see a bigger picture of her, her soul, mind and spirit. He knew now that the kind of love he felt came only once in a man's life. It was a treasure beyond compare. If he did get out of here, then somehow he was going to win her back.

So many times in the past days and nights he'd closed his eyes and pictured her face. The slant of her almond eyes, the way they crinkled up when she laughed, the curve of her lips and the delicacy of her cheekbones. Lying on the hard stone floor, he tried to warm himself by imagining her body curved into his. He could smell her skin, her hair, feel the smoothness of her breasts in his hand. He thought how many soldiers must have had such images in their heads on the eve of a battle, knowing they might not return, and wondered too if it was that which gave them the courage to fight.

Daphne hardly said a word to Baz as he drove her down from London into Kent. She was rarely thrown by any problem, somehow the solution always seemed to spring up at her effortlessly, but if this girl Mick had caught was Charlie Weish, then everything she'd planned was in jeopardy.

The scheme to dispose of Andrew Blake was already underway. Within minutes of talking to him back in Shepherd's Bush on Friday, he had told her enough about his troubled relationship with Charlie and his background for her to see that a carefully faked suicide was the perfect way of getting rid of him.

Right now she had a young man in her employ, of similar colouring, age and build, posing as Andrew, using his identity, cheque-book and wearing his clothes, moving from guest-house to guest-house along the south coast. In each one he was carefully building up an appearance of a man in distress. He would be last seen close to Beachy Head. Meanwhile Andrew would be taken there too, dressed again in his own clothes, and thrown off the cliff.

So maybe this girl down at The Manse wasn't Charlie Weish and she was worrying unnecessarily. But if it was, how did she find the place?

The only people who knew Daphne owned it were her own two brothers. The solicitors who'd handled the cash purchase of it back in 1964 knew her as Mrs Jennifer Randall. The telephone, rates and every other service were in the same name and she never had visitors there.

Nine years ago it had been her intention to turn it into a grand country house hotel. It had seemed perfect then, within easy reach of London, but remote enough for reclusive weekends and holidays. She'd intended to extend the stables, add a swimming pool and gymnasium. But a shortage of funds had halted her plans, and as time went on and her circumstances changed,

512

she found she'd lost the impetus to start such a venture, and now only spent occasional weekends there. Thanks to a sudden boom in property prices, however, she was about to put it up for sale. She would stop seeing it as a mistake when she made a good profit.

'What are we gonna do if it is 'er?' Baz said suddenly, interrupting her thoughts.

'I'll have to find out how she found the house before I can decide that,' she answered crisply.

Baz turned in his driving seat to look at her, his expression one of extreme anxiety.

'Don't look like that,' she said sharply. The twins often reminded her uncomfortably of their mother. Not in looks – they'd got their father's squat features, his brawn and his knack of getting women to keep them. It was more the weakness in their mouths, the pleading in their eyes, she'd seen her mother with that expression so many times when Danny came back from the pub drunk. 'I mean talk, that's all. I got the boy to open up, didn't I?'

'Yes, but—' he stopped abruptly. He shared his brother's views about his sister, sometimes he could swear she wasn't human. He wanted to say that at the end of the day it would be he and Mick who'd be chucking the boy off the cliff, and she'd be sitting safely miles away. He had a feeling if this girl was Charlie Weish she would end up with a similar fate too. But right now it probably wasn't a good idea to irritate Daphne with incidentals. She was, when all was said and done, the brains in their family. But for her, he and Mick would have nothing.

'Trust me,' she said, laying one cool, beautifully manicured hand on his and giving him that heart-stopping smile that reminded him of when they were kids. 'Haven't I always done the best for all of us?'

Mick saw the red Mercedes coming up the lane from the study window and ran downstairs to open the door. He was surprised the lad didn't call out again, he'd made enough noise first thing this morning to wake the dead.

As Baz drove in and stopped, Mick opened the passenger door for his sister and bent down to speak to her. 'It is 'er! Charlie Weish,' he said. 'I done exactly what you said. I kinda made out I felt sorry for 'er. But it's gotta be just a fluke she came 'ere. She can't know about us or she wouldn't 'ave told me 'er real name.'

Daphne sat there thinking as Mick rattled out the whole conversation. 'What yer gonna do, sis?' he asked finally.

'Give me time to think and change my clothes,' she said. 'You two go through to the kitchen and wait for me there.'

Daphne waited until her brothers had gone through the door from the hall into the back of the house, then, taking off her shoes, she tiptoed across the hall and up the stairs. She didn't want the boy to know there was a woman in the house too.

Her bedroom was a vast and beautiful room at the front of the house, furnished with opulent antique furniture, which included an exquisitely carved seventeenth-century four-poster bed. The room reflected her aspirations at the time she'd bought the house. She had wanted to be lady of the manor then, with horses in the stables, crystal chandeliers in the hall and drawing room and servants kowtowing to her. But that dream vanished when Ralph refused to marry her. Without his wealth to pour into the place she had never got beyond transforming this room.

The rest of the house was an acute embarrassment to her – still so many empty rooms left as they were from the time it was an isolation hospital in the Twenties, the back garden overgrown. It was impossible to heat adequately, every window at the back needed replacing, all she'd managed to do was create a façade of country house living by keeping the front neat and tidy. She hated the place now and couldn't wait to get shot of it.

Stripping off her black business suit, she stood for a moment in front of the cheval mirror wearing only her black lacy underwear and appraised herself. She was forty-six, but her body was still almost as good as when she was twenty: firm, full breasts, a tiny waist, curvy hips and long slender legs. All her adult life people had remarked on her beauty and likened it to Elizabeth Taylor's. She could see the similarities – the black wavy hair, eyes that dominated her face – yet felt she had the edge on the actress for there was no vulnerable little-girl weakness in her perfect features, she was also taller and slimmer.

Moving nearer to the mirror, she examined her face closely. There were a few fine frown-lines on her forehead, and tiny puckers round her eyes and mouth; she would need to do something about them before long.

Bringing herself back to the job in hand, she went over to the walk-in wardrobe, switched on the light and began rummaging through the rails to find something suitable to wear to deal with this girl.

Back in her days of owning property in Paddington she had often adopted a disguise to get information about her tenants. In her time she'd been a district nurse, an official from the National Assistance Board, even a canvasser from the Labour Party. This was why being Martha Grimsby for an afternoon posed no problem to her. Yet she couldn't see how a disguise would help this time, not if the girl was wily enough to find this place.

As an idea came to her, she pulled out a pair of slacks and a black sweater and slipped them on. She would keep out of it. Mick might be as thick as two short planks, but he had already got the girl to reveal her real name, so that suggested she believed his story about being Mrs Randall's gardener. After being locked up for over two hours, she'd be frantic; with a little friendly persuasion she might very well be ready to spill out exactly how she came upon this address, and how the police were reacting to her boyfriend's disappearance.

Daphne smiled to herself. Once she had that information, a solution would present itself, it always had before.

Charlie leapt up from her chair as the door opened at last. In the two hours she'd been waiting she'd gone from extreme fright to indignation at being locked up like a criminal, and then sunk into a kind of numb state because she thought she'd been forgotten.

But on seeing the man again, still alone, she felt angry. 'Where are the police?' she shouted at him.

'You can't keep me here like this. I haven't done anything.'

'I'm sorry, love,' he said, shrugging his shoulders. 'They've just rung me to say they've got a big job on and they'll be along soon. So why don't you come on upstairs with me, 'ave another cuppa and we'll have a little chat. If you can give me a good enough reason for poking around in the garden, I might just drive you down to the station and let you go without waiting for them.'

Charlie's anger was wiped out. He was just a working man doing the best for his employer, he was being reasonable, so she must be too.

'Okay,' she agreed and forced herself to smile. She wondered if she could persuade him to give her something to eat too, it was half past three and apart from the bar of chocolate she'd had nothing to eat since the night before.

Yet as he led her up a narrow bare wood staircase into the main part of the house, and they didn't arrive at the big Victorian hall Rita had described, she felt disorientated and uneasy. He led her down a long, gloomy magnolia-painted corridor, with several doors leading off it, but everyone of them was shut. She surmised by the modern panelled doors on her right that they opened on to rooms at the back of the house. Therefore the more solid, older ones on the left led to the front. The corridor gave it a very institutional, spooky appearance, and it struck her as a peculiar home for an old lady living alone.

Right at the end of the corridor the man opened a door on the left-hand side. ''Ere we are at last,' he said jovially. 'Mrs Randall's dining room.'

Charlie was soothed by the sight of a tray of tea on the large oval antique table and its matching spoon-backed chairs, also by the view of the front garden through the windows. 'It's a very big house for an old lady,' she ventured as he pulled out a chair at the side of the table for her.

'Yeah, much too big,' he said, sitting down at the end of the table with his back to the door. 'Mrs Randall spends most of 'er time these days at her daughter's place, that's why I 'ave to be so careful.'

The bone-china tea service, the lace-trimmed tray cloth, was all appropriate for the room and indeed for the age of the woman he worked for. Yet on a moment's reflection it seemed strange to Charlie that a working man would choose to use it. The gardener at 'Windways' wouldn't have dared take anyone beyond the kitchen, and if he was making tea it would have been a mug.

It crossed her mind that he could be an intruder himself! Suppose he'd actually been burgling the house when she startled him? But she dismissed that thought as ridiculous; although he looked and sounded like a stereotype of a burglar with his bulging muscles and his missing front tooth, he was too relaxed, too at ease for that. As he poured the tea, he chatted companionably about how he wished he could find time to tackle the back garden, but just keeping the front nice was too much work.

Looking around her at the many large paintings on the walls, all in ornate gilt frames, she noticed there was no theme to them. Portraits were mixed with views, animals and seascapes. Her father would have dryly commented that the owner had no real interest in art but merely bought a job lot as an investment and had them framed identically. Likewise, the large silver salver and three different-sized tureens on the sideboard looked as if they'd been placed there to create an impression of country house living.

'Now, how about telling me why you really came in here?' the man said suddenly as he handed her the tea. He smiled disarmingly at her and his blue eyes were twinkling. 'I've been around the block a few times, Charlie, so don't try to kid me. From the field at the back you can see the road clearly, so no one but an idiot would push their way through that fence and brambles. And you ain't that, are you?'

Charlie smiled weakly. After being so long on her own and frightened out of her wits for most of the time it felt good to find he wasn't the bully she'd taken him for at first.

'No, I'm not stupid, just nosy,' she said. 'Okay, I did come in purposely, but only because I saw the front of the house and it looked so posh I wanted to see the back too. I found I couldn't see anything through the bushes, so I wriggled through a small hole. Once I got inside I was baffled as to why the back garden was so overgrown. I thought maybe the house was empty, so I couldn't resist taking a peep in the windows.'

He smiled again and patted her hand almost affectionately. 'That's better, now we're getting somewhere. But that's not all, is it? I've got a feeling someone told you something about this house, and that's why you looked for it. Am I right?'

Charlie was tempted to tell him the truth, to be

done with it all and get back to London, yet a sixth sense told her not to.

'No, no one told me anything. Why, is there something strange about its history?' she said, looking at him inquiringly.

'Not that I know of.' He shrugged. 'But you said you lived in London, so why come here? It ain't a place people usually go for day trips.'

'I had a holiday somewhere near here when I was a kid,' she said impulsively. 'I just remembered it being pretty and wanted to see it again. But I must have taken the wrong road from the station, because I couldn't find the cottage we stayed at.'

He smiled again, and now his rather cold blue eyes looked warmer. 'I did that once, tried to find a place out in Essex I'd been to. Got meself well and truly lost.'

'I hope you didn't wind up in trouble like me?' she laughed.

'Well, I didn't go traipsing round anyone's garden,' he said, raising his eyebrows reprovingly. 'Now, do you live with your mum and dad, Charlie?'

'No, in a flat.'

'On your own?'

It was an innocent enough question but aware she was vulnerable enough here in a strange house miles from anywhere, with a man who hadn't even told her his name, she didn't think she'd better portray herself as a loner.

'No, with three other girls,' she said. 'It gets a bit noisy there too, that's why a day in the country seemed a good idea.'

'Did you tell them where you were going today?'

All at once she felt uneasy. 'Yes, I did,' she lied. 'In fact if I don't get back by the time they get in from work they'll be worried about me. I couldn't phone one of them at her work could I?'

When he didn't reply immediately Charlie looked hard at him. He was rubbing his chin as if thrown by the request.

'I'll pay for the call,' she said quickly. 'Please?'

He still didn't reply and his eyes moved sideways. Charlie assumed he was actually looking towards the phone as if pondering on her request. Yet there was no phone in the corner to which he glanced, only a small hatch, the kind for passing food through from the kitchen.

'The phone's not working,' he said.

'You said you'd called the police?' she retorted indignantly.

He looked flustered. 'I went out to phone them.'

At that alarm bells began to jangle in Charlie's head. It would have been fair enough if he'd refused to let her use the phone, but why lie to her? Had he forgotten he said the police phoned him back just recently?

All at once all the oddities she'd noticed about him and this house bound themselves into one large mass. Maybe it didn't belong to Daphne Dexter, but there was something very strange about the whole set-up here. The hairs on the back of her neck were standing up, and she felt threatened. 'I need to go to the toilet,' she blurted out. It was the only ruse she could think of which might give him a chance to prove he was harmless. 'Where is it?'

Again his eyes flitted to that hatch. All at once she

realized why. There had to be another person on the other side of it listening to them.

A cold chill ran right through her. It could of course be the owner of the house and that she'd just wanted to hear Charlie's explanation herself before deciding what to do about her, but such devious behaviour wasn't typical of old ladies.

She had to know for certain. Leaping up, she rushed to the hatch and pushed it open before he had a chance to stop her.

As the two doors fell back Charlie recoiled in shock. It wasn't an old lady there, or even another man, but a dark-haired woman with vivid blue eyes.

Their eyes locked for only the briefest split second before the woman slammed the hatch shut, but Charlie instinctively knew who it was.

Daphne Dexter.

Coming face to face so unexpectedly with the woman she was sure was responsible for all the misery in her life suddenly made her feel faint. But as the man grabbed hold of her arm to haul her away from the hatch, she realized she was now in a very dangerous situation.

'I know who you are, you bitch,' she yelled at the top of her voice. 'Don't even think of hurting me like you did my mother because the police are on to you.'

'Take her back downstairs, Mick,' she heard the woman call out.

Stunned and scared as Charlie was, when the man grabbed her arm more tightly, she knew she had to fight from being taken back to the basement. She had already checked the barred windows in that room and they were as strong as the vaults in a bank. She had no doubt now that the man was one of the two who'd helped maim Rita and crippled her mother. She had to get away from up here and save Andrew.

'Don't lock me up again,' she pleaded with him as he manhandled her bodily out into the corridor. 'I'll do anything you say, just let me stay up here.'

She knew that sounded daft after what she'd just yelled at Daphne, but she was only playing for time. The front door was right in the middle of the house, so by that she guessed the middle door in the corridor led to it.

'If you think we want you up here yelling and screaming you're off your rocker,' he said, his face turning bright red with the effort of lifting her. 'Now, just be a good girl and come quietly.'

'Don't hurt me then,' she whimpered, making herself go all limp. 'Please don't hurt me!'

Whether it was this sudden subservience, or just that the corridor was so narrow, she didn't know, but he put her down and took up a position in front of her, dragging her along by only one arm. His grip was like a vice, yet while the other was free, there was still hope. She didn't attempt to struggle, just followed him meekly.

'I know you've got Andrew here in the cellar, that's why I came,' she said softly. 'Put me in with him, will you? If we're going to be killed, I'd rather we went together.'

Maybe it was her calm tone of voice, or even shock that she knew Andrew was here, but he turned to look at her as she hoped he might. She caught hold of his arm with her free one, insinuating herself closer

523

to him. 'I love him, Mick, wouldn't you want to see the person you loved one last time?'

That statement must have softened him marginally because she felt his grip on her arm weaken. Looking right into his cold eyes, she pleaded with her own. 'Please!' she whispered. 'It's not much to ask, is it?'

For just a split second she allowed herself to picture that scene on the lawn at 'Windways', to hear again her mother's agonized scream as her knees were crushed. She couldn't be absolutely certain he was one of the men who crippled her, but that didn't matter. It was pay-back time anyway.

Her knee came up like a sledge-hammer, hitting him right in his testicles. He staggered back, letting out a fearsome bellow of pain, but she was off past him, running up the corridor to the middle door.

As she grasped the brass knob she heard the kitchen door open, and another man's voice, but she didn't even dare look in that direction. She flung the door open and hurled herself across the wide hall towards the front door.

'Don't let it be locked,' her mind screamed, and miraculously it wasn't. She could hear feet thundering behind her, and she had no intention of being caught again.

Down the steps taking them two at a time, straight across the lawn to the bushes. She knew the wall behind them was four feet or so high, she had never been any good at gym at school, yet sheer terror drove her blindly through the bushes to vault over the wall.

Daphne slumped down on one of the kitchen chairs after returning from seeing her brothers drive off to catch the girl. She was trembling from head to foot, her heart was beating much too fast. She opened Baz's pack of cigarettes he'd left on the table and lit one, inhaling deeply to calm herself. 'Why on earth did I allow myself to get panicked into this?' she rasped aloud.

She took another deep draw and tried to gain her equilibrium. She knew why. Jin was the only man who'd ever made her behave recklessly, and even though she thought she'd put all that behind her a long time ago, it only took a mention of his name from Spud to start it up all over again.

Before she met Jin, she'd believed love was a weakness only fools succumbed to. But he'd turned her upside down and inside out, she'd let her defences down and become vulnerable. She would have done anything for him, but when he walked away from her, back to the wife and child he wouldn't and couldn't leave, that love turned to savage hate. She had to destroy him.

Sitting watching his daughter through a crack in the hatch had brought back all that passion she'd felt for him. Over the years, despite having seen the child as a baby countless times, she'd made herself picture it looking like Sylvia. Maybe she'd never convinced herself it was a blue-eyed blonde, but she'd taken pleasure imagining it had the same submissive and vulnerable nature, so that in time she would be exploited in the same way her mother had been.

Yet the girl she saw sitting in her dining room was all Jin. The same calm demeanour, the same steady, sloe-eyed gaze which gave nothing away. Her glowing skin, raven-black hair and defiance was all his. If she had any of her mother's nature she would have sobbed out everything to Mick, but instead she stuck tenaciously to her story and had the wits to work out she was being observed.

Finally when she knee-ed Mick and escaped from him, the girl had proved she had Jin's quick thinking and courage too. He had never bowed down to anyone, he was his own man always.

In the last two years, with all that passion and hatred spent, in reflective moments she occasionally pondered on what had made her so ferocious. Jin might never have returned the love she felt for him, but he'd been a caring, sensitive lover and a friend too. He'd set her up with the Lotus Club and when he said he wished her well, he had meant it. Yet that hadn't been enough, she'd wanted all of him, his heart, mind and soul. When she couldn't have that, there was nothing left but plotting her revenge.

She did it too, even though it took many years. She took his money, crippled his wife, spoiled the kid's life and destroyed his good name.

'But you've come back through her to haunt me, you bastard,' she hissed through her teeth. 'Well, I haven't finished yet. No one gets the better of me.'

Andrew sat down on the top step of the cellar stairs. He was very confused by all the sudden noise and charging about he'd just heard. First he'd heard a car pull up outside, then another man had come back into the house with the one who had brought him the food earlier. There was silence again for some time, then all at once he heard feet rushing across the hall and out through the front door. This was quickly followed by a man's heavy footsteps, then a woman's, and she shouted to someone called Mick to 'pull himself together and find her'. Finally the second man came past the cellar door, and he was groaning, his steps uncertain and slow. The car roared off from the drive outside, its wheels spinning on the gravel, and then the woman had come back in.

He couldn't be absolutely certain – after all the woman had been shouting – but she sounded like Martha Grimsby, her voice had the same low pitch. But who was the 'her' the men had been sent to find? He might not have heard one woman coming earlier if she was wearing soft shoes, but surely he couldn't have missed two of them?

Had this other woman attacked one of the men and run off? Surely they didn't have other prisoners in this house other than himself?

One thing was certain out of all this, things were escalating upstairs and before long they'd have to come and deal with him. If someone else had managed to get away from them, it was about time he put his mind to how he might escape too.

He had already tried kicking and pummelling at the cellar door many times, but without shoes on his feet it hadn't even so much as quivered. Now he knew that the door opened outwards, he couldn't even resort to the old trick on the films of standing behind it and slipping out like that.

'If only you had some sort of weapon,' he said aloud.

He gripped the top step, wondering if he could pull off one of the treads and use that, but it was rock solid. He worked his way down trying each one, but they were all the same. It was only as he got to the bottom and looked across at the wine rack that he suddenly saw that as a possibility.

If he could get it off the wall and be waiting in readiness at the top of the stairs with it when the men came back to get him, he might be able to force his way out with it like a battering ram and evade knives or fists.

'That's it,' he whispered to himself, refusing even to contemplate that he had no idea of the layout of the floor above, or where the front door was. 'It might just work.'

Standing in front of the rack, and catching hold of it firmly, he tugged it fiercely. It didn't budge.

The light in the cellar was dim, his feet were icy again through standing on the stone floor for so long, but by climbing up the rack, he discovered it was only held in place by four rusting screws along the centre of it.

Bracing himself at one end, he tugged again, and this time he felt a faint movement. He tried again and to his delight saw he'd loosened the first screw. Focusing his strength on each screw separately, slowly he managed to weaken each one.

He was hot and dizzy now with the exertion. He took a rest for a minute or two, then went back to it. Taking up a firm position in the middle, concentrating his mind entirely on the project and possible freedom, he heaved again, summoning up all his last remaining strength. The cracking, crumbling sounds of the screws coming loose from their fixing in the brick was like hearing beautiful music.

Another minute and he had it free. He was exhausted, but jubilant. Turning it sideways, he slowly hauled the heavy iron up the stairs to the door. He wanted to whoop with joy when he saw it in place. It almost filled the doorway from top to bottom, leaving enough space on the hinge side for him to barge through with it.

Chapter Eighteen

Charlie had only been running for a few minutes after escaping from The Manse when she realized she wasn't being chased any longer. Already severely winded, her first reaction was relief, but that was quickly followed by terror when it occurred to her that it meant the men would soon come in their car.

She couldn't remember seeing any houses between here and where the farmer picked her up on his tractor, and the lane was narrow, with tall hedges on both sides. If she continued along it she was a sitting target. Seeing a break in a hedge, she quickly scrambled through it, and she had only taken a few steps when a red car came past. It passed too quickly for her to see the occupants, but the speed it was travelling at seemed to confirm it was them.

Still panting, Charlie sat down to get her breath and consider what she should do. But suddenly she found herself crying. Reason told her it was just shock, she had after all just been through a terrifying ordeal and she still wasn't safe now. Yet it didn't feel as if it was the fear of imprisonment and maybe even death that was troubling her, but rather that woman's face.

She may have only caught the most fleeting glimpse,

yet she could picture her as clearly as she could her own mother. It was an outstandingly beautiful face. How could a woman look like that, yet be so evil? She could understand now why her father had been tempted into an affair with her, yet that was the only thing she did understand, everything else was still as mysterious as it had been this morning.

'Not quite,' she said aloud. 'You know for certain Andrew is locked up there, or that man Mick would have looked puzzled when you asked to be put in with him.'

That thought focused her mind. She had to phone the police quickly to get Andrew out of there before he was moved. At the same time it was imperative she didn't get caught herself. It was obvious that the men would soon turn the car around and come back when they'd been as far as they knew she could get on foot. The fields here were very open and if she was out in the middle of one she'd be spotted instantly.

Tentatively she stood up and looked around her. Unfortunately she was on the wrong side of the road to look down the hill towards Borough Green, and on this side the ground sloped upwards, and she could see no houses at all. She hadn't any idea how far the nearest village was either.

She looked at her watch and was surprised to find it was half past four. She had been up in that dining room for longer than she'd imagined. The smartest thing to do seemed to be to go back towards the house, keeping inside this hedge, as they'd be bound to imagine she'd continue the way she'd started. With luck there might be a house up that way too.

*

Andrew pricked up his ears at the sound of car tyres on the drive again. He had been sitting up by the cellar door with the wine rack for what seemed like hours, afraid to move in case the men came back. He sensed it must be close to dusk now as he'd tried turning off the light again to check and there was only a faint grey shadow rather than the brightness earlier. As the front door opened with a click, he also heard soft footsteps coming from the other direction.

'Why have you come back without her?' a woman's voice asked from somewhere to his left.

'She weren't anywhere on the road,' a man replied.

'You idiots,' she hissed back at him. 'Surely even you two could see she was bright enough to hide in a field? Get out again, on foot this time, checking behind the hedges. You can bet your life she doubled back when she saw you go past.'

'Okay,' the man said. 'But what if –'

'You *will* find her,' the woman cut him short. 'And quickly. You know as well as I do there isn't another house along there for three miles.'

The front door slammed abruptly. All at once the house was silent again.

Andrew was absolutely certain now that the woman was Martha. That deep husky voice had played on his mind over and over again when he'd woken up to find himself in here. But who could the woman be that they were looking for?

A chill ran down his spine.

'Not Charlie, surely,' he exclaimed. He tried to quash the thought, telling himself that if *he* didn't know where she was living, how could they have found her? Yet he'd told Martha she was coming back from Yorkshire on Friday night. Could they have met the trains and snatched her too?

He began to tremble with fear. It was bad enough to find himself in this predicament, but to think he'd put her life in danger too was unbearable. 'Please God, don't let them catch her,' he whispered. 'I don't care what happens to me, but don't let her be hurt.'

Rita arrived home just after six to find the flat just as she'd left it that morning, her own breakfast things still in the sink, Charlie out and no meal ready. Tired after a long day with Mrs Haagman behaving as though it was her fault they were short-handed, her initial reaction was one of irritation. It was only later as she sat by the fire with a bacon sandwich and a cup of tea that it occurred to her Charlie couldn't have returned from her early morning walk. The note she'd left was still in the same place, with nothing more added, and she certainly would have tidied up if she'd been here.

Thinking that she might have gone over to Jack Straw's Castle to check over Andrew's things again, or even got a message that he had turned up, Rita rang the pub. The landlady said Charlie hadn't called, and that she had in fact rung her twice during the day to find out if there was any news but got no reply. Rita became worried then, she couldn't think of any-one else her friend was likely to visit, and someone as desperate for news as she was would stay close to the phone.

She looked out of the window. It was growing dark and cold too. Charlie would know she'd be worried about her, so why hadn't she telephoned her at work if something unexpected had come up?

It was then that the conversation of the previous night popped into Rita's head. Had Charlie been quizzing her about that house with the intention of going to find it? It seemed a ridiculous notion – surely no sensible person would go off on such a wild goose chase – but the more Rita thought about Charlie's desperate state of mind, the more convinced she became that this was exactly what she had done.

Rita sat for some time weighing up the implications of this. Just thinking about what had happened to her in that house brought back all the old terror and although she tried to tell herself that Charlie couldn't possibly have found it with such a sketchy description and that even if she had, it was unlikely Daphne Dexter would be there, still the thought persisted that her friend was in trouble.

But what should she do about it? If she rang the police and said Charlie was missing they would tell her just to wait and see if she came home later. To get them to investigate down in that area of Kent she would need to tell them everything she knew about Daphne Dexter, and that would be like opening Pandora's Box.

It wasn't just a question of finding Andrew and Charlie. To ensure the woman was locked away permanently where she could never hurt anyone again, Rita knew she would have to agree to go into the witness box, and that meant her own past would become public knowledge.

She could perhaps live with her parents cutting her out of their life again, but what of Paul? What would it do to him to discover that his older sister was in fact his mother and that she'd been little better than a prostitute?

She didn't think she could bear that. Yet if she sat here and did and said nothing, it was possible Andrew and Charlie could be maimed like she was!

Suddenly she saw a vivid picture in her mind. She was lying on that bench, bound and gagged, and Daphne Dexter was looking down at her, the long knife poised in her hand.

'Maimed!' she exclaimed aloud. 'If that woman's got hold of Andrew because he's stumbled on something about her, she won't want to maim him, but kill him. And Charlie too!'

She saw then that she had no choice – even being cast off from her son was preferable to the thought of two young people with their whole lives ahead of them being killed. Snatching up the phone, she dialled the number for Bow Street.

Charlie's plan hadn't worked out too well. She should have continued the way she was going originally. She was making her way through a small wood just beyond The Manse when she heard men's voices coming up behind her, less than forty yards back.

She was hidden from them at that point, but she couldn't run on or they would have heard her. The only thing she could think of doing was to climb up a tree and hide. Fortunately the one nearest to her was easy enough to scramble up into, and she'd already discovered today that fear gave her strengths she didn't know she had. But once up in it she felt so vulnerable. The wind had got up, it was very cold, and she wasn't even sure she was concealed enough. The men walked right beneath the tree, poking into the undergrowth with sticks, and she was so scared she could hardly manage to hang on.

She had no choice but to stay in the tree because she had no idea which direction the men took once they got through the wood. Slowly the light began to fade from the sky, and although she welcomed darkness because it would conceal her once she climbed down, she still had no idea how much farther she had to go to get help. Every minute she delayed gave Daphne Dexter more time to get Andrew out of that house.

Finally she could stand the suspense no longer and she climbed down. Her foot slipped at one point and she cut her hand on a sharp broken branch trying to catch herself. She jumped the last six or seven feet, landed heavily on her knees and hobbled out of the wood.

A faint light in the distance became her goal. She'd lost track of where she was in relation to the road, and the field she went through had just been ploughed, so it was heavy going across furrows she could barely see.

The ploughed field led to one with cows, and she slipped in a cow-pat and gashed her hand again, this time on a stone. Two more barbed wire fences, and finally she came to a five-foot-high stone wall. She followed it along and a few minutes later she was hammering on the front door of a small detached house.

'Please call the police,' she blurted out the moment the door was opened by a tall man in spectacles. 'The house over there,' she pointed back the way she had come, 'The Manse it's called. They've got my boy-friend locked up. I'm afraid they're going to kill him. I've just escaped from them.'

She had never been so frustrated in her life as when the wretched man made her repeat what she'd said. Even then, instead of going straight into the house, he came outside and looked over the garden wall in the direction she said she'd come from.

'Look, please hurry,' she implored him, catching hold of his arm. 'Just ring 999, I'll explain to them. Andrew could be in terrible danger when they find I've got out.'

Later that night she was to understand why he didn't act immediately. He was a retired school teacher and he and his wife had been eating their evening meal when they were interrupted by frantic hammering on their door. It must have been alarming to find a wild-eyed, dirty Chinese girl with blood all over her hands on his doorstep shouting about prisoners in a house across a field. She couldn't really blame him then for thinking she was an escaped lunatic.

'The Manse, you say.' He spoke slowly and deliber-ately, looking at her with undisguised disbelief. 'Surely not, the woman who owns it is rarely there.'

Charlie lost her temper. 'Don't question me. Ring the bloody police,' she shouted. 'I'll stay out here if you're scared of me. But for Christ's sake get on to them now, before it's too late.'

'Okay, calm down,' he said. 'Now, what's your name?'

'Charlie Weish,' she snapped at him. 'Tell them that I know Andrew Blake is in that house, with two men and a woman called Daphne Dexter. Andrew's been missing since last Friday when they abducted him from London.'

He moved then, perhaps realizing at last that such a wild story had to be true. But he left her outside and closed the door firmly behind him. In the dim light Charlie could barely see her watch, but she thought it was nearly half past seven, three hours since she'd been in that dining room. By now the Dexters would almost certainly have whisked Andrew off somewhere new.

She was on the point of screaming in frustration when the door opened again. The man held the receiver of the telephone out to her. She felt like a leper being offered sustenance through a hatch.

'You'd better explain,' was all he said.

The relief at actually being in touch with police calmed Charlie a little. She explained as quickly as possible what had happened and urged them to go straight to The Manse immediately.

It was only once she'd handed the receiver back to the man that he suggested she came inside. 'You'd better take your shoes off,' he said, looking down at her mud- and cow manure-caked shoes. 'And I'd better get my wife.'

While Charlie was removing her shoes, back at The Manse Daphne was beside herself with anger when her brothers finally came back empty-handed from their search. It made no difference to her that they'd walked miles, she had been alone, living on her nerves and afraid that the police would arrive any minute.

'You are fools,' she shouted, her face and neck

turning purple with rage. 'I can't trust you with the simplest job. First Mick brings her in here, and then lets himself be bollocked. Now you can't find her.'

'I wish I hadn't brought her in 'ere an' all,' Mick retorted. His testicles were still throbbing and they were badly swollen. 'But it ain't no good goin' on about that now. What we gonna do with the lad?'

'Let him go,' Baz said wearily. He had already discussed this with Mick on the way back here. In his opinion a charge of abduction wasn't too terrible, certainly not as bad as murder.

'We can't let him go,' Daphne snapped back. 'We'll get him out now, drive him down to Sussex and I'll think of something then.'

'But the girl might have got to the police by now,' Baz argued.

'They won't take her seriously,' Daphne said. 'They'll drive round and when they find no one here they'll think she's got a screw missing.'

Neither of the brothers was convinced by their sister's opinion, and they had come to the conclusion earlier that she was behaving very irrationally, but they both wanted to get out of here as soon as possible. Perhaps on the way down to Sussex they could talk Daphne round to letting the lad go free.

'Okay, let's get on with it,' Baz said, moving towards the door.

Andrew was tense with terror on the cellar stairs. He'd heard the men come back in and there was the sound of faint yet angry-sounding voices in the distance. But pleased as he was that they presumably hadn't found the girl they were looking for, he was cold and hungry again, without any idea of what was really going on or where he was, and he felt he was on the point of collapse. As he heard footsteps coming towards the cellar, he tried to brace himself to carry out his plan, but he was afraid he no longer had the strength even to lift the wine rack, much less bludgeon his way out with it.

'You've got to,' he whispered to himself. 'Just think of Charlie!'

As the heavy footsteps came closer, he lifted the wine rack, tucking his arms through it securely, then momentarily closed his eyes and pictured Charlie as she had been down on the beach at Slapton Sands that first time he'd kissed her. Gleaming black hair blowing in the wind, almond eyes closing as he took her face in his two hands, and her soft lips ready for his.

He could taste the sweetness of that kiss, smell the salt in the air, feel the silkiness of her cheeks in his hands. As the key turned in the lock and a chink of light appeared, he charged, roaring like a bull imprisoned for weeks.

It was Baz who opened the door. Mick was standing just to his right looking up at his sister who was going on up the main stairs. Neither of them was alert, they were in a state of shock with their minds only on getting out of the house as fast as possible.

Baz was caught by the full force of Andrew's charge, staggering back as the huge, unexpected weapon hurtled out and virtually impaled him against the wall on the opposite side of the hallway. Mick was trapped on the other side, too startled for a moment by the surprise and the roaring noise the lad was making even to move.

'You bastards!' he heard Andrew scream out as he ran towards the front door.

'Stop him!' Daphne yelled from her position on the stairs, and she came clattering down them.

As Andrew reached the door and scrabbled to open it, he was more aware of the woman in black bearing down on him than of the two men trying to get the wine rack out of the way. Seeing a large vase on a table beside the door, he grabbed it and hurled it at Daphne. He got the door open as the vase crashed to the floor, and he didn't look to see if he'd managed to hit her, but sped down the steps and headlong straight across the lawn.

Andrew was a good sprinter. At school he'd been noted for his speed. But after being cooped up for so long, half starved and with the added difficulty of darkness, he wasn't so fast. Even over the wind he could hear someone in hot pursuit behind him and he headed straight for the bushes. They were thick, and he had to fight his way through them. He could hear the panting of the man chasing him and sheer terror gave him an added boost of strength to vault over the wall behind the bushes. Finding himself on a road, he turned left and belted up it, running for his life.

'Watch out,' PC Knowles yelled at the driver of the police car as the headlights suddenly revealed a man hurtling towards them. 'Brake!'

In Andrew's terrified state he saw the approaching car's headlights as another peril, and froze. He heard a squeal of brakes and as two men jumped out of the car, another dizzy spell caught him and his legs gave way beneath him.

Chapter Nineteen

Just after nine the police telephoned Charlie at Mr and Mrs Harding's house to give her the news that Andrew was at the police station and that they would be sending a car round to collect her shortly too.

As Charlie had convinced herself during the long tense wait that any news would be bad, she could hardly believe her ears. 'Is he hurt?' she asked in a trembling voice.

'Not at all,' the police officer assured her. 'He's weak with exhaustion and lack of food, but a square meal and a good night's sleep will put him straight. All he wants right now is to see you.'

Charlie had a million questions she wanted to ask, but the Hardings were sitting side by side on the settee looking very anxious, so she thanked the policeman and put the phone down. 'They've got Andrew safe and sound, and they are sending someone up to collect me,' she said excitedly, beaming at them both. 'Thank you so much for everything. It must have been an awful shock to you when I hammered on the door. But I'll be out of your hair in a little while.'

Mrs Harding had been kindness itself. Although a rather prim little woman of over sixty, she'd fed Charlie soup and sandwiches, washed and dressed the many cuts and scratches on her hands and face, found her a clean pair of trousers belonging to one of her grown-up children, and been very sympathetic. She'd even phoned Rita to tell her Charlie was safe.

Mr Harding had been more distant. While his wife seemed to understand the emotional torture Charlie was going through as she awaited news of Andrew, and the need to talk about her ordeal, he appeared to be only concerned that sinister activities were going on less than half a mile away, and that Charlie had brought a breath of it into his home.

'We're so glad Andrew is safe.' Mrs Harding got up from her seat and gave Charlie a warm hug. 'My goodness, we'll be able to dine out on this story for months.'

Ten minutes later a police car arrived to collect Charlie. She turned to Mrs Harding at the front door and kissed her cheek. 'Thank you for taking care of me,' she said. 'You've been so very kind.'

'Just drop me a line and tell me the outcome,' the woman replied. 'Good luck, Charlie.'

Down at the police station Charlie was ushered into an interview room where Andrew was waiting, feeding on tea and sandwiches. He leapt to his feet to hug her, but for a moment they were both so choked with emotion they couldn't speak.

'I'll leave you for a few minutes,' the police constable said from behind them. 'Make him finish up those sandwiches, Charlie, he's half starved.'

Charlie watched like a mother hen as Andrew returned to his food. She thought he looked terrible. He face was gaunt and grey, eyes haunted and red-rimmed. With several days' growth of beard, filthy overalls and his feet bare and dirty, he was a pitiful sight. But her heart welled up with love and concern for him.

'I never knew plain cheese sandwiches could taste so good,' he grinned as he finished up the plateful. 'Now, tell me exactly how you ended up there too. The police haven't told me anything about that.'

'They don't know much about it yet either,' she grinned. 'And I'm not telling you that until I hear about whether the police caught the Dexters. I assume the two men were her brothers?' She hadn't thought to ask the policeman who brought her here, she'd been too caught up in the story of how Andrew used something as a kind of battering ram to get out.

'I didn't know who they were.' He shrugged. 'The police haven't got any real proof about that yet either, because they got away,' he added.

'Oh no,' Charlie gasped.

'That was my fault,' he said ruefully. 'You see, I collapsed in front of the police car and delayed them. By the time they got to the house, everyone had gone. But they're organizing a search warrant right now, and apparently some bigwig from London is on his way down here.'

Charlie was aghast that they'd got away, but sensing Andrew was not only blaming himself already for this but was somewhat confused, she kept it to herself. 'You were incredibly brave and clever to get away from them, if you hadn't they would almost certainly have whisked you off somewhere else before the police got there,' she said. 'But that doesn't matter now. We're both safe and together again.'

'I thought I was never going to see you again,' he said in a quavery voice. 'I've never been so terrified in my entire life. You see, I thought they were going to kill me.'

That statement made Charlie realize he was still in deep shock. She had recovered the moment she knew he was safe, but then she'd been through so much less than him, and she'd known a great deal more about the Dexters and that house than he had. She guessed it would take some time before he could come to terms with it all. Setting aside all her questions, and everything she had to tell him, she moved over to hug and reassure him.

'I came looking for you because I love you,' she whispered.

Andrew pulled away from her. 'I stink,' he said, his eyes suddenly downcast.

'Do you think that matters to me?' she said gently, stroking his face. 'You've spent four days alone and starving in a cold cellar, not even knowing where you were or why they were doing that to you. Another man would have cracked, but you fought your way out of there. You're the bravest man I've ever known.'

He cried then. As she held him tightly against her shoulder, out came a muffled and often garbled account of how it had been for him. Charlie could understand his terror and confusion completely, but when he sobbed out how pathetic he was, telling her of his ingratitude to his parents and his conviction he was never going to see them or her again, she cursed Daphne Dexter for reducing a strong and brave man to this.

'Listen to me,' she said at length, lifting his face up

and holding it in both her hands, looking right into his eyes. 'You aren't pathetic, far from it, and you started all this for the best and most pure motives, for me. It's over now and you are safe, and all the nasty things which happened between us are all wiped out and forgotten too. I'm going to ask someone to take us home, I'll bath you and put you to bed. Tomorrow I'll feed you till you burst, and we'll talk about it all. Don't you dare crack on me now, I've got too many plans for us.'

He smiled wearily, but Charlie thought he'd taken what she said on board.

As Charlie and Andrew were being driven home much later in a police car, Daphne Dexter was in the car park of her London flat in St John's Wood, hastily packing clothes and other valuables into the boot of her red Mercedes.

White-hot anger was the fuel she was running on, against herself for allowing herself to become rattled by a student posing as a researcher, against Charlie for outwitting her, and against her brothers for their cowardice. They had jumped into their van the moment Andrew Blake leapt over the garden wall. She had assumed they were going to head him off, but instead the gutless wonders drove off at speed down towards the Maidstone Road and left her high and dry.

She had looked after them since their mother abandoned them – but for the fear of them going in an orphanage, she would have run away the first time her father raped her. She'd fought to keep them with her when he was found dead; she'd begged, stolen and prostituted herself to give them a better chance in life. She'd been the one who'd fed, clothed and housed them even as grown men. She'd tolerated their stupidity, covered up their ineptitude, bailed them out of trouble more times than she cared to remember, just because she had always known it was they who attacked and ultimately killed her father.

But the last strands of affection and gratitude she felt towards them had gone now. Maybe she had intended to leave them, but she would have seen them all right financially – now she could hardly believe their loyalty to her was so fragile. It was a very good thing she hadn't lingered at The Manse. She'd snapped off the house lights, shut the front door, and was just getting into her own car when she heard the police siren in the distance. A few more seconds and she would have been cornered.

As far as she was concerned her brothers didn't exist any more. She was off to Spain for good. A quick phone call had ensured that the emergency plans for liquidating her business operations she'd made some time ago would be put into place. She was a rich woman, she had no need ever to work again. She would have a good life in Spain.

Yet beneath her anger Daphne was scared. Jin had once warned her that if she ever tried to hurt Sylvia or his precious daughter he would come gunning for her. It seemed to her after today's events that his spirit was alive and well, in that damned Charlie.

Detective Inspector Hughes and PC Farrow were watching the tall, slender woman pack her car. Sitting in Hughes's black Jaguar in a side street opposite the

Wellington Road, they had a clear view of the well-lit glass entrance hall, the car park and the one exit.

As soon as they got the message from the Kent police that Andrew Blake and Charlie Weish had been found, they had driven straight here to the address Hughes had discovered earlier in the day. As Hughes saw it, there was little point in rushing down to check out The Manse once the birds had flown.

Oswald Hughes, or Ozzie as his friends and family called him, might very well have become a villain himself, but for his father and the war. He grew up in a Bermondsey tenement, one of nine children – their father was a porter at Smithfield meat market. All his early adolescent years were spent working in a warehouse by day, cruising the streets at night, fighting, petty pilfering and aiding and abetting older criminals. But his father was a great deal tougher than him, and honest too. When he saw the way young Ozzie was going he gave him an ultimatum: either join the army, or find himself an outcast from his family. Young thug that he was, Ozzie cared deeply for his family and admired his father, so he reluctantly enlisted.

He was somewhat surprised to find he liked army life – the comradeship with other men, sport, adventure and the orderliness of it. He rose to Sergeant in record time. Every good quality he had – intelligence, courage, toughness, plain-speaking and a strong sense of fair play – were expanded by his experiences during the war of leading the men under him.

When the war ended he had a quite different slant on life. He saw that Britain might be the victor, but his country was on its knees. Those same slimy sods who'd avoided conscription and gone into black-marketeering were now set to move into serious crime. He saw apathy among the older people, bewildered ex-servicemen, children running wild, vice of every description rising to meet the demands of a frustrated nation suddenly freed from the fear of death and destruction. He knew then that what England needed most was a strong police force, to bring back law and order. He thought that he could serve his country better by joining the police than staying on in a peace-time army.

Twenty-eight years on Ozzie felt the police were fighting a battle with one hand tied behind their backs. The public insisted they wanted a strong force, yet flew into a state of alarm when a copper clouted some young ruffian. Murder, robbery with violence, rape, thieving and drugs were all on the increase, the prisons were overcrowded and the courts couldn't cope. For every pathetic petty criminal who got caught and locked away, there were probably six real villains who got away with their crimes.

But disillusioned as he often was, Ozzie still stuck tenaciously to his principles. His job was to catch criminals and put them away, whatever, and however long it took. He was shrewd, crafty and patient. He'd had a hunch two decades ago that Daphne Dexter needed watching and he'd never given up on it.

Last Friday afternoon when Charlie Weish had come into the police station with her tale of Andrew Blake's disappearance and her conviction that Daphne Dexter was behind it was like striking gold. He had always been convinced this cunning and very beautiful woman was behind many unsolved crimes, but although he had compiled a thick dossier on her activities, business interests and acquaintances, he had been unable to find any concrete evidence to charge her with.

Ozzie hadn't let on to Charlie during their interview that he knew both her parents, or indeed was perfectly aware that DeeDee and Daphne Dexter were the same person. Experience had taught him to keep his own counsel and let others tell him what they knew.

As a young copper back in the early Fifties, his beat had taken him up and down every street and alleyway of Soho. The Lotus Club was a place he popped into regularly, it was a good club, and Jin Weish was a decent sort. He remembered once walking in just as Sylvia and DeeDee did a strip together and they almost brought the house down. Sylvia was the saucy blonde one, all flirtatious blue eyes and sexy wiggles, whilst DeeDee was dark-haired, sensuous, supple and kind of dangerous.

Ozzie was pleased when he heard that Jin had married Sylvia. In his many visits to the club he'd got to know her very well, as he had many of the girls in Soho. For all her sauciness, there was something very vulnerable about her, like Bambi in a jungle. She needed a strong man beside her and it had always been patently clear that Jin worshipped the ground she walked on. Later Ozzie was even more pleased to see how seriously Jin took to fatherhood. He bought a house well away from the corrupting sleaze of Soho, and tucked his wife and child away in it.

The only mistake Jin made was to allow DeeDee to slip into Sylvia's old shoes as manageress. Almost overnight, well before she got him into her bed, she changed things at the club. The old characters of Soho were no longer welcome to drink there, nor were policemen. She took on waitresses and strippers who were in fact hookers, and took her cut for every man they took home. Ozzie imagined that as his profits rose Jin was probably delighted to discover what an ambitious schemer the woman was.

That one club became two, then three, and somewhere along the line DeeDee, who now called herself Miss Dexter, got her claws right into Jin. Ozzie could understand it in one way – she was gorgeous, she smouldered with sensuality, giving all men the idea that one night with her would be worth risking everything for. But he'd always considered Jin Weish too worldly and astute to be susceptible to womanly wiles.

Ozzie never did get the full story of how Dexter managed to end up with Jin's clubs when he moved to the West Country. Rumour had it that she blackmailed him into it, but he didn't believe that totally as Jin had never been a villain, or a fool. In Ozzie's opinion Jin just had the right priorities. He wanted a cleaner life for himself and his family, and to distance himself from a woman he knew was trouble.

At first it was just fond memories of Jin and Sylvia coupled with a hunch that Dexter had criminal tendencies that made Ozzie keep tabs on her. She bought property in Paddington, and although he heard she put the frighteners on her tenants to keep them in line, there was nothing tangible enough to warrant a proper investigation. Miraculously she sold all these places just before the Rachman scandal, and moved on to more genteel parts of London.

About the same time Daphne Dexter's name was linked with Ralph Peterson, a very wealthy businessman. There were many mentions of them in the gossip columns, at Ascot, first nights at the opera, and at parties given by Mayfair socialites. They made a handsome couple and Ozzie thought that perhaps love had mellowed Daphne.

Two years later Peterson was knocked over and killed close to his Mayfair club late one night. An eye-witness claimed that he had moved to look out of his window on hearing the sound of an engine revving up. He was just in time to see the car hit a man, throwing his body up over the bonnet. The driver didn't stop, but reversed back over the body, then drove off at speed towards Oxford Street. The witness said there were two men in the car, but he could only remember part of the registration number and that the car was black.

It was Peterson's spinster sister who insisted Daphne Dexter was responsible. She said her brother had fallen out with the woman some two months earlier and at the time he'd expressed fear she might retaliate in some way. The partial registration number did match Barrington Dexter's black Jaguar, but by the time the police acted, any marks, blood or threads of Peterson's clothing which might have been on it had been washed away. The twins had an unshakeable alibi for that night too, so nothing could be proved. When it transpired that Peterson had left a large sum of money to Daphne in his will, officers more senior than Ozzie took the line that Peterson's sister was hysterical with jealousy and bitterness. They discounted her claims on the basis that any man who felt threatened by a woman would immediately cut her out of his will. But in Ozzie's view it was far more likely Daphne was motivated more by revenge at being jilted than purely money, but also guessed there was a strong chance Peterson wouldn't have got around to changing it immediately.

Ozzie watched her even more closely from then on. He noted that Jin's old clubs had turned to seedy clip joints, then they became peepshow dives and latterly discotheques. Ozzie was on the Drugs Squad by then, and he was one of the men in the raid on the Purple Pussy Cat in Wardour Street where a large quantity of acid and amphetamines were found. Dexter ought to have done a stretch for that – it was common knowledge that the drugs were sold openly there – but somehow evidence was tampered with, suggestions made that the drugs had been planted by the police. She escaped scot-free.

When Dexter moved away from Soho and opened her property office Eagle Incorporated in Mayfair, it appeared she had turned straight. But Ozzie wasn't convinced. Was it coincidence that an old lady who was the only sitting tenant in a house in Holland Park Avenue was brutally beaten up by burglars one night shortly after Dexter's company had bought the property? Nothing could be proved, but the old lady moved out soon after, the house was divided up into luxury apartments and each one sold for more than the entire house had cost. Again and again there were whispers that people who'd been foolhardy enough to get in Dexter's way ended up in hospital with grievous injuries. Ozzie had interviewed three of these mysterious victims, none of whom could explain satisfactorily how they got their injuries. Two were married businessmen, neither of whom had any obvious link to Dexter, the third was an ex-call-girl who certainly did know her, but denied it. But all three of them shared the same kind of fear. Ozzie could only surmise their silence had been bought by threatening someone close to them.

Some of Ozzie's senior officers had remarked that he had a bee in his bonnet about the woman and advised him to stop wasting his time on her. But when Jin disappeared two years ago, they too became interested, in fact the investigation was taken out of his hands entirely. Ozzie couldn't prove a thing, but to his mind that so-called investigation stank. He didn't believe for one moment that Jin was capable of running off and leaving Sylvia and his daughter with a mountain of debt. It wasn't his style. The two men who attacked Sylvia Weish in her garden could well have been the Dexter brothers, yet he could find no record of them having been brought in for questioning, or their sister. He came to the conclusion someone had been paid off.

So when Charlie came to him with her story of her boyfriend's disappearance, Ozzie's first emotion was elation because for once it looked as if the woman had made a serious mistake. A prostitute, a drug addict or another villain could go missing and who cared? But a bright young student with a decent family was a different ball game, and even back-handers wouldn't help this time.

Of course that elation vanished in the face of the girl's distress, and the knowledge she was prepared to shield those who had given her information humbled him. He thought she was a great deal like her father, and his last thought as she'd left his office was the hope that before long he'd be able to prove to her that her father had always been an honourable man.

He admired Charlie even more now since talking to the Kent police. She'd managed to find Dexter's hide-out, and she'd outwitted her by escaping. Now he was going to bring Miss Bloody Dexter to justice. He felt certain that once he had her in custody there would be dozens of other people like Rita Tutthill queuing up to add to the charges against her.

'She seems very calm,' Farrow remarked. He was a lean, blond, twenty-three-year-old with only eighteen months' experience on the force, so he was somewhat surprised to find himself on a case like this with such a senior officer.

'Arrogant more like,' Hughes chuckled. He had selected Farrow tonight because the lad reminded him of himself when he was that age – cocky, tough and quick-thinking. 'She thinks she's fire-proof.'

He had to hand it to Daphne Dexter, she was cool, elegant as always in a dark suit, her hair pinned back in a sleek chignon as if she'd just come from a business meeting. He could of course pick her up right now, he had more than enough to charge her with, but Hughes liked cat-and-mouse games, and besides, in her flight she might lead him to her brothers.

'She's leaving, sir,' Farrow said.

Ozzie waited as the Mercedes came up the car-park slope to Wellington Road and turned down towards Baker Street. He left it a minute or two before following; at this time of night with clear roads it would be easy enough to keep her in his sights. He didn't need to be right on top of her and alert her to a tail.

'Bugger me, she's not going to Dover after all,' Farrow said some time later as they saw the Mercedes tail-lights turn off towards the A11 at Aldgate. 'Where'd you think she's going, sir?'

Hughes thought for a minute. During his investigations he had discovered Dexter owned a property in Marbella in Spain – in fact it was the only property he could find which *was* in her real name – bought some years ago with the money she'd inherited from Peterson. Even her London apartment, and the house in Islington where her brothers lived, were owned by her company. So he had assumed Marbella would be where she would flee to. Yet he'd expected her to take the most direct route via Dover.

'Harwich is my bet,' he replied grimly. He wasn't pleased, it would be a long drive with plenty of opportunity on the empty roads for her to notice she was being followed. 'We'll keep following for a bit, just to make sure. Then you'd better phone in from a call-box and get them to alert the Harwich police. I wouldn't put it past her to be tuned in to police radio.'

'You poor loves,' Rita said as Charlie and Andrew came into her flat, their faces grey with exhaustion. Rita was in her nightclothes, but she'd sat up waiting for their return. 'What can I get you? Tea, food?'

'Nothing, thank you,' Charlie said. 'You go to bed. Andrew just needs a bath and sleep, that's all. We'll talk about it all tomorrow.'

'Take my bed.' Rita's small pale face was furrowed with lines of anxiety. She felt she would never sleep again until Daphne Dexter was behind bars. 'I'll sleep in yours.'

While Charlie was being questioned by the Kent police, she had been told that her friend had given their colleagues in London a great deal of information about the Dexters. Charlie knew just how tough that must have been for Rita to relive her ordeal again. She so much wanted to talk to her now, console her and reassure her that she and her son would be protected until Daphne was convicted, but Andrew's needs were greater right now.

'We're safe now, all of us,' was all she could say, and she took a step forward to hug her friend. 'The local police are keeping an eye out here. But she wouldn't dare try and hurt any of us again, not now.'

Rita stepped back and smiled bravely at both of them. 'I'll run the bath for Andrew,' she said. 'Sleep tight, both of you. If you need anything, just call me.'

Charlie lay awake for a very long time, curving her body round Andrew's protectively. He had fallen asleep the moment he'd got into Rita's bed, long before Charlie got in beside him. She thought that tomorrow they would laugh about how ironic it was that on their first time ever in a double bed they weren't even capable of kissing.

But her mind just wouldn't switch off. Her thoughts flitted from all the people who had to be informed Andrew was safe, how they would get some clothes for him, to thinking about how soon she would have to go back to work. Yet above all those relatively unimportant things were all the unanswered questions. Had Daphne Dexter killed her father, was it

557

definitely her brothers who hurt her mother? And how long would it take for the police to catch them and find out for certain?

Charlie woke to hear Rita in the kitchen. She looked at the clock and saw it was seven in the morning. Andrew was still sound asleep, he didn't look as if he'd even turned over in the night. She got out of bed and crept out to the kitchen to find Rita sitting at the table smoking a cigarette. She looked as if she hadn't slept at all, her eyes were puffy with black circles beneath them.

'I didn't bring you any tea because I didn't want to wake you,' Rita said, looking up with a wan smile. 'But there's some in the pot.'

Charlie poured a cup and sat down beside her. 'I'm so sorry I dragged you into all this. I bet you wish you'd never met me.'

'Don't be silly,' Rita retorted. 'I don't wish any such thing. I was frantic with worry of course, but because I care about you, and I suppose I still am because it's not all resolved yet.'

Charlie remained unconvinced. She could see a haunted look in her friend's eyes. 'Was it awful talking to Hughes?' she asked.

'Not as bad as I expected.' Rita shrugged. 'He's a decent bloke, shame all coppers aren't like him. But of course that was the easy bit, the worst will be giving evidence in court.'

Charlie hadn't thought that far ahead yet. 'You don't have to. They'll get enough on her to send her down without you getting involved,' she said.

Rita grimaced. 'I do, Charlie. Hughes pointed out that so far they have only Andrew's abduction to charge them with. Unless there is a more serious charge they wouldn't even be able to hold the three of them long enough to get evidence into your dad's disappearance. Hughes is convinced they killed him, Charlie.'

'He is?' Every hair on Charlie's head stood on end at hearing this. Hughes had seemed so nonchalant about everything she'd said to him, and even after all she and Andrew had been through yesterday, not one of the police down in Kent had actually agreed they thought the Dexters had intended to kill them. 'Then why didn't he say so?'

Rita put her hand over Charlie's, her face soft with sympathy. 'I'm sure you can see why. He saw, just as I did when I first met you, that you were hoping against hope that Jin would turn up some day. Now I've promised to give evidence it means he can return to people who were questioned two years ago, and try and persuade them to tell him more too.'

Charlie began to cry.

'Now, come on!' Rita shook her shoulder. 'You should be glad about this! You must relish that bitch getting her come-uppance. I know I do.'

'I do relish it,' Charlie sobbed. 'It's just so awful that Mum died believing Dad had run out on her. And what about you? A court case will be terrible for you. I hate to think that through me you have to go through all that pain.'

'It is awful about your mum,' Rita agreed. 'Terrible too to think that your childhood was suddenly ended by that woman's viciousness. But that's why I have to do it, Charlie. I can't hide my head in the sand any longer. Besides, Hughes said that if the Dexters are convicted I could make a claim for compensation against them. It might mean a nice little house for me, and security at last.'

Charlie was even more touched by her friend's show of bravado. She knew perfectly well Rita hadn't been swayed by the possibility of compensation.

'Money won't make up for everyone knowing about you,' Charlie retorted. She looked right into her friend's eyes and dared her to claim it would.

Rita laughed. 'Oh yes it will,' she said flippantly. 'Money soothes all hurts.'

Charlie had to smile. She somehow knew Rita would stick with that reason until the bitter end. She had more guts than anyone she'd ever met.

'It's a good job I know what you really are, Rita Tutthill,' she said, wagging a finger at her. 'If you get any trouble from your parents and son when it all comes out, I shall personally go and visit them and tell them a few home truths about you.'

Rita smiled. 'I believe you would too. But now I'd better get ready for work.'

Charlie's eyebrows shot up. 'Work! You can't go in, you look exhausted.'

Rita laughed. 'Exhausted I may be, but apart from the fact the Hag will stop my money if I don't, work is the best way I know to get through difficult times.'

To Charlie that encapsulated everything she admired about her friend. She didn't lie down and feel sorry for herself when things were tough, but got on with her life with courage and fortitude. Charlie thought she must take a leaf out of her book.

'Tell the Hag I'll be in tomorrow,' she said. 'That's if she hasn't had the impudence to sack me already.'

'Charlie, even you couldn't be that lucky,' Rita rolled her eyes comically. 'Now, go easy on poor Andrew today. He's had a tough time and needs to recover before you start feasting on his emaciated body.'

Charlie laughed. She had a feeling Andrew would have made a complete recovery by the time he woke.

She was right. Rita had hardly closed the front door behind her when Andrew woke and immediately pulled her into his arms. 'This was what I thought of most of the time I was in the cellar,' he said. 'Holding you, loving you. I think if I hadn't had that I might have flipped.'

He was savage the first time, so rough and forceful that it took her breath away. Yet her own need was as great as his and she responded with equal savagery, clawing at his back and biting his shoulders. To have him in her arms was all that mattered. They had been granted a reprieve.

An hour or so later they made love again, but this time it was slow, tender and loving. They kissed, stroked and licked at every inch of each other, two minds with the same goal, to wipe out the hurt and misery, to begin on a new road.

'Saying I love you isn't enough,' Andrew said, his face pressed deeply into her breasts. 'I adore you, I worship you, but that sounds like something out of a church service. I wish I could find the right words to explain just how I feel.'

'"I love you" is enough for me,' she whispered, tears of joy flowing down her face. 'I never want to be parted from you again.'

'That's a tall order,' he laughed, and moved back on to one elbow to look at her. 'Am I supposed to take you with me to college?'

'You know what I mean. To spend every night with you. For yours to be the face I wake up to.'

'We can't have that straight away,' he sighed, flicking his hair from his eyes and looking very apprehensive. 'I'll have to go home to my parents for a few days. I phoned them last night from the police station, Mum was in a terrible state. Dad said she'd been distraught right from when they first heard I'd gone missing.'

'I suppose they'll be against me,' Charlie said in a small voice. 'I mean, it's all my fault, isn't it?'

'They aren't that kind of people,' Andrew reprimanded her. 'Mum is Beryl's sister, remember, and in many ways they are very alike. Aunt Beryl has always spoken so highly of you, Mum feels she knows you already. I just wish I'd taken you to meet them before all this happened though. Still, never mind, I'll ask if you can come up at the weekend to meet them.'

Charlie didn't think his mother would welcome her with open arms after what had happened. Would any mother really want a half-Chinese girl with a tainted background for her only son? But she didn't say this, time would tell if she was right.

'You'd better phone them now,' she said instead. 'And Carol at the pub. We'll have to arrange to get you some clothes too.'

'You are a little worry-guts,' he smiled. 'Will you promise me that once we're married you'll leave all the worrying to me?'

'Marry you!' Charlie feigned astonishment. 'Now, that's going a bit far!'

'It's the only way I know of having you with me for ever,' he said. 'Not to mention being able to sleep with you anywhere and everywhere without raising eyebrows.'

'I might have known sex was at the bottom of it,' she laughed. 'You get your degree first, sonny, then we'll see!'

As Andrew was speaking first to his parents, then to Carol on the telephone, Detective Inspector Hughes and PC Farrow were checking out the queue of cars waiting to board the Harwich ferry.

It was a cold grey morning, with high winds whipping the sea over the harbour wall, and both men were tired and dispirited. A puncture halfway to the port delayed them for almost an hour, so Dexter could have turned off in some new direction for all they knew. But they'd continued to Harwich anyway and arrived here an hour or two ago only to discover that although the dock police had been notified to look out for and apprehend Daphne Dexter, for some reason they hadn't received details of the car she was travelling in. To find such a major blunder was infuriating, but fortunately all the ferries had been delayed because of high winds, so there was still a chance she might be travelling under an assumed name and that she was in fact still here, trapped in the long line of cars waiting on the dock.

'There she is!' Ozzie exclaimed jubilantly as he spotted the red Mercedes tucked in between a grey Rover and a black Ford. 'Thank fuck!'

'Should we get some back-up?' Farrow asked, looking around him nervously. He couldn't see any dock police anywhere, just a few passengers stretching their legs before boarding.

Ozzie grinned. 'Back-up! For one woman? She can't move that car, and where's she going to run to? She's a smart cookie, but unless she's sprouted wings during the night she's got no chance. Nip through the line of cars now and be ready just in case she tries to get out that side.'

A shiver of expectancy ran down Ozzie's spine, wiping out his tiredness. As he walked towards the car he could see she was alone and engrossed in putting on lipstick. She clearly thought she was almost home and dry.

Checking first that Farrow was in place, Ozzie tapped on the passenger door. The woman looked startled, then frowned, as if knowing the face looking in at her was familiar, but unable to place it. She opened the window and smiled, but her blue eyes were as cold as the North Sea. 'Yes?' she said.

Ozzie leaned his entire weight against the car door. With his right hand he reached in and withdrew her car keys from the ignition, with the left he held out his warrant card. 'Detective Inspector Hughes. You are under arrest, Miss Dexter, for the abduction of Andrew Blake. You are not obliged to say anything, but anything you do say will be taken down and used in evidence against you.'

'I beg your pardon,' she said haughtily, the consummate actress right till the end. 'My name is Sandra White. You clearly have the wrong person.'

'Save all that,' he said, flicking both his warrant

card and the keys into his pocket, and bringing out his handcuffs. 'I've had my eye on you for twenty years, right back from when you were a stripper. I probably know more about you than you do yourself.' Opening the car door he grabbed her right wrist, clicked the handcuff round it, and attached the other to his own. 'So get out! The game's up.'

At half past two that same afternoon, six officers from the Sussex police raided a tiny isolated cottage on the South Downs three miles from Seaford and arrested Michael and Barrington Dexter.

The address had been passed on to them following Daphne Dexter's arrest in Harwich. It had been found in her handbag, written on an old envelope, and although she wouldn't admit what it was, the police had been certain it had earlier contained a set of keys to the property.

Convinced by the speed with which the police had found them that their sister had turned her brothers in to escape justice herself, once Mick was in custody, and separated from his twin, he began talking. He admitted his sister had ordered him to Tittmus Street to collect the unconscious Andrew in his van. He said he had no idea why she wanted the student locked up at The Manse, and that he and his brother had purposely let the boy get away because they wanted no part in whatever she was up to. He admitted that he had caught Charlie in the garden and questioned her, but he claimed there had never been any intention on their part to hurt her.

While searching The Manse, the Kent police found a large quantity of valuable imported goods. Both the twins denied knowing anything about the goods, or that they'd ever met Jin Weish. As for crippling Sylvia Weish, they claimed they didn't even know where Dartmouth was.

By six that evening, Hughes and Farrow were on their way back to London and home. Hughes was completely exhausted, but elated and triumphant that all three Dexters would be appearing in Sevenoaks court the next morning. He had a strong hunch those goods would be proved to be the property of Jin Weish. Although he was a long way off charging them with the man's murder, he felt he had enough strong evidence to encourage reluctant witnesses and informers to speak out.

Charlie and Andrew learned of the arrests at nine that night when Detective Inspector Hughes telephoned Charlie.

'Rest easy tonight,' he said with laughter in his voice. 'All three of them are locked up and even the slickest lawyer won't get them bail tomorrow in court.'

Charlie was eager to hear all the details, but Hughes couldn't be drawn. 'I'll be wanting to see you soon to get statements from each of you,' he said. 'But for now I just want to thank you and Andrew and Rita too. But for your courage and persistence there would be no case against these people. I am indebted to you.'

When Charlie arrived at work the next morning, Mrs Haagman called her into her office immediately. 'Sit down,' she said, her dark eyes as cold and expressionless as they had been on Charlie's first day there. She was wearing a charcoal-grey suit which made her look even more forbidding. 'Before we go any further, I want the whole story about what has been going on. Right from the beginning.'

Charlie wasn't in the mood for questions or any confrontation. Yesterday's elation had vanished when she woke up to a hangover today from the previous night's celebrations. Andrew had left for Oxford to see his parents first thing in the morning and she was feeling flat and sad. Common sense told her she had to pick up the strands of her life, and that was bound to mean explanations to her employer, but she resented being called upon to do it immediately.

'You can take that surly look off your face,' the woman snapped at her. 'I invested good money in sending you on that course, and I have every right to know if you intend to stay here or skip off somewhere else. How can I judge your state of mind when I don't even understand what exactly happened to you?'

Charlie had to concede this was reasonable, even if the woman had no charm or grace. As simply as possible she related her story right from the beginning. To her utmost surprise Mrs Haagman's face softened as she listened. When Charlie finished Mrs Haagman sighed, but she didn't speak immediately.

'I see now,' she said eventually. 'Charlie, I lost both my parents in the Holocaust when I was a child, and I've never trusted anyone since. I don't want your misfortunes to affect you that way. It would be a wicked waste.'

Charlie felt chastened. She sensed Mrs Haagman rarely told anyone such things about herself and as such she felt she had to reciprocate with total honesty.

'I appreciate your sympathy,' she said. 'I also appreciate you sending me on the training course.

You do have a right to know if I've got other plans for a new job. Well, I haven't, not right now, everything's up in the air at the moment and I can't think straight yet.'

'That sounds as if you feel you might want to leave?' the woman said.

Charlie squirmed. 'To be honest I don't know that film processing is really my scene, not as a career. But I haven't got any other plans. I'll have to be a witness at this trial, Andrew's about to go back to university for his final year, there's dozens of ifs and maybes.'

There was a moment or two's silence while Mrs Haagman looked thoughtfully at her. 'I think, if you want my opinion,' she said at length, 'that in the long term you should consider a business of your own, not a career working for other people. You are a bright girl, Charlie, but you've got something which separates you from all the other bright kids who come to work here in their college holidays. You have determination, guts and fire in your belly. Maybe it only comes to those who have had early hardships, I don't know, but wherever it comes from, use it.'

Charlie could only stare blankly at the woman. If anyone had ever suggested she ought to treat the Hag as a good role model, she would have laughed at them. Yet here she was not only admiring her, but perhaps even liking her a little.

'I wouldn't know where or how to start a business,' she protested, a bit embarrassed.

'You start off with thinking what your real interests are,' the woman half smiled. 'I chose photography after my foster mother gave me a batch of photographs of my family back in Germany and it made me realize how important photography can be. Your interests might be fashion or cooking. It doesn't matter what they are, as long as you care enough about the subject. You say you don't know how to start – well, there are night-school classes to teach you such things. But meanwhile you stay and work for me. Yes?'

Charlie thought Mrs Haagman was clever. By offering sympathy, then sound advice, she was now compelled to commit herself to staying here for the time being. 'Okay,' she agreed.

Mrs Haagman smiled, the first time Charlie had ever seen her do so. It lit up her entire face, revealing another, warmer side of her.

'You work all the rest of this week, but if you can arrange it with your young man, you may take next week off as a holiday and spend it with him. When you come back you'll be refreshed, ready to take over as my manageress, calm enough to cope with that trial and all it will entail. Come and talk to me if you need to.'

At lunchtime Charlie related the gist of the conversation to Rita, who was equally astounded.

'So she's human after all,' Rita sniggered. 'And so what business are you going to go for then?'

Charlie had been thinking about this all morning as she worked. 'I don't know that I will,' she said thoughtfully. 'I mean, just because she suggested it doesn't mean I have to. But I could fancy antiques.'

There were several antique shops in Church Street and Charlie was always drawn by them. From what she'd observed the owners of these shops weren't experts by any means, they just bought and sold what they liked. It struck her that if they could do it, so could she. After all, she had been brought up with antiques. Furthermore there was her little stash of treasure down in that vault in Exeter, to which she had hardly given a thought since she moved to London, but it could provide the capital to get started.

'Antiques!' Rita laughed. 'Oh, come on! Why not an undies or dress shop? You'd be good at that with your looks.'

Charlie just smiled. There was nothing like someone scoffing to make her more determined.

Chapter Twenty

'Don't be scared,' Andrew said, squeezing Charlie's hand tightly as they walked up the road to his parents' house. 'Dad's been a bit weird ever since I got home, but Mum's fine and she's looking forward to meeting you. If Dad is prickly with you, just ignore it. He'll soon come round.'

It was Friday night, just four days since their ordeal at The Manse. Charlie had come by train after work and Andrew had met her at Oxford station. The visit was only for two nights as on Sunday they were going down to Salcombe together.

Charlie gripped the bunch of flowers she'd bought for Mrs Blake a little tighter. She *was* scared. Whatever Andrew said, she felt sure his parents were going to be hostile towards her.

Although it was too dark to get much of an impression of the Cowley housing estate as a whole, there were enough curtains left open to see that Andrew's neighbours lived much the same way as the people she'd got to know in Mayflower Close back in Dartmouth. It was a solid working-class community, with unimaginative and somewhat cramped homes, yet scrupulously clean and cosy.

Mrs Blake opened the front door as they came in

through the wooden gate and in the light from the hall Charlie was heartened by her strong resemblance to her sister. Like Beryl she was short and plump with the same profusion of laughter-lines round her blue eyes; the only real difference was that Mrs Blake was clearly aware she *was* middle-aged. Her hair was a soft brown sprinkled with grey and she wore a tweed skirt, slippers, a pale pink sweater and an apron round her middle.

'So this is Charlie,' she said with a warm, wide smile. 'It's so good to meet you at last, dear. Come on in, the supper's just ready.'

Mr Blake was tall, thin and slightly stooped, his face heavily lined and his thinning hair very grey. He looked older and more severe than she had expected. Charlie's first thought as he shook her hand without smiling was that he was going to be difficult to win over.

Their home was much as she'd imagined: small rooms, traditional Axminster carpets, a chintzy three-piece suite in the sitting room, and a great many framed photographs of Andrew from babyhood upwards taking up every spare surface. It was only now seeing the *Lady with the Green Face* print hanging over the fire-place, which Andrew had told her about so long ago, that she saw the irony of it. When the Blakes bought it, they couldn't possibly have imagined that one day their son would fall in love with a real Chinese girl.

Mrs Blake thanked her for the flowers, took her coat and ordered Andrew to take her bag upstairs, then led her into the dining room at the back of the house. 'I do hope you like fish,' she said. 'We always have it on Fridays.'

Charlie assured her she did and was asked to sit down. Mr Blake took the seat by the window, and Mrs Blake hurried off to bring in the food.

'Smoked haddock! Great,' Andrew said as he came in and took a chair opposite Charlie, grinning broadly at her. 'Mum's been indulging me with all my favourites since I came home. We've had treacle pudding and Spotted Dick.'

'Well, you looked so thin,' his mother retorted, and her eyes held a trace of lingering anxiety. But as if reminding herself it was advisable to forget the events of the previous weekend she smiled warmly at Charlie. 'Still, I expected him to look worse. I can't imagine what it must be like to go without food for so long.'

The conversation during the meal was strained. Charlie had expected that they would immediately talk about the recent events, perhaps even air any grievances or ask for explanations, but they didn't mention it. Mr Blake politely asked if the train had been crowded, his wife spoke of the last time they'd been to London when they'd had to stand the whole journey home. Andrew said nothing at all and it occurred to Charlie that he was every bit as ill at ease as she was.

'You are a very good cook, Mrs Blake,' Charlie said appreciatively as she finished up what seemed an enormous plate of delicious fish, mashed potato and runner beans. 'Perhaps I ought to take some lessons from you, I can't do much more than basics.'

'Beryl said you couldn't cook anything when you first went to stay with her,' Mrs Blake replied, and although she smiled, there was a hint of sarcasm in her tone.

Charlie thought for a moment before replying. It seemed likely to her that the recent events must have thrown a new and damaging slant on everything this couple had previously heard about her.

'I couldn't,' she agreed ruefully. 'To be truthful I couldn't do anything much for myself. But I soon learned. Ivor Meeks and Beryl were great, sometimes I wonder how I would have coped with Mum without them.' She paused for a moment, wondering if she was actually making things worse.

'I know you must both be very apprehensive about me,' she continued. 'Especially after what Andrew went through. But please ask anything you want to know, about me or my parents. It's only by bringing things out into the open that we can move on.'

Andrew looked anxiously at his father when he cleared his throat. Charlie could sense the man's disapproval of her, all the time she'd been speaking he'd studiously avoided looking at her.

'Say what's on your mind, Mr Blake,' she said quietly. 'I know it must be hard to bear your only son getting involved with a girl whom trouble seems to follow.'

'It's this court case,' he blurted out, still not meeting his eyes. 'I'm afraid it might affect Andrew's career.'

'Oh, Dad! Don't be so ridiculous,' Andrew exclaimed.

'He isn't being ridiculous,' Charlie said quickly. 'Only concerned for you.'

Andrew grimaced. 'He's got the idea that your father is the main issue in the trial. I can't make him see that unless the police find firm evidence that the Dexters killed Jin, or crippled Sylvia, he'll hardly get a mention. I can't imagine why Dad supposes anyone would pillory me for trying to help my girlfriend find out the truth about a crime that robbed her of both her parents.'

'Nor I,' Mrs Blake said, and she reached down the table to pat her son's hand. 'In my view my Andrew will be something of a hero, and I'm very proud of him.'

Mr Blake made no further comment. His eyes were cold, his mouth set in a disapproving straight line. Charlie's heart sank. If the man wasn't prepared to talk over what was really troubling him, what on earth could she do or say to improve the situation?

On Saturday morning Andrew took Charlie on a tour of Oxford. The sun was shining but it was very cold, and a strong wind shook the trees and sent down flurries of gold, brown and russet-coloured leaves to the pavements.

Charlie thought Oxford was the most beautiful city she'd ever seen. The mellow gold of the majestic university halls, the serene gardens, the wide meandering river with its many bridges and overhanging willows, all moved her. She was here at last in Andrew's home town, seeing all the places he'd spoken of so often, yet even with his warm hand in hers, hearing the pride in his voice as he introduced her to old friends, she felt unbearably sad and forlorn. After supper the previous evening Mrs Blake had asked her friendly questions, showed her Andrew's baby photographs and told her many family stories, yet his mother's efforts to be welcoming were overshadowed by her husband's continuing brooding silence.

Andrew took the line that it didn't matter what his father thought. He even joked that his mother ruled the roost and her approval was all that was necessary. But to Charlie, who had been brought up with the Chinese conviction that fathers were the foundation stone of the family, it did matter.

'Breakfast's ready,' Mrs Blake called up the stairs on Sunday morning. 'Hurry up or it'll get cold.'

Charlie came down a couple of minutes ahead of Andrew who was still shaving. Mrs Blake was already sitting down and pouring tea. The table was laid for only three.

'Do start on your bacon and eggs,' Mrs Blake said. 'Edward's had his already. He's used to an early start, you see. Even on a Sunday he can't lie in.'

Andrew came into the room buttoning up his shirt, his hair still wet. He must have heard the last part of what his mother had said because he frowned at her.

'Dad could have waited for us just for today. We haven't got much more time together. Our train goes at twelve.'

Mrs Blake looked embarrassed. 'I'm sorry, Andrew. I did suggest it but you know how he can be when he's in one of his moods! Anyway, I'd thought it would be nice, just the three of us.'

'Miserable old sod,' Andrew muttered, but sat down and began tucking into his breakfast as if he hadn't eaten for a week.

Charlie found she'd suddenly lost her appetite, even though just a few minutes ago she'd been ravenous, and excited about seeing Ivor and Beryl later in the day. It was bad enough that Mr Blake was avoiding her, but even worse to think her presence in this house was driving a wedge between him and his wife and son.

Andrew launched into a description of a dream he'd had about circus horses. 'What does that mean?' he asked her.

'I haven't a clue.' Charlie had to laugh. Andrew's knack of finding bizarre topics to move conversations in a different direction always amused her. She thought he would make a good diplomat. 'Maybe that you are about to start a new career as a ringmaster?'

Mrs Blake said she thought it was a warning that someone was about to crack a whip to make him work harder, and changed the subject to one of their neighbours' son who was emigrating to South Africa. But throughout the conversation she kept glancing out of the window. Charlie guessed that her husband was out there in his shed and that she was cross with him because of it. Later, while helping Mrs Blake to clear the table, Charlie asked if she thought it would be a good idea to go and speak to him.

'I wouldn't do that, dear,' the older woman said with a disapproving cluck. 'I'm afraid he can be quite disagreeable when he wants to be. Follow Andrew's line and just ignore him.'

'I can't do that,' Charlie said quietly. 'His opinion matters to me. I can't leave here without trying to find out exactly what it is that bothers him about me.'

Mrs Blake rolled her eyes with some impatience. 'If you think you can get anything out of him, try it by all means. I've never managed it.'

Charlie almost lost her nerve as she went down the garden and Mr Blake pointedly shut the shed door as he saw her coming. But she took a deep breath and pushed it open again. 'I know you don't want to speak to me, Mr Blake,' she said. 'But I can't go down to Salcombe without clearing the air.'

He was standing at a workbench, potting up some plant cuttings. His sideways glance at her was chilling.

'I understand why you don't approve of me,' she said, edging her way right into the shed. 'I'm Chinese. My dad sounds like a rogue, and I got your son into danger. But I'm not leaving here until I've pointed out the good things which have come out of Andrew getting involved with me.'

The man paused in his potting up and raised one eyebrow. For a brief moment Charlie saw a strong resemblance to his son. 'Good things! Being exposed to seeing a suicide? Worrying himself about you when he should have been concerning himself with his exams? Preferring to work in a pub all summer instead of coming home here? Frightening his mother so badly I thought she might have a heart attack?'

'I couldn't help it that Andrew happened to be with me when we found Mum,' Charlie said with some indignation. 'Without him I'd have gone to pieces. You should be proud of the way he coped.'

He shrugged and pursed his lips. 'I suppose so. But he might have neglected his work.'

'But he didn't, did he? He went back to university. His support with letters and phone calls helped me cope with going back to school and sitting my exams. He didn't bunk off to come and see me, not once, nor did I try to make him do so. As for not coming home for the summer, wasn't it better that he worked and kept himself rather than sponging off you two?'

'But it was you who set him off on this mission to

578

find your father,' he spat out. 'If you only knew the half of what he put us through!'

'You think I don't know!' she exclaimed, her voice rising at the man's narrow and intolerant view. 'I was away in York when he hatched up his plan. I came back to find him missing. But I didn't sit there wringing my hands and crying. I went to find him. Because I love him more than anything or anyone. But there's no point now in recriminations, or dwelling on what might have happened, it's the good which came out of it which is important.'

'I can't see one good thing,' he said stubbornly and bent over his pots.

'Oh, can't you?' She stood up, hands on hips, angry now because he was so stubborn. 'While Andrew was in that cellar he spent most of his time thinking about all the sacrifices you and his mother made for him. He was terribly sad because he didn't think he'd shown you enough appreciation. He made up his mind if he got out of there to work harder and get a first-class degree to make it up to you. Isn't that a good thing?'

When the man stood up straight with a stunned expression on his lined face, she saw Andrew hadn't told his father any of this. She knew why. The man wouldn't listen.

'Look at you!' she snapped. 'Have you once sat down with him since he got back here and asked him about it? No, you haven't, have you? You were far more interested in putting him off a girl who might hold back his career. Never mind that he loves her, and she him. All you can see is my slanty eyes, the colour of my skin. You're afraid of me.'

'I am not,' he said, but he couldn't meet her eyes, not even now.

'You are, and that hurts more than anything,' she said, her anger suddenly fading and being replaced by despair. 'You see, I found all the qualities I most admire in Andrew. He's courageous, warm, compassionate, sensitive, clever and ambitious. I expected he'd got them all from his father. You see, to us Chinese, fathers are revered. That's why it was so important to me to find out what really happened to mine. And why I care so much about your opinion of me.'

She slumped back on to a box and burst into tears.

Edward Blake was not an emotional man. He had been brought up to believe a man's role was to provide and protect. Discussing feelings and suchlike was a female thing. When the police called to tell him his son had gone missing and there was a possibility he'd been abducted, he'd been terrified. For the first time in his life, he'd felt like sobbing. Yet he didn't give into it, crying was for women.

Throughout that endless Sunday and Monday as he'd helplessly watched his wife breaking down, convinced it was only a matter of time before Andrew was found dead, he'd found it soothing to put all the blame on this girl. He put all the information he had about her together, and before long he'd built her into a kind of she-devil who had purposely set out to entrap his son.

But now, stung by the truth in the girl's angry words, and seeing her tears, he felt chastened. The policeman who had informed them when Andrew was found had praised her courage and determination. Dora had expressed the view only this morning that he should open up his eyes, recognize that she wasn't some empty-headed floozy, but a bright, well brought-up girl who had managed to keep her integrity despite everything life had thrown at her. Perhaps he had allowed his imagination to get the better of him.

'Don't cry,' he said in a gentler tone. 'You're probably right in saying I'm afraid of you, but not because you're Chinese. That doesn't matter to me.'

'Well, why then?' she sniffed.

'Perhaps it's because I'm afraid you are going to take Andrew away from me and his mother,' he said awkwardly. 'He's been everything to us, I suppose you could say without him we have nothing else.'

'Why do you imagine I'd take him from you?' Charlie's sympathies were aroused at that bleak statement. 'I have no family of my own left. The truth is I'd kind of hoped I'd become part of yours.'

At that last poignant statement, Edward looked at Charlie, really looked at her for the first time since she'd arrived on Friday night. All at once he felt ashamed for prejudging her. There was no guile in her eyes, just a plea for understanding. She was just a kid, a pretty, sweet and well-mannered one at that. It wasn't right for him to assume she would corrupt his son, just because he believed her father was a crook and her mother crazy.

'Maybe one day when you've got children of your own you'll understand my fears,' he said and half smiled.

'I'd like you to explain them to me now,' she said.

Edward sighed and perched on the edge of his

581

workbench looking at her. 'Well, I was just like Andrew as a young man, full of fire and ambition. But times were hard then, and I found few doors opened to sons of farm labourers. I had to reconcile myself to doing my stint in the army during the war just like every other able-bodied man, then afterwards I ended up in Cowley Motors where I've worked ever since. It hasn't been the kind of life I dreamed about as a boy, a mundane grind mostly. I wanted a great deal more for my boy.

'That's why I was so proud when he got a place at the grammar school. Even prouder when he went on to university. Can you understand what it's like for a working man like me without one qualification to his name to imagine his son with letters after his?'

Charlie got up from her box, wiped her eyes with the back of her hand and touched Mr Blake's arm tentatively.

'Yes, I can,' she said, looking up into the lined face which seemed to portray all the hardships in his earlier life. 'But Andrew is where he is, because of those dreams and all that support and love you and his mother gave him. He knows that too, and loves you for it.'

'Does he?' The man looked doubtful. 'He's so independent, so sure of himself. He laughs at Dora and myself, sometimes I feel we're an embarrassment to him.'

'He doesn't,' she said, shaking her head. 'If he laughs at you sometimes, it's only out of affection. He knows your true value.'

Suddenly the man smiled, and all at once he looked so like Andrew it made Charlie smile too. His lips turned up at the corners just like Andrew's did, and his eyes were the same bright blue, even the lines on his face seemed to disappear.

'You should smile more often,' she said teasingly, and impulsively smoothed his cheek. 'It takes years off you, and makes you as handsome as Andrew.'

He caught her hand in his and squeezed it, his smile growing wider still. 'I'm beginning to see why he fell for you.'

'So are you going to come back in the house until we have to leave for Salcombe?' she asked cheekily. 'And do you think you might invite me here again?'

He gave a rich belly laugh. 'You know I'm fifty-five, Charlie. Not that old, but I look in the mirror these days and see a man that's lost his looks, hair and some of his strength. But I didn't know until just now that I'd also begun to lose some of my wits.'

'Well, this is better,' Mrs Blake said a little later as she came into the sitting room with a tray of tea and found her husband and son laughing at something Charlie was saying. 'Are you going to let me in on what's going on?'

'Charlie was just telling us about the woman she works for,' Mr Blake said. 'She sounds like a cross between Attila the Hun and a pantomime dame.'

'You can talk, dear!' she retorted.

Andrew spluttered with laughter and his father joined in. Charlie sat back in her chair and just smiled with happiness. Everything was going to be all right.

On Friday evening later in the week, Beryl came into the bar where Ivor, Andrew and Charlie were, and said the phone call she'd just answered was for Charlie.

The last few days in Salcombe had flown by. Although it had been cold, the sun had shone, they'd taken long walks, and been out each afternoon in the *MaryAnn* with Ivor. Evenings in the pub had been so jolly, playing card games and darts with the locals, listening to all the gossip and in turn relating the story of Andrew's abduction to an eager audience. The story had taken on the light of an exciting adventure rather than a trauma, both Charlie and Andrew had portrayed the Dexter twins as a pair of bumbling fools rather than hardened criminals, their sister Daphne as a kind of Disney-like Cruella DeVille. They were both happily looking forward again, Andrew to his imminent move into the shared house and his last year at university, Charlie to taking up her new position at Haagman's and enrolling for evening classes in business studies.

Charlie put her drink down on the bar and stood up. 'Is it Rita?' she asked. That was the only person she could imagine phoning her in Salcombe.

'No, at least not unless she's got a gruff voice and calls herself Hughes,' Beryl said with a smirk.

'Hughes the policeman?' Charlie gasped. 'What can he want me for now?'

'Oh, I expect it's only a loose end or two,' Beryl said soothingly. 'You'd better take it up in my sitting room, you won't be able to hear over the noise down here.'

'Hullo, Charlie,' Hughes said as she picked up the phone upstairs. 'Sorry to interrupt your holiday, but I had some news for you that couldn't wait.'

'That sounds bad,' she replied, her heart sinking. 'Has the Dexters' lawyer got them out?'

'No, it's not that,' he said. 'And with what we've discovered there's no chance of that either. We've found a body, love, and we believe it's your father – we will of course be checking dental records.'

Charlie sank into the chair by Beryl's desk as her legs seemed to give way beneath her. 'Where was it?'

'In the Thames,' he said. 'Ironically, quite close to the river police's station at Wapping. If it hadn't been for a witness coming forward we would never have found it, as it was in a stretch of deep water and heavily weighted, but fortunately this witness was able to pinpoint almost the exact spot. Divers brought it up early this morning, the pathologists are examining it right now.'

'How long had he been there?' she asked, her voice cracking with emotion.

'We can't say yet, not accurately. But the witness claims he was killed on the 20th June back in 1970. As everything else he told us has proved to be true, for now we are accepting that as correct.'

'So he had been dead for over three weeks when Mum was crippled,' she said in a whisper.

'It looks that way,' he said. 'We'll be charging Daphne Dexter with his murder and her brothers as accomplices. According to our witness, she shot him several times in the head and chest, and then the brothers disposed of his body.'

All at once the comical image of the Dexters which had grown funnier all week departed. They *were* savage, ruthless, and cold-blooded killers. Charlie began to sob. She had always thought that firm proof of her father's death would be better than living with uncertainty, but instead she found it was devastating.

'I'm so very sorry,' Hughes said in a soft voice. 'I know you'd never given up hope he would turn up alive and well one day. I wish too I could have found a gentler way to break it to you. But you can take heart in the fact he didn't run out on you and your mother, Charlie. I have firm evidence he was on his way back to you both. Those goods you saw at The Manse *were* his, the Dexters took them. As I see it, your father was stitched up in every possible way.'

'What happens now? Can he have a funeral?' She tried to stop her tears, to pull herself together to ask the right questions, but instead of seeing her father as he was the last time they were together, all she could imagine was a gruesome, weed- and mud-covered skeleton lying on a marble slab in a mortuary.

'Yes of course, sweetheart. Once all the formalities are over.'

Charlie couldn't speak, overtaken by a burst of sobbing. She could hear Hughes trying to soothe her, but his kind words didn't help.

'This witness. Why didn't he come forward before?' she asked eventually.

'For very similar reasons to your friend Rita,' he said. 'He's a very sick man, he might not even make it as far as the trial, but when he heard the Dexters had been arrested he felt compelled to speak up.'

'Who is he? Did he know my dad? I mean, before he saw him killed?'

'Yes, he did.' Hughes sounded hesitant. 'Very well, and admired him. That's what has been preying on his mind, and I think what finally gave him the courage to come to us.'

'Could I meet him?'

There was a sudden silence at her impulsive question. 'You can't, Charlie,' he said eventually. 'You must know the police can't allow witnesses to collude with one another.'

'I don't want to collude with him about anything, I'd just like to hear first-hand his views on my father. What harm could that do?'

'No, Charlie,' he said firmly.

All at once anger pushed back her grief for a moment. 'Look here, Mr Hughes,' she snapped. 'I've been robbed of both my parents because of those Dexters. Don't you think I'm entitled to at least know the whole story?'

'But you'll get that at the trial.'

'Oh, will I?' she said sarcastically. 'You've already said this man might not make it that far. What if all I get to hear is a dry statement about the actual murder? That's not what I want to know. I want to be able to *see* the whole picture, about what my dad was doing, before it all happened, where he was going, what he was thinking about, how he looked. Can't you understand that? I need to have something to hold on to after I've buried him.'

Silence fell again, and Charlie gripped the telephone receiver tightly, willing him to agree. 'Just slip me his address,' she pleaded. 'No one ever need know about it. Please.'

Ozzie Hughes found himself in a moral dilemma. Should he shield his key witness, or support the one truly innocent person in this whole case?

His witness was dying of stomach cancer. In his time he'd been one of the biggest rogues in the East End. His silence about Jin's death had been bought with threats to his only daughter. But she was now married and living in Australia.

Charlie, on the other hand, was young, honest and with her whole life ahead of her. If she could get Kent to tell her about her father, his relationship with Daphne and exactly how she plotted her revenge on Jin, then maybe the girl could put the tragedy of losing her parents behind her.

It seemed to Ozzie that the dice was loaded in Charlie's favour. Even if it might mean he would face disciplinary procedures if it ever got out.

'Okay,' he sighed. 'I'll give you the man's name and address. But don't harass him, and don't ever let on to anyone that I gave it to you.'

'Not even Andrew?' she said.

'Especially Andrew,' he said firmly. 'Promise me?'

She promised, and took down the East London address of a man called Dave Kent.

'I'll be in touch one evening early next week,' Hughes said finally. A few hours ago he'd been jubilant that he now had enough evidence to make sure none of the Dexters ever walked London's streets again. Now he felt only sadness that his triumph was won with this girl's pain. 'I'm really sorry about your dad, Charlie. He was a good man.'

It was only after Charlie had put the phone down that it occurred to her that Hughes must have known Jin. She wondered why he hadn't admitted it before.

That evening was the strangest Charlie had ever

known, so many different emotions, love, hate, sorrow, bubbling up from within her, and yet a kind of odd relief too that the uncertainty was over. She could give her father a funeral. The Dexters' reign of terror was finished.

But as Ivor, Beryl and Andrew all talked around her and at her, grief was the emotion she felt most keenly. There was no faint hope now that her father was alive and well somewhere, perhaps waiting for the right moment to come back into her life. Anger welled up within her at what her mother had endured, their beautiful home gone forever. She wanted revenge. To stand by and gloat as that fiend of a woman was slowly tortured. Prison, even if she got a life sentence, wasn't barbaric enough.

She drank a great deal that evening, silently and grimly, refusing to go upstairs with Andrew and allow herself to be comforted. She needed to keep the flame of hate burning inside her for now. Tears were for the weak. Until she finally laid her father to rest she would remain dry-eyed.

Charlie didn't remember Ivor and Andrew taking her home to the cottage. The next thing she knew it was morning and Ivor was standing by her bed holding out a mug of tea and a couple of aspirin.

'I think you might need these,' he said gently. His eyes were bleary and he smelled of drink.

'I don't feel too bad,' she said as she sat up gingerly to find she was fully dressed apart from her shoes. 'But I suppose I ought to feel terrible if I couldn't even take my clothes off. I hope I didn't behave too badly?'

'You were a silent drunk,' he said with a chuckle.

'That's the kind I'm always most wary of, and why Andrew and I didn't attempt to undress you. But then we were all three sheets to the wind, Beryl included.'

Minnie came padding in and sloped up on the bed. Somehow her mournful expression and her cheek at getting on to the bed, even in front of her master, said she sensed something momentous had happened to Charlie and she wanted to offer comfort.

'I think I'd better take you for a walk,' Charlie said, stroking the dog's ears tenderly. 'I'm not fit company for humans, but a bit of fresh air and you might make me better.'

Ivor sat down on the bed too, his eyes as sad as his dog's. 'I'm so sorry, Charlie. For once I can't think of anything else to say. You were having such a good time too, before you got this news.'

Charlie turned to look out of the little window beside her bed. The harbour was hidden by the roof of the shack in front of the cottage, but the sea beyond was azure blue, and a stiff wind was whipping up white horses.

'Perhaps it's best I heard here, with all the people I love most around me,' she said with a sigh. 'But I think I'll have to go back to London later today. I'll get my head together quicker on my own. Andrew can stay on for a day or two.'

When she got back later from her walk with Minnie, Andrew was in the cottage, talking to Ivor. He hadn't shaved, his hair was tousled and he looked a bit fragile. His eyes widened in surprise to see her rosy-cheeked and clear-eyed.

'Ivor says you want to go back to London on your own,' he said. 'Are you sure?'

Charlie nodded. Although her first thought this morning had been purely to have a quiet Sunday alone before going back to work on Monday, while she'd been out walking it had occurred to her it might also be a golden opportunity to visit Dave Kent. She knew it was going to be very hard keeping it from Andrew, she had always told him everything. But if she could just see the man, before Andrew got back, maybe she could do it.

'I need time alone, and the police might want to see me. You could come back on Monday or Tuesday. I've got to go back to work anyway, and you haven't got anything on until Wednesday when you go to sign the agreement for that house.'

'You could give me a hand, Andrew,' Ivor suggested, making them both a mug of coffee. 'That's unless you've got other plans. The roof on the shack needs a bit of attention and I'm too old to be leaping about up there.'

Charlie had expected Andrew would protest, and when he didn't she realized Ivor must have had a word with him before she got back. As always Ivor was very intuitive and after a brief chat he went out leaving them alone.

'How are you really feeling today?' Andrew asked, pulling her on to his lap and cuddling her into his shoulder. 'You look fine, but are you?'

'I feel as if I've just run through a minefield,' she said. 'Can you understand what I mean? Imagine running and hearing mines exploding all around you and thinking you'd had at least one limb blown off.

Then suddenly you are safe. You find you are all in one piece. But then you look back and find everything else is destroyed.'

'Not everything. I'm still here,' he said, holding her tightly. 'And Ivor and Beryl. We'll wipe it all out for you between us.'

Charlie just let him hold her for a while, loving him for always being so caring, and it struck her that he was the really important person in her life, and that she must keep that in the forefront of her mind. 'At least it's resolved now,' she said softly. 'I can give Dad a proper funeral. That's something.'

'You ought to contact a solicitor pretty soon,' Andrew said thoughtfully. 'Please don't take this the wrong way, but now they've found your dad's body, it puts a different light on everything. He shouldn't have been made bankrupt for one thing, his life assurance would have paid off all his debts. That insurance company must be made to pay up.'

'I hadn't even thought of that,' she said in some surprise. 'Who will they pay it to?'

'Well, you, of course,' he said, smoothing her hair. 'You are his heir and you're entitled to it. I expect they'll take forever, mind you. When my grandfather died they spun it out for a year. That's all the more reason to put the wheels in motion soon.'

It did seem terrible to think of insurance money at such a time, worse still to think she might benefit from her father's death. But Charlie sensed Andrew was thinking more of entirely clearing her father's name than anything else.

'I don't fancy speaking to Mr Wyatt. I still haven't

forgiven him for rushing off after Mum's funeral,' she sighed. 'But I suppose I'll have to.'

'No, you don't, you can use any solicitor, a London one if you like. They'll get all the papers from Wyatt. It's a good way of teaching him a lesson.'

'Or getting a bit of revenge,' she smiled, suddenly feeling a whole lot more optimistic. 'I think I could really get into that.'

On Sunday morning Charlie set off to the East End to see Dave Kent. She had arrived back from Salcombe around eleven at night and she and Rita had stayed up till late talking about the latest developments. Charlie wished she was able to confide in her friend about seeing this new witness, but fortunately Rita had already planned to go home to Essex the next day to see her family, so there was no need to tell any lies.

Finding the right clothes for the occasion had been difficult. Jeans appeared much too casual, her one and only suit too formal to visit a sick man in the East End. Finally she settled on the same maroon wool maxi-skirt and jumper she'd worn on her first night with Andrew, and as it was very cold, a short brown fur jacket Beryl had passed on because it no longer fitted her.

Her heart sank as she came out of Stepney Green tube station and saw a sign for the Ocean Estate straight across the road. She had somehow expected it to be small houses, but in fact it was a series of giant blocks of flats, even more forbidding than the ones Angie had lived in at Mornington Crescent.

As she got closer, she was heartened to see this estate was better maintained, the grass was a lush green, surprisingly rubbish-free, and the children's playgrounds were freshly painted. Children rode past her on bikes, and one directed her to the second block along and informed her she needed the third floor.

It was only as she walked along the long landing to his front door that she was suddenly frightened. She had no way of knowing if Hughes had warned Kent she might call. As he was a sick man he might still be in bed. And of course there was always the possibility that he'd be antagonistic at finding her on his doorstep.

The door finally opened just as she was about to ring the bell a second time.

'Mr Kent?' she asked timidly. He was a big man, probably in his fifties. Completely bald, wide shoulders but with a chalky white flabby face. He was dressed in a stained blue sweater and jeans that looked much too big for him.

'Who wants him?' he asked in a curt, gravelly voice.

'My name is Charlie Weish,' she said. 'I believe you knew my father, Jin.'

He just stared at her for a moment. The whites of his eyes were very yellow and the irises pale brown, which gave him an odd, cat-like appearance.

'You're Charlie?' he said eventually. 'I didn't expect you to be so grown up.'

Although his expression showed neither surprise, pleasure nor wariness, she was encouraged. His remark suggested he'd known her father for a very long time. 'Can I come in?' she asked. 'I promise I haven't come to make trouble, just to talk to you.'

He hesitated for a moment, then nodded and opened the door wider. 'You'll have to excuse the state of the place,' he said. 'I don't get many visitors.'

As he led her into the living room Charlie saw that he had been living alone for some time. The room was dusty and tired-looking. All the furniture – a large three-piece suite, a dining table with matching chairs around it – looked expensive, but worn. An artificial flower arrangement on the table was faded almost white by sunlight, perhaps put there many years ago by a woman in his life.

Photographs of children had still more smaller ones tucked into the frames, a well-loved teddy bear sat on the television like a reminder of happier times. The large Westminster clock on the mantelpiece had stopped at ten past two. The room was tidy, no cups, plates or full ashtrays lying around, yet there was evidence of Dave Kent's ill-health, many bottles of pills and medicine on the coffee table and a faint smell of sickness in the over-warm room.

'How did you find me?' he asked, and sat down heavily, then apologized for his rudeness and said he couldn't stand for long.

'I persuaded a friend in the police force to give me your address,' she said, gingerly sitting down opposite him. 'I know I shouldn't really be here. But I had to see you. I need to know about my father.'

He looked puzzled, even confused. Charlie had no way of knowing if he knew anything at all about her, so she quickly ran through the important points of her story.

'So you see I know *now* that he was killed and by whom, the police told me that. But that isn't enough for me, Mr Kent. In the two years since Dad disappeared I've pondered and thought about him all the time. I've been angry with him and felt betrayed because I loved him and couldn't understand why he ran out on us.

'Now they've found his body, thanks to you coming forward, I just want to know why, and how it happened. I know the police could probably tell me most of it eventually. But they are strangers, aren't they? They didn't know *him*, and they weren't there.'

He looked at her silently for what seemed ages.

'Please,' she begged. 'I could cope with his funeral so much better if I knew exactly what happened. I promise you I won't tell anyone.'

He sighed deeply, and ran his hand over his bald head. 'Okay, love,' he said. 'You've got a right to know, but you'll have to excuse me if I seem a bit slow. It's the medicine I'm taking.' He paused as if trying to think where to start. 'I did know your dad well. We weren't mates exactly, but we liked and respected each other. Jin was never a rogue, not like I was, but he was a dark horse, not a man you'd take for a ride, you know what I mean?'

Charlie nodded. If the man had claimed they were real friends she wouldn't have believed him. Jin had never been the chummy sort, not with anyone. 'So when did you meet?'

'Must have been sixteen years since,' he said thoughtfully. 'I went in his club a few times and we got chatting about Hong Kong. See, I'd been there for two years when I was in the navy. Anyway, I got in a bit of bother up in the West End one night, there was a crowd of us blokes, all tanked up, someone got knifed and the filth nicked me for it and banged me up. Next thing I know, they say I can go. Seems Jin had seen what had happened, knew they'd got the wrong man and he come down to the nick and said so. Well, I owed him one then, didn't I? I fully expected him to call in his card before long, that's the way most of those blokes work it. But he never did.

'A couple of years passed. I went up to his club one night and found he'd gone, packed up and left the place to Miss Dexter. I asked around, heard a few tales about her blackmailing him and the like, and because I knew all the Dexters from way back, and knew what they were, I kind of wanted to help him, know what I mean?'

Charlie was already warming to this odd-looking man. On closer inspection she'd become aware that once he must have been quite a giant, but his illness was slowly eating away at him. She could see folds of loose skin on his neck and hands. It saddened her.

'Well, to cut a long story short,' he went on. 'I asked around and heard Jin had gone into the import business with foreign goods. I got a whisper he used a shipping company down in Tilbury and I left a message for him there to say I might be able to help him out sometimes. We got together. I had a couple of trucks in them days and an old warehouse down at Wapping. We started to do business. He bought the stuff out East, got it shipped back here, then I stored it for him and delivered it to his buyers.

'Everything was hunky-dory then. Jin was pleased because he could concentrate on the buying and selling. I was more than happy to do the donkey work because it was regular and clean. The shipments were getting bigger and bigger, and we were both making a lot of money. But unknown to me, and maybe yer dad too, at that time, the f-ing Dexters were out to get him.'

'Did you know that Dad had an affair with Daphne Dexter, Mr Kent?' Charlie interrupted.

'The name's Dave, love,' he said. 'Yeah, I knew about the affair, leastways I heard it on the grapevine. But I didn't really believe it until he told me himself some years later. It must have been early in '65, because I remember we were hanging around waiting for a delayed shipment of stuff from Hong Kong and it was brass-monkey weather. Jin had booked into a flash hotel because you and yer mum were coming up to London to join him. He'd bought tickets for a panto-mime and all sorts. See, he weren't one for staying in posh places, not on his own. Usually he got a room in a local guest-house. Anyway, he come in this par-ticular morning with a face on him. I asked what was wrong, as you do, and he said he'd had a bit of bother the night before.'

'I think I remember that night,' Charlie interrupted again, remembering how her father had rushed out of the hotel leaving her mother crying. 'He had a phone call from someone. I've worked out since it must have been Daphne.'

Dave looked at her sharply, perhaps surprised she'd dug that deeply. 'Your dad never talked about himself, or his problems, he were a very private man, but he was really rattled that day, and I guess he had to confide in someone. He said Daphne had insisted on seeing him, otherwise she was going to cause a scene in front of you and yer mum. We had a bit of a heart-to-heart. He told me how it all came about.'

'Tell me what he said, Mr Kent.' Charlie was on the

edge of her seat now. She felt she was finally going to get the truth.

'He said it was the thing he most regretted in his life. How it came about was that he'd left Daphne to run his club a great deal after you were born. Partly because he wanted to be with you and yer mum, but also because yer mum weren't too well. Daphne increased his profits quite a bit and he was grateful. Anyway, he took her out one night for dinner as a kind of thank-you, and one thing led to another.' He broke off, Charlie could see he was embarrassed.

'I can understand that,' Charlie said, wishing to put him at ease again. 'She's still a good-looking woman, she must have been gorgeous when she was younger.'

Dave half smiled in agreement. 'She put me in mind of Elizabeth Taylor, just one look at her was enough to make any man lust after her. But for all her beauty, you could sense she was an evil bitch. I'd met her first when she was about sixteen, she were as hard as nails even then, ready to do anything to make a few bob. One of her tricks was to lure men into back alleys where her brothers were waiting to rob them. That's why it was so surprising she was capable of falling in love.'

'She loved Dad?' Charlie gasped.

Dave gave a rueful weak grin. 'Yeah, she did. Mind you, from what yer dad said, Daphne's idea of love weren't quite like other people's. Once she got her claws into poor Jin she weren't going to let him go, she wanted to possess and control him, for him to leave Sylvia and marry her.'

'Did he love her?' Charlie asked. 'Don't give me any bullshit, Dave. I need to know the whole truth.'

Dave shook his head. 'No, he never did, not even briefly from what he told me. He might have liked her, admired her strength and stuff, but he was sucked into a situation he couldn't get out of. As I see it, he soon found out how dangerous and jealous the woman was, her brothers were loonies. She had only to snap her fingers and they'd be off to hurt Sylvia, burn Jin's club down, or anything. So he just tried to keep the peace.'

Charlie sighed in understanding. She'd already seen plenty of evidence of what the woman was capable of when she was crossed.

'So in the end, Jin did a deal with her. He gave her the Lotus Club. It were a right little gold-mine, and on the strength of that she borrowed enough money to buy the other two clubs off him too. He went off to Devon. He thought that would be the end of it.'

'But it wasn't?' Charlie said.

Dave shook his big bald head. 'No, it weren't. He had a few years of peace, got his show on the road, and forgot her. But she must've been keeping tabs on him all along, and I suppose when she got the wire he was making big money again, she decided that by fair means or foul she was going to get him back in her clutches. That night you remember was the time she surfaced again. She blackmailed him into meeting her by saying she was going to spill the beans to Sylvia.'

'Poor Dad,' Charlie sighed. 'Why didn't he just tell Mum outright? Mum had always known anyway.'

'Your dad was no coward, if that's what you're thinking,' Dave said quickly. 'If he handled things badly that night it was only to spare Sylvia and you public humiliation. When he went out to meet Daphne later it was purely to keep her well away from the hotel, and to tell her to get lost, once and for all. And that's exactly what he did. But Daphne ain't human, she had not only made up her mind that Jin would leave Sylvia and marry her, but she had big plans to run drugs through his import business. He was furious with her about the drugs, and warned her that if she found some other patsy to do it with, he'd grass her up. Jin despised anyone who dealt in drugs more than anything. He'd seen what opium does to people back in China.'

'But he always seemed quite cool about drugs to me,' Charlie said. She didn't want this man to make out her dad was a saint just for her benefit.

'He was a cool man in every respect,' Dave said sternly. 'I expect he took that line with you because he knew kids are always more curious about something when their folks come down hard about it. But take it from me, love, your dad would never get involved with drugs. Not even if there was millions in it.'

Charlie smiled. She was so glad she'd come now. She suggested she made them both some tea and Dave smiled back at her with real warmth.

'You're a lovely girl,' he said. 'Your dad always said you were. Only time I ever heard him boast was about you. He'd be right proud of you now.'

The cleanliness in Dave's tiny kitchen left a lot to be desired. While Charlie waited for the kettle to boil she washed up a few plates and wiped over the surfaces. She wondered what was the matter with him, and if he ever had any help from anyone.

Dave heard the noises coming from the kitchen and guessed what she was doing. It touched him more than anything had in a long time, and all at once he knew for certain he'd done the right thing in grassing up the Dexters, even if it was against everything he'd been brought up to believe in.

He looked around his living room and saw what little he had for a lifetime of ducking and diving. Even during his time in the navy he'd been a thief and a con-man. When he came out he'd progressed to burglary, extortion, ringing motors and just about any crime that didn't involve violence. Sometimes he thought now that was his only saving grace, at least he could go to his death knowing he'd never intentionally hurt anyone.

It had been Jin who straightened him out and showed him a way to make an honest living. Those years they'd done business together had been some of the happiest times he'd known. Ten quid earned straight was better than a bent hundred, he found. He could remember golden days down in the warehouse at Wapping, sitting with a bottle of beer and his sandwiches looking at the sun on the river, content in knowing that even if the police were to storm in and check the contents of the hundreds of packing cases, they'd find nothing but exotic artefacts, all bought legitimately and paid for.

Jin taught him to appreciate the beauty of Chinese lacquerwork, jade and the patience and artistry those Oriental rugs had been woven with. Dave didn't even mind that those items would end up in the kind of snooty people's houses he'd once envied and earmarked to rob. Or that for the first time in his life he had to work hard for twelve hours a day. He had peace of mind and self-respect.

Dave winced with the pain in his stomach, the cancer was eating away at him, but it was too early yet for his next dose of medicine. Besides, it made him too woozy and he had a great deal more yet to tell the girl.

Charlie came back from the kitchen with two mugs of tea. She could see Dave was in pain and she asked if she could get him anything.

'No, love,' he said. 'I'm fine. We'd better get back to business.'

'Can I just ask what Daphne had over you that you couldn't speak out before?' she asked.

'My daughter, love,' he said with a deep sigh. 'See, me wife left me, years ago. I brought Wendy up on me own since she was five. The apple of me eye as they say. She'd got a little one too, got herself in trouble when she was sixteen. My grandson Grant is seven now, and they're both safely in Australia with Wendy's new husband. But back at the time Jin was killed, they were still living here with me. Daphne put me straight. One word from me and Wendy would cop it. What could I do? I knew she'd get someone to do it, even if she was in a prison cell herself. I couldn't take the risk, not with my own kid.'

'I think the Dexter twins must have threatened my mother with something like that too, because she wouldn't tell the police anything after they crushed her knees,' Charlie said.

'I think with hindsight that she'd been their victim for a very long time before that,' he said thoughtfully. 'You see, that night we were speaking of earlier,

Daphne was savage. She warned Jin that if he didn't play ball she'd make him sorry in more ways than one. I'm a good bit older than the Dexters but I come from the same manor, and I'd watched them all grow up. I knew they wasn't the type for loose talk, especially her, she got where she is by pulling evil strokes.

'A couple of years before Jin died, he told me that Sylvia was acting strange. She didn't like him going away, and when he had to, she hardly went out of the house. He said she wouldn't tell him what was wrong, and he thought she was suffering from depression. I reckon one of them Dexters was dripping poison in yer poor mum's ear all along, hoping to unhinge her. Sylvia and Daphne had been good mates once, so she'd have known her weak points. You can bet the evil cow used them.'

Charlie had a sudden mental picture of her mother lying in bed at the nursing home, telling her about those letters she steamed open and the phone calls for Jin. She told Dave about it, and how in that period before her father went away for good, she took the brunt of her mother's misery.

'So that bitch was chipping away at her all the time, knowing full well Sylvia was too weak and too afraid of losing Jin to speak out,' Charlie said angrily. 'No wonder she gave up entirely once Dad was gone! She'd got nothing left to hang on to.'

'Only you,' he said sadly. 'And I know just how that bloody well feels. See, I kinda took it out on my Wendy, after Jin was killed. I was so scared for her I didn't want her out of my sight, but when she was with me, I was brooding and uptight about everything. She used to ask me all the time what was wrong, what had she done? But I couldn't tell her anything. I reckon that's what started my cancer. See, that's what's wrong with me now, Charlie. I used to be seventeen stone of pure muscle. Look at me now! Your body can't fight back when your mind is sick.'

Suddenly everything about her mother's moods fell into place for Charlie and she was sickened to think that she'd put it all down to selfishness. Because of those Dexters and their terrible threats, Dave had succumbed to cancer, her mother to mental illness. She didn't know which was worse.

'I'm so sorry, Dave,' she said, reaching out and touching his arm tentatively. 'I think if Dad had known what would happen to you and Sylvia because of him, he would have done what she wanted.'

'But he didn't know,' Dave shook his head. 'That's the whole point, Charlie. He was innocently going about his business, totally unaware Daphne was still on his case.

'Jin told me he'd done a huge deal when he came back from Hong Kong in the autumn of 1969,' he went on. 'He confided in me that he'd have to pull out all the stops to raise the money for it. He said if everything went to plan he was going to sell up in Dartmouth, and take you and yer mum out to South Africa to live. He wanted a new start for all of you.

'As God is my witness, I never said a word to anyone, but I reckon one of the three young lads in the warehouse must have been a Dexter plant and he heard, and passed it on to them. It had to be something like that because the way it all came about Daphne must have had inside information to plot Jin's downfall to the last detail.

'Anyway, towards the middle of May the following year, Jin was getting very edgy. He had sent off the dosh for these goods, but the shipment was delayed en route, and he was getting frantic for cash. He went over to Holland to do some other small deal which would give him a quick turn-around.'

'That's where he was when he last phoned us at home,' Charlie said.

'Right,' Dave said. 'Well, I didn't speak to him, or see him from the time he left for Holland until the night he was killed. Like I said, I had a couple of lorries, and I did work for people other than him too. I was coming back from Leeds on June the 19th and I broke down on the way – by the time I got back to London it was two in the morning, but I had to go and unload and lock the stuff up in the Wapping warehouse because someone would have thieved it otherwise. I let myself in with me key and found the Dexters were all in there with Jin.'

Dave suddenly slumped back in his armchair and closed his eyes. 'Are you all right?' Charlie asked, moving out of her chair to go over to him. She sat on the arm of the chair and put her hand on his forehead. It was hot and sweaty. 'Don't go on if you're feeling ill.'

He didn't answer, but took her hand in his and pressed it to his lips for a moment. 'So help me, sweetheart. If there was anything I could have done to save Jin, I would've done it, but I was trapped too,' he said in a hoarse whisper.

To Charlie's surprise he began to speak as if he was mentally reliving the events of that night. 'It had been stifling hot all day. As I drove through the city, it suddenly started to rain real heavy, with thunder and lightning. I left the lorry a bit further up the road from the warehouse, and ran like the clappers through the rain to get the doors open, so I could then back up to the unloading bay and get the stuff out. The main doors were locked from the inside, so I had to go in the small door on the side, then down the dark passageway which led to another door in the warehouse.

'I wasn't alarmed when I saw a chink of light shining around this second door, all of us was always forgetting to turn it off when we locked up at night. I just shut the door to the street behind me and went on down the passageway.

'I was just fishing around in the darkness for the right key when I heard footsteps. Suddenly the door was flung open and I found myself face to face with Baz Dexter.

' "What the fuck are you doing here?" I said, mad as hell. He had no business there at any time and I hated the geezer anyway. But before I could say anything more, he kneed me in the groin.

'I doubled up with pain, and before I could shout or even blink, the bastard's brother Mike came through the door too and the pair of them forced me back against the passageway wall. I'm pretty handy with me fists, but these two had me too tight to fight them, and I was winded. Then all of a sudden bloody Daphne appeared in the doorway, and she had a gun in her bleedin' hands.

'My first thought was that they was after the stuff in me truck, and under the circumstances, with a gun pointed at me, they was welcome to it. It were only a sodding load of spices anyway. I even tried to make a bit of a joke about it, but all of a sudden I cottoned on that they was up to something else, and I'd interrupted them. I tried to say I'd go and make out I'd never seen them there, but they was having none of that. Next thing I know they're hauling me up the stairs to the floor above and slung me down on the floor.

'The twins gave me a good kicking, then they tied me hands and feet. After that they just walked out and left me lying there in the dark. Not a bleedin' word about what it was all about, or what they were going to do to me.

'Now this room upstairs is like a loft and it goes right over the whole warehouse to the river at the back. In the old days goods used to be hauled up from the boats with an old pulley thing. Now the river's too silted up for big boats, so all we used this floor for was storing lighter stuff we could carry up, and at that time there weren't no more than a few boxes left there. But the floor is only old planks, and there's cracks and holes everywhere. Lying there face down, I could see the light from below, and heard voices, so once I'd got me second wind, I wriggles over to a biggish one and looks down.

'I got the shock of me life when I see Jin down there. I thought he was still in Holland! He's sitting there on the floor against a packing case, his ankles tied together and his hands behind him. I reckon he must have come back earlier in the evening, probably hoping I'd be there, because he was still wearing his dark business suit and his briefcase was a few feet away from him, spilled open, like they'd been going through it.

'"Leave Dave out of this," I heard him say. "He's done nothing to you and he's got a family to support."

'I heard Daphne laugh at him, though I couldn't see her because she was out of my line of vision. "A gentleman to the last," she said, kind of sneering. "If you'd just forgotten your stupid principles for once in your life, it wouldn't have come to this."

'"My principles might be stupid to you," he said in that cool way he had. "But to me a man has to live by a decent code of behaviour otherwise he is no different to an animal. I told you Daphne, right at the beginning that I loved Sylvia and I would never leave her. I never lied to you or promised anything I didn't fulfil."

'"You could have had everything with me," Daphne shouted back at him and she must have stepped forward because suddenly I could see her clearly. She was holding the gun with both hands, pointing it right at Jin. Her face was in shadow, but by the shake in her voice and the wavering of the gun, I could tell she was cracking. "Look at me! I'm beautiful, rich and desirable. Sylvia's a pathetic mess unless you're beside her to hold her up. How can she compare to me?"

'"There is no comparison," Jin said. I couldn't believe he could sound so calm, tied up with the gun waving in front of him. "She's gentle, kind, and loving and she's the only woman I've ever loved. All the happiest moments in my life have been spent with her and my daughter. She would have loved me even if I'd stayed a waiter for my entire life. You wouldn't have looked at me twice unless I had a full wallet."

'"Well, much good she did you," Daphne screamed

out like a hell cat. "How will she keep herself and that kid in that fine house by the sea when you're gone? She'll crumble, you poor fool, when she finds there's no money left. And there won't be any. I've seen to that."

'I couldn't believe what I was witnessing,' Dave said, turning to look at Charlie. 'Me stomach was in knots. I knew Daphne had set him up and she was going to shoot him. Yet Jin just looked up at her as if he pitied her.'

' "What made you so vicious, Daphne?" Jin asked then, like he really hoped she'd tell him. "Sylvia was your friend, the only real one you've ever had in your entire life. She loved you like a sister."

' "I hate her because she got you," she roared at him. "And I hate you for still loving her even though she's pathetic."

'Jin just shook his head sadly as she raised the gun again. "Just tell me before you shoot me," he said, "will killing me make you happier? Have you finally got all you wanted?"

'I waited for her answer, but the gun rang out, and I pressed myself closer to the hole in the floorboards to see more clearly, hoping it was just a warning shot to make him beg. But I could see she'd already done for him. Jin was slumped over to one side, his white shirt already turning bright red. She shot again, and again. But I couldn't look any more. I was struggling not to be sick. The smell of cordite was thick and strong, the smoke was coming up through the cracks in the floor.

'I heard the twins shouting at one another, but I couldn't hear what they were saying over thunderclaps. Lightning lit up the loft, and I was terrified they would come up and get me next. I knew I couldn't be brave like Jin was. I was crying like a baby for his mother.'

Charlie was crying too. She moved from the perch on the arm of Dave's chair and knelt in front of him, sliding her arms round the man's waist, and leaned her head against his chest.

'I'm sorry, love,' he said in a whisper a little later. 'Maybe I shouldn't have told you the last bit?'

Charlie lifted her head and found he had tears rolling down his cheeks. 'I'm glad you did,' she whispered back. 'It was terrible, but I needed to hear it.'

She made him more tea and helped him take his medicine. His pale face had a grey tinge now and she said she ought to call his doctor.

'No,' he said, taking her hand as she knelt by his chair. 'I'll be fine in a minute. Just let me have a couple of minutes to pull myself together.'

He dropped off to sleep in his chair. Charlie sat watching him, her heart filling up with sympathy for him because he was so sick and alone. It occurred to her that had her father ever brought her to this flat to meet Dave, she would have been horrified that he mixed with such men. She'd been a heartless little snob then, valuing people only by how well they spoke and their material success. Judging by what Jin had divulged to Dave, this man had been of more importance to him than any of those so-called friends back in Dartmouth. She just wished her father had realized that for her to become a well-rounded human being like himself, she too needed to meet people from all walks of life.

As Dave continued to sleep she considered quietly letting herself out and going home, but she couldn't bring herself to. Instead, she found a duster and quietly went around the room using it. She looked at the photographs and saw his daughter Wendy in every stage of her development from a small baby to a glowing bride on her father's arm. He had been a big, rugged man with thick fair hair and a wide, proud smile, then, and as she looked back to the sick ghost of the man in the chair, her heart filled with compassion for him. Maybe he had been a bit of a rogue, but he had been a good father, and friend, he deserved something a great deal better than a slow, painful death alone.

By the time Dave woke again in the late afternoon, Charlie had stripped his bed and remade it with clean sheets, cleaned the bathroom, and then went on to iron a pile of shirts she found in the bedroom. She'd also found out a great deal more about the man's character.

He was domesticated, or he had been until illness had recently halted it. He had a modern automatic washing machine, the airing cupboard was full of clean linen and soft, fluffy towels, even the equipment in the kitchen bore out that he had once been in the habit of cooking proper meals. But it was his daughter's old bedroom that affected her the most, for his love for her shone there. It was a pretty blue and white room, with a flounce round the dressing table, a Degas print of ballerinas on the wall, a few old dolls, all dressed properly, sitting on a shelf alongside some well-thumbed Enid Blyton books. Charlie guessed there had once been a cot there too, perhaps later replaced by another single bed for her little boy. Wendy must have taken away most of her possessions, but enough was left behind to see Dave liked to keep her here in his mind, the room ready for her.

'How are you feeling?' Charlie asked as Dave stirred and rubbed his eyes. 'Can I make you something to eat?'

He seemed a bit confused for a moment. He frowned at the newly ironed shirts on a clothes-horse by the fire and looked at his watch. 'You're still here?'

'I'm not that easy to get rid of,' she said with a smile. 'Even Daphne Dexter couldn't manage that! Now, what about food?'

Later, after a cheese omelette and chips Charlie rustled up for them both, Dave seemed much better. 'You're so very like Jin,' he said thoughtfully. 'Not just in looks, but that calm, inscrutable quality he had too. That's good, Charlie, if you ever go into business you'll be every bit as smart as he was.'

She told him her idea of maybe going into antiques and he smiled. 'You'll be a real whiz at it, I know you will. So don't let anyone put you off.'

They talked about a great many things, of Charlie's childhood in Dartmouth, of how she managed after Sylvia died and of Andrew. Dave told her about Wendy and her husband Martin and showed her photographs of their home in Sydney. 'I went out there at Christmas,' he said, his face glowing as he described her house. 'Martin loves Grant as if he were his own kid, and they're hoping to have a little sister for him too some day.'

'Do they know how ill you are?' Charlie asked.

He shook his head. 'If I was to tell them they'd come

home. I don't want that. I'd rather they remembered me as I was.'

'You must write and explain that then,' she said, not liking to use the phrase 'before it's too late'. 'If you don't, she'll be riddled with guilt if anything happens to you. She might not have someone to go and see, like I found you, to tell her about you.'

'I wouldn't want her talking to someone who told her such nasty things as I've had to tell you,' he said with a grimace.

'It might have been nasty, but I'm still glad I know about it,' she said. 'But getting back to that nastiness, can you just tell me the last part? Especially what happened to you.'

'They left me up there,' he said. 'I was convinced they were going to come for me and shoot me at any minute. What with that, and the thunder and lightning, I was scared witless. Through the crack in the floor I watched the twins bundle Jin up in a tarpaulin. I heard them open the back door out on to the river, we had a rowing boat tied up out there, and they heaved him into it at high tide. I managed to wriggle over to the window and watched them. They rowed out and dumped him. I was flabbergasted at that. The river police have a station just four or five hundred yards away, but I suppose they took the risk because it was such a stormy night, and no one was likely to be out watching. When they got back, they hosed down the blood as cool as cucumbers.'

A shiver went down Charlie's spine. If they were that calm they'd probably disposed of others before who got in their way. 'Then what?'

'They came for me,' he said. 'It was first light by

then. Daphne just stood there looking down at me for some time before she even spoke. I nearly shit meself! Her brothers were covered in blood, but she looked like a bloody beauty queen, even after what she'd done. Not a speck of blood on her dress, not a hair out of place. Then she gave me her ultimatum. Forget what I'd seen, or Wendy would get it. I was to go downstairs, and open up the warehouse and start unloading as if I'd just got back with the lorry. She said she would give me further orders in a day or two. I had no choice but to agree.'

'Of course you didn't,' she reassured him; faced with that predicament she thought she'd have chosen the same path. 'But what happened about Jin's shipment of goods?'

'She must have got that picked up,' he said. 'As I hadn't spoken to Jin I didn't know where it was arriving or when. I reckon he must have had all the documents in his briefcase that night. Maybe that's what he came there for, to tell me about it, or they might have picked him up somewhere else. I never found that out. I never saw his car either, so they must've got that too and got rid of it. So you see no one but me ever knew Jin had come back, everyone thought he was still in Holland. My business plummeted then without the work I used to get from Jin. In a few months I was in trouble. Then I got an offer for the lease of the warehouse. I knew she was behind it, but I had no choice but to let it go. I couldn't bear to be in it anyway, not after what I'd seen happen there.'

'So she ruined you too then?' Charlie sighed. She felt so much for him, it must have been a living hell.

'Not quite, I still had me trucks. I got a bit of work

with them and I still had a few thousand I'd got for the lease. But then I blew most of that on Wendy's wedding which was in the spring of '71. You can't imagine how glad I was when she told me they were going to emigrate. I wouldn't have put it past Daphne to do something to Wendy just to make sure I still kept me mouth shut. I started to feel ill soon after the wedding. I sold off the trucks, and packed it all in, then I went out to see Wendy before I got too bad. Please God she'll never see me like I am now.'

Charlie privately thought she ought to see him, but she kept that to herself.

'Did the police ever come to see you about Jin?' she asked instead.

'Just once,' he said. 'It was just after your mum was hurt. I felt so sick about that, love. I never met her, but after knowing your dad stuck by her, right to the death, I knew she had to be pretty special. But what could I do?' He shrugged his shoulders. 'I just told them what I'd been instructed to say, which was the same all the blokes who worked here said too, that the last time I saw him was when he was off to Holland.'

'Did anyone tell them Jin was expecting a shipment of goods?' she asked. 'It seems funny to me they never picked up on that.' She mentioned that Hughes had found the stuff now.

'I never said anything. The other blokes at the warehouse were just young lads who didn't know about anything until the day it arrived. The Fuzz went through the place, but there was nothing there to see, Jin never left papers, not unless it was delivery notes for us. But that stuff was valuable, Charlie, really good stuff, jade mostly and carpets. Your dad was the main man dealing in it, so they wouldn't have been able to sell it on easily without attracting attention. But I don't reckon nicking his gear was her real purpose, ruining him was. If you hadn't stuck your oar in, I expect she'd have sat on it for years, gloating over it.'

'It was a fiendish plot,' Charlie sighed. 'It's hard to believe anyone could be so ruthless.'

'The only thing which keeps me going is the thought she'll die in prison,' he said with a chuckle. 'She'll fight everyone, she'll get striped and worse. Soon she'll go right off her rocker.'

Charlie knew she must go now. It was nearly nine at night and she wanted to get back before Rita. She gave Dave her telephone number. 'If you need anything, a meal cooked for you, the flat cleaned or just a chat, call me,' she said. 'I can't thank you enough for all you've told me.'

'Let's just hope I make it to the trial,' he said with a feeble grin. 'The police have got my sworn testimony, but I want to be there to see that woman go down. I just wish they hadn't abolished hanging.'

'Me too,' Charlie agreed. 'I'd gladly put the noose around her neck myself.'

She leaned over him to kiss him, and he caught her face in his two big hands and held it for a moment looking at her. 'You're your father's daughter all right,' he said. 'He put me on the straight road, away from crime. Whatever comes up in that trial, you just hold your head up, love. He were a good man. One of the best. Keep that in your head, and follow the instinct he's given you. He'll be watching over you.'

Chapter Twenty-one

The Dexters' trial began at the Old Bailey on 2 April 1973. Charlie's nineteenth birthday had passed back in February, Andrew's twenty-first just a week ago, but they hadn't celebrated either occasion. They were waiting for the outcome of the trial.

It had been six long, tense months, starting with Jin's funeral down in Dartmouth. Charlie had imagined that burying her father alongside her mother in the town he had loved would ease the pain of losing him, and finalize everything, but instead it released a new deluge of grief for both her parents.

Ivor comforted her by saying she'd bottled up her real feelings about them from the time when Sylvia was attacked and Jin didn't return home: he said it was good that she was allowing all that hurt and sorrow to come to the surface at last. Charlie thought he was probably right, but that cold, grey October day of the funeral was the start of a long, bleak winter. She coped with her sorrow by working long hours at Haagman's and two nights a week at a business studies class. Keeping busy and avoiding looking back was Rita's way of getting through bad times. Charlie found it worked for her too.

Andrew had moved into the house in Sinclair Grove

in Brent with his three friends, but Charlie had remained living with Rita. This was partly to appease Mr and Mrs Blake, who held the belief that unmarried couples sharing a house were 'living in sin', partly so that Andrew would have fewer distractions from his studies, but mostly for Rita's sake. Back in November she had told her parents the full story about her part in the impending trial, and urged them to tell Paul she was his real mother. As she had half expected they showed no sympathy or understanding, but flew into a rage and demanded she get out of their house and never come back. Since then Rita had written them many pleading letters, but they returned them all unopened. Charlie felt compelled to stay with her then – Rita had been there for her when she needed support and Charlie wanted to help her now.

She had been very touched when a letter arrived at Haagman's from Meg, Beth and Anne. They had read about her father's body being found and felt they had to write and offer their condolences. There was a paragraph from each of them – Anne and Beth urged her to get in touch, maybe meet up for a drink sometime; Meg said simply that she was very sorry for all the hurt she'd caused her; that she knew Charlie wouldn't ever want to see her again, but just the same she wanted her to know how much she felt for her about her father.

Charlie wrote back to thank them. She wasn't sure yet whether she'd keep in touch, but it felt good to know they hadn't forgotten the good times they'd shared, and that Meg did have a heart after all.

Dave Kent was getting sicker week by week, but he remained stubbornly determined to give his evidence at the trial. An unlikely friendship had grown between him and Charlie in odd evenings they spent together at his flat, unbeknown to Andrew or Rita who thought she was off at another class. Maybe she was a substitute daughter for Dave, and he was a substitute father for her, but through his many amusing, gritty stories about the years he worked with Jin, Charlie had found the solace she needed and an understanding of both men's characters.

While Dave had been quick to point out that Jin had always been the brains behind their operation and he merely the brawn, they had both learned new skills by working together. Dave had taught Jin to drive a lorry, Jin had taught Dave simple book-keeping and to appreciate the beauty of his artefacts. Although Jin wasn't exactly one of the lads, he hadn't been as aloof as Charlie had imagined. He helped with loading and unloading and always mucked in with the cleaning up, making tea and other mundane chores. But it was hearing about the boyish side of her father that touched Charlie the most. Dave, laughing, described a time when Jin let off Chinese crackers in the empty warehouse, and how the men leapt around yelling as the whizzing, crackling fireworks came at them. One hot afternoon he goaded all the lads into jumping into the river with him for a swim, then doubled back, locked the warehouse doors with their clothes inside, and left them no choice but to run naked around the side of the building to retrieve them.

She learned too of Jin's youth, of how as a young boy, alone in Hong Kong, he wheedled his way into working for English naval officers and their families, just so he could learn from them. His fierce ambition to get to England drove him to take any job, however tough. By day he cleaned houses, tended gardens, ran errands, at night he worked in bars, saving every penny he made. It was clear to Charlie that Jin had been a great influence on Dave, that once he discovered Jin's youth had been far grimmer than his own, he tried to emulate the man's honesty, good manners and dignity.

But the hardest part of the past six months had been having so little time to spend with Andrew. It wasn't enough just being with him from Friday night till Sunday morning, then it was all fiery passion but no chance really to relax and talk. If he was anxious about the trial, he didn't speak of it, and she had the added burden of keeping all she'd learned from Dave about her father from him and Rita too.

'Penny for them?' Rita asked as they travelled to work together on the Central Line on the morning of 2 April. As always the rush-hour tube was packed solid, and the girls were pressed up tight against each other.

'I was just thinking that in a couple of hours the jury will be sworn in,' Charlie admitted.

'I bet Daphne's pooping her pants right now,' Rita giggled. 'Being stuck in Holloway all these months must have brought her down a peg or two. I doubt she got a chance to lord it over anyone there.'

'Part of me wishes I wasn't a witness at all, or working, so I could sit through the whole thing and give her the evil eye,' Charlie said with a trace of wistfulness.

They both knew the trial might last for weeks. As Detective Inspector Hughes had hoped, other victims had come forward in the past few months. In all probability Dave and Rita's vital evidence would be heard early in the trial, but Charlie and Andrew's, being less important, would mean they might have a long wait.

'I don't. I want my chance to speak out,' Rita said firmly. 'I just hope they call me quickly. I'm so jumpy I don't think I'll be able to eat or sleep until it's over.'

On an impulse Charlie kissed her friend's cheek. 'What's that for?' Rita sniggered.

'For being so brave,' Charlie said simply. Today was the first time Rita had admitted how jumpy she was, yet she'd already been through so much. One of the worst things was having to submit to being photographed naked. Charlie thought she would die of embarrassment if pictures of her body were to be passed around the court, but Rita had even managed to laugh and joke about that.

'I wish I'd been brave enough to go to the police when it happened,' Rita whispered, her small face clouding over. 'If I had, you probably wouldn't be standing on this tube with me now. You'd be off at university, with two proud parents sitting at home.'

'Maybe,' Charlie said softly. 'But then I'd still be a spoiled brat who couldn't boil an egg. I wouldn't have Andrew, you, Beryl or Ivor behind me.'

Rita said nothing more until they got out at Tottenham Court Road. But as they rode up on the escalator she turned back to Charlie. 'I thank the day I met you,' she whispered, putting her hand on Charlie's shoulder. 'You've given me back more than you could ever know. So stop worrying about me, or how I'll hold up under cross-examination. I'll be fine.'

622

By Wednesday, once the prosecution and defence had laid out their cases, all the national newspapers had picked up that the Dexter trial was going to be a sensational one. That morning as Charlie was rushing into work she had spotted a billboard on a newspaper man's stand which said 'Dexters in the Dock'. It was so busy at Haagman's she had no time to buy a paper, much less read it, so it hadn't been until she finished work, with an hour to kill before her evening class, that she got her chance.

Charlie was astonished to find the list of charges against the Dexters ran into almost two columns. Apart from their crimes against Jin, Sylvia, Rita and Andrew, there were three other women who had been maimed, a bank manager who had been blackmailed, an estate agent who'd been hospitalized, several ex-tenants who had been victims of a terror campaign, and the hit-and-run murder of Ralph Peterson. This last one was a total surprise. Hughes had told her very little about any of the charges, but he hadn't mentioned this one at all.

It was just on nine in the evening before Charlie got home, bursting with this new development, but Rita was glued to the news on television. Without turning her head she waved a greeting. 'I missed the six o'clock news,' she said. 'I'm just waiting for them to go through all the charges. Sit down and watch it with me.'

Charlie was shocked into utter silence as the main news began with a report on the Dexter trial. Somehow the calm, measured tones of the television reporter listing the charges against the accused made them seem even more brutal than the sensationalized report she'd read earlier in the press.

There were pictures shown too of the Wapping warehouse where Jin died, of 'Windways' and its garden, The Manse and Ralph Peterson's Mayfair apartment, of the various clubs Daphne had owned, including the Lotus, and then of the many properties she'd bought up. With each picture came a little background information about its connection with one of the victims.

Rita leaped up to switch off the television as the newscaster moved on to a story about the new Value Added Tax which had replaced purchase tax as from 1 April. She stood there for a moment, her back to Charlie, and her shoulders were heaving.

Charlie was surprised at such a reaction. 'It wasn't so bad,' she said, getting up and putting her arms round her friend to comfort her. 'They didn't say anything more about you than your name.'

'It's not that.' Rita sobbed. 'I didn't know until I saw that that she'd killed Ralph too.'

'You didn't either?' Charlie explained how she'd read it. 'I thought Hughes would have told you.'

Rita shook her head. 'I knew of course that he was killed in a hit-and-run accident, I read it in the paper a couple of years after she tortured me. I laughed at the time Charlie, *laughed*. I thought it served him right for not sticking by me. I never thought the Dexters had anything to do with it, not an important man like him.'

'Well, at least they struck across all social classes,' Charlie said dryly. 'From poor immigrants to nobs.'

Rita gave a sort of giggling sniff. 'I don't quite understand why it upset me,' she said.

'I do,' Charlie said, taking her friend by the shoul-

624

ders and drawing her to her. 'You had all the big dreams about him. And you didn't just use him, I know that. You really cared for him, didn't you?'

An affirmative sniff came from her shoulder. 'I thought as much,' Charlie said. Rita was a great one for playing down her real feelings. Having been rejected by her parents at an early age she'd learned to cope with all hurts and disappointments by pretending nothing touched her. 'Well, as I see it, he probably truly cared for you too. That's exactly why Daphne had to knock you out of the running. Now, that's something to comfort yourself with on a cold night, isn't it?'

Rita stood up straight, wiped her eyes with the back of her hand and smiled. 'You've got more sense at nineteen than I've got in my mid-thirties,' she said. 'You know something else?'

'No, what?' Charlie giggled.

Rita's eyes suddenly came to life, sparking with glimpses of the young Suzie Charlie had seen when she talked about that era. 'I got a message earlier that I'm being called on Friday. But I'm not going to do it looking like a Sunday school teacher. I don't give a shit, whether it weakens my testimony, I'm going in there hair done, face on and all flags flying. I'll bloody well make that bitch wish she never picked on me.'

Charlie was surprised at Rita being called quite so soon. She was also uncertain if the prosecution would appreciate her turning up looking anything other than drab and beaten down. Yet if it made Rita feel more confident, she thought she ought to encourage her.

'Well have a dress rehearsal right now then,' Charlie said. 'Come on, let's look in your wardrobe.'

Ironically, it wasn't in Rita's wardrobe that they found the right outfit. Everything Rita owned was either too dreary, sleazy or out of date. But amongst Charlie's clothes was a classic Chanel cream dress and jacket that had belonged to Sylvia. It was one of the things like the blue velvet jacket she thought she might sell one day. It fitted Rita as if it was made for her. The dress reached just beneath her knees, and with her brown high-heeled shoes she looked perfect.

'And you don't look like a tart in it, before you ask. Just beautiful and stylish,' Charlie remarked as Rita swirled around in front of the mirror. 'I think Mum and Dad will watch over you wearing it. The reason I kept it was because Dad loved Mum in it.'

A sudden vivid flashback shot into Charlie's mind, one the dress and jacket had never evoked before. She was fourteen, her parents were in their bedroom getting ready to go out, and she'd gone in there to ask them something. Sylvia was wearing just the dress, her blonde hair piled up on top of her head, and she looked sensational. Jin was fastening a string of beads around her neck and just as Charlie looked in, he kissed her neck and said he loved her.

Sylvia turned to him, held his face in her two hands and kissed his nose.

'All the best moments in my life have been spent with you,' she said.

It was strange that she should only remember it now, but then as Beryl had said at Sylvia's funeral, it took a while for all the memories to surface. She hoped that in time many more good, happy ones like that would replace the sad ones. She told Rita about it, and her friend wiped an emotional tear from her eye.

'Hair loose or up?' she asked after a minute or two, piling it on top of her head.

'Loose, it's too beautiful to hide,' Charlie said bossily. 'Get it trimmed and set tomorrow evening. But now we've got to try the makeup.'

Rita did her face with her old makeup, the way she used to eight years earlier. She suddenly looked like a streetwalker.

'No.' Charlie snatched the bottle of foundation and eyeliner from her. 'They are too heavy. Tomorrow we'll get a light foundation and a soft eyeshadow. And lie down on the bed so I can pluck your eyebrows, they're a mess.'

A couple of hours later when they were about to go to bed, Rita caught hold of Charlie's arm. 'If I go to court like that, how can I go back to being like this again?'

'You can't,' Charlie smiled. 'And you won't want to. This is going to be the new Rita, for good.'

The following evening Charlie came out of Haagman's to find Andrew sitting astride his scooter waiting for her. Her face lit up with pleasure and she ran to kiss him. 'What brought you up here?' she asked.

'That witness who saw your father killed was cross-examined today. I thought I'd whiz you home so we could watch it on the news together.'

Charlie would have been delighted to see Andrew, whatever the reason, but his sensitivity and his urge to protect her were moving. He didn't know she was already aware of everything the man had to say, he was just afraid she might watch it alone and become upset. She hoped he would understand when she finally did tell him about her secret relationship with Dave. It was so sad that Andrew might never get an opportunity to know him as well as she did.

As Andrew wound his way through the evening traffic in Oxford Street, Charlie clung on to him and wondered if Dave's ordeal was now over. The last time she'd seen him had been ten days ago. His weight had dropped to beneath ten stone, his diet was liquids only, and he was in constant pain. She didn't think he could hold on much longer. But he had to get through until the verdict. And until his daughter got here.

Charlie knew it wasn't really her place to interfere, but two weeks earlier she'd been so worried about him she'd taken the matter into her own hands and written to Wendy, telling her everything. She'd asked her not to phone her father, because this might distress him, but just to come. Wendy had telephoned her the minute she got the letter, and crying over the phone she'd said she couldn't come immediately, however much she wanted to, as her husband was working away from home and she had no one to leave her son Grant with, but she'd get here as soon as she could. Charlie just had to hope that wouldn't be too late.

They got back and switched on the TV just in time to hear Big Ben striking six. Dave Kent's appearance in the witness box was mentioned first in the summary of the news; they had to wait some time before the newscaster came back to the subject.

Charlie was a little disappointed. All the newscaster reported was the bare bones of the story, how David

Kent, the owner of the warehouse, was tied up and left in a storeroom where he witnessed Daphne Dexter shoot Jin Weish and subsequently saw the Dexter twins row a small boat out into deep water in the Thames and drop the body in. Under cross-examination by the defence it was brought up that he had a criminal record himself, and it was suggested that on a dark, stormy night, tied up in an upper storeroom, he couldn't have seen all he said he did. They also asked why he later sold the lease of his warehouse to the Dexters, if they had done all he'd stated.

It was only as he was filmed leaving the Old Bailey, pale, drawn, so thin and all alone, refusing stoutly to pass any comment to any of the reporters milling there other than to say he had told the truth, that Charlie felt her heart breaking and forgot herself.

'The jury must believe him. Don't they know he's got nothing to gain by lying? He's dying, for God's sake,' she sobbed.

Andrew looked at her in surprise. She had told him back in Salcombe that Hughes had said this witness was very sick. But that outburst sounded very much as if she knew much more than she'd told him. 'Have you been holding out on me?' he asked indignantly.

Charlie had planned to wait until the end of the trial before she told him. But now, afraid that the defence had twisted Dave's story so that he sounded like the villain, she couldn't hold it back any longer. Sobbing, she told him what she knew.

Andrew rocked her in his arms as he listened. He understood she felt compelled to keep her promise to Hughes and not tell him, he was also touched by her compassion for this sick man, yet it still hurt to think she had kept so much from him for so long.

'I've grown very fond of him,' she said finally, sniffing and drying her eyes. 'I just hope he makes it till his daughter comes back and until after the trial so you can meet him too.'

'You mustn't go anywhere near him again, not until then,' Andrew warned her. 'You can bet your life reporters are camping on his doorstep right now. If they spotted you, it could turn the case upside down.'

'I don't see why. I didn't know him when it happened. Besides, Rita is a witness too, and we aren't banned from speaking to her.'

'Well, that couldn't be helped,' Andrew said. 'You worked with Rita and came to live with her, before all this started. As for me, my whole object of getting involved was because of you.'

'It doesn't seem very logical to me, we are on the same side after all,' Charlie said with a pout. 'I wonder if it came out in court that he was protecting his daughter, and how ill he is?'

'I'm sure it did,' Andrew replied. 'No doubt they'll print every word in the papers tomorrow. You'll have to wait till then!'

The following morning Rita came swirling into the kitchen as Charlie and Andrew were finishing their cornflakes. 'How do I look?'

'Wow!' Andrew exclaimed. 'You look sensational.'

'That's not quite how I wanted to appear,' she said, her voice suddenly cracking with nerves.

'He's not strong on subtlety,' Charlie said quickly.

'What he means is, you look wonderful. And you do. Classy and very feminine.'

In fact Charlie could hardly believe her eyes, Rita was simply stunning. She had been to a late-night hairdresser's the previous evening. They'd cut a few inches off her hair, and now it shimmered under the kitchen light, a cascade of loose, coppery waves. The expensive dress and jacket looked as good on her as it had on Sylvia, the new delicate makeup enhanced her naturally pale skin giving it a pink glow.

Charlie could see now that Rita was right to go looking like this. The defence lawyers might try to discredit her by bringing up that she was a night-club hostess, but every member of the jury would look at those photographs of her scarred body, then at her sweet face and lovely hair, and despair that such a pretty woman had missed out on happiness, love and marriage.

'I wish I could come with you, to hold your hand,' Charlie sighed. 'But you'll be in my thoughts all day.'

'And mine,' Andrew said, getting up to plant a kiss on Rita's cheek. 'Now would you like a lift on my scooter?'

Rita hooted with laughter at his joke. 'Now, with my old image I might have taken you up on it. But today I think I'll swan off in a taxi. I am after all getting my expenses paid. Besides, looking like this I might pull some famous barrister while sitting around waiting to be called.'

'That's the spirit,' Charlie laughed. 'You go in there and knock them dead. Make sure you make lots of impudent faces at the Dexters too.'

*

Jin Weish's photograph was on the front page of two of the tabloids that morning, giving Charlie something of a start as it was a photograph she'd taken herself in the garden of 'Windways' a year before his death. He was wearing an open-necked shirt, sitting by the summer-house, smiling, with a glass of beer in his hand. Sylvia had loved it, she said he looked just the way he had when they first met, boyish and happy, and she'd rushed to get it enlarged, and pinned it up in the kitchen. Charlie could only imagine that the police had taken it at the time of his disappearance and distributed copies of it around London, for she hadn't seen it since. Yet even though it was an unexpected jolt, she was glad the papers had used it, for it was a far more endearing image than ones taken at smart dinner and cocktail parties. He looked the way she wanted to remember him, just Daddy in the garden.

The copy which accompanied it centred mainly on the evidence Dave had given in court the previous day, but Charlie was cheered further to read that a forensic scientist who had been called to the witness box immediately after Dave had confirmed that it was possible to get a good view of the warehouse through the crack in the floor above, and also that the window was an excellent vantage-point, night or day, to see a long stretch of the river. He went on to say that the heavy weights retrieved with the body came from a Victorian scale and were missing parts of a set found recently in the warehouse. Also the angle that the bullets had penetrated the body was consistent with the information disclosed to the police. There was also a paragraph about Dave bringing up his daughter alone, and the threats made against her which bought his silence.

Charlie was on edge all morning wondering how Rita was holding up in court, but she didn't have to wait for news for as long as she expected. Everyone in the laboratory knew about Rita's role in the case. She had told them about it at the same time she informed her parents, but when she swept into Haagman's during the early afternoon, every member of staff's mouth dropped open in astonishment at her dramatically changed appearance. All work stopped as they clamoured round her for news; even the Hag came out of her office.

Charlie leapt to her feet. 'How did it go?' she asked anxiously.

Rita gave a cynical half-smile. 'You'd have been proud of me, I wrung the last drop of sympathy out of the court as I described what she did to me. When the prosecution chap led me into saying that I'd lived like a hermit for the last eight years, in terrible fear for my son, I could see the jury were all on my side, a couple of the women were even dabbing at their eyes.'

'Great!' Charlie exclaimed jubilantly.

'But the defence barrister was an absolute bastard,' Rita went on, her smile fading. 'He twisted everything. He suggested it was me who was jealous of Daphne Dexter, not the other way round, and I was using her and her brothers as a convenient scapegoat, when my scars could have been made by someone else.'

'He didn't!' Charlie burst out, unable to believe anyone could suggest such a thing.

'He did. I felt like screaming at him, especially when

633

he went to great pains to sway the jury into thinking the word of a girl who had dumped her unwanted baby on her parents, and made a living from using men, wasn't to be believed.'

'Poor Rita,' Charlie said in sympathy, but to her surprise her friend laughed.

'Poor Rita nothing!' she said, her eyes twinkling with merriment. 'As I came out the Old Bailey, a reporter from the *Daily Mirror* came up to me. He's offered me money for the exclusive rights to my story.'

It was typical of Rita's character that she'd find something to give her the strength to bounce back. But Charlie wondered how much deep hurt she was concealing. She intended to tackle her when she got home.

That weekend passed in a bewildering and exhausting fashion. Charlie got home from work just in time for the six o'clock news and saw Rita filmed as she left the Old Bailey. The newscaster spoke only of her being a key witness for the prosecution and there was a brief description of her mutilation as they showed film of the cellar at The Manse.

'See! They didn't even say anything nasty about you,' Charlie said triumphantly. 'And you looked like a film star!'

Rita just laughed and said she'd already had two phone calls, one from the *Mirror* and one from the *News of the World*, and she'd said she'd call them back in a few days to discuss money. Moving on swiftly from that she said there had been a message that Charlie and Andrew were to be called earlier than they'd expected to give their evidence. They were to be at the Old Bailey at nine-thirty the following Tuesday.

'About the deal with a newspaper,' Charlie said, realizing Rita didn't intend to discuss it. 'You will be careful that they agree to print what you want, won't you? I mean, it's a real chance to set the record straight, so Paul and your parents can see how it really was for you. Don't sell it to someone who might portray you in the wrong way.'

'I'm quite capable of working that out for myself, bossy boots,' Rita grinned. 'Neither are you the only one with a brain.'

Charlie laughed. 'Well, that's settled then. Now, what did the Dexters look like today?'

Rita shivered. 'That was the worst bit,' she said, grimacing. 'The brothers didn't even look at me, they kept their eyes down at all times. But she never took her eyes off me. It brought that night back so vividly. I swear she was trying to warn me she could still get to me, even from prison.'

'But she can't,' Charlie assured her, glad that Rita was finally admitting how she really felt. 'That's just bravado. She hasn't got any friends now. I bet they haven't got one witness on their side.'

'They have,' Rita retorted. 'The chap from the witness service who looked after me told me. And they are pulling out all the stops to show what a grim childhood they had.'

'That won't change the jury's thinking,' Charlie said with a shrug. 'Both my parents had terrible ones, it didn't turn them into killers. But anyway, tell me how you thought Daphne looked, compared with how she used to be?'

'Well, she doesn't look like Elizabeth Taylor any more, more like Bette Davis on a bad day,' Rita grinned. 'She looked gaunt, her skin kind of yellowy. I couldn't help thinking what a shame it was your mum didn't hang on. She might have got some degree of comfort from seeing her old enemy brought to her knees.'

It was then Charlie decided to tell Rita about Dave Kent, and all he'd passed on to her about the relationship between Jin and Daphne.

'He might say your dad was a dark horse, you're even more so,' Rita exclaimed. 'Never mind going into antiques, you ought to be a private detective!'

Saturday's and Sunday's papers were full of the case. Andrew went out and bought all of them, and they read every word. Meanwhile the phone never seemed to stop ringing. Journalists, old friends of Rita's, distant relatives, they all wanted to know the inside story. But Rita remained very cool and said she wasn't allowed to discuss the case until it was over.

It was late on Sunday evening after Andrew had gone home that Rita suddenly began to cry.

'What on earth's wrong?' Charlie asked. She might be one for bursting into tears, but Rita wasn't.

'Just all those people who haven't bothered with me for years suddenly making out they care,' she said bitterly, dabbing at her eyes. 'But not a word from my parents.'

Charlie didn't know what to say. She knew exactly how Rita must feel – she hadn't forgotten or forgiven the way those people in Dartmouth reacted to her when her mother was in hospital and her father disappeared. Some of them had the cheek to come fawning round her again at her father's funeral, but she'd given them all short shrift.

She moved over to sit by her friend and cuddled her. 'Try not to let it get to you,' she said eventually. 'The people who phoned are just vultures. And your parents are blinkered. But Andrew and I both love you because we know your worth, so does everyone at work, even the Hag is on your side. Sod your parents, Rita, they don't deserve you anyway.'

'It's not them so much, it's Paul's feelings I'm worried about,' Rita replied. 'I don't even know if they explained it to him.'

'I expect they did, no one would willingly let a sixteen-year-old boy find it out by accident. And unless he's very unusual, I bet this has made him far more curious about you. I reckon he'll turn up here before long to see you.'

'I don't think so, you can bet Mum and Dad have poisoned his mind.'

'Mum did her best to poison mine about Dad,' Charlie said. 'But she didn't succeed, kids are smarter than adults realize. Paul won't think it's so terrible being illegitimate, or you working in a night-club – this is the Seventies, remember, nobody gives a jot about that sort of stuff any more. And then there's the story you're going to sell, that will tell the whole truth.'

Rita smiled weakly. 'I used to be the mother figure around here,' she said. 'How come our roles are reversing?'

Charlie laughed. 'As you are so fond of telling me, I'm just a bossy boots who thinks she knows everything.'

*

On Tuesday morning Charlie was awake at six, shaking with fear at the thought of the day ahead. A week ago she had been eagerly awaiting it, but until she heard Rita's experiences she hadn't fully appreciated how unpleasant the defence lawyers could be.

She met Andrew at nine outside the Old Bailey. He too looked drawn and anxious, and it was strange to see him in a suit and tie, he looked so much older than in his usual jeans. She kissed him and asked him where he'd got the suit.

'I borrowed it from John,' he said with a weak smile. 'It makes me feel as if I'm going to a funeral. But you look lovely.'

She was wearing a plain black dress with a red jacket over it. Red made her look confident, even if she wasn't inside.

'Have you got the collywobbles?' she asked as they went for a quick cup of coffee before going in.

Andrew grinned. 'The screaming ones,' he admitted. 'But by this afternoon our part in all this will be over. Let's get paralytic tonight.'

Just walking up the steps and through the imposing door of the Old Bailey made them even more nervous. It was as quiet as a church but with its shiny dark grey marble floors and pillars it had the unexpected opulence of a palace. They were met by a small wiry man from the witness service, who introduced himself as Brian and explained it was his job to look after them. He led them up a wide staircase, and smiled at them both when they paused to gawp in surprise at the fantastic frescoes on the domed ceiling.

'Uplifting, aren't they?' he said, and pointed out his favourite which was a scene from the Crimean war.

'Somehow it always reminds me how *great* Britain was, and still is. Our system of justice is admired the world over.'

As she walked past Charlie noted the inscription, 'Moses gave unto the people the laws of God,' and it gave her a shred of comfort that laws that had stood for so many centuries couldn't be just pushed aside by the likes of the Dexters.

'You'll be in Court Two,' Brian said, waving his hand to show them which of the many doors that was, then promptly whisked them into a small room where they would wait with him until they were called to the courtroom.

'Now, there's nothing to be scared of,' he said reassuringly as they sat down. 'Some of the questions the barristers put to you may seem odd, even irrelevant at times, but that's just because it's their job to dig out the whole truth, not just from you two, but from everyone else involved in this case. Sometimes the judge might ask you a question directly, if he wants something clarified. You address him as "My Lord".'

As they waited Brian chatted, asking Andrew about City University and what he intended to do when he got his degree. Charlie was aware the man was doing his best to put them both at their ease, but she found it impossible to join in the conversation for listening for any sounds outside their door.

It was so very quiet, as though they were the only people in the entire building. Brian explained when she finally managed to voice this that the jury filed into the court from another direction, the prisoners were brought up from the basement through yet another way, and even the public gallery was reached separately.

They hadn't been in the room more than fifteen minutes when the usher called Andrew in. Charlie thought he was very cool; he grinned at her, squeezed her hand and marched out smartly. She wondered whether he was really as scared as she was.

The waiting seemed interminable. Brian offered her a newspaper to read, but her eyes seemed not to be able to focus on it. Just occasionally she heard tip-tapping feet pass by outside the room, and there was a constant hum of traffic from out in the road, but there was nothing at all to take her mind off watching the hands of her watch creep round and wondering what she was in for later.

Finally, soon after eleven, Andrew came back smiling reassuringly. Brian had already warned her that she mustn't try to discuss the case until after she'd given her own evidence, so all she could do was grip his hand as they both drank the coffee brought to them.

The wigged and gowned court usher came for her at exactly eleven-thirty.

'Good luck,' Andrew whispered as she left. 'Speak up and don't let them intimidate you. I'll be waiting for you here.'

Charlie's nervousness increased the moment she walked through the doors. Although the courtroom wasn't anywhere near as big as she'd expected, it made her feel very small and insignificant. Everything was of heavy dark wood, from the panelled walls, to the dock, the jury benches and the raised bench at which the judge sat. His red robes were the only splash of colour in the entire room, and although at first glance the court appeared to have a glass roof, the image of natural light was faked, it was just lights set behind glass. There were so many people too, apart from all those engaged in the trial, wearing wigs and gowns and seated in the well of the court. Almost every seat in the press benches was taken, and Charlie could hear coughing and whispering coming from the public gallery which was above the jury benches and out of her line of vision.

Her voice shook as she took the oath – she was only too well aware of Daphne Dexter studying her insolently from the dock to her left. Despite what Rita had said about Daphne's appearance, from Charlie's swift glance at her she thought the woman looked pretty good. She was wearing a black jacket and a white blouse, her dark hair pinned up in a bun.

It was difficult to tell which of the brothers was the one who had caught her in the garden, as they were so staggeringly alike, both dressed in dark suits and white shirts, with short-cropped dark hair, an identical burly build and square jaws. But neither of them looked at her; they were both studying their laps.

The prosecution barrister was a short, stocky man with glasses and traces of a North Country accent. Charlie had been told by Brian that his name was Underwood, and he took her straight into the events of the day Sylvia was attacked. Charlie described where she was when she first heard the car draw up, and how she was getting dressed when she heard her mother scream, and what she saw from the window before running to call the police.

Underwood then led her onto the aftermath, her mother's loss of mobility, her depression and misery through losing their former home. It was clear to Charlie by his penetrating questions about how they lived in Mayflower Close until the day Sylvia took her life, that he wished to establish in the jury's minds the full picture of the havoc that had been wreaked on both women through the vicious attack and Jin's disappearance. There were no interruptions throughout these questions, yet when Underwood asked Charlie when she first heard about Daphne Dexter from her mother and what was said, the defence leapt up to say this was hearsay. The prosecution claimed what she had said was vital evidence and the judge ruled Charlie could go on.

'My mother only ever called her by her nickname DeeDee,' Charlie said, going on to repeat the rest of what she'd been told.

'What was your mother's attitude to this other woman in your father's life?' Underwood asked.

'Bewilderment that her old friend had done such a thing. Anger, jealousy too of course, but she seemed to be very frightened of the woman as well.'

Charlie found she was regaining her confidence as his questions seemed so sympathetic. She found she wasn't even thrown by the many times the defence interrupted with claims that his opposite part was leading the witness.

There were no further interruptions from the defence as she was asked how she met Rita, and how it came about that Andrew set out to try and solve the mystery of her missing father. Finally just the part about her ordeal in The Manse remained. Underwood asked her first if the man who locked her up was in the court today. She agreed he was one of the two men in the dock, but could only guess which one because they were so alike. Then Underwood asked if the woman she saw through the dining-hatch was in the court. Charlie said she was and pointed to Daphne.

The look Daphne gave her was one of pure loathing. Her lips curled back and her vivid blue eyes flashed with menace. Even in the safety of the court Charlie felt shaken and it brought it home to her how terrible it must have been for Rita to face her again.

The prosecution's questions ended with how she escaped, then it was the turn of the defence. Cunningham, the defence barrister, was entirely different to Underwood. A handsome, tall, well-built man, with olive, glowing skin. His voice was cultured but loud and commanding. Although he smiled at her, it didn't reach his penetrating dark eyes. Right from the very first question Charlie felt uncomfortable. It seemed he was setting out to ridicule her.

'Tell me, Miss Weish,' he said condescendingly. 'If your father had last telephoned as you say on the evening of June the 17th, saying he'd be home within a week, why didn't your mother report him missing when she heard nothing more from him?'

Her reply explaining he was often delayed sounded feeble.

'You said you had never seen these two men who attacked your mother before, but surely only someone who knew her and her habit of sunbathing well, would come straight into the garden to find her? Can you explain that?'

'No. But I think my mother knew who they were, though she never admitted it,' she replied.

He smirked. 'So they could have been debt collectors, even old lovers?' he suggested, then before she could deny this, moved straight on to ask if the two men in the dock were the same ones she'd seen that day.

'They could have been,' Charlie said. 'They are the right build and age, but I couldn't see their faces clearly because the sun was in my eyes.'

'A good percentage of men in England must be the right build and age,' he said to the jury. 'Please note that there was no positive identification.'

After many questions about the high standard of living Charlie and her mother had enjoyed at 'Windways', he moved on to probe deeply about how they lived in the council flat, asking about her job in the hotel and how she coped with schoolwork and looking after her mother. Charlie wondered why he had to ask all this, she'd already been through all the relevant details with Underwood, but this man continually kept coming back to the subject of her mother's depression and how difficult it must have been for a schoolgirl to cope. At one point he commiserated with her lack of social life, and when he came to ask about her mother's suicide his questions were so gentle and sympathetic she began to cry.

Underwood jumped up then with a protest. The judge ruled that the defence must stick to questions relating only to the charges laid against the accused.

Yet when he moved on to her meeting up with Rita Tutthill he seemed scornful again. This he described as 'providential', giving Charlie the feeling he was trying to insinuate that although it might have been pure chance that she met someone from a similar background to her own mother, she was in fact being manipulated by this older woman for a sinister purpose.

His line of questioning seemed very odd. It wasn't until he asked about her first visit to the police regarding Andrew's disappearance, and got her to admit she felt angry that no one seemed to care about either Andrew or her father, that she suddenly saw his real aim. He was in fact attempting to prove to the jury that she had a persecution complex and maybe was unhinged too.

'Isn't it true, Miss Weish, that far from coming to London after your mother's death to start afresh, you came on a crusade? You were bitter that the police hadn't apprehended your mother's attackers or found your father, and you were prepared to listen to tales from anyone sympathetic to your grievances.'

'No, that's not true,' she retorted. 'I came to start a new life for myself and although I always intended to try and find out what had happened to my father, I was so happy and busy for the first few months I hardly thought about him.'

'Quite so, Miss Weish,' he smirked. 'You put it aside temporarily until you met up with Miss Tutthill, but once she'd fired you up with her story about the accused, you became convinced, without a shred of real evidence to support it, that they were responsible for both the attack on your mother and your father's disappearance. Isn't that true?'

Put like that she had no choice but to agree.

He was very clever, she had to allow him that.

Looking back later she saw he had slanted every single question to portray her as a badly used, grieving innocent, who was punch-drunk from the hard knocks she'd been dealt and in her desire to discover the truth about her father had fallen prey to believing anything she was told, regardless of whether the source was questionable.

Charlie felt angry that she wasn't being given any opportunity, even by the prosecution, to show what she was really made of. When she was asked which of the twins had locked her in the basement and she couldn't tell him, that anger finally boiled over. 'Does it matter which one it was?' she shot back at him. 'You know perfectly well both men were in on it.'

She received a rebuke for this, but when she was asked how she could be positive that the woman she'd seen only briefly through a small hatch was in fact the same woman as in the dock, she was beyond caring what sort of impression she was making. 'I've got two perfectly good eyes, and a first-class brain,' she snapped back at him. 'And Daphne Dexter's face is unforgettable.'

All at once it was over and she was asked to step down. For a brief moment she was tempted to stand her ground and shout out to the whole court that these people in the dock robbed her of both her parents. But the realization that would only make her look foolish stopped her in the nick of time.

'Let's go home,' Andrew said after he'd hugged Charlie silently for several minutes while she blurted out the gist of her humiliation. Earlier that morning they had planned to go into the public gallery during the afternoon to watch, but that didn't seem a good idea any longer.

'The defence barrister was a swine to me too,' Andrew said. 'He sneered at me and called me a boy scout. He even suggested I was never in that cellar! That was ridiculous. He might be able to cast doubt on some of the crimes the Dexters are supposed to have done, but how can he deny what they did to me?'

'I think it's just all a game to those lawyers,' she said weakly. 'I don't think they really give a toss about justice, all they want to do is score points and show off to one another.'

Brian commiserated with them. 'Don't take it personally,' he said. 'If you were ever to sit through a complete trial you'd understand how the system works. Now go on home and forget about it. Your part in it is over now.'

They hadn't anticipated there would be a crowd of reporters waiting for them outside in the street. As they came down the steps, they all lunged towards them, cameras flashing.

'What was it like, Miss Weish, to come face to face with your father's killers?' a woman called out.

Andrew tried to drag her on, urging her to say nothing, but after being portrayed in court as a pathetic character, Charlie was intent on asserting herself.

'I've been face to face with them before, remember,' she said in a loud, clear voice. She blinked as another camera flashed at her.

'Do you think Daphne Dexter will be found guilty of murder?' another voice called out.

'If she isn't, there's something wrong with British

justice,' Charlie retorted. 'But if by some fluke she does get off, she'll have me on her back for the rest of her life.'

Andrew flagged down a passing taxi and bundled her in. 'Now, that wasn't the most sensible remark to make,' he said dryly as he leapt in behind her. 'Every paper in England will be quoting you tonight.'

'Good,' she smiled, as she sat back on the seat. 'I meant it!'

The trial dragged on for three more weeks. It no longer hogged the headlines, as it had at first, and worse still, what little was reported seemed to suggest the defence were scoring the most points.

It appeared to Charlie and to Rita that their intention was to build up the idea that the Dexters were the victims of a malicious vendetta. As so many of their alleged crimes had been committed years earlier, against people of dubious character who were often proved to have some sort of grudge against the accused, it sounded all too possible to anyone who hadn't suffered at their hands.

The hit-and-run murder of Ralph Peterson was a case in point. His sister, a spinster in her sixties, staunchly insisted her brother was a man of high moral standards, and claimed he had parted company with Daphne Dexter because he discovered she owned several strip clubs. He had also expressed his fear to her that the woman would retaliate with some kind of violence against him. When asked why, then, Peterson had still left money to Daphne, she said she thought he'd forgotten to change his will after they fell out.

Under cross-examination she admitted she had always disapproved of her brother's relationship with Daphne because, as she put it, 'She was low-class and a gold-digger.' It also transpired that she had hired a private detective with the sole purpose of discrediting Daphne. Miss Peterson's testimony to her brother's 'high moral standards' was further shot to pieces by the defence drawing attention to his predilection for young and racy women, listing not only Daphne and Rita but two other club girls he'd also 'kept company' with.

The defence brought on a witness who was the manager of a peep-show club owned by Daphne, and produced a document which showed that Peterson had loaned Daphne money to open a new strip club. He also claimed Peterson regularly came into all her clubs to watch the shows.

The police had bungled the investigation into Peterson's death. Although they were given a description of the hit-and-run car, and part of the registration number, by an eye-witness, they didn't check it out immediately. Barrington Dexter's car matched the description and the partial number, he had also had a recent repair to it, consistent with driving at someone at high speed, but by the time the police acted, any traces of blood or fibres from Peterson's clothes which might have been on the car had been washed away.

Finally, on the Friday of the fourth week of the trial, all the witnesses had given their evidence. On Monday the prosecution and defence would make their closing speeches.

On Saturday morning Charlie was over at Andrew's

house, busy trying to clean the filthy kitchen, when to her surprise Dave Kent called her there.

'Hello, darlin',' he said in his now very familiar crusty voice. 'Sorry to intrude when yer with yer fella, but I kinda twisted your mate's arm to give me the number.'

Charlie had last spoken to him just after she gave her evidence and he had been very low then because he was being pestered by reporters. She knew just what that was like now, she'd had a basin full of it herself. But at the time he had insisted she wasn't to call on him. As he put it, 'We don't want no bloody toe-rags putting two and two together and making a hundred.'

'How are you?' she asked tentatively, afraid he was going to tell her he was in hospital.

'Never better,' he said joyfully. 'But then I've got you to thank for that, getting Wendy to come over.'

'She's there?' she exclaimed. When his daughter hadn't turned up when Charlie last phoned she was afraid she wasn't ever going to.

'Right here by me side,' he laughed. 'And bloody lovely she looks an' all.'

'You aren't mad with me then for sticking my nose in?'

'Sweetheart!' he chuckled. 'When I answered the door last night and saw her standing there, all me principles flew out the bleedin' window. She showed me the letter you wrote her too. Christ, Charlie, you've got one helluva way with words. I'd have been sitting here for a twelve-month before I could put it the way you did.'

'I'm glad something ended happily,' she said, trying to gesture to Andrew what had happened.

'It's all gonna end happily,' he laughed. 'I'm going with Wendy on Monday to hear the closing speeches, even if I need a wheelchair to get in there. We'll be knocking back a few celebration bevvies on the way home too. Why don'cha join us?'

Charlie had already decided she couldn't bear the strain of attending even though Mrs Haagman had offered both Rita and herself the day off. But hearing Dave's happiness and his firm belief the Dexters would be found guilty changed her mind.

'Okay, I'll see you there,' she said. 'Now, how are you feeling?'

'On top of the world right now,' he said. 'I know I'm right near the end now. Next Friday I'm going into a hospice. I reckon it's only pure bloody-mindedness which has kept me around this long. But don't you worry your pretty little head about that. I shall be flying out on a cloud of glory.'

On Monday morning Charlie, Rita and Andrew joined Dave and Wendy in the front row of the public gallery with only a few short minutes for introductions and a brief chat before the court rose.

Wendy was prettier and younger-looking in the flesh than she'd appeared in snapshots. Her short fair hair was bleached by the Australian sun, her small uptilted nose was freckled, and it was clear by the expression in her tawny eyes and the way she constantly tucked her arm through her father's and held his hand that she was savouring every minute of the short time she had left with him. Dave looked so ill,

651

even thinner than the last time Charlie had seen him, the skin on his face hanging like a bloodhound's. But his smile was bright and he said he felt pretty good.

The prisoners were brought up and all conversation stopped. The twins looked just the same as they had when Charlie was in court before. They shuffled in, eyes down, faces pale and expressionless. But Daphne almost swaggered in, and it was clear she'd made a special effort with her appearance. She wore the same black suit as before, but with a turquoise blouse beneath which picked up the colour of her eyes. Her dark hair was loose too, falling in a sleek bob to her shoulders. She looked the picture of elegance and confidence.

The jury came in, and finally the court rose for the judge.

Brian Underwood's opening speech was calm and measured. He took up a stance by the jury and addressed everything to them. He started out with a plea for them to look at all the charges separately, to study the evidence and the testimonies of witnesses carefully, weighing them one against the other before they came to their final decision. 'You may think that on some charges only one person is guilty, that is, the hand that wielded the gun, knife, or other weapon. That isn't so, the three accused worked together, therefore they share a "Guilty" or a "Not Guilty" verdict.'

Charlie caught hold of both Andrew and Rita's hands as Underwood ran through the evidence on each of the charges. With regard to Jin Weish's murder he said, 'We don't know exactly how Jin Weish came to be in the Wapping warehouse on the night of the 20th June 1970, maybe he was taken there by force.

But it certainly wasn't chance. Not when three other people who had no business to be in that building, were there, armed with a gun. Yet we do know for certain that he was bound, then shot several times, at close range in both the head and chest, wrapped in a tarpaulin, weighted down, rowed out into the river and his body dumped. We also know for certain that the goods Jin Weish was awaiting at that time were stolen, to be recovered over two years later in a house belonging to Miss Dexter.

'Mr Kent, our witness, owner of the Wapping warehouse, saw the entire murder from a position in the room above. From him we heard that Daphne Dexter, driven by an extreme jealous rage because Weish wouldn't leave his wife for her, had planned not only to kill him, but also to ruin and bring disgrace to him and his family.

'Should you believe Mr Kent's testimony about the identity of the murderers and the events he witnessed? I believe you must. Not only were many of the details he gave us verified by experts, but I ask you to bear in mind that a man with a terminal disease has nothing to gain but clearing his own conscience by telling the whole truth. If you had doubts about him because he kept this secret for so long, just ask yourself now, would you have reported this crime if in doing so you put your own child's life in danger?'

Charlie looked along the bench at Dave and he smiled encouragingly.

Underwood then moved on to the charge of grievous bodily harm to Sylvia Weish. He pointed out emphatically that while there might be a lack of any real proof it was instigated by Daphne Dexter and carried out by her brothers, the jury must bear in mind the words 'in all probability'. Miss Dexter had stated she intended to decimate Weish's character and destroy everything he had achieved and loved. Crippling Sylvia Weish at such a time was a perfect way not only to wreak revenge on her personally, but also to create the suspicion that Jin Weish had disappeared because he was involved in serious crime.

Going on to each of the other charges, he reminded the jury how many of the witnesses for the prosecution were victims who had lived in fear for their own lives and those of their loved ones, yet had bravely put aside that fear, albeit belatedly, to see justice done. When he spoke of Rita Tutthill he was at his most eloquent. 'A young and pretty woman, whose only crime was to fall for a man Daphne Dexter had set her cap at. Did such an act warrant being tied down naked to a table, to be scored painstakingly with a butcher's knife, from her shoulders to her knees, like a piece of pork? One could perhaps understand a single thrust of a knife in a moment of jealous rage. But the scars on Miss Tutthill's body must have taken several hours to achieve. The monstrous cruelty of such an act must prove to you all that the accused are merciless, barbarians, remorseless in their desire to inflict pain on anyone who dared oppose or challenge them.

'Miss Tutthill was too afraid for her child to go to the police, or even to seek medical help. You have seen the photographs of the mutilation to her body, but let me remind you again, these scars were inflicted eight years earlier than the photographs you have seen. I beg you not only to imagine the pain such torture brought, but the terrible mental scars she still bears to this day. Her life since that fateful night has been a sad and lonely one, yet when she met young Charlie Weish and realized that Jin Weish's one-time mistress was none other than her torturer, she felt compelled to speak out if only to protect her young friend from similar hurt.'

Charlie's eyes filled with tears, and sensing Rita was crying too she caught hold of her hand and squeezed it tightly.

'Bearing all these atrocities in mind, can any of you now doubt Daphne Dexter chose to dispose of Ralph Peterson too?' Underwood's voice rose. Pausing for a moment to allow his words to sink in, he strode up and down in front of the jury, his hands clasped behind his back. 'Peterson had jilted her when she had her heart set on marrying him – almost certainly the attraction was his money. My learned friends for the defence would have us believe this is too weak a reason. I agree that for most of us reasonable people it is. Yet we have already seen and heard that Daphne Dexter is not a reasonable woman, but a vengeful, cunning and jealous woman.

'The defence went to some pains to discredit Peterson, yet he was a man of sixty-three who had amassed his fortune by building several highly reputable companies, with never the slightest hint of a stain on his character. Wasn't it far more likely that Miss Dexter engineered the evidence of his trips to peep-show clubs, and indeed lied to him about what she was using his loan for?' He paused again, looking hard at the jury.

'Now, the question of the twenty thousand pounds

he left Miss Dexter in his will. Proof he still retained some affection for her, as the defence have claimed? I think not. That will was dated nine months prior to his death. Miss Peterson said that her brother didn't express anxiety about Miss Dexter until seven months later. I ask you all to think when you last updated your will. A year ago, two? It isn't a high priority to most of us, is it?

'I believe Miss Dexter always knew the contents of that will, and guessing Peterson wasn't the type to think of rushing off to change it immediately, ordered her brothers to wait outside his Mayfair club late at night, and knock him down and kill him. At one stroke she rid herself of a humiliating failure and gained a considerable amount of money.'

Charlie looked along to Dave and saw he was grinning. He made a thumbs-up sign to her.

'Finally we have the abduction of Andrew Blake.' Underwood looked as if he was enjoying himself now; his face was more animated, his hands, which earlier had been clasped behind his back, were now making involuntary gestures.

'There can be no doubt in any of your minds that when Daphne Dexter drugged him, stripped him of his own clothes and drove him from Shepherd's Bush to her house in Kent, that she fully intended to murder him. What else was she intending to do with him, if not that? He was the boyfriend of Charlie Weish. She felt that in his investigations into the disappearance of Jin Weish, he was getting too close to the truth for comfort.

'Our learned council for the defence would have us doubt Blake was ever in that cellar. They produced a witness who said that on the first night of his so-called abduction he stayed at a guest-house in Eastbourne. Yet in a statement made to the police soon after their arrest, Barrington and Michael Dexter admitted they drove the unconscious Blake to The Manse that same Friday evening on instructions from their sister.

'We also heard from the police that another young man was in fact fraudulently using Blake's chequebook and his identity along the south coast, during the entire weekend while Blake was incarcerated. I would suggest this was a ploy to create the impression Blake's balance of mind was disturbed well before his "faked" suicide. Happily Blake escaped, as did Miss Weish, but I would like you all to think on what might have happened to these two young people if they hadn't managed it.'

Charlie's spirits had soared as Underwood summed up the case for the prosecution. She couldn't see any way that the defence could bring up a stronger argument. But the moment their man stepped forward, her heart sank. Just his height, good looks and bearing made little bespectacled Underwood with his North Country accent look inferior.

He smiled warmly at the jury in the manner of a man who had not a moment's doubt about his ability to sway the minds of others. He opened up with the standard plea that while the jury made their deliberations they were to bear in mind that if there was any 'reasonable doubt' against any of the charges, they must find the accused 'Not Guilty' on that count.

Starting with the charge of Jin Weish's murder, he launched into an assassination of the victim's character. He suggested that a man who had arrived in

England in 1949 with nothing but the clothes on his back, yet leapt from waiter in a Chinese restaurant to owning three Soho night-clubs, and then on to an extremely successful import business, was hardly likely to have achieved all this without skul-duggery, cutting corners and making a great many enemies.

'Are we really supposed to believe that a man as determined and successful as Weish obviously was would really give his most lucrative club to an ex-mistress, just to get her off his back?' he said with a look of amusement. 'Ask yourself too, why a woman as dynamic and beautiful as Miss Dexter, who had the world at her feet, would be so riddled with jealousy she'd plot for years to ruin an ex-lover and then execute him herself. It is a ridiculous idea.'

He paused just long enough to allow the jury to ponder on his words. Then, moving away a little and turning again, he raised his voice an octave.

'Jealousy is an emotion we've heard a great deal about in this court for the past few weeks, but I put it to you members of the jury that many of the witnesses whose evidence you have heard were motivated to come forward by just that emotion. How odd too that all these "terrified victims" living in fear of their lives – often it is reputed for years – all found their courage as soon as they heard the Dexters had been arrested! Isn't it far more likely that these "victims" with their sad little stories, perhaps with some petty grudge against the accused, entered into a feeding frenzy, and relished five minutes of fame, while getting back at those they were jealous of?'

Charlie wished she could see the jury's faces, but

they were hidden from view below the public gallery. She felt that each of them was slowly being turned around, and forgetting everything Underwood had put to them.

'I don't for one moment doubt that Mr Kent did see someone shoot Jin Weish, wrap up his body and row it out into the river. But we only have his word for it that it was the Dexters. Can we believe the word of a man who not only keeps quiet about this heinous crime he has observed, but happily sells his warehouse a few months later to the very people he claims committed it?

'As for the attack on Sylvia Weish, witnessed by her daughter, there isn't a shred of evidence that this crime was committed by either of the Dexters. It could have been anyone who had a grievance against Jin Weish,' he said firmly.

As the barrister went on through each separate charge, Charlie was astounded at how the man could discredit every witness with some sort of grudge motive. The bank manager who claimed to have been blackmailed and beaten up in an alley one night when he refused to pay any longer was dismissed as being 'as crooked as a corkscrew', later sacked by his bank for misappropriation of funds. The tenants who'd been intimidated were passed off as whining inadequates who were evicted fairly and squarely for non-payment of rent. As Charlie knew so little about what had passed when these people took the stand, she couldn't judge whether any of this was true. But she did know for certain that the Dexters had killed her father and maimed Rita, and she wondered how the man could sleep at night knowing that through his clever words the jury might let the Dexters back on to the streets to begin another reign of terror.

When he got to Rita's mutilation, Charlie felt like shouting out abuse at him, only Andrew's warning look and his firm hand on her arm prevented her.

'Can we really believe that Miss Dexter, a sensationally beautiful woman in her thirties, who has already proved herself an astute businesswoman, would be concerned about a club girl making eyes at her man?' he said scornfully. 'I think it is far more likely the jealousy was all on the side of the younger woman who knew she couldn't possibly be anything more than just a temporary plaything for a man like Mr Peterson.

'I suggest that the scars Miss Tutthill bears were executed by one of the many men she must have used in her days as "a good-time girl". That when she met young Charlie Weish, a grieving, bewildered girl whose deranged mother had so often brought up the name of "DeeDee", Miss Tutthill found she had the ideal audience to tell a different tale about her tragedy. She slotted fact and fiction together, conveniently using Daphne Dexter and her brothers as the scapegoat and villains. I have nothing but admiration for the determination Miss Weish showed in trying to uncover the mystery of her father's disappearance, but she was led along the wrong path by people who used her gullibility for their own devious ends.'

All at once Charlie knew that the justice she'd hoped for so long had failed her. Shrugging off Andrew's hand on her arm, she jumped up, pushed past the row of people on the bench and made for the courtroom door. Once outside in the fresh air, and seeing another pack of reporters, she ran down towards Ludgate Hill and kept on going, sobbing as she went.

'Where on earth has she gone?' Rita asked Andrew as they came out of the court and made their way downstairs, looking for Charlie. Soon after her hasty departure the judge had summed up the evidence and now the jury had retired to consider their verdict.

'I don't know,' Andrew replied, looking anxiously around the crowd of people who had been with them in the gallery.

'I think she was cut to the quick by what that defence geyser said,' Dave said in a strained voice behind him. 'I know I was.'

Andrew had almost forgotten Dave in his anxiety to find Charlie. He turned to see Wendy virtually holding her father up; he was ashen-faced, suddenly and dramatically weakened by what he'd heard in the court.

Charlie's disappearance no longer seemed so important. 'Come and sit down,' Andrew said, slipping his arm around Dave and supporting him over to a bench. 'I'll go and get you some water.'

Andrew returned a few minutes later to find Dave slumped against his daughter's shoulder, his face grey, his eyes almost closed. Rita had gone off to find medical help.

'He's all in,' Wendy said, her sunburnt face contorted with anxiety. 'I must get him home, it's been too much for him.'

'Just let me get my wind again,' Dave croaked. 'I'll be fine. Just wait for the verdict.'

Andrew held the plastic cup of water to Dave's lips,

but a sixth sense told him the man was much too ill to be taken home.

'Just wait for the verdict,' Dave repeated, but his words were barely audible.

Rita came hurrying back with a middle-aged woman in a nurse's uniform. She told them that she was one of the Old Bailey's medical team, and sat beside Dave to take his pulse.

'He must go to hospital immediately,' she said, looking at Wendy. 'We do get quite a few people taken ill in here, but this is more than just shock. Bart's is very close, they'll take good care of him.'

An ambulance arrived within minutes of being called. Dave was lifted on to a trolley and wheeled out past the scores of reporters waiting in the street. As Wendy got in beside her father, she called out to Andrew, 'Find Charlie and bring her to the hospital. I know Dad will want to see her.' She didn't have to say 'one last time', it was written all over her face.

The ambulance pulled away with the sirens blasting. Andrew looked at Rita questioningly. 'Where do we look for her?'

Rita was still smarting at what the defence had suggested about her, and she was acutely aware that journalists were not only photographing her but had taken pictures of Dave Kent being carried into the ambulance. She felt incensed by such insensitivity. Charlie's disappearance was an excuse to let her anger out.

'I don't bloody well know,' she snapped. 'Just when I think she'd learned to behave like an adult, she reverts to being the spoiled little girl again. Maybe she even believed what that creep said about me.'

'Of course she didn't,' Andrew said alarmed by Rita's anger. 'But I'll have to go and find her.'

He went over to the journalists and asked if anyone had seen Charlie come out. On being directed towards Ludgate Hill, he grabbed Rita's arm and took her with him. He didn't think she should be left alone at such a time.

Charlie was close to Blackfriars Bridge, sobbing her heart out as she looked over the Embankment wall at the Thames. Since her father's funeral back in Dartmouth she had comforted herself that he was back in a place he loved, but now, as she looked into the dirty, green-grey water, she was reminded that this was his real grave – the river had washed over his body for over two years, his flesh disintegrating into it, then flowed with the tide out to sea.

The anger which had made her run out of the court was replaced now by despair. For six months she had placed all her faith in British justice, but all she'd received was humiliation. By tomorrow the whole nation would be hearing her father was a crook, her mother a deranged ex-stripper, Rita, Andrew, Dave and herself all liars. Where could she go from here? All her illusions were shattered, she had no strength left to fight any more battles. The river looked just like her thoughts, muddy, slow and tainted. She might just as well fling herself into it and be done with the struggle.

'Charlie!'

She involuntarily turned her head at the sound of her name, to see Andrew running across the road, with Rita tottering behind him on her high heels.

Charlie was dismayed. Now she was being robbed of the one act which might give her permanent peace.

'Come with us,' Andrew called out as he came closer still. 'Dave's been taken to hospital. Wendy wants you to see him. I think it's the end for him.' He was right in front of her now, panting furiously, his blue eyes wide with concern for a man he'd only met for the first time today.

'What on earth were you thinking of, coming down here?' Rita shouted out breathlessly before Charlie could even get her thoughts together.

Charlie glanced over her shoulder at the river. 'I don't know,' she whispered. 'I just couldn't,' she broke off, unable to say the truth, that she couldn't cope any longer.

'Are you all right?' Rita asked. All at once her anger at the girl faded.

Charlie pulled herself together, suddenly remembering that Rita's character had been more cruelly attacked than anyone's. 'I'm fine now,' she managed to get out. 'What's this about Dave?'

Andrew put two fingers in his mouth and whistled down a taxi cruising past. 'Come on,' he said. 'To the hospital. I'll tell you on the way.'

Dave was in a small room just off the main Casualty Department. That he'd been put to bed immediately in a quiet place suggested that the nursing staff knew there was little they could do for him.

Rita stayed outside, but Andrew went in with Charlie. Wendy was on one side of the bed, holding her father's hand, a nurse was on the other taking his pulse. Dave was conscious and he tried to smile as he saw Charlie.

'Glad you came,' he whispered.

'I'll leave you for a few moments,' the nurse said, and indicated the bell. 'Ring if you need me.'

'Oh, Dave.' Charlie moved into the place left vacant by the nurse. 'I'm sorry I ran off without saying anything, I just got upset.'

'Me too,' he said weakly. 'That defence man was a slime ball. But we ain't finished yet, we got to wait for the verdict.'

'Dad made me ring the court and ask them to phone here when the jury comes back in,' Wendy said, her eyes swimming with tears. 'I keep trying to tell him it doesn't matter any more.'

Charlie knew Wendy meant she would rather her father rested and regained his strength than concern himself with what was going on in the jury room, but then she probably didn't realize that only willpower had kept Dave alive this long, and a 'Guilty' verdict would mean he could die a happy man. His dogged single-mindedness shamed her. She had given up even before hearing the verdict.

'It's going to be "Guilty",' she lied, knowing she intended to tell him that even if it wasn't true. 'I spoke to the Clerk of the Court and he said we weren't to worry.'

Dave looked at her hard. His eyes seemed to tell her he knew that wasn't true. 'Let me speak to Andrew,' he whispered. 'Just for a minute on our own.'

As Wendy and Charlie left reluctantly, Andrew moved closer to Dave, wondering what the man had to say to him.

'I wish we'd had time to get acquainted,' Dave said with some difficulty, his breathing laboured. 'But I feel as if I know you from what Charlie told me. If they do get acquitted, will you do something for me?'

'Of course,' Andrew said, leaning closer so he could hear better.

'Make Wendy get back to Australia fast, no hanging around clearing up the flat and stuff. Then get yourself and Charlie somewhere safe too. You understand what I mean?'

Andrew felt his legs tremble. Although he was certain the Dexters wouldn't have the gall to come looking for any of them, it was still a frightening thought. 'I will, I promise,' he said.

'Good lad.' Dave attempted a weak smile. 'Your Charlie's a gem. You look after her and treat her right.'

While Rita and Andrew stayed in the waiting room, Charlie and Wendy sat either side of Dave's bed. He drifted in and out of consciousness, but the girls talked to each other across the bed so he would know he wasn't alone. How they had managed to hold a conversation Charlie didn't know. They were strangers until a few hours ago, the only thing they had in common was the sick man lying between them, and that was a subject which couldn't be discussed now. So Wendy talked about her life in Australia with Grant and Martin, and Charlie told her about Salcombe and Ivor, steering the subject away from anything to do with her parents. They were both very aware that as each hour passed Dave was gradually growing weaker.

Now and again as Wendy was talking, Charlie found herself slipping back in time to her childhood. Walking down Beacon Road towards the ferry, her father holding one hand, her mother the other, swinging her up in the air and laughing at her squeals of excitement. Sitting by the fire with them both on a cold winter's day toasting crumpets. Swimming at Slapton Sands with them, and her father diving under the water pretending to be a shark and biting their legs. Unimportant little memories perhaps, yet reminders of happy times together as a family before Daphne Dexter cast her evil spells on their peace and security.

It was only now as this man lay dying, his daughter talking to remind him she was beside him, that she saw the importance of such memories. They were the evidence she needed of her parents' love for one another, and her. The headstone in the cemetery which marked their graves only marked their deaths, their lives were inside her heart and in her memory. Whatever the outcome of this trial she must remember that, and put aside bitterness. Rising above all the grief, hurt and pain and becoming a happy and successful woman was the only way to compensate her parents for their sacrifices.

At half past three Andrew came rushing in with the news that a message had come to say the jury were going back in. He suggested that he and Rita should go back to the court, and Charlie urged him to hurry back with the verdict.

Dave rallied a little then. 'How many hours have they been out?' he asked.

'About four and a bit,' Wendy said, stroking his forehead.

'Not long for something like this,' he whispered and drifted off again.

The wait was agonizing. Charlie sat rigidly on her chair, watching Dave, offering up silent prayers that if the verdict was 'Not Guilty' he'd die before Andrew got back. Yet she knew the man's will would keep him going; every now and then he would clench his fists as if reminding himself he had unfinished business.

She so much wished too that she could find something to say to Wendy to make this less painful for her. She could feel the girl's sorrow, see the desolation in her eyes. But while Dave's heart was still beating, how could she offer words of comfort without drawing even more attention to his approaching death? They each held one of his hands, bonded silently together by their feelings for this man.

'His hands feel so soft,' Wendy whispered. 'When I was a little girl I used to ask him why they were so rough and hard. He laughed and said, "All the better to smack you with." But he never smacked me.'

'I did,' Dave said hoarsely a few seconds later, as if the remark had woken him. 'I smacked your face when you told me you were pregnant. I've always been ashamed of that. Grant was the best present you ever gave me.'

'I don't remember the smack,' Wendy said, bending to kiss him. 'I only remember knowing you would always look after me, whatever I did.'

Charlie bit back tears, wondering what she would have said to her father if she'd got to him before he died. She didn't recall any smacks, angry words, only the way he always swung her round in his arms every time he came home.

Over an hour had passed since Andrew and Rita left. It was nearly five now and the rush-hour traffic would be heavy. But an hour seemed far too long to hear a verdict and get back. Could they be afraid to come back with bad news?

A doctor and nurse came in to examine Dave again, and the girls waited outside.

'Go on back in,' the doctor said as he came out, folding his stethoscope and putting it in his pocket. His grey eyes were gentle with sympathy and he touched Wendy's shoulder comfortingly. 'I'm afraid there's nothing more we can do but keep him comfortable and free from pain.'

It was quarter to six when Andrew rushed in panting. His wide smile of triumph said it all.

'Guilty?' Charlie asked, jumping up.

'Guilty on all charges,' Andrew gasped out. 'Life imprisonment for all three of them.'

Charlie wanted to scream with delight, but she had to restrain herself to just a wide grin.

'Did you hear that, Dad?' Wendy laid her hand on her father's cheek and pinched it gently. 'Guilty on all charges.'

His eyes opened wide, the pale brown irises and the yellow whites all blending together to give that curious cat-like look Charlie had noticed on their first meeting. His mouth curved into a smile.

'So they believed me,' he said. 'Thank you, God.'

He drifted off again and Wendy asked them if they would leave. 'You've done your bit for him,' she said resolutely, but her lip was trembling and her eyes glistening with tears. 'It's time you went.'

Charlie bent to kiss Dave, her eyes welling up. The grief she felt at that moment was as keen as she'd felt at her father's funeral. 'You're a good man,' she whispered. 'I can't thank you enough for giving me back my dad. I'm going to miss you so much.'

She went round the bed and hugged Wendy, too choked up to speak, then quickly turned and followed Andrew out, struggling not to break down.

Rita was waiting, and as Charlie came towards her, she ran and flung her arms around her. 'We did it,' she said, her voice squeaky with excitement. 'We got them what they deserve.'

It was the strangest moment for Charlie. She shared Rita's jubilation, together they'd struck out for justice, and today they'd seen it done. But she couldn't scream and shout with joy when the man who had been instrumental in bringing that verdict was dying.

'It's wonderful, marvellous, and no one was braver than you,' Charlie said softly, hugging her friend with tears rolling down her cheeks. 'You're the best friend anyone could ever have.'

She wanted to get away from the hospital, to feel her joy unrestrained, but as soon as the three of them were outside the main doors, Charlie stood still. 'I can't go,' she said. 'You two go on home on your own.'

'But Wendy doesn't want you there, and we should be celebrating,' Andrew argued. 'I want to tell you about Daphne's face –'

Charlie cut him short. 'It's not going to be long,' she said. 'And I'm not going in there again. I just want

670

to be waiting for Wendy when she comes out. She hasn't got anyone else.'

Rita nodded in understanding. 'We'll see you back at the flat then.'

It was half past seven when Charlie got home. Dave had died just half an hour after Andrew and Rita had left. Wendy said he woke again, told her he loved her and just slipped away.

They had sat together in the waiting room, cried and comforted each other for some time, until Wendy said she must go back and see a friend of Dave's who lived near him. As Charlie saw her into a taxi, Wendy said she would phone the following evening.

Andrew hugged Charlie as she related what had happened. 'Well, that puts paid to any celebrations,' he said in a husky voice, his eyes soft with sorrow. 'I've already rung Beryl and my folks. They'll be opening a bottle of sherry, Beryl's probably giving everyone drinks on the house by now. But we'll have to wait.'

Charlie thought for a minute, leaning her head on Andrew's shoulder. She felt drained and exhausted, yet as Wendy had weepingly pointed out, her father had gone out on his cloud of glory just as he hoped.

'We will celebrate,' she said, looking up and smiling. 'That's what he would have wanted us to do.'

Rita beamed and rushed out into the kitchen, coming back with a bottle of sparkling wine. 'I couldn't run to champers,' she said as she poured three glasses. 'Maybe when I sell my story!'

'To Dave,' Charlie said, lifting her glass. 'For his courage and honesty.'

671

'Dave,' Rita and Andrew repeated, clinking their glasses.

'A second toast,' Charlie said with a smile after they had all taken a large swig. 'To golden futures for us all.'

'To golden futures for us all,' Andrew and Rita said. 'And happy-ever-afters,' Rita added with a wide smile.

They topped up their glasses and sat down. 'And now,' said Charlie. 'Tell me about the bitch's face.'

'She just crumpled,' Rita laughed. 'She couldn't believe it! I never knew revenge could taste so sweet.'

'She went all tense first,' Andrew said, standing up to demonstrate. 'She kind of puffed up, like this.' He took a deep breath and held it, his neck stiff and his eyes almost coming out of his head. 'She looked around at the jury like she really didn't believe what she'd heard, then it was like someone stuck a pin in her. She just seemed to shrink before our eyes. Rita laughed really loudly. I had to put my hand over her mouth.'

Charlie looked from one joyful face to the other and laughed too. 'What about the twins?'

'They just stared, then bent their heads,' Rita giggled. 'I felt like yelling out it was too late to say their prayers. You could have heard a pin drop in the court. But then, once they'd been led away and the judge went too, it all went wild. People were cheering and crying, I went down and hugged Underwood, and sneered at Cunningham. I wanted to kiss every member of the jury, but they'd been led out by then.'

'I wish I'd been there,' Charlie said enviously, yet with a pang of guilt she remembered the thoughts she'd had down by the river. That seemed so long ago now, and so pathetic.

'Underwood was very sorry you weren't, he told me to tell you to try and put it all aside now. He wished you every happiness.'

While Andrew and Rita reminisced gleefully about things which had been said in the courtroom, Charlie sank into reflection. It was so very sad that Dave had died, yet he had passed away content and without pain. Rita would never lose her scars, but facing what had happened to her had freed her. What of herself, however? She'd avenged both her parents' deaths, and discovered so much about both of them, but what now?

Looking across to Andrew, all at once she saw the answer. His dark hair was flopping in his eyes, his face was radiant with happiness as he talked to Rita. He had been beside her throughout all this, making her laugh when she was sad, calming her when she got overwrought, loving her with passion and tenderness. All these past months she hadn't projected her thoughts beyond the trial, almost as if she was on a path through woods which ended with a brick wall.

But there was no brick wall. She had stepped out of the woods on to a far wider path bathed in sunshine. She had Andrew by her side, Rita as a friend for life, she had almost got through her business studies classes, a great deal of money would eventually come to her from her father's life insurance, and she had those treasures still in the vault in Exeter – something she had never told Andrew or Rita about.

Suddenly she felt lighter, warmer and bubbly inside. 'Let's go down to the pub,' she called out, making Andrew and Rita turn in surprise. 'I want to get totally legless, and kiss the whole world.'

'Well, you can start with me,' Andrew said, catching hold of her hands and pulling her up to her feet. 'Cunningham might think I'm a daft boy scout, but I've got the most beautiful girl in the world, and he's been defeated!'

As Andrew kissed her, tears of joy prickled at Charlie's eyes. Of all the good things in store for her, he was the best of all.

'Have I ever said how lucky I think I am to have you?' she asked, smiling into his eyes.

'No, you haven't,' he said, grinning a little sheepishly. 'But I had intended to remind you.'

Chapter Twenty-two

January 1977

Detective Inspector Ozzie Hughes parked his car at the end of Church Road, Paddington, slipped on his sheepskin coat and walked back studying the shops as he went. It was a bitterly cold afternoon and already dark, but many of the small shops still had their Christmas displays in the windows, and with the bright lights from within, it looked festive and cheering.

Hughes had come to this area because of Charlie Weish but today he wasn't on duty, just out shopping for a silver wedding anniversary present for Ursula, his wife. Shortly before Christmas, Ursula had shown him an article in a magazine about shops which specialized in unusual gifts. She had been attracted by a very pretty early Victorian candelabra, which was available at 'Charlie's' in Church Road. Ozzie felt it had to be more than a strange coincidence that a shop of that name was right in the same street where Charlie Weish had once lived with Rita Tutthill. He had decided to check it out.

Over the last four years, Ozzie Hughes had often wondered how life had treated Charlie since the

Dexters' trial. Normally he never gave witnesses, victims or even villains another thought once a case was brought to a satisfactory end. But his association with Jin Weish at the start of his career, all those years he'd spent investigating the Dexters, and indeed his admiration for Charlie's spirit and determination, had kept her in his mind. He'd smiled back at the time of the trial when he read in the newspapers how Charlie had vowed that if Daphne Dexter was acquitted, she'd be on the woman's back for the rest of her life. He reckoned she would have been too. She'd been like a little terrier from the outset.

No one had been happier than himself when the Dexters got sent down for life. He considered it one of the high points in his career, if not *the* highest. Other criminals had already stepped forward to take their place, sometimes he felt he was swimming in treacle, but it still gave him a rosy glow to think of Daphne Dexter locked up in Holloway.

Ozzie stopped dead in his tracks when he spotted the shop across the road. It was impossible to miss, painted a rich dark green with brass spotlights above the two large windows, and he stood for a moment appraising it. Even from the distance he was from it, it beckoned to be visited, for it was like an Aladdin's cave stuffed with curios, furniture and huge oriental ginger jars. A stuffed bear wearing a Santa Claus hat and a tinsel collar standing in one of the brightly lit windows added an appealing and comical touch which was irresistible.

As he watched a couple came out, the man carrying what looked very much like an Edwardian lady's writing desk. They laid it in the back of an estate car, covered it with a blanket and then drove away.

Ozzie walked across the street and peered in through the window. A girl in a red dress was bent over a desk at the back of the shop writing something down. Her hair gleamed like black satin under the shop lights, swinging forward and concealing her face, but it was unmistakably Charlie.

As she straightened up and turned, Ozzie's heart gave an odd little flutter to see that the pretty young girl he remembered had grown into a very beautiful woman. She looked so elegant yet dramatic in red. Her high cheekbones seemed more prominent, and her skin was like pale gold. When she spotted him, she inclined her head to one side, as if considering why he looked familiar. Then suddenly she smiled and ran to the door to open it.

'Detective Inspector Hughes!' she said. 'Are you casing the joint, passing by, or actually looking for me? Whichever it is, do come in, it's freezing out there.'

Ozzie hadn't had a moment of shyness since he was a lad, but the unexpected warmth of her welcome, the way she grabbed his hand and drew him in, threw him for a moment. A little awkwardly, he explained about the article in the magazine.

'So you didn't hear on the grapevine that I'd followed in Dad's footsteps then?' she asked, her almond eyes alight with real interest.

'No,' he admitted. 'I often wondered about you, but heard nothing. You look as if you are doing well.'

'I am,' she said, but there was no trace of smugness in her face. 'Now let me make you a cup of tea and

677

then we can chat. I'm sure I can leave a senior police officer alone in my shop without a few goodies ending up in his pockets?'

While she nipped out to the back of the shop, Ozzie roamed around looking at everything. She had an enormous stock, antiques mixed superbly with reproductions and many oriental items which looked ancient, but probably weren't. Locked glass cases held jewellery and smaller valuable items, small trinkets were grouped under spotlights. Everything was displayed to perfection, from an old wicker doll's pram full of plants to a buttoned-back chair seating a collection of old dolls and teddy bears, and a dresser loaded with pretty china. He thought he could be in here for a week and not see everything.

'Now, sit down and tell me how you are,' she said as she came back with tea and fruitcake. She put the tray on the desk and cleared a chair for him. She perched on the edge of an old club fireguard.

'I'm the one who asks the questions,' he laughed. 'Anyway, there's nothing new in my life, just plodding along as always.' He spotted a wedding ring on her finger. 'You got married!'

'Yes,' she laughed. 'To Andrew, of course. Just after he got his honours degree.'

Just the way she had to mention the 'honours' said how proud she was of him.

'And what's he doing now?' Ozzie asked.

'Working for IBM. He's a bit of a hot shot,' Charlie said. 'Always off to Japan and America to study the latest in technology. But he's at home at the moment, and I'm really happy because he won't be going away again until the spring.'

'So how did all this come about?' Ozzie waved a hand at all the stock. 'Early influences?'

She nodded. 'I guess, but I've had to learn as I go along. My basic rule of thumb is only to buy what I like.'

They chatted for some little time about antiques and Ozzie said how much his wife would like the shop. 'How did you manage to get it though?' he asked curiously – at his rough estimation the stock alone must run into thousands of pounds.

'Dad,' she said simply. 'He was a very canny buyer. You remember the stuff the Dexters stole from him? Well, that's what really got me going.'

'But I thought it was mostly rugs and jade?' he said.

'It was. But I auctioned it once it became mine.'

Over their tea she explained how she started off the summer after the trial with a stall in Chelsea antiques market selling bric-à-brac. 'It was a real hand-to-mouth business,' she giggled. 'Lots of fun, but I wasn't getting anywhere, and Andrew and I wanted to get married. We did it on a shoe-string anyway, down in Salcombe, with just a week's honeymoon there afterwards, and found a couple of rooms in Paddington which we furnished from junk shops. Then just before I was twenty the money finally came through from Dad's life insurance, but I was shocked to find I wasn't allowed to touch it till I was twenty-one. That made me really mad! We needed it right away, our rent was so high we had a job to make ends meet, and I had nowhere to store anything. It seems preposterous to me that I was expected to wait another whole year.'

Ozzie chuckled. At his time of life a year meant nothing, but then he had seen from the outset that this was a young lady who expected immediate action about everything. 'So what did you do, hassle them like you did me?'

'I certainly did,' she said, her eyes twinkling. 'And I read everything I could get my hands on about inheritance. Finally I managed to discover a bit of a loophole, that the executor would be allowed to use his discretion if the heir was in need. Well, I was in need, wasn't I? I needed, and was entitled to, a proper home. I reckoned if I was to use the money to buy a freehold property, they couldn't refuse.

'When this place came up for sale I knew it was perfect. There was a lovely spacious flat upstairs, I could run the shop, and it was a good investment. So I kept jerking the executor's chain until he agreed.'

She told him about how initially she had hardly anything to sell, but then she got the news that her father's goods were now hers. 'Oddly enough they were only too glad for me to have them! It would cost a fortune to keep them in store otherwise.

'I went through it all carefully, but it scared me because it was all so valuable, more like you get in Bond Street shops. I couldn't launch into a business straight off with that kind of stuff. I knew I'd get ripped off, if not burgled, the moment I displayed it,' she admitted. 'So I got some advice from a retired valuer I knew, and he arranged for a reputable auction room to handle it.

'It turned out to be the smartest thing to have done. The sale went beyond my wildest dreams, so I invested half the money, and took a couple of months off travelling around buying stuff I really could handle. Gradually it turned into this.'

Ozzie thought Jin Weish would have been very proud of her. 'How old are you now, Charlie?' he asked. It seemed incredible to him that someone so young could be so astute.

'Twenty-three next month,' she said with a grin. 'Looking back, I'm glad I didn't get that insurance money for so long. Having to wait and use my wits taught me a thing or two. Once we did get the rest, we went a bit wild. We did the flat up, bought a nice car, had an expensive holiday in America. But by then the shop was paying its way too.'

Ozzie thought she was understating her success, both she and the shop glowed with it.

'So where do you go from here?' he asked.

'At the moment I'm really happy just how we are,' she said, looking around her with obvious contentment. 'Maybe in a few years we'll buy a house in the country, and have some children, but I get a buzz out of buying and selling. I know everyone round here, it's a great place to live and work.'

'Are you still friends with Rita? Is she still in the flat across the road?'

Charlie smiled with affection. 'We'll be best friends for ever. But no, she's not in the flat any more, she bought a guest-house in Broadstairs two years ago with the compensation she got from the Dexters. It's a lovely place, right on the sea, and she's the perfect landlady, she cossets her guests as if they were her family.'

Ozzie smiled wryly. He could just imagine Rita as a landlady – her days as a night-club hostess had been good training for her. 'Is there a man in her life now?'

Charlie laughed. 'Several. But the important one is her son Paul. He's at Nottingham University now, studying horticulture, but he spends all his holidays with her and when he gets his degree he'll find a job somewhere near her. She really did get her happy ending.'

'No more nightmares about the past for either of you then?' he said gently.

'Not now,' she said, suddenly very serious. 'I've had black moments, sudden spells of anger that Dad and Mum aren't here to see what I've done and be proud of me.'

'How do you cope with that?' he asked, reaching out and taking her hand in his.

She looked down at his big hands holding hers and half smiled. 'I tell myself I'd have nothing of my own if they were still alive. I'd probably be married to a "good catch", some boring ex-public schoolboy making his way up his daddy's company. You see, I came to realize that was what Dad wanted for me. That house in Dartmouth, my good school, it was all to that end.'

'All parents who've had it tough as a child want that for their kids,' he said reprovingly. 'I know I want something better for mine.'

'I don't mean I blame Dad and Mum for wanting it,' she said quickly. 'I'm very grateful they gave me such a good foundation. But its rather tragic to think that if they had lived, and they'd continued to shield me from the harsh realities of life, one day they might have looked at that self-centred, egotistical daughter of theirs and been dismayed at how she turned out.

The saddest thing to me is that it took their deaths for me to discover who they really were, and for me to find out that I liked the parts of them they'd kept hidden far more than the false image they had created for my benefit.'

Ozzie smiled. 'You are so very like Jin,' he said. 'He was a deep thinker too.'

'Why didn't you tell me you knew him right from the start?' she asked.

Ozzie shrugged. 'I'm first and foremost a policeman,' he said. 'Had I let it out that first day I wouldn't have been able to do my job properly. But I can tell you now that I liked him and your mother very much. They'd both had appalling childhoods, almost certainly many people had tried to corrupt them, yet they found one another, clung to each other and somehow together managed to rise above all the ugliness of Soho with their integrity intact. That's where you get your strength from, Charlie. And don't you ever forget it.'

Charlie moved from her perch to hug him. She had been touched that such a senior policeman cared enough to look her up, but now he'd told her his opinion of her parents it was confirmation of her suspicions that he'd made sure the charges against the Dexters stuck, for a little more than mere duty.

Ozzie held her silently. He had a lump in his throat, but he was so very glad he'd come in here today. 'Now, about this present for my wife,' he said huskily after a few moments.

Charlie had only just locked the shop after Hughes left, when Andrew came home. He flattened his face

683

against the window with his tongue out so he looked like a lunatic. Giggling, Charlie unlocked the door again.

His old student image had gone: hair neatly cut, a dark suit, and an expensive leather briefcase in his hand instead of the battered canvas bag he used to hump his books around in. But the essential boyishness was all still there in his twinkling blue eyes and his ready smiles. He might be IBM's golden boy destined for an illustrious career, but he still didn't take himself very seriously.

'How's my little Lotus Flower tonight?' he said, kissing her lingeringly. 'Is there enough in the coffers for us to go out to dinner?'

'I should think so,' she laughed. 'But why do you want to go out? Is my cooking still so bad?'

'Not at all. But I thought a celebration was in order. I've got to go to Hong Kong next week, and you can come with me.'

Charlie just stared at him for a moment. She'd wanted to go there for years.

'Really?' she gasped, a wild excitement welling up inside her.

'Now, would I say such a thing if it wasn't true?' he asked, laughing at her flushing face. He'd been married to her for three years, known her for five, yet he still got a kick out of seeing her lovely eyes dance with excitement. 'Two weeks in a swish hotel. I won't be working all the time, so we'll be able to shop, hunt out stuff for the business, and we can put out feelers about your dad's family.'

He knew that last item would thrill her, it was something she'd wanted to do ever since the trial. She threw herself into his arms, wriggling with glee.

'I love you, Andrew Blake,' she said, covering his face with kisses. 'You're the best thing that ever happened to me.'

'We'd better ring Beryl, we said we were going down there for the weekend and we won't really have time for that now. Do you want to do it now, while I have a shave and a bath?'

'Okay,' she replied kissing him again. 'Make yourself scrumptious. I expect I'll have plans for you later tonight.'

'Going immediately,' he said, playfully pushing her aside. As he got to the stairs at the back of the shop which led up to their flat, he looked back. 'How about a taster before we go out?'

Charlie stuck her tongue out at him. 'Shave and then we'll see,' she said.

Once Andrew had gone, she sat down by the phone, pausing for a moment's reflection on how lucky she was. Andrew was her love, her best friend, a rock to lean on, and her clown when she needed one. She had a beautiful home, security, dozens of friends and a job she loved.

The business had been built on love, the foundations laid during the trial while she took the business studies course, the inspiration and the capital from her father. Andrew's father and Ivor had built the shelves, Dora Blake made all the exquisite lace-trimmed cushions which Charlie not only sold but made the shop look pretty. Andrew had rewired it and organized all the lights which gave it character. Beryl and Rita were her scouts for country house auctions where she got most of the best items. Even Charlie's flair for display was an influence from Sylvia; as a small child she'd watched her mother arranging pictures or ornaments until they looked just right. The buying and selling was her own part, and she loved it.

The love they'd all put into it showed. Charlie knew people sensed something extraordinary the moment they looked through the window. It brought them back in, time and time again.

She wondered what her father would say if he knew that she'd never sold his treasures, that those valuable miniatures adorned the chimney breast in her sitting room, the jade and silver in a glass cabinet, her mother's jewellery in the safe, worn occasionally when she and Andrew went somewhere smart.

It had been tempting to sell them when she and Andrew first got married. The two rooms they found were cramped and squalid and they couldn't afford anything better. But Andrew had stopped her. As he so wisely said at the time, 'They are all you've got left of your parents. They represent everything they strived for when they bought "Windways", and what they wanted for you.'

That was one of the things she loved most about Andrew. He was far-sighted, thought things through. He understood what was truly important, like love, family and inner peace.

On their wedding day, his father had made a little speech, and said he was overjoyed to have a daughter at last. And that was what she'd become to them; Charlie even called her in-laws Mum and Dad. When they came to stay for weekends, Mum liked nothing better than to serve in the shop, while Dad pottered around mending and fixing things. They said their trips to London to see their children were the high spots of the year.

On top of that they had Ivor and Beryl too. Ivor had given Charlie away at the little church in Salcombe. He trimmed his beard, had his hair cut, and even bought a new suit. Every time they went down to visit them he asked how much longer he was to wait for a grandchild. He said his dream was to take him or her out in the *MaryAnn*.

Charlie picked up the phone, smiling to herself as she glanced at her watch, it was just after six. In the Victoria Inn Ivor would be sitting on his favourite stool with a pint, Beryl would be leaning on the bar talking to him.

'So you're off to Hong Kong, eh!' Ivor said as he took over from Beryl. 'Well, that beats Salcombe in January. Give my regards to Wan Chai, I had some great nights in the bars there.'

'I'm hoping I might be able to trace Dad's family,' she said reprovingly. 'Not looking at the places he got inspiration for his own club.'

'All right, Miss Toffee Nose,' he chuckled. 'But that's exactly where you might get a lead. There's a bar called the Red Dragon, anyone will direct you to it. It's owned by a chap called Red MacDonald. Scots, as you'd imagine, with a Chinese wife. Remember me to him, we were buddies. He'll put you on the right track.'

After a brief chat Charlie put the phone down and went upstairs. She met Andrew on the landing wearing nothing but a towel around his middle, clean-shaven and smelling of soap.

'That outfit suits you,' she said, running her fingers down his bare chest. 'Don't get dressed. I'm feeling a bit peckish.'

Andrew took her hand and led her into their bedroom. It was a huge room at the back of the building, decorated and furnished in a Moorish style with the large, low bed surrounded by sumptuous drapes, fur rugs and kelims on the walls. Charlie had found a local craftsman to make Arabesque-style shutters for the windows and matching doors for the fitted wardrobes.

Andrew lit four candles, then turned out the main light. The room immediately took on the character of a scene from the *Arabian Nights*.

'What would my Lotus Flower have me do to her?' he said, coming up behind her to kiss her neck, at the same time unzipping her dress.

'I don't mind, just lots of it,' Charlie sighed, already aroused by his lips on her skin. Many of her friends had said that after a year or two of marriage she'd get bored with love-making, but she hadn't. It was still as exciting as it had been in the early days of snatched opportunities in Andrew's attic room in Jack Straw's Castle.

'I think then we'll have the seduction of the new concubine,' he murmured, dropping her dress to the floor and lowering the straps of her slip from her shoulders and cupping his hands round her breasts. 'It takes a very, very, long time, because she needs gentle arousing.'

'Umm,' Charlie sighed as he slowly and sensually stripped her of panties, suspender belt and stockings. She could feel his erection against her buttocks, but she knew in this particular game he wouldn't remove the towel around him for ages.

He moved away from her, picked up one of the fur rugs and laid it on the bed, then picking her up in his arms laid her down on it.

The soft fur against her bare skin, the candlelight and Andrew's practised caresses turned the snack she had expected into an erotic feast. The holiday next week, the business, everything disappeared but the need to love one another.

It was over an hour later, as they lay sleepily in one another's arms, that Charlie thought more about Hong Kong and what Ivor had said. Maybe Jin had no family left to trace – somehow she couldn't imagine he never tried to find out what had happened to them. But Red MacDonald might know someone who knew her father and could tell her about his early life. Yet even if they discovered nothing, it would be wonderful to see the place where Jin had learned his English, and his manners. She too needed to get in touch with the Chinese part of her.

Andrew cuddled her tighter. 'Thinking about finding family?' he asked.

'Umm,' she said, remembering too that she hadn't yet told him about Hughes's visit. 'Maybe there won't be any.'

'Will that make you sad?'

She thought for a moment. 'A bit, I expect, but if I do feel dejected I'll just remind myself how much I've already got.'

'You mean your outstandingly brilliant husband, your luxurious home and a few bob stashed away in the bank?' he said, leaning up on his elbow to grin down at her.

'Well yes, I appreciate all those good things,' she

laughed. 'But just having them isn't what makes me happy. Mum had them too, remember, and it didn't make her happy, did it? I'm just so lucky I feel secure enough inside that if anything bad should happen again in the future and we lost the house and the money, as long as I still had you, it wouldn't break me.'

'I'm relieved to hear that,' he grinned. 'I'd need someone to cling to if we lost everything else.'

'That's it in a nutshell,' she laughed. 'We know because of all we've been through to arrive here that we'll always have each other. The wind can blow, evil people can come along and foul things up, but at the heart of it all is us two, clinging together. Nothing and no one can tear us apart.'

'Unless of course it's hunger,' he said, wriggling away from her. 'I cling much better on a full stomach, and right now a fillet steak, chips and mushrooms is luring me away.'

Charlie leapt out of bed and ran towards the bathroom. 'Five minutes and I'll be with you,' she shouted back at him. 'I can stand a steak coming between us, as long as it's big enough for two.'

Number one bestselling author

LESLEY PEARSE

Now in hardback for the first time

TILL WE MEET AGAIN

'You killed two people,' Beth said. 'You're likely to spend the rest of your life in prison because of it.' Susan looked up again. Her eyes had just a faint spark in them now. 'It was worth it,' she said.

When they were children, Beth Powell and Susan Wright spent every August together in Stratford-upon-Avon. Susan was shy and plump, Beth was tall and skinny. Both girls were loners because of their unhappy family backgrounds: Susan had a live-in granny suffering from dementia and Beth a vicious bully of a father. But alone together, never admitting their problems, they were happy. Until fate intervened and separated them.

It's twenty-nine years later when they meet again.

Susie is a down-and-out who has shot two people in cold blood and Beth is the lawyer allocated to defend her. And as Beth prepares her defence by trawling through her old friend's tragic past, she has to face her own demons. Yet the love both women had for one another as children is still there, even as the evidence against Susie mounts up. A love which must be stronger than the traumas of their past. Because, for one of them, there can be no happy ending...

Coming in August 2002

ISBN 0–718–14515–1

MICHAEL JOSEPH
an imprint of
PENGUIN BOOKS

By the same author

ROSIE

Rosie Parker is no more than a child when her mother dies during the war. Left to the less-than-tender mercies of her father Cole and her brutish step-brothers Seth and Norman, she sees housekeeper Heather Farley, when she arrives, as a possible replacement mother and her salvation. But when Thomas Farley comes looking for his sister several years later, he discovers Heather has left the Parkers in mysterious circumstances, abandoning her small son. As the terrible truth about Heather's disappearance comes to light, Rosie is compelled to leave the farm and make her own way in the world. And if that means being exposed as the daughter of a murderer, that's a risk she'll have to take ...

By the same author

NEVER LOOK BACK

Moving from Victorian London to the plains of the Wild West, from New York to the gold rush of San Francisco, *Never Look Back* is the story of beautiful intelligent Matilda, who rises out of poverty to forge a new life for herself in the land of the free. Escaping poverty, she travels to America with Giles, a Presbyterian minister, his wife and their young daughter. There she loses her heart and learns the lessons her childhood never taught her – that we are all created equal, that tragedy afflicts those who don't deserve it, and that true love comes when we least expect it. Above all, she discovers that life must go on and that she must never look back . . .

refresh yourself at penguin.co.uk

Visit penguin.co.uk for exclusive information and interviews with
bestselling authors, fantastic give-aways and the
inside track on all our books, from the Penguin Classics
to the latest bestsellers.

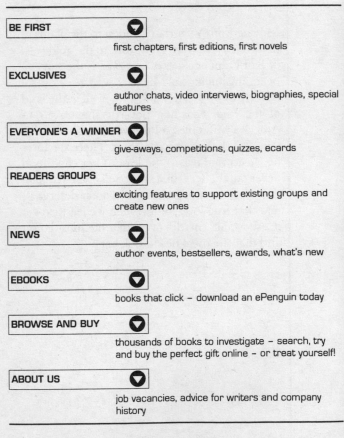

BE FIRST ▼

first chapters, first editions, first novels

EXCLUSIVES ▼

author chats, video interviews, biographies, special
features

EVERYONE'S A WINNER ▼

give-aways, competitions, quizzes, ecards

READERS GROUPS ▼

exciting features to support existing groups and
create new ones

NEWS ▼

author events, bestsellers, awards, what's new

EBOOKS ▼

books that click – download an ePenguin today

BROWSE AND BUY ▼

thousands of books to investigate – search, try
and buy the perfect gift online – or treat yourself!

ABOUT US ▼

job vacancies, advice for writers and company
history

Get Closer To Penguin . . . www.penguin.co.uk